THE E-ZINE OF CLEA

CW01203278

ANTHOLOGY ONE

Staff:

Brendon Taylor, Charlie N. Holmberg, Jeff Wheeler, Kristin Ammerman, Steve R. Yeager, and Dan Hilton

We'd like to thank our First Readers:

Susan Olp, Ashely Melanson, Mike Abell, Greg Garguilo, Elicia Cheney, Junior Rustrian, Tyson Dutton, Crystal Fernandez, Krysia Bailey, Melissa McDonald, Loury Trader, Hollijo Monroe

The stories in Deep Magic are works of fiction. Names, characters, organizations, places, events, and incidents are either products of the author's imagination or are used fictitiously.

Copyright © 2018 Jeff Wheeler

Cover design by Steve R. Yeager

Deep Magic logo & cover design by Deron Bennett

Copyediting by Wanda Zimba

E-zine design by Steve R. Yeager

www.deepmagic.co

CONTENTS

THE APOTHECANT

By Brendon Taylor | 18,800 words

DANAI WALDERS HAD climbed every peak in the mountains surrounding the Brasin valley by the time she was twelve. Now seventeen, she continued to climb almost daily. Her strong fingers and nimble feet had earned her a reputation for being part mountain goat, while her stubborn mind and disregard for rules or parental commands earned her a reputation for being part ox. Both were well deserved. All of her nicknames, which were admittedly terrible, played on one or both of these traits, and all came from her father: she-goat, nanny ox, and the mule spider. Danai's favorite nickname was the one he had begun calling her the summer before everything in her life changed: Pugnox. Her father, who had a love of words and language, explained that it was derived from an old tongue, and referenced someone who was stubborn and liked to fight.

Danai counted it as good fortune that no one but her father had ever called her Pugnox, and she had not heard the name since her mother died five years earlier. She would walk a path of burning embers to hear her father call her any of those ridiculous nicknames once more. Losing her mother to the blue moth plague was devastating. That tragedy alone would have been more than a young woman should have to bear, but it was also that summer when her father contracted the same illness. She went from having two loving, attentive parents to having one ill father in constant need of medication and bed rest. Yet, she also learned to be strong and to be content with little, and she was still able to find happiness in the world inside and out of her shanty of a home.

She had even found a job that provided enough income to cover their needs and that was actually the perfect job for her. She worked for the apothecant, Merdrid Knaevel, who knew more about herbs, poultices, and healing than the physicians from the big city. Thanks to Merdrid, Danai's father received medication each month that kept the plague at bay and allowed him a brief respite from the pain.

It was her father's poultice, the poultice that would treat him and seven other members of the valley who likewise suffered from the blue moth plague, that put Danai on the tallest peak over the Brasin valley on a late spring morning. Little purple flowers from the elusive pintiach tree were an essential ingredient. This time of year, only the most adept climber could retrieve them. Hence, Danai's value to Merdrid was realized. The elderly, portly Merdrid huffed when walking up the short flight of stairs from the cellar. Climbing a mountain was unthinkable. Not only was Danai able to climb any mountain around, but her mind stayed focused on the specific flower, root, or berry Merdrid required, and she nearly always returned with the correct item and amount. If she did not find what Merdrid wanted, it was because it was not there to be found.

Notwithstanding the cool of the morning leaving tendrils of fog around the tall evergreen trees in the valley below, Danai felt rivulets of sweat roll down her back between her shoulder blades. Her muscles strained to pull her body up the vertical face of granite. She felt a sharp shift followed by a terrifying crumble as her left handhold gave way. Her body swayed as she sought purchase with her right foot, and the fingers on her right hand gripped their hold more tightly. A few whispered counts helped calm her nerves. She felt the gentle breeze and warmth of the sun, and forced thoughts of aching arms and shoulders out of mind. Focusing on each place to put a hand or foot, she continued her ascent. A short while later, she reached the ledge where a large cropping of pintiach bloomed beautifully.

Danai filled her belt pouch with purple flowers before she gathered a handful of heather berries and sat in the sun with her waterskin to relax. The pintiach flower was the last ingredient Merdrid needed for the poultice that would relieve her father's pain, and even enable him to wake and speak for a few precious moments. His disease left him with little energy and almost no ability to communicate. The windows of clarity the poultice brought when first applied were the only golden treasures Danai had. She loved Merdrid for giving those to her.

The tartness of the berries lingered on her tongue, and the red from their juices stained her fingers. They were some of her favorites. She thought about gathering enough for a pie, but decided against wasting the time it would take to gather that many. Besides, she had no bag or sack to hold them. And her pockets would be a soggy red mess if she tried to climb down with berries inside. Ultimately, thoughts of hearing her father speak that evening pushed all other ideas out of her mind. As soon as her limbs regained their strength, Danai slipped over the edge of the rock wall and methodically descended.

The ancient brass bell that dangled from a wire hook above Merdrid's door clanged as Danai entered the apothecary. Danai had mentioned to Merdrid several times in the years she had been her assistant that the bell looked worn and dirty. Merdrid always defended the bell with a smile, declaring the age and wear were called patina, and that it made the bell even more valuable than a new one. Danai liked the bell, but the smell of the shop was what made it her second home. It was like freshly turned soil, harvested vegetables, ripe fruit, and a flower garden in bloom. At least, in Danai's mind that was how it smelled. If she was honest, she would also admit it smelled a bit like a burlap bag of moldy mushrooms and mud from a barnyard.

"I'm in the back, Sis." Merdrid's voice cracked.

"Coming." Danai hustled down a root-crowded aisle.

Merdrid scraped the underbark from a section of kiltenmoss brush with a short, stout bone-handled knife. Her favorite. "You look a shabby mess! Sweaty face, hair mussed, and blouse untucked." The older woman chuckled without moving her eyes from the section of bark. It was one of several odd things about Merdrid. She always seemed to see Danai without needing to bother herself with actually looking.

Danai glanced up and saw strands of her blond hair dangling in front of her eyes as she unconsciously tucked in the loose tail of her shirt. "You didn't even see me, Merdrid. That was a lucky guess."

"It is my business to know everything that happens in my shop. Of course I saw you." Merdrid put the knife and bark down on the table and smiled with a nod as her eyes confirmed what she had said. "Just be glad that I was too courteous to mention your smell." The older woman waved a short-fingered hand in front of her nose as if to ward away the smell and squinted.

Danai's own nose dipped toward her right armpit, and she took a half step back. The older woman was right. "Perhaps I should take a quick bath before working in the shop."

"Perhaps you should. But if you leave the pintiach flowers on the table, I can prepare them for the poultice while you bathe." Merdrid pulled her heavy stone mortar from the shelf under the table and gathered the bark shavings into its bowl.

Danai chided herself for momentarily forgetting the importance of the day. "What makes you so sure I found the flowers?"

"Sis, I already told you. I know what happens in my shop." Merdrid looked serious for a moment, with her stone-gray hair carefully pulled into a bun secured by two mixing rods. "Besides, you would not have been smiling so much had you not found them."

Danai could not argue with that. She loosened her belt pouch and placed the flowers gently on a clean section of the table near the bark. "When will the poultice be ready?"

"By nightfall if we stop yapping and you clean yourself enough to get some work done." Merdrid winked as her hands worked the pestle in the mortar. "Danai, let me give you two compliments before you go. You have earned them."

Danai had started turning toward the front door, but stopped. Compliments were rare from Merdrid, and always sincere.

"First, I have never seen a young woman who stays as consistently cheerful as you, when life gives you few reasons to be so." Merdrid's look was serious.

"Well, I get to climb all over the valley and am blessed to work with . . ."

"Hush!" Merdrid stopped her. "I'm giving you a compliment. Let me give you the second one." Merdrid paused long enough that Danai began to feel the urge to fill the silence, but she forced herself to stand still. Seemingly satisfied, Merdrid continued. "Second, I have never seen a young woman willing to sacrifice so much of herself for her family. What you do for your father is truly remarkable, Danai. These two things make you very rare, not unlike the pintiach flowers from your pouch."

"Thank you." Danai remembered the way her mother taught her to receive a compliment when she was a little girl. This seemed to please Merdrid.

"Am I correct to believe that you would do most anything to help your father?"

"Of course!" Danai nodded.

Merdrid paused for a moment, and Danai made herself stay still. "Sis, what if I told you I have been working out a way to heal your father completely from his illness, but it would take a bit of a sacrifice from you?" The look in Merdrid's eye was a mix of sparkle and something else.

Danai's stomach clenched with ice. She had long beaten down any hope that her father might recover, since Merdrid and everyone else in the valley assured her that was not possible. Yet, Danai knew that Merdrid would not mention a possible cure unless she had found one. Merdrid would never hurt her like that; she was certain. Still, she did not want to open herself to that level of pain, and let hope creep in where she had safely locked out emotion for so many years. "You are serious, aren't you?" Danai's voice was a whisper.

Merdrid's mouth turned into a small smile. "You know I would not say such a thing unless I thought it was possible. Only possible, mind you."

The front door bell clanged as a customer walked into the shop. Danai clenched her hands into fists at her sides, angry that they might be interrupted right then. She glanced over her shoulder and saw the most handsome face she had ever seen. A dark-haired, tall man, about twenty years old, in a crisp gray uniform with green-and-gold trim walked toward them with an older well-dressed man behind him. Her nose dipped once more toward her armpit, and she frowned.

Danai refused to think of herself as beautiful. When she was a child, she always felt beautiful, in part because her mother's compliments were effusive. Mother always praised her for her golden hair and gorgeous eyes. Danai believed her at the time because Mother was a beautiful woman. She too had blond hair and blue eyes. She too had a dimple in her left cheek. The biggest difference beyond the gentle wear of years was that Danai's younger face bore a smattering of freckles across her nose and cheeks. Mother had promised those would fade by the time Danai became a woman.

Mother had not been right about the freckles fading; however, Danai believed her beauty had faded—her hair seemed paler, her eyes less dazzling. Even her dimple now looked too deep to be pretty. Danai wondered how much of the way she had viewed herself as a girl was shaped by her mother, or if she had truly been prettier as a child. Certainly a person's looks can change, but she felt that was one more unfortunate turn of events that followed the summer her mother died. She knew she was not ugly, but believed most people would describe her as plain or pleasant. Neither term was what a young woman strived to hear.

She decided right then that if she was going to meet this handsome soldier, it would not be as grubby or smelly as she then was. She might not turn all of the young men's heads in the valley, but that did not mean she would stop trying to look her best.

Merdrid hustled in front of Danai and whispered as she went by, "Slip out the back and get cleaned up. We can talk more later."

With another quick glance at the man in uniform, Danai sighed and did as she was bid, sincerely happy the shop had a back door.

Danai would not want to admit it, but she sprinted the two cobblestone blocks to her home tucked behind the town well. She almost forgot how weak the front door was and nearly broke it off its hinges as she bounded into the small main room.

"Father!" Danai dropped onto the stool next to her father and held his hand.

He startled from sleep, and looked at her through drooping eyelids.

Danai could see his concern. "I have great news! Do not worry. The poultice will be ready tonight, but that's not even the best part." She smiled and waited to make sure his eyes confirmed that he was alert and listening to her. Satisfied, she went on. "Merdrid hinted that she may have found a cure or at least a more effective treatment for the plague." She reconsidered whether she should have told him about the possible cure, but decided she was right to give him a little hope. This way, he could be ready to talk about the possible cure when the poultice was ready that night. She also thought about telling him of the handsome soldier, but decided to keep that bit of news to herself.

Father's eyes closed for a moment and he seemed to shake his head from side to side. Danai decided he must be overwhelmed, as she was, at the hope of a cure. She stood and pulled her hand from his. "I need to clean up and hurry back to the shop. Merdrid needs me." She poured the remaining water from their bucket into the pot and stoked the wood-burning stove to at least take the chill off. "I will fetch fresh water to fill the tub and get you a drink while the pot heats."

Several minutes later, the tub was a little more than a quarter full and the water in the pot was at least not cold. Danai helped her father sip down a glass of water, smiling and telling him about her climb that morning. It would have taken a full pot of boiling water to make the tub temperature comfortable, but Danai could not wait that long. After she added the water from the pot, the tub water went from icy to frigid. At least she would stop sweating. She pulled the curtain for privacy and made quick work of the task. She had taken colder baths before, but they had been accidental and involved mountain springs.

Before leaving, Danai changed her father's bed pot and helped him take a few more sips of water. She brushed long strands of graying brown hair back from his eyes and felt the heat coming off his forehead. He had a low fever, which was not unusual, so Danai ground some bitter bark into his water and helped him drink. It was not a high fever. She had long experienced his conditions and knew which signs should cause her to worry. This fever would likely respond to the bitter bark within a few minutes. She felt guilty about leaving, but could not get the image of the handsome soldier out of her mind. Besides, she had a hunger to know more about Merdrid's cure.

Danai kissed her father gently on the forehead and promised to be back by evening. She grabbed a hard roll to eat on the way and rushed out the front door like a rabbit with a coyote on her tail.

Danai swallowed the last of the roll as she ducked into the narrow dirt alley leading to the back of Merdrid's shop. Her blond hair pulled back into a tight ponytail dripped down her back, soaking a circle on her blouse. She regretted not taking a little time to dry it after the bath. At least she smelled fresh, like the soap Merdrid gave her for her birthday last year. Jinderberries and honeyblossom. Merdrid was going to tease her mercilessly. Danai only used the sweet-smelling soap on special occasions, and with her birthday coming tomorrow, she would likely get a fresh cake of the special soap. Danai peered through the window in the back door, hoping to see the handsome soldier, while she caught her breath. Instead, she saw Merdrid crumpled on the floor by her worktable.

Merdrid sobbed. The sound halted Danai and broke her heart. The sweet, grandmotherly woman who had cared for Danai and her father for the past five years had been a rock. Danai placed a gentle hand on Merdrid's back and knelt beside her. For a minute, Merdrid's body shook with sobs, and Danai consoled her without words.

Finally, Merdrid looked up, eyes swollen and red, cheeks wet and shiny. "I have failed you, Sis."

Confused, Danai scooted to where she could see Merdrid better. "You've never failed me, Merdrid. What happened?"

"The soldier and the emissary." Her voice quavered as she struggled to put words together. "They came on a mission from King Evenricht. They took it."

Danai patted Merdrid's leg and leaned in. "What did they take?"

The older woman took a deep, stuttered breath. "My mortar."

Danai cocked her head to the left. "Is that all?"

"Yes."

"You must have another mortar in the shop. If not, we can get another from the merchant." Danai used her best comforting voice, one she might use if she was coaxing a wayward goat into a pen.

"You don't understand, Danai." Merdrid's tears were now flowing from eyes that showed anger and loss. "Without that mortar, many of my potions, powders, and poultices will lose their effect."

The last of her words lingered in Danai's mind. She just sat there, going numb at the thought that her father's poultice would not work. "But why is that mortar so important?"

"I was going to explain this to you before your birthday tomorrow, and I feel horrible that this is how you found out." Merdrid's eyes released their tinge of anger and showed nothing but compassion toward Danai. "My recipes are sound, and the cures and crafts I make would be of high quality without the mortar, but some of them require something more than herbs, roots, and berries provide."

Merdrid continued. "The mortar is made of a special stone that came from a very rare and deep mine—the mine caved in a very long time ago. The stone that was found is called by several names: hearthstone, bloodstone, oathstone, and mantle rock. It has the power to bind people to their oaths and give power to those who vow to use it for their promised purpose. This power is called, *vivos sanguine* in an old tongue, or *vosang,* for short. It means 'life blood.'"

Voice quivering, Merdrid went on. "The truth of the stone remains unknown to most, but not to the emissary and his protector. The king sent them to gather any remnants of that stone and hold it in a treasury to add to the king's wealth. Unfortunately, where it is now going, it cannot help people who are in dire need. Like your father."

There it was—the fear carving a hole in Danai's heart, put into words. It was an old wound that was tearing open. Danai's eyes blurred with her own tears.

"Oh, Sis. I am so sorry. You must think I am a fraud. I am embarrassed that I needed something beyond my own abilities to help my patrons." Merdrid looked away and crossed her arms tightly. Silence loomed for many long seconds. Merdrid continued. "I didn't want to let them take it, but they threatened to arrest any who stood in their way or prevented them from taking the bloodstone. I was so afraid that I did nothing to stop them."

A wave of darkness and despair threatened to overwhelm Danai, but what kept it at bay was the image of her father lying on his bed, suffering from fever, and straining in vain to talk to her. She would stay strong for him, at least until all hope was gone. "I will get it back for you." Danai's words were dry and brittle like old parchment.

Merdrid coughed out a little laugh. "Danai, I wish you could, but they will already be heading south to the highlands of Gretford. I overheard the young man tell the older that the horses were ready. Even as fast as your feet are, they cannot keep up with the king's horses."

Danai thought a moment. "The highland road winds its way through the cedar woods on the east slope of the valley. That way will take them the rest of the day to reach the rim of the highlands to our south." Danai wiped the wetness from her own cheeks, relieved that the plan in her mind had somehow stopped the tears.

Merdrid shook her head gently. "Even if you follow them on foot, it will take you until midmorning tomorrow to reach the rim. By then, they will be farther down the road. Besides, the soldier wasn't alone. He had a knot of five others with him. No doubt they will be watching the road behind. Even if you did catch them, how would you wrestle the mortar away?"

Danai offered a weak smile. "The answer to the first problem solves the second. At least I hope so. If I climb the table steppe on the southern slope, and continue over the face of the rim, I could be there by an hour after nightfall. Well, if I leave right away, I could." Merdrid shook her head, but Danai continued. "I have made the climb many times and know it well enough to finish the ascent in the dark. The solution this plan offers is that it places me in the roadway beyond the shelter of the tall pines. It seems unlikely the men would camp out in the open of the highlands when they have tall, sheltering pines to protect them from the vicious winds that abuse anyone who lingers on the long plateau. They will be watching the road behind them, but might pay less attention to someone coming from the road ahead."

Merdrid labored to stand, pulling herself up with the help of a firm grip on the worktable. It wobbled a little, but held together. She shuffled slowly toward a high shelf holding a row of bottles of various sizes. She reached up on her tiptoes to grab a slender red bottle with a cork stopper. "I'm a fool to let you go. But I know how stubborn you can be. Besides, your interest in this matter is every bit as important as my own." Merdrid grunted a little as she turned, and favored her left knee. "I might as well offer what help I can." She held the bottle out to Danai.

Danai had asked about the bottles before and had received little information for her queries. "What is this?"

"That particular elixir will help you get into camp unseen and get out safely as well. It has a powerful memory block, so none of them should remember seeing you if they do catch a glimpse. I warn you that your own memory might also be shaded. Unfortunately, it won't help you find the mortar, so that part of the job will be up to you."

Danai gripped the cork stopper to pull it free.

Merdrid yelped. "Not now, girl! There is one dose in that bottle and you want to drink it no more than ten minutes before entering the camp, which will give the potion long enough to take effect. Mind you, those effects will only last for a couple hours, so you must be sure when you drink it you are ready."

Danai could feel the blood flush her cheeks. "Sorry, Merdrid." She was ready to sprint up the face of the southern steppe. Then, she remembered her father. What she was doing was dangerous, and if she failed, they both were in dire trouble. She wanted to tell him good-bye, but knew if she went home, she would only worry him. Still, he was expecting her to be home that evening with the poultice. Even if she succeeded in recovering the mortar, she would not return until morning. He would need help before then.

"Sis, I can see your thoughts linger with your father. That is one of your tender strengths." Merdrid's weak smile comforted Danai, who was just glad to see the older woman had stopped crying herself. Merdrid continued. "I will visit him with supper and sit with him while you are away."

Danai thought her eyes were getting plenty of water today. "Thanks." She choked out.

A few minutes later, Danai set a fast pace to the south, shouldering her pack, with a full waterskin at her hip.

* * *

Shortly after dusk, when the few street lamps in the sparsely populated Brasin valley had begun to flicker, Merdrid waddled up the cobblestone roadway to the shanty where Danai and her father lived. She carried a maplewood bucket with too many cracks to be watertight, which held a bowl of soup on bottom and a napkin full of rolls on top. After a perfunctory knock (Merdrid knew Danai's father could not respond, much less get up to answer the door), she entered. The home was pitiful. Small, adorned with furniture that seemed to stay upright by force of will alone, and smelling of illness. She reached a stubby-fingered hand into one of her several belt pouches and flung a large pinch of powder into the air. The powder ignited into a sizzle of sparks that quickly dissipated. Although the powder seemed gone, the smell of lilacs lingered in its place. Merdrid nodded contentedly.

"Well, well, Haimer. You are looking rather ill tonight." She said in a matter-of-fact tone.

Haimer lay in bed, eyes open and wary. His mouth tried to move and muscles in his neck strained, but words and sound failed him.

"Fret not, good man. I am here because Danai is on an errand for me. We had a run of unfortunate luck this afternoon that required her help to make it right." Merdrid sat the bucket on a table near Danai's father and pulled the items out one at a time. "I promised her I would bring you dinner and explain that she would be out late tonight." Merdrid sat on a stool, but it groaned loudly enough that she put it aside and knelt on the floor near Haimer's head. "I won't be surprised if she is not back before you fall asleep for the night."

Tears leaked from Haimer's eyes and he squirmed in the bed.

"Steady. Don't worry so. Danai will be home tomorrow morning when you wake up, I have no doubt. Trust me when I assure you that I have a very keen interest in that young woman. Almost as keen as yours." Merdrid's smile did little to comfort the man. She pulled a spoon from the bottom of the bucket and dipped it into the creamy soup. As she waited a moment for the soup to cool, she said, "Once Danai is back, we will complete the poultice, and then you can have a nice visit with her." Steam still wafted up from the spoon as Merdrid lowered it to Haimer's mouth. Her other hand

11

gently steadied his shaking chin, and she smoothly slid the spoon in and tipped it up.

Haimer's shaking slowed a little and his eyes relaxed.

"Did you expect my cooking to taste foul? Perhaps I should be offended." Merdrid chuckled at the man. "One doesn't get so portly as this without knowing how to make food that tastes good." Merdrid turned sideways on one knee to exaggerate her girth.

The more spoonfuls she put in, the more content, then tired, his eyes seemed. Merdrid chewed on a roll. If she had to answer honestly, she would have admitted she always intended the rolls to be for her. A half hour after she arrived, Haimer was asleep and she had fulfilled her promise to Danai. At that point, she went above and beyond her promise and cleaned the bed pot for Haimer.

Merdrid popped another roll into her mouth, gobbling this one whole as she quickly put her things away, leaving the bowl in the bucket on the table and reaching into another belt pouch. Certain the man was asleep, Merdrid popped a pickled root into her mouth and pulled a wide, shallow silver bowl out of her pack. The surface of the metal gleamed and reflected like a freshly polished sword. She set the bowl on the floor, then pulled a dull brown bottle out of her robe pocket. The contents were bloodred as she poured them into the bowl. The liquid in the bowl turned clear when she added a bottle of water. Checking Haimer once more, she squatted on the floor and began to hum a catchy tune.

* * *

Danai cursed as the darkness made handholds more difficult to find. She had pushed herself near her limit in arriving beyond the southern steppe and more than halfway up the face of the mountain before true dark was upon her, but upon her it was. She was pleased that her waterskin was still bulging with water. She had used enough to avoid a light head or exhaustion, but still had plenty for the rest of the climb with some left for the return trip. Clouds had moved in near dusk, which would make the climb harder, but might aid her when she found the men's camp.

The urgency of acting—her father's dire need—had put her on her path to find the handsome soldier's group with little thought or planning. She had one potion she did not really understand, the cover of night, some skill in moving quietly through wilderness, and a knowledge of the area. The things she lacked filled her mind and sprouted doubts like cattails on a meadow pond. She had no weapon aside from a short-bladed root knife. That was just as well because she did not know how to use a weapon or fight. She did not know the strength of the men she sought, other than the fact that there were at least six soldiers counting the handsome one. She did not know if they would even camp, nor was she certain they would be coming along the highland road anywhere near where she would emerge. She also did not know where the mortar would be kept and how she might secure it. What if it was in a locked wagon? Would she be able to find the key and pilfer it?

The doubts offered one benefit. They occupied her mind so she could climb quickly. Often she found that when her brain worked on a problem, her hands and feet seemed to find their own way up a slope. Even in the dark. No more than an hour after true dark, she neared the rim. Danai decided it was time to worry less and focus on the task before her. The wind had picked up, and gusts buffeted her body against the rock face, then threatened to pull her off. She slowed to be more certain in her movements and made sure she had three points of contact with the rock at all times.

Coyotes called from peaks along the ridge. She was not terribly close to them, but just hearing their cry was like a splash of icy water to the face. When she was twelve, a pack of coyotes had followed her as she was on a climb by herself. Her father would scold her every time she came home from a climb alone, telling her to make sure she had a companion, but she never cared to find one. They would slow her down and make her talk when she did not want to. The evening the coyotes followed her, she regretted being alone, but not enough to change her practice. They followed for nearly an hour, getting closer and closer until she reached the safety of the valley. Ever since then, the cry of a coyote sent a shiver along her spine.

Finally, Danai pulled herself over a jagged ridge and onto the plateau above, hearing a tear of fabric as she made it to safety. It was a pretty big rip on the stomach of her blouse. Her favorite blouse. She shook her head in disgust. She had worn the blouse because she wanted to look nice for the handsome soldier. It had been an impractical choice for a work shirt and an even less suitable choice for climbing attire. She only had three other blouses, and resolved to mend this one when she got home.

As she stood, a gust of wind pushed her toward the cliff, but she was ready and leaned into it. Scanning around, she found a small cropping of rocks and quickly sat on the downwind side to catch her breath and drink a little water. It was then that she felt the first stinging droplet of cold rain. She mentally added "only bringing a light jacket" to the list of problems that was growing. Danai took solace in the fact that she had made it to the top of the climb before rain fell. It would have been a much larger problem if she were still on the wall.

Moments later, with her light jacket offering a meager defense against the rain and cold, Danai found the highland road and turned left. She stayed to the side of the roadway, where her form would be more difficult to spot. In the dark and rain, she would be even more concealed.

After looking for what seemed like an eternity, she was relieved to reach the beginning of the woods. The next stretch of roadway would be the most likely place for a camp. Danai slowed, walking quietly despite the muting rainfall. The drops became bigger, though still cold, and soaked her clothing to the skin and drenched the ground below all but the thickest of evergreens.

The smell of wet earth was comforting, but the chill numbed the comfort and Danai's fingers. She breathed on her hands, hoping her warm breath would restore feeling. A little farther down the road, Danai decided that if the rain continued and she got any colder, she would be unable to open the stopper on the bottle Merdrid had given her. She reasoned she had to be near the camp. Trembling fingers found the bottle and pulled it out. Relieved that it had not been damaged when she scrambled on the rocks, she walked slowly for a short while, looking around and listening. Hoping to find the camp. After thinking it through a little longer, she pulled the stopper and swallowed the contents. It tasted like vinegar and mint and would not find a place in any of Danai's cooking recipes.

For the next few minutes, she looked at her hands, felt her face with them, and even bit on one of her numb fingers. Why hadn't Merdrid explained what the potion would do? She could not perceive a difference in herself, but Merdrid had warned that it would take a while to work.

Time continued to pass, and Danai worried that she had gone too far down the road, mumbling to herself, "Why would I have thought they would camp right along the road? Far more likely, they would be well off into the seclusion of the woods."

"Far more likely indeed." A deep male voice behind her answered.

Danai nearly added to the wetness of her clothes at the shock she felt, and did jump more than a little. It was only due to her quick reflexes that when she spun to see who belonged to the voice, she did not fall in the mud. Gone was the soldier's crisp uniform. Gone was the charming smile she had imagined on his face. Gone was the feeling of security she associated with the king's soldiers. The man before her was still handsome, but a heavy cloak with a hood covering his head draped him in darkest black. His eyes, which she had not been able to get a look at in the shop, were dark and serious. He was tall. More than a half foot taller than she, and that placed him above most men in the valley. His shoulders seemed broader than before, but that might have been because of how close they were in the nighttime storm, or it might have been the thickness of his heavy cloak. She envied the warmth that cloak would provide. In contrast to the wetness on her outside, Danai's mouth felt like a desert—she said nothing.

The soldier shook his head, right hand on the pommel of a long-bladed knife on his right hip. "You were at Merdrid's shop today, weren't you?"

Danai almost laughed as she realized she had run away from the shop earlier so he would not see her. She had not wanted him to see her smelling foul and grubby from a climb. As it turned out, he had seen her there and probably recognized her so easily now because she was once again dirty, shirt torn, likely smelling of sweat, and drenched on top of it. So much for making a good first impression. She simply nodded, not trusting how foolish she might sound if she spoke.

In contrast to Danai standing stiffly at the side of the road shivering in small bursts, the soldier seemed comfortable, relaxed perhaps, or maybe just ready to act however he needed. He said, "Is there another road that we did not know about? Or did you come over the face of that cliff?"

Danai cocked her head slightly to the side. Did the man seem amused? "I climbed the face." She was relieved her voice did not falter.

"Well, I'm glad to see you can speak. This would take much longer to get through if we could not converse."

Danai retorted without much thought, "I think you mean, you *heard* me speak. You cannot *see* the words."

He offered a mirthless chuckle. "I meant what I said. A good soldier sees as much as he hears when he is speaking with someone. I can see by your expression that you were startled and not entirely happy to see me. I can also see you are frightened, but determined, by the way you hold yourself."

"Can your keen eye see that I'm freezing?"

The soldier folded his arms in front of his chest. "Yes, I can see that too. But you were the one who scaled her way into the highlands at night with naught but a light jacket." He stepped a little closer. "Now we are going to discuss what you hoped to accomplish tonight. Will you tell me?"

The rain grew colder and the wind blew harder. Treetops swayed back and forth like hands waving in a parade. Danai did not know what to say, so she said nothing.

"We don't need to make this any worse than it needs to be." He pointed toward an enormous evergreen a short distance away. "Sit under those boughs and you won't get any wetter." He waited for her to start walking and then followed.

The span of branches grew just above the man's height and offered a large circle of dry needles and dirt. Danai no longer cared that she was a mess, and sat on the dry ground, knowing that her backside would be covered in mud and needles. She hugged her knees to her chest, hoping to get feeling back into her fingers and toes. She was not very good at lying, so she decided not to spin one here. "You took something that I need to keep my father alive."

The soldier stood near, and raised both eyebrows. "You admit you came to steal the bowl?"

"No, I came to take back what you and your boss stole from mine." She kept her tone even, and tried to keep her emotions under control. She must have regained a little feeling in her behind, because she realized several needles were poking her there.

"Do you really believe all of that? You believe that your father will die without Merdrid getting the bowl back, and that she is its rightful owner?"

Danai shifted her weight forward and brushed the seat of her pants to clear away the offending needles. "I do. I have gathered ingredients for my father's poultice for years. He suffers from the blue moth plague, which killed many in the valley five years ago when it came. Without Merdrid's poultice, the last several survivors will die. Without the mortar, she cannot infuse the poultice with the power needed to fight back the plague. You have no idea what that plague did to my father." Danai decided that the soldier did not need to know about her mother dying from it. That was one more wound in her heart—one that would remain there as far as this man was concerned. "Whether Merdrid owns the mortar I had not considered; all I know is that she has had it as long as I have known her."

Not far from where they were speaking, a treetop creaked in the wind and snapped. It fell to the ground with a thud. "You willingly serve her then?" The man's head shook slowly from side to side.

"Yes. She has given me work and enough money to keep my father and me fed and sheltered. She also cares for him free of charge. Without Merdrid, my life would have been far worse. In the last five years, she has given me no reason to doubt her." Danai felt the truth of her words shiver down her spine. She would have been an orphan without Merdrid.

The soldier studied her for a while. "Your words ring true, but I cannot see how that is possible. We will need to talk a little longer, but you have at least interested me enough not to arrest you on the spot. My name is Kleed, Kleed Rancic."

Danai raised her chin in defiance. "Arrest me? For what? I have committed no crime."

"You came to steal the king's bloodstone."

Danai rose to her knees. "Perhaps I came to ask you to return it to its owner."

Kleed chuckled, and seemed to do so with genuine mirth. "We both know your intent. But you are generally right that mere intent to commit a crime is not enough to warrant an arrest." He ushered her to sit back down. "However, as one of the Kingsworn, my commission gives me certain rights. Any who hinder the recovery of the bloodstone are in violation of the law. That is my authority to arrest you. But as I said, I do not intend to do that just yet."

Danai could not believe the arrogance of the soldier. He was actually smiling. "You call the mortar bloodstone. I have heard this name, but I know very little of what that means." Perhaps if she stalled, she would figure a way to get out of this hog's pit of a mess. Besides, the potion should be helping her any minute, though she wished she knew how.

"Miss, I will ask the questions. However, if you will start by giving me your name, I will consider your request."

Danai fought the urge to roll her eyes. "I didn't actually ask a question or make a request. My name is Danai Walders."

Ignoring her near eye roll and verbal impudence, Kleed continued. "Thank you for your name, Danai. I cannot tell you about the bloodstone. And I cannot believe you risk your life for one, not knowing what it is. What I do want to find out is how a beautiful, smart young woman came to align herself with Merdrid."

"I already told you that Merdrid took me in and gave me work. She tends to my father and gives me moments of time each month where my father is much like his old self. Merdrid is strict, but fair, and she has a sweet side." Her cheeks heated at his insincere compliment.

Kleed chuckled once more. "I wonder what you will think of her a month from now, when she has no bloodstone to continue her 'work' in the valley."

Danai scowled, "If that happens, I will likely lose myself completely. My father will be dead and my heart with him." She wondered why she ever felt attracted to the man who was now robbing her of her last treasures. "Why do you think Merdrid is so awful? Even if the mortar came from a rock that belongs to the king, she uses it to heal. In her hands, it does good for the king's subjects in that valley." She pointed sharply in the direction of the Brasin valley.

Kleed breathed deeply for a moment, tapping one finger on his chin. "I will tell you this much. I have seen the truth of the woman, a truth that cannot be hidden from me. That truth does not square with your opinions of Merdrid. I fear she may have you bound in something so tightly that you can only see the truth she wants you to see. I considered arresting her this day, but she did nothing in her shop to prevent our recovery of the bloodstone. However, now that she has sent you to steal the stone . . ."

Danai tried to think. Not only was her freedom and her father's life at stake, but her actions would likely pull Merdrid into this quagmire. Those thoughts did not help her; she must think productively. *How did he know to lead me to this tree, when almost all others failed to protect from the storm?* She looked around and saw the answer: footprints and wet spots existed where neither she nor Kleed had been, at least not since she and he arrived at the tree together. She feared the man had followed her down the road, and may have even see her drink the potion. But the prints and wet spots showed he had been here, watching the road from here. The camp must be close by. She had been quiet too long. She looked up and let her lip quiver, which was easy to do as cold as she remained. "First, you tell me I am smart, and then insult my intelligence by telling me you can see the truth of a woman in an instant when she has fooled me for years. Then, you try to flatter me by telling me I am beautiful, when I know I am plain. Perhaps these tricks work on many girls, but I know who I am and I know what I believe. I am not one to be moved by false compliments and bold promises." Danai knew she was laying it on a little thick, but also knew there was truth in both her words and feelings. She really did despise it when men used lies and compliments to get what they wanted from a girl.

Kleed's mouth hung open for a long second. "I meant what I said on both counts. I can see the truth of Merdrid because of something unique that has nothing to do with my intelligence. And, Danai, don't bandy with me about your looks. Plain is a daisy. You are a rose." Kleed's head tilted a little askew and he rubbed the back of his neck.

Danai looked around without trying to be obvious, hoping to find a rock that might be used as a weapon if she needed it, and found none. She also looked into Kleed's eyes and saw he was earnest. She shook her head. How much would she have given when she first laid eyes on the man to hear him genuinely say what he said now? Now, she was looking for a way to hit him on the head and get free of him. Not only was life not fair in the Brasin valley, but it sometimes made little sense.

Lightning and thunder joined the rain all around them, shaking the ground and flashing brightly for a split second before leaving them in the dark once more. Kleed continued. "You truly believe you are plain." He took a step back and reached down the back of his cloak. "I think I may have found the answer. Sit still for just a moment." His hand came out, clutching a leather cord. He slipped it around his head and removed a pendant of dark gray stone with golden flecks, cut into a circle and polished until it shone like burnished metal.

Once the pendant cleared Kleed's head, Danai felt something within her chest move, like her insides were all trading places. Whatever she felt must have paled compared to what was happening to Kleed. He swayed and dropped to his knees. When he looked up, his expression had changed into what appeared to be hopefulness. Keen hopefulness. At least, that was the modest characterization Danai chose to use. "Are you well, Kleed?"

"Oh, yes." His smile was gorgeous.

Danai thought it unfair that he had such a perfect smile on top of all the other blessings he had been given. But she knew she should be thinking of something else. Her mind refused to work how she wanted. "Tell me how you know my opinion of Merdrid is wrong, Kleed."

He winked at her. "Say my name once more and I might."

Good heavens! Danai thought. Why is he acting so bizarre all of a sudden? *The potion!* Good golden lake of the gods! Why did Merdrid give her *this* potion? "Kleed . . ."

He interrupted before she could continue. "I wear a bloodstone that lets me see things as they really are and prevents other bloodstones from affecting me." He held up the pendant.

Danai decided her mind, as muddled as it was, worked far better than Kleed's was working. "Tell me what you know about bloodstones. Please, Kleed?" She batted her eyelashes like she imagined girls did when they flirted. She made herself blush by doing it.

"If I tell you, can I give you a kiss?"

Danai arched a single brow and said softly, "Why don't you tell me and find out." She almost made herself vomit.

"All of the bloodstone found in this kingdom came from one place, the king's mine to the far south. All bloodstone from that mine belong to the king. It is his decree that the stones be found and gathered that underlies my commission. A person can make an offering through a bloodstone, and if the offering is accepted, the blood of the one making the offer seals it in an irrevocable covenant. The power or blessings offered to the oathmaker are called *vosang*. The power comes from the dedication of life and blood of the offeror to serve the purpose of the promise."

"Who accepts the offer?" Danai's head was swimming.

Kleed continued. "Some say it is the gods themselves. And it must be an offering that is balanced on both sides. The stone I have protects the wearer from the power of other stones, but it was made by my offer to bring other stones to the king. I know that once an offering is accepted, amazing powers can be gained. That is why they are so dangerous and why the king wants them kept safe." Kleed crawled toward Danai. "May I kiss you now?"

The offer sounded really good. Somewhere in her mind, Danai knew it was not real, that what was happening came out of a bottle, but she did not care right then. She smiled and leaned toward him. They clasped hands, and Danai felt the cool smoothness of the stone pendant. Lightning flashed, thunder broke, and the trees swayed as they came together for a kiss. The ground seemed to buck, and everything went dark. Danai fell, but was unconscious before she hit the ground.

* * *

Unaware of how much time had passed, where she was, or even if she was really alive, Danai awoke. Her head felt as though it was being used to prop up the drooping corner of Merdrid's shop as a makeshift cornerstone. It throbbed in time with her heartbeat. Her thoughts seemed to lurk at the bottom of a rather thick pea soup, and wanted nothing more than to stay lost in the depths of unconsciousness. The first thing outside of herself that she realized was some source of bright light beamed as though to burn through her eyelids and melt her brain. And her mouth was so very dry.

"Ah, you live again, Sis." Merdrid's familiar and soothing voice beckoned her.

Danai felt a blanket covering her, and she struggled to pull it over her head with her left hand; something was in her right hand, but she did not know what. Both hands and arms felt as though hundreds of tiny pins were pricking them and robbing all strength. She grunted something in reply that fell far short of a recognizable word.

"Don't play the turtle on me, Sis. I need you to come out and drink the tea I have prepared. It will help you feel better. Then we can talk about all that we need to do today." Merdrid's voice was still sweet, and in remarkably good spirits.

Danai heard the part about tea and feeling better. She also realized Merdrid seemed happy, which was noteworthy in itself. "Close the drapes." She managed to say.

The sounds of scuffled steps moving away from Danai preceded the room going dark. Merdrid's voice spoke from across the room, "It is nice and dark now, Sis."

When Danai lowered the blanket, she realized she was in her own room at home. It seemed strange to find Merdrid at her bedside. "I'm . . . sorry . . . Merdrid." She managed to say around the throbbing spasms of pain in her head.

"Don't be foolish. What have you to be sorry for, dear child?" Merdrid's cheerfulness grated her nerves.

"I didn't get it." Danai felt the object in her right hand. It was circular, very smooth, and attached to a string. She thought she should recognize it by feel, but her mind was not working properly, and any effort to recall the prior night made her head hurt worse.

"Please let me get some of this tea in you." Patience was almost as foreign as cheerfulness with Merdrid. This was a rare day.

Danai obliged and took the steaming cup. It was made of gray stone and had a few chips, but no cracks, which made it the best one in her home. She felt a tinge of embarrassment at her meager living quarters, but tried to forget her pride. The tea was warm, but not hot, and the bitter bark that she expected to find was well masked with a generous amount of honey. She felt better just drinking something warm. The object in her hand had a hole in it—like a ring. She almost pulled it out to inspect, but then decided not to at the last second.

"What didn't you get?" Merdrid asked, sitting on a wobbly stool next to the bed.

It took Danai a moment to recall her own statement and realize what Merdrid was asking. "The mortar." Her eyes focused on Merdrid's shoes, which looked a little muddy.

Merdrid's chuckle filled the room and Danai nearly fell off the bed. "Of course you did not fail, Danai." Merdrid leaned down and picked the mortar up from the floor, holding it where Danai could see its dark gray form with flecks of gold, the inner bowl glistening like it had been polished with wax. "I warned you that the potion might addle your memory, did I not?"

Danai strained to remember getting the mortar, or even entering the camp, but could not. She wondered if she had met the handsome soldier, but try as she did to recall anything from the night before, no memory materialized. One question lingered in her mind above the others. "How did I get home?"

"I suspect you ran down the face of the mountain, for you got home at the break of dawn." Merdrid indicated with her hands to drink more of the tea. "The potion you drank was strong indeed. I would not be surprised if you had dreams you believed to be true. Reality and dream could easily be mottled together, Sis."

There was something about the potion that beckoned unpleasant thoughts in Danai's mind. She was unhappy about the potion, but could not remember why. Then there was the handsome soldier, and her thoughts about him were uncertain. She drank the rest of the tea and tried to piece together the missing memories from the night before. "Are we safe? Will the men come back?"

Merdrid's smile sank a little. "I fear that they will. That is why I believe we need to move forward more quickly than I wanted with my idea about your father. We can try the cure on him today, and then if it works, we can quickly apply it to the others who suffer from the plague. Do you still want to help him?"

Danai's head hurt a little less, and the strength in her arms was slowly coming back. "Certainly. Is he okay?" Danai felt guilty that she had not thought to ask about her father earlier. She had never failed to check him throughout the night since he had become ill. She started to get out of bed to check on him, but Merdrid's gentle touch stopped her.

"He is well enough, Sis. I promised I would watch over him while you were on my errand, and I did so. He even ate a little soup last night." Her smile returned, albeit a little weakly.

"Thank you."

"You are welcome, as was he. It was a trifle compared to what you did for me, Danai. I will remember you all my days for that great service alone." Merdrid started to rise, taking a rather long time to get her body upright. "You need a little rest, which the tea should help you with. I need to go to the shop to gather ingredients and a few items necessary for the cure. I will wake you when I return. I do not trust the safety of the shop—so we will put the cure together here at your home, yes?"

"Of course," Danai said. "But I have more questions about last night."

"We can talk when I get back. I won't be long—get some rest." Merdrid smiled brightly before she shuffled out of the room.

Danai waited until Merdrid left the home, and then sat up on the edge of the bed, her vision darkening and dizziness threatening to empty her stomach, but after a little while, she was able to slowly rise to her feet. She looked down into her hands and saw the pendant. Gold flecks in dark gray, the same colors as the mortar, glistened from the shiny ring tethered to a leather cord. Seeing it made her think about the night before, and a picture involving the pendant tried to form in her mind, but never came together. After trying to sort her thoughts for a couple of minutes, she decided to try later.

With considerable caution, Danai moved slowly across the floor. She poked her head out the door and saw her father sleeping on his bed in the main room. His low snore greeted her like a familiar friend. His brow was wet with perspiration. Danai remembered him having a bit of fever the day before, which must have broken. Merdrid probably helped him more in the night she was here than Danai helped him all month. Danai's brow creased as she realized she could remember her father's fever clearly, but so little of what happened after she reached the highlands last night.

Satisfied that her father was doing all right and not wanting to disturb his sleep, Danai slowly returned to her own bed. Perhaps a little more rest would help her think clearly. She was yawning as she got back under the warm covers. Before she fell asleep, she put the stone ring in her large pouch on her belt that hung from the bed-post.

* * *

At the camp in the woods near the highland road, dawn brought order to the soldiers who had spent the night on alert, searching for the girl who had brought near ruin upon them all. The apothecant's assistant had somehow subdued Kleed, but she had done worse to the emissary. The old man remained unconscious, his head wound still weeping blood. The men had looked for her most of the night, but could not track her in the storm. It had taken them an hour to find Kleed after she darted into their midst, stole the artifact, and slipped into the night like an arrow.

In the clear light of morning, Kleed organized them, his temper fully engaged. The soldiers stood before him in line, at attention. "You wasted half of the night running in circles. She made fools of you. She made fools of us all. But the day will undo much of the harm done in the dark. By nightfall, she will be in chains, the mortar in stow, and we will be back on the road to the city." He spat.

He went on. "Pack everything but the tent. We will let the emissary rest. Tyngrid and Ellisen stay with him and notify me of any change in his condition. Keep his wound dressed and help him be comfortable. I will check in before we leave, but I want him kept here until he is fit to travel. You will keep the carriage and join us in the valley when you can." He turned to the others. "Move out. Now!"

Kleed felt like an idiot himself. Danai had taken more than his pride. She was not yet a woman, and she had lured him to take off his protective pendant. Now he would go back into the valley where a truly dark practitioner of the *vosang* lived, with only his skill and sword as defense. He checked himself. He was giving the girl too much credit. It was his arrogance and pride that had cost them. Had he put her in chains when he found her and conducted a proper interrogation, the emissary would not be on the verge of death. If the emissary did not live, he had no doubt their commission would end with the emissary's burial and his own court-martial.

* * *

The next time Danai woke, she felt substantially better. Her pounding headache had reduced to a slightly annoying thrum, and the rest of her body was merely stiff. Humming from the main room caught her attention. Humming. Merdrid had never hummed that Danai could recall. Standing came easier, but this time Danai looked down and realized she was in her sleeping slip. Her cheeks warmed as she tried to recall whether Merdrid had seen her in the slip. Nobody other than her parents had ever seen her in her slip. She quickly dressed in some trousers and a blouse and secured her belt in place, remembering the pendant in the large pouch. She took a quick peek to see if it would jar more memories into place. It did not.

As she was getting ready to leave her room, she saw a clump of clothes and shoes in the corner. It was what she had worn the day before. Around the clump was a puddle of water on the stone floor. She remembered stinging rain and instinctively pulled her arms around her body, remembering her limbs and back aching from the cold.

"Danai, are you awake, Sis?" Merdrid called from the other room.

Danai tried to keep a picture in her mind of the storm so she could tease out more memories later. Before she left the room, she grabbed her only other pair of shoes, which were sturdy, though not pretty, and made from old burnished saddle leather. "I'm coming."

When Danai entered the main room of the home, she saw Merdrid standing at the worktable from the shop, with rows and piles of herbs, roots, and what appeared to be bugs on its top. Next to the herbs were three round black bottles with neat labels on them; Merdrid's short, stout knife; and the mortar and pestle. Danai could not help but notice and realize the pestle was also made from dark gray stone with flecks of gold. The room was a little hazy with smoke coming from two trays of burning incense. Merdrid scooted around the table and across the now crowded room with a package in her hands tied with a red ribbon. She smiled and said, "Happy Birthday, Sis."

Danai had completely forgotten it was her birthday. During the past five birthdays, she could count on Merdrid getting her some small gift, but she would have otherwise been forgotten. She took the present and fought back tears. "Thank you, Merdrid. Thank you for remembering." She fussed with the paper for a moment, then looked at her father and saw that he was still sleeping. "I want to wait and open it when Father is awake."

Merdrid frowned briefly and then nodded, "Of course. It is not much, mind you. So don't go building it up in your mind."

"Has he been up today?" Danai cleared a space on their only shelf and set the package down.

"Oh, yes. I cleaned his pot not more than an hour ago and gave him some of the tea I gave you. He has been fighting fever and it was starting to come back. I told him you were resting too, and I'm sure he was relieved to know you are safe at home." Merdrid walked back around the table and started shaving a root with her knife. "It is no doubt for the best that we are making the cure today. He grows weaker with time and struggles to fight the lingering effects of the plague."

"What can I do to help?" Danai took her yellow well-used apron from a peg near the back door and put it on.

"I started a fire this morning. Why don't you fetch a half pot of water to put on the stove and stoke the belly until the sides glow like a church boy's cheeks at a tavaranga dance."

Danai laughed out loud. "I haven't heard that one before."

"You probably haven't seen the tavaranga dance either." Merdrid winked at Danai as the young woman walked out the door with the water bucket.

After getting the fire stoked and making sure the pot was on the hottest part of the stove, Danai walked over and gave Merdrid a hug. The older woman only came up to Danai's chin and felt soft like a pillow all around. "Merdrid, what can you tell me about last night?"

Merdrid returned to scraping short, thin curls of giathen root into a shallow dish. "Unfortunately, I don't know much more than I told you before. After you left, I made dinner and brought it to your father. I fed him and then attended to a couple things before spending the rest of the night here until you came home near dawn." Merdrid seemed satisfied with the root scrapings and moved to a large bluish-colored nut that she grated into the same shallow dish. "You were soaking wet and nearly frozen when you came in. I built the fire to warm you, but you lacked the strength to stand in front of it. You changed out of your wet clothes in your room and then I warmed the blankets near the stove and tucked you in."

Having been outside, Danai could tell it was late afternoon. "Did I say anything about what happened?"

Merdrid frowned, "No, Sis. Nothing more coherent than 'brrrr' came out of your mouth until after you slept."

They worked quietly for a long while after that, with Danai working by Merdrid's side, restocking the incense, stoking the fire, and stealing looks at her father resting on his bed. They were used to working together without having to talk.

Danai considered asking about the pendant, but had a nagging feeling that she should not. She still struggled to make sense out of her memories while cleaning the knife for Merdrid. She had only remembered the coyotes howling and nothing else beyond what she had already sorted out. "I recall you saying that I would have to make a sacrifice for this 'cure' to work. Is that right?"

Merdrid started putting several of the ingredients into jars and little boxes, then stowing them in a large leather pack. "I did. I am sorry—I forgot we were interrupted when we were discussing this before. And you need to know what you will have to give for the cure to work." She continued to clean the work area until all that remained were the mortar and pestle; knife; seven shallow dishes with various herbs, shavings, and fibers; and the three bottles. "But before we do that, you should open your gift. I think your father is going to continue sleeping for a while, which is for his good. The cure is at a resting point, where there is little we can do until the shoots and nuts that are cooking in the pot have softened. This might be the best chance you have before we finish the cure."

Danai smiled and nodded her approval. She retrieved the package from the shelf and made quick work of the ribbon, saving it to use in her hair. It would make a beautiful bow. The paper came off next, and she could see red satin fabric inside with glittering stones in a row. They turned out to be the adornment along the waistline of a gorgeous dress. When she saw the neckline, she felt her cheeks redden. It would not go far below her neck, but it would hint at much more than she was used to. "It is beautiful, Merdrid. Absolutely beautiful." She held it up against her body and swished from side to side. The full skirt would fall just below the knee. All she could think of was when she would ever have occasion to wear such a dress.

"I know it is not something you are used to wearing, and you probably can't think of when you would." Merdrid waited until Danai nodded, then continued. "And I will be mortified if you wear it to climb mountains. Yet, now that you are eighteen, there are some dances and other gatherings I think you might attend. Trust me when I promise that the dress will get more use than you now imagine." Merdrid winked again. That was twice in one day.

"As long as you don't expect me to do the tavaranga dance in it. Whatever that is."

"I would be happy to teach you if you want." Merdrid started to move as though she was going to demonstrate the dance.

"Good golden gates of heaven, Merdrid. No, no, no. I have no need to redden any church boy's cheeks." Danai laughed a little.

"No? Well then, how about you try your dress on for fit, and then I will tell you more about the cure." Merdrid waved her hands to usher Danai toward her room.

Danai spent several minutes wrangling the dress into roughly the right position and thinking she wished she had time to bathe before wearing the dress. She was relieved that her feet and legs had been cleaned since her long climb the night before, and her hands were clean as well. Gripping the sides of the dress with both hands and squirming a little, she was able to put everything into the right places. She smoothed the fabric with her hands and enjoyed the feel of it on her fingers. A lattice of cream-colored ribbon on the back still needed tightening and tying, but she really wanted to see how she looked.

Feeling a bit nervous, she walked quietly to the polished oval mirror on the wall. It was not large enough to see herself from head to toe, but she could at least see herself from the waist up. As usual, she was a little disappointed by the plainness of her face. The band of freckles across her nose and cheeks were too many. The dimple looked wrong, and her eyes were too small. Her blond hair hung in waves, which always happened when she slept on wet hair. She could feel in places it was not fully dry. The dress was still beautiful, but her shape was thin and lacked the curves that men seemed to like. She offered a sigh and decided to make a smile. Her smile was nice, and it made her face look better than anything else she could do.

Merdrid called from the main room. "Are you going to come out so I can see?"

"In a minute." Danai said absently, pulling her hair up and trying to picture how she would look if she tied her hair like that with a ribbon. As she did, a bit of the fog on her memory cleared and she remembered the handsome soldier's mocking smile and words, telling her she was beautiful. No, that was not right. She thought he had been mocking her, but he seemed so genuine. Kleed. His name was Kleed.

More memory cleared. He had told her that he was able to see her for who she was because of a bloodstone. She moved to the bedpost where she had hung her belt when she changed out of her regular clothes and reached inside. Her fingers felt the smooth ring of stone tied to a leather cord. She pulled it out and returned to the mirror, telling herself she was foolish to hope that if she put the pendant on, she might see something different. Yet, Kleed had seemed so earnest. Yes, that was the word she remembered feeling last night. Shaking her head, she decided she had nothing to lose and slipped the loop of leather over her head.

Danai felt as though a heavy, wet coat had dropped from her, and rays of sun warmed and invigorated her whole body. She nearly fell to the floor with the forces moving her. She gripped the small table below the mirror and looked at her reflection. Gasping audibly, she saw her mother's beauty, enhanced by youth, and bright blue eyes looking back at her. She grinned weakly and the face in the mirror grinned back. The dimple. Her mother's gorgeous dimple, and not the misshapen, too deep dimple she was used to seeing, appeared on her face. Blond, dull waves were replaced by golden luster framing her face. Tears began leaking down her cheeks at the memory of her mother living in the image before her now.

"Are you all right in there?" Merdrid asked. The sound of feet shuffling toward the doorway followed.

Danai quickly removed the pendant and wrapped the cord into a small ball. She was relieved to find the dress had a pocket on the right side. She slipped the stone and cord into the pocket, hoping it would not bulge noticeably, and kept her back to the door. "Yes, Merdrid. I just saw how pretty the dress is on me and I'm being far too vain. I could use a hand tying the ribbon."

Merdrid entered the room and clucked in appreciation. "Yes, yes. That is a perfect fit." Her strong, steady fingers gripped the ribbon and began tightening the lattice. "Tell me if I pull too hard."

Danai stole a look in the mirror and her plain self was back. She worried that the bloodstone might have changed how she looked, and was relieved in part that it had not. Yet, another part of her began to wonder why she looked plain without the stone and so different while wearing it. The stone had also removed many great weights from her that all fit snugly back around her now that the pendant was off. The *vosang*. She imagined that must be the source of what seemed to bind her mind and weigh her down. The pendant pushed it all away. She longed to put it back on, but there was more to figure out first.

Merdrid finished working with the ribbon and stepped back. "Okay, Sis, please turn around so I can get a good look."

Danai turned around slowly, warily. The woman who had helped her father for all these years and been her mentor. The woman who had provided work to Danai, which kept her in a home, with food and clothes. What had this woman done to her? She remembered Kleed's warning that the older woman was not what she seemed. Danai forced herself to look into the other woman's eyes, and tried to keep her expression neutral. Like a puzzle piece clicking into place, Danai believed whatever had been done to her had been done by Merdrid. But why? What Danai longed to do most of all was put the pendant on and see Merdrid for who she really was.

Doubts crept in. What did Danai know about the pendant? Only that which Kleed had told her. Perhaps the pendant made her see what she wanted to see, and made her feel as though she were weighed down with webs of *vosang*. She tried to make her mind believe that it was more logical to trust Merdrid, who had done so many kind things for her family for all those years.

Merdrid had finished looking her over and was staring into her eyes. A twinkle that seemed something other than happiness shone in Merdrid's. Merdrid's smile was also unusual. More unusual than the simple fact that she rarely smiled. That alone was odd given the fact that she nearly lost her mortar and likely had the king's emissary and protector combing the valley for them. Why was Merdrid so happy? Danai also wondered why the men had not shown up at her door yet. Too many questions.

Merdrid's voice was low and serious. "You look breathtaking, Sis. I think you are ready to talk about the cure." The older woman turned to walk into the other room. "Come along, dear. It's time."

As Danai entered the main room, she saw the worktable had been cleared of everything except the mortar and pestle, two black bottles, and an earthen bowl that now contained all of the ingredients that had been prepared. The concoction was a thick brown goo, and Danai tried not to think of what it looked like. She felt sorry for whoever would have to eat it. Perhaps it was to be applied to the skin, she hoped. Her eyes lingered on the bottles and she remembered the potion in the red bottle Merdrid had given her.

The details came back to her. The potion had been an amour potion of some kind. When it took effect, Kleed acted like he loved her, desired her, and would do anything to have her. Then she remembered the kiss. It was her first kiss, and it was to a man she did not really know. She knew she too had been effected by the potion. But it had done more to her than just make her willing to kiss Kleed.

Danai's thoughts were interrupted by Merdrid, who now stood next to the mortar. "Sis, the cure is nearly ready, but I need you to do something, give something of yourself that might sound like a lot to ask. With the Kingsworn in the valley, I fear I will have to move on, so it is well that we have prepared the cure this day."

The reality of what Merdrid had said hit Danai like a blast of winter wind. Whether she trusted Merdrid or not, the older woman had been at the center of her life for five years, and she could not imagine what she would do without Merdrid. She started to object, but couldn't find the words.

"Hush, Sis, let me finish. We both know those men will not give up now that they know I have a bloodstone. Besides, if I can heal the last survivors of the plague, then my work in the valley is complete. You know enough to continue the work of healing in the valley, and I will leave the shop to you."

Danai stood statue still, not knowing what to think.

"Let's get on with the cure then, shall we?" Merdrid asked. Without waiting for an answer, she went on. "The bowl on the table holds all of the ingredients but two. The first is the potion in this bottle." She held up one of the black bottles and swirled the liquid inside with a sweeping motion. "Once I pour the potion in, the last ingredient will need to be added within an hour. If it is not, the cure will sour and lose its efficacy. Once the last ingredient is added, the cure will be stable for a full day, but last no longer than that."

Danai thought of the other people sick in the valley and realized it would take her almost a full day to reach them all. She also knew that a horse or carriage would be useless to reach two of those suffering from the plague, as they lived in the upper reach of the west end of the valley, and a climb was needed to get to their houses. She had taken them the monthly cures herself since Merdrid was unable to climb. She knew she would have to be the one to administer the cure.

"You have done a marvelous job in getting the monthly doses of remedy to those in need. I am sure you realize that with the time constraints we will be under, my body cannot make the trip."

Merdrid paused, looking serious and perhaps a little sad. "That is where the problem lies. The administration of this cure requires the use of a bloodstone and talent in the *vosang*."

While Merdrid paused, her words ignited a firestorm of thought in Danai. Would she have to take the oath on the bloodstone that Merdrid had taken? Could she even do it if she was willing? What impact would making an oath have on her life? Merdrid had warned Danai that she would have to make a sacrifice.

Yet, the question that underlay them all was the one Merdrid asked, "Sis, do you trust me?"

Even as Danai nodded yes, a thread of doubt grew to a strong cord within her. "What must I do, Merdrid?" The sound of her voice was distant in her ears, and she felt numb.

"The only way the cure will reach everyone is if your ability to climb and travel is combined with my talent in the *vosang* in one body. We are going to have to trade places for a while."

"What does that mean?" The numbness was accompanied by a chill that made Danai shudder.

"It means, we both have to enter a covenant, seal it with blood in the mortar, and allow the *vosang* to put my mind in your body and your mind in my body." Merdrid's tone was serious and somber, but there was a hint of eagerness.

"Is that even possible?"

"Yes. But it requires willing sincerity by both of us, and a sacrifice that is balanced on both sides. For myself and the Creators, they will be satisfied that the change will allow me to continue the work I have covenanted I would do. For you, it allows your father and others in the valley you love to be healed and live. There is symmetry in that bargain. Will you do it?" Merdrid's hands rubbed together as she watched Danai.

Danai needed time. She needed to think this through. But time was short and dwindling like the last rays of sunlight on an autumn evening. "How long will we be switched?" Somehow she knew that whatever Merdrid said would be a lie.

"Only for one day, Sis. After I have healed them, we can meet in a safe location and change back." Merdrid's eyes were hawk-like. "You could stay here and care for your father. I have put protections on your home that should keep the Kingsworn away for a while."

Of the many things that bothered Danai about the idea, the one blocking other thought was that Merdrid would have a familiarity with Danai's body that should be reserved for self and spouse alone. Closely following that concern was the realization that she would have that same familiarity with Merdrid's body. Danai could not escape the nagging belief that if the switch worked, she would never go back to her own body. Yet, even if that were true, if it meant saving the lives of eight people, including her father, the price might be worth paying. She looked over at her father, his pitifully weak form lying in bed, wet with sweat, just behind Merdrid. Then, another chilling thought hit her, what if the cure was ineffective or an outright lie. If that was true, then her future was dark as the bottom of a bear's den in winter. Her father would die, her boss would be an outlaw, and she'd have nobody to turn to for help. She felt very alone, abandoned.

"Cheer up, Sis, things will work out just fine," said Merdrid.

"I need to know the truth before I agree to do it." Danai resolved to a course of action and felt some warmth extend out to her limbs.

Merdrid's expression was serious, but her smile remained. "The truth about what?"

Danai folded her arms across her chest and stood tall. "About many things."

Merdrid smiled more broadly. "I thought you trusted me; you just so much as told me so. Perhaps it is you that cannot be trusted. Let me ease your doubts. I will give you the truth to the question that is on your mind right now, and by my blood and the power of the stone, I will give you the rest of the truth after we have entered our covenant. You want to know if the cure will really work. The answer to that question is yes."

Danai studied the older woman's face, trying to discern truth and lie. The best she could tell, Merdrid was telling the truth.

"If you doubt me, why don't you put that pendant on again and I will tell you once more." Merdrid chuckled mirthlessly.

Danai felt like she had been punched in the stomach. Her heart broke at the realization that she no longer knew whether anything she thought she knew about Merdrid was true. She wanted to hold onto it all, but that would be foolish childishness. Danai had defended Merdrid to Kleed. Worse yet, Merdrid knew about the pendant. She wordlessly pulled the stone and leather from her pocket. It was not much shelter from the crumbling of her world around her, but it was something. Her hands trembled as she put the cord over her head. Again, she felt as though the weight of an ox were lifted from her shoulders and strings wrapping all around her body were snipped away. Her mind quickened and she gasped.

Merdrid's smile returned. "Oh, but you are a beautiful young woman, Danai. Ask your question so I can assure you I speak the truth."

Danai could see Merdrid clearly for the first time. The loving, plump apothecant was as much an illusion as was her own plainness. Where a gentle old grandmother just stood, a mean-faced hag of a woman remained. Her body was frail, skin so old and thin that the veins stood out like lines on a map. Her hair was wispy and brittle, devoid of color. Her teeth were most troubling, sickly and jagged. Danai had never seen anyone who looked so old or so terrifying. "Will the cure work?" She gasped, realizing if she traded places with Merdrid, just how much of a sacrifice it would be.

Merdrid's smile showed too many teeth. "Yes, Sis."

The last word had seemed so endearing the past five years, but now sounded like a curse in Danai's ears. A spreading warmth near the pendant let Danai know in her heart that Merdrid's words were true. "Will you administer the cure after we trade?" Danai had to know the answer to that question.

"I kept my promise to give you truth to one question, the one you wanted answered the most, but the rest of the truth comes after we have completed our covenant." Merdrid folded her bony arms and said no more.

Danai was not sure when she had started crying, but felt tears rolling down her cheeks. "If I cannot be sure the cure will be delivered and applied to all of the people from my village, I will not agree to the switch."

"You seem to think that your position in this bargain is superior. But do you consider the fact that a knot of soldiers is at this moment combing the valley not only for me but you? Search your memories now and you will see that those soldiers want to capture you every bit as much as they want to recover the mortar from me." Merdrid's eyes blazed like a flame about to devour a child's wooden crib.

Danai had the sickening feeling that Merdrid's words were true. She searched her memory of the prior night, now free of fog. She remembered vividly all that happened until the moment that she and Kleed kissed. She saw herself and Kleed both falling to the ground. Something in the potion that had drawn them together had ignited when they kissed. She passed out, as did Kleed, but soon after she awakened and stood. She had Kleed's pendant in her hand and carefully tucked it into her belt pouch. The rain fell like a dark curtain all around her. She used the storm as her cloak and found the camp that was nearby. Her memories were not the typical kind that played from her own perspective and were narrated by the thoughts that had been in her mind as the events happened. These memories were like watching a play involving herself and everyone else who appeared in the memories, with none of her own thoughts present. It was as if someone else directed her steps. She was a puppet and someone else pulled the strings, and there was no doubt who the puppet master was. She saw herself enter the emissary's tent, search through his packs, and find the bowl. The emissary returned and caught her with the mortar. He called for help, but she struck him on the head with the heavy stone mortar. The older man fell, blood pouring from the wound on his head. Danai ran from the tent, soldiers in pursuit, and slipped into the dark of the night, losing all pursuers in the storm.

Danai closed her eyes in a quiet prayer that the emissary and Kleed were alive, and asked the Creators to restore each of them to health. She also prayed in her mind to find a way out of this horrible situation. In her mind, she knew that Merdrid had been putting strings on her for a long time, and pulling them.

Merdrid broke the silence. "You see the truth now. You murdered the emissary and the soldiers saw you do it. They search the valley now and will not give up. They want the bowl from me, but from you, the demand will be your life. Deny my request and I will walk away with my mortar and my cure. I may lose out on the chance to trade places with you—you will have your life and your body, but only until the soldiers find you. Then they will take your life, and without the cure, all eight people in this valley suffering from the plague will also die. You can imagine how long you will be safe from Kingsworn searching for Merdrid and her assistant when my wards no longer keep them away. And I imagine young Kleed will be motivated like a bronco with an ember under his saddle to find the girl who stole his bloodstone and murdered his charge. Which of us loses more if our deal is not consummated?"

Danai realized that Merdrid's words rang true. "Please. I have served you for five years without fail. If I give you my body, I know you will not come back. If I give that much, please pledge in the covenant that you will heal all of the sick before you go." Danai realized the beautiful dress she wore was proof that Merdrid intended to do no climbing once the trade was complete. The dress was not a present for Danai, but Merdrid's choice of what she would look like after the trade. Danai refused to consider what Merdrid would do with her body if the switch were made.

The old woman's smile became a smirk. "You know I will not. I will leave this valley within the hour. For your service to me, I will ease your mind two ways. First, fear not that you will be trapped within the form you see now—I have a supply of potion at my shop that will last several years. The potion sustains my life and alters my appearance. I can be the portly Merdrid you know. Or, I should say, you can be her. Second, I will tell you the last ingredient to the cure once the trade is complete, and perhaps I stretched the truth about needing the *vosang* to administer it. The paste will be viable for at least a week, and you simply need to feed it to those who suffer. The dose is one thimbleful. There, I have given you more than I promised. It is my last offer."

Danai's tears flowed freely. "Your lies and deceit are like the leaves on a head of lettuce. I fear that if I accept anything you say, I will end up peeling all the leaves away and find nothing beneath." The trap now sprung seemed inescapable. "But what choice do I have?"

Merdrid nodded solemnly. "There is but one choice—you know what you must do. Let us make the switch, I will deliver the last secret of the cure to you, and I will leave. You can tell the soldiers how I beguiled you, took the bloodstone mortar and the pendant, and fled the valley. They may keep a presence here for a while, but they will have to conclude that it was Danai who was most wicked and the true target they seek. You will be in the clear, with your father and others in the valley restored to health, and you can live the rest of your days working as the valley apothecant, who saved everyone from the blue moth plague."

Danai had already decided she would give her life to save the eight people in the valley. She knew her decision. "I will do it."

"It will take but a moment to prepare." Merdrid reached down into her pack and pulled out a long vial made of dark green glass. It had flakes of some kind within, but Danai could not tell their color through the dark glass. Merdrid continued. "First, you must remove the pendant."

Danai reluctantly pulled the cord over her head and felt the weight of *vosang* lay on her shoulders. The fog returned to her mind, though it was less dense than before. She saw Merdrid as the older woman she knew again, feeling nothing but loathing for her. Danai's fingers shook again as she set the pendant on the table.

Merdrid pulled the stopper out of the vial and shook a few flakes into the bowl of the mortar. The light caught them as they fell, glittering a brilliant gold. Next, Merdrid took up the stout-bladed knife. "Don't worry, Sis; it will only take a little blood." The older woman reached out and grabbed Danai's wrist, pulling her hand over the mortar. Danai did not resist. The blade of the knife flicked against the side of her wrist, stinging like a wasp, and blood started dribbling into the mortar. True to her word, after a few dribbles, Merdrid placed a cloth against the wound and released her grip. Merdrid then added her own blood.

Merdrid then spoke several words in a tongue Danai did not recognize, and she wondered if they were names or a whole different language. Instantly, the room felt colder, despite the fire burning in the stove. Danai was left with the distinct impression that they were not alone. She looked around, but saw no one there.

The air grew thin and chilly; Danai gasped to find breath that satisfied her lungs. Merdrid's words became recognizable and little puffs of fog left her mouth with each syllable. "I make this oath of my own free will, and commit my blood to seal it. By the power of the *vivos sanguine*, my body shall be hers and her body shall be mine. By my oath, I shall make this transfer to continue my work and dedication to your cause throughout all the days that blood may flow in my new body."

Pressure swelled in Danai's head; it ached and throbbed. She nearly fell to the ground, but held onto the tabletop with both hands to stay upright. The pressure within her mind seemed to gather into a single entity, and became Merdrid's consciousness. It was a strong, dark presence, ugly and brutal. She felt violated, like Merdrid was pilfering through her secret thoughts and memories. *"Stop that!"* she thought.

"You need to say your oath out loud, and leave this body. Once you are gone, your memories will be with you." Merdrid's words bit like a venomous snake.

Danai realized something, *"You knew this would work because this is not the first time you have stolen another's body."*

Merdrid's mind dwelled on a memory of this same oath with another girl. Even though she had not thought the words, Danai could see the image for a fleeting moment. That realization led to another. If Merdrid's life were extended for all of Danai's days, she would use those days not to heal, but to take lives and manipulate people to suit her own desires, or the desires of whatever being reached out to them through the bloodstone.

"Say the oath, or I will kill you and your father right now." Merdrid's words stabbed, and her head ached with each syllable.

"What is the last ingredient to the cure?" Danai expected the wave of pain that followed her question. She was not disappointed. Merdrid's mind slammed her consciousness like an anvil falling from the sky. Danai thought she might die that very moment, but she did not. As Merdrid's mind pressed against her own, Danai sought images or thoughts that would betray the answer to the question she had asked. For a split second, she saw the closer of the two black bottles with neat labels in Merdrid's consciousness. As Danai recognized the bottle, Merdrid's thoughts howled and ravaged against her own.

Mentally, Danai curled up into a ball and cried out in thought, *"I will not give up my life to save eight if it means you will spend a lifetime using my body to commit the atrocities I know that you have done and would do again."*

That thought brought up more images, but Danai refused to see them. Whether they came because Merdrid wanted her to see what she had done, was capable of doing, or as an involuntary response to what Danai had said, Danai did not care. She was done letting this beast of a woman control her life. She realized her eyes had been closed. She forced them open and saw Merdrid's face contorted into a mask of rage, mouth in a snarl, teeth bared and gnashing. Her eyes were the most terrifying part about her, they seemed rolled back into her head, showing nothing but the whites.

Danai forced her hands to move, defying the pain ripping through her mind. She grabbed the pendant and tried to raise it.

"No!" howled the older woman. Merdrid lunged over the table with unbelievable speed and force, arcing into the air with her rotund body behind her and bearing down with the stout-bladed knife in her right hand.

Danai was frozen with fear, worrying that her mind would not move her limbs fast enough. All she could do was hold her hands up to ward off the attack, still holding the pendant cord. As Merdrid landed on her, the cord slipped around the old woman's head and the blade of her knife sunk into Danai's left shoulder.

Pain seared into the shoulder and her arm went limp.

Merdrid was up in an instant. Her ancient, hideous form was back and the rage on her face was feral and evil. "You want me to see the truth of anything? I know the truth. You think I need protection from your *vosang*? You have none!" She mocked, spittle spraying with each sentence. Then she stopped, cocking her head to one side.

The coldness in the room receded. The sense of dread and hopelessness lifted a little.

The creature that was Merdrid clawed at the pendant, trying to rip it off her head. Danai still held the cord with her right hand. She held fast and pulled down as Merdrid tried pulling up. The old woman howled and ravaged at Danai, but the younger woman took the blows and scratches. Soon, the attack weakened and waned. The older woman aged before her eyes. Her skin cracked and her eyes seemed to sink into her skull.

Danai coughed and said, "This bloodstone not only shows the truth, but also protects the wearer from the *vosang*. Apparently, it protects you even from your own."

Before Danai had finished the words, Merdrid's shell of a body crumpled to the ground beside her, all the *vosang* extending her days beyond what nature would allow sundered.

Danai's body ached and stung where she had been scratched and battered. Her shoulder pulsed with sharp pain. The knife was still buried in the flesh. Even though she hurt all over like she had never hurt before, her mind was clear and her own. It was free of fog, and Merdrid was gone from there too. She gripped the handle of the knife and pulled it quickly out. The pain dropped her to the ground, and she stanched the flow of blood with the cloth that had been wrapped around her wrist.

Danai looked down at the dress and laughed. It felt odd to laugh, but that was the sound coming out of her. She would never do the tavaranga in that dress. The fabric was scratched, torn, and soiled with blood and other things she could not immediately identify. Danai wadded the stanching cloth into a ball and placed it under the fabric of the dress covering her shoulder, to hold it in place.

Panic gripped her for a moment, and she checked the worktable for the cure and the black bottle she needed. With relief, she saw them still on the tabletop. Merdrid must have leaped completely over the table, without touching anything on it. Small, tender mercy, she thought.

Danai was less pleased to see the mortar still in place, holding flecks of gold suspended in a mixture of blood. She considered throwing the whole thing in the fire of the stove, but she really did not want to touch it at all. Using her right hand, Danai lifted the black bottle to her mouth and bit into the cork. With a turn of her head, she pulled the cork free and poured some of the liquid into the earthen bowl holding the pasty concoction. The liquid smelled of oil and spices. She did not know the exact amount to add, but relied on instinct to decide when she should stop pouring. It took several tries and a lot of wrangling using her knee and body to pin the bowl, but eventually Danai was able to stir the mixture thoroughly with a wooden spoon.

After digging through Merdrid's pack, Danai found the dosing spoons, and chose the one equivalent to a thimble. Merdrid always had unusual standards of measurements, Danai thought absently. Danai scooped out a spoonful and took it to her father. She was unable to rouse him to wake, but did prop his head in an upright position and slipped the cure into his mouth. She carefully poured a little water in, and hoped he would not choke.

Hard knocks at the entryway nearly made her drop the water bottle. She looked and saw cracks of light slipping through the door, which would buckle under any more strain.

"Open for the Kingsworn!" A deep voice beyond the door demanded.

Pangs of fear froze her. Was it Kleed? Did she hope it was him or not? She could not think clearly, but it had nothing to do with the *vosang* this time. "Give me a couple seconds. I am coming." With care, she negotiated the room, now cluttered with things Merdrid had brought, and Merdrid's dead body. She said a silent prayer before reaching the door.

Kleed was about to pound on the door again when Danai pulled it open. His face, still handsome, but now fixed with stern purpose, took her in from head to toe. She then recalled how she looked in the low-cut dress, tattered in places, with a wadded cloth soaked in blood bundled at the shoulder, and wounds covering her front. Kleed's voice was frosty. "What is going on in there?"

Danai's nerves hindered her mouth from forming words, but slowly they came. "You can come in . . . I will explain everything." She meant it. She wanted to clear everything up, and face whatever consequences followed. Her only fear was what would become of her father.

Once inside, Kleed ushered in several other soldiers. None of them were prepared for the chaos they met—clutter, death, and illness—and the room reeked of smoke from the woodstove, incense, pungent herbs, and roots, combined with the odor Merdrid's body was exuding. On the whole, it was somewhere between unpleasant and disturbing.

Danai tried to explain about Merdrid giving her a potion that was infused with *vosang* that made Kleed and her behave most peculiarly the night before, and then rendered her unconscious, allowing Merdrid to control her actions thereafter. She got no further than that when Kleed stopped her.

Kleed shook his head, "I would like nothing more than to believe that story, but I witnessed what you did to me yourself. By your own oath, you swore for Merdrid's honesty and said you were aligned to her unconditionally. Now you want to pin all of the evil that you did on her. My gullibility was stretched past its limit last night and will not be tested today. We are going to gather everything up from this shack and take you and whatever that is"—he indicated the husk of Merdrid's body on the floor—"back to Brasin City and sort this out at the Grand Court." He refused to meet Danai's eyes, looking away contemptuously.

A weak, whisper of a voice spoke from the corner, "Why don't you put your pendant back on and see if what she tells you rings true." It was Danai's father. She hurried to the bed, tears flowing once again at seeing him speak. He was incredibly frail, but looked better than he had in five years.

The idea was sound. Moments later, Danai helped Kleed pull the bloodstone from the head of Merdrid's corpse. Kleed insisted the leather and stone be washed in boiling water, but while they waited, Danai's father related the story of what happened once Danai returned at dawn. He told how Merdrid had laid a trap for her. He even told about the scrying the old woman had done in the middle of the night in the silver bowl of water. Everything he said confirmed Danai's accounting. Once the pendant was adequately cleansed, the story was told again by both Danai and her father. It was late when they finished.

While they talked, the other soldiers put the room to order, cleaning out the mortar and securing the potions and concoctions in Merdrid's pack. Danai did not object to them taking whatever they wanted, with the exception of the cure. While Danai's father spoke, Danai was able to change out of the dress and into her last clean outfit. She needed to do laundry, and committed to doing so if she was not arrested. The soldiers even helped dress her wounds after she changed. The first good news she received was that the emissary was alive. His wound was serious, but not life threatening. He waited in the carriage outside of the home, resting in the company of two soldiers.

By the time both Danai and her father had completed telling Kleed everything, he was convinced they told the truth. Merdrid's long use of a bloodstone was clear, and Danai's lack of any use of *vosang* was irrefutable. Danai decided she liked the way he looked at her by the time they were finished talking. He took a break to relate his oral report to the emissary and let him decide what to do with Danai.

She waited a long while, enjoying being by her father's side. She helped her father drink some water and eat a little bread. Oh, how she had missed him. He was about to fall asleep when he opened his eyes and looked up into hers. "You did well, my beautiful Pugnox."

She even missed that horrible nickname. "I love you too, Father." But he was already asleep.

She was fighting off sleep herself when Kleed returned. "We will carry Merdrid's remains to the edge of town and burn them. Some practitioners of these dark works leave threads that extend beyond death. Burning the body may help sever those. Then we will leave the valley and return the bloodstone to the king. You will have no charges set against you. However, I may have to come back and ask additional questions if the examiners request it."

"I would welcome you back. Thank you." Danai realized she meant it.

As the soldiers carried the body through the doorway, led by Kleed, something fell from the clutched hand. The soldiers did not see it. At first, Danai thought it was the knife that had stabbed her shoulder. Then, she remembered pulling the knife out herself. When she walked over, she saw the familiar gold flecks in dark gray stone of the pestle. She considered calling out to the soldiers, but did not. She eventually put the pestle away in a box that was put in a drawer. She would decide what she wanted to do with it later.

About Brendon Taylor

Brendon is an attorney during the workweek, a writer when he can find time, a food and camping enthusiast often, a frustrated Miami Dolphins fan each fall, and a loving husband and father all of the time. He has been at Merrill & Merrill, chartered in Pocatello, Idaho, since he became an attorney in 1999, after graduating from Washburn Law School in Topeka, Kansas. He was an original founder of Deep Magic in 2002 and has written many articles, short stories and contracts since its inception.

IMPERIAL GHOSTS

By Arinn Dembo | 13,000 words

THE SEVERAN FUNERAL Garden was the planet's largest public park. Bordered on all sides by the imperial city of Nova Roma, its grounds extended for several hundred kilometers, featuring ornamental terrain of every kind. In its green commons were thousands of monuments to the dead. Standing tombs stood shoulder to shoulder with shrines and reliquaries. Fountains murmured alone in empty clearings. The dark forests were crowded with stone angels and obelisks to mark the passing of royalty.

It was a fine playground for a young empress, with a million places to hide. On one particular morning, a child crept through the weeds, hardly stirring a blade of grass as she prowled on her hands and knees. She was stalking an old man, who had taken shelter in the shade of the trees. A born hunter, she came silent and deadly on his right flank: the daisies nodded wisely around her head, stirred more by the morning breeze than by her passage.

The old man watched her from the corner of his eye as she circled through the shrubbery behind him, waiting for her pounce.

"Boo!" she crowed, leaping from the shadows.

"Awk!" The old man clapped a hand to his chest, in the time-worn gesture of heart-clutching terror, which all old men know.

It was most gratifying. "I scared you!"

"You most certainly did." The old man hid a smile.

"Did you fink I was a ghost?" She was only four, and still struggling with the fricative sounds of the old Imperial tongue.

"Oh yes." It was the truth.

"I came here to see the ghosts too. But all I found was you!"

"I'm sorry to disappoint you. Most of the real ghosts sleep during the day. They only come out at night."

"Oh." She squinted up through the boughs of the trees. "I'm not allowed to stay out after dark." The tapestry of spring leaves overhead was still broken here and there, scattering cool light over her face like silver coins.

The old man looked up as well, pleased by the breeze and the birds high in the tangled branches. It was a good morning . . . and the garden was far more wonderful with her in it.

She turned to him at last, remembering her manners. "What's your name?"

"I am Tiberius." They had met before, although she would not remember the occasion.

"I'm Cleona." Even at her age, her voice rang with pride.

He inclined his head graciously. "I am very pleased to make your acquaintance."

She cocked her head at him, eyes narrowing with calculation. "Are you one of my uncles?"

"I suppose so. My sister and your father are related, although distantly." Tiberius met her level gaze without flinching. "Why do you ask?"

Although there was very little resemblance between them otherwise, the eyes of the old man and the little girl were very much the same: bright copper and piercingly intelligent. "I have lots of uncles. And cousins." Her gaze was steady and grave. "Mommy says I shouldn't trust them. Some of them are bad."

"Really? That's a shame."

"Are you one of the *bad* uncles?"

He smiled ruefully. "I suppose that would depend upon whom you ask, my dear. My own nephew was not fond of me. I mean you no harm, however—which does set me apart from most of your relations, I suspect."

"Someday I'll be empress. Everyone will want to sit in my chair." She paused. "I can't let them, though."

"Yes. This is very true." He patted his old stone bench, cracked by ivy and mottled with lichen. "This one is better. Far more comfortable."

"Really?" She eyed the bench dubiously. "It doesn't look better."

"Why not try it?" He stood up, offering the bench with an elegant half bow.

Cleona said nothing. With a very serious expression, she climbed up onto the offered bench and sat. She made a pretty picture there. Someone had given her a miniature naval uniform to wear, brass buttons shining and gold piping along the collar and sleeves. Her boots swung a few inches above the ground; she looked down and rocked back and forth a few times, testing the feel of cool granite.

"What do you think?"

"It's all right." Her tone was thoughtful. "Hard, like chairs in a temple. I think it would hurt if I had to sit here a long time."

"The throne is much the same." When she opened her mouth to protest, he held up a hand to forestall her. "It *looks* soft, Cleona— that's why everyone wants to sit there. But looks can be deceiving. That golden chair grows harder the longer you sit—and it's sometimes very hot as well."

"Your chair won't *ever* get hot, Uncle. It's *very* cold." She looked up at him, curious. "Even though you were sitting here a long time. Why didn't it get warm?"

He stood in the shade of the tree and held out one of his dark hands toward her, palm up and open. "Take my hand, Cleona, and you will understand."

She hopped down off the bench and went to him, very slowly. Some instinct made her stop a few feet away; she reached for his extended fingers from a good distance.

Her little fingers flickered as they passed through his, disappearing within the seemingly solid boundary of his milky flesh. Her eyes went wide and her mouth popped open; she snatched her hand back and stared at her fingers in disbelief, as if they had somehow betrayed her.

When she looked up at him again, still gaping in astonishment, Tiberius raised one eyebrow and smirked.

"Boo!"

The little girl ran away yelling. It was most gratifying.

* * *

Many years passed before the child came back. When she did, she was taller, and she carried a heavy book in her arms. The play uniform of a little girl had been traded for the tight-fitting suit of a real military cadet, and her hair had darkened from the pale yellow wool of early childhood to neat cornrows of dark summer gold. The strands closest to her brown face were plaited neatly and tucked behind her ears.

When she saw him, standing on the broken path beneath the trees, she stood her ground. "Hello, old ghost."

"Hello, young niece."

"You can't hurt me." She was still afraid. She took a slow step toward him, holding the book against her washboard chest as though it were an aegis of life.

"True," he agreed. "Not directly, at any rate."

"I've read about you." The sound of her own voice seemed to steady her. "You're nothing to be afraid of—only a trick of the light. You may move and talk and seem to live . . . but you're not alive. Not really."

His eyes twinkled with amusement. "Is that so?"

She faltered. "You're not a person . . . j-just the echo of a person."

Tiberius made a sour face. "Are we having a conversation, child, or are you holding a lecture?" He made an impatient beckoning gesture with one hand. "Let's have a look at this book of yours. Sounds as if it's full of hogwash."

Still young enough to be obedient to her elders—even the dead ones—she held out her prize.

Tiberius laughed. "Come now—you know that I can't hold it, dear. Show me the cover, please." She turned the unwieldy tome over in her arms and he leaned forward intently. "*The Imperial Ghosts*," he read aloud. "*A Walking Tour of the Famous Funeral Gardens of the Severans*. The date escapes me . . . I never could fully grasp the new calendar."

She stepped away from him again, folding the book back up in her arms. "There are three shades named Tiberius listed; I came here today to find out which one you are. But I suppose that if you predate the current calendar, you can only be Tiberius the Third . . ."

"I'm afraid you're mistaken." He cocked his head, glancing at the spine of the book again. "The author of your guide—Diodorus, is it?—has apparently misled you."

Her eyes narrowed with distrust. "How so?"

Tiberius turned and walked away through the trees, hands clasped behind his back. When the girl didn't immediately follow, he looked back over his shoulder. "Coming?"

She hesitated. "All right."

She picked her path over the broken pavement carefully, following him up out of the dark trees and into a wild hillside meadow.

Tiberius waded through the sunlit grass ahead of her, the folds of his simple robe gathered in one hand, and made his way to the crest of the hill.

Someone had built a sundial at the summit, a great flat disk of silver under the open sky. The standing arm, which had once told the hours, was bent, a thick wedge of steel folded down and melted, but the hours of the day were still deeply incised into the base.

"We can talk here." Tiberius sat down between the eleventh hour and the stroke of noon.

The girl sat down cross-legged between two and three o'clock. "Good. Tell me what's wrong with my book, then."

The old man laughed. "Straight to the point! Fair enough. In the first place, there are more than three Tiberiuses in the garden of your ancestors. There are actually eight of us, if memory serves."

"Eight? How so?"

He smiled, looking away down the green slope. "Your great-grandfather was Tiberius the Twelfth, was he not? A good man and a middling emperor. One of the last Severans to be buried in the garden. He's in one of those little tombs down there."

He pointed to a line of strangely geometric mounds at the foot of the hill. Cleona sat up straighter, shielding her eyes; the white marble pyramids were wound so tightly with kudzu that they looked more like tiny tropical mountains than anything built by men.

"He rises very rarely. And nowhere near here, of course. I've seen him once or twice by the waterfall holding a reader in his hand."

Cleona looked down at the cover of her text. "He must have died after this book was written. It *is* over two hundred years old."

"We also have Tiberius the Seventh and his cousin Tiberius the Eighth. They played here as children—I still hear their laughter on the night of the winter festival." He cleared his throat. "A tragic story, that. Turbulent times. . . . Neither of the boys ruled for more than a year." The old man crossed his arms suddenly, as if he were cold, although the summer afternoon around him sang with heat. "I remember the night they brought the little one to the garden," he muttered vaguely, as if to himself. "There's nothing more terrible than a tiny coffin in a shallow grave."

Silence followed for several moments, which the girl finally broke. "You said eight Tiberiuses."

"That I did. Tiberius the Tenth was lost in one of the colonial rebellions, but someone built a monument for him at the western gate. It was cleverly done; the architect saw the place where his ghost appeared and built the shrine around the haunting. There was a reflecting pool lined with colored tiles; when you stood close and looked down into it, you could see the gas giant that swallowed his ship, just as if you were looking down from a low orbit."

"Sounds beautiful."

"It was. He used to appear there on summer evenings, reenacting his daily exercises. Crowds would gather at the gate to watch him. Tiberius Chilo was a great martial artist. When he danced his kata across the water, it was something to see."

"Can you take me there?" her eyes sparkled eagerly. "I've read about his campaigns—he was a fine commander."

"I could." He shrugged sadly. "But the pool is long dry, and the tiles have all fallen now; his ghost is hardly more than a flicker these days."

"Oh." Her golden lashes dropped. "That's a shame."

"It is," he agreed mildly. He crossed one bony leg over the other and sat back at his ease, fingers laced around one knee. "Now . . . how many would that be so far?"

"Four. And I know about Tiberius the Third. His burial chamber is supposed to be one of the biggest in the garden."

The old man made a face. "Yes, it is. A horrid little man, Tiberius Orthrus. He had to make that vault of his extravagant. He wanted to take it all with him when he went." He pointed his sharp chin at the book in her lap. "If there's any truth at all in that thing, you'll know that his reign was a bloody disaster—and never more so than when he lay dying. He couldn't bear the thought that anyone might enjoy his possessions when he was gone. He had everything that wouldn't fit into his tomb destroyed. It was an appalling waste."

"What do you mean?"

"Every beast in his menagerie was butchered, even though he wanted only the rarest specimens to join him in the grave. Hundreds of his servants were poisoned, but only fifty were dressed and mounted to serve him after death." He smiled to himself. "On the day they buried him, they tried to strangle all his concubines as well . . . but his wife put a stop to that, thank the gods."

The girl leaned forward, pleased. "She was my namesake, Cleona the First! Where did you hear that story? There aren't any concubines in *my* books."

The old man gave her a lopsided grin. "No, I don't imagine so. Royal historians don't usually chronicle royal scandals, unless they want to part company with their heads." His bright eyes flashed with amusement. "And it *was* something of a scandal, you know, when the sixteen-year-old new empress refused to obey her husband's wishes, even while his ghost stood by wringing his hands and blustering about postmortem retribution. It was even more scandalous when she married off all those women to landed nobles over the next few years." Cleona's eyes widened at this, and he winked at her merrily. "Cleona always said that she was repaying a favor—that the concubines had done her a great kindness when her husband was alive. I expect that they kept Orthrus out of her bed."

"But . . . how did she persuade her nobles to marry commoners?"

Tiberius laughed. "Oh, they didn't take much persuading, my dear! Orthrus had fine taste, and half of his intended victims had been culled from the noble families. They made stunning, accomplished wives . . . and even if a man was inclined to disobey the royal edict, how could he turn down a bride deemed fit for the emperor? It would be a dangerous insult to the throne!"

"I never knew any of this." She shook her head. "Amazing."

"Yes, she was. I admired her a great deal." He closed his eyes and turned his face toward the sun. "Cleona always had an eye for situations that could be turned to her advantage."

"She was only empress for fifteen years, though." The girl was clearly disappointed.

The old man chuckled again. "Oh, her reign was considerably longer than that, my dear! Don't be fooled by the superficial details of succession. Cleona held power in her own name for fifteen years, in her son's name for close to fifty, and in her grandson's for another twenty after that. The poor man cried like a child at her funeral— he was terrified to rule the empire without her."

Cleona giggled. "Really?"

"Really." He yawned. "Now, where was I?"

"Tiberius the Tenth," she said promptly.

"Ah yes. Well, Tiberius the Sixth and Ninth are also here in the garden; they were laid to rest in the family catacombs. The entrance to those passages collapsed four hundred years ago, however, and the area is badly overgrown. No one could find it today . . . unless I were to show them where to look."

She laughed. "Well, that's seven . . . but you still haven't said which Tiberius *you* are, old ghost."

He met her eyes, no longer smiling. "I thought you would have guessed by now. Being a student of history. But we will make formal introductions, if you insist."

The old man stood up and faced her, planting his bare feet in the grass. When he drew himself up to his full height, the girl paled. It was a frightening transformation; in one breath he went from an old man in his dressing gown to a white-haired wolf, captured for eternity in the winter of his life. He was a legend, a man to be feared . . . and when he put on the grim mask of authority again, she knew him right away. She'd seen the same stern face many times in marble, and even stamped in gold.

"Oh no." Her voice was hushed with horror. "You must be—"

He cut her off with the tiny formal bow of imperial courtesy. "Tiberius Marcus Severan. Also known as Tiberius Atroxus and—"

"Tiberius the Great," she finished. She stood up, knees shaking, and backed slowly away from him. "You're the Tiberius who—"

"Yes, yes," he interrupted testily. He sat back down on the sundial, turning away from her—a weary old man once more. "No need for a catalog of my crimes. I'm sure the bloody tales have lost nothing in the telling, even in your generation."

"No. They certainly haven't." She hesitated. "I've known about you since I was six years old. My father told me the story when he executed my uncle Kaeso."

Tiberius shook his head. "Charming. Still the family ogre . . ."

"No, no—it wasn't like that. My father admires you. He told me that I shouldn't be afraid to follow your example, if I have to. He says you don't live long as emperor unless you're willing to cut a few throats . . ."

"Oh my. Better and better—I've become the patron saint of imperial fratricide." The old man put his face in his hands, and his shoulders trembled with some suppressed emotion. "If your father follows my example, my dear, I'd step lightly in years to come. You never know when he'll decide it's *your* throat that needs cutting."

She waited a few moments before speaking again. "So. Is it all true? What they say about you?"

He sighed heavily. "Probably. I don't know exactly what you've heard, but you're young yet; most of my nephew's riper fabrications are unfit for such tender ears. For the record, however—in case you hear differently—I was never a rapist or a cannibal."

She stood quietly for a time, and the song of cicadas grew loud in the silence. "You're very lucky."

The old man turned to look at her, incredulous. "How so?"

"You're here to defend yourself." She came and sat down beside him. "You're not at the mercy of history."

He sat for a long time, back bowed. "I'm not at the mercy of *historians*. History is another matter."

He was talking to himself, however. By the time he looked up again, she had gone, and the meadow grass was brown and pinched by cold, poking up in tufts from a blanket of dingy snow.

* * *

On a pleasant autumn evening the child returned, emerging from the trees just as the first star appeared. Fifteen years old, she was rising like bamboo. Her corona of rust-colored hair had been cut close to the scalp, and her severe uniform could not hide the march of time. The gangly child she had been was steadily retreating before the tall, vigorous woman she would become—a bittersweet sight for an old man who had first loved her as a toddler chasing butterflies.

"Hello, Uncle." Nervously she tugged the hem of her jacket down, then reached up to touch the two bronze tabs of rank on her collar, as if to be sure they were in place—an unconsciously military gesture. He had seen it many times in junior officers waiting for a review. "I need your help."

"Hello, Niece." Sitting on the edge of a dry fountain, Tiberius looked up into her eyes. "How did you find me here?"

She stopped, brow creased by a slight frown, and looked over her shoulder at the dark forest behind her. "I'm not sure. I wanted to see you, and—"

"It doesn't matter." He rose from his seat. "What help can I give you today?"

"I'd like you to show me a way out of here." She stepped forward eagerly. "A secret way that only ghosts know."

He raised an eyebrow. "And what use would you make of such an egress?"

She put her gloved hands in her jacket pockets, but not before he saw the glint of fire and gold. "Does it matter?"

"Probably not. But I am curious. And I'm afraid it's against my nature to give away information for free."

She rolled her eyes. "You're a Severan, all right."

"Of course." He paused for a moment. "This is not the place to escape your family, Cleona. Quite the opposite."

She kicked at the fallen leaves viciously, sending up a shower of purple and brown. "I'm choking to death in that palace, Uncle. I have to get out. The new security measures are driving me mad. Everywhere I go, a dozen eyes are watching me." She flung out her open hand, encompassing the whole garden with a contemptuous gesture. "This is the only place I'm allowed to be alone—and there are still guards posted outside all the gates."

He nodded. "You've tried bribes, of course?"

"Of every kind."

"Threats?"

"Only the ones I could carry out quickly." She shook her head. "Believe me, old man—you were not my first choice!"

He smiled blandly. "And what pressing business do we have in the city, may I ask?"

"That's none of your affair."

"Ah. A lover, then." She was wise enough to avoid his eyes, but he saw the flicker of light beneath her lashes. "Come now, Cleona. If you hope to hide this sort of thing in the future, you'll have to do better than that. You're as easy to read as a child's primer . . . even for an old ghost like me."

"You're not just any old ghost, Tiberius Marcus." Her look was sour. "No one else has guessed—I'm sure of that."

"Oh really? How long has this little romance been going on?"

A wind stirred in the trees, and the rattle of dry leaves nearly drowned her soft reply. "Since the spring."

"Mm-hmm. And the new security measures at the palace—when did these begin?"

"Two months ago, when I went back to the academy." She turned and looked him in the eye. "I know what you're going to say, but you're wrong. My father is not the emperor you were."

"Perhaps not. But he is your father, which gives him a distinct advantage." He shook his head. "If Glycon has chosen to pretend ignorance, he's a subtler man than you believe. But rest assured, child—he knows about this little affair of yours."

"Impossible."

Tiberius did not dignify that with a response. Instead he turned and strolled down a narrow corridor of thorns, leaving the fountain behind him. Although darkness was falling, his body was still very bright, as if he were standing in the full light of day. Ash-winged moths circled his wooly head, a fluttering crown; his glow was so strong that it drew insects like a flame.

Cleona followed close on his heels. "We were very careful," she insisted. "We never met in public. We were never seen together. The room was—"

He rounded on her abruptly, cutting her off. "Enough, girl. You'll be empress someday; it's time you learn to lie to others, not yourself."

Her jaw worked, biting down on her first reply, but her gaze never wavered. "Very well." Her voice was clipped short by anger. "We'll assume you're right, even if you aren't: my father knows. And making me a prisoner in his house—that would be his subtle way of telling me he doesn't approve?"

"Yes. I believe you have the gist of it. He doesn't approve, or he thinks it's gone on long enough—it all comes to the same thing." Tiberius turned and walked away again.

She came after him doggedly, hissing curses as the brambles whipped her face. "It's no use running from me, Uncle! I'm going to keep up—ow, bloody hell!—regardless of where you go."

Tiberius pressed his lips into a harsh line and kept moving. The path took several sharp corners as he went, through tunnels of knitted thorns. After a bewildering series of turns, a ruby-red glow began to leak through the black leaves of the hedge; there was an open space ahead. Tiberius stepped out into the clearing and nearly vanished, swallowed by a rolling fog the color of blood.

Cleona stumbled out after him and grinned, as if she'd just beaten him at some child's game. "Topiary maze! But it needs trimming." Looking around her, she seemed to take in the crimson mist for the first time. "Where are we?"

He pointed upward, where the fog swirled thick against a strangely curving ceiling, like smoke in a glass. "The Red Temple. The heart of the garden."

She reached out and tried to touch the canopy with her hand; the tips of her fingers disappeared, and then reappeared as she quickly pulled them back. "Strange. What is it?"

"A sheet of energy. They called it a baldachin, in my day. Very few people had them, even then; they are relics of the First Empire."

"Interesting. What does it do, exactly?"

"This one is fairly harmless—it only keeps out prying eyes," Tiberius replied. "Light and heat pass through from above, but cannot pass through from below. It has no effect on physical objects or living things—but I always feel a tingle as I duck under it."

"A useful device." She passed her hand through it again. "Why would someone waste it here, in the middle of a cemetery?"

"To protect a very special place. One which would otherwise be visible from the air, when strangers flew over the city at night."

Cleona looked around her. "Most definitely. Where's all the light coming from?"

"Go see for yourself."

She walked slowly past him, moving toward the source of the red glow. There was a little shrine there, its back set against the black briars; the red light was spilling forth from its columns and walls. Moving closer, she could see a whole structure built from a radiant stone, which glowed the bright vermilion of eyelids closed against the sun.

In the portico of the building, four caryatids served as columns, each an exquisitely lifelike image of a woman in a flowing gown. Every sculpture was of the same lady, but she had been captured in different moods: once in a laughing dance, her supple arms entwined above her head; once in reflection, a small bird perched on her finger; once with a silent word of welcome hanging on her lips; once with hands crossed over her breasts, her head bowed in grief.

As if in a dream, Cleona climbed the steps toward the stone women; she took off one of her black leather gloves and touched the vivid cheek of the nearest with her brown hand.

"Warm," she breathed. "And the patterns . . ." Upon closer inspection, the shining stone was veined with milky pink and deep maroon, mottled with whorls of crimson.

Turning, she saw that Tiberius had come up behind her. "Is it really—?"

"Yes. Heartstone marble. Several tons of the stuff." He pointed to her still-gloved hand, half-hidden behind her back. "I thought you might like to see it, since you wear a bit of heartstone yourself."

She gave him a sad smile and pulled off the second glove, letting a golden bracelet dangle freely from her wrist. "I *am* transparent. I should have known better than to hide anything from you, Tiberius."

"A gift from your lover?" The bracelet was a slender chain of gold, set with two tiny red beads; they shone brightly against the black fabric of her sleeve.

She looked down at the pearls of pink light, touching them with her fingertips. "Yes. These little things cost him a fortune." For a moment her face shone brighter, flushed with its own incandescent flame. "You understand the symbol?"

Tiberius nodded gravely. "Two hearts aflame. A very eloquent gift. Has your father seen it?"

"He might have. If his spies have found all my hiding places." She lowered her wrist and looked at him squarely. "Why?"

"It would explain a great deal. Consider the nature of heartstone. The rock absorbs energy from the sun during the day, storing it within; at night, it releases that energy and gives us the heat and light we prize. But what happens if the stone is always kept in a dark place, away from the light?"

She dropped her eyes. "It doesn't glow. It goes cold and black."

"It may be that your bracelet has more than one meaning. It's a rare and precious gift—but loses its fire if you keep it hidden. Love can be the same: thriving in the open, dying in the dark."

"No." Her voice was steady, but her eyes were troubled. "I'm sure he never meant to say that."

"Perhaps he didn't—but if I was your father, I'd worry. Is the boy from a poor family, by any chance?"

Her lashes trembled. "Why does that matter?"

"You said it yourself, Cleona; the bracelet cost him a fortune. Only a very rich man could afford to buy such a trinket casually. If he isn't the spoiled son of wealthy parents—and I can see by the look on your face that he isn't—he must have sacrificed a great deal to give you such a gift. So one must ask: what did he hope to gain?"

Her smile was strained. "Are you the ghost of an emperor, or a monk?"

He rolled his eyes, making no reply.

"I'm cold. I don't want to talk about this anymore." She sat down on the steps of the shrine, drawing her knees up to her chest, and wrapped her arms around them.

He studied her carefully. After several seconds of silence, he spoke. "I can't tell what you're thinking, Cleona."

She raised her eyes, glittering in the red glow. "I think you're a horrible, suspicious old man. And that you've forgotten what love is . . . if you ever knew."

"I won't deny it." He walked past her, up the steps of the temple. "In life, I was the living god to four hundred billion souls. If I loved anyone, it was my people."

"Loved your power over them."

"Power." He held the word in his mouth like old wine. "Yes. I know much more about power than love." He paused on the top step. "If you're cold, we can go inside."

"It's sealed with a solid slab. I don't think I'm strong enough to move it."

"It doesn't take strength." He extended his shining brown fingers toward the door. "Can you read Solari?"

"A little. My father forced me to learn it when I was eight." She made a face. "Don't ask me why; I've always hated those old dead languages."

"Come here."

She stood and peered at the door. The inscription was so worn that it would have been invisible, if not for the ghostly light of Tiberius; his bright hand dimmed the marble, teasing it back to sleep just enough to bring out the faint shadow of the letters.

"Read it aloud."

"But some of the words are gone." She glanced at him, reluctant. "I can't make them all out."

"The last line is all that matters . . . the others are only there for the sake of art."

Haltingly, she repeated what was still legible of the verse, fingers trailing along the lines as she struggled to pronounce the archaic words.

"I was a child beneath her touch
A man when breast to breast we clung,
A spirit when her spirit looked through me
A god when . . . our lifeblood ran . . .
Fire within fire, desire in deity."

Something shifted within the wall, and the door began to slide, screaming in protest as it ground against dry bearings. Cleona slipped in before it was half-open, shrugging through the narrow crack like a cat.

Tiberius hastily followed. Within the tomb, the red glow was much deeper and darker, the veins of stone bright as the cracks in cooling lava. It was a single room, empty except for a plain heart-stone altar. On the broad platform, a shining man and woman lay sleeping, curled up nude together—the golden woman lying on her side, her head pillowed on her lover's arm, while the man cupped her with his polished obsidian body and wound his fingers into her hair.

Cleona bent close, her pale face underlit by the radiance of the sleepers. "They're not breathing." She spoke softly, as if afraid to wake them. "Who are they, Tiberius?"

"I don't know. The man was a Severan emperor. He wears the crest." He pointed to the pendant hanging from the man's neck, threaded on a heavy chain of gold.

"She died before him," the girl said suddenly. "He built the tomb for her, in grief. It must have taken a very long time—years to gather all the stone, years more to have it carved so perfectly—but when he finally passed, he had himself buried here beside her." She rested her white hand on the dark tabletop, gentle and reverent. "The two of them are lying together under this—just as we see them here."

"Perhaps." He was shaken by the conviction in her voice. "We can't know. The two of them are too ancient . . . even when I was a child, none of the ghosts in the garden remembered their names."

She looked up suddenly, and he saw the glistening tears on her face. "Help me, Uncle. Please. I know you don't understand, but I have to see him." She put a hand to her chest, her voice rising in pitch like a tortured harp string being wound tighter and tighter around its peg. "I've never felt a pain like this—I'm dying . . ."

"Don't . . ." He reached for her, and she stumbled back, startled. Tiberius withdrew his hand slowly, still holding out the open palm. "Don't cry, Cleona." He hesitated, awkward and ashamed. "I'm sorry."

Her eyes were enormous golden coins, brimming with tears.

"Of course you must go to him. Some feelings . . . are too strong to be denied." He seemed to be speaking to himself. "Let me show you the way out. I never meant to torment you."

"Uncle! Thank you, thank you, thank you!" She rushed toward him, as if to catch him up in her arms. For a moment he could almost feel her embrace—wet cheek pressed into his hollow chest, the smell of warm clean hair—but when he looked down, she had run right through him. There was nothing to do but turn and follow her out into the dark.

* * *

Winter came early one year, and brought war with it. For several nights running, the skies above the garden blazed with battle, and the snow shimmered with a thousand colors of flame.

Tiberius found her on the eastern wall, standing at the parapet of a crumbling tower. She was dressed all in white, a tight-fitting environment suit and a long winter coat; her hair was coiled beneath a cloth cap. He admired her profile silently for a few seconds, dark and still against the burning sky; the imperial crest was hooked to a collar under her chin, sparkling.

"Your father has died." Tiberius observed. "Congratulations—or condolences. Whichever you prefer."

She didn't look away from the battle. "Hello, Uncle. I'll accept the condolences, for now. It's a bit early for anything else. Half the empire has risen against me."

Another voice spoke in the shadows, sly and dripping with irony. "Oh, he knows what that's like. Don't you, 'Uncle'?"

The old man turned toward the corner of the room. "Decimus. Why?"

"War." The speaker slouched out into the light, smiling. He was young, no more than thirty, black and beautiful, his lean body dressed in a close-fitting red shirt and breeches. His face would have been handsome, were it not so cruel. He had large bronze eyes and sharply sculpted cheekbones, his broad sensual mouth framed by a well-cut mustache and beard. "Wars and fires always wake me. I sleep the rest of the time—everything else is so intolerably boring."

Cleona had turned swiftly, her pistol drawn; she held it pointed at the center of the stranger's chest. "Do you know him, Tiberius?"

"Know me? He grew me from a bean." Decimus turned back to Tiberius and laughed out loud. "You should see your face, old man! She's a pretty piece of stuff. Who is she? Another of your protégés?"

"Is he dead?" Cleona asked. Her voice was hard as ice; Tiberius smiled silently beside her. She cocked the ancient pistol and it whined eagerly, building up a charge. "If not, he soon will be."

"Oh, I'm dead all right," Decimus said bitterly. "Uncle Tiberius saw to that."

The old man shook his head in disgust. "That was your doing, boy—no one else's."

Cleona holstered her pistol and turned her back. "You ghosts can take your squabbles elsewhere. I have worries of my own."

" 'You ghosts'?" Decimus stepped toward her, head tilted to the side quizzically. The old man moved to bar his way, but he wasn't quick enough; in a twinkling, the man in red was beside her, peering down into her face.

"I remember you now." He bared his teeth in delight. "I saw you once before—crying about your little pet pilot."

Cleona jumped. She backed away, casting a quick glance at Tiberius.

"He's dead, you know." Decimus purred, eyes slitted in pleasure. He leaned in close, as if to kiss her. "He's been blown to atoms. Vaporized."

The old man took a menacing step forward. Decimus giggled, dancing away.

Cleona frowned. "What is he talking about, Tiberius? Is there something I should know?"

"Nothing." He gave his nephew a warning look. "He's mad. Best to ignore him."

Decimus grinned. "Don't listen to him, girlie." He peeked over the old man's shoulder. "He's a rotten old liar. Always was."

Tiberius turned his back on Decimus, trying to put himself between the two of them. "There are other towers, Cleona. You can see what's going on just as easily from there."

Cleona raised an eyebrow at Tiberius, her face a mask of humorous disbelief. "You expect me to run . . . from that?" She indicated Decimus with a contemptuous flick of her eyes. "Hell, I wouldn't run from him if he were alive, much less now."

Decimus snarled. "Run. Then you can pretend that your boy is alive for a few minutes longer." He laughed to himself. "What was his name again? Castus?"

Cleona froze, a bit of the color draining from her cheeks.

"No, no," the younger ghost mused, stroking his chin thoughtfully. "That's not right. Cassius? Castor? Something like that, wasn't it?" He shook his head, mumbling to himself. "It was so hard to make out, with all the sniveling . . ." Suddenly he snapped his fingers. "Casca!"

Her jaw suddenly stiffened in fury, and she turned to Tiberius with eyes blazing. "How exactly does he know that name?"

"I'm dead. I know the names of other dead people." Decimus smiled like a skull, tapping his temple with one finger.

"I am not to blame," Tiberius told her quietly. "I do not confide in him now, any more than I did when he was alive. But he is a resident ghost. He could skulk about . . . overhear things."

"Indeed he could!" Decimus hooted with delight. " 'Oh, Casca! Why, why didn't I take you off the line?' " he simpered girlishly, trying to imitate her voice. " 'How will I ever live without you?' "

Cleona turned her amber eyes toward the younger man, with an expression of undisguised loathing. "History books sometimes lie, but the garden does not. You really are an awful thing, aren't you?"

Decimus leaned back against the wall, eyes closed and head half-turned toward his shoulder. He shivered with pleasure, listening to the distant scream of energy weapons in the dark. "Such a pretty child," he sighed. "She carries herself well; doesn't she? I'd dearly love to hear her scream." Tiberius shook his head in disgust, and the younger man smiled brightly. "Isn't this fun, Uncle?"

"I've never shared your enthusiasm for petty cruelty."

Decimus laughed and folded his arms. "And yet you taught me everything I know."

"Indeed. That is why it pains me to see you. As always." Tiberius closed his eyes, weary with the weight of centuries.

"Does it?" Cleona's voice was tender. "Are you suffering, because of him?"

Tiberius turned toward her. "Does that matter?"

"Yes." Her eyes shimmered with flashing spears of war light, but her voice was kind. "It matters to me."

"Then yes." Tiberius waved a hand. "It causes me genuine grief to see him. He shames me. He is a reminder of mistakes I can never unmake."

"Oh, please." Decimus rolled his eyes. "As if *you* had feelings!"

"That will be quite enough." She wheeled on the younger ghost. Her voice held such a ringing note of command that both men jumped at the sound. "I think it is time that you were laid to rest once and for all, Decimus Severan."

Decimus sneered. "Dead is dead. What more can you do to me?"

"There is death, and then there is *damnatio memoriae*."

The handsome face twisted, racked by a sudden spasm of emotion. "No. No one would do such a thing. It is blasphemy."

"Someone would do it, or it wouldn't have a name." Cleona turned to Tiberius. "And you will show me how it is done." She turned her left hand palm upward and slowly closed the fist, clenching the gloved fingers like claws. "We will tear him out of this garden like a tumor."

Tiberius looked down into her eyes, his heart so full of fierce love that he thought it would burst his chest like a mortar shell. "As you wish, my sovereign."

Something like sweat had broken out on the younger man's face. "You're bluffing. If anyone could do that—"

"I would have arranged it before?" Tiberius shook his head. "That was always the trouble with you, Decimus—so little imagination." He smiled. "I haven't been sleeping for all these years. I know where they buried you."

"And when he leads me to your tomb, I will end this." Cleona spoke with firm and gentle assurance. She walked toward Decimus, steps slow and predatory. "Regardless of what I must do. I will rip apart your vault like paper. Throw your bones into the street for stray dogs. Leave your mother's jewels in the gutter for beggars. Smash your sister's skull under my boot like a wedding glass . . ."

"You can't do that!" Decimus roared back. He struggled to master himself; when he spoke again, his voice had dropped back to a low, insinuating hiss. "And you wouldn't. This place is sacred!"

Tiberius gave a bark of laughter. "Is it? Perhaps it was when there were priests to tend it. You killed something far greater than yourself, Decimus, when you put those old men to death.

"No." Decimus put his hands to his head, as if to shut out their voices. "You can't. I'm family! Family!"

Cleona shook her head. "No. You are not. I will decide what that word means from now on." She turned on her heel, her white coat whirling, and disappeared into the snow.

* * *

The sweet drone of bees roused him from torpor many years later. Like an aging bear, Tiberius rose and followed his nose; he wandered out into the garden, drawn by the smell of fine perfume.

She stood against a wall thick with blooming lianas, leaning close to breathe in the fragrance of a trumpet-shaped flower. Her gown was long and dark, its velvet hem sweeping the ground; her hair fell, sleek in whip-thin honey braids, down to the small of her back. One of her hands was pressed there above her rump, as if to ease a nagging pain. When she turned, he saw that her other hand rested on a pregnant belly.

She smiled. "There you are."

"Here I am." He cocked his head to look at her, staring so long that she laughed from embarrassment.

"What is it, old man?"

"You. You look . . . lovely."

She chuckled. "Maternity clothes. Small wonder you like them—I feel like something out of a museum."

He nodded. "The old styles suit you." He put the back of his hand to his mouth, clearing his throat. "To what do I owe the pleasure of this visit?"

She looked up at the summer sky; it was full of gleaming darters, swooping occasionally to snatch a smaller insect out of the air. "Nothing in particular. A warm day, a few canceled appointments. I wanted to get away from people for a while."

"Ah." He was unable to hide his disappointment. "Well, I won't trouble you, then . . ."

She laughed brightly. "Don't be silly, Tiberius. You don't count as people!"

He gave her a wry sidelong glance. "If I were alive, I might take that remark personally."

"Then it's lucky you aren't." She smiled and beckoned to him. "Come, old man—walk with me."

He led her through the garden slowly, finding the low and easy ways through woods and fields. For the most part she seemed to have no difficulty, although she would stop from time to time, distracted by something she found beautiful.

They came to a giant marble chessboard on a hilltop, still standing as if in the middle of a game; it looked as if two colossal players had abandoned it suddenly, called away on pressing business. Each piece was a perfectly exact and life-size sculpture of a human being, placed according to his or her role in life—priest and pilot, emperor and heir, guard and servant. Although several pieces lay smashed on the ground, she laughed to see the sculptor's sense of humor in those still standing: the cook raising his ladle for a taste of the soup, the maid checking the bottom of her shoe, the priest picking his nose.

In another place, they found a collapsed earthen wall, beaten down into the grass by many seasons of rain. Countless bones had tumbled out of the broken clay, and the ground was littered with rotten fabric and glinting gold. As they approached, a black bird was hopping among the old remains, pecking at some bright thing that had caught its eye; it rose flapping at they drew near, carrying in its beak a royal finger bone with a signet ring still attached.

At last Tiberius looked back along a dark forest path and saw that she had fallen behind. Her face was flushed, brow shining; he paused in the center of a low stone bridge, clasping his hands behind his back, to give her a moment to rest in the shade.

Cleona breathed deeply, one hand still holding her stomach. "The baby's awake." She ran her palm over that ripe hard curve. "I felt her move."

Tiberius turned away, afraid his face would betray him if he looked her in the eye. "Must be . . . all the exercise."

The silence between them was long, but peaceful. Tiberius watched the stream rush by beneath his feet, fascinated by the bright quick water; it was so hypnotic that she had called his name three times before he looked up again.

She was standing very still, looking to the path ahead. "Tiberius." She spoke more softly this time. "Someone is coming."

He turned to look. A plump old matron was walking toward them through the forest, wearing a turquoise dress and a light shawl over her gray hair. In one hand, she carried a clear plastic bag of candies; the other was folded behind her back.

She stopped halfway across the bridge, looking up at them with friendly brown eyes and a beatific smile. "Excuse me." Her tone was perfect, befuddled and a little embarrassed. "Have you seen my little cousin? He's gotten away from me, it seems."

Cleona smiled warmly. "What does he look like?"

The old woman blinked and looked down with a rueful little smile. "Oh, he's just a little boy . . . about six years old? He was wearing a yellow jacket."

"We haven't seen him," Tiberius said, drawing away from the woman with a shudder.

"I've got to find him before it gets dark," the old woman said sensibly. "He'll get lost out here on his own . . ."

"We can't help you," Tiberius said quickly. "We have business of our own to attend to."

"Well, if you *do* see him, tell him to go back to the fountain and wait. Tell him his auntie is very worried . . ."

Cleona put out a hand to forestall her as she turned to walk away; Tiberius shook his head.

"Let her go."

The girl frowned at him, annoyed. "Don't be silly, Tiberius." She turned to the old woman again, mouth open to call her back, but the words died unspoken.

As the old woman walked away, the hand behind her back was visible: her fingers were folded around the hilt of a dagger.

Cleona paled. "What—?"

"The Empress Prisca. The boy she's looking for is Zeno, the legitimate heir to the throne. She found him not far from here, and made use of that knife; if that scene is about to be reenacted, I'm fairly certain you don't want to see it."

She shivered. "And I was going to help her *look* for him."

"You had no way of knowing."

"Poor old ghost." She sounded genuinely sad. "Just imagine being forced to murder that child again and again, for centuries— never knowing that the two of you are both long dead."

"Yes." He shuffled nervously. "Terrible."

"It's funny, isn't it?" Her tone was dreamy. "How different the modern ghosts are from the older ones?"

He turned and looked at her oddly. "Different?"

"Come now, Tiberius. I've spent more time in the garden than you think; I *have* noticed it."

"Noticed what?"

She made a face. "I used to come here for afternoon walks, after the war. Did I ever tell you that?"

He startled, surprised.

"I found it very hard at first, having to sit in session with the senate all day. I would run to the garden just to get away from it; I knew no one would dare disturb me here, especially if I brought flowers for my father."

"Clever. Devotion must come before budgets and taxes."

"I always wondered if I would see you here. But you never appeared."

"I'm sorry I missed you. I enjoy your company."

"Of course, I saw a lot of other ghosts." She gave him a searching look. "They aren't like you, Tiberius."

"I suppose not." It was a subject that obviously made him uncomfortable.

"Some of them . . ." She trailed off for a moment, frowning. "Some of the newer ghosts really *are* just echoes, aren't they—like a recording, a holographic film. They only appear when you come near a certain spot; if you back just a few steps away from them, they disappear again. You can make them appear and disappear several times just by walking back and forth. Like flipping a light switch on and off."

He frowned. "You shouldn't do that sort of thing. It's disrespectful."

She looked down over the railing of the bridge. "The older ones, though . . . they seem more like people." Cleona looked at him again, and he struggled to keep his expression blank. "Dead people, of course. But genuinely human . . . not just a taped message. Do you understand what I mean?"

"I suppose so," he said reluctantly.

"You can actually talk to them. I spent several hours that summer talking to Quintus Valerius—I kept meeting him by the north wall."

Tiberius nodded. "His presence is strong there."

She was studying him carefully as she spoke, watching for any hint of reaction. "Whenever I met Quintus, he was always wearing the same clothes. If I asked him his name, or his reason for being in the garden, he would always give me the same basic information— but the way he said it would vary. Just as you would expect, if he were a living man. He never knew me; no matter how many times we had spoken before, I always had to introduce myself. He couldn't remember any of our previous conversations."

"And then there's old Tiberius." He completed the thought for her.

"Then there's you." She held him with her serene copper eyes. "Quintus and the others . . . all seem to be asleep somehow. When I speak to them, I'm always waking them from the same dream."

"The dream of being alive."

"Exactly. Ask them a question; they'll answer—they even have questions of their own, once you've started a conversation. But if you want to know what year it is, or what they're doing in the garden, they'll say it's 1393, and they've just come for a little walk, and they have to get straight back afterward for dinner." She shook her head wonderingly. "Quintus actually seemed to think that I was the ghost; when I told him my name, he assumed I was Cleona the First."

Tiberius smiled. "That's a natural enough mistake. You accused me of being Tiberius the Third when you were ten; I was quite insulted."

"Why? Because he was a bad emperor?"

"No, because he was short and ugly!"

She laughed out loud. "Well, I'm sorry, then." Her eyes twinkled merrily. "You certainly aren't *short* . . ."

He put his fingertips to his chest in mock offense. "You, madame, are clearly no judge of masculine beauty. I'll have you know that I was considered quite handsome in my day; my profile was much admired."

She grinned. "No one tells an emperor that he's ugly, Tiberius. I'm sure they told Orthrus he was lovely as a rose and tall as a mountain—and prodigiously endowed with manhood as well—if that's what they thought he wanted to hear."

He inclined his head. "A point to the lady."

"Anyway, don't change the subject." She paused, frowning a little, and rubbed her belly absently as she continued. "You are different, Tiberius. You're aware of the passage of time—you know where you are, and *when* you are. You learn new things, and remember them over the years: you can tell stories about emperors who died centuries after they buried you. And you always recognize me as your niece, even if I've gone from twenty-one to thirty-one since our last meeting."

He gave her a wry lopsided smile. "I'm surprised that you've given this so much thought. Did you have a point to make?"

"The point is, you're not just a ghost. You, Tiberius, are alive."

He made a dubious face. "Let's not exaggerate, dear."

She shrugged. "To me, a man who thinks, feels, and learns is alive—regardless of whether his body is made of flesh or light. Perhaps I'm too simplistic, but philosophical points don't really interest me. What *does* interest me is the difference between a ghost like you and one like Quintus."

Tiberius regarded her silently. "Your question has more to do with the workings of the garden in general than with me in particular. If you're not interested in philosophy, I may as well say 'I don't know'—because I have only theories and speculations to answer you. No firm facts."

She turned away, another ripple of disturbance passing over her face. Tiberius, looking down, saw her hand pressed hard to her stomach. "I'll take your theories and speculations."

"All right. Then I'll answer your question. But before I do, I have a question of my own."

She gave him a little shake of the head. "Always bargaining!" She took a few steps along the bridge. "Ask your question, but we should move on; I'd like to be back to the palace before dusk."

"As you wish." He led her through the trees casually, following the course of an old road, its pavement long ago shattered by twisting roots. "I'm curious to know why you chose a body birth for your heir. Surely it's not necessary. Even if they don't have incubators nowadays, you could still use a surrogate to carry the child. Why would you adopt such an antiquated mode of reproduction? Is it the fashion these days?"

She shook her head, smiling. "No, it certainly isn't the fashion. Not for those who have a choice."

"Why, then?" He ducked under a branch, leading her over a mound of jumbled rock. "It seems an unnecessary risk—body birth is dangerous and damaging to your health, even under the best of conditions."

"True." She paused, bending a little to pick her way down the incline. "Believe me, there are times when I regret my decision—times like now. The baby's kicking like mad; it feels as if she's dancing on my liver."

Tiberius looked down at her gravid midsection again, dismayed; seeing his expression, she laughed out loud. "Don't look so worried, old man! It's a fetus, not a parasitic growth. It's perfectly normal for a baby to kick and wiggle at this stage; she's just becoming more active, that's all."

"I . . ." He looked into her eyes. "I'm sorry." He finished lamely. "I don't have much experience with this sort of thing. I suppose I find it . . . disturbing."

"Well, you're not alone. Just about everyone is looking at me strangely these days. There's no such thing as a pregnant empress, apparently." She sighed, running her fingers through her hair. "I've had to make up a variety of excuses for this 'outlandish behavior.' At this point, I think they're all ready to dismiss me as another mad Severan, and let it go at that."

"Well, I don't need to hear the excuses. What was the real reason?"

She gave him a sly look as she continued up the trail. "The truth? I warn you, you'll think me a fool."

"I can keep such thoughts to myself."

"The truth is, I wanted to love her. My heir. There aren't many body births among the nobility, but I've seen the bond that exists between plebian mothers and their children—it's very deep."

"And you felt that this bond was somehow . . . physical?"

"It is. I can feel it."

She looked down at her belly for a moment, running her hand over it lightly. Tiberius abruptly realized that the hand she placed on her stomach was not for her benefit, but for the child's—an indirect caress for the unborn.

"I've become the vessel for her life, Tiberius." She looked up at him and smiled. "I know you won't understand it. You never had any children of your own. But she's part of me, a piece of my living body—not just some detritus thrown together out of my cast-off cells. I feel intimate with her in a way that I could never be with something growing in an incubator—and I feel somehow subordinate to her as well, as if my own survival and interests were secondary to hers." She sighed, brushing a strand of hair away from her face. "Strange thought, isn't it?"

"Is she a clone of you? Did you use a consort, get a donation from someone—?"

Cleona flushed a little, quickening her stride. "She has a father. I used DNA from a man—new blood to mingle with the old. The Severans need that from time to time, you know, or we'll all turn into feeble-minded mules."

"A man . . ." Suddenly he halted in his tracks. "Good gods. It was Casca; wasn't it?"

The weight of sadness descended on her visibly, bowing her head as she walked. "He was an officer. His genes were still on file at the war office. It was just a matter of getting to them."

"Oh . . . oh, my child. I am so sorry."

"Don't be." Her eyes were strangely luminous. "I'll see him every time I look at her. And I'll love her . . . for his sake and mine." She smiled. "Casca will live again."

Stricken, Tiberius said nothing more.

"What about my question? We had a deal, didn't we?"

"I . . . I feel foolish talking about it now. Perhaps you could come again some other day. We could talk about the garden then."

"Bah. You're just stalling. Pay up, old man—I don't like to be cheated."

Tiberius cast around for words, fighting to swallow the pain in his chest. "The garden is very old. It was old beyond record or recollection when I was a boy. But back then, there were gardeners —priests—who spent their entire lives here." He licked his lips nervously. "It was very beautiful. Nothing like the mess you see now." He made a vague gesture, indicating the wild wood and the undergrowth, the choking weeds and broken obelisks by the road-side. "The gardeners kept things up. They planted and pruned, weeded, watered . . . there were wonders here, beautiful things kept alive by their hands. Exotic birds, lovely fish . . . in this area, there was an arboretum. Trees from five hundred different worlds, each one a treasure in its own right." He smiled. "Have you ever seen a helium tree, Cleona?"

"No." Her face was pinched with distress. "Never even heard of one."

"Are you all right? You seem—"

"It's fine. She's a busy little devil today, that's all. Giving me a bit of a pain." She gave him a weak smile. "Please, don't let me interrupt."

"There was only one of them. It was my very favorite. Lovely bark—white as snow. The flowers were strange; they came out in fall instead of spring, fleshy little things that looked like ears. The local insects didn't care for them. The gardeners had to climb a ladder and pollinate them by hand, with a little paintbrush."

"Why did they call it a helium tree?"

He smiled. "The fruits. They came out every spring. Great, glorious metallic bunches of them, each one as big as a man's head, in every imaginable color: green, blue, pink, gold. The gardeners would let me climb up and shake the branches, and masses and masses of them would rise on the wind and sail away."

She laughed. "So they really were filled with helium?"

"Yes. When I was older, they explained it to me; the helium fruits were seed pods, designed to rise into the upper atmosphere and explode. The cold at those heights was favorable to the seeds somehow—I think it caused them to germinate—and then the wind would scatter them." He glanced at her face; the natural rosy luster of her golden cheek had been replaced with clammy gray pallor. "Cleona, perhaps we should—"

"Talk," she gasped. "It helps keep me moving. I have to get back to the palace, Tiberius; I think I'm getting that 'morning sickness' I've been reading about . . ."

"Yes. Right. The old gardeners." He quickened his stride. "Well, I befriended them. I spent hours here. The ghosts weren't just 'taped messages' back then, as you say, but living spirits, like me . . . interested in gossip, fashion, current events, full of opinions and advice. They were my friends; I knew them better than my living relations." He glanced at her quickly, then barreled heedlessly on. "The old men could see I loved their garden for its own sake, so they confided in me a little—even though, in their eyes, I was no one special. Just a future emperor . . . one of many subjects for a great art form. To them, the greatest art form of all."

"Art. So, the gardeners made the ghosts? For the sake of art?"

"No, not exactly." He was distracted by the sound of her increasingly labored breath. "But they helped. The garden itself made the ghosts. The garden is the artist."

She stopped suddenly, bent double with a grunt of pain; he stopped with her, grimacing in sympathy. When she looked up at him, her eyes were hot, golden, fierce as a hawk's. "Talk," she commanded.

"It's all under our feet," he said helplessly. "The woods, the water, the tombs ... those are only surface trappings. The most important parts of the garden are all underground. Beneath everything you see here, there is one great machine—an engine of the First Empire, built before the Fall." He shifted uneasily from one foot to the other, looking down at her. "The gardeners thought that it was built for our benefit. Designed to make the Severans better emperors. They thought if we could learn history from those who'd lived it, we would be less likely to repeat their mistakes."

She straightened and began to walk again, slowly. "You don't sound ... as if you agree with them, old man."

"They were men of faith. They thought the builders of the garden were men like them, driven by high ideals and lofty visions." He shook his head. "I was a man of power, and I thought that power of such magnitude doesn't need to hang a halo on its motives. If I could have built a thing like this—a machine that would record and preserve a human soul—I would have. Just because I could. And for the sake of vanity. Who better to live forever than me?"

She laughed unevenly, stumbling a few more steps onward. "It's funny to hear you use a word like 'soul,' Tiberius. You sound ... like a priest."

"Stop a while," he begged. "Let me find you a place to sit and rest."

"No." She turned and staggered off the trail. Holding her stomach with one hand and leaning against a gravestone with another, she bent low in the bushes to be sick.

"We can't talk about this any more now. For heaven's sake, girl!"

She spat repeatedly into the weeds, ignoring him for several seconds, and then straightened again. "Tell me how it went wrong," she croaked. She was moving more slowly now, but seemed somehow calm—as if she had passed through a crisis. "What happened to the gardeners?"

"My nephew." He still winced at the memory. "Decimus didn't like the tomb they built for me: he said the man who had murdered his mother and siblings deserved a wooden box, if that. So he had my mausoleum demolished, and executed them for 'sentimentaliz-ing.' "

"The machine." She breathed the words, suddenly struck by understanding. For the first time in several minutes, she looked him in the eyes. "It needed them, didn't it? Without the gardeners to care for it, it began breaking down."

"Yes."

"It made . . . bad recordings."

"Not bad. Just . . . incomplete. When a living person comes into the garden, the machine still tries to do its work—but now it can only capture part of the whole. Sometimes it's just the dimensions of the body, the vibrations of the voice, a fleeting gesture. Other times it forms a more complete picture, including all that a person was thinking and feeling at that moment. So we have Quintus Valerius on a summer day, when he walked by the wall: a single man, frozen in a single moment, knowing only what he knew then."

"Summer," she gasped. "Summer, by the wall. That's why I only saw him . . . a few times."

"Yes. The garden will not place him out of his proper context; he remembers coming here in a certain season, on a cloudless day. He will only appear if the light, the wind, and the clouds are right . . ."

Cleona cried out, clutching her abdomen in agony. When she looked up at him, her eyes were glazed with confusion; shadows stood out sharply against her skin. "Tiberius?" She looked down at herself, bending to gather her skirts with both hands. "I think . . . I think that I . . ."

Cleona raised the hem of her dress; a slow dark trickle of blood was running down her brown thigh. She looked up at him in mute supplication—as if to ask that he take this back, unmake it some-how.

"I'm sorry." His voice broke. "So sorry, child."

Her eyes rolled up toward the darkening sky, lashes closing over white sclera. When she fell, he couldn't catch her.

* * *

The highest point in the garden could almost be called a moun-tain. For those hardy enough to climb to the summit, the towering bluffs offered a complete view of the imperial city—from the white walls of the palace to the dingy roof of the meanest bayside tene-ment. Tiberius could not bring himself to make the climb often, but when he smelled the salt on the wind and saw the broken clouds above, he knew that it was time to go.

There had once been a trail up the mountainside, an exhausting switchback snaking back and forth all the way to the top. Time, rain, and erosion had destroyed the easy way, however; now he could only climb directly up the mountain, scuttling up slopes of broken tallus and clinging to steep rock faces like an old gray spider.

She was waiting for him when he reached the end of the climb, sitting cross-legged on a boulder. "I wondered if you would come!" she cried, shouting down the wind.

He straightened up slowly. "I knew you would be here today. I didn't want to leave you alone."

She turned away and looked out at the sky; clouds raced across the horizon, beams of bright light slashing down amid the falling rain. "Tell me how long I've been dead."

He went down on one knee beside her, his robe whipping in the wind.

"Go on, tell me. I want to know. Tell me how long I've been dead—and who did *that*."

She jabbed an angry finger at the lands below, but there was no need to point. The city was in ruins; vast swaths of it had been reduced to pools of glass, with the half-melted skeletons of many high towers still standing, twisted and naked, like trees drowned in a flood. Elsewhere there had been heavy bombardment, and sweeping fires that eradicated everything but a few low broken walls. Whole districts had been replaced by impact craters, and whatever was left standing was windowless and gaunt with long neglect. The streets were white with human bones. Nova Roma was dead—and she had died by violence.

Cleona trembled, her gray cloak whipping in the wind. "How long?"

"It happened fifty years ago. The last survivors were forced to abandon it when biological weapons were used against them—this whole planet will remain uninhabitable, until someone finds a cure." He looked down at the devastation. "If anyone ever does."

"What do you mean, 'if'?"

He held out his trembling hand, and somehow this one gesture seemed a general indictment: of the city, of the empire, of the species that had destroyed them both. "We are in decline, Cleona. War is devouring us, and with it will come darkness and ignorance —just as it did before. Those who create a virus today that will target and eradicate all human life may die before they can teach the next generation how to cure it."

She made a halfhearted nod, unwilling to argue. "And how long has it been since . . . me?"

He stood silently for a time, trying to read her face. "Over six hundred years. Give or take a few. I'm afraid I never really understood the new calendar."

She looked at him and smiled. Years had creased and folded her skin, but the eyes had not changed; they were still bright, beautiful, heartbreaking golden brown. "Shame on you, Tiberius." She shook her head.

"Why?"

"You're lying. And what's worse, I caught you at it—your naive little niece!"

He smiled back feebly. "You're not so little anymore, old woman."

"Apparently I'm not anything anymore." The wind caught the lip of her cowl, blowing it back from her face; coarse white dreadlocks spilled around her shoulders. She turned again to look down on the ruined city, its streets and squares slowly succumbing to an invading army of trees. "Was this my doing, somehow? Is that it?"

He shook his head, unable to speak.

She studied his expression carefully, and then nodded to herself. "It was."

"Don't blame yourself. There was nothing you could do."

"Stop. You, of all people, cannot forgive me for this." She shook violently. "I've killed the empire, the one thing you loved . . . how can you help but despise me?"

"Everything dies." He offered the words gently. "It is the way of things."

"Succession." She spat the word bitterly, ignoring him. "That's what started this war." She wrapped her arms around herself, shrinking against the wind. "All those years, old man, you tried to tell me: get rid of a few more cousins, good or bad—you'll be glad you did! And this is the final proof." She put out a trembling hand toward the city. "You were right, and I was wrong."

"No. Just the reverse, Cleona."

She squinted at him, surprised.

"You tried to prevent this. The heir that you conceived was poisoned in the womb—they murdered her before she was even born. Don't be ashamed that you refused to play that game; you should be proud that you stood above it. It was an ugly, stupid way to live." He pointed to the broken ruins below. "And this is the way it always ends."

"My, my." She cocked her head, deeply amused. "You've certainly changed your tune, old man. You were always a great proponent of the game."

"I practically invented it. That wreck below is as much my doing as anyone's. I wanted to build a great empire, one that would last forever—but I laid the foundation in blood." He turned away from her. "It's a shame I didn't ask the gardeners for help. They could have told me that nothing stands long, rooted in bad soil."

She reached out a weathered hand. "Tiberius . . . There's nothing we can do to change things now."

"Yes. I know." He swallowed, staring dry-eyed at the destruction below. "No one knows it better than I."

She remained silent for some time, sitting beside him on the bluff. When she finally turned to him again, she wore an almost girlish smile. "Do you ever wonder how things might have been, if we had both lived at the same time?"

Tiberius looked away, hiding his face from her. "No, Cleona."

She frowned. "Really? Never?"

"No. I think it was a blessing that we met when we did."

She drew back, mingled hurt and bemusement in her eyes. "Why do you say that?"

"I was a different man when I was alive. I would have hurt you." He turned away. "And I've done enough harm to the things I love."

She reached tenderly for his cheek, but her fingertips met no resistance; they passed through him like a dream. She was fading, the wind and rain wiping her away. Grinning at her own predicament, she quickly kissed her withered palm and blew it toward him. "Something to remember me by." Her voice was so faint it was almost inaudible.

"No need." He smiled. "We'll meet again."

* * *

The Severan Funeral Garden is the planet's largest public park, bordered on all sides by the imperial city of Nova Roma. It is a fine playground for a young empress, with a million places to hide. On certain spring mornings, when the sun and wind are right, a child still creeps through the weeds there, stalking an old man. He goes to the same place year after year, to tell her his name—because although the two of them have met before, he knows she will not remember the occasion.

About Arinn Dembo

Arinn Dembo is a writer and game developer currently living and working in the Greater Seattle area. Her short stories, poetry, and novellas have appeared in the *Magazine of Fantasy and Science Fiction*, *H.P. Lovecraft's Magazine of Horror*, *Weird Tales*, *Lamp Light Magazine*, and several collections. Most recently, she contributed three stories to two anthologies, which were both nominated for the 2015 World Fantasy Award, in different categories: *Gods, Memes and Monsters* by Stoneskin Press, and *She Walks in Shadows* by Innsmouth Free Press.

As a narrative designer in the computer gaming industry, she has provided world-building and background fiction to a number of popular PC titles. She is the English-language screenwriter for the Japanese animated series *World Trigger*, based on the manga series written and illustrated by Daisuke Ashihara, and her military SF novel *The Deacon's Tale* and her short-story collection, *Monsoon and Other Stories*, are both available from Kthonia Press.

The author holds a degree in anthropology and a second in classical archaeology. The inspiration for this story comes from her academic work in Roman studies and is dedicated with love to her younger daughter, Freya.

THE BEESINGER'S DAUGHTER

By Jeff Wheeler | 21,600 words

IT WAS A story Rista never grew tired of hearing, yet she shivered with fear each time her father told it. The hearth crackled and cast an orange glow across the small cabin space, lighting her siblings' faces as they stared at the storyteller, transfixed. The mood had to be right before Rista could convince her father to share the stories of his adventures from the past. As the oldest, she felt it was her duty to incite the tellings.

Her father was a good storyteller, with a baritone voice that was just a little too soft, forcing her to lean forward to catch every word. His gray thatch of hair showed his age, which always made Rista secretly sad, but his hazel eyes twinkled as he leaned forward, a little smile making his lips crooked.

"We had traveled four days to reach Battle Mountain," he confided, "after crossing the Arvadin. Four days of serpents. Four days of kobold raids at night."

"Not Twig!" little Camille said indignantly. "He couldn't hurt anyone!"

At the mention of his name, a little kobold no taller than a strutting rooster peeked his head around Father's back. He was small, even for a kobold, and he blinked at Camille and skittered into her lap, then around her back, and finally rested his lizard-like snout on her shoulder, making her giggle in hysterics.

Rista wanted to swat him down for ruining the story. "Shhh!" she scolded. "Let Father tell the story! Twig, get down!"

The kobold blinked at her, his little shoulder wilting at the rebuke, and then he curled up in Camille's lap while she stroked his knobby horns. Little Twig had joined Father's adventure all those years ago and had not grown an ounce bigger in all those years. He was the runtiest little excuse of a monster. The only reason he had survived so long was because he was cowardly in the extreme, jittery as a squirrel, and clever enough not to fight anything bigger than her little brother, Adam.

"As I was saying," Father went on patiently, his eyes twinkling, "we reached Battle Mountain. It's a desolate land, full of jagged rocks and scrub. Not a single tree. The peak comes out of the middle of the flatlands. It's huge."

"Are there any bees then?" piped in Brand, the second oldest, who would be leaving with Father in the morning to move the hives.

"Sshhh!" Rista hissed impatiently.

"There *are* bees in that forsaken land," her father said, giving Rista a subtle hand gesture to try to calm her down. She hated such interruptions. "Carpenter bees. The big black fat ones. Practically the size of hummingbirds."

A chorus of shivers went through the siblings, including Rista. She was the Beesinger's daughter, and had grown up loving bees of all sorts—except the nasty black carpenter bees. She wasn't afraid of bumblebees, yellow jackets, honeybees, wasps, or hornets. But the giant bees had terrified her as a child, and now that she was seventeen, she wondered if she would ever conquer her fear of them in order to become a true Beesinger herself.

"When we reached Battle Mountain, the fortress of the Ziggurat dominated the base of the rocks. I've never seen something so big, yes—even bigger than King Malcolm's palace! The kobolds had been working on it for centuries, driven by their slave master. Now, how could we get in without being seen?" He tapped his chin thoughtfully.

"Twig could get in," Camille said proudly, and the little kobold lifted his head from her lap with a toothy grin and a little purring noise.

"But that was *before* I found Twig," her father said, wagging his finger. "The Ziggurat was built above caves in the mountain. So we searched the base behind it, looking for another way in. That was before the king's army arrived. Well, I found a little cave—a small one that Twig could fit through, but so could I." He patted his own belly.."I was thinner back then. I crawled on my stomach to see how far it went. It was so dirty and dusty, I could hardly breathe or see, and it was full of cobwebs." He used his arms and hands to gesture the words as he spoke. "I used my cudgel to clear some away and then scoot in a little farther." He paused, eyes twinkling again, and Rista felt the shivers already starting to go up her back.

"I had a piece of magic, given to me from the Enclave. It's that small clear stone full of borrowed light. I've shown it to some of you before. It was so dark I couldn't see well, so I reached into my pocket, opened the pouch that hides the light, and pulled it out." He mimicked the action, withdrew the small oval stone, and then opened his palm. The clear stone began to glow dimly. The light had been much brighter when Rista was young. The magic in it was fading. "*That's* when I saw the spiders," he added softly and with a wicked grin. "Black widows—everywhere. I'd crawled into the middle of their nest."

Rista hated spiders, especially black widows. She saw the faces of her siblings twist with disgust and fear. Twig suddenly leaped from Camille's lap and skittered around the hearth with his usual disruptive antics.

"Twig!" Rista complained while her siblings giggled. The tiny kobold scrabbled up the Beesinger's arm, up his shoulder, then down his front before nestling on Father's lap. He stared at the light from the crystal as it began to fade, his red-orange glassy eyes shimmering with the light. His long snout of teeth grinned at it. Rista loved the little monster—even though she sometimes called the kobold a little runt in front of her siblings and friends. Twig could be very exasperating on occasion.

"What did you do?" Camille asked fearfully. The freckles on her nose crinkled. "I would have screamed!"

"I'll tell you *that* story . . . when I get back," Father said. "Tomorrow morning Brand and I are taking hives to Apple Hill. Rista is going to take care of you." He gave her an affectionate smile and gently rubbed the knobs on Twig's head.

"Maybe you should take Twig with you for protection?" Rista suggested jokingly.

"No, Twig's your protector!" Father said, rubbing the kobold's bony back. Twig's snout spread into a wide, crookedly toothy grin. The kobold loved being praised, even if it was unearned. He hissed something in his guttural language.

"And what will he protect us from?" Rista taunted. "Mice?"

Father didn't reply to her insult. He was a patient man. He had been sadder since mother had passed away bearing the twin boys.

But Rista had never tried coaxing him into marrying again, and he'd never shown any interest, saying his hands were full with twenty hives, five children, and an energetic kobold. He was about the plainest, most ordinary man you'd find anywhere in the kingdom. He never boasted of his accomplishments. And he never talked about how he'd defeated the Overlord of Battle Mountain. He—a simple Beesinger.

* * *

Rista was up when Father and Brand were ready to leave. They had loaded four hives onto a wagon the day before and were going to head out while the hives were still asleep. Because of her father's innate magic, he could calm the most ferocious swarms and was occasionally called upon to do so throughout the kingdom. He was up before dawn every day, tending to the small farm and capturing honey from the hives, which was sold to a merchant down the hill and distributed to the farthest reaches of the kingdom. The merchant earned most of the profits, which Rista thought was unfair since he leveraged Father's reputation. A Beesinger's honey was said to be the best, and her father was the most famous Beesinger of all. But he refused to profit from reputation rather than his own hard work and didn't care that he made other men rich.

She found him in the yard with his cutting axe resting against a spoke, rubbing fronds of mint on his hands while Brand checked the axles and the horse tack. She walked up to her father, hugging a warm shawl to her shoulders.

"It's two days to Apple Hill, two days back, and four days of letting the bees do all the work," Rista said. "Do I spy your fishing poles back there?"

Her father grinned. "Yes, Brand packed those just in case there's time." He smiled at her and then opened his arms for a hug. He smelled so strongly of mint that it made her smile. He was strong, sturdy, and boring. But he gave the best hugs.

"You have plenty of food," he said, pulling away and then tugging on her blond braid. "My sister Natalie said she'd cook if you get tired of it."

"I can cook," Rista said, a little offended. She sighed, cursing herself. Part of her wished that Brand were staying behind and she were going with him. The farm was dull, and she could use a change of scenery. She'd love to go down the hill to the village, but she couldn't leave Camille in charge of the twins, even though she was almost twelve. It was Rista's duty, as the eldest, to look after the others. At least Aunt Natalie lived close enough.

"You're a good cook, Rista," Father said, tipping her chin and then kissing the top of her hair. "We'll be back soon."

"I'll miss you, Father," Rista said, giving him another squeeze. "Be careful."

He was the most careful person in the world. He nodded to her and grabbed his axe, which often served as an alpenstock while he walked. "Watch after things, Twig," he said with an important voice. "You're in charge of protecting Rista. I think I spied some field mice on the western fence. Make sure you set up a patrol."

The kobold was lounging on the porch and yawned lazily and then set his snout back down on his arms. He made a few uncommitted clicking noises and then closed his lantern-like eyes.

"The wagon is ready, Father," Brand said, holding the lead rope.

"Thank you, Son. Good work." They mounted the box, and soon the wagon lumbered away. Rista folded her arms and hugged herself, watching it go and realizing that the next fortnight would be unendurably boring. Nothing exciting ever happened.

That was true for the first day.

* * *

It was nearing sunset the following day when Twig came skittering through the window of the cabin in an absolute terrified panic. He was clicking and growling so fast and hard that, even struggling, Rista couldn't make out his words at all, though she could usually understand him if she tried.

"What is he saying, Camille?" Rista asked, setting plates on the table and feeling a little impatient. "Is there a skunk nearby?"

Camille was probably Twig's next favorite, and he scampered up her leg and gesticulated with his bony little arms and pointed to the door urgently.

"No," Camille said, her face suddenly worried. "He saw a bear coming."

Rista's stomach dropped. "Of course. A bear! It had to come the day after Father left. What kind of bear was it? A black bear?"

Camille made a series of grunts and clicks. Twig understood the speech of humans, and Rista refused to speak to him in his own language. But Camille had taught herself and was quick to understand what Twig meant.

"I think it's a grizzly," she said worriedly.

Rista frowned, suddenly worried. "Adam, Ben. Bar the windows. Camille, bar the door. It'll be after the hives, no doubt. Why did it have to come now?" The children were quick to obey her. It was unusual for a bear to wander this far down the Arvadin Mountains, but it had happened before. However, Father had always been there, and he knew what to do in such times. He had a longbow and arrows as a final resort, which Rista wasn't strong enough to use. But it was his magic that allowed him to summon the bees themselves to frighten away unwanted visitors. The cabin was secured quickly and she felt her nerves starting to calm. She reached out with her senses, trying to see if the bees were aware of the danger yet. But they were all back in the hive by this late hour. They wouldn't know about the danger until the claws arrived. Bears were drawn to honey, and she hoped the beast didn't wreck too many hives to satisfy its cravings.

With the windows shut, it was dark inside, so she quickly trimmed the wick of an oil lamp and lit it. The children clustered around her, and she did her best to soothe them, putting on an air of confidence. It was inconvenient but not truly dangerous.

Then she heard the bear snuffling near the door of the cabin and felt Camille suddenly squeeze her waist, her eyes wide with terror, her freckles twitching. The twins were silent, staring at the small gap beneath the door.

"It's all right," Rista soothed. "It can't get in."

Suddenly a hard knock sounded at the door, jolting them all. Camille shrieked and started to whimper. Twig began running around in circles frantically and then cowered behind the flour barrel. Rista's heart was shuddering in her chest, but she was a clever girl. Bears did not knock.

She gestured for Camille to take the twins to the loft ladder as she walked forward. "Wh-who is it?" Rista asked, angered by the tremor in her voice.

"Ilias."

At the sound of the man's voice, her fear suddenly vanished, replaced by intense and immediate relief. This changed everything! Ilias was from the Enclave, he was the wandering protector of the valley, advisor of the king, and he was an Eyriemaester. His creature, an enormous gold eagle, could often be seen flying over the valley and keeping watch over the kingdom.

Rista lifted the crossbar from the door and hurriedly opened it. The man standing in the doorway filled it and still had to stoop. He looked young, like a man in his midthirties, but he was a being who was over a thousand years old. One did not age living in the Enclave. In fact, the aging process reversed until a person was in the prime. He was clean-shaven with wavy bronze hair and piercing blue eyes. Rista hadn't seen him since she was six, and he had seemed like a giant back then. Surprisingly, he was even taller now. He wore an impressive tunic with a leather band across his chest, holding back a dark cloak. She noted a wide bulky satchel hanging from the band as he looked at her with concern and worry.

"Hello, Rista," he said, his voice calming. "Where is your father?" He gazed around the interior of the cabin, searching quickly.

"He's . . . he's gone to Apple Hill," Rista stammered. "What's wrong?"

Ilias frowned. Then he looked back and made a gesture. Ilias had not come alone, and Rista's heart hammered with excitement. "Inside, quickly," Ilias beckoned.

"There's a bear," Rista warned.

Ilias smiled and chuckled. "The bear is with us. It'll guard the farm while we talk. This is Lielle of the Enclave," he said, gesturing to the woman who entered next. Rista stared at her in shock and surprise. She was the most beautiful woman Rista had ever seen. She had red hair that was braided back and she entered with a sculpted bow and an arrow already nocked. Her skin was flawless, showing her to be of the Enclave as well. Rista had never met her before, but she had heard her father tell of Lielle and her fox. She was the best hunter in the valley. Rista had suspected that her father had, long ago, secretly cared for her. But Father had never revealed his true feelings to his daughter, keeping them sealed like a walnut hull. The other man who came, she did not recognize, but he was nearer to her age, and so Rista did not think he was part of the Enclave.

"This is Gabe Doer," Ilias said, and Rista blinked in surprise.

"You're the son of King Malcolm Doer," Rista said, impressed. He was the king's youngest.

Gabe looked at her, wrinkling his brow, and cast his eyes around the small cabin as if it were a pitiful thing. "We can't stay long, Ilias. They'll track us here."

"I know, I'll be brief," the Eyriemaester said. "Lielle. The door." The redheaded girl secured it and then went to a window and unbolted it, again preparing her bow to shoot.

"You are in great danger, Rista," Ilias said urgently, putting his strong hand on her shoulder. "We travel at night to avoid being seen in the day. Something stirs in Battle Mountain. I must find your father. Where is he?"

Rista's heart churned with excitement. "What is it, Ilias?"

He shook his head. "Best if you don't know. Is there a place you can go for shelter? The village perhaps? They will track us here."

"Who?" Rista asked eagerly. Her heart was hammering, but she felt part of her coming alive as if for the first time. Was her magic awakening at last?

"I cannot say and it would be better if you didn't know. You said your father went to Apple Hill? When did he leave?"

"I see something," Lielle said from the window. "It was just a shadow."

Suddenly the roar of a bear came from outside. Lielle drew back the bowstring and sent an arrow into the burgeoning dark. "Got it."

Gabe was looking at Ilias fretfully. "We can't stay here, Ilias! We don't have time!"

The Eyriemaester let out a deep breath. Then he looked into Rista's eyes. "Do you have the magic, child? Are you truly a Beesinger's daughter?"

Her heart leaped. "I do have it," she said eagerly. "I've not fully . . . not fully mastered it yet. But I can calm or summon a swarm like my father can. You are returning to Battle Mountain? You needed my father, but could I come instead?"

Ilias gave her a look that was impressed. "How old are you, Rista? The last time I saw you, you were . . . ?"

"I was only six. I'm seventeen now. If you need Beesinger magic, then bring me with you!"

Gabe scrunched up his face. "It's too dangerous."

"I'm not *afraid*," Rista huffed, glaring at the young man. "My aunt lives nearby. Twig can take my siblings there, and then she can take them to warn the village in the morning."

Ilias looked to Lielle and then back at Rista. "I'd almost forgotten about little Twig," he said with a humorous chuckle. Rista pointed to the flour barrel and saw the little kobold trembling.

"Your father is the one I hoped to find, Rista," Ilias said, putting his hand on her shoulder. "Since the Great War, the Ziggurat has been left desolate. But something stirs within. An evil that begins to summon creatures into its service. I thought your father had destroyed the Overlord. But it may have only been asleep. Will you come with us, Beesinger? Yours is a subtle magic. And subtlety is what we need most."

Rista could not refrain from grinning. "Of course I will come with you," she said. "Twig, take Camille and the boys to Aunt Natalie's cabin." She was so excited she could hardly contain herself. "You said we must travel at night?"

Ilias nodded approvingly. "You have your father's courage. I will do all in my power to protect you from harm. Gabe, tell Damon Papenfuss we're leaving. We may have to fight our way clear. Lielle, make sure these children make it safely to their aunt's."

"I'll take them instead," Gabe said. "If you get attacked, she'll be better in a fight. I'll meet you at Weathercress Hollow tomorrow night. The bats will lead me to you."

Ilias looked at the young man and then nodded. "We must go quickly. Now."

The bear roared again from the yard outside.

"Douse the lamp," Ilias hissed.

* * *

Her father's cabin was nestled in the foothills of the Arvadin, amidst a thick wood of twisted oak trees. The oak provided much cover as Rista and her companions began hiking up into the mountains. Lielle remained in the rear, often stopping to loose an arrow at some creatures following them. By morning, the woods had changed from oak to cedar and pine. From an outcropping of rock, just as the sun began to gleam over the snow-capped peaks, Rista looked down into the valley and saw the distant spires of Stanchion castle amidst the rivers that crisscrossed the lush green and provided a fertile basin for growing. The castle looked like a child's toy from the heights, but she had been there frequently enough to recognize the deception. Stanchion and the town encircling it made up the largest city of the kingdom.

"Weathercress is that way," Lielle said after catching up to them, pointing to a series of hulking boulders. "Papenfuss should be waiting there with Kylek."

Ilias craned his neck, looking up at the eastern sky toward the sunshine. "We need to get out of the light. Lead the way, Lielle."

The huntress nodded sternly and scrambled over the rocks.

"Where is her fox, Ilias?" Rista asked in a soft tone, walking alongside the legendary man. She'd heard many stories from her father about Lielle and her sly fox and how close they could get to an enemy without being seen.

Ilias glanced down at her and then pointed back down the trail. "Keeping an eye open for Gabe, who should join us before long. I thought he might catch up to us ere now." He gazed back down the valley and shook his head. "The Arvadin has its own dangers."

"I thought the king's men patrolled the passes?" Rista said. "They used to be infested with kobolds, but that was long ago."

Ilias nodded sagely. "What hunts us will not be stopped by soldiers," he said meaningfully. "These mountains are the lair of many creatures. Our enemy, Rista, is a Serpentarium." Ilias's expression hardened. "Have you met one?"

Rista shuddered. "I've not."

They followed after Lielle and found the entrance to a cave, which was nothing more than a series of boulders that had crashed down from the mountain and nestled together, forming large pockets. As they reached it, Rista smelled a rank odor and saw a giant of a man, with a fraying gray cloak covering his bulk. His face was ravaged with scars, one of his cheeks so deformed that it made his eye unnaturally big. He was the ugliest man Rista had ever seen, his wounds clearly caused by bear claws. Behind him was a huge grizzly, its snout resting on its enormous arms. Rista had never been so near such a bear and felt the terror wriggling inside her, telling her to flee. The bear growled at her, sniffed, and then looked away.

"Damon Papenfuss is a Warwick," Ilias explained as he nestled amidst the rocks. Rista was grateful for the chance to sit. Her limbs were exhausted from the arduous night journey, but she was determined not to complain. All her life she had wanted to go on an adventure. She was the kind of girl who ran outside during storms to watch the lightning. When she set her mind to something, she was relentless.

The giant hunched over his knees, arms crossing in front of him.

"Where are you from?" Rista asked him.

"Kingvale," he grunted. He said nothing else and looked annoyed.

"Master Papenfuss is not one for much talk," Lielle said, flashing Rista a warm smile. "Fortunately Gabe makes up for it."

"Tell us what you know of enmitical magic," Ilias said to Rista in a kindly way. "Your father is a renowned Beesinger. I'm sure he has trained you in the lore?"

Rista nodded eagerly. "He has. There is a place where man and beast coexist as companions. The Enclave. It is surrounded by the Enemist. Once you cross it, once you enter the fallen world, there is enmity between man and beast. But some have learned to conquer the anger and fear and can bond with a certain creature. Eyriemaesters bond with hunting birds. Eagles, for example." She saw Ilias's approving smile and felt a flush of pride. "Some bond with foxes or other creatures. Very few can bond with dangerous animals, like grizzly bears." She looked at Papenfuss again, suppressing a shudder. Obviously his attempt to tame Kylek had not gone so well at first.

"And some can even tame insects," Ilias said. "Bees, for example. They are called Beesingers. It takes courage to enter a hive swarm. Have you done that?"

Rista took a deep breath. "Not exactly," she answered. "I've summoned a swarm, but I've not entered one to try and calm it. Bees are difficult to calm once they are frenzied."

Ilias glanced at Lielle, a knowing look passing between them. Then he turned a kind smile to Rista. "I hope you will not have to do that then," he said thoughtfully. "I hope we are wrong about what is happening at the Ziggurat. It has been uninhabited for years, since your father went with us to defeat the Overlord. But we have seen from the skies that there is an enemy afoot. A Serpentarium by the name of Mattson Kree. Only the bravest men attempt to tame poisonous snakes. The Arvadin and the wastelands to Battle Mountain are full of a breed of serpent that is distinctive because they have an *atrox* at the end of their tail from whence they get their name. When they are angry or threatened, the atrox rattles quickly, making a sound. The strongest atrox can slay an eagle."

Rista blinked at him and felt the thrill of danger down her back.

"She's smiling," Lielle said with a snort. "These beasts are dangerous, but they only venture out during the day. Mattson Kree controls them, and they are hunting us. Their poison is deadly. Back at the Enclave, there is magic that can heal a poisoned bite. We have brought a way to heal it with us, but it is a distant journey to get more."

Rista was so curious she blurted out a question. "And you think Mattson Kree is trying to revive the Ziggurat? Instead of enslaving kobolds, he will infest us with these deadly snakes?"

"Yes," Ilias said. He smiled again. "You're quite clever, Rista. I was hoping to have your father on our side, but you will do quite well."

"But what can I do?" Rista asked. "How is Beesinger magic going to help?"

Lielle gave Ilias a warning look.

"I'll explain that later," he said. "I think I hear boot steps. Gabe is joining us."

The announcement was followed shortly after by the young man as he scrabbled down a rock and hunched over to join them in the cave. He turned to Rista first. "Your siblings are with your aunt."

"Will she send word to Father?" Rista asked. "To tell him where we've gone?"

Gabe gave her an enigmatic look, then glanced at Ilias. "I think it would be too dangerous if he followed us. Don't you, Ilias?"

The Eyriemaester nodded gravely. "Best if we rest now." He reached over and patted Rista's shoulder. "Get some sleep. We'll start up again just before sunset."

* * *

It took a long time before Rista fell asleep. The exhaustion of the climb into the Arvadin was overwhelmed by her excitement at being with such famous individuals. She hadn't heard her father talk about Damon Papenfuss before, but clearly he had earned his way into Ilias's company. The Doer family were known to her. The king valued her father's wisdom. She was also impressed by how handsome Ilias was, even though he had lived for centuries in the Enclave. Her father had chosen not to live there, although he had been invited. She still couldn't imagine why he had refused such an honor.

She rested with her head on her arm, trying to get comfortable, and dozed in and out of sleep. The daylight made it difficult, but she was tired enough that sleep eventually overtook her. She was awakened middream by a clawlike touch on her arm.

She blinked her eyes and saw Twig's snout right by her face. She was so surprised by it that she nearly started.

"Tw—" she started to say, but the kobold gesticulated wildly at her not to, emitting a series of low clucks and hisses. The kobold glanced at her sleeping companions, and Rista saw that Lielle was gone.

The kobold motioned for her to follow him and quietly climbed up the rock at the mouth of the cave. He squatted there, his little scaly legs looking like a rooster's. He urgently motioned for her to follow.

Rista was confused and looked back at her slumbering companions. What was Twig doing in the middle of the Arvadin? Why wasn't he protecting her siblings? Was it because her father had ordered him to protect *her*? What good could the kobold do on such a quest! Twig soundlessly moved around the rock and then peeked back at her, gesturing emphatically for her to follow.

She felt frustration welling up inside her. She did not want Twig along on her first adventure. She'd be worried sick about him dying. He was truly the most defenseless little nuisance. She almost gestured for him to go away, but tightening her mouth into a frown, she quietly rose from the dirt and slipped away from the cave. The sunlight blinded her momentarily, and she shielded her face from it. Twig gestured again and then pointed, and she saw Lielle hunched down amidst some rocks with her bow, her back toward them as she watched the trail. Rista saw some eagles circling high overhead and wondered which one belonged to Ilias.

Rista followed Twig over another boulder where they would be out of sight of the cave and Lielle.

"Twig," Rista whispered with exasperation, "you need to go back and wait for Father! Why did you leave?"

The kobold said something in his guttural language. He was trembling with fear, which was typical of the cowardly thing.

"I didn't understand," Rista said, shaking her head. Where was Camille! Her sister was much better at communicating with him. "Slow down. Say it again." Twig shook his arms warningly, his head cocked and listening. Twig was like a frantic bird.

He repeated the same thing and Rista still wasn't sure she understood.

"What?" Rista asked again. "You're not making any sense."

The kobold growled and stamped his little foot. Very slowly, he stated it again, and Rista's mouth went dry.

" 'That's not Ilias.' Is that what you said?" Rista asked. Her stomach began to twist into knots.

The kobold nodded vigorously and began chittering again.

"No, no, slow down! Slow down!" Rista was growing more and more concerned. "What do you mean, it's not Ilias?"

The kobold gripped her arm and started to tug her.

"You want me to leave?"

Twig nodded violently again and chittered away in his peculiar speech. It was difficult, but she was starting to comprehend the urgent warning.

"Because you've met Ilias. And you know this isn't him. He doesn't *smell* like him. He smells like what?"

Twig repeated the word in a low clicking sound.

"He smells like snakes," Rista whispered, and then she realized, to her growing horror, that she had possibly been abducted.

Suddenly Twig bolted, vanishing around the rock so fast that Rista blinked and the kobold was gone. She heard boots and quickly stood, coming face-to-face with Lielle.

The huntress had a wary look in her eyes.

"What are you doing away from the cave?" she demanded. "It's daylight still."

Rista's stomach was flopping uncontrollably. "I . . . I needed to find some . . . some privacy," she stammered.

Lielle arched an eyebrow, then she jerked her head toward some trees and brush. "Over there. Be quick."

As Rista walked ashamedly toward the shelter, she realized why they were traveling at night. The clues were suddenly making sense. It was so that the *golden eagles* wouldn't see them. She felt like such a trusting fool. Rista glanced back at Lielle and realized it wasn't truly Lielle. She hadn't seen the huntress's fox because there wasn't one. She couldn't believe she had fallen for such a trick.

When she reached the privacy of the ferns and brush, she squatted low and hid herself, then searched around. Twig suddenly appeared next to her, one of the fronds brushing his face.

"Good, Twig," she whispered gratefully, feeling her heart gush with gratitude. "You're sure about this?"

The kobold nodded his snout emphatically and made a low growl in his throat.

"I need to get back to Father, Twig. Will you help me?"

Twig nodded eagerly again, showing a row of tiny teeth.

Then she heard it. The drone of bees. It was coming from the crook of a tree. An idea began to come together in her mind of how to escape her captors.

* * *

As Rista approached the hive, she tried to soothe her chaotic emotions. The sickening feeling of being deceived had rattled her, but she knew she needed to tame her emotions or she'd never be able to use her magic.

Enmitical magic had its roots in emotions. It involved conquering the self, specifically the conquering of fear. The fear of animals and creatures existed because of the Enemist. The sound of the bees humming around the hive normally filled people with abject terror. But not Rista and not her family. She had been raised around the droning sound and even as a child, before her father had taught her the magic, she had lain on the grass and watched bees collecting nectar from flowers. Her childlike innocence and lack of fear made her willing and eager to reach out her little finger and pet the fuzzy end of the bumblebees she'd find. When one would land on her open palm, their little legs would tickle, but she had no desire to squash it or run away shrieking. Creatures of nature could sense human emotions. They could sense when there was a state of enmity and they responded accordingly. A Beesinger could reach a hand into a honeycomb without getting stung because the bees understood the intent and willingly shared the sticky, sweet treasure they created by their own primal instincts.

Twig remained at the edge of the copse to watch for pursuers while Rista closed the gap to the gnarled tree. The hive had been erected in a huge knot of a dead tree, and she saw blurs of gold and black darting and dancing through. There was still daylight and much work to do, so the hive was active. Rista swallowed, approaching it cautiously, one hand stretched out, invoking the magic within her. The frenzied hum started to subside. Many scout bees came out to investigate and hovered around her, some landing on her arm and palm, some in her golden hair. She felt the tickling sensations again, unable to help the smile that came. These were honeybees, and she sensed their curiosity in meeting a Beesinger. The magic she bore made them trust her immediately, and soon the drones were flying around, treating her as if she were a normal part of the forest and not a threat.

Rista had only tried her skills at Father's man-built hives and was grateful that she was strong enough in the magic for this to work. There was a difference in the mood of these bees, naturally. Her father's bees had been trained and raised for generations to make honey and fertilize trees. They cooperated with the Beesingers and had for generations. Bees of the wild were a little less structured in their thinking, but the instincts were still the same. She was welcomed as part of the colony and closed the distance to the hive. Gingerly, she reached into the hive to fetch a chunk of honeycomb. Father had taught her that honey contained nearly all the nutrients needed to stay alive and that a Beesinger could live off the land almost indefinitely.

The gooey hunk dislodged easily and she brought it out. The honey was sweet when she tasted it.

Twig made a chittering noise, warning her that Lielle was coming.

Rista had walked deliberately to the tree, leaving a clear trail to follow. She turned her attention back to the hive and reached out to it with her magic. Bees were primitive and could only understand basic concepts. Over time, a Beesinger could train bees to follow complicated instructions. This was not such an opportunity. But there was much she could do. Each bee had wandered far from the hive to collect pollen, and she could read the hive mind to understand the land surrounding the hive almost as if they'd made a map of the terrain. She closed her eyes, searching for a place to hide, and found one that the bees like to frequent. It was a fallen log with decaying wood that was hollowed out. It wasn't very far.

After gaining the knowledge she needed, she began to alter the magic. She let her fear and worry begin to build inside her, instilling in the hive the sense of a threat. Humans were coming to destroy the hive, she thought to the bees, and they understood her. Humans would wreck all their hard work and destroy their home. The tone of the hive changed instantly to one of hostility. The buzzing grew louder, more dangerous. Bees hurried off to spy for danger and to summon others to defend the hive. The sounds they made were immediately noticeable. The magic would not last for long if a threat didn't materialize. Bees had short attention spans.

Rista motioned for Twig to follow her as she stole around the tree and quickly fled the area. Bees followed her, of course. She was part of the hive and the queen had sent some to protect her. She relished the feeling of the magic as she became part of the hive mind herself. The sunlight shone down on her and she knew she needed to find the shelter quickly. After nightfall, it would be easier to escape her foes. But first she would listen to them as they hunted her and see if what Twig had warned her of was true. Twig was fiercely loyal to her family. Even though he was a tiny, almost useless little monster, he had hunted her deep into the Arvadin to save her. A few hundred paces away from the hive, she found the hollowed log and quickly settled into it. It was small, but so was Rista, and she wedged herself in to get out of sight.

"Rista?"

The voice called from far away. It was Lielle.

"Rista? Where are you?"

She hunkered down inside the log and waited. Then the bees began to sting.

"Rista! Ouch! Rista!" The tone changed to one of anger.

"What happened?" shouted the voice of the man she thought was pretending to be Ilias.

"The little brat tricked me," said the woman. "There's a beehive over there. Ugh, they sting! They're swarming. I've been stung three times already. I'm going to slit her throat, Kree."

"No, we need her," replied the man angrily. "Fuss! Get up here. Send Kylek to destroy the hive. Gabe! You two. Go around and encircle where she may be hiding. She can't have gone far."

"She's not far," the woman snarled. "I'll find her."

"We *all* will," Mattson Kree said. "You go that way. Gabe, you go that way. Fuss . . . destroy the hive now!"

Twig scampered inside the fallen log. His orange-red eyes were alight with mischief and his crooked-tooth grin showed his inner cunning.

"Good, Twig," Rista whispered, rubbing the knobbed horns on his head. She hugged the kobold. Her pride was tempered with growing fear. She was not under the protection of Ilias. She was being hunted by a Serpentarium.

* * *

Rista remained perfectly still as Papenfuss's bear destroyed the beehive. She'd heard his pained snarls and growls, listened to the sound of mighty claws raking the scabbed bark. The bees began to scatter with the destruction of their home, the queen being the first to leave. All the energy of their efforts and defense were useless against a bear. She had bought herself some time, and watched as the sun dipped into the valley far below. The shadows of the trees were getting longer. Her body was cramped and uncomfortable. She heard the sounds of her pursuers. They were making no effort to be quiet. It was clear that their friendliness had all been an act, a deception to convince her to come with them willingly.

They called out to her, issuing threats. They threatened to go back down the mountain and hurt her family. Rista clenched her teeth with fury, not fear. She knew they'd say anything to get her to reveal herself. The Arvadin was an enormous mountain range that was like the spine of the world. There were many places a person could hide. Her best hope of concealment was remaining still.

The shadows thickened as night began to descend. This was her opportunity. Her pursuers were spread out around her, tromping and marching in the woods. In a few more moments, the dusk would make it very difficult to see. From the hive mind, she had learned the lay of the land and had mapped out a course that she would follow in the dark. From the commotion her enemies were making, she could almost see in her mind's eye that they had wandered far afield, not realizing how close she was to the original hive. She'd hoped they would get past her.

Twig's head, which had been resting on her shoulder, popped up. The eyes blinked twice and then he suddenly rose and crept out of the stump. His bony little hands and claws gripped the decaying wood.

Then the kobold jumped away as a snake leaped at him.

Rista shrieked with fear. The snake was an atrox, with a diamond-shaped pattern down its back and length. The fangs had missed the kobold by a hair. The rattle on its tail began to whir viciously, and Rista scrambled to get out of the log. Her heart felt like it was going to jitter its way out of her chest as she fled in terror. The atrox slithered after her, moving with fluid grace and speed that made her mind go nearly black with panic.

She scrambled over the log on the other side, lost her footing, and went down. She saw Mattson Kree standing by a tree about a dozen paces off, arms folded imperiously and a malevolent smile on his mouth.

Rista's knee was throbbing, but she scrabbled to her feet to flee the other way, when she was grabbed roughly from behind. Rista reached and grabbed a fistful of flaming-red hair and pulled hard, her body reacting to the desperate situation without thinking. She found herself clutching an abandoned wig and then felt the naked edge of a blade against her quivering throat.

"You think I *won't* slit your neck?" the woman hissed in her ear.

"Trea," said the Serpentarium in a scolding voice.

"I was stung five times because of her!" railed the other. She grabbed Rista by the wrist and jerked her arm up behind her back, sending a jabbing pain into her shoulder that made her knees wobble. "Five times!"

Gabe bounded over another log and landed nearby with a smirk on his face and then sheathed his daggers.

Rista felt like crying because she'd been caught so easily, but she refused to give them the satisfaction.

"And who are you really?" Rista demanded the boy. "Not the king's son!"

"Actually, he *is*," Mattson Kree said smoothly, closing the distance. "That part wasn't a lie." He walked up to her, his expression now cold and calculating. "You've got spirit, Rista. And you do your father credit for one so young. I had thought to fool you all the way to Battle Mountain."

The atrox slithered up to them, the noisy tail still making its fearful rattle. Then Mattson Kree bent down and scooped up the giant snake, fondling it and giving Rista a crooked smile. The head hissed and gaped its jaws at Rista, and she fought against Trea, increasing the painful throb of her arm. The atrox hissed, its pink, fleshy mouth wide, the fangs dripping venom. Rista had never felt so much fear, never had her mind gone so utterly black with panic.

"Five stings on poor Trea," the Serpentarium mocked. "Well, since you like to cause pain, girl, I'm sure you can handle *taking* it."

"What do you want from me?" Rista whimpered, unable to break free. She saw the grizzly skulking toward them from the woods, the huge Damon Papenfuss coming from behind.

"I really just need you alive, that's all," Kree said with a biting coldness in his voice. His eyes were like the snake's, utterly devoid of sentiment. "Until your father is dead. I can't have him ruining all my plans like he did to the Overlord, now can I?" He looked up at Trea, who was still gripping Rista and holding the knife to her throat.

"I think one bite is worth five stings. Will that satisfy you, Trea?"

"For now," huffed the angered woman.

Rista stared at them both in fear and horror.

"Not on the leg, or she won't be able to walk all night," Mattson Kree said menacingly. "How about her arm then? You think a little bee sting hurts, Rista? I have magic that can purge the atrox's venom. But you need to *feel* it working first. You think you're so clever? I control every atrox in these mountains. They mostly hunt at night. You think slipping away from me will save you? You think your insignificant *bee* magic is going to save you? Trust me, little girl." His tone went flat with ruthless intensity. "You have no idea what I'm capable of."

His eyes flashed with hatred and he nodded to the woman pinning Rista. Trea untwisted Rista's arm and exposed the meaty portion just below the elbow. The snake's fangs flashed down, sinking into Rista's arm. It was painful, like getting jabbed by pins. But then the venom began to turn her blood into fire.

Trea dumped her on the ground as the convulsions began to shake through her legs. As the pain began spreading throughout Rista's body, the Serpentarium casually gathered up the snake and gently lowered it into the leather satchel he wore around his neck.

Rista's eyes bulged with pain, but she wouldn't cry out. The pain in her arm grew worse and worse.

She could not sense any bees around for miles.

* * *

The atrox venom was the most painful thing that had happened to Rista. She knew it would kill her if left unchecked. After Mattson Kree was satisfied she had suffered enough, he offered relief in the form of a glass vial with a stopper. Inside the egg-shaped crystal was a murky liquid. He brought the vial to her arm and looked as if he would pour it on her skin. Instead, the vial began to glow and the murky liquid seemed to suck the venom out of her bleeding punctures. She stared at it, quivering with pain and agony, but fascinated by the magic being wielded. The flaming sensation began to calm and then it was gone, expelled from her body. The murky contents of the vial were darker now, swirling malevolently. He crouched by her, his eyes devious as he showed her the vial, and then he stuffed it into a pouch at his waist and stood.

"I know you have magic, Rista," he said in a threatening tone. "I would encourage you to use it to keep any bees from getting near us. Your father will likely send them to hunt you. If I hear even one insect close enough, believe me—you will regret it. Keep them away from us and you will not get hurt anymore. Do we understand one another?"

"Why should I help you at all?" Rista said angrily, clenching her fists. "You said you would kill my father."

His eyes narrowed. "There are many ways one can die, child. Remember that." Then he turned to the others. "The sun is down. We need to be at the top of the pass before dawn to destroy the guards stationed there. Onward."

Rista rubbed the swollen bite marks on her forearm. As she walked, she searched the shrubs and vegetation for a sign of the kobold. Twig was nowhere to be seen.

After nightfall descended, they hiked by moonlight up to the craggy heights of the Arvadin. The trees became denser, thick with pine needles and cone-shaped tops. The mountains grew steeper as they climbed, but they headed toward a gap between two peaks that still contained chunks of snow and ice. The air grew steadily thinner and Rista found herself gasping for breath to keep up with her captors. Papenfuss and Kylek took the lead, lumbering up the trail. The girl, Trea, no longer wearing the wig, scowled at Rista every time she happened to glance back at her. She kept her longbow ready and covered their trail to make it more difficult to follow. Gabe walked alongside Mattson Kree, conferring with him in low tones, but eventually he dropped back to walk alongside Rista.

"So you *are* the king's son," Rista said with malice.

"The king's *youngest* son," he replied casually. "The most useless. The least wanted. I have a better chance becoming master of Stanchion castle allying myself with this lot than I ever had before."

"Your father is a good man, an honest king!" Rista said angrily.

"A fat lot of good it does him too," Gabe replied with a chuckle. "And what do *you* know about politics, Rista? You live far away from court. The factions surrounding my father, constantly wheedling and maneuvering. He can hardly get anything done with all the opposition he faces. A king should have power. Not be a slave to the people." He chuckled derisively.

Rista's insides boiled with anger. "And I suppose you think life would be better under the heel of another overlord? Mattson Kree may grant you your father's throne, but you'll be his puppet."

"Oh yes, I'm sure you've got it all figured out," Gabe said with a snort. "Your father is reputedly the wisest man in all the realm. And look how easily we abducted *you*. Everyone knew that he was going to Apple Hill. Everyone knew that he left you all unprotected. So wise . . . yet so blind. Are you just like your father?"

Rista bridled at his taunt, but she tried to keep her voice calm. "And what of the Enclave? Do you think they will sit still while your *master* seeks to reclaim Battle Mountain? Surely the *true* Ilias will come."

Gabe sniffed and shrugged. "That is a problem, Rista, when your eagles can see so far away. But they can only see during the daylight. They don't see what happens in the dark." He was walking closer to her now, his voice dropping lower, almost conspiratorially. "It is a different world at night. A world of bats. A world of croaking frogs. A world of shadows and drunks and laughter and dicing and all sorts of other evils that would make a young woman like you blush. Even the bees cannot sting at night."

She folded her arms, feeling a strangeness in her belly as he spoke. His tone was almost confiding.

"That's not true, you know," she said, shaking her head. "Bees *can* sting at night."

"Really?" he said, surprised.

"Think on it, Gabe. The time people are most likely to be stung are when the bees are out of their hives and people are out of their homes. At night, both are inside. But if you jammed a stick into a hive in the middle of the night, they'd come out fighting."

"Humph," Gabe said with a chuckle. "You may be wiser than I thought."

He butted her with his arm and then hiked to catch up to Mattson Kree. And proceeded to warn him about what she had just told him. She gritted her teeth and wished she could summon a swarm into his shirt.

* * *

The night began to peel away and they had still not reached the summit. Rista was exhausted and felt her eyelids drooping. Mattson Kree looked impatient and angered by the delay. They were waiting for Trea to return from hiding their trail. The Serpentarium had his boot planted on a jutting rock and stared up at the mountains almost in defiance.

"How much farther to the summit, Papenfuss?" he asked.

The bearlike man shrugged. "It's not much further, but we'll be seen approaching in the light."

Trea came jogging up from the hill, a worried look on her face.

"What is it?" Gabe asked her in concern.

"I saw someone," she said.

Everyone turned to face her. "Saw someone or *something*?" Mattson Kree clarified.

Trea rubbed her arm, keeping her bow flush against her body. "A man. He's coming up to the pass."

Rista's heart leaped and a small smile crept onto her mouth.

"Tell me what you saw," Mattson Kree said patiently, his eyes narrowing.

"A man with gray hair," Trea said. "He was hiking quickly with a walking stick. There was something scrabbling alongside him. A raccoon or a small dog."

Twig. Rista smiled even wider.

"Is it the Beesinger?" Gabe asked Mattson Kree.

"I have to assume that it is," he answered darkly. "He doesn't need footprints to track us." He rubbed his mouth. "Well, he's come a lot sooner than I suspected."

A thrill of hope tingled inside of Rista. Her father was coming. But what could he do against so many?

"What do we do?" Gabe asked. He had a worried sound in his voice.

Trea spoke up. "If we wait here during the day, he'll catch up to us well before nightfall. If we keep going, we'll be seen by the soldiers."

"I know," Mattson Kree said angrily. "I'm not worried about the soldiers. There are enough atrox in these mountains to kill them all. This is what we do. Papenfuss, you will wait here and ambush the Beesinger with Kylek. We'll go ahead and clear the pass."

"We'll be seen!" Trea said worriedly, pointing to the skies. "Let's all wait for the Beesinger and ambush him together."

Rista felt worry trembling in her stomach. There were four of them against her father, and he was old. There was also Twig. And of course, she would do what she could.

Mattson Kree shook his head. "He'll be no match for Papenfuss, let *alone* a grizzly."

Rista had to do something. She saw them conferring closely, ready to make a decision that would kill her father. If she could run ahead, she could warn the soldiers and bring them down to help. Although she was tired, the sudden panic lent her strength, and she glanced up the trailhead, wondering how far the gap in the pass would be. Trea had her bow, and she had no doubt the woman would shoot at her, but she had to try something!

Rista glanced once more at the trail and prepared to bolt when suddenly Gabe was standing next to her, gripping her arm with his hand. She tried to shake him loose, but he clenched her so tightly it hurt.

"That wouldn't be wise," he whispered to her.

"What are you doing, Gabe?" Mattson Kree demanded.

"She was about to run! You were all looking the other way and I saw her. We'd better gag her, just to be safe."

"Do it," the Serpentarium ordered, glowering.

Gabe withdrew a wadded rag and stuffed it into her mouth and began tying it roughly behind her. "I like your hair," he whispered, tightening the knot. "It's like sunshine."

She gave him a withering look and he only chuckled at her, returning to grip her arm.

"You are so naive," he scoffed, making her even angrier. She'd lost her chance to warn her father and cursed herself for being too slow. She should have bolted the moment the idea struck her. But Gabe was watchful. She'd remember that. She kicked him in the shins out of pure spite and anger, and he winced, startled.

"She does have a stinger after all," he mused, then pulled her along toward the others. She watched helplessly as Papenfuss and Kylek began to lumber down the mountain. The worry in her stomach turned to sickening fear. No human could outrun a bear. Her father had made sure he had taught his children that.

* * *

Mattson Kree walked ahead of them now, climbing up the steep slope toward the gap. Gabe marched with Rista next to him, one hand on her arm to keep her close to him. He kept glancing nervously back at Trea who was scouting for signs of what happened down the trail.

The Serpentarium's fancy cloak was brown with dust and dirt from the hike. He looked sternly ahead, his brow furrowed in concentration.

"He's summoning them," Gabe whispered to Rista.

She couldn't answer him because of the gag and was wondering why he was even bothering to tell her.

"He is powerful. And ruthless. He'll do what he says he'll do. His goal is to destroy the Enclave and put himself the master of it." He pursed his lips. "He just may accomplish it too. If anyone could, it would be him."

Rista tried to jerk her arm away again, but he wouldn't loosen his hold.

"He is enemies with the Enclave," Gabe continued, as if she were holding an equal part of the conversation with him. "He tried to earn his way there, to be admitted. He learned about serpent taming, which admittedly takes a great deal of courage. The homestead where he grew up was situated on a viper's nest. No one knew it." He chuffed to himself, shaking his head. "Killed his entire family. He was the only one who survived. His aunt raised him." Gabe rubbed his jaw. "He grew and mastered his fear of snakes. He was determined to reclaim the abandoned homestead. And he did. He surely did. He began to develop a reputation of taming atrox and helped other families rid their properties. For a fee. He was doing everyone a great service, so he thought. But the Enclave refused to admit him. They saw something unworthy in his motives, I think. By denying him entrance, they provoked him. He learned at a young age that when you set your mind to something, however impossible the ambition, you will succeed if you do not falter. He's the sort of man who could overcome my father's kingdom and set himself as a tyrant."

Rista looked at him, again confused at why he was talking to her in such a way. He wasn't boasting. He was speaking in a low, conspiratorial voice, almost as if he were trying to confide in her.

She wanted to ask him questions but the gag prevented it.

"Watch how he uses his power," Gabe said, nodding. "Pay attention."

Rista kept her eyes fixed on Mattson Kree. He unlatched the satchel he carried and then hefted out the enormous atrox. The man's face brightened as he held the serpent. He seemed to be speaking to it, whispering to it in a strange, encouraging way. Then he set it down on the ground as he kept walking toward the ridge ahead of them. Rista felt something brush against her and saw with terror another atrox slither past. They were emerging from the woods and brush all around them, flocking to the Serpentarium as if he were invoking them.

"He's been summoning them for a while," Gabe whispered. "See how they come to him. The mountains are *full* of atrox."

Gabe kept Rista back a few paces as she watched the serpents writhe and slither around their master's legs. They came in a horde, first dozens, and then hundreds, until the entire trail was full. Some hissed and reared at each other, as if fighting to be closest to him. It was like a river of snakes, and it horrified Rista to see it. She was trembling uncontrollably at the sight and felt Gabe's hand tighten on her arm. They were walking amidst the river of snakes also and she saw the uncomfortable look on his face. He wasn't enjoying it either.

Then the shouts of men started up again. The soldiers saw the threat. There were cries of pain. Rista cringed as she heard the noises, the groans of men, the shrieks of fear. This was awful magic. This was the stuff of nightmares.

The serpents converged on the gap ahead and all the while he walked, the Serpentarium smiled with glee and satisfaction. He reached the top of the ridge and stopped, staring down at the scene before him. He chuckled to himself, satisfied at what his power had invoked.

Gabe and Rista reached his side, and she stared down, growing sick at the vision of soldiers wearing the tunic of Stanchion castle spread out on the ground, some still twitching as the venom overwhelmed them in moments. The sight horrified her and made her tremble. There were at least two dozen soldiers. Some had perished while trying to climb up on boulders. All were slumped and fallen.

The serpents had done their work quickly. The river of snakes would have been able to handle ten times that number. In fact, she realized with horror, it would be enough to stop an army. She thought she'd be sick. She knew she'd have nightmares.

The cruel look in Mattson Kree's eyes as he glanced at her spoke of his willingness to do anything to achieve his goals.

"What now?" Gabe asked solemnly.

"We await word of the Beesinger's death," he said coldly, and his look made Rista even more afraid.

* * *

It was an agonizing wait and Rista took a long time falling asleep in one of the tents used by the soldiers. She couldn't stop thinking about the soldier whose tent it was. She had been raised on her father's stories of adventure, but now she understood a part of the sadness that was always in his eyes. Gabe was positioned outside to guard her, but she was so tired and heartsick, she eventually fell asleep.

A tug at the gag awakened her and she blinked her eyes quickly, confused and trembling. She felt little claws digging at the bond and suddenly the gag loosened. She turned her head and saw Twig. Her heart leaped with excitement.

Rubbing her eyes, she tried to contain her emotions. Gabe was no longer patrolling the door. She heard his voice outside, talking to Trea and Mattson Kree.

"What do you mean he's dead?" the Serpentarium said with fury. "He's an aging man, how did he manage to kill Damon Papenfuss?"

Trea's voice was full of worry. "Kylek turned on him. Kylek killed him!"

"That doesn't make any sense," Gabe said. "One person's magic cannot be used against another form of animal."

"I know that!" Mattson Kree snapped. "It's not possible. Tell me what you saw. What you *saw*, Trea!"

"It happened very fast," the woman said. "Papenfuss sent the bear down to kill him. It was quite a distance from me, so I couldn't see it well. Kylek is huge! He roared and came down to fight and then suddenly ... I don't know ... he was distracted. He kept swatting his face."

"Bees," the Serpentarium said with a shiver of revulsion in his voice. Rista peeked through the tent and saw the emotion of fear in his eyes.

"Of course it was bees!" Gabe snapped. "He's a Beesinger, after all! But bears have thick hide. They destroy hives all the time."

"The bear was distracted. Then the Beesinger went around the bear and charged at Papenfuss. He's no match for the giant, but suddenly a swarm struck him. I saw it. He was crying out and swinging his arms. The Beesinger hit him with a pack. A bag. Something. He clubbed him in the head but kept running. Then Kylek came and attacked Papenfuss. He killed him. I saw it! Then the bees started coming up the mountain and after me, so I ran. We have to get out of here! He's brought a whole swarm with him!"

Rista heard the story and rejoiced. She turned to Twig and asked what happened. The kobold gave her a toothy grin. He was proud to tell her the story but it was difficult for her to understand. Twig had just come from her father, who had sent him ahead to help her escape. Father had used honey. He knew the bear's instincts for sweets would overcome its will for a few moments. Her father had used the confusion of bees to distract it from him and then smacked Papenfuss with a small beehive he'd discovered in the woods, making him drip with honey and bees. The swarm had interrupted Papenfuss's control of his own magic, and his own bear had attacked him to get more honey.

She grinned with triumph at her father's ingenuity. She was so proud of him.

"Grab the girl!" Mattson Kree said angrily. "Bring her to me."

Twig looked panic-stricken, and Rista quickly grabbed a blanket and smothered the kobold with it to conceal him. She went to the tent and stepped out.

"Where's the gag?" Gabe demanded.

"I was tired of it," Rista snapped. She glowered at the Serpentarium, but her mind was working fast. "Well? Are we going to stand around at the summit or go to Battle Mountain? I think my father's planning to defeat you there."

The taunt was probably ill-advised, but she did not regret it.

"We'll see who wins," Mattson Kree said angrily. "I still have *you*, after all."

"There's a bee on your shoulder," Rista said, nodding at him.

The man jerked back, eyes wide with the involuntary spasm, and flapped his arms almost comically. It confirmed Rista's suspicion. Mattson Kree was terrified of bees.

* * *

After crossing the highest summit of the Arvadin, the terrain changed drastically. The western slopes had been lush and full of trees. Rista's father had explained to her that the leeward side of the mountains was stark and barren, for although it did get storms, it did not get as many because of the height of the mountain range. Different creatures infested the rocky, scraggy country—creatures like lizards, serpents, vultures, and even roaming bands of kobolds.

As Rista walked, she sensed the presence of bees, but they were distant and the colonies were small. There were more carpenter bees in the desolate land, their size and hardiness better suited for the rough landscape. Rista sensed them, but she didn't like them. There were also a variety of wasps clustered around the mud pits that were the remains of dried-out ponds. The earth was cracked and parched, the ground hard on her legs and ankles.

The march down the other side was quick and uneventful, and before them stretched a massive plain with another range of mountains in the far distance. The peak of one of the distant mountains was shaped like a pyramid. Battle Mountain. Pockets of scrub and brambleweed stretched for leagues in front of them. The plains were barren of trees, save for a few stunted mesquites. There was nowhere to hide, unless you were small like Twig. Rista tried to spot the kobold to make sure he was following, but she couldn't discern him from the foliage, which would have perfectly hidden the creature's movements. Her thirst became a concern, but Mattson Kree had filled several water flasks up on the mountaintop and they had claimed those left behind by the slain soldiers.

As she plodded on the dusty road, the sun scorching high above, she would occasionally glance back to see if she could also spot her father. But there was no sign of pursuers, no sign of the massive eagles that patrolled the valley on the other side.

"Why do you keep looking back?" Gabe asked, dropping back suddenly to walk alongside her. "Do you think he's going to suddenly run up and save you?"

"I don't know what he's going to do," Rista replied stiffly. "But he's smarter than the lot of you."

"You think so?" Gabe asked with a wry smile.

"Why are we traveling during the day and not the night now?" she asked him, feeling the dust and dirt all over herself. Each step kicked up more plumes of it.

"Once we crossed the mountains, we became less of a target for the Enclave. It's very far to the south. If they did know about us, it would take weeks before they could get here."

"What about your father?" she challenged.

Gabe shrugged. "Again, it will take weeks before he learns about the soldiers on the pass. What clues will they have? Bite marks. They won't know who was behind it. They don't know about us. They don't even know about Mattson Kree. But they will." He glanced ahead at the Serpentarium who maintained a bold, tireless stride. He was speaking to Trea in a low voice. There was no effort to hide their trail.

"What is his plan?" Rista asked conspiratorially.

Gabe glanced back at Mattson Kree, then at her. He dropped his voice even lower. "Do you really think I'm going to tell you? I thought you were smart, Rista."

She elbowed him sharply in the ribs, which startled him and he grunted. Mattson Kree glanced back angrily and Gabe rubbed his side and stepped away from her, giving her a sulky look.

"My father will stop you," Rista said hotly, her voice cracking.

Mattson Kree looked back at her again, his look sly. "I'm counting on it," he replied ominously.

* * *

They walked until well after sunset. Rista's legs were tired and aching, but she never complained of the fatigue. The mountains in the far distance seemed no closer at the end of the first day. It was like they were walking in sand that pulled them backward ten paces for every five they went forward. After it was dark, Mattson Kree directed them at a sharp angle to the one they had been traveling. They made camp in the dark, with no fire. The earth was hard and sharp with stones and cracked edges. The diminutive shrubs weren't gentle either. Rista cleared a space to stretch out on her blanket.

Gabe walked by and tossed another rolled-up blanket to her. "It gets cold at night," he offered by way of explanation. She took it without thanks.

Mattson Kree sat nearby, his back straight.

"I saw no sign of him during the day," Trea said in a dark tone. "Not even a smudge on the horizon. He could be camouflaged, though."

Mattson Kree shook his head. "He may have waited for the dark to follow us."

Trea wrinkled her nose. "Why do you think that?"

Mattson Kree extended his arm, pointing.

Rista turned back and she saw it too. There was an orb of light shining in the mountain, winding down the trail they had come from.

"He stands out like a beacon," Trea said angrily.

"He's doing it on purpose," Mattson Kree said, chuckling. "He's a clever man, Trea. We shouldn't underestimate him. He defeated the Overlord, after all." The Serpentarium turned his gaze to Rista. The moon showed just enough of his face that she could see his sardonic expression. "How did he defeat the Overlord?"

Rista huddled beneath the blanket Gabe had thrown to her, feeling a spark of hope and a deep reservoir of defiance. She leaned forward, glancing from one to the other, keeping her voice low. "Do you *really* think I'm going to tell you? I thought you were smart, Mattson Kree."

Gabe stifled his snort of laughter and tried inadequately to disguise it as a cough.

Mattson Kree's face hardened. "I grow weary of your insolence. Perhaps you'd care to feel an atrox's fangs again."

Rista lifted her chin. "I'm not afraid of you."

"But you are afraid of serpents," he said knowingly. He opened the flap of his satchel and the snake lifted its head out and then coiled on the dusty ground in a heap. Rista's skin shivered at the sight of it, despite all her efforts to control her fear. Cold sweat leeched from her skin.

"You cannot help yourself," Mattson Kree whispered. "It's the enmity magic. Little children are unaffected by it—until they are hurt. Children are afraid of nothing. But soon they learn, and it is pain that teaches them. The scalding handle of an iron skillet. The sting of a bee. We are a weak and vulnerable race. A sack of watery blood and soft organs enmeshed in brittle bones." His voice took on a mystical quality as he gazed at her, his eyes fierce and determined. "All the while, the Enclave exists in a state of peace. They have immortal bodies that cannot age and die. They sing their fat songs and drink their ancient wines and pluck the strings of their melodious harps." He said this with derision. "They could be the rulers of the valley. They could knock down Stanchion castle with an earthquake. Yet they refuse to participate in the world at large. They let kingdoms rise and fall. They let us squabble and fight, and they do nothing to intervene. Nothing until humanity is too wretched and irksome and only *then* will they be *bothered* to lend assistance.

They could make the world like the Enclave. Instead, they huddle within its confines, sipping its precious magic, free of fear." He leaned forward, his arm resting on his knee. "But they will fear me."

"You cannot get into the Enclave," Rista said, her voice trembling. She wanted to be brave, but there was an atrox coiled in front of her, its forked tongue flicking at her. Mattson Kree sat behind it, his eyes probing into hers.

"Can't I?" he whispered smoothly. "But you misunderstand my goals, Rista. I don't want to go *into* the Enclave. I want to stop them from coming *out*. A serpent population will continue to grow so long as there is plentiful food. Trust me, my dear. I have thought this all through. The Overlord had the right plan. He had the right protections. He just underestimated the folk wisdom of a Beesinger. That is why my plan begins there. Your father should have gone to the Enclave while he had the chance. No one will *ever* go in there again."

There was a hint of madness in the man's eyes, and Rista feared it. He was ambitious and confident. He was convinced he would succeed. But Rista wondered how many would die for his ambitions to be fulfilled.

Mattson Kree leaned back, stretching out his long legs, resting on his elbows. "Get some sleep. The Beesinger is still a league away, if not more. Don't try to escape, Rista. These plains are full of snakes. And they are hunting your father just as they are protecting us. If you try to leave this camp, you'll be bitten. I may or may not save you a second time."

* * *

It was the middle of the night and the moon had gone down. Only the stars offered some meager light. Rista blinked awake, afraid, feeling a tap on her shoulder. She lifted her head and found the kobold leering down at her. He pressed a clawlike finger to his snout.

Rista nodded. The atrox was gone. In the dim light, she saw the satchel was flat, empty. The Serpentarium breathed in and out, deep asleep. Trea was nestled again him, her face buried against his side, her arm around her shoulder. It made Rista frown. Looking over her shoulder, she spotted Gabe on his blanket, away from the other two. Part of her wanted to rouse him, to persuade him to come with her and escape these two.

Twig gestured for her to follow him. The kobold slunk low to the ground, keeping an eye on the sleeping forms and listening for sounds of trouble. Rista got to her feet and grabbed her half-full waterskin. Each movement felt loud and distracting and she winced at herself. Twig grabbed her hand and led her away from the camp, each step as soft as the wind, while her boots scuffed on the dirt and pebbles. Twig guided her away from the stunted shrubs, weaving and crossing. The kobold would suddenly stop, sniff, and then pull her a different direction. He was helping her avoid the snakes, and she was grateful.

Once they had crept far enough, the kobold tugged on her hand and began to move more quickly. He was taking them east toward Battle Mountain.

"Why are we going this way, Twig?" she whispered.

The kobold tugged and pulled again, chittering softly. They had not gone far when a cry went up from the camp.

"She's gone."

"What?" Mattson Kree growled.

"I said she's gone!" It was Gabe's voice, full of worry.

"How did she get past the serpents?" Trea asked.

"Can you see her footprints?" Mattson Kree demanded.

"Not in the dark. I need light."

"Can't risk it," he answered angrily. "The Beesginer will be watching."

"How did she get past the snakes?" Gabe demanded. "Do you think she went back?"

"It won't be long before my *pets* catch her," Mattson Kree said with savage fury. "Stay here. She can't get far."

"Let me light a torch!" Trea pleaded. "Let me hunt her."

"No," shot back Mattson Kree. "Snakes don't need light to hunt."

* * *

The sun slowly brightened the eastern sky and was on the verge of being seen. Rista was cold and tired from the night walk and she was hungry. But the fear of capture and being bitten had kept her moving. She shivered, rubbing her arms vigorously, and was grateful for the sun. She had only drunk two mouthfuls of water, wanting to preserve what little she had.

They were still walking east because that's where Twig insisted on leading her. Twig had tried to explain, but she couldn't understand his gibberish like her sister could. She regretted not taking the time before it was needed. She caught her dirty braid with her fingers, looking at it and then tossing it back over her shoulder. Her hair was no longer golden blond, but dusty brown. She felt the dust all over her body and longed for a stream or something to clean herself in. The dust was even in her teeth, which was uncomfortable and aggravating.

As the sunlight began to crest the mountains, she turned her gaze backward and dreaded what she would see. The plain was so flat there was no way to hide herself, but that also meant her enemies could not hide themselves either. What had they done after she'd escaped the camp? She had gone all night and not heard sounds from her pursuers, although she did hear the noise of an atrox rattle several times, but Twig guided them away from the path.

During the night she had also seen the strange light in the distance. She thought it was her father's light stone and that he was using it to see his way. But it had disappeared during the night, and she'd lost all connection with her father. Just seeing the pinprick of light had been comforting. And then it was gone and she felt alone again. Except for Twig.

The dawn revealed her pursuers.

They were several miles behind her but much closer than she had thought possible. Yes, the serpents were still hunting her, leading them to her. And she was going to Battle Mountain, the place they wanted to go anyway, and she didn't understand why Twig was leading her there. She had wondered if Mattson Kree, Gabe, and Trea would separate to find her, but no—they were sticking together.

Rista kept walking, enduring the thirst and hunger the best she could.

"Stay out of sight, Twig," she reminded the kobold. Had they figured out that Rista was no longer alone? They couldn't consider the little kobold much of a threat.

A familiar hum sounded in her ear. She turned as a bee came zigzagging up to her. It landed on her hand. It was a honeybee. The relief she felt hearing its drone and feeling the tickling sensation on her palm made her want to cry. Invoking her magic, she saw where its hive was and her stomach growled. Honey was just what she needed.

"Come on, Twig," she said with courage. "I think we could both use some breakfast." Then she turned her magic to the bee and began to follow it back to its hive.

* * *

The beehive Rista found was small and nestled in a dense shrub. With her magic, she kept the swarm calm and extracted a hunk of gooey comb to satisfy her hunger. The sound of the bees was soothing to her nerves and she kept glancing over her shoulder as she watched her pursuers coming after her. They were gaining ground, and she felt the urgency to leave and wondered if she would be able to outpace them throughout the day. The honey was sweet and delicious and she licked her fingers after discarding the comb.

Twig picked it up and wolfed it down, grinning at her with point-ed teeth.

She heard the rattling of an atrox coming from behind her and felt a surge of fear. Twig chittered at her to run and so she rose and began briskly walking toward Battle Mountain, which loomed in the distance. Her stomach, although sated, was wringing with worry as she walked. She could see Mattson Kree, Trea, and Gabe stalking after her, rising above the thin brush and earth, coming after her with determination and purpose. She could find no trace of her father. Was he lying down in the brush, low against the horizon to conceal himself? He could be anywhere in the vast desolate plain.

The sound of the serpent faded behind her, but she did not slow her pace. Twig bounded and scuttled ahead of her, testing the air, sniffing and smelling. This arid land was his domain.

As the sun rose higher in the sky, it became unbearably warm, and Rista's thirst became more pronounced. There were no rivers or streams in the barren landscape. She did not want to risk losing all her water, so she endured the discomfort. The sun beat down on her skin and hair and made the land in front of her shimmer with the peculiar distortion that made the horizon look wet. Glancing back, she saw that her pursuers were closing the distance more, and so Rista increased her pace. She looked for signs of other people, but there were none.

Past midday, she saw strange shapes ahead in the plains and wondered if her eyes were playing tricks on her. There were long poles sticking out of the ground at various angles. It was like a grove of skeletal trees, except made of poles, and she couldn't understand what she was seeing.

Twig began muttering in his strange, guttural tongue.

"I don't understand you," she said, her voice a little croaky from lack of use.

The kobold repeated himself and she understood a few words. "What is it? Did you say the dead?"

The kobold nodded vigorously, pointing to the shapes. And then Rista remembered there had been a battle fought in the plains forty years ago. It was part of her father's tales of his adventures and he had called it the barrowlands. The Overlord's massive kobold army had been defeated by the King of Stanchion. The kobolds were small and cunning but outnumbered the humans significantly.

As she approached, she began to discern the shapes. Soldiers had fallen with spears transfixing them. There was nothing but dust, bones, and the rusted shells of armor now. The unforgiving heat and windy plain had scoured the remains. As she drew closer, she saw some burial mounds, but there had been a vast battle and there were many skeletons remaining, mostly that of kobolds. Twig ventured near and began searching the debris, picking up broken sheaths and snapped arrows. He examined many, scuttling from one mound to another for anything interesting. Rista entered the barrowlands cautiously, weaving through the burial mounds and gazing at the shattered remnants. It was desolate and depressing how many lives had been lost in the Overlord's attempt at conquest. It made her think of what Mattson Kree was attempting again. There were no kobolds around now, the battlefield had been picked over multiple times. Strange how Twig, so small and fragile, had survived the outcome when his more hardy brothers had perished in the war. Twig picked up another broken arrow, examining it with a melancholy slump to his little shoulders. Her heart yearned with pity for him.

Turning again, she saw that her pursuers were even closer now, their march had increased, and Rista set off again. She had to keep ahead of them until nightfall. The dark was the only protection she had, and she could change directions and try to circle back around them. They had more food and provisions than she did. But she knew her father was in the wastelands somewhere, likely watching them all. He was a smart man, the smartest man she knew, and he was probably working on a plan to help her. She had to keep away from Mattson Kree. And find water. She rubbed her arm across her face and felt no sweat. Her body needed to be replenished. Her strength would fail before her enemies' did.

Twig chittered in warning and then she heard the atrox rattles coming from ahead, so the kobold rushed back to her and pointed another way. She followed his direction and suddenly another set of atrox noise announced that way was blocked too. Rista's stomach lurched and she turned around, going back the way she'd come and trying the other path.

More noises—more atrox blocking the path.

Rista began to worry even more. Then she saw the snakes slithering toward her, coming from all directions, converging on the barrowlands in hundreds if not thousands. Her stomach wrenched with panic.

"Twig, what do we do?" Rista said in desperation. The kobold was panicking, searching for a safe way to flee, but all escapes had suddenly vanished. The sun beat down mercilessly, and the loathsome noise of the atrox drew in like a net around them. Rista stopped, looking around in each direction for a way to escape. The slithering motion of the snakes made her frightened, especially the memory of the venom and how it hurt when one had bitten her earlier.

Mattson Kree had let her walk ahead, she realized. But he also realized that finding her in the dark would be nearly impossible, so he had set up a little trap to catch her before dusk. A cold fear burrowed into her bones. She hadn't escaped her pursuers at all. She'd pushed herself hard all that day for nothing.

A huge, fat atrox was nearing her, so Rista hurried to a mound and grabbed one of the broken spears to use as a weapon. She climbed up on it and prepared to defend herself.

"Twig, you have to hide!" she said. "They might have seen you. Hide in one of the mounds. Bury yourself in the ground. You have to get away from here!"

The kobold scolded her and said he wouldn't leave. He grabbed one of the snapped arrows and brandished it.

"No, Twig!" Rista said. "You have to hide. Now!"

The large atrox was coiling at the base of the mound. Soon they'd converge on all sides. Rista jabbed the spearhead at the serpent and it hissed and reared its head at her, exposing sharp fangs. She wrestled with her fear and jabbed at it again.

"Now, Twig! Now! Obey me!"

She knew that Mattson Kree wouldn't kill her. Not yet, anyway. But Twig had helped her escape. There was a strong chance they had seen the kobold coming along, and they already knew about her father's kobold, from the cabin. They'd kill Twig without remorse and she *couldn't* let that happen.

The kobold snarled and poked its pitiful weapon at the snake.

Rista stomped her foot, startling Twig. "Hide! Now!"

The kobold hesitated.

"Please, Twig! If you don't hide, how can you help me later? You need to hide! They'll be here soon."

The kobold looked defiant. He was fiercely loyal to her and her family. He was willing to give his life to protect her.

The atrox started slithering up the mound and another appeared behind them. Rista jabbed at the snake again, driving it off, and then hurried to the other side to repeat the maneuver.

"Please, Twig. You're very brave. But I need your help. I need you to hide, to help me later. I need you to find Father and guide him to us. Please! Go find Father and help him! Get far away from me. Please!"

A third snake had reached the mound.

"Go!" Rista nearly screamed at him.

The kobold glared at her, grunting something, and then sped off the mound, dodging past the snake and moving low to the ground, reaching one of the burial mounds and digging inside it to conceal himself.

Rista was relieved for a moment and then realized her situation was getting worse. The atrox swarmed around the mound she was on and came at her from all sides. She swung the spear at them, jabbing with the point. Some snakes got close enough that she poked them with the spear. Rattles and hisses erupted around her as she felt her strength waning. In the hazy distance, she saw Mattson Kree, Trea, and Gabe advancing relentlessly.

Rista had a deep well of stubbornness inside her. She fought off the atrox far longer than a girl her age should have been able to. Her head was dizzy with the effort and her body weakened by thirst. Her sturdy boots protected her from several atrox bites as they lunged at her. They seemed to take turns climbing up the mound, but she realized that Mattson Kree was controlling them. They had herded her to a mound and now prevented her from leaving. The area around the mound was a river of snakes with the strange diamond-shaped pattern on their backs. As she fought them, her fear of them began to wane. These were animals caught under a magic's power. It was unnatural for them to converge like this, but Mattson Kree's power controlled them absolutely. They were forced to do his bidding, just as the bees did hers.

The sun had begun to sink in the sky by the time Mattson Kree and the others arrived. The sea of atrox parted to allow them through. An antagonizing smirk was on the Serpentarium's face.

"It was quite a chase, Rista," he said smoothly. "I'm sure you are very thirsty."

She nodded at him, feeling weak and trembling. Her throat was so parched she could hardly talk. "Are you going to kill me?" she asked defiantly. "I will always try to escape from you."

Mattson Kree shook his head. "No, I won't kill you, Rista. Not yet. But I can't let that pesky kobold run loose anymore. I believe it helped your father last time." He looked at Trea and Gabe and then pointed. "It's burrowed in that mound over there. The snakes can smell the creature. Kill it."

Rista started with panic. "No!"

Mattson Kree smiled at her, a chilling smile. He gestured for the two to obey him. Trea looked pleased by the order. Gabe looked conflicted.

"No!" Rista said, staring at the mound where she had seen Twig enter. It was the same one the Serpentarium had pointed to. "You can't!"

"I don't make idle threats, Rista," he said coldly. "I'm not sentimental like you and your father. Do it!"

Trea and Gabe stalked over to the mound. Gabe motioned for her to go one way, he went the other. The serpents slithered away from them, some hissing at them in annoyance. Rista was anguished. This was her fault! She tried to rush off the mound, but Mattson Kree caught her in his strong arms and held her against him. She tried to wrestle herself free, but he was twice her size and she was exhausted by the ordeals of the day.

"No, I beg you! No! Not Twig! He can't hurt you! Leave him alone!"

She watched in growing desperation as the two motioned to each other. Gabe grabbed a spear from the burial mounds. Trea had an arrow nocked in her bow.

"If it runs, I'll get it," she said.

Rista grew frantic. She leaned down and bit Mattson Kree's hand. His grip tightened reflexively, startled by the pain, but he did not release her. Instead, he squeezed her so hard she couldn't breathe. Spots began to dance in front of her eyes.

"I see it," Gabe said warningly, moving slowly like a hunter. "It's wedged inside a skeleton." He cleared some of the dirt and tangled rags away.

"Get it!" Trea shouted.

Rista released her bite and Mattson Kree relaxed his grip so she could breathe again. There were bite marks on his hand and blood oozed from the wound.

"Gabe, no!" Rista wailed.

Suddenly the man's spear jabbed out, a quick and powerful stroke sinking into the mound. Gabe held it with both hands, using all his weight.

"I got it!" he said triumphantly. He cleared some of the dirt away with his boot and peered into the mound. Then he looked at Mattson Kree, and a brief look of shame clouded his expression, replaced by a cold shrug. "It's dead."

Trea stalked around the mound with her bow and examined the spot where the spear still quivered. Rista felt tears of disbelief flooding her eyes. No, no, no, no!

The hunter peered into the mound, squinting, her bow ready. Then she relaxed the draw and straightened. "The kobold is dead," she said with a malicious smile.

Rista hated her. She hated them all.

"Blood for blood," Mattson Kree said, releasing Rista and chafing his bitten hand. Then in a gruff voice he said, "Gabe, tie her wrists with a lead rope. One of us keeps a hold of it from now on. We each of us take a turn. Rista is our new *pet*."

A quivering sob came from Rista's throat as she stared at the spear in the mound.

"Are we camping here?" Gabe asked, twisting his pack around and producing a rope from it.

"No, we're going to walk all night," Mattson Kree said. "We'll reach Battle Mountain by dawn if we do. I want to get there before the Beesinger and set my trap. His daughter is the bait. Don't weep, Rista. This is where the kobold *should* have died forty years ago."

As Gabe wrapped her wrists with the rope, she stared at him with hatred in her eyes. He had a contrite look, but he said nothing to her as he obeyed the orders.

* * *

For the first time since her abduction, Rista began to worry that things would not end well. She had clung to her conviction that her father would outthink and outsmart Mattson Kree and that her first adventure would be the dawning of a great future. As she stumbled and doggedly walked through the bone-chilling night, there were no specks of light coming from behind that showed that her father was near. They had only slept a few hours until sunset and then continued the march. She felt alone, sick with grief at Twig's murder, and vulnerable. The cold skies glittered overhead and she stared at them, sending her thoughts into the aether.

Father, can you hear me? Father, I'm frightened. I don't want these people to hurt you. She felt tears sting her eyes at the very real possibility that the situation might end poorly for all of them. Her father was only a Beesinger. How did that power compare to a man who could rouse the fury of serpents? Had her father been bitten already? Was he dying in the wastelands, his body to become like the skeletons of the barrows? The thought triggered horrible emotions, made her squirm against the bonds at her wrists.

Gabe glanced back at her, still holding the lead rope. He shook his head in silent warning not to test the ropes. She wanted to spit in his face. Rista wanted to yank the dagger from his waist and stab him with it. Her heart felt like ashes after a great fire had burned away the hunk of wood. She'd wept for hours, quietly grieving for the kobold, wondering how she would break the news to her sister and brothers. They'd be devastated.

Father, can you hear me? she thought pleadingly. *I could not bear it if I lost you. You are always so patient with me. I know I've not been the best daughter. I've tried to learn the magic. I've tried to make you proud of me. But I fall short so many times. If . . . if one of us must die, it would be better if it were me. I couldn't take your place. You should go back and warn the king at Stanchion. You should make sure the others are safe.*

Her boot kicked a rock and sent it skittering into a stunted shrub. Her muscles were aching and tired. The night was deep and absolutely still. The sound of the insects was gone. Only the wind and the crunch of their boots could be heard. But she wished her thoughts could reach her father. She wished for a way to speak to him.

Father, can you hear me? I'm sorry for being so stubborn. I'm sorry I neglect my chores sometimes and you have to do them. I've seen you, scraping the scrap bucket for the pig. I've gotten angry with you for doing it for me. I should have been grateful. All your life you've tried to teach me to be responsible. She bit her lip, aching inside.

Father, can you hear me? Sometimes, sometimes I wished that you would have chosen to live in the Enclave. You were offered the chance and turned it away. I never understood why. It's such a rare honor. But you don't care about things like that. You don't care that everyone thinks you are famous for defeating the Overlord. You're just a Beesinger, and you try to help people. I've never realized how proud of you I am. Please, Father. If you are out there tonight. Go back to Camille. Go back to Brand. Go back to Adam and Ben. I can face whatever horror Mattson Kree will do as long as I know that you won't die. Please, Father! Go back!

Yet even as she made her silent wish, even as the plea left her thoughts like a blossom on the wind, she still hoped her father would find a way to save her. She was all out of ideas herself.

* * *

The morning broke over Battle Mountain and the crumbling Ziggurat. It was Trea's turn to keep hold of Rista's rope, and the older woman gave her a scornful look as Rista sat on the dusty ground, eating from a broken crust of bread. The bread was hard and chewy, but it was something to fill her hollow stomach.

As she chewed, Rista stared at the majestic sight and could not believe her father's stories had done it justice. Father was a good storyteller and had painted the scene in her mind so many times. Battle Mountain was a V-shaped pinnacle in the midst of the plains. It rose to a towering height, with jagged cliffs standing starkly, the upper heights dusted with snow year-round. But at the base of the mountain, amidst the rock and debris, had been hewn a majestic castle called the Ziggurat. It was carved into the rocky face of the mountain, a series of archways and designs that were centuries old. Two enormous sculptures had been chiseled and assembled outside the main gates. These were of giant kobolds, each holding shields in front of them. The snouts were fierce, with battle helms atop each. The Ziggurat was a monument to the industry of the kobolds and had been painstakingly shaped to symbolize the apex of their power. The Ziggurat was carved with symbols of skulls and horrid eyes. It looked like an unholy place, like a screaming skull made from stone where the bone had been carved with tattoos.

Rista stared at the desolate place, the ruins of a vast empire that had nearly overthrown the kingdom of Stanchion. The kobold hordes had once ruled the entire wasteland and claimed the Arvadin Mountains where they'd launch raiding parties into the valley. These were stories from her father's youth. Rista had seen the remains of the battles fought decades before, a silent testament to the horrendous conditions. The Overlord had ruled the kobolds with an iron fist. He had made them mighty.

"Get up," Trea said angrily, yanking on the lead rope. "Rest is over. We need to get inside before the heat of the day."

Rista had expected to see the Ziggurat teeming with people, but it was nothing more than a graveyard. Her wrists were swollen and sore, and she stumbled as she tried to get up. Gabe took her elbow to help, and she shot him a threatening look and jerked her arm away from him.

He gave her a sardonic look, held up his hands, and backed away.

"Why are we here, Mattson Kree?" Rista asked, nodding toward the mighty Ziggurat. "There is nothing left but stone and bones."

The proud man was staring at the fortress with a look of intense interest. His arms were folded, his boot resting on a small rock.

"It is a symbol," he said, not looking at her. "This fortress will be glorious once again. There was a time when the plains were lush with rivers. The army of Stanchion made culverts to direct the water from the melting snows away. There used to be waterfalls down the face there," he added, gesturing with his finger. He shook his head as if in a dream. "This place was a symbol of power for a thousand years. Slaves were brought here from realms far beyond the borders your puny imagination can fathom, Rista. It was the nest of power. It was the cradle of civilization. It will be reborn."

Rista stared at the gloomy facade, Kree's words conjuring images in her mind. "But it is nothing now. There is no one here. Where are the kobolds?"

"Scattered," Mattson Kree said. "Driven far and wide. But they will come back. They will return and serve the master of the Ziggurat. They will serve *me*. And they will see that I am more terrible than the Overlord ever was. They will be restored to their birthright, and we will raze Stanchion to the ground." He turned and looked at her, his eyes livid with ambition. "And when I am the new overlord, we will trap the Enclave inside its mists for all time, never to molest or cause trouble again. My reign begins today."

Rista stared at him, saw the determination in his eyes. He was a handsome man, but the swelling pride made him look frightening and enraged.

She heard a familiar sound, the drone of a carpenter bee. It was a heavy, shivering sound that never ceased to make Rista's skin crawl. Carpenter bees were enormous, all black with huge leathery wings.

A look of fear shot into Mattson Kree's eyes. He snatched the rope from Trea and pulled Rista close to him, drawing a curved dagger shaped like a fang from his tunic. He held the dagger near her neck.

"Use your magic, Rista," he said, a small quiver in his voice. "Make it go."

The blade was close; its edge was as polished as silver. There was unmistakable fear in the Serpentarium's eyes.

She nearly provoked him to kill her, to save her father. But she reached out with her magic to the bee as it came closer to the camp.

Did Father send you? she wondered. Its presence could have been random. She read its mind and learned that its hive was based in the Ziggurat. There were hundreds there. An idea began to sharpen in her mind.

"It's just a scout," Rista said.

"Send it *away*," Mattson Kree hissed.

Rista reached out to the insect in her mind and bid it return to the hive. She bid it to warn the others that danger was coming. She swallowed.

The drone of the bee faded as it turned and zigzagged away. There was a bead of sweat on Mattson Kree's brow that hadn't been there before. He licked his upper lip, then tugged at the lead rope, slowly lowering his fang-shaped dagger.

"You keep them away from us," Mattson Kree warned, tugging her until his face met hers. He held the knife close to her cheek. "For every sting of a bee, I will start carving my vengeance into your skin. In the Ziggurat, they used to offer sacrifices of human blood. There are things worse than death, my dear. You defy me, and your father will grieve at how I get my revenge on you. Stay close to me, Rista. And remember—keep the bees away from us!"

Rista swallowed, but she felt a growing confidence. The Ziggurat was the hive of carpenter bees. She hadn't known that. Her father had never told her. She did not think it a coincidence that the enemy's lair was guarded.

* * *

There were barrow mounds leading up to the Ziggurat steps, full of the bleached skeletons of man and beast. The war against the Overlord had brought together many with enmitical magic, and Rista's father had told her of lions and cougars and bears that had mauled through the ranks of kobolds. The final battle had been fought on the steps of the Ziggurat, and as she approached them, it was as if the ghost of the battle rang out in her mind. She imagined seeing the swarms of arrows coming down from the battlement walls, of catapults and trebuchets that had hurled death down on Stanchion's army. So many had died, her father said, to crack the Overlord's power at last.

They climbed the massive steps, and she noticed that many segments had been shattered and turned to rubble. Scorch marks could be seen descending from the arched windows, where flaming oil had been poured down on the attacking army. The shouts were gone but there were still echoes of violence all around. Rista picked her way up the broken steps, her leash held fast by Mattson Kree. He had a cunning look on his face, as if he were visiting hallowed grounds. The fierce look in his eyes showed a perverse pleasure.

Trea led the way, an arrow nocked in her bow as she scouted ahead. Gabe trailed behind, looking backward constantly to the flat plain where there was no sign of her father or anyone else. There was no army marching to stop them. Nothing but the eerie quiet of the wind and the silent maw of Battle Mountain.

When Trea reached the top of the steps, she released the tension of the bow. "No one is here," she said, her voice ricocheting off the stone.

"He will come," Mattson Kree said solemnly. "Do not doubt it."

Rista and Kree reached the top next. The platform level was pockmarked with crumbled stone. Huge boulders interspersed the area where they had been flung down from the heights above. Rista craned her neck to see the black gaps, imagining the ramparts crawling with hordes of kobolds. The thought made her heart throb for Twig.

"How long do you think before he catches up?" Trea asked, nodding back to the plains.

Mattson Kree chuckled. "He'll come at night, of course. That is the only way to approach the Ziggurat unseen. There is a cleft of rock on that side where the sewage used to flow. That's how Ilias and the others snuck into the Ziggurat before. Lots of spiders, they say." He gave Rista a knowing look. "I've heard the tales, lass. I've heard all your father's stories. They grow more elaborate with each telling as the crowds passed it on, I'm sure, and it's hard to know whether you can believe a drunk. But I have paid coins to hear the tales, especially the ones told at Stanchion palace when the king traveled here with your father. It was a desperate gambit. But all the tales agree that your father was the most clever man in the valley. That he figured out that the Overlord kept his soul trapped in a bone. It is necromancer magic. The bone could have been hidden anywhere, yet your father found it. By destroying the bone, he destroyed the man."

Mattson Kree gazed up at the face of the fortress, a gleeful smile crossing his lips. "My soul is not tied to a bone, Rista. Not yet." He gave her a meaningful look. "But it will be. Come, we must perform the incantation before he arrives."

Rista heard the drone of carpenter bees as they approached the shattered doors of the Ziggurat. Huge battering rams had been used to smash open the doors, and the remnants were still there amidst the rubble. The rain and snow had made the rams decay, but Rista sensed that they were the source of the carpenter bee colony. She saw the black-stained wood and heard the rumble and buzz.

"Looks like only the bees survived," Mattson Kree said. He brought Rista close to him, almost like a shield, and brought the dagger to her neck. "Keep them calm, girl. Settle down the hive."

"Why are you so afraid of bees?" Rista asked him, reaching out with her magic to engage with the hive. She started to sow thoughts of agitation and wariness. The noise of the hive began to grow louder.

"I said calm it," Mattson Kree warned.

A soothing feeling came over the hive and the buzzing sound calmed. Rista was surprised because she sent in provoking signals. Then she sensed her father's magic.

"Someone's in there!" Trea said, swinging the bow around toward the black gap of the ancient doorway. "I just saw him move in the shadows!"

"Wait," Mattson Kree said curtly. There was the sudden clomp of boots, and Rista's father appeared in the doorway holding his favorite wood-cutting axe in his grip. He looked haggard and serious, his gray hair unkempt and wild. She had never seen him so stern and angry before, and even though he was older and softer around the middle, he still looked dangerous. Her heart thrilled at seeing him, unbelieving that he had made it to the Ziggurat ahead of them, but by the ashen look on his face, she saw he had barely slept and had pressed harder than they had.

"Father!" Rista gasped.

"Silence!" Mattson Kree hissed, bringing the edge of the dagger to her throat. The Serpentarium was rattled, clearly surprised to see the famous Beesinger waiting for them.

Rista stared at her father and she knew he was going to sacrifice himself to save her. She saw the desperate look in his eyes, the worry, the fear. He would die to save her. She couldn't let that happen. In her mind, she tried to summon the bee swarm to attack her and their enemies, but her father's will was like iron, and the bees obeyed *him*. She pressed her own magic against his and felt it start to budge.

"I'm surprised, Beesinger," Mattson Kree said challengingly. "Not often can someone do that to me. Put down the axe."

"I don't think so," the Beesinger said, stepping forward. Trea's bow was quivering. She waited for an order to loose the arrow. Her father was wearing dust-stained travel garb, not a chain hauberk, and he did not have a shield, just the stocky axe.

"It is three against one," Mattson Kree said. "The odds are stacked in my favor, and I have your daughter's life in my hands. Don't be a fool to risk it unnecessarily."

Her father walked forward still. "Yes, it is three against one," he agreed. "But I thought we may as well try talking first. I'll be quick and simple. You came here prepared to kill my daughter. I know that. I just want you to understand what will happen if you do. I will kill you." He hadn't shaved in days, and a wild, terrible look was in his hazel eyes. "The only way you live through this, as far as I can see, is if you let Rista go and take me captive instead. I'm the one you wanted. That's what this is about. Let her go."

Mattson Kree's face hardened. Rista's hands were bound. There was a knife at her throat. One cut and she would be dead. She forced her thoughts on summoning the swarm of black carpenter bees. She didn't care if she got stung now. The hive began to groan with her efforts. She pushed her magic against her father's.

"Rista, *don't*," her father said softly, gesturing with one hand calmingly.

"No, Father," she said. "I won't let you do this."

"You will both do as *I* say!" Mattson Kree hissed. "Calm the bees."

"I'm trying to," her father said with a nervous tone. "She's riling them. Rista, *don't*."

Rista ignored her father and used her magic to provoke the bees further. Several fat ones appeared from the rotten husks of the battering rams and began hovering. Then others began to join.

"Stop it," Mattson Kree warned in her ear.

Rista continued to feed the bees with the signal of danger. The drone was growing louder and louder, taking on an agitated, dangerous air.

"Rista," her father pleaded. There were tears in his eyes.

I won't let you sacrifice yourself for me, she thought, staring at him. *I love you too much.*

"Mattson?" Trea asked with growing dread.

In a moment the bees would attack them. Her father's grip on them was slipping away as Rista's power surged.

"I love you, Father," Rista said, staring at him, blinking back her tears. She felt courage unlike anything she'd ever felt before. Courage and resolve. It was like stepping off a cliff, knowing she'd fall to her death.

"No!" Mattson Kree roared in panic as the bees lifted like a cloud from the stumps.

"Gabe, now!" her father shouted.

Everything happened at once.

Rista blinked with surprise as she saw Twig land on Trea's arm with a tiny little blade. The kobold used it to sever the taut bow-string, and the longbow nearly exploded in the girl's hands as the pent-up force bucked her backward. The kobold skittered around her, stabbing viciously with its puny weapon as the girl shrieked with terror and pain. The Serpentarium was startled, but only for a moment. He swung the dagger around and sliced at Gabe across the face as the young man was severing the lead rope. Rista saw a nick of blood on his cheek, but the rope went limp and she realized she was free. She dived forward, hands still tied, and rolled.

Gabe was helping them? Rista couldn't comprehend it, but she saw Mattson Kree's face wilt with rage at the betrayal. He raised the knife high over his head and lunged after her to plunge it down into Rista's heart.

And that's when the swarm of bees reached them.

Rista was stung once, twice, three times and thought it was Kree's dagger, but he was flailing his arms as the swarm reached them. A heavy weight landed on her, crushing her to the broken floor, and she realized it was Gabe, covering her body with his own. Beneath him, she could see as the cloud of bees attacked Mattson Kree, and then she stared in shock at the look on his face. He was clawing at his throat, gasping for breath. There were huge welts on his cheeks and temple from the multiple bee stings. His face turned purple as he choked, and she recognized what she was seeing. Her father had explained to her that some people couldn't endure bee stings—that it made them choke to death. Her father had been called on a few times over the years to treat them, and his magic was powerful enough to draw out the bee's venom and save the child's life if he got there fast enough. She watched in horror as the Serpentarium dropped to his knees, strangling to death, as the black bees swarmed and stung him. Gabe was limp atop her and she watched the bees attack him still. From her position, none of the rest could reach her.

Then Rista reached out her will and she calmed the violent swarm. She had never done that before with black bees because of how terrified she'd always been of them. But she felt no fear now. And the bees, sensing her change in mood, began to quiet instantly and return to the hive.

Mattson Kree's purplish face was terrible to see, his eyes clouding over. His quivering fingers reached and opened the satchel he still had around his shoulders. Lifting the flap, he heaved out the massive atrox, and it began to rattle and hiss threateningly as its master fell flat against the stone, catching himself momentarily on one arm before slumping to the stones.

A moment later, her father's axe severed the atrox's head. He grabbed the convulsing end and the atrox's body wound around his arm, coiling tightly as if even in death it were trying to kill him.

The Beesinger stared down at the decapitated snake, then at the dead man, and a slow smile of relief brightened his face.

As Gabe lifted himself up, Rista could hear the noise of running and saw that Trea was fleeing the Ziggurat. She'd left her broken bow behind and Twig was dancing atop it, holding up his puny little dagger with his puny little arm and shaking it and hissing after the fleeing girl. A black bee buzzed around the kobold.

"Twig," Rista croaked in relief, tears stinging her eyes.

Gabe had welts on his face and hands and he looked to be in a great deal of pain. But he used his dagger and severed the bonds at her wrists.

"There you are, Beesinger," he said with a wincing look, rising to his feet and pulling Rista up with him. "Safe and sound."

Rista's heart nearly ripped open with happiness. She rushed to her father, weeping with gratitude as she hugged him.

"I'm so sorry, Father!" she babbled, hugging him, smelling the scent of mint along with the dirt and sweat.

He stroked her hair, hushing her soothingly. "It's all right, Rista. It's all right."

Twig chattered away down below and Rista released her father and then dropped down. She turned to Gabe. "What happened back at the barrow mound then? I mean . . . you've been on our side the entire time? You could have told me!"

Gabe smirked at her, still looking uncomfortable with his sting wounds. "But that would have taken all the fun out of it. Besides, I had to be convincing for Mattson Kree."

"You *are* Gabe Doer?"

He nodded. "Yes, I'm the king's son. Why don't you explain it, Beesinger? I'm not keen on talking now. Do you have any salve? This *really* hurts."

"I do," her father said humbly. He put his arm around Rista's waist. "Thank you, Gabe. I owe you."

The man shrugged. "It's the least I can do for my father. His scouts should be at the Arvadin by now."

"Hopefully," her father said. "We're short on food, and even *I'm* getting tired of eating honey."

* * *

It was well after nightfall and father had built a bonfire on the tiles outside the Ziggurat. The first reason was for warmth, but the second was so that the light from it would be seen across the valley and help would arrive. They'd buried Mattson Kree's body under a heap of stones, as well as the head of his atrox. Her father had warned them both about getting too near the severed head and explained that even a decapitated atrox could bite someone. They roasted the meat from the serpent's body and had it for dinner that night.

Twig nestled in Rista's lap and she stroked his scaly head with the knobs and horns. "So you only *pretended* to kill Twig," she said to Gabe after the story had been told a second time. "He did know that you were in league with us?"

"He *did* try to leave you a clue, but you didn't understand," her father said with a small laugh. "We'll have to brush up on kobold when we get back."

Rista smiled and patted Twig on the head. "You're a brave little kobold," she said.

Twig began to purr and closed his orange eyes with a toothy grin.

"How did you get to the Ziggurat before us? We saw the light from your orb behind us. Did you overtake us then?"

"That was your brother," her father answered. "I went another way to the Ziggurat and came around from that side," he said, pointing. "Your brother came down the mountain and then hid the orb and went back for help. He wanted to come along and help rescue you, Rista. But I wasn't going to risk *two* of my children."

Rista shook her head. "I still don't understand how Gabe and you know each other. How did he communicate with you? I'm confused."

Gabe tossed another hunk of wood from the battering ram into the fire. "I'm my father's spymaster," he explained. "My gift with enmitical magic is with bats and rats, as you know. Nocturnal creatures. Back when your father fought alongside my father, he made a suggestion. People are always looking to cause trouble. I developed a reputation for being discontented—on purpose—to attract to me that kind of people, like Mattson Kree. Last year, a scheming duke tried to convince me to join his rebellion. I went along with it to find out who the ringleaders were. Then told my father. I thought Mattson Kree was trouble the moment I first met him. He was an ambitious and capable man. I came along, before knowing who his target was. Now that I understand his reaction to bee stings, I can see why he feared your father and you so much. It was his biggest weakness. His vulnerability."

Rista nodded. "So you hadn't spoken to my father directly."

"Not at all. If you recall, I was standing *behind* Kree and Trea at the end. I smuggled Twig with me after leaving the barrowlands and showed him to your father to alert him that I was on your side."

"So when I told Kree that it was three against one," her father said with a gleam in his eye, "I should have said it was *four* against one. I didn't know about Twig until the end."

Rista laughed at that and smiled as Twig's eyes opened again sleepily.

"So you stole ahead of us because you guessed where he was going," Rista said.

"It was rather obvious," her father said meekly.

Rista shook her head. "Well, I feel like a fool for not realizing *any* of it."

Her father shook his head. "No, Rista. You had information that I didn't. I thought it was going to be a fight at the end. You were trussed up and vulnerable, but I knew you could use your magic. I thought the odds of all of us surviving were rather small. The swarm frightened away that woman, and the stings killed Mattson Kree. It was your plan that worked best in the end. I'm proud of you, Rista."

She flushed with his words of praise. The fire was so warm and she was exhausted by the ordeal. Sleepiness stole over her and she yawned. She hadn't fully slept in days.

"Stop, you're making me yawn too," Gabe complained. He lifted the blanket around his shoulders and then curled up by the fire, his back facing it and them. "Good night, Beesingers. I don't think I've ever eaten atrox before. I don't think I'll care to in the future."

"Thanks again, Gabe," her father said. He scooted closer to Rista and then reached out and patted her back. After a while, he pitched his voice low and stared at her. The firelight played over his face and whiskers.

"You've always asked me why I never joined the Enclave," he said softly. "Not many get invited. Fewer still turn down the honor."

She stared at him, feeling a strange prickle go down her back. She listened intently.

He glanced at the flames and then back at her. "Part of the reason was because I felt I didn't deserve the honor," he said. "It was Twig that helped overthrow the Overlord."

Rista stared at him in surprise. The kobold was fast asleep.

Her father nodded. "After I crawled through that mess of black widow spiders, I discovered Twig. He was so weak and insignificant. The smallest runt of a kobold you ever knew. He was the Overlord's drudge. But I befriended him and treated him well. And he showed me where the Overlord kept the bone. I snapped it, like a *twig*." A crooked smile came to his mouth. "That's where the nickname came from. The real hero of Battle Mountain is that little creature in your lap. Without him, we would have all died. So that's the first reason I didn't feel worthy to be part of the Enclave. I've never told you that story before because the king and I agreed that it was a secret best kept." He paused a moment. "But the *main* reason I didn't join the Enclave with Ilias and the others was the same reason the king didn't."

He reached out and poked the fire with a long stick.

"Why?" Rista asked softly. She reached out and put her hand on his knee.

He was trying to master his emotions. Rista waited patiently.

"I learned something about the Enclave during my travels with them. They live in an immaculate city surrounded by dazzling waterfalls and beautiful woods. There is music and poetry and delicious food. When one goes to the Enclave, it reverses all aging and sickness. It restores you to a younger age. You can, in fact, live forever." He tapped the stick on the ground and then crushed the embers on the end into the stone. "*But* if you live there, you can't have children." He glanced at her and shrugged. "More than anything else, I knew I wanted to be a father someday." Then his hazel eyes fixed on hers. "That is a privilege worth more than Beesinging. I'd rather be back *home* right now more than anywhere else in the world. I'm glad you'll be coming back home with me, Rista."

He brushed a tear from his eye and then reached out and squeezed her hand.

Rista's heart was so full she couldn't speak. And so they held each other's hands and stared at each other and listened to the crackling fire, not willing to disturb the magic of that moment with words.

About Jeff Wheeler

Jeff took an early retirement from his career at Intel in 2014 to become a full-time author. He is, most importantly, a husband and father, a devout member of his church, and is occasionally spotted roaming hills with oak trees and granite boulders in California or in any number of the state's majestic redwood groves. He is also one of the founders of *Deep Magic*.

SALT AND WATER

By Charlie N. Holmberg | 12,000 words

THE SOUND OF his dying breath played a broken melody on the strings of Chellis's thoughts. The silence of the tiled chamber amplified the haunting song; only the occasional shifting of chains disturbed it.

She tried not to weep, for only when she stopped crying long enough—promising no wasted tears—would they release her back to her chambers. A chamber that sat empty, for the Hagori whom she served had killed little Temas.

Chellis had suspected ulterior motives from the Hagori when her unexpected bunkmate arrived two months before, and a child at that, only eight years of age. A Hagori orphan, not even a Merdan like herself. But after a week of Temas's smiles and songs, Chellis had come to believe that her dian—her "caretaker"—had come to pity her. That her dian felt guilty over the beatings and the harsh words all dians used to make their Merdans cry. That perhaps she thought eighteen months of loneliness had been too harsh, even for a slave.

Another tear squeezed between Chellis's eyelids, absorbed by the spongy blinders pressed against her face. A lie. Another lie, but that one crueler than the rest. The Hagori had merely waited long enough for Chellis to grow attached to the boy, to love him, before slitting his throat right there in her chambers. And then her dian had snapped the blinders over her eyes, unwilling to risk wasting a single drop of Chellis's lifesaving tears. Healing tears that only a Merdan stolen from the sea could weep.

She shifted in the chains that suspended her over the shallow vat —chains that bound her arms and ankles to the wall behind her. The edge of the vat dug painful, deep lines into her scaled knees, its gaping mouth waiting for any tears that might escape the blinders. The manacles dug into the scar tissue over her wrists. Her shoulders were numb from supporting her body, which leaned forward with only the chain preventing her from toppling into the vat itself. Her webbed feet tingled. The small fins around her ankles felt like ice, though no ice could be found in the desert home of the Hagori, save within the empty cavities of their chests.

Chellis breathed through her nose, trying to calm the convulsing muscles in her abdomen. Trying to dry out the hurt and relieve the twisting barb that mangled her spirit and sliced her soul. She blinked against the wet sponges in the blinders and willed herself still.

Suspended over the vat with silence her only companion, Chellis could almost smell the sea. She let her tired mind believe that she did, let it whisk her away to the wide-open waters, blue as sky, where she swam weightless among whales and alongside her kin. So few in number, the Merdans. The slave fishers' relentless hunt for them dwindled their people and shredded their families. The Hagori only saw the Merdan as a balm for their war. Not once had the warmongers tried to barter for the lifesaving tears. They'd only taken.

Three sets of footsteps entered the collecting room, echoing off the tiled walls so loudly it seemed an entire army had come for her. Chellis distinguished the soft sounds of her dian's sandals from the heavy boots of the guards. She held still as her dian reattached the fine chain leash to the metal collar encircling Chellis's neck. Only then did the guards unlock the manacles around her wrists and pull her back from the vat. Blood surged into Chellis's webbed fingers. She bit her bottom lip to keep from crying out. The soft bones in her knees wrenched and popped as the leash hauled her upward. Blood flowed into her feet, marking every new bruise along its path.

"Hold still, Naki," Lila-dian warned, calling Chellis by her Hagori name. The two guards stood close enough that Chellis could feel the shroud of heat rising from their skin, smell the cactus oil in their beards. It made her itch—made her want to scream and swim away —but Chellis held still, unsure that her weak legs and sore body could withstand another lashing. Not today.

Lila-dian carefully pulled the blinders from Chellis's face and scraped her eyelids to remove any dried or excess tears. Chellis opened her eyes slowly, wincing at the light, blinking away the blurry images twirling in her vision. They settled, too pale and too bright.

Lila-dian placed the blinders in a rectangular, waterproof case held out by the guard on Chellis's left, who carried it from the collection room like a Hagori infant, newly born and weak-necked.

Chellis's eyes adjusted. The collection room was small and round, a white-tiled cylinder with one exit, one bench, and one large vat that swallowed the center of the floor. Two stations, marked with large metals Ts, bordered the vat. These were where Merdans knelt to cry their tears if their dian expected a flood of them. For Temas, Chellis had given them a flood.

She glowered at Lila-dian, who met the expression with an empty face. May the cursed woman slip in Chellis's tears and be swallowed by the ocean itself.

He was only a boy.

Chellis dropped her gaze as Lila-dian wrapped the leash around her own forearm. It had been such a horrid wound on Temas's neck. If only Chellis could have dodged the guards. If only she could have reached Temas's limp form, perhaps she could have wept enough to mend his severed windpipe and seal the split skin. Maybe she could have saved him.

But no Hagori boy was worth more than a soldier on the front. No. Her tears—tears shed for Temas—would be used to mend murderers and nourish the men and women who permitted the killing.

If only Chellis could die herself . . . but the warmongers kept too close a watch for that.

Lila-dian yanked the chain and tugged Chellis toward the door, the remaining guard trailing behind them. Each step grated her skin, which had gone dry from her long suspension over the vat. The fins stretching from Chellis's ribs to her upper arms chafed as though coated with sand. The scales over her shoulders would surely flake free if she lifted her arms. It wouldn't be the first time she'd lost scales. But the Hagori didn't care. Merdan scales were worthless in their coffers.

Her bare feet padded down the marble hallway, just a step behind Lila-dian. Chellis stared at the back of the woman's knees, clothed with the fine beige cotton of her uniform. Chellis sported only a short-skirted, shapeless dress, threadbare and patched in three places. She hated that dress. In the sea, she had worn nothing. No clothes, no chains.

Temas.

She didn't want to go back to the room where Temas had died. To the empty bed devoid of his warmth, or the hot nights deprived of his delicate snores. Chellis bit her tongue. *I will not cry. I will not.* She wouldn't go back to the vat, even if Lila-dian did something else horrendous to her.

Lila-dian tugged up on the chain, halting Chellis's stride. The guard took a post a few feet from the door to Chellis's chambers as Lila-dian's stubby fingers selected a key from a small ring fished from her pocket. The bolt locking the door snapped back, and Lila-dian shoved Chellis through, pushed her head down, and unhooked the chain from Chellis's collar.

The walls shaped the room into a perfect square, just large enough to fit a cot on one end and an oval tub on the other. Merdan bodies were not made for the desert, so they had to soak in saltwater—a Hagori potion that felt nothing like the sea—once a day. Over the vat, Chellis had been swabbed with the solution twice. In her room, only her dian could turn on the water.

That's when Chellis saw it—the rusty, almost-brown stain on the thin, dingy carpet. Uneven circles of old blood, one as wide as her fist, some droplets barely more than mist.

Blood. Temas's blood. It stained the carpet. No one had even bothered to clean it up.

"You'll have a later meal because of the new rotation," Lila-dian said as she wound the leash around her left hand. "Sit quietly until I return with it, and I'll let you bathe before bed."

The bloodstains formed shapes before Chellis's eyes: abalones, stars, eyes, mouths. In them she saw Temas's smile as he told a joke Chellis didn't understand.

"Naki?"

Dead. They had killed him, and her dian had blinded her from the scene as soon as the tears began, face as smooth as the marble floors in the hallway.

"Naki, are you listening?"

Chellis straightened, ripping her gaze from the blood.

"Do you need to go back to the vat?"

Chellis met her dian's dark eyes and did something only a Hagori did.

She lunged for them.

The attack surprised the dian and knocked her off balance. They both tumbled to the ground, Chellis on top.

Chellis didn't have nails, but she pressed the tips of her thumbs into Lila-dian's eyes. The Hagori woman cried out, signaling the guard at the door.

"I hate you!" Chellis screamed in Hagori, slapping her dian's face one way, then the other. "I hate you, I hate you!"

Lila-dian screamed. The guard's rough hands seized Chellis's shoulders and jerked her back, but not before Chellis grabbed two fistfuls of Lila-dian's dark hair. The guard heaved Chellis up and away, and the hair tore free from the dian's scalp.

Chellis flailed in the guard's grip, still clutching the hair in her webbed fingers.

"I hate you!" she shouted, tearless. "The Moray devour you in pieces! *He was only a boy!*"

Two more guards scrambled into the room as Lila-dian blubbered and scrambled to her feet. One of them drew a leather-wrapped club and whipped it across Chellis's crown. The room spun. Her limbs died. The guard holding her dropped her to the ground, and Lila-dian spat onto her cheek.

At least, Chellis thought as her heavy eyelids closed, *at least I didn't cry.*

* * *

Chellis lay on the floor of her room just three feet from her cot. The Hagori had manacled her wrists, binding her arms behind her back. Metal cuffs hugged her ankles as well, crushing the fins there, and a rough, taut rope bound her knees to her collar, forcing her to remain in a curled position. She could throw her weight enough to roll from one side to the other and relieve her shoulders, but nothing could soothe the painful arch of her back, nor the hunger that had become almost sentient in her stomach, rolling and growling, futilely struggling to claw its way into the dark, dry world.

She didn't know how much time had passed when the chamber doors opened—the room bore no windows, and blinders covered her eyes, though she had withheld her tears, save a few.

She listened as carpet-muted footsteps filled the room. Three . . . no, four pairs, followed by voices softly mumbling Hagori. Two pairs of feet moved toward her, and deft hands removed the blinders from her eyes. Chellis blinked. A Hagori man stepped out of the room to bottle what little she had wept.

A key pushed into the chains binding her wrists, and an unfamiliar voice—a man's voice carrying a Hagori accent—said, "Move slowly when these come off. You'll be sore."

Chellis strained to see who spoke behind her, but the rope binding her neck to her knees wouldn't allow it. Heavy steps—a guard—neared, but the voice stopped them.

"It's all right," he said.

The guard replied, "She's gone wild. I think it's best if—"

"I said it's all right," the voice repeated. Chellis saw the man's tan arms as he leaned over her to loosen the rope. He had a small, straight scar on the knuckle of his right index finger. "You can go; I'll handle her from here."

"But, sir—"

"Stand outside the door if you must," he said, reaching for Chellis's feet. She held very still as he unlocked the manacles there. "But I'll not have you scaring her."

Though free from her binds, Chellis waited for the guards to retreat and shut the door before extending her aching legs and rolling over to see the stranger.

"Careful now," he said. His hands posed to help, but he didn't touch her. Chellis's back cracked as she sat up. She winced and rubbed her wrists.

The man scooted away from her. He was young—younger than Lila-dian, but older than Chellis's usual guards—and unlike most Hagori, he wore his hair short. But like all Hagori, he had dark brown eyes and tan skin. A bronze loop pierced his left ear halfway down the cartilage. His full lips didn't sneer.

"My name is Ahad," he said. "I'll be your new dian."

Still massaging her wrists, Chellis eyed him, silent.

"Lila-dian has been reassigned," he explained. "Are you hurt?"

How could she not be?

Ahad stood up without an answer and moved to the door, where a tray of food sat on the floor. It held the usual bowl of mixed-seafood slop—whatever the citadel chefs didn't use in their delicacies—and a wooden cup of true seawater. Ahad . . . dian . . . placed it before Chellis and moved to the tub on the other side of the room.

He measured tall for a Hagori, very tall, and had a narrow build. He wore the dian's uniform of a gray wrap-like shirt and loose beige pants that bound tightly to the calf.

He inserted his key into the wall by the tub spout and turned on the water.

Chellis's skin ached as she saw the crystal liquid pour into the tub, but her nose drew her eyes to the bowl of food. No amount of defiance could subdue her hunger. She clasped the bowl with both hands and lifted it to her mouth, swallowing whole chunks of fish hearts and shrimp heads. She coughed, almost choking, and ate more.

Lila-dian would have scolded her for "manners." Ahad-dian said nothing.

She guzzled down the seawater, relishing the briny taste on her tongue.

Her stomach churned.

The cup toppled from her webbed fingers and smacked against the tray. She pressed one hand to her stomach and the other to her mouth. She swallowed as the slop sloshed in her belly.

Poison? Lila-dian had poisoned her food twice before, leaving her retching for a full day. Just to harvest tears.

Chellis glowered at Ahad-dian, who held a small sack of salt in his hands.

He merely smiled at her.

"Eating so much on an empty stomach will make anyone sick," he said.

She stared, palm pressed to her lips, willing her stomach still. Not poisoned?

Ahad-dian poured salt into the bath and shut off the water. "Do you understand me?"

Chellis's stomach settled somewhat, and she dropped her hand from her mouth. Of course she understood. The Merdans all learned Landwalker languages, Hagori and Nakanese and Trinnish, in addition to their own dialect and signed speech. Did the slave trainers know so little about her dwindling people?

She merely nodded.

Ahad-dian stepped away from the tub, but gestured to it with his hand. "If you want it. You look . . . uncomfortable. You scared the others. Fear leads them to neglect; you'll have to forgive them."

Chellis eyed him, mulling over his words. No Hagori spoke so politely. Even Temas hadn't. Was it a new dian tactic? What more could they possibly do to her?

"What's this?" Ahad-dian asked, moving toward her. She backed up into the cot, but he stopped halfway across the room, crouching down on the carpet.

Her eyes followed his, and her ribs involuntarily contracted around her heart.

The bloodstains. Temas.

Ahad-dian lifted a five-inch switchblade from his belt, identical to the knife Lila-dian carried. The knife that had left long, thin scars down Chellis's back and breasts. Chellis held her breath.

"Not Merdan blood," Ahad-dian commented, almost more to himself than to her. Merdan blood flowed blue and left gray stains —stains that blended well with the dingy carpet. "And too old for Lila."

He glanced at her, his eyes curious. She saw a dark sort of light in their depths. Sympathy? But no Hagori knew that emotion, especially dians.

He stabbed the tip of the blade into the carpet and dragged it around the stains, cutting a square piece that revealed stone underneath. He stood, returned the knife to his belt, and stuck the carpet under his arm.

"What on earth did she do to you?" he asked, though he looked ahead at nothing in particular. When his dark gaze shifted to Chellis, he said, "You're welcome to the tub, Naki. I can't leave the room, but it's there."

Chellis's skin itched. She stood, wincing again at the stiffness of her joints, and padded toward the tub. She discarded her rough dress and slid into the water, sighing as its coolness climbed up her skin, soothing away chafes and flakes.

"No one will expect harvesting from you today," Ahad-dian said. "And hopefully not tomorrow. Your health might be forfeit, but even the overlords won't risk your life. And they won't question my judgment. They haven't in the past, at least."

Chellis smoothed back her thin hair and studied the dian with wide eyes. Ahad-dian seemed sincere. Had the great Moray finally heard her pleas and granted her a fraction of relief?

"I recommend you rest after you bathe, Naki," Ahad-dian said. "You'll need it."

"My name is Chellis," she dared to say.

Ahad-dian straightened, his eyebrows raised. "So you do speak."

Chellis sank deeper into the water.

Ahad-dian offered a small smile. "A strange name," he said, "but if you prefer it, I will use it."

She had that option? "I do."

"Chellis, then," he replied. "I recommend you rest after you bathe, Chellis."

How strange to hear someone else say her name. Her true name. Even Temas hadn't done that.

* * *

For two and a half days, Chellis had peace.

She did not leave her room, she did not see Lila-dian, and she did not cry, save for a short time the night after Ahad-dian's arrival, when she wept once more for Temas. She hid her tears in the seams of her dress and over her own scrapes and bruises. Though Lila-dian didn't know it, she had taught Chellis how to weep in complete silence.

Before two and a half days could become three, Ahad-dian came to the small chamber with a kelp-green card in his hand—a Merdan summons. Or, rather, an irrefutable command for more tears.

Chellis eyed the card, her throat tightening. But Ahad-dian said nothing of it, merely set it on the tub rim. He sat beside it. Chellis, on the cot, picked knots from her hair with her fingertips.

"What is the ocean like?" Ahad-dian asked, leaning forward and resting his elbows on his knees. "Your ocean, not ours."

Chellis blinked. She searched the question for tricks, but she found none. Then again, Ahad-dian had proved himself—so far—a dian who didn't employ tricks, unlike Lila-dian.

She answered, "It is all the same ocean."

"Is it?" Ahad-dian countered, his voice sounding like feathers on a morning breeze. "On a map, maybe. But my ocean is the surface, the layer of water that parts before the bow and reflects the sky. The water that breaks when I cast a line, that ripples around the string. Your ocean is all the layers beneath, where the ripples don't touch. It's the sand and the coral and all the dark miles I don't see. Please, tell me. What is that ocean like?"

Chellis's hands dropped from her hair, and she studied the Hagori man. Perhaps for too long, but he didn't chide her for it. He met her gaze, his expression unwrinkled.

"You are not a dian," she said.

He laughed. "Then what am I?"

"Not a dian."

His back straightened. He rubbed one hand over his shaved chin. "Not always a dian, but dians are made, not born. I've been a dian these past three years."

Chellis inched forward on her cot. Only Temas had ever spoken so many words to her. She nearly forgot the summoning card on the tub rim. "Why?"

Ahad-dian smiled, but it was a sad smile that didn't move his cheeks. "Because I cannot fight. I have Widow's Blood—I bleed until there's nothing left."

Chellis narrowed her eyes. "But our tears would heal the wound."

"A waste of tears. Too many for one man," he replied, and shrugged. "And so I became a dian."

"I would heal you," Chellis said, glancing to the card. "But I don't choose who receives my tears. Not anymore."

"I'm sorry," Ahad-dian offered. "But why do you say I am not a dian?"

"Because you say 'please.' And because you apologize. Because, so far, your words are too soft for a dian."

He chuckled.

Chellis lowered herself to the floor and folded her legs under her, careful not to pinch the fins leafing from them. "The ocean is vast, with no walls. No up and down, silent save for song. It is light and free and peaceful, like swimming in sleep itself. It is cool and comforting, filled with life. There are no cages, no locks. No wars. It is a holy space."

Now Ahad-dian studied her. She wondered what he saw. He said, "You must miss it terribly."

"It sings to me through the desert, through the citadel," she said, glancing to the walls around her. "It ails me more than Hagori hands."

"They do wrong to hurt you."

The words shocked her, yet dared Chellis to embolden her speech. "They do wrong to keep me at all."

Ahad-dian did not respond. He picked up the green card and held it in his hands. "I've tried guntha weed—the liquid in its leaves burns the eyes and makes them tear. I've tried salt and lemon and onion, but the tears that fall are just that. Tears. They can't heal. They're not the right kind of tears, the ones that form from deep within. Only those have the power to heal men."

Neither of them spoke for a long moment. Chellis's eyes remained on the card. When she lifted them, she saw that Ahad-dian watched it too.

"Let me try," she pleaded, curling her webbed fingers into fists. "Let me try it on my own, no whips or words, no incentives. Let me cry my own tears."

Ahad-dian gazed at her. "Can you?"

She nodded, already feeling the sting in her eyes. "I have enough in my heart to give you what you need."

She looked to the missing square of carpet where Temas's blood had spilled.

"All right," Ahad-dian conceded, pulling blinders from his belt. "I will let you try."

He hooked the fine chain leash to the back of the iron ring that had encircled Chellis's neck since the Hagori slavers pulled her from the sea. He did not jerk the chain or keep it taut, merely held its end as he guided Chellis into the marble hallway, past the two bulky men who still guarded her door.

As taught, Chellis remained a step behind Ahad-dian, which wasn't hard, considering his long stride. However, even within sight of the guards, Ahad-dian slowed until she walked beside him. Turning the corner, she fell back, and again he slowed. Chellis watched his face as they neared the collection room, but it remained smooth, unreadable.

The collection room lay empty—Chellis had not seen another Merdan since her capture. The dian tried to time it that way.

Her breath quickened as she reached the left platform, the muscles in her thighs tensing in remembrance of her last long visit chained over the vat. But she had told Ahad-dian she could do it without prompting. She couldn't let him change his mind.

She knelt. Ahad-dian removed the leash and replaced it with the heavy chain suspended from the wall. His warm fingers embraced her wrists—carefully smoothing down the fins there—and cuffed them in manacles, which also affixed by chain to the wall.

Then he knelt beside her, biting the inside of his cheek. Their eyes met, and he slid the spongy blinders over her eyes, blocking out the light.

Ahad-dian moved away, and for the first time since becoming a slave, Chellis felt cold.

She leaned over the vat, her chains clinking only once.

And she remembered.

She thought of Temas crouching on her floor, trying to teach her a children's game with rules that kept changing. She heard his cry as soldiers seized him, the flickering light in his moon-wide eyes, the gargle from his lips as the blade raked across his neck.

She heard Lila-dian's voice: *fish-whorer, scubweed, fish fodder.* She felt each choking jerk of her collar, each open-handed slap across her face, each lashing that bit into her skin like the coils of a jellyfish.

She breathed saltwater, felt the cool embrace of the sea as she followed the shadows of her dwindling kin. The fiery agony of the harpoon piercing her calf and dragging her to the surface. The rough hands of the Hagori pulling her, tying her, crating her.

She lived every lonely night, every curse, laceration, burn, and break. She felt the walls of her chamber press against her every side, laughing at her, suffocating her.

And she thought of Ahad-dian, imagined him being beaten for walking alongside a Merdan, for feeding her too often, for letting her heal. She imagined him chained and shackled and dragged away, replaced by a darker, crueler dian.

The thoughts flooded her mind, and Chellis wept.

* * *

Chellis wept for hours, but she could not mourn everything at once; the next summons would demand more, and the next, and the next.

Choking back her sorrow, Chellis let it dry in the back of her throat. Ahad-dian removed the soaked blinders, and men with rough hands collected every stray tear for the Hagori arsenal.

The green card demanding Chellis's contribution to the war came again two days later, and once more, Ahad-dian allowed Chellis to cry for herself. She did, but not as heavily as before. She feared—and she saw that Ahad-dian feared—that she would be unable to continue filling the expected medicinal supply based on memory alone.

The summons card appeared in Ahad-dian's hand less than a day later. He crumpled it in his fist.

"Too soon," he said with a scowl. "They'll kill your kind off with demands like these."

Chellis eyed the card, yet oddly she didn't fear it, not with it clutched in Ahad-dian's hard-knuckled fingers. "Why?" she asked, drawing her knees to her chest, adjusting herself on the cot.

"The war is getting bloodier," Ahad-dian groaned. "More soldiers killing one another, and the Vitian lines haven't budged in a month.

The slavers aren't pulling in new Merdan, so the king wants the ones we have squeezed dry."

Chellis frowned. *At least more aren't being caught,* she thought. Or were all her people already enslaved?

"I can't ignore *this* one," he mumbled.

Chellis stiffened. Had she translated his words correctly? "Ignore . . . this one?"

He didn't look at her. "You've received four summonses this week. I didn't report for the second."

Chellis's heart beat harder in her chest. Before she could ask why, Ahad-dian answered, "It's too much for one person."

She stiffened. No Hagori had ever referred to her as a "person."

"I don't want to hurt you, Chellis," he said, but his eyes focused on the card, not her.

Chellis shivered. She stood, stretching out the fins that lined the sides of her legs. "You're not a dian," she said. "No dian would speak as you do."

He actually smiled. "I'm certified. But I haven't been . . ."

His words caught. He licked his lips and retrieved the chain for Chellis's collar.

"Come with me," he said, reaching over her shoulders to attach the leash.

"Where?" she asked.

But he didn't answer, and Chellis dared not speak as they passed the guards outside her door. However, Ahad-dian didn't lead her toward the collection room, but away from it. Past other guarded doors and down a hallway that reeked of spoiled fish. Up a narrow set of stairs that Chellis faintly remembered having passed before, shortly after her arrival to the prison.

They stopped at a thick door. Ahad-dian thumbed through the keys on a small brass ring pulled from his belt and opened it.

She cried out, then clamped her hands over her mouth the stifle the sound. *Sunlight.* She trembled as her eyes traced the golden rays pouring through the barred windows of the citadel.

Ahad-dian guided her forward, then out another door. Soft, hot air grazed her skin. The brick floor was hot and dusty under her feet, like the skeletons of sunbaked anemones.

Outside. Chellis stood outside.

Her lips parted and she dropped her hands as she took in the courtyard, its angled paths formed with more brick, its thorny gardens filled with wood chips colored rose and indigo. It smelled clean and fresh, but the still, arid air burned her nostrils and gills. It felt like fine sand filtering through her lungs, and once more Chellis craved the sea.

But the *sun*.

Tears sprang to her eyes, and seconds later a blinder's spongy pockets pressed into them.

"Please don't cry," Ahad-dian whispered into her ear, his breath tickling her skin. "Not yet."

She nodded and breathed deeply. Ahad-dian removed the blinders. Chellis spied a guard to her left and lowered her gaze.

Again Ahad-dian led her forward, keeping the chain taut, perhaps to ease the guard. The brick began to burn her scaled feet. Ahad-dian moved so she could walk on wood chips or, when the landscaping permitted, patches of trimmed limp grass.

He stopped as two guards approached. They spoke in a dialect Chellis didn't understand. Ahad-dian answered in a similar fashion, making sharp gestures toward Chellis. After a minute, the sun growing hot on her skin, the guards nodded and let them pass.

They walked until the sunlight became uncomfortable and threatened to dry out her skin. Ahad-dian had to talk to another set of guards, again in that unfamiliar dialect, before leading Chellis onto an elevated walkway over a narrow ravine. Chellis dared to lift her head and look around, taking in the desert landscape around her, the short, tall cliffs that provided backdrop for the citadel and its neighboring buildings, the wild cacti beyond the cultivated gardens, women in veils and long dresses working to pull weeds or sweep walkways. Chellis did not see their reaction to her; all kept their heads down.

They started down a set of stone stairs. The rock blistered her feet, but Chellis did not complain. Even if Ahad-dian had merely meant to take her for a walk, she didn't want it to end. She didn't want to return to that cramped room full of sour memories.

She peered around, looking for guards. She only saw them afar, so she asked, "Where are you taking me?"

Ahad-dian released a long breath through his nose. "I won't tell you yet, unless you want the blinders."

"It will make me cry?"

He seemed uneasy. "I think so. I suppose I should hope so, for the sake of the summons."

Chellis nodded, her leash clanking against her collar. Ahad-dian led her through a covered corridor carved from the rock face itself.

He used another key to open another door, and Chellis found herself in a sandstone-tiled room lit with skylights carved into the ceiling. Two guards, one at the left wall and one on the right, watched them, and an older dian sat at a simple table in the room's center.

The dian behind the table perked up. "She looks very young to be wasted."

"This is for collection purposes," Ahad-dian replied. He showed his green card.

The dian looked uneasy. "Has it been approved?"

"Of course," Ahad-dian replied, and Chellis wondered at the lie.

Ahad-dian said something else in the unknown dialect, and after a moment, the dian nodded and gestured to the door on the left.

As they neared, Ahad-dian whispered, "You were right about my not being a dian, in a sense. I've never been assigned a Merdan before. I manned that table up until the time Lila-dian transferred."

Chellis pressed the heel of her hand against an uneasy tightness blooming in her stomach. It was the same weightless sensation she got when a bull shark lingered nearby. "What did he mean, 'wasted'?"

Ahad-dian opened the door and led Chellis inside. A long, white-tiled hallway met them. "I shouldn't tell you."

"But you will."

"It's when the Merdan can't cry anymore," he whispered, so hushed Chellis had to lean in to hear him. "Something happens to them. We go overboard, or they're away from the sea too long. Something in them breaks. I've studied it, but I haven't found a cure."

Chellis stopped in the hallway and grabbed the center of her leash before it could pull on her collar. "Stop crying? Break? What do you mean?"

Ahad-dian looked much older in the brighter lighting.

She said, "They can't meet their summonses?"

"The tears don't fall," Ahad-dian said, solemn. "They just . . . don't fall."

Blood drained from Chellis's face, running like hot wax down her neck. "And . . . they're here? The others?"

He nodded.

Her heart leaped at the thought of seeing her own kind after eighteen months, but the hope quickly churned bitter. "They're not in the sea? You don't return us to the sea?"

Ahad-dian hesitated, then said, "Come," and guided Chellis down the hallway.

It opened up into more corridors carved into the rock face and lit by skylights, too high to be used for escape. Ahad-dian guided her down the corridor farthest to the left. They passed under a shadowed arch. Ahad-dian paused and gestured down another narrow hallway.

"It's difficult to get the Merdan to cooperate," he murmured, "but down there are the breeding rooms."

Chellis's blood drained even further, pooling in her gut. "Please tell me I misunderstood you."

But Ahad-dian shook his head. "The king believes it's easier to, excuse my phrasing, 'make our own' Merdan than hunt them from the sea."

Chellis quivered. She turned toward the hallway, took one step forward, and stopped. "Then . . . they use children . . ."

"I don't know," Ahad-dian confessed. Chellis didn't realize he had moved until the leash tugged on her collar. She followed behind him, away from the breeding rooms, on numb legs.

The corridor brightened and opened up onto a large atrium in the mountain, lit by several skylights. The corridor had metal railing, and below, Chellis heard the clinking of iron and the groans of men. The sick feeling in her middle intensified, and she peered over the railing.

Below, several long tables sat in rows, lined with men—mostly Merdan men—wearing tattered smocks and dresses like her own. They held small hammers in their webbed hands. On many, the webbing had been ripped from between their fingers to better help them hold the tools.

Upon the tables Chellis saw strange shapes of bronze work, things that looked similar to the armor the Hagori guards wore day and night. The slaves, chained together at the ankles, labored to shape and mold the armor: breastplates, gauntlets, leg coverings, whatever the pieces were called. An overseer on a small horse road by one table, dumping water from a battered pitcher onto the heads of the Merdan as he passed. Many had lost their scales.

Chellis's hands rushed to her mouth, and tears sprang to her eyes. "Why are they here?" She asked, almost shouted. A few slaves turned to look at her, but Ahad-dian clamped the Moray-forsaken blinders over her eyes. She turned toward him, blind. "Why are they here, and not in the sea?" she shouted.

Ahad-dian's too-warm hand clasped her upper arm between delicate fins and pulled her down the corridor. "Come," he said.

Chellis shook her head, tears running from the corners of her eyes, greedily drunk up by the blinders. "Why are they not in the sea, Ahad-dian?" she asked, her voice choking on his name. "If they can do no more to heal the Hagori, why enslave them further? Why not send them home?"

"I don't know," he murmured, very close to her ear. They stopped. Somewhere shaded, for the air turned cool. "I've petitioned it myself, but no one cares for the opinion of a solitary dian."

"Then the others—"

"The others don't care, Chellis."

She shook her head and sobbed, more tears escaping from her eyes. Her legs weakened, and she crouched down, feeling loose dirt under her fingers.

"It makes no sense!" she said, and her words echoed against the rock around her. Hugging her knees, she wept for her broken people, forbidden to return home. So many scaled faces had labored over those tables. How many of her kind still swam the oceans as freemen?

She cried until her eyes felt too dry, despite the soggy sponges pressed against them. Ahad-dian gripped her shoulders and helped her stand, then carefully removed the blinders from her eyes. He boxed them, stuck the box into the back of his belt, and wiped a stray tear away with his thumb.

"Come," he said, pulling her from the alcove they had taken refuge in. Chellis didn't follow at first. Ahad-dian waited until she obliged. Her bare feet left dragging prints against the sandy floor of the prison.

They didn't retrace their steps.

"What more is there?" Chellis asked, her voice trembling in her throat. "What more is there for me to see?"

"If we can double this," Ahad-dian replied, staring straight ahead, "perhaps I can relieve you of summonses for a time. Let you rest."

Chellis quickened her step. "How can I rest when I know my people are being treated so cruelly?"

He glanced at her. "You already knew, Chellis."

Chellis hissed between her teeth, but said nothing.

The cool rock under her feet gave way to dusty carpet. The ground dipped downward, and fewer skylights lit their way. Everything looked as at dusk.

Someone, somewhere, screamed.

Chellis froze. "Ahad," she whispered, "where are you taking me?"

His shoulders slumped. "I will not hurt you, Chellis."

"Where are you taking me?" she repeated.

He chewed on the inside of his cheek for a long moment before pulling her forward. "Some are bred, some are put to work. Mostly the men."

The sickness within Chellis spread out to her limbs. "And the women?"

The scent of roses and seaweed filled her sinuses. Chellis looked up, seeing thin fabric like the Hagori women's veils draping the ceiling. She peered down another narrow corridor, lit by lanterns hanging on the wall.

Ahad-dian pulled on the chain, calling her attention. Chellis turned just in time to step out of the way of a heavyset Hagori man walking with a Merdan woman under each arm. One looked half asleep, the other downtrodden, like her head weighed too much for her neck to support. Both women wore draping clothes that hid their breasts and wrapped around their hips, but exposed everything else.

The Hagori man led both Merdan women down the dim hallway and into the second room on the right. Chellis heard him chuckle before shutting the door.

She backed up into a cloth-strewn rock. "This isn't . . ."

Ahad-dian pulled a second pair of blinders from his belt, but he held them as though they were a dead animal. "If nothing else," he whispered, "I thought you should see . . ."

Another scream, but that time it sounded closer. Close enough that Chellis's blood shot through her veins, heating her skin from the inside. A Merdan woman, naked, bolted from the fourth door on the left, near a hanging lantern. Shouting in Merdani, "Help me! Moray eat my soul!"

Chellis stepped away from the wall and squinted through the shadows, the scales running up the outside of her arm prickling. That voice. She *knew* that voice.

A Hagori man rushed from the room, dressed only in slacks, and seized the Merdan woman by the wrist, crushing her fin. She cried out. He grabbed her by the waist, which forced her to turn toward Chellis.

Chellis's heart crumbled to ashy pieces. "Gaylil," she whispered.

Ahad-dian asked, "What?"

"Gaylil!" Chellis screamed, pushing off the rock and bolting down the hallway, wrenching her leash free. Her legs were ill-trained in running, but she pushed them, passing doors and lanterns as she sailed toward the Merdan woman, tears catching the air as she went.

Ahad-dian shouted her name.

A guard turned from the opposite end of the hallway.

The half-dressed man saw Chellis and flung Gaylil into the wall. Gaylil, recognition in her eyes, clamped her hands over a gash in the back of her head. It stained her fair hair blue.

"Gaylil!" Chellis screamed, but just before she reached her, rough hands grabbed her from behind. Not Ahad-dian's hands, but guards' hands, Hagori men she didn't know. They wrestled her back. One drew a knife.

"No! *No!*" Chellis screamed, flailing in their grips, kicking out her legs. "Let her go! Gaylil! She's my *sister!* Ahad-dian!" she cried. "Someone, *help me!*"

A loud thunk echoed inside her skull, and—

* * *

Chellis hadn't seen light for three days.

The edge of the vat dug into her knees. She couldn't feel her hands or feet, but sometimes, when she shifted, the faintest tingling reminded her they were still there.

Her head throbbed in time with her heart, and her mouth and throat were as sandy as the Hagori desert. As sandy as the cavern floor where she had seen the abuse of her people and the absolute injustice of the Hagori. Villains, tyrants, whoremongers. May the great Moray consume them all and dig the entire nation a grave in the deepest recesses of the ocean, where even the Merdan dared not swim.

She heard Ahad-dian arguing with someone in the hallway, for the second time since awakening with blinders strapped over her eyes and her body bound in the shackles that supported her as she dangled over the vat. He argued low, he argued high. She couldn't make out most of what he said, but she didn't care.

"I don't want to hurt you, Chellis."

But you did. Worse than anyone.

Gaylil. Chellis hadn't seen her sister for three years. Chellis hadn't been there when the slavers took her. She hadn't seen her sister's blood in the ocean or heard her water-muted screams as the Hagori dragged her onto their boat. She had only heard of it. Heard of it and mourned.

To find that those land-ridden sharks had her. How Chellis hated them all.

She heard footsteps, a stride she had memorized over the past three days. Ahad-dian knelt beside her and pressed a cool rag, wet with saltwater, to her leg, a sad treatment for her dry skin.

"I'm so sorry," he whispered. Chellis could not count the number of times he had uttered those words since Gaylil. "You'll be released soon, I swear it, even if I have to cut the chains myself."

Chellis didn't answer. Despite feeling like a desert herself, another tear absorbed into the blinders.

Ahad-dian sighed. "For some reason I thought it would . . . I didn't expect . . . your sister. Oh Chellis, I'm sorry. I'll look into helping her, I promise."

Help her how? Chellis thought, bile churning where her throat met her stomach. *Let her do hard labor instead? Let them kill her or throw her into the desert, or drop bits of her body into the Merdans' slop?*

What will happen when they finally break me too?

She pressed her lips together, refusing to utter a word.

He moved the rag and touched her outstretched arm with his warm hand. Too warm. "I'm sorry," he repeated. "Please forgive me, Chellis. Please."

But Chellis didn't, and after several long minutes, Ahad-dian's footsteps retreated back into the hallway.

* * *

Hours later, four pairs of heavy footsteps entered the collection room. A Hagori's gloved hand gripped a fistful of Chellis's hair and pushed her head forward until she choked against the collar.

Her handler removed the chain on her collar and replaced it with the standard leash before jerking Chellis's head back so another could remove the blinders from her eyes. The light of the collection room burned, and the guard holding the blinders cursed as a few tears dropped into the vat. A second guard quickly collected them using a rubber spatula.

Chellis blinked spots from her eyes. Cold spiked her center when she did not see Ahad-dian among her visitors. Three guards, one dian—a broad-shouldered woman with light hair for a Hagori. Her small mouth twisted as though she had just eaten bluefish. She stood stiff as a coral as the third guard finished unchaining Chellis's wrists and ankles; Chellis winced as blood rushed back into her deadened limbs.

The dian released her hair and snatched the leash, jerking it hard against Chellis's windpipe. Chellis sputtered and coughed, nearly teetering into the vat, her dead feet and screaming knees unable to support her. The dian jerked the chain again so that Chellis fell onto her rump. Pain flashed up her backbone. She caught herself on tingling hands, jarring rusted shoulders.

"Get up," the dian snapped. Her voice sounded low and quick, the way a barracuda would talk, if it could.

Chellis scrambled for a footing, forcing her stiff joints to move. Her heart slammed from one side of her rib cage to the next. "Ahad-dian," she rasped, "where is Ahad—"

The back of the dian's gloved hand smashed against Chellis's jaw, shoving her onto her left side. Again she nearly slipped into the vat, but a jerk of the leash prevented it.

Chellis gasped for air as her head spun. Her pulse throbbed along the side of her face, and her jaw popped as she opened and closed it, tasting blood in her cheek. She swallowed it.

"Your papers say you've been here eighteen months, and yet you still speak out of turn?" The dian snapped. "Disgusting. To your feet, Merd!"

She jerked back on the leash until it cut into the already chafed ring of scar tissue around Chellis's neck. She gasped and struggled to stand. She steadied her feet against the tile, but she didn't straighten completely—her back wouldn't allow it, not yet. She had stayed too long in those chains, but surely a dian wouldn't be offended by her crippled stance.

She bit on her tongue and blinked rapidly to keep herself from crying. *By the Moray, they've transferred Ahad-dian, or worse.* Had he gotten in trouble for their excursion? Is that what he had been arguing about in the hallway?

She dared a glimpse at the new dian, who was speaking to the second guard. *Please, no.* Don't let the woman be her new caretaker. Give her Lila-dian, but not that woman. Not that dark squid among sharks.

"Fine," the dian said. She didn't look at Chellis, merely jerked the chain and started for the door. Chellis's hips ground in their sockets as she staggered after her, trying to keep pace with the impatient strides. Her belly growled. The dian sneered and jerked the chain again, nearly knocking Chellis into the wall. A scale fell to the spotless marble floor—from where, Chellis couldn't tell. She'd lost so many.

Four guards took their posts outside Chellis's quarters. The dian threw Chellis inside; Chellis's toe caught on the missing square of carpet and she tripped forward, landing on her knees. She quickly knelt and slumped her shoulders—a passive position Lila-dian preferred—hoping the new dian would give Chellis something to eat, or at least turn on the bath.

She did neither.

One of the guards from outside stepped into the room, and the dian shut the door. From a sort of sheath buckled to her calf, she pulled a short leather whip. She tugged on either end to test its durability.

Chellis shrank back. She hadn't been whipped for . . . months. A chill raced through her blood despite the stuffiness of the room. She tried to swallow, but her time over the vat had dehydrated her. Surely the dian would let her recuperate before giving her a beating!

"Please, where is Ahad-dian?" she asked, knowing each syllable grated on the dian's ears. "Where is—"

The woman stepped forward and belted the whip across Chellis's face. White light danced in Chellis's vision, and then she found her face pressed to the floor, a cool drop of blood tickling her chin.

"Do not speak out of turn, Merd," the dian said. "You have a ripe problem with that, in addition to your other failures. You are not to speak unless spoken to. You are not to leave the care of your dian. You are not to converse with other Merdan. You are not to engage with other Hagori save your dian, and especially not in altercation."

She turned toward the guard. "Time me for a quarter hour."

The man nodded, and the dian raised her whip.

* * *

"I knew they'd do this."

Chellis came to herself, acutely aware of her surroundings; the lightening of the room as someone turned up the lamp by the door, the taste of iron and sea in her mouth, the burning strikes littering her body. Her hunger, her thirst, her aches.

Her relief at hearing his voice.

Ahad-dian crouched beside her and smoothed hair from her face. "I'm so sorry," he whispered. "They called me for a disciplinary council. I knew that if I left you . . . oh Chellis." He looked her up and down, fingered the flaking scales on her right shoulder. He smelled like Hagori spices, though the only one she could name was cardamom.

He stood and pushed his key into the wall by the tub, turning on the water there. Chellis strained to watch him and noticed a tray of food by the door. She pressed a hand to the carpet to push herself up, noticing for the first time that the fin running along the outside of her wrist had been torn in two. That would hinder her, if she ever swam again.

Ahad-dian returned, crouched, and scooped Chellis into his arms. He carried her to the tub and gently laid her into the still-rising water. It stung, for a moment. She cupped the water in her hands and drank until Ahad-dian handed her the glass of seawater.

"Slowly," he advised, his speech slightly slurred, like he'd missed days of sleep. Perhaps he had.

She drank, relishing the brine coating her insides. Ahad-dian added a packet of salt to the water before shutting it off. Then he did something dians didn't do.

He left the room.

Chellis watched, waited, feeling an invisible fisher's line stretching from her chest to the door. When Ahad-dian didn't return, she checked her wounds. They didn't feel as sharp in the water. She didn't have enough of her own water to cry and heal them, but Ahad-dian had already assumed that. He returned with a small white case Chellis recognized as a first-aid kit. The blue water droplet painted on its side denoted its use for Merdan, as did its tiny size.

"Here, now," he said, kneeling beside the tub. He pulled out a gray handkerchief—more of a rag—and doused it with the foul-smelling yellow contents of a cloudy bottle. He pressed the rag first to Chellis's forehead, then to her jaw. She watched his face as he worked, the crease marring his forehead, the fine, permanent lines between his brows.

And his eyes, dark as a midnight thunderstorm, focused solely on their work. On her.

"I know what it's like, in a way," he said, hushed, the wet rag stinging a shallow cut on her elbow. "To be a slave, I mean."

Chellis held very still.

After several breaths, he said, "Being born the way I was—with Widow's Blood—people treated me differently. My mother coddled me, always afraid I'd get hurt. I wasn't allowed outside, like you. Wasn't allowed to take off my shoes unless I was in bed. She even tested the temperature of all my meals until I was twelve.

"But my father, my brothers, they were different," Ahad-dian continued. "They treated me like . . . well, like I was a Merdan. Please don't take offense at that." He glanced at her. "I barely know my brothers, even my younger ones. They saw only the disease. But they never hurt me. Not like this, not physically. I would have died if they had."

He rewetted the rag and leaned over the tub sill, pressing the cloth to the side of Chellis's neck. Chellis lifted her wet arms and wrapped them around his.

He froze.

"Thank you," she whispered, her nose pressed against his unpierced ear.

A second passed, and another. Ahad-dian shifted, palmed the rag, and returned the embrace, his sleeves soaking up the water along Chellis's back, his wrist pressing into another laceration there.

"I'm sorry, Chellis," he said. "I never meant for this—"

"I know. But you've done more for me these past two weeks than any other Hagori I've known, even before your war. Thank you."

She released him, and he pulled away, not bothering to wipe away the saltwater along the side of his neck.

"You are not a dian," Chellis said.

He chuckled under his breath and ran his free hand through his hair. "I know. God above, I know."

He resumed his work, and Chellis leaned forward so he could treat her back. He had nearly finished when he said, "You aren't a slave, Chellis. Or you shouldn't be. None of them should be, but you most of all."

She turned toward him.

He held the rag in one hand and the cloudy bottle in the other, but did nothing more. His eyes focused on the rim of the tub. "It's all I can think about, after taking you there," he murmured. "I'm out of excuses to defend it, to defend myself. It's a war over land, did you know that? A border dispute because the river dried up. Six years of war because of a river. My older brother died for a few miles of infertile desert."

Chellis fingered her split fin. "I'm sorry."

"Gaylil's been here for four. I looked up her records."

"Almost four," Chellis replied.

"Older sister?"

"Younger, by three years."

Ahad-dian nodded. "How many others have been captured?"

"I don't know," Chellis said, drawing her knees to her chest. "Gaylil and my father before me. But since . . . I don't know."

"How many siblings do you have?"

"Just her. We aren't a numerous people."

Ahad-dian whistled. The sound faded, and he remained quiet for a long moment, still holding the rag and bottle. "It isn't right."

Chellis didn't respond.

He shook his head and dumped the rest of the bottle's contents onto the rag, then pressed the rag to the stripes along Chellis's right arm. "It isn't right," he repeated as he worked his way down.

Chellis soaked in the saltwater for a long hour. Ahad-dian helped her from the tub, gave her a new, rough-spun dress to wear, and sat in silence as she ate. She slept for a time, and when she woke, Ahad-dian still lingered in the room, sitting cross-legged on the floor with his back against the door, rubbing his chin, his eyes looking somewhere beyond the walls.

She fell asleep again, but when she woke, it was to a hand pressed against her mouth, the lamp in the room turned low for the night.

"I don't want to raise any alarm," Ahad-dian whispered to her. "Chellis, can you walk?"

She nodded against his hand.

"Good," he said. "We have a long way to go."

He stood and pulled the fine chain leash from his belt. Chellis sat up and rubbed a sore spot on her hip.

"Where are we going?" she asked. "Back to the collection room? So soon?"

Ahad-dian hooked the leash onto her collar.

"The sea," he answered.

The room fell away from Chellis's vision and she stood in a realm of shadow, empty save for Ahad-dian and the chain that connected them.

Tears filled her eyes. "The . . . sea?"

Ahad-dian wiped the tears from her lashes with a knuckle and placed them over the lashing on Chellis's jaw—the dull pain there vanished within seconds, healed. "I can try," he whispered, "but if it doesn't work, neither of us will have a second chance. Do you understand?"

She nodded, a surge like a volcano bursting from the deepest parts of her. The shadows around her reformed into her chambers. Chambers she might never have to see again.

"What do I have to do?" she asked.

Ahad-dian held up a summons card. "I stole this. A midnight summons is believable, given the high demand for Merdan tears. This will, at the very least, get you past the guards outside your door. I'll have to hope my standing can get you out of the citadel. From there, we run."

Chellis nodded. "Anything. I'll do anything."

Ahad-dian let out a long breath and wrapped the leash around his wrist, tightening it. "Act as subservient as you can, and forgive me if I fail."

Ahad-dian didn't flash the card as he pulled Chellis from her chambers, much rougher than usual. The guards must have noticed, however, for they didn't ask questions. Chellis didn't see them for herself; she kept her gaze fixed on the floor. Once Ahad-dian led her around the corner, he snapped blinders over her eyes. He guided her down the hall. Chellis heard someone moving toward them, and Ahad-dian jerked the leash as though Chellis had been walking too slowly. He didn't need to explain; Chellis whimpered and quickened her pace, hoping that whatever stranger saw her would see only another worthless Merdan on her way to the vat.

She knew when they passed the collection room. She had walked the path to and from it enough times with blinders to gauge its location. Ahad quickened his step, then, and shortened the leash. She didn't know the citadel's layout beyond the collection room. Not by heart.

The marble turned cold beneath her feet, then hot. She heard men talking, a conversation that stopped as she passed by, then resumed as she and Ahad-dian rounded another corner. Ahad-dian paused, and she heard the subtle jingle of keys.

A voice made her scales rise.

"Where is Naki appointed this time of night?" Lila-dian asked, her soft footfalls nearing. She paused a moment and added "And I thought *I* beat her hard. I'm surprised you have it in you, Ahad-dian."

"I don't," he replied, spitting the words. "This wound-licker is beyond saving. I'm taking her to be drained before she's turned over for labor. If I didn't know any better, I'd think you set me up for this."

The accusation rubbed Chellis like sand under her skin. She focused on her breathing.

Lila-dian snorted. "The better. Save me a piece for my collection."

The soft footfalls moved away, and Ahad-dian opened the door, pulling Chellis up a set of steep, high stairs.

She was panting by the time they reached the top of them. "What," she asked between breaths, "is draining?"

"I made it up," Ahad-dian said, fumbling with his keys again. "But Lila has never worked outside maintenance. She wouldn't know." A lock clicked. Ahad-dian pulled the blinders off Chellis's eyes. The stairwell was dark, save for a high, horizontal window that let in a few speckles of starlight. "Come," he said, opening the door.

Chellis stepped into a wide marble hallway with circle-top windows lining one side, letting in the warm desert breeze. Every other lamp in the hallway had been lit, casting an orangey glow over the stone. One hand on the leash and one on her upper arm, Ahad-dian led Chellis down the hallway and through the first junction on the left.

Ahead of them walked a cluster of guards. Their eyes narrowed at Ahad-dian, but instead of trying to walk past them, Ahad-dian cursed and pulled Chellis back into the main hallway. Two of the guards shouted after him.

"What are you doing?" Chellis hissed as Ahad-dian broke out into a run, tugging her alongside him.

"I can't lie to those ones," he huffed, taking the next left, then a right. He slowed, scanning his surroundings before hurrying to another set of stairs. "I'm a dead man," he said.

He half dragged Chellis up the stairs and took a hard right down a poorly lit hallway, slowing when they neared another, tired-looking guard outside an ornate door. The guard said nothing as they passed, but Ahad-dian picked up the pace again when the previous guards' shouts echoed up the stairwell.

He cursed again.

Chellis writhed from his grasp. "Where are the waterways?" she asked.

He wiped his palm over his forehead. "What?"

"The waterways," Chellis repeated, the shouting getting louder. "Where the river branches off to feed the citadel. I've seen them before. The moat."

Ahad-dian's eyes widened.

"We don't have time, Ahad! Where are they?"

Ahad-dian seized her arm and ran down the hall. Chellis struggled to keep up with his long strides; her legs were not made for running, and they hadn't had decent exercise for eighteen months. Ahad-dian tugged her left, guards' footsteps echoing behind them. Someone all in gray, carrying a candle, started at the sight of them; Chellis darted forward and slammed both hands into his chest, pushing him as hard as she could. He dropped the candle and hit the wall, banging his head. Ahad-dian pushed Chellis forward, then out an open window onto a narrow precipice some four stories above the earth.

Below them flowed the moat, silver by the light of a crescent moon, covered by the curving roofs of a balcony to the left and a walkway to the right. They left a ten-foot gap of water between them. If Chellis jumped and hit one of the roofs, she'd break.

"I don't know . . . how deep," Ahad-dian said.

"There, the window!" a man shouted inside. An arrow flew between Chellis and Ahad-dian, tearing through the gray fabric of Ahad-dian's shirt. He hissed as the tear filled with crimson.

"Hold your breath," Chellis said, wrapping her arm around Ahad-dian's waist.

She kicked off of the precipice and fell into silence.

The cool water hit her like a storm-tossed wave, and Ahad-dian's weight thrust her down far enough that her shoulder blades grazed the moat's cement floor. She swam with the current, avoiding the surface. An arrow sailed past them, leaving a line of silver in the dark water.

She pulled Ahad-dian forward until they reached the cover of the exterior walkway, then brought him up for air. Hagori could hold their breath for only a minute at best, and Chellis didn't know how much air he had gotten on the way down.

Not much. Ahad-dian gasped, his long limbs flailing without grace. Chellis held him up, the base of the walkway only inches above their heads.

Ahad-dian took a deep breath, and Chellis took his arm and pulled him down into the water.

The fresh, unsalted water rubbed her like unsanded wood, yet its depths invigorated her. Her bruises and abrasions turned to memory beneath the current, and her fins opened and propelled her and her dian forward, around the corner of the citadel. She swam until the moat forked. Ahad-dian pointed to the right, and Chellis swam through the channel until Ahad-dian tugged at her, desperate once more for air.

They rose to the surface, and almost immediately Chellis heard the shouts of angry guards, saw the waving of torches on the looming citadel. Ahad-dian gasped several times before diving back under, kicking his sandaled feet to swim.

They met a grate, and Chellis pulled Ahad back to the surface.

"Climb," she ordered.

He did, finding footholds in the grating. An arrow whizzed by, dangerously close to his head.

Chellis shoved Ahad-dian from the top of the grating to the other side, and his body splashed into the water. She submerged, swam back, and then propelled herself forward as fast as her limbs would allow—the unused muscles remembered the movements, even if they protested it.

She burst from the water, arcing up and over the grate, and dived into the water on the other side. She grabbed Ahad-dian's belt and swam as hard as she could, urging both of them forward. If Ahad-dian were to swim alone, his slowness would kill him.

They swam. Even with Chellis's help, Ahad-dian had to begin swimming at the surface to prevent hyperventilation. Chellis came up every five minutes or so to gauge their surroundings, though she could hold her breath for ten. Each time the guards' cries sounded a little quieter, their torches a little more distant.

Finally, Ahad-dian could go no farther, and he lifted himself onto the river's sandy banks.

"I can feel it," Chellis said, wading in the water, her breaths searing but alive. "The sea. I can feel it."

Ahad-dian breathed heavily. "Good," he said, more voice than air. He clutched his left shoulder.

Chellis pulled herself onto the bank and moved his hand, then gasped at the amount of blood running down his arm. It soaked his entire sleeve, and he'd been free from the water only a moment. In the starlight, he looked ashen and pale. Too pale for a Hagori.

"Ahad," Chellis whispered.

"Widow's Blood," he said with a tired grin. "I told you . . . it doesn't stop."

"Lean over," Chellis said, pushing him onto his good arm.

"Chellis, you can't—"

"I can certainly cry for you, Ahad," she said, the tears already coming forth. "If I can cry for anyone, it would be you."

The vision of Ahad-dian bleeding out and dying on the sand filled her consciousness. She thought of his arrival as her dian, his kindness, his risk to bring her there. It was more than enough. Chellis pressed her forehead to Ahad-dian's shoulders and wept into his wound, watching the skin seal itself with every drop.

She laughed. "There," she said.

Ahad-dian sighed and lay back on the bank, still ashen.

"Ahad?"

"Thank you," he breathed, "but I've still lost too much. I can't go any farther. Not tonight."

"I'll carry you," she said, taking his hand. She searched for the citadel, but didn't see it. "Twenty miles to the coast from the citadel, isn't it? We must be halfway there. I can *hear* it, Ahad. We're so close."

He chuckled. "I can't live in the ocean, Chellis. You must go on alone. That was always the plan."

Chellis's heart stopped beating for several seconds, or so it felt. "We'll stay on the coast," she said, almost whispering. "You and I, land and sea."

But Ahad-dian shook his head. "I have to go back."

New tears coursed down Chellis's cheeks. "But why?"

"Gaylil," he said. The name pricked her skin as though lightning carved it there. "I have to . . . get Gaylil."

"They'll kill you."

"I think I can do it," he said, pushing himself into a sitting position again. "I have to get her too."

Chellis shook her head. "You can't save all of them, Ahad! Neither of us can! Not until this war . . . not until my people can gain allies. I'll go back to them. I'll find them and report my stories. Surely someone will listen to our plea for aid, if they haven't already." She squeezed his hand. Perhaps in her absence, someone had rallied supporters. Surely her people didn't swim around complacent, awaiting a man-given fate. "We'll save them together, but I need time."

Ahad-dian smiled. "War takes time. Gaylil may be dead by then, Chellis."

She shivered.

He cupped the side of her face with a sand-covered hand. "Believe in me. I have friends in the city. No one will expect me to come back. I'll sort it out, make a stronger plan. I'll save her, and I'll save you."

Chellis blinked away another tear, letting it fall, useless, to the sand. "You really want me to leave you on the bank of the river, with our enemies following behind? Come with me, Ahad."

"I can't. Not yet."

"Then when?"

He tilted his head to the side, studying her.

"One month," she answered for him. "Enough time for you to recuperate and plan. Enough time for me to learn what has happened to the remnant of my people. Do you understand?"

She stood, squinting through the darkness. She pointed toward the squat mountain range far to the west, a black wedge against a blue-black sky. "Spear Peak. I don't know what your people call it. The far end of the range, where the rock turns dark. One month from this night, Ahad. Meet me there." She turned toward him. "Promise me."

He nodded. "I promise, Chellis."

She knelt down in the sand beside him, searching his eyes for truth. The night was too dark for her to see it, but she believed him.

"Promise," she repeated, and she leaned forward and kissed him, her lips against his. One tradition that meant the same in both their cultures, she knew.

At that moment, he smelled like the sea.

She pulled away. Ahad smoothed her hair behind her ear and whispered, "Promise."

Chellis nodded and imprinted his face onto her memory. One month.

Leaving her savior on the bank, Chellis dived into the river and swam for the ocean.

About Charlie N. Holmberg

Charlie Nicholes Holmberg was born in Salt Lake City, Utah, to two parents who sacrificed a great deal to give their very lazy daughter a good education. As a result, Charlie learned to hate uniforms, memorized all English prepositions in alphabetical order, and mastered the art of Reed-Kellogg diagramming a sentence at age seven. She entered several writing contests in her elementary years and never placed.

In summer 2013, after collecting many rejection letters and making a quilt out of them, Charlie sold her ninth novel, *The Paper Magician*, and its sequel to 47North with the help of her wonderful agent, Marlene Stringer. Someday she will own a dog. (Did she mention her third book, *The Master Magician*, totally made the WSJ bestseller list? Because it totally made the WSJ bestseller list.)

Charlie is also a board member for the Deep Magic e-zine of science fiction and fantasy.

THE WAXING DISQUIET

By Tony Pi & Stephen Kotowych | 6,000 words

METEMIS TOUCHED RED honey to Gilani's lips, hoping play would distract his love from the worries of recent days. "The Wicks foretold that we'd share a sweeter kiss."

His jest coaxed a smile from her. "Did they?" Gilani spun out of reach, leaning coy against their shywood tree. Her dress of white linen danced with the breeze. The orchard atop the terraced hill was their usual trysting place, and the bright pink blossoms filled the sultry air with perfume. Here, they could escape the waxing disquiet in the city, the rumors of war, and indulge instead in one another . . . if only for a breath. "Did they also augur that I'd ask you to serenade me?"

Metemis laughed. "Shall I praise your smiling eyes? No, I sing of them too often." He pushed a dark curl behind her ear, and was pleased she wore the earrings he'd given her, mosaics of greenstone and opal, signifying devotion.

But then, over her shoulder, he saw the city in the distance.

Ziroi was fringed by the fire of the setting sun. Farmland ringed the city like petals, while aqueducts and gardens checkered it like a rushlight board. From the hive pyramid at its heart, paper lanterns rose by the thousands, slow and silent like a plume of fireflies.

The beacons tore Metemis from his flirtatious mood. Did they signal war at last with Tekura?

No, war lanterns would burn sunflower yellow. These glowed lavafruit red.

Gilani tightened her grip on his arm. "The queen."

All Ziroi whispered that Her Royal Grace would soon succumb to her long illness, and of late, the tallies of the Wicks had tipped toward the same conclusion. Crimson meant the moment was nigh.

Buoyed by the west wind, the lights wended between the Hundredhand Pillars and disappeared beyond the terraced hills. By morning they would summon all the queen's subjects to the city for her last Grand Census.

"I must return to the pyramid." Metemis pulled his feather-fringed cloak around his bare shoulders. "There will be many tests to oversee in the coming days."

Gilani sighed. "Go, Tallyminder. And I will to my own tasks." She replaced her beaded headdress. "My roads will soon grow fat with travelers, and too many are in ill repair."

"No, come with me." Metemis took her hand. Gilani was a sixth-cell hundredhand, so it was Metemis's prerogative as a like-ranked tallyminder to administer her test in private, safeguarding state secrets from the masses. "I'll speed us through so that we may deal with the myriads at leisure."

* * *

Already, citizens gathered in the Plaza of Two Moons to pray, to mourn, and to make report. Swarms of people milled around the hexagonal base of the hive pyramid, a sea of humanity from the lance towers to the north and the bazaar domes to the south. The crowds sang mournful praise songs for the queen as dozens of breechclouted hawkers peddled honey sticks with their calls.

"How do you think this Grand Census will influence the next queen?" asked Gilani.

"Same as the lesser ones, I suppose," said Metemis, thinking of the surveys he proctored in six-week, six-month, or twelve-month cycles as he rose through the ranks. He shook loose a pebble from his sandal. "The Wicks will reckon and augur the brightest future for us, and the new queen will use this tally to guide us. There will be suggested alliances, trade pacts. *Wedding matches* made." He squeezed her hand.

Centuries of knot-histories had shown that the candle equations matched strength to strength and mind to mind with great foresight, as they were sure to do shortly for him and Gilani. Even strangers called to marry soon discovered they fit each other like the Wedded Moons now rising above Ziroi. The Wicks had paired Metemis's own parents that way.

Together they climbed the pyramid's steep outer steps, past hexagonal cavities set into concrete and stone. The Queen's Sting were lighting signal fires in some cells, while other cells housed humming beehives.

"What will your Wicks say about Tekura?" Gilani asked.

Metemis stiffened. They had argued over this twice before. "The Wicks perceive patterns that escape us. If they say we must war with Tekura or Somaros or some other city, then it must serve our best interest."

Gilani frowned. "Not everyone in Ziroi agrees. The Wicks have more and more to say about how we live our lives. Is it any wonder that factions have sprung up to oppose the queen?"

"Oh? Revolutionaries in every shadow?"

"Don't mock. If the new queen doesn't make changes, then resentment will only fester."

"And what would you have Her Royal Grace change?"

"In the early days, people lived their own lives and made choices without relying on projected outcomes. The Wicks did nothing more than help farmers calculate the best time to plant and when the rains would come."

"Why endure such chaos when there's order?" answered Metemis. They stood midpoint between the royal tiers above and the lesser rings that served the myriads below. He took Gilani's hand, but thought better of kissing her cheek. "Such a fierce spirit! But think of the heights our city has reached thanks to the guidance of the Wicks over the centuries. Think of where they'll lead us."

* * *

Ventilation shafts peppered the floor of the sixth ring, each wider than a man. The scent of sweet candle smoke wafted from the holes, as did the rumbles and creaks of giant fans, and the water-wheels that powered them.

At the gate, Metemis grazed palms with a pair of Queen's Sting guards in greeting. They lowered their venomlances and allowed Metemis and Gilani to enter the honeycomb corridors. At the sanctum door, Metemis placed a combination of weights on a mahogany balance lock. When the hands of the scales pointed to the right symbols chosen for the day, the gatekeeper rolled open the door.

In the quizzing chambers beyond, Metemis's acolytes were already testing citizens of the upper echelon. His own such chamber was grand, large enough to administer two tests at once. The two quizzing tables backed one another like the slopes of a single mountain, lit by caryatid candles.

This chamber was for the Grand Census only, and had more questions than the cyclic surveys. Each question was carved into its own stone pan, awaiting answer candles of the right weight and burn speed. Even the order in which the test taker chose to answer questions and the time taken meant something to the Wicks.

Metemis dismissed his acolytes. He removed Gilani's necklace and unbraided her namestone into its three unique parts, placing them on their respective name pans to mark her identity. He lit her calendar candle with flame from the caryatids and set up her initial candles for her.

As Gilani started in, Metemis prepared his own tallyboard and began with the questions of love.

Single still, yet seeking. In love, hoping for children. He retrieved the answer candle he wanted from the proper bin, and touched flame to its wick. The balance pan dipped as he placed his answer. The strings and scales hidden underneath the tallyboard began to slowly feed the Wicks their information.

Next, questions of loyalty, of his personal wealth and status, and of his faith in the four castes. Unlike the tests taken by the myriads, there were no questions about harvests or livestock. The last questions he took were about what the next queen should champion.

Metemis couldn't help but glance at Gilani on the sly, wondering how she answered. But she never looked away from the tallyboard, her brows drawn together in concentration.

When he lit his last candle, Gilani was still searching the bins for more. He retreated to the calculation antechamber, where the tallylooms worked unceasingly.

Click-clack went the wooden hooks, tying knots in coarse hemp twine, the knot-history of their answers. Some answers would be visible to Metemis here before being sent to deeper wickwork chambers, there to be woven into a greater plan. He didn't think of it as cheating; his servants were there to ensure against a chance breeze blowing out a candle, or an accident knocking something out of alignment. Such acolytes were everywhere, keeping the Wicks lit and calculating.

Gilani set her last candle.

Metemis was pleased to see that his own knot-history was woven together with a red silk marriage thread, signaling he was finally to wed. And Gilani's—

His stomach lurched. The Wicks were never wrong, but . . . it just couldn't be. Gilani's knot-history was being woven with a white chastity thread.

It took a few moments for Metemis to trust that his legs wouldn't give out if he took a step, but he soon emerged from the calculation antechamber. He kept his face and manner calm. There was no need to alarm Gilani.

Yet.

Surely they were meant to marry. Who had the Wicks chosen for him?

* * *

The hive pyramid was abuzz with people of upper-cell ranks, including several members of the Inner Circle draped in their distinctive jaguar pelts. A cacophony of voices from below wafted up the great air shafts. The tally was well underway, and in days, the results would be set. Their fate would be final.

Gilani squeezed his hand, bringing Metemis back to himself. "I said: 'When shall we have the answers, do you think?' "

He had missed her first query, and had led her on a circuit of that level of the pyramid. "Oh, soon enough," he said. "There's still much tallying to come."

He should take her home. He needed time to think.

They descended three rings to the Arcade of Hanging Flames. The stone chamber was long and valley-like, busy with first-cell acolytes leaping and climbing ledges and ropes as they maintained the heart of the Wicks.

Narrow stone bridges ran above Metemis and Gilani, allowing the acolytes access to swinging candle pendulums and knot-history hooks. The arcade reverberated with the whoosh of flame relays, the bobbing of scales, the snap and twang of countless strings.

Their fates could already be burning their ways through this hall to the marriage looms.

Metemis helped Gilani cross the gulf of candle flames. Once a first-cell acolyte himself, working the catwalks and the high candles had given Metemis strength, balance, and agility that he worked hard to maintain, though he was now sixth-cell and long separated from such demanding physical tasks.

"Should we have our union ceremony in the Plaza of Two Moons?" asked Gilani. "Marry where we met. Pleasing symmetry, no?"

Until that moment, Metemis would have agreed.

They'd met in the rain. Metemis was escorting several heavy wagons bound for the hive pyramid with a shipment of upgraded parts for the tallylooms. As a hundredhand and Mistress of the Roads, Gilani was overseeing the repaving of several large sections of the Plaza of Two Moons, and with the cobbles torn up, Metemis's wagons became stuck in the mud.

As they stood yelling in the downpour, enumerating each other's shortcomings and those of their respective castes, he fell in love with this passionate, challenging, talented woman.

He'd never doubted that love, or that the Wicks would match them for marriage when the time was auspicious. But now? How could the Wicks not pair them? How could there be any woman he was more suited to than Gilani?

"I've always dreamed of marrying atop the hive pyramid."

Gilani laughed. "Why did I even ask? I knew you'd insist on a pyramidion ceremony. Such a stickler for tradition."

Metemis smiled, and hoped it didn't betray his sadness.

* * *

His bride-to-be was named Lawa. That was all he knew of her, save that she belonged to the Queen's Sting.

Wedded to a stinger. What would *that* be like?

Metemis had deduced which loom would braid his marriage record, and it was early enough in the census that he hadn't needed to comb through ten thousand pairings. He memorized the measurements of the woman's identity weights as his knot-history was married to hers, and found the matching name in the archives.

He'd made inquiries among contacts in the hive-pyramid guards, and discovered that Lawa was well-known within the ranks and something of a rising star. She was rumored to be in line for the rank of Inner Circle, guarding the new queen herself.

She was known to frequent the Plaza of Games on her off-duty hours, and that was where Metemis found her the following morning, playing rushlights.

He watched her for three-quarters of an hour, beating one opponent after another. She beat one old codger in six turns—six turns! Metemis had never seen the like. He wondered why they kept lining up to play.

Lawa's honeyed hair and musical laugh might have been the reason, or how she glowed even when wrapped in the simple blue tunic of a Queen's Sting. Her sash, fringed with ocelot fur, marked her as sixth-cell of her caste.

She was beautiful, yes. But could he love her?

Metemis slipped the gamesmaster a few extra honey sticks to play next, and walked away as the gamesmaster shouted down the objections of the old men.

"I wondered when you'd work up the courage," she said, setting up the board afresh. "You've been watching me long enough."

"I didn't blend in as I'd hoped, then?"

Lawa laughed. "Don't worry. I study my opponents beforehand, too. I'm Queen's Sting, sir," she said, with mock officiousness. "Nothing escapes us. Mind if I make the first move?"

"If you need such advantage, I won't object."

She lit the fresh rushlights and began her turn, angling some lights in their brackets to slow their burn, marching others upright down to the next tier of the board and toward Metemis's rushes.

"What brings you to the games today, Master Tallyminder?"

Metemis adjusted the angle of his defender lights, and moved several others from the corner tower of the board to the lower tiers. "It's the Grand Census." His gaze lingered on Lawa's namestone necklace, and its obsidian eye beads peering back at him. "I'll be busy with the tally for the foreseeable future. I thought an early-morning game might clear my head for the day's work."

"Even if you're sure to lose?"

"Am I?"

She made a combination move across the east quadrant of the board, sacrificing two rushes to burn down four of his, and gaining the right to tip two of his defenders horizontal across the board so they burned faster. The rest of his rushes were now in danger of conflagration as flame crept along the length of the horizontal pieces.

He frowned and thought of the game she'd won in six turns.

"Do you want to bribe Tzisu now for our rematch," she mock-whispered, nodding to the gamesmaster, "or wait until you officially lose?"

He did like her sense of humor, and her competitive streak.

He made what he knew was a futile attack on her western quadrant, losing rushes in a two-for-two trade. She countered with a smoke defense, blowing out her own nearest rush and trading it for his farthest rush. He was vulnerable now in his center and on three quadrants as flames began to lick at his remaining rushlights.

She'd have him in eight turns.

Métemis laughed and doused the board with white sand. "I concede, Mistress Stinger. You have the better of me."

"Lawa," she said, extending her hand formally. Protocol required Metemis to kiss her hand, but he surprised himself with a moment of giddiness as they touched for the first time. He laid a soft kiss on her knuckles; her skin was perfumed with nicte flowers.

"I've enjoyed our game, uh—"

"Forgive me. *Metemis.*"

"You must excuse me, Metemis. I've business in the plaza."

"I must be getting back to the pyramid. May I accompany you?" he asked.

Lawa nodded. Smiling, they linked arms.

* * *

They spoke of the weather as they made the short walk to the Plaza of Two Moons, and of the myriads from outside the city now swarming the square, standing in long queues to answer the census. They spoke of the dying queen and which of her daughters would replace her.

"What do you make of talk of factions opposed to the queen?" Lawa asked as they passed a group of hivemasters and their families arguing loudly about which was their proper queue.

"Truthfully, I don't know much about politics or what such factions want," said Metemis as they stopped by the central candle clock in the plaza. All he knew of such groups was speculation that some agitators sided with Tekura or Rheb to stir trouble in advance of war. "And I was just the other day saying to someone, 'Without the queen what do we have?' The Wicks help guide her in leadership—who else can claim that? To do otherwise would be . . ." He searched for the word.

"Chaos?" Lawa ventured.

"Exactly."

Lawa smiled.

He thought order must be important to a Queen's Sting, sworn as they were to protect the queen and her realm. He knew his own inclination to order was a trait that made him an ideal tallyminder. It came as further proof of the Wicks' verdict about him and Lawa.

The candle clock read the fourth hour since sunrise. Metemis had to return to the tallylooms. "When you come to the pyramid to take the census, ask for me," Metemis said by way of leave-taking. "I am Her Royal Grace's Chief Tallyminder. I will conduct your tally personally."

"Alas, I've already taken it," said Lawa. "On the first night, while the lanterns were still in the air."

She had been in the hive pyramid as he completed his census, Metemis realized. She could have been in the next quizzing chamber. No mistake or confusion by the Wicks, then. This was the woman he was to marry.

The attraction wasn't like it had been with Gilani, not as sudden or intense, but he'd be lying to himself pretending it didn't exist. Could you feel giddy and guilty, excited and in mourning all at once?

But Gilani! The Wicks were all so unfair to her.

"I do hope we will meet again, Tallyminder," said Lawa. Rising to tiptoe, she pressed her lips gently to his cheek. The sweet scent of nicte lingered when she withdrew.

She disappeared into the throngs crowding the plaza. Probably another of her skills as a Queen's Sting.

As people swarmed through the plaza, a natural break opened in the crowd. There, sitting on a stone bench near where they'd first met in the rain, sat Gilani.

She had seen everything.

* * *

"Was that the woman the Wicks paired you with?" Gilani asked, sitting still and upright, looking quietly sad.

He sat next to her, for it felt like the whole plaza had tilted and threatened to slide from under his feet.

"I knew something was amiss after we took the census," she said, matter-of-fact. "Something troubled you. I rose early, worried about you. I went to your canton, but you were leaving your great-house in a terrible hurry. I called, but you didn't hear me. So I followed. When I saw the two of you playing"—her voice broke—"then I knew what the Wicks wanted for you. For us." She looked away.

"Gilani, I—"

"What did the looms decree for me? Where should I find my new love?"

He had no answer for her.

"I see." She exhaled a shuddering breath.

"I never wanted this. I expected the Wicks to let us finally wed. But when I was matched with someone else . . . I've spent my whole life in service of the Wicks. I couldn't understand how they could be so wrong. I *had* to see her."

"Was she everything you hoped for?"

"I love *you*." He meant it. But he loved Lawa too, or thought he could. When he was still an acolyte, Metemis saw a tallyminder trip once in the Answer Hall, sending pendulum candles swinging out of control as he crashed to the floor. His heart did the same now.

How could he feel this way about two women at once?

"And your precious Wicks?"

He shook his head. "I've never known them to be wrong before, but—"

"There are those in Ziroi who don't share your faith in the Wicks or their prognostication," said Gilani with obvious venom. "There are other wicks, other weaves."

"Just simple tallylooms, not *the* Wicks." He'd tried many times to explain the distinction to Gilani.

Gilani scoffed. "The Wicks are just a complex series of tally-looms, harnessed together to calculate greater sums than any could individually. You've explained again and again, *painstakingly*. So why not a series of smaller looms and weaves, spread across Ziroi, that calculate vast sums of information the way the hive pyramid does? Oh, more slowly, to be sure. But just as reliably. And what if they calculate different outcomes, what then? What does that mean for the certainty of your Wicks, and your Queen?"

"*My* Queen?" said Metemis. What was it Lawa said about factions opposed to Her Royal Grace?

Gilani stood and smoothed the front of her dress. "I don't care who sits on the throne. What I want is to control our own destiny. Don't you want us to marry?"

"Well . . . yes. But . . ."

Turning her back to the milling crowds, Gilani withdrew a small jute drawstring bag from her satchel and placed it in Metemis's hands. He felt the shape of candles within: several votives of differing lengths, a waxspur gear for a tallyloom. But it felt wrong. The difference was subtle, but the candles were heavier than they ought to have been. Fine grains of sand fell onto his hands through the loose mesh of the jute.

"Where did you get these?" he demanded. To give Her Royal Grace's Chief Tallyminder a set of *weighted* candles clearly designed for abuse in the Wicks . . .

"A *friend*." Gilani pulled him close, her lips almost touching his chin. "If the Wicks didn't pair us—*us*, Metemis!—then how could it be all-knowing? We are the Wedded Moons, you and I, a perfect match. All I want is for us to be together. The *candles* make that possible."

He understood. Substitution of the sand-weighted candles in key mechanisms of the Wicks would mean altered calculations. Done properly, Metemis could rig the Wicks to match him with Gilani. It might delay the final results a few days, perhaps accidentally tabulate some of the living as having died, maybe even upset marriage matches for others. Could he trade their happiness for his own?

He couldn't believe this was happening. Lawa had warned him of factions, but he'd never suspected Gilani possessed a rebel heart.

He realized he was squeezing the jute bag and relaxed his grip. Was he really considering *treason*? What of his duty to the queen and to Ziroi? What of the oaths he had sworn to the Tallyminder caste?

"It must be tonight," Gilani said.

How could she know that the census would be complete by sundown? Who were these "friends" she had mentioned? The calculation looms would be prepared then, proper candles selected and set in place, timed and weighted to ensure accurate tabulation of the knot-histories.

And Metemis would oversee it all.

"I'll wait by the fourth-cell gate on the west side of the pyramid," Gilani said. "If you come, I'll know that our destiny lies together."

* * *

Metemis stood in the shadows of the great tallylooms, sand-weighted candles in his hand, still unsure what he intended.

The air in the Answer Hall was muggy and glowed with the amber light of a thousand candles dotting the curved hundred-foot stone walls, as hot and humming as any hive. All around him fourth- and fifth-cell tallyminders prepared the looms for the Grand Tally.

Only the Queen's Edict remained, those final census answers and last wishes (both grand and small) she would give in life. Once entered, they would shape the advice the Wicks gave the new queen.

And they could also override specific calculations as the queen desired. This was the great secret that only the sixth-cells and the Inner Circle knew. It was hard at first to accept that anyone—even the queen—could interfere with the calculations of the Wicks. The edicts allowed the monarch to input different variables, he was told, to test outcomes. But Metemis immediately understood the possibilities for abuse. The calculations had been sacrosanct in his mind before that initiation, and so to discover that they could be subject to politics or to whim?

He felt again the weight of the jute bag and considered his former naivety.

The Queen's Edict was how he would effect a change in the weave of the Wicks to alter his fate. Only a small treason, one that would go unnoticed, he told himself.

He needed to bypass the guards to the Queen's Edict Chamber. But a resourceful tallyminder had ways to gain entry, particularly one as knowledgeable as the chief tallyminder.

Metemis stole from the Answer Hall and out through one of the hexagonal openings that ringed the hive pyramid's exterior. This one held one of the hundreds of beehives that dotted the structure. As bees danced around him in the waning daylight, he squeezed past the great stone hive. The air was humid. Far beyond the farmers' fields, lightning played between rain clouds over the jungle.

He laid his crimson-and-feather cloak on the stone, a terrible breach of protocol, but one that made for an easier climb. Kicking off his sandals, he anchored one foot in the narrow seam between two great blocks. Taking a deep breath and using all the strength and agility he'd worked to maintain from his days as a first-cell acolyte, he drove up from that anchor point and leaped at a ledge one level above. His practiced hands found purchase, and for a moment he hung hundreds of feet above the ground. Using his momentum, he swung his leg up and over the lip of the platform and pulled himself to safety.

The yawning mouth of a narrow ventilation shaft greeted him, and the hollow rushing sound of air being drawn in encouraged Metemis to pause and catch his breath. He made a silent prayer and continued his climb.

* * *

Metemis emerged on the lowest of the royal tiers and crept through the royal corridors. He had studied the edict systems and knew what to do. Coding in his name, pairing it with Gilani's, replacing the marriage string, using the weighted candles. One of the queen's true edicts would be cast aside as a translation error, with none the wiser.

A minor indiscretion was all, he told himself. He would make it up to the new queen sixfold in return.

The Edict Chamber was small but magnificent. A high honeycomb vault of polished white marble rose above him, illuminated by the light of flickering candles in the hexagonal recesses in the walls. The queen's judgment table was crafted from smoky quartz, amethyst, and even metal, the rarest of the rare. Metemis marveled at the burnished metallic inlays of bees. Several *pounds* of metal, from the look of things.

He'd never seen so much metal in one place.

Candles were already burning, which meant the queen had set her decrees. He had only a twelfth of an incense-hour to make the switch. The trick was a well-timed switch, swapping out the candle without tilting the scale catastrophically.

Metemis put his hand in his satchel and cupped the weighted candle.

"Don't do it, Tallyminder," Lawa's voice echoed behind him. "You've lost this game too."

Heart pounding, Metemis turned. Lawa's sad eyes reflected guttering candlelight. Her right hand leveled a venomlance toward his bare chest.

"Lawa, I—"

"Spare me. The Queen's Sting sees everything. We've been watching your *beloved* for months," said Lawa. "But we didn't know whether you were loyal to the Sand Lions too. When the Wicks matched you and I for marriage, we knew a moment of crisis had come that would force her hand. Are those the candles she gave you? I'll have them now." She motioned for him to toss them.

He gripped the jute bag tight, and felt sharp sand trickle into his palm. Did Gilani belong to the Sand Lion faction?

"You knew of our pairing?" Metemis asked as he fumbled his hand inside the small bag, playing for time. If he could gather enough sand . . . "How? No one's seen those knot-histories but me." He pulled a waxspur gear from the bag and tossed it to her. She let it clatter to the marble floor.

"The whole bag," she said.

He threw it to her feet and she stomped the votives with the heel of her boot.

"You'd be surprised how many of your acolytes are Queen's Sting. Our own looms processed your knot-histories the night you made them, and our guards in the hive pyramid reported back your inquiries about me. Do you think I really spend my free time playing rushlights with old men?" She flashed her sly smile, which stung Metemis as hard as any venomlance ever could.

"But what if the Wicks *can* be wrong?" Until the last few days, he would never have believed he'd say those words. Everything was upside-down.

"Our looms gave us the same output from the same census answers. The error isn't in the weave, but in *you*. I would gladly have —" she stopped short.

"What now?"

"Hope that the new queen is more merciful than her mother. Time to go."

As Lawa stepped toward him, Metemis flung a fistful of sand into her eyes.

Lawa cried out and jabbed her lance toward him. Metemis side-stepped it but lost his footing and crashed into a bank of edict candles. A part of him wondered what edicts he had disturbed, but the need to flee took charge.

He reached the air shaft and climbed down as fast as he dared. One slip and he'd fall a half-dozen tiers to his death. But what would he do, now that he was a hunted man?

The chance for a future with Gilani—or even Lawa—was gone.

At least, in *this* city. Hope flickered back to flame. Gilani had been marked as a traitor, too. Perhaps they could find shelter in the mountains of Rheb, or in Tekura by the coast. A man of his skills might find service tending their wicks and weaves.

He emerged from the shaft, but not where he expected. This wasn't the tier of the Answer Hall. Had he gone down the wrong vent? He had to reach Gilani before—

A slender shadow landed on the same stone platform. Lawa's hard kick to his abdomen doubled Metemis over, and he collapsed backward through the hexagonal passage into the hive pyramid.

Metemis scrabbled on the cold stone, trying to get his wind back. An almost deafening hum surrounded him. The space was dark and echoed like a vast chamber. He felt cross breezes and bees zipping around him.

He was in the Royal Apiary, the queen's own hives and a muse-um of all Ziroi knew of beekeeping.

Scrambling to his feet, Metemis pressed deeper into the darkness to escape Lawa. He felt his way through the room as fast as he could, though delicately so as not to disturb the hives. Moving row to row meant moving through centuries of Zirojan history, from woven skep baskets to rough hives of unbaked clay and dry straw to fired pottery and finally to the tall ceremonial hives of stone that dotted the exterior of the hive pyramid.

A shattering body blow knocked Metemis to the floor, smacking his head hard on the stone. Thrumming tendrils of pain drove forward from the back of his skull.

Lawa was on top of him, trying to bind his hands. He pitched her off with the last of his strength. Lawa reeled backward into the skep hives, tumbling with them in a terrible crash.

An angry roar rose from the hives. The bees Lawa had disturbed swarmed around her in a savage cloud as she thrashed and stepped back by instinct.

Her foot found empty space, and she fell with a cry.

"Lawa!" Metemis grabbed for her, but he was too late. She vanished into the dark pit.

Fiery stings assailed Metemis as the bees found him. He ran to escape the swarm, heart pounding. Could Lawa have survived the fall? Some of the low shafts had safety nets, but not all. Not knowing her fate was almost as painful as the stings.

He emerged from the tier and found reprieve from the bees outside in the smoke of a beacon fire. He was stung in the face, on his arms, on his bare chest and back. His wounds throbbed, yes, but that wasn't what had him trembling. He ought to turn himself in, beg the pyramid guards to search the shafts and see if Lawa might still be alive. He thought of Lawa's musical laugh, of the brief time they had spent at rushlights, and wept.

He should face judgment for his crimes.

But the Queen's Sting knew about Gilani. If they captured her . . .

Hers was the one life he could still save.

* * *

Metemis walked as calmly as he could manage toward the fourth-cell gate, hoping none of the guards would see his swelling face. Gilani sat on the steps near the gate, and he fought the urge to rush forward and take her into his arms.

She stood when she recognized him, her horror evident at his swollen face. With care, she led him down the pyramid steps.

"I've failed you," whispered Metemis through fattened lips. "I've failed you."

He said no more until they were lost among the alleys west of the hive pyramid. He whispered of his confrontation with Lawa. "Our names may already be braided with black for death. We haven't many choices."

Gilani led him into a garden of flowering cacti. "There's another way."

"Sand Lions."

Gilani nodded. "My *friends* will keep us safe. We can continue our work in Tekura. Live on, work on, and dream on together."

What was it she had said before? There were *other* tallylooms in Ziroi.

"All those questions you asked me, about how the Wicks worked. You've been feeding them—the Sand Lions—information to refine their wicks and weaves."

She beckoned him to follow. "I'll have answers, my love, once we escape the city."

He had dismissed other tallylooms as lesser devices, but if Lawa was to be believed, then the Queen's Sting had one that rivaled the Wicks. What if the Sand Lion faction did likewise? The scale of such a project was unfathomable outside of the hive pyramids of each city-state. A similar system would require space, manpower, stores of candles, waterwheels to work the fans and the looms . . .

But *what if?*

Despite himself, his mind raced to consider ways the Wicks could be made smaller, better. Spread swarm-like across an entire city, as Gilani had suggested. Would he have the freedom to tinker and improve upon the technology?

A thought chilled his heart. Perhaps all this time he, Lawa, and Gilani were hapless pawns in a game of rushlights between wick-work giants, with his loyalty as the prize.

It felt right to be here with Gilani, on the knife's edge of a new life together. Yet for all that had happened between him and Lawa, he still prayed silently that she had survived the fall.

With a hesitant hand, Metemis brushed Gilani's hair from her ear. She still wore them, his opal-and-greenstone gifts.

He reached behind her neck and undid the clasp of her namestone necklace. He undid his own, too. How many of these had he processed through the Wicks? How many fates had he helped decide?

Metemis pitched both necklaces into the thickest patch of the cactus garden. The unbraided stones scattered among the spines.

He kissed Gilani. Despite the hurt, her kiss was sweet.

About Tony Pi & Stephen Kotowych

Tony Pi and Stephen Kotowych first met ten years ago, when they attended Writers of the Future. Since then, between them they have amassed a John W. Campbell Award for Best New Writer nomination, a Writers of the Future grand prize win, and multiple appearances as finalists for the Aurora Award for short fiction, Canada's top SF prize. As individuals they have published dozens of stories in venues like Clarkesworld, Interzone, Intergalactic Medicine Show, Beneath Ceaseless Skies, numerous anthologies, and had work translated into a dozen languages. This is their first—but hopefully not last—collaboration. And in a case of life imitating art, the "candlepunk" computers described in the story recently served as the inspiration for two University of Toronto engineering teams' final projects in mechanical design. Tony and Stephen were thrilled to see their creation come to life!

PIRATE READERS

By James Van Pelt | 4,300 words

KELSIE TAPPED HER desktop rhythmically, switching the display's background image each time. As long as she interacted with the interface, it wouldn't flag her as being inactive. Mr. Dettis, the instructional coach, was helping a student across 'the room from her, so she wasn't worried he would direct her to spend more time on task. He moved with studied efficiency. Short, wiry, a mouth that never smiled. Close-set eyes. She checked her achievement status update: 27 percent through eighth-grade social studies, 42 percent through math, the same with science, 11 percent through Spanish, 14 percent through ninth-grade literacy, and only 33 percent through seventh-grade PE. It seemed as if it had been days since any of the numbers had moved.

School was *so* boring! More than that; it was claustrophobic. Almost no place to go where she wasn't watched—where she wasn't evaluated and measured. For being such a big building, it was the smallest place she knew.

Dettis followed the same route going from station to station, narrating in a monotone as he went. "Tom is working on an algebra problem. Tina has finished annotating a poem. Kipp is . . . asleep." Dettis nudged the student's shoulder. Kelsie knew she had at least six minutes before he'd check with her again. She slipped a book from her backpack, a forty-year-old paperback she'd bought online. Strictly illegal in school, of course, since her reading rate and comprehension couldn't be measured, as it was when she read electronically. Also, she wouldn't keep a progress log, nor would she write chapter by chapter predictions of what would happen next in the book. In short, she was pirate reading, an offense that had cost her detention three times that year.

She opened the old book delicately, careful with the yellowed pages, then sighed with contentment at the first sentence: "Petrified with astonishment, Richard Seaton stared after the copper steambath upon which he had been electrolyzing his solution of 'X,' the unknown metal." She glanced at the chapter's subheading: "The Occurrence of the Impossible." That's what she wanted, the impossible, or at least a world where the impossible was a legitimate concern. At school, everything related to her "individual strengths and weaknesses," her "long-term goal," and her "growth plan." All reading was mandated or chosen from the "developmentally appropriate independent reading list," mostly political nonfiction.

"What's the book?" whispered Gilbert, a tall, plump boy who wore his black hair short. He tapped his desktop too.

"It's about space travel," she whispered back.

"Oh." Gilbert looked disappointed. "That's my alternate career track, communications satellites."

"No, not commercial applications. People going to space, like to other planets. It's an adventure with characters. It's . . . interesting."

"Why read? You can watch a movie."

"I get two recreational movie hours a week, just like you. The school suggests documentaries. That's not enough."

Gilbert glanced over Kelsie's shoulder, straightened, and turned his attention to his work.

Kelsie slipped the book between her legs and called up the multiple-choice questions on the chart displayed on her desk. Question number one was "According to the graph, which month will Farmer McDonald have to increase his water requisition to save his crop?"

"Kelsie is reading a chart," Dettis announced. She sighed with relief.

At lunch, Gilbert lined up behind her. "Where do you get books like that without your parents finding out?"

Her tray popped out from the dispenser along with her nutritional goal card: "I will consume no more than 140 grams of carbohydrates today." She looked doubtfully at the main course, a pile of oily-looking brown rice with little orange cubes that might have been carrots.

"Don't browse for books. That's a tip-off for sure. Search for household decor. There's a subcategory for a den or study. Some people buy books for the retro look. Don't get leather-backed facsimiles. They cost a fortune and there's nothing inside them. But if you look under "budget decorating," you can order books with real pages. They sell them by the pound. You can also check antique stores, but they're pricey again."

"I don't know," said Gilbert wistfully. "I set up a fake name on our account at home when I was nine, and I downloaded some cool stuff. There was a graphic novel, and this great story called *Little Brother*. I don't remember who wrote it, but the school caught me. Mom and Dad were furious. 'You're derailing your education,' Dad said. If they catch me again, I'll be chained to my desk."

"That's the best thing about these." She held up the book. "No trail. I've been reading in my room at night. I have a curfew, and my parents can tell when my lights are on, but my e-reader gives me enough light to see my book, and no one knows."

"Clever." Gilbert studied his tray, which held steamed vegetables and a serving of limp lettuce. "I'm cursed by a slow metabolism. If this doesn't work, they're going to feed me cardboard. Do you have any extras?"

"Food?"

He blushed. "No, books."

She fished in her backpack, made sure no one was looking, and passed him another copy. "I have this title twice. Tell me what you think when you're done."

That night, Kelsie read under the covers about Dick Seaton and his rival Marc DuQuesne. She found herself smiling at the science, which was terrible, but also hopeful. Seaton built a spaceship, the *Skylark,* to rescue his kidnapped fiancé and 'Peg' Spencer. There were battles and aliens and marriages. When Kelsie fell asleep, she dreamed about floating above far planets, about suns with strange light, about looking out her window and seeing possibilities.

* * *

"That was so good," said Gilbert. He had put the book in a bag to return to her, but seemed reluctant to hand it over. Kelsie didn't know the short girl with spiky red hair standing beside him. "Bernice wondered if she could borrow it. And I wanted to know if there was a sequel. I was going to look it up, but the instructional coaches notice and change my reading lists. I searched for information on sailing once, and for months, all my reading excerpts were about boats. I just wanted to know the difference between port and starboard."

Kelsie nodded. Everyone's curriculum was based on aptitude and interest. She'd started reading science fiction a year ago and had used her computer to look up Connie Willis, a writer who used to be famous. After that, her reading selections at school became science fiction, which would be a good thing, except that the selections were never the entire work, and reading that way wasn't fun. She remembered in particular a two-paragraph section from Ursula Le Guin's "The Ones Who Walk Away from Omelas," but the questions weren't on what Kelsie felt about the story or her thoughts; they asked what rhetorical strategy Le Guin used, and then there were a bunch of questions about mood and tone. She had really wanted to read the whole story, but she couldn't find the complete tale without provoking extra excerpts she would have to respond to.

She'd asked Mr. Dettis why they were never assigned novels, and he said, "You do not need a long work to learn how to analyze text. Novels take too much time."

Nothing in her life encouraged her to read less than her literacy class.

Bernice lent *The Skylark of Space* to Debra who lent it to Richard. Richard returned the book to her with rubber bands around it to keep the pages together. In the meantime, Kelsie tracked down the sequel, which was confusingly called *Skylark Three*.

She passed it to Gilbert while Mr. Dettis went through a presentation on maximizing multiple-choice test scores.

"How old do you think he is?" whispered Kelsie.

"Forty-nine. It's on the school's profile."

Dettis reminded them to start by eliminating the least likely answers, a strategy Kelsie had learned her first year in school. "Why in the world would he take a job like this?"

"I saw him at the mall once with his family. He's really a pretty nice guy. He's budded, you know."

" 'Budded'?"

"Yeah. My mom teaches in the elementary school. They give her an earbud that coaches her as she teaches. They're monitoring her performance, and they feed her scripts. She says that it's the school trying to guarantee students receive the best education, but I don't think she likes it."

"Ew, that's terrible."

Both her and Gilbert's desktops chirped a warning that they were not taking notes. She turned to her display and wrote, "Ignore bad choices."

At lunch, Gilbert, Bernice, Debra, and Richard sat with her.

"I almost got caught last night," explained Richard, a pale, blond boy who chewed his fingernails when he was nervous. "I was in bed. My sister came in. I didn't even hear her. Fortunately, my back was to the door. She didn't see it."

Debra said, "My parents have books in the living room. They're all in French or something. Dad dusts them on the weekend when he cleans house. I've never seen him read one, though."

"There are other authors who write this kind of stuff, right?" said Bernice. "I love the space part of the story, but the women don't do anything. I could imagine parts of it excerpted, and one of the answer choices would be, 'demonstration of sexist assumptions.'"

Kelsie bristled. "That's possible, but a likelier one would be, 'reflection of the time's cultural attitudes.' Here, try these." She gave Bernice *The Shore of Women* by Pamela Sargent; Debra took Frederik Pohl's *Gateway*; Richard received Lois McMaster Bujold's *Dreamweaver's Dilemma,* and Gilbert got the *Skylark Three* title. "When I buy them by the boxful, I don't get to choose what's in it. I have other kinds of books. There's Western, fantasy, mystery, thriller, and horror. Do you want to mix it up?"

They shook their heads.

Kelsie shrugged but understood. "We'll stick with science fiction for now."

* * *

Kelsie's dad met her at the door when she came home. "I found these in the basement." He pointed to the paperbacks he'd stacked on the dining room table. "We have talked about this behavior before, young lady."

Kelsie tried to act casual. She laughed. "It's an industrial arts project, Dad. Multimedia. I'm learning how to work the carving laser. Paperbacks are cheap, they carve easily, and I can assemble the whole thing with paper glue. It's way better than the aluminum structure some kids are doing."

"Did Instructional Coach Dettis assign this?"

"No, he's academic. This is vocational."

"Wouldn't paper burn?"

"Charred edges are a feature of the piece."

Her father looked carefully at her while stroking his chin. "I think you're putting one over on me."

Kelsie held her breath.

"If you can push your achievement numbers up at school, I won't tell your mom about the 'art supplies'."

In the next month, the pirate reading group added two more members. Bratton liked Larry Niven's *Ringworld* so much that he paid her rather than return it, while Tyra asked only for horror titles. Kelsie gave her Stephen King and Clive Barker, but when Tyra got a taste of Lovecraft, that's all she wanted.

Kelsie found Dorothy Haley at the bottom of the box under a James Patterson title (there were a lot of Patterson books). Haley wrote *Red Star Triumphant.* The cover showed a silver-blue spaceship crossing a bloodshot sun. Kelsie hadn't finished by dawn and was still reading when called for breakfast. She padded to the top of the stairs and called down. "I have a headache, Mom. I think I should stay home today." After the usual checking of her temperature and the inevitable, "Maybe I should take her to the doctor," which Kelsie assured them would not be necessary, she went to bed. Soon, both parents left for work. Kelsie opened the book, which was newer than many the company sent her. She buried her nose in it. It even smelled good. Stomach down on the bed, her chin lapped over the edge, she let the book rest on the floor. Jewell Ripkin, the *Innisfree*'s captain, had lost touch with her crew while exploring the giant derelict ship they'd discovered. Kelsie turned the pages, drifting from her bedroom.

Captain Ripkin trusted her sensors that told her the air within the ship was breathable. The first lungful was a welcome change from the suit that recycled what she breathed. Now, helmet off, ship sounds were clear. Somewhere, a light ringing, like a thimble on metal, caught her ear. What could be making the noise?

Kelsie read until she realized she was hungry. It was nearly five o'clock. Her parents would be home soon.

At school, Gilbert leaned into her cubicle. "They caught Tyra. She's in the principal's office now."

"Is it about pirate reading?"

"I heard Dettis talking to her. She used vocabulary in her last essay they couldn't account for. He said, 'Where'd you get *cyclopean*, *eldritch*, and *gibbous*?' "

"What was she supposed to be writing about?"

"Rhetorical strategies in George Washington's inaugural address."

"Gibbous?"

Gilbert said, "Yeah, I don't know how either."

Kelsie stiffened. Getting caught would be her fourth strike. If Tyra told who gave her the book, Kelsie would be moved to a high-supervision academy. Instead of Dettis visiting her a few times an hour to check on her progress, she'd be in a constantly monitored class. No time to call her own at all. She envied the kids who learned independently. Most didn't leave their homes except for field trips. They could read all they wanted as long as their learning objectives were met.

She said, "You've got to hold my book. If they search my backpack, I'm done for."

Gilbert shook his head. "She could give us all up. Either Tyra stays quiet, or we're sunk, even if we don't have books on us."

Kelsie tried to focus on her desktop, her heart pounding. It was a history lesson. She was supposed to read three excerpted articles about Joseph McCarthy and the Cold War, watch a short video, listen to a speech, and then write an essay that synthesized the material into an original argument. She'd done this kind of prompt numerous times. After she submitted it, her desktop would instantly spit back the piece with all mistakes marked, questions about her thoughts ("What did you mean in paragraph two?" "Can you strengthen your third argument with another reference?"), and a graph that showed where her essay scored compared to both her previous writing and to other students who had responded to similar assignments.

She couldn't remember the last time she'd written about anything that mattered to her.

But maybe if she looked really involved in the essay, Dettis wouldn't stop at her station. He wouldn't put his hand on her shoulder and say, *Can you come with me?* to ask her about the books.

Dettis didn't talk to her.

At lunch, Tyra said she had sat outside the principal's office for an hour. When she went in, he said that there had been a mistake and that she could return to her desk.

"Weirdest thing ever," Tyra said.

Gilbert said, "We were just lucky. We should dump the books and pretend to be normal kids."

Kelsie looked down the table at them, her little pirate reading group. Bernice, Debra, Bratton, and Richard hadn't said anything. She didn't know how they felt. She thought about how much she looked forward to discussing what she read with them and hearing their reactions to books she'd shared. Gilbert was probably right. There was no way they wouldn't get caught and her role in the group exposed.

What would Captain Jewell Ripkin do?

* * *

At home, she sat on the top stair to the basement. Her parents wouldn't be home for hours. Kelsie had laid the books out on the floor. Not counting the ones she would never give away (she'd found another Dorothy Haley book called *Bone Singularity*), almost two hundred paperbacks stared up at her. She could shut the group down, read the books herself, even the non-science fiction ones, and never share. At least she could still be a pirate reader. She sat for a long time before packing them into the boxes and hiding them again.

Late at night, lying awake in the dark, she realized what Ripkin would do. There was only one solution.

Her backpack weighed heavily on her shoulders as she walked into school. The students who learned best early in the morning were already there. Others, whose biorhythms peaked later, were yet to arrive. A couple of instructional coaches passed her in the hall. She couldn't tell if they were budded, but the coaches when they weren't in their classrooms always sounded livelier. She suspected they didn't put the earbuds in until they were in class.

Kelsie went to the girls' locker room first, a place where there were no video cameras. Lockers only locked during classes, so she picked one in the corner, where whoever used it would have more privacy, and she put a book in it. That morning she'd used a permanent marker on a blank name tag to write, "It's against the rules to read this book," and then drew a little skull and crossbones. The sticker went on the back to save the cover image. She put another one in a locker on the other side. The third book went into a stall in a bathroom. She looped strings through the fourth and fifth books to hang in a coat closet.

When Kelsie headed to Dettis's room, the backpack was five books lighter and she felt as if the gravity in the school had changed. She was Captain Ripkin on the bridge of the *Innisfree*, rocketing forward. Those books couldn't be traced to her. She thought of them as idea grenades she'd rolled into the building.

The feeling only lasted until she saw one of the books she'd brought in the trash can. At lunch she saw another thrown out, and when she left school for the day, the janitor swept a paperback with his big push broom along with dust, dirt, and paper scraps. He pushed the mess into a dustpan. The "It's against the rules to read this book" sticker was clear just as the book tumbled from sight.

Kelsie walked home, her head hung down. Nobody read the books. They were just thrown away! But the longer she walked, the better she felt. Sure, three books were lost, but maybe the other two found homes. Maybe even now some kid was reading it, free from curriculum, reading just for fun.

She prepared five more stickers and put them on the books. If she placed five a day, it would be forty school days before she ran out.

That night, she dreamed about long space voyages and heroes, about acceleration couches and airlocks. In her dream, she stood at the spaceship door, looking out on a strange landscape and smelling a distant sea. She woke happy. By the week's end, she'd dropped twenty-five books in the school. Were people finding them? If they were, they hid it well, but she felt good while doing it.

Mr. Dettis stopped at her desk before she'd even opened the program to where she'd stopped yesterday. "I need you to come with me." He held a paperback under his arm. Kelsie didn't need to see it to know a pirate reading sticker was on it. She started to speak.

He frowned and shook his head.

Dettis led her from the classroom toward his office. Silent, Kelsie followed, convinced that everybody they passed knew she was in trouble. Moving to the high-supervision education unit would be bad enough. Only the worst kids needed that kind of instruction, but her parents would be furious. She clutched her hands in front of her. Maybe if she ran?

Mostly she felt the weight of *Bone Singularity* in her backpack. She'd just started it. If Dettis confiscated the book, she didn't know if she could get another copy. It would be like "The Ones Who Walk Away from Omelas," but a thousand times worse.

A long-haired boy, looking miserable, sat in a chair outside of Dettis's office. He didn't glance up as they passed through the office door. She settled into a stiff wooden chair without a seat cushion in front of Dettis's desk. Dettis closed the door behind her. He moved behind his desk, then carefully dug into his ear. A flesh-colored button popped out.

"Okay, now we can talk." He opened a cabinet and pulled paper-back books out by the handful, stacking them in front of her. "You're not the only pirate reading group in the school, you know."

"What?"

More books joined the first ones. They weren't titles she recognized. "There's a fantasy group going pretty strong. I've identified four readers in that crowd, and another that leans toward techno-thrillers. There's three in that, but you're the only one doing guerrilla distribution." He put the book with her sticker in front of her. "What do you have to say for yourself?"

Kelsie thought about dozens of replies. Some were questions like, "Have you read books?" or "Don't you remember being a kid?" And some were defiant. "You can't control what I think" or "Nobody cares about what you have us read."

What she went with was, "How did you find out?"

"Word use in your essays, the same way I caught Tyra. I had to add words to old vocabulary lists to make it look like she had been exposed to that language before, just like I did for you." Dettis spread the rest of the books, covering his desk. "They're beautiful, aren't they?"

"Excuse me?"

"Beautiful, the books." Dettis picked up one with a hooped object floating in space called *Ringworld*. "I remember the first time I read this one."

Kelsie sagged back in her chair. "Whose side are you on? You're an instructional coach."

"Only when I'm wearing this, Kelsie." He pointed to the earbud on the desk. "Before I got one of those, I was a teacher. Completely different job." He handed her the familiar *Ringworld*. "You might like this one."

She held the book on her lap. The edges were soft. It was a much-read copy. "I can keep bringing books to the school?"

"If you don't get caught." He returned the books to the cabinet. Four more cabinets just like it lined the wall. Did books fill them all? "And you've got to improve your progress. Read what you want anywhere but at school."

"I don't know." Kelsie thought about *Bone Singularity*. Even now she wanted to take it from her pack to see what Dorothy Haley did on the first page. It also was all she could do to not open *Ringworld*. "That will be hard."

"There's nothing I can do. I would if I could, but I can help you with this. I can give you title suggestions. I can find authors for you. All the pirate readers can benefit if you'll be smart and work in the system."

Kelsie squeezed the book. Where would it take her? What other books could Dettis guide her to? "You're a pirate librarian!" she exclaimed.

He laughed. It was the first time she'd seen Mr. Dettis look happy. "I guess I am." He closed the cabinet and locked it. "So here's the deal. Don't read in class. Don't let anyone see you bringing in books. If you find something really good, let me know. Oh, and I've got someone I want you to meet." He opened the door to let the long-haired boy in.

"Troy," Dettis said. "This is the girl I told you about, Kelsie. Ask her the question."

Dettis picked up his earbud, but didn't put it back in. "Go to class when you're done."

He closed the door as he left. Troy looked embarrassed. His long hair covered his eyes. "Hi."

"Hi," she said.

"Mr. Dettis said you liked science fiction."

"I do."

"I . . ." He swallowed hard. "I wrote a story, actually a bunch of them, with spaceships and aliens in them. On my own. Not for school. Mr. Dettis said you might read them and tell me what you think. He said you were my audience."

Kelsie was dumbstruck. If reading without the school knowing was hard, writing had to be twice as difficult. He would have to write it all by hand. No computer could check it.

Troy pulled a notebook from his backpack and held it out to her. Inside, the first page contained just a title in a tidy script, "The Jupiter Dilemma."

"You're a pirate writer," she said.

Troy blushed. "It's what's in my head."

His handwriting covered page after page. He'd even drawn illustrations. Characters in space suits. Rockets balanced on long exhaust tails. A comet streaking above an alien mountain range.

"I'm honored," said Kelsie. "Thank you for sharing your work with me."

"I have other notebooks." Troy moved the hair away from his eyes. They were deep blue.

Suddenly, the school didn't feel so small.

About James Van Pelt

James Van Pelt is a part-time high school English teacher and full-time writer in western Colorado. He's been a finalist for a Nebula Award and been reprinted in many year's-best collections. His first young adult novel, Pandora's Gun, was released from Fairwood Press in August of 2015.

James blogs at http://www.jamesvanpelt.com and can be found on Facebook.

THE MOST REASONABLE HOUSE IN FAERIE

By Dafydd McKimm | 7,000 words

"Tobias," my dear friend Loosestrife said to me one afternoon as I perched on his drawing-room mantelpiece contentedly smoking my pipe. "I have, of late, as you well know, gone up in the world. My investments are yielding excellent returns, the cloud-mining venture alone has brought me enough wealth to build this magnificent stately *brugh*, and my trousers have never been finer—look you here at these new breeches that I purchased only yesterday at Honeysuckle and Garlic's." I peered over the bowl of my pipe to appraise them. "Do you remember that particularly clear evening back in June? Well sir, these breeches are sewn with the starlight from that very night! Mr. Honeysuckle assures me that they are the finest he has ever made, and therefore, it follows that they must be the finest that you—or indeed anyone—has ever seen."

I do not, as a rule, encourage Loosestrife with too many compliments—he is quite self-assured enough as it is. But I did have to admit that they were indeed a magnificent pair of trousers.

"I have a *brugh* to rival anything within a thousand leagues (even Baron Vetchling's Citadel of Midnight pales in comparison to my abode), fine clothes, and even a friend who rides my coattails—everything a man of station is meant to have."

I balked a little at the last remark, but my face was sufficiently obscured by my pipe, allowing Loosestrife to continue unhindered.

"The one thing I lack," he said, assuming a pose that accentuated his trousers to their fullest glory, "the one thing that will secure my position for good, is a servant—a human servant!"

My response to this particular remark was far less easy to obscure and resulted in the spilling of hot tobacco (in no trivial amount) onto my second-best smoking jacket.

"Why, my dear Loosestrife!" I cried, hastily brushing the tobacco away. "The last human servant in Faerie died a decade ago, and you know as well as I do that the paths between their world and ours have been sealed since the debacle at Cottingley."

"Then how, if I do not have a human servant, am I to show myself of equal station with all the barons, earls, marquesses, viscounts, and dukes of Faerie, when even a lowly squire was expected to have at the very least a basic serving staff of changelings?"

"Times change, dear friend," I said, giving my pipe a philosophical series of puffs. "I'd put it out of mind if I were you."

But my friend would not—indeed, could not—put it out of mind. He thought about the problem night and day. He dreamed of it when he should have been dreaming of more genial things— dawnlight-trimmed jerkins or suits of the finest gossamer or obtaining a more articulate horse, to name a few. He pondered over the problem at breakfast, leaving his honeycomb all but untouched; he hardly danced at all at parties, preferring to mope pensively in corners; and he was constantly distracted at the gaming table, a state of mind that caused him and his unlucky partner (yours truly) to lose a not insubstantial sum (as well as nearly several limbs) to some very unforgiving gentlemen of the trollish persuasion.

One day, however, when I was again installed on his drawing-room mantelpiece and enjoying immensely the pleasures of my pipe, Loosestrife exclaimed "Ah-ha! I have it!" so loudly that I almost set myself ablaze.

"What do you have, sir," I shouted, "that has almost burned me to a cinder!"

"The answer to my servant problem!" he cried.

I listened as intently as a man who has twice only narrowly escaped ruining his second-best smoking jacket could, before replying that, though I was sure the plan would have some amusing results, I thought it follysome and best left unrealised. Loosestrife replied that my lack of encouragement was making his ears ring, and I should either desist or find another house in which to smoke my pipe.

* * *

"This," Loosestrife explained to me, several days later while pointing to an illustration in an ungainly, leather-bound tome that he had bought at some cost from the septennial market at Fool's Errand, "is what the anatomists call the *osseus*. I believe I have made a fair representation of it out of these twigs and branches, do you not think?"

"Indeed," I replied, "though the artist seems to have omitted this nest of song thrushes in his representation."

Loosestrife waved my objection away. "Details, Tobias. Mere details."

"And for the head I see you have procured one of Widow Dark-rain's turnips."

"Not just any turnip, my friend. This turnip has won first prize at the Lammas fair three hundred years in a row. It cost me a pretty penny, I can tell you. And as you can see, I have carved all the requisite holes for the various sensory organs."

"And what about the *musculi*, and the *arteriae*?" I asked, flipping now myself through the book.

"A good question, my dear Tobias," he said. "For the *musculi*, I have these mice, freshly collected from the pantry, and for the *arteriae*, I have used a mixture of ivy from the front of the *brugh*, while for the finer vessels, these bulrushes from the stream at the bottom of the garden."

"And the skin . . . the *corium*?"

"Offa's Dyke! I had not thought of it. What does human skin look like?"

"Well, it is all wrinkled and grey, like an old pear, or a walnut," I answered. "Or so I remember being the case when last I saw a changeling servant at one of Tom Thistletop's solstice soirees."

Loosestrife raised the more hirsute of his eyebrows. "Very well," I said, unable to suffer such bushy disbelief, "or so I have been told by people who attended Tom Thistletop's soirees. In any case, I've been told their skin has a distinct droopiness about it and is mottled and veined like a well-aged cheese."

"Cheese, you say?" Loosestrife now raised the lesser of his eyebrows, which, joining its brother high on my friend's brow, transformed his expression to one of glee. "Now that is fortunate, as I just so happen to have a wheel of Old Cob Deadnettle's cheese maturing in the dairy (from the time he insisted on going everywhere as a goat, remember?)"

He hurried off and in a moment came back with a great wheel of pungent blue cheese.

"Poof!" I cried, wondering what Old Cob Deadnettle must have been eating during his time as a goat. "Yes, that's the type of thing."

Several minutes and much smeared cheese later, we surveyed the creature. "A fine specimen!" said Loosestrife, wiping the cheese from his hands.

"But it is completely immobile, my dear Loosestrife," I observed. "It lies there like a dead toad! How is it to perform its duties in this state?"

"You are right, Tobias," he replied. "We must animate it with what humans call a soul! An *anima*! How shall we do it, do you think?"

"Does this book of anatomy not mention where one can find a soul?"

"No, it is all joints and vertebrae and cartilages—it makes no mention of souls. Indeed it is quite dull and, if I may say, painfully lacking in anything ineffable."

It was now my turn to have a moment of enlightenment. "My dear Loosestrife," I cried, "I think I have it. Humans are known for prizing reason above all things, are they not?" He nodded most vehemently. "Then let us imbue this creature with reason!"

"Well said, my friend! But where to get this reason that the humans possess in droves? I see very little of it around here. Indeed it strikes me that in Faerie it is practically nonexistent!"

"I have the answer to that too."

"You do?"

"Yes, indeed! Books!"

"Books?"

"Books are where humans get their reason—all their strange ideas and punctilious sciences, their anatomy and philosophy, and empirical geography—books!"

"But where shall we find such books? No respectable Faerie would have such drivel in his library. Why, my library practically overflows with grimoires, gramaryes, and cantripædiæ. But the books you speak of? Not one, sir!"

I pondered for a moment, taking several puffs of my pipe. Eventually I said:

"The fairer sex are known to dally in reasonable things, are they not? I know a lady who delights in all things reason and logic. Quite

DEEP MAGIC ANTHOLOGY ONE

a splendid creature, though she does tend to be a little too level-headed at times."

"Her name?"

"Miss Marjory Greenteeth who lives over the hill at Wit's End. She, I know, has a large collection of thoroughly pragmatic books."

"Then let us visit her at once!" my friend exclaimed. "There is not a moment to lose!"

* * *

Marjory Greenteeth lived in a large, once-grand château of moss-covered stone at the rear of a windswept estate overgrown with thin, dreary hawthorn trees.

"Good grief," said Loosestrife. "What a terribly humdrum place."

"I assure you, Loosestrife," I said, "that the Greenteeths are a family of the highest breeding, though one admits that they have perhaps fallen on rather difficult times of late."

Loosestrife acknowledged this with as much grace as a man who has recently gone up in the world could and proceeded to pull the tasselled bell cord that hung at the side of the somewhat haggard front entrance. Chimes rang within the château, peal after peal echoing through its many wings and galleries. After a moment, the door was opened by a portly man of gruff appearance with whiskers that reached most way to the ground (had the man been better dressed, one might have assumed that his beard was a modern fancy of the aristocracy; however, by the state of the house and the man's poorly mended clothing, one could safely hazard that his bearded long-windedness was down to nothing more eccentric than an inability to afford a barber). It was also quite clear that this particular gentleman was trying, and failing, to conceal a small, though undoubtedly potent, cannonette behind his back.

"Good day, sirs. How may I be of service to you?" said the man, looking the two of us up and down. "You wouldn't happen to be creditors, would you?"

"No, sir," said Loosestrife. "My name is Loosestrife Foulweather and this is my companion, Tobias Tamlane. We are here to speak with Miss Marjory, your daughter."

"Marjory, you say! And what, may I ask, do you want with her?"

"Why, sir, we merely wish to—"

"Don't fancy marrying her, do you?"

"I beg your pardon, sir?" said Loosestrife.

"I said"—he raised his voice—"don't fancy marrying her, do you?"

"Sir, I have not come here to marry your daughter, merely to borrow some of her books!"

"Pity, pity . . ." he said, his moustaches drooping. "Are you sure I can't persuade you?"

I leaned over and whispered in Loosestrife's ear: "He'll never let us in at this rate! Agree to marry his daughter and be done with it."

Loosestrife considered it and returned his gaze to Mr. Greenteeth. "I will consider the matter, sir. But I can do no more than that while standing here shivering on your doorstep."

"Wonderful! Oh, wonderful!" said Mr. Greenteeth. "Come in! Come in, do! I believe my little Marjory is in the library; allow me to escort you there at once!" With that, he led us through the many ill-lit corridors (ill-lit more from shame at the state of the wallpaper than a lack of candles, I'm sure—though I cannot imagine that candles would otherwise have been in abundance either) and up several dilapidated staircases that creaked and moaned and lowed as if there were a menagerie of broken-limbed creatures trapped below, and every step we took was agony to them.

As a man who had recently gone up in the world, my dear friend Loosestrife viewed the decrepitude with great interest. "I was under the impression, sir, that you had once been a man of great means and wealth."

"You are quite right, Mr. Foulweather, you are right. My home was once a paragon amongst *brughs*, a paradise, with intricately woven carpets, ornate tapestries, brocaded sofas; commodes, armoires, and chiffoniers of ebony, walnut, and oak; glasses of crystal, services (both dinner and tea) of silver and gold—Oh! Mr. Foulweather, it would have melted your heart."

"And human servants, I'd warrant, too?"

"Oh yes! Butlers, footmen, cooks, maids of almost every variety, ostlers, gardeners, hall boys—I had to part with them all, each and every one. All long dead now, though, of course. Now my house is served by nothing more than a troupe of diligent house spiders, who, in all fairness, do keep away the flies. Cobwebs and dust, sir! That is what decorates my *brugh* now."

"But what happened, Mr. Greenteeth?" Loosestrife asked.

"Relatives!" came the grave reply. "Accursed relatives descending on us like rats! And dependents, and second cousins, and third cousins, and uncles and aunts, and many of them twice or three times removed! They ate and spent and borrowed me out of house and home, sir. Why, I had to sell everything to pay off my creditors."

"Mr Greenteeth. I am most sympathetic," said Loosestrife.

"Thank you, Mr. Foulweather. Your sympathies are kindly received. Now, if you could lighten my burden by taking my daughter as your bride, you would indeed be doing me a great service. I cannot promise much of a dowry, but if you truly desire the books that you wish to borrow, I may be able to make a permanent exception of them."

Loosestrife considered this for a moment. He had not bargained on leaving Mr. Greenteeth's house with a bride as well as books, but as he was going up in the world, he could not stay a bachelor forever—it simply wasn't done. If he was to have a fashionable house with a fashionable servant and all manner of fashionable rooms and table settings and dinner sets and tea services and curtains made from expensive cloth, then it would only be fitting that he had a wife as well.

"Very well, sir," he said at last. "I accept your offer with glee."

"Wonderful! Wonderful! Ah, here is my rather modest library, and your new bride reclines within."

Mr. Greenteeth opened the library door and stepped aside to let us enter.

On one of the room's threadbare armchairs sat a pretty young woman with an enormous pouf of midnight-black hair that smouldered with the multicoloured iridescence of opals.

"May I help you?" said the lady.

"Good evening, Miss Greenteeth. My name is Loosestrife Foulweather and I am here to request some of your books, and it has recently been agreed, your hand in marriage."

"Oh, erm, no thank you," she said, and turned her head back to the book she was reading.

Loosestrife looked at Mr. Greenteeth, who shrugged and rolled his eyes, so he returned his gaze to the lady and once again cleared his throat. "Miss Greenteeth—Marjory—may I call you Marjory?"

Marjory ignored him.

"Marjory," he continued regardless, "your father and I have come to an agreement that you should be my wife, and in return he will grant me permanent leave to borrow some of the books in your library. Is that not agreeable to you?"

"Not particularly." said Marjory, not looking up from her book.

Loosestrife looked at Mr. Greenteeth again, who this time took the hint and piped up: "Marjory, dear, you must do as your father wills."

"I will do no such thing," said Marjory. "A woman should be able to choose whom she marries, if and when she sees fit to do so."

"Oh, such reason! That's what I get for allowing you to indulge yourself with all those dreary human books."

"If I am to marry this comparative stranger, father dear, then there must be some advantage to it. As far as I see, my books are here; they are my pleasure, so here I shall remain."

"Ah, but Marjory," said Loosestrife. "I see you have a fondness for human books, yes?"

Marjory nodded, almost imperceptibly.

"You have a fondness for humans, then. But have you ever actually seen a human, Marjory?"

Marjory looked up briefly. "Only when I was a girl," she said, and returned her gaze to her book. "Before father sold them all. I barely remember them."

"Well, then. If you come with me, you shall see a real human servant. I have, you see, made quite some progress in constructing one myself. Would you like to see it?"

Marjory's eyes did not leave her book, but she began to bite her lip, and a faint quiver could be detected in her lower jaw. After what she must have considered an adequate pause, Marjory raised her head and said:

"Very well, then, I do believe I should like to see that."

* * *

"Behold, my dear," said Loosestrife when the formalities of marriage had been dealt with, and Marjory and her books had been installed in the house, "our human servant!"

"It doesn't look very human," said Marjory, looking at the strange and ungainly mass of lumps that lay on the tulipwood commode in Loosetrife's back parlour.

"My dear, that is because you haven't seen a human since you were a little girl. Your memory of them is rather fuzzy I imagine."

"But I have seen illustrations," she said.

"Pedantically accurate renderings no doubt, devoid of the most basic fanciful embellishments."

Marjory gave a dissatisfied humph and began to prod at the lump of inanimate matter with an elegant finger.

"Now, now, my dear," said Loosestrife. "Do you not have any wifely duties to perform? Making . . . erm . . . tea? . . . or darning something, perhaps?"

Never having had a wife before, my dear friend had little idea of what duties were expected of them.

"No," came the curt reply, "I do not."

Loosestrife began to protest, but Marjory continued: "What exactly are you going to do with my books?" she asked. "You can't teach this lump to read, surely. It can't even open its eyes."

"We shall imbue him with an *anima*! Wife, fetch my cauldron!"

"Fetch it yourself."

Loosestrife blanched. ". . . Very well." He fetched the cauldron from its cupboard, placed it on a tripod so as to avoid scorching the carpet, and reluctant to risk asking any more of his wife, requested that I proceed with providing the heat—a task that I confess to thoroughly enjoying—whereby I commenced hurling my finest and most vehement insults at the pot until it very nearly boiled over with rage.

"Easy now, Tobias," he said. "Perhaps you could temper your insults just a modicum, lest the sensitive fellow explode. There are also," he added, "ladies present." To which Marjory responded with an insult of her own that set the poor fellow's ear's smoking.

After he had doused them in cold water, and checked that my insults were keeping the pot at the optimum temperature, Loosestrife opened the great chest of books provided by Mr. Greenteeth and picked out a series of leather-bound tomes: "Aristotle's *Organon*." He nodded and dropped it into the cauldron. "Euclid's *Elements*, *An Essay Concerning Human Understanding* by a Mr. John Locke, and—aha!—*Mrs. Beeton's Book of Household Management*, for, I think, practical purposes."

The cauldron began to simmer gently. "Now, where is my distilling apparatus?" he said. "Excuse me, my dear, while I go look in the cellar."

Loosestrife left the room once again, leaving Marjory and myself alone in the room. I, having effused enough foul language at the cauldron to keep it bubbling for several hours, and knowing full well that my capacity for small talk with young ladies is somewhat nonexistent, retreated to the mantelpiece above the small fireplace, where I soon fell into contemplation, cradling my pipe.

Marjory, on the other hand, looked altogether vexed. A frown had taken residence upon her forehead and lay there like a stubborn cat. "Why, you can't have Locke without Hume, and what about Rousseau and Kant? They've been omitted altogether! And Mr. Spinoza too. And why Aristotle but no Plato? Euclid without Newton, too, is an omission." She began to rummage around in the chest, pulling out book after book. "Oh! And here we have Paine, Hobbes, Montesquieu! They must all go in."

When Loosestrife returned with his distilling apparatus, he found the chest all but empty.

"Dearest," he said, with a forced smile, "where have all the books gone?"

"Oh, I added them to the mixture," she said. "It's far better this way."

"I see," replied Loosestrife, scratching his head. "I do fear, however, that this human will be too reasonable by far." The viscous liquid in the pot belched as if in agreement. It had turned from a thin, watery yellow to a deep and profound gold.

"Oh, do stop being such a stuffy old bore!" said Marjory. "Where is your sense of adventure!"

"Here, here," I said, not out of any particular desire for adventure, but it is always necessary for one's opinion to be heard; it prevents one from being mistaken for a piece of furniture.

"Come now, Husband," Marjory said, patting him on the shoulder tenderly. "Is the *anima* ready? It looks wonderful!"

Loosestrife did not quite know what had gone wrong. His new bride was far more involved than he'd imagined, and his human servant was soon to be a savant rather than a loyal worker. Indeed, he was rapidly learning that being married was a lot more trouble than he'd imagined. But he supposed it was simply the price of going up in the world.

"Well, my dear, it needs distilling, which will take a few hours. But, perhaps I can convince the apparatus to hurry the process along."

"Would you, my love?" said Marjory. "It would please me ever so much."

Loosestrife blushed. "Very well," he said, and began to set up the copper still, bribing it with promises of honey brandy and dew liquor in the very near future. He decanted the liquid from the cauldron, which looked far more potent than he'd expected, into the flask, and in the blink of an eye, it had evaporated, condensed, and fallen, drop by golden drop, into the collection bottle.

Loosestrife took the bottle and proffered it: "Would you, my darling, care to do the honours?"

"Why, my dear friend, certainly!" I said, rising from my chair and tapping out my pipe (I believe, in hindsight, that I may have misread the situation).

"I think he means me, Tobias."

"Madam," I replied, not willing to be gotten the better of, "you may be Loosestrife's wife, but I have been decorating his house for decades. This honour must surely go to me."

We turned to Loosestrife, both of us with severely affronted faces.

But Loosestrife merely sighed, saying, "I do not like this going up in the world one bit."

* * *

Slowly the creature sat upright, its eyes shining with the lancing light of a summer dawn, which faded, soon enough, to the bright amber of sun-baked wheat. It coughed, emitting a twitter of bird-song as it did so, flexed its muscles with a squeak, and set its feet gingerly on the ground.

"Careful now, my dear Loosestrife," I said, eyeing the creature with a mixture of suspicion and awe, "it may bite."

"Nonsense!" he replied, and proceeded to clear his throat before addressing the creature in a loud and commanding voice: "Good morning, servant. My name is Loosestrife Foulweather, your master and, I flatter myself, your creator . . ." The creature blinked, but did not speak, unable, it seemed, to comprehend.

Marjory, without taking her eyes off the creature, leaned over to her husband. "Can it understand you? Why does it not speak?"

"Leave it to me, my dear," he said, patting her on the shoulder. "It would do you good, man, to address the lady of the house and I as Master and Mistress. I am all for quiet servants, but a mute one who cannot even utter the most basic formalities is quite out of the question! Come now. Speak up."

But the creature still did not answer. Instead, something behind Loosestrife was engaging its attention.

"What? What is it? Is there something behind me? Is Tobias doing something amusing behind my back?"

But the creature was not looking at me either, and after a moment, it pushed past all three of us and became very interested in Loosestrife's walnut games table.

"What is it, man? Have you never seen a games table before?" said Loosestrife, wrinkling his brow in frustration.

I pointed out (with the utmost discretion, of course) that the creature had likely not seen a games table before, or indeed, any table, as it had but moments before come into animation.

"Yes, well—ahem—I suppose not. Now listen here—"

The human turned suddenly and looked at Loosestrife with its eyes of summer wheat and said with a twitter, "This is not right. This table has no legs! How is it standing? The laws of gravity clearly state that it should fall to the ground!"

Loosestrife pressed his hand to his forehead. "The table, you *utterly* reasonable human, stands on my orders. It needs no legs to do so."

The human ran now to the walls. "And the walls, the cornices, the lintels, the door posts . . . they defy the geometry of Euclid!"

"The walls do as they're told. I find them more aesthetically pleasing when they are thus contorted."

"And this cauldron. It remains red-hot, with no source of heat? The laws of thermodynamics declare this to be impossible!"

"By oak and ash and thorn, I have never encountered anyone as frustratingly obtuse as you! The cauldron remains hot because Tobias here hurled enough insults at it to keep it fuming for several hours. Do you know nothing, man?"

"I know only reason, sir," said the servant.

"Useless! Utterly useless!" he said, throwing up his hands. "He understands nothing, Tobias. Nothing! We shall have to destroy him and start again. Where's my cheese knife?"

Marjory, however, would have none of it. "Husband," she said, "if I may interject."

Loosestrife was busy searching for his cheese knife, but he nodded that she should continue.

"If indeed this servant is to be but a symbol of your going up in the world, then surely it matters not that his domestic skills be lacking. Surely the more logical he is, the more impressive he will be to your guests. Why, you now own the most reasonable servant ever to serve in Faerie! Surely you wouldn't want to hack at that accolade with your cheese knife!"

"Well, no, I suppose not. Yes . . . yes. Jolly good point, my dear. Obtuse! You shall remain in my service, for now at least. Perhaps there is something to be said for this reason of yours after all, my dear."

* * *

Over the next several days, owing most certainly to the presence of such a reasonable creature as Loosestrife's new human servant, the *brugh* and its contents, which had once been so grandiose a work of fancy, began in many ways to change. Loosestrife found, to his great consternation, that his snuff box quickly ran out of snuff, even though he had expressly forbidden it to be empty. He found that the pillars of his house began to creak and groan, as if they could not abide the strain of their whimsical contortions. The fireplaces became cold and sooty, coming to realise just how unreasonable it was to be expected to provide warmth without sufficient fuel and kindling. Only the bluebells in the garden continued to defy Obtuse the servant's inscrutable logic, pealing as usual each morning, and providing my dear friend with his only comfort. Even Loosestrife's horse (a gregarious rabicano stallion named Claptrap) stopped speaking to him, for Obtuse had explicated in no uncertain terms that a horse's anatomy did not allow for such a sophisticated expression of so wide a range of phonemes. All in all, and despite his wife's protestations, Loosestrife was quite dissatisfied indeed with his new servant. He was of half a mind to cancel the grand ball he had arranged to show off his new status as a man who had gone up in the world, having invited several prominent faeries of excellent breeding and station: the aforementioned Tom Thistletop, of course, several lords and ladies, and even the Duke of Long Wind, who, though his conversation was known to be tedious in the extreme, was nonetheless (as it was often noted in the society papers) descended from King Auberon himself. In the end, of course, the desire to prove his social buoyancy in the presence of such fey and fair warmed any cold feet that may have troubled him.

When the guests arrived several days later, however, the house was almost unrecognisable by any respectable Faerie standard. The walls were straight, the beams of the roof were arranged all in a structurally sound criss-cross arrangement. The tables had legs, or else lay supine on the floor. The fireplaces were filled with coal, the clocks on the wall all ran at the same time, the mirrors reflected only what was put in front of them—even the cutlery no longer did as it was told, and had become complacent and lazy, needing to be operated entirely by hand. It was by far the most reasonable house that anyone in Faerie had ever seen.

Loosestrife had planned on converting the cosy little morning room at the front of the house into a majestic high-ceilinged ballroom, with lambent parquet flooring, marble columns, and several enormous chandeliers, but Obtuse had laboured the point that the dimensions and volumes of reality would not allow for such a thing, and the room had retained its original size, with little if any room for dancing. It was so poky in fact that the Countess de Winter's voluminous gown of frost not only knocked over rather a lot of Loosestrife's china ornaments (which in order to impress Obtuse insisted on smashing when they hit the floor) but also began to melt in the heat from the fireplace.

"Now listen here," Loosestrife said after sneaking out to the serving pantry to scold his frustratingly scrupulous servant, "I want no more of your incessant reasonability tonight—you must be somewhat reasonable, of course, otherwise they will not believe you to be human, but please do your best not to be so pedantically logical. You have quite ruined my house, I have several very important guests in attendance, and I shall be very much displeased if you make this evening even a modicum less successful than it ought to be."

At that moment, Marjory appeared at the door to the pantry.

"Marjory, my dear!" Loosestrife exclaimed. "Why, but a moment ago I saw you chatting to Martin Willowlimbs. What in all the realms could have possessed you to so hastily abandon one of our most important guests? Was his conversation not frivolous enough?"

Marjory smiled. "Quite, quite, he has a very fanciful way with words indeed, which kept me quite entertained. However, I had to tear myself away to consult with Obtuse here about the small matter of the canapés. You see—"

But Loosestrife simply waved his hand in dismissal. "I leave all that up to you, my dear. But do remember to hurry back. I have been told that my company is entertaining, but even I cannot be expected to singly keep a whole parlour of faeries enthralled for an entire evening."

And with that he left to attend to the guests.

* * *

Having returned to the far-less-than-adequate ballroom and taken up my customary position on the mantelpiece, I was pleased to overhear the following conversation between the Countess de Winter and the aforementioned Martin Willowlimbs.

The Countess: How strange this house is, my dear Martin. I have never seen the like. Why, everything is so orderly! I must confess it to be the dullest house I have ever seen. And they say Loosestrife has gone up in the world . . .

Willowlimbs: Indeed, Countess, his wife, too, speaks of the most dreary topics. She's almost as bad as Long Wind.

The Countess: Is that the Greenteeth girl? Yes, what a strange slip of a thing. How unfortunate for her father to be so overcome with relatives like that.

Willowlimbs: How do you deal with them, my lady? I hear you have a large family yourself, and yet your wealth does not seem to have been leeched from you.

The Countess: Oh, swiftly, and sharply. They ask for much less money when they have no heads, you see.

Willowlimbs: Indeed, indeed, a wise course of action.

Loosestrife: Enjoying yourself, Squire Willowlimbs, Countess?

Willowlimbs: Quite, quite, my dear Loosestrife. But tell me, what is this strange way you have renovated your *brugh*? It is, uh-ha, somewhat dreary, is it not?

Loosestrife: Ah! You noticed. Well, my dear squire, Countess, you shall find out the cause of it soon enough. I have something of a surprise for you all, you see. Proof positive that I have indeed gone up in the world.

Tom Thistletop: A surprise, you say?

Jack Catkin, Marquess Arumhall: What's this about a surprise I hear?

Loosestrife: Now, now, everyone, your lordship, my lady. All in good time.

Lady Arumhall: Oh, Loosestrife, don't make us wait. Come now, show us your surprise.

Countess: Yes, do.

Willowlimbs: Go on, be a good fellow and show us!

Loosestrife expelled a long, considered sigh. "Oh, very well," he said with apparent reluctance (although he could not, in truth, have hoped for a warmer reception to his surprise).

He marched to the head of the room, and stood on a stool in front of the fireplace. He picked up a miniature bell from the mantle, and when he shook it, it rang as loudly as the tenant of any belfry (it, too, must have escaped the attentions of the servant, Obtuse), dampening the chatter of those in attendance beneath the weight of its peals. The music stopped, the dancers came abruptly to a halt.

"My lords and ladies, dukes and duchesses, gentlemen and crones. As you are all aware, I have recently found myself going up in the world. From humble beginnings as a simple weaver of lightning thread, I worked diligently, investing my earnings in many sundry ventures, which have, as good fortune would have it, made me a man of not inconsiderable wealth. I built this most excellent *brugh*, acquired a friend who rides my coattails, and decorated my abode with the most frivolous furniture in all of Faeriedom. I have held parties and gatherings well-received and attended by the most prestigious guests"—here he paused to smile benignly upon them all—"but one thing I have been missing, one thing that will convince even the most staunchly feudal among you, that I, Loosestrife Foulweather, have a place among you."

He rang a service bell. "I present to you, Obtuse, my new human servant."

Gasps rose up from the crowd.

"A human servant! Why, there hasn't been a new human servant in Faerie since Cottingley."

"Offa's Dyke! This is marvellous. A new servant in Faerie—why, I haven't seen a human in decades!"

"Thistletop won't be happy about this. He's always been proud of being the last faerie to have had a working servant. Now an upstart from the shires has one! And not he! Such a scandal! Such a marvellous scandal!"

So were the mutterings of the Faerie gentry while they awaited the arrival of the human servant. But when minutes came and went and no human servant appeared, Loosestrife began to show the merest hairline fracture of concern.

"Tobias, would you tell my wife to fetch Obtuse, please," he asked of me, sweat beginning to bead on the larger of his eyebrows.

"Your wife, Loosestrife?" I replied. "I know not where she is."

"She is not here?"

"No, my friend, she is not."

"Fornicating fauns! Then I'll go and get them myself." He grasped me by the shoulders and hauled me off the mantle. "You keep the guests entertained," he said in a voice hoarse with panic, before rushing to the serving pantry to find his wife and servant. But no one was there. He rushed to his quarters, but no one was there. He rushed to every corner of the house, but his wife and his servant were nowhere to be found. Only, nailed to the front door he found a letter, written in two separate hands.

In a script clumsy and smelling slightly of cheese was written: *To my former master, Every man having been born free and master of himself, no one else may under any pretext whatever subject them without his consent. I bid you farewell.*

And below it, in the clear, sensible hand of his wife: *To my former husband, I wish to be treated as a rational creature, I wish to feel the calm and refreshing satisfaction of loving, and being loved by, someone who can understand me. Adieu.*

Loosestrife sat down upon a very reasonable seat in the very reasonable drawing room of his now thoroughly reasonable house. The guests slowly departed, and he said not a word to them as they left, though they certainly had plenty to say about him (of which I shall not repeat here for fear of setting your ears alight). He sat in the chair for many hours, while I, once more, took up my position on the mantle.

When the sun began to rise, he sat there still, and it wasn't until the rays fully illuminated the world outside the house that Loosestrife realised he no longer looked out on Faerie, but rather on a strange and uniform landscape of closely tended gardens and dull square houses, lined up in neatly regimented rows as far as he could see. The sound of bells rang across the brightening morning from the tower of a nearby church, and strange dark forms wandered hunched along the streets, boarding oddly shaped carriages, which rumbled and roared in the morning air and left clouds of grey fog in their wakes.

A knock, suddenly, came upon the door.

"Marjory? Obtuse? Is it them, do you think, Tobias?" he asked me, rising from his chair and rushing from the drawing room before I could answer.

How peculiar I felt in that new morning light, as though my whole body had ossified—from exhaustion, I surmised, following all the recent excitement.

I heard him open the door. And a voice, not Marjory's, nor that of Obtuse, came galloping down the hall.

"Mornin', Mr. Fowler. How are you today?"

"Excuse me, miss, I . . ." Loosestrife began, but the voice had already entered the drawing room (now much smaller than I recalled it ever being before) and revealed itself as belonging to a young woman wearing what appeared to be a sky-blue housecoat. Loosestrife followed her, and I must admit that now, in the fullness of the morning light, I could see how the strain of last night had changed him. His face was wrinkled and veined much like the cheese we had used to coat Obtuse's wooden frame, and his posture was as crooked and contorted as the walls of his house had once been.

"Now, then," said the woman. "I'll give you your medicine first, and then I'll make you a nice cup of tea. Then we'll get you washed and dressed; how does that sound?"

"What is she talking about, Tobias?" he asked me, his eyebrows quite nearly leaping from his head.

The bluebells outside rang in the wind—but wait, it was not the bluebells; the ringing came from the intruder. She dug about in her pocket and lifted what looked like a pink snuff box to her ear.

"Hi, babe," she said, apparently addressing an infant that had somehow entered the room unannounced. "Yeah, I'm at Mr. Fowler's house now. Yeah, I'll be done in about half an hour, all right? I'll drop it round for you after I'm finished."

"Tobias! What on earth is going on here! Who is this woman?"

"What's that, babe? No, that's just him talking to that flippin' Toby jug on top of the fire. Yeah, yeah, all right, babe. T'ra."

(I have done my utmost to transcribe her eccentric way of speaking, but I make no claims on its accuracy. It was indeed a most babbling and incoherent dialect.) She continued:

"Right, then, Mr. Fowler. Let's get you that cup of tea, shall we?" She smiled a sweet smile, and left the parlour. I heard her going down the hallway to the kitchen.

"Tobias," Loosestrife said to me, quickly approaching the mantelpiece. "I think this may be our replacement servant. Oh, yes. Oh, yes! Now everyone will see how I've gone up in the world. Another party, do you think, dear friend?"

To this I said nothing. Having experienced quite enough excitement of late, I thought it best not to encourage my friend any further in his fancies. I merely stared, and chewed on my pipe in silence.

About Dafydd McKimm

Dafydd McKimm was born and grew up in the glove-shaped valleys of South Wales but now lives in the East Asian metropolis of Taipei, Taiwan. His short fiction has appeared or is forthcoming in Daily Science Fiction, 600 Second Saga, Flash Fiction Online, and Syntax & Salt. He tweets, now and again, @DafyddMcKimm.

THE WIZARD'S GRANDDAUGHTER

By Christopher Baxter | *11,500 words*

DWYN FELT HER spells react to the explosion before she heard it. She dropped the flask she'd been about to fill and darted to the window just as a dull boom rattled her cottage. Across the garden stood her grandfather's tower. Guided by her spells, flames roared out of the narrow chimney that poked up from the steep roof. The rest of the tower seemed unharmed, not a stone out of place.

The wards should have protected her grandfather, but she wasn't positive she'd gotten everything right; they had been very complicated to create. She turned to sprint for the door. Then she paused to ensure that her pots were all simmering at safe levels—she felt guilty for taking the time when her grandfather might be hurt or worse, but if she didn't, then she risked a second explosion right there in the cottage. It only took a moment to satisfy herself that everything would be safe, and then she took off down the hall.

A foot from the front door, Dwyn tripped and nearly fell, barely catching herself against the wall in time. As she opened the door, she glanced back to see what she'd tripped over—it was a stack of newspapers, the South Wales Echo. Several matching stacks stood along the wall. When had her grandfather left those there? She'd just cleared the room out the night before.

She sprinted along the gravel path between her home and the tower. Out of the corner of her eye, she could see a few of her neighbors peeking over their fences. They were used to odd noises from the high wizard's tower, but that one had been louder than most. A car had stopped in the street, and the driver was leaning out the window with his bowler tipped back on his head.

Dwyn yanked open the tower's heavy oak door. A narrow stair-case ran up along the curved outer wall, made even narrower by the stacks of papers, boxes, and clothing as high as her waist that crowded the left side. She cursed her grandfather's traditionalism as she scrambled up the four flights to the top. Most wizards those days lived in simple houses or flats in the city—why couldn't he?

"Grandda?" she shouted as she burst into the uppermost room of the tower. "Grandda!" She couldn't see him over the piles of junk that filled the place. Somewhere in the room, his old radio was blaring, dry old newsreaders discussing the Molotov-Ribbentrop Pact in dusty but deafening voices. But when their speaking paused, she could just barely make out the sound of coughing and grum-bling. She sighed in relief. If her grandfather was grumbling, he was probably not seriously hurt.

She took a moment to catch her breath, relief warring with irritation and guilt. She shouldn't let him make potions anymore—disasters would just keep happening. Then she snorted and shook her head. How was she supposed to stop him?

She edged down the one relatively clear path through the stacks of junk, occasionally tiptoeing in a vain attempt to see her grandfa-ther. It didn't look like anything in the room was on fire; the wards had worked, though they'd left more smoke in the room than she'd have liked. The explosion had also knocked things into the narrow pathway through the junk—an old burlap doll here, a bundle of brown weeds there, and a box of dried plum pits beyond that.

Dwyn carefully stepped over it all, fanning herself with her hand. Whenever she went in there, the piles of junk seemed to loom in toward her, crowding her space, and the smoke made it even worse. The blaring radio was beginning to make her head pound. She bit back curses. That was it; she was going to clean the whole tower out.

Coming around a curve in the path, she finally found her grand-father. He was standing next to a table that sat beneath the window, using an old shaving brush to painstakingly sweep fine purple dust off a stack of newspapers.

"Grandda, are you all right?" Dwyn asked as she climbed over a toppled crate. He couldn't hear her over the radio show, which had moved on to a discussion of the looming threat of war on the continent. She bit her tongue in irritation; that was the last thing she needed her grandfather to hear about. She pushed her way to the radio, a tall, decade-old standing model that poked out of a pile of junk a few feet from her grandfather, and switched it off. "Grandda!"

Her grandfather jumped and turned to face her with a reproachful frown. "Dwyn, there you are," he muttered, his voice gravelly with a heavy, singsong Welsh accent. "Did you meddle with my protective wards?" He waved a gnarled hand over his head, gesturing to the smoke. "This should have cleared out by now."

Dwyn sighed. "I replaced your wards years ago, Grandda. I told you about it—you had let them fade."

"My wards were fine," he grumbled, hunching his shoulders and turning back to the stack of newspapers.

"Are you hurt?" Dwyn took the old man by the shoulder and turned him to face her. He was a little bit shorter than she was, wrinkled and tan—at least, she hoped he was tan and not just dirty. His hair was disheveled, as though he'd only gotten halfway through combing it before giving up, and he'd missed several small patches of white whiskers when he'd shaved that morning. Dwyn stifled another sigh and straightened the ragged green robes that he wore —the man looked like a beggar.

"I'm fine, Dwyn, leave it alone," her grandfather said, pushing her hands away and turning back to the stack of newspapers. "If you want to help, you can get the fae dust off these papers."

"Grandda, they'll fall apart before you could ever get them clean. Just throw them out."

"Well, I can't throw them out until I've read them."

Dwyn leaned over his shoulder to look at the top newspaper: the UK Wizard's Times from June 25, 1919. "They're over twenty years old."

He didn't reply; she was pretty sure he'd heard what she said and was simply ignoring her. Rolling her eyes, she turned to his workstation.

"What happened, then?" she asked, eyeing the dented, cracked cauldron on his workbench. A towel had been hastily shoved beneath it to sop up the mud-thick brown goop that was dripping out.

Her grandfather didn't reply.

"Grandda, what exploded?"

"What?" Her grandfather turned to her, his brow furrowed. "Oh, this blasted cauldron cracked and leaked the potion I was brewing. I'll tell you, I'm angry about that—I just got it back from

McKaeton, and he promised me that it was patched up perfect. Overcharged me too."

"Blacksmith McKaeton moved back to Glasgow three years ago, Grandda."

Her grandfather blinked, his face startled. "Oh. Well . . . it must have been another blacksmith, then."

"Why aren't you using the new cauldrons I bought you for your birthday?"

"Well, my old one is good enough," he grumbled, returning to his newspapers.

"Obviously it wasn't." Dwyn leaned forward to sniff the puddle of brownish potion on the workstation. Icebark, fourth clover, and . . . mandrake? No, something else, something with a strong scent. Was he trying to make a shapechange potion? "Grandda, which potion is this?"

"The clearthought potion, of course. I managed to salvage enough to fill a flask, though."

Dwyn's stomach dropped and her headache seemed to spike. He'd been trying to make clearthought, and he'd ended up with that? She followed the puddle to where it leaked off the back of the workstation, and found the twisted remains of a rusty steel bucket on the floor there. So the potion had leaked into the bucket and reacted with whatever it held, causing the explosion. She picked up the bucket and then frowned, studying the charred remains of plants within it.

"Grandda, was this bucket holding anything other than powderpods?"

"No. I picked them the other day," he said, not looking up.

"There's not much that would have reacted with powderpods," she said, frowning. She turned to search the shelves above his workstation. "What was in that potion?"

"You know what goes in clearthought, Mair. Nothing in there caused the explosion."

"Something caused it," Dwyn replied. She didn't bother, anymore, to point out when he called her by her mother's name.

"I'll tell you what it was," her grandfather said, pointing out the window at their neighbor's house. "I caught those goblin neighbors of mine nosing around my garden last week, trying to steal some of my ingredients. I'm sure they messed around with the powderpods and got something else in them. Goblins are always doing things like that."

"The Jameses aren't stealing from you, Grandda." She pulled a tray of dark green leaves from one of the shelves and sniffed it. They had a strong scent—the smell she hadn't been able to identify in the potion. "What is this?"

Her grandfather stared at the tray for a moment and then turned red. "Well, that's just some of the starleaf that I found in my lawn."

"Grandda . . ." Dwyn closed her eyes and took a deep breath before continuing. "We discussed this—it's not starleaf, it's a weed!"

"I know starleaf when I see it."

"Where're the points on the leaves, then? Where're the silver veins?"

Her grandfather turned away with his lips pursed stubbornly.

"It's a weed, Grandda," Dwyn continued. "It's a weed that's been growing in your yard and soaking up stray bits of magic. It's what made the potion explode." Shaking her head, she dumped the weeds off the tray and into the dustbin beside the workstation.

"Dwyn, don't!" her grandfather shouted, hurrying forward and snatching the bin from the floor. "Maybe I wouldn't have to scrounge for wild starleaf if I still had any in my garden."

"Scrounge . . ." Dwyn gritted her teeth, fighting for calm. "The starleaf needed to be harvested before the full moon, Grandda! You're the one who taught me that! I kept asking if you were going to pick it, and you never did. Half of the crop went bad before I harvested the rest."

Her grandfather mumbled something under his breath as he began picking the weeds out of the dustbin and placing them carefully on the tray.

Dwyn shoved the tray aside. "And then—then I brought you half of what I picked. You said you didn't want it, remember? I had to force you to take it, and what did you do with it then? You left it in the sunlight and it withered!"

She realized suddenly that she was almost shouting, and went quiet, breathing heavily. She rubbed her temples. How had her mother dealt with him for so many years?

Her grandfather simply pulled the tray back into place and re-sumed picking leaves from the bin. After a moment, Dwyn sighed and turned away.

"I'll bring you some starleaf later," she said, "and we'll dig through this place and find the cauldrons I gave you. Are the other potions ready? I'll take them down."

"I'll take them," her grandfather replied. He dropped the dustbin and shuffled past her to a half-buried chair near his completely buried bed, grabbing a small leather satchel that was balanced precariously on the edge. "I need to make sure the lad knows the proper dosages." He tromped from the room.

Dwyn took a deep breath, reminding herself how glad she was that he wasn't hurt, and followed him down the stairs. She eyed the stacks of junk along the wall; it couldn't have been more than two months since she'd last cleaned it out. Where did he even get all that stuff?

A young man was sitting on the grass outside with his back against the fence—she hadn't even noticed him earlier, or the rusty bicycle that leaned on the fence beside him. The lad's hair was a dark brown, a little lighter than Dwyn's, and when he scrambled to his feet, he was just a few inches shorter than her.

"Is everything all right?" he asked, wringing his hands.

"Everything's fine," her grandfather replied. He held up the satchel. "Here are the potions for your father." He proceeded to list off when the young man should give his father doses of which potion, as though he expected the lad to remember it all from the one lecture. Dwyn shook her head—his instructions made little sense, anyway.

The young man nodded, wide-eyed, and bowed once her grandfather finished. "My whole family gives their thanks, High Wizard," he said. "Our local hedgeman has tried to treat him, but it wasn't helping. I couldn't believe it when he told me I could go to the great Arliss Bobydd himself!"

Despite her frustrated mood, Dwyn smiled slightly at the look on her grandfather's face—he was beaming. He stood up a little straighter and adjusted his robes. "Yes, well . . . I'm always happy to help. If anyone else in your village falls ill, you just come back to me."

"Thank you, sir!" The lad hesitated, biting his lip. Just as Dwyn's grandfather began to turn away, the young man blurted, "Why is everyone talking about war, sir?"

Dwyn's grandfather blinked. "What?"

"It's just . . . won't the Peace Ward—"

Dwyn stepped between them and placed a hand on the lad's arm. "How far is your village?"

"Oh—I'm from Llanelwedd," the lad replied, glancing back and forth between them. "About seven hours away on my bicycle."

"So you probably haven't eaten since you left home, have you? In what . . . eleven hours?"

"Oh . . . well, no."

"Come inside and have a meal before you go, then. That's a long ride to make on an empty stomach." Dwyn forced a smile and gestured to the cottage, pushing the boy along before he could bring up the rumors of war again. If her grandfather heard about that, he'd want to run off to the continent to fix things, and no one would be able to convince him that he wasn't able to anymore.

Her grandfather was frowning, but he didn't follow them. Grumbling, he turned and headed back into his tower. Dwyn sighed; that good mood hadn't lasted long.

The young man hesitated, glancing down at the satchel he still held against his chest. "I just . . . I worry about keeping my father waiting for his medicines."

"We'll get you something you can eat while you ride, then." Dwyn took him by the arm and began pulling him toward the cottage.

The lad looked up at her with a frown. "Miss, can I ask you something?"

"Certainly."

"If the Peace Ward is still protecting us, then why is everyone so worried about war?"

Dwyn winced and glanced over her shoulder involuntarily. Her grandfather was nowhere in sight . . . not that he would have been able to hear them if he was. "Wards don't last forever," she replied, turning back. "They fade over time."

The young man's eyes went wide. "So . . . there could be a war?"

"Don't worry." Dwyn tried to make her tone reassuring. "We can always make another peace ward."

"Would the high wizard do it again?"

"Well, he's retired now," she said. "But I'm sure that Lord Wizard Churchill will make one if things come to that."

The young man nodded. His shoulders relaxed a bit, and he smiled as they entered the cottage. "Thank you, Lady Wizard."

"I'm . . . not actually a full wizard. Just a student."

"Are you the high wizard's assistant?" the young man asked as she sat him down at the kitchen table. "Is that why you live here?"

"I'm his granddaughter," she replied, digging through a pouch at her waist. "This was my mother's cottage until she passed last year."

"Oh. I'm sorry." He was silent for a moment. "Can you do magic too?"

She pulled a small handful of suspension powder from the pouch. "Yes, I can." She tossed the dust in his face and whispered some words of power in Old Welsh.

The lad barely had time to react; his eyes went wide and then he stopped moving, frozen in place.

Dwyn took the satchel from his hands and opened the bag, wincing when she saw the potions inside. Only one was anywhere near the right color, a dull green that could almost be mistaken for the vibrant wellrest potion that its label said it was. The virulent orange potion that was labeled "Elixir of Healing and Restoration" should have been a rosy pink, and the brownish goop her grandfather claimed was a clearthought potion should have been pale blue.

She glanced at the boy, making sure that the suspension spell had taken effect properly, and then left the kitchen. A knock at the door interrupted her before she could reach her workshop. She groaned and turned back, hoping it wasn't another petitioner. A glance through the peephole showed her neighbor, Mrs. Reilly. Dwyn opened the door.

"Good morning, Dwyn," Mrs. Reilly said, smiling. The middle-aged woman had prematurely silver hair and was wearing a pale green long-skirted summer dress. She held up a worn disk of wood carved with spell knots. "I'm not imposing, am I? I was hoping you could get me youth charm working again. Me husband'll be getting back from sea this week, as long as things on the continent haven't gotten any worse, and I want to be sure I'm looking me best for him."

Dwyn gave a thin smile and took the charm. "I'd be happy to. Come in." She stepped back to let Mrs. Reilly in, and shut the door behind her. "I just need to take care of one other thing first, if that's all right."

"Oh, of course, dear, take your time."

Dwyn turned and headed to her workroom, trying not to feel irritated. She really was happy to help Mrs. Reilly—the woman was always so kind and solicitous, and Dwyn would have to be completely thoughtless not to appreciate her. It was just that she wasn't getting done any of the things she'd planned to do that morning . . .

Mrs. Reilly followed her down the hall and stood in the doorway to the workshop, looking around with a curious eye. Dwyn set the youth charm on her carving table and then turned to her row of simmering cauldrons. She carefully removed all the flasks and vials from the satchel—old and poorly washed, every one of them—and placed them on a stand beside her sink. She would pour them out later, after she'd made sure that none of them would damage the plumbing or cause trouble if it washed out into the river. Most of them were probably harmless, but . . . you never knew.

"What're all those, then?" Mrs. Reilly asked as Dwyn began filling new flasks with the potions she'd been brewing before the explosion interrupted.

"Potions for a petitioner," Dwyn replied without looking up. "Clearthought, wellrest . . . a few others."

"Oh, I didn't know you'd begun taking petitioners!" Mrs. Reilly hesitated a moment. "I . . . thought students weren't allowed to do that. Aren't you still on leave from the academy?"

Dwyn paused her pouring without looking up, a familiar sinking feeling settling into her stomach. "No, not anymore."

"Oh, dear." Mrs. Reilly placed a hand on Dwyn's shoulder. "They wouldn't extend it?"

"It's all right." Dwyn took a deep breath and resumed pouring. "It really is. They'd already given me a year's leave, after all. It wasn't really reasonable of me to hope . . ." She trailed off with a shrug.

Mrs. Reilly leaned down and gave Dwyn a gentle hug. "I'm so sorry, dearie."

Dwyn shrugged. "It should be all right, really. I found some of my grandfather's old spellbooks buried in one of the lower tower rooms—the books he was just positive the Jameses had somehow broken in and stolen. I've been studying some of the spells he designed, trying to learn them myself. It will give me an advantage if I . . . whenever I reapply to the academy."

"Well, that's good, I suppose . . ." Mrs. Reilly sat down quietly in a chair by the wall.

Dwyn forced a smile. "Anyway, no—I'm still not taking formal petitioners. I'm just . . . helping my grandfather with one of his."

"Helping him?" Mrs. Reilly glanced at the dirty potion flasks that Dwyn had removed from the satchel. "I take it he doesn't know you're helping?"

"Well . . . no." Dwyn corked the final flask and began loading them into the satchel. "I hid eavesdropping spells in the protective wards I put on his tower last year. I just listen in when a petitioner comes and then switch his concoctions out for the proper ones when no one's looking."

Mrs. Reilly bit her lip. "You know, Dwyn . . . there are homes for older people, when they become this troublesome."

"Oh, I've thought of that, believe me," Dwyn replied. More and more every day, she'd thought of that. "But . . . I couldn't do that to him."

"They're not so bad, these days," Mrs. Reilly said. "Especially after all the work your grandfather did for the kingdom back in the day; I'm sure his pension could get him in a prime, government-run home where they'd take wonderful care of him. He's the High Wizard Bobydd, after all!"

"That's the problem, Mrs. Reilly." Dwyn frowned at the older woman. "He's the man who single-handedly ended the Great War, the greatest Welsh wizard since Gwydion. Everyone knows it. I can't put the legendary Arliss Bobydd in an elderly home. Even before word of it got around, he would be so ashamed; he wouldn't really be alive after that."

Mrs. Reilly sighed. "Is it really much worse than living a lie, thinking he's still living up to his old reputation when he's not?"

Dwyn hesitated, staring down at the potions in the satchel. She wondered that every day. "Yes, it would be worse than this," she finally replied. A year ago, when she'd come home from school, she wouldn't have hesitated. "He spent his life building that reputation, and he deserves to keep it. The only times I really see him happy now are when he thinks he's helping someone, or when he gets talking about the old days, and I won't take that away. If . . . if I have a hard time because of it"—she shrugged her shoulders —"that's just too bad."

For a moment, she thought that Mrs. Reilly was going to cry. "Well, that's right compassionate of you, Dwyn. Your mother would be so very proud." Mrs. Reilly hesitated, biting her lip. "But . . . and I hope I'm not being too forward saying this . . . but I don't think your mother would want you to give up everything you cared about. She was so proud of you, going off to the academy so young. All of those offers of employment you had and whatnot."

Dwyn leaned her head into her hands. Her temples were throbbing again. "I know, I just . . . I don't know. What do you think I should do?"

"Oh, I wish I knew, dearie." Mrs. Reilly hugged her again, patting her hair. "I just don't want you to feel like you have to give up what you want. You can, if you think that's best—but you don't have to."

Dwyn nodded. She would think over it some more later, when her head didn't hurt so much.

Mrs. Reilly squeezed Dwyn's shoulder and then stood. "I'll come back for me charm later, dearie—don't worry about getting it done right away." She turned and headed for the door.

Dwyn tucked the last potion into the satchel, the clearthought. Years before, her mother had convinced her grandfather to take a little of it every morning. It had helped him keep things together for a while. But the potion no longer helped enough to waste the resources.

"Mrs. Reilly?"

The older woman stopped in the doorway. "Yes?"

"How did my mother deal with all this, while I was at school?"

"Oh, dearie," Mrs. Reilly smiled. "She talked with me. When I stop by for the charm, you can let out all your frustrations. It'll do you good." She waved and left.

Dwyn smiled. She took a deep breath and then returned to her work, penning a list of instructions for using the potions. Then she returned to the young man in the kitchen, placing the satchel back in his arms. After checking to ensure she was standing where she had been before, she let the power fade from the suspension spell with a whisper. The young man blinked once or twice, and then his brow furrowed.

"All right," she said, turning to her cupboards before he could ask what had happened. "How about some pasties? I've got some with meat and potatoes, and some with raspberry. That should get you through the day."

She looked over her shoulder at the young man. He blinked a few more times, visibly confused, and then he nodded. "Um . . . yes. That sounds wonderful, thank you."

"Of course," she replied, pulling the pasties from the icebox and placing them in a small basket. She handed the young man the note of instructions. "Now, I know my grandfather went over the instructions for those potions very quickly, so I just wanted to make sure you remembered what to do. Give your father a spoonful of the restorative and the wellrest potions before he sleeps each night, and let him sip at the fortitude potions whenever he's feeling weak. Give him a teaspoon of the clearthought potion each morning—

that will help him focus through the day until the fits pass—but don't give him any more than that. If he has too much, his mind will become overworked and he'll go into a coma. Understand?"

The young man nodded, wide-eyed as he looked over the note. Dwyn smiled and handed him the basket. "You'll do fine. Let us know once your father's doing better."

He smiled and stood. "Thank you so much, ma'am." He bowed, clutching the satchel and basket. "I can't believe we got help from Arliss Bobydd himself! I'm going to have to tell my whole town about this. Thank you!"

She smiled again and led him to the door. The young man's gratitude made her feel a bit better about things. As he hurried down the walk to his bicycle, however, she noticed her grandfather on his hands and knees in front of the tower, picking weeds out of his lawn and placing them carefully in a basket.

Dwyn sighed and leaned against the door frame, rubbing her forehead to try to clear her head. Her plans had been to spend the day researching some new spells, but it didn't look like that would happen. The morning had been taken up with potion making, and she needed to replace the tower's protective wards since the old ones had used up all their energy containing the explosion.

She turned to head back to her workroom and immediately tripped over the stacks of newspapers by the door.

* * *

Dwyn made the physical focus for the new wards out of tungsten wire and oak branches, weaving in small bits of other materials here and there while constantly double-checking her work against one of her grandfather's old spellbooks. The design for the wards was his, discovered when he'd been younger and somewhat more . . . stable. Like all of his spells, it was intricate and amazing and difficult.

The strenuous work was already beginning to give her a headache when she heard her grandfather enter the cottage. A moment later, he turned on the radio and turned it up loud enough that the news-readers seemed to be shouting. She groaned and rested her head on the worktable. Then she continued working, trying to concentrate through an ear-pounding discussion of the king and queen's visit to the United States. When the topic shifted toward German aggressions on the continent, she stormed out to turn off the radio and discovered that her grandfather had already returned to his tower, leaving the radio on behind him.

As she worked, Dwyn realized where she'd gone wrong when she'd made the wards the year before—her eavesdropping spell had interfered with some of the more delicate functions of her grandfather's design. It took her most of the day, but she eventually adjusted the design to incorporate both spells without interfering with the functionality of either.

Immensely proud of herself, she waited until her grandfather left for the market and then took the focus up into the tower. Using Welsh words of power, she projected her magic through the focus, casting glowing replicas of the ward into the walls, windows, floor, and ceiling—she left no surface unprotected. The images would be visible only to other wizards who knew how to look for them, but her hidden spell wouldn't be visible at all.

By the time she was finished, she was exhausted and beginning to feel jittery and stifled from the looming piles of junk. Her stomach rumbled as she climbed down the stairs; she needed some food and a nap before she finally picked up on her personal studies. When she entered her cottage, she was greeted with the scent of fresh bread and roasted lamb. A steaming pot of stew sat on her stove, a loaf of bread was keeping warm in her oven, and a note of encouragement from Mrs. Reilly sat on the table.

Her grandfather returned home about a half hour after dark. Unsurprisingly, his bag was stuffed with odds and ends—from a roll of natty twine to a horseshoe that looked as though it had been sitting in the mud when he found it. And six newspapers. She didn't complain until he tried to stash his newfound treasures in one of her kitchen drawers. She led him to the storage room at the back of the cottage and helped him stash the things there.

"An old woman in the market asked me whether I thought there was going to be war with Germany," he muttered as he sorted through a box of broken charms.

Dwyn froze for a moment and then forced herself to continue tidying the messy storage room. "Oh, really?"

Her grandfather nodded absently. "I felt bad for her—memory gone like that. She must have thought it was still before the Great War."

Dwyn breathed out in relief. "Poor thing."

Her grandfather put the box away and began sorting through the newspapers he'd bought. As he lifted the first one, Dwyn noticed the headline on the second: "Kaiser Seeking War?" She snatched the newspaper before he could read it and tossed it on top of a larger pile.

"That's not where that goes—" her grandfather began, but she hustled him out of the room to the kitchen table.

"Mrs. Reilly made us some stew for supper," she said. "I'll dish some up for you."

"Oh . . . Mrs. Reilly." He shook his head, scooting his chair closer to the table. "That woman is after my apples."

Dwyn paused in spooning out the stew, confused. "What?"

"Every time she comes by, she always asks about the apple tree on the edge of the garden. I know she's planning on sneaking in and stealing them once they're ripe—that's what she did last year."

"No," Dwyn said, more firmly than she'd intended. She pointed the ladle at him. "Mrs. Reilly has been nothing but sweet to you, and she was a great support for mother during her last years. I don't want to hear you badmouthing her."

"Well, I'm sure she does lots of nice things," her grandfather said. "But that doesn't change the fact that she stole my apples. I caught her sneaking in!"

"You caught her? You saw her in your garden?"

"Well . . ." Her grandfather stuck his chin out stubbornly. "No, I didn't, but Mr. James did. He told me she was in there."

"Mr. James? The one you've been accusing of breaking into your house?" Her grandfather opened his mouth to reply, but she cut him off. "No. I'm not going to listen to this, Grandda." She set his bowl of stew on the table with a thunk. "Just eat your dinner."

After that, he didn't speak to her for the rest of the evening; all her life, that had been his most common response when someone offended him. It had stopped bothering her years before.

Dwyn retreated to her workshop, looking forward to finally being able to study. Then she remembered the flasks and vials of potion that she'd confiscated from the young man that morning. They were still sitting by her sink, awaiting disposal; and it looked like one of the vials was beginning to melt. It took her several hours to safely negate the magic of the potions and dispose of them. By the time she finished, it was nearly midnight. She regretfully patted the spellbooks she'd been hoping to study; they'd have to wait until morning.

When she came out of her workshop, she found her grandfather asleep at the kitchen table with his head on his arms—he did that more and more often of late, falling asleep wherever he sat. It worried her. She was trying to decide whether or not she should wake him, when a knock came at the cottage door.

She frowned and made her way quietly to the door, where she peeked through the peephole. A thin man in an old-fashioned black suit stood on the porch, holding a bowler under his arm. She couldn't make out his face, but she could see several cars on the street behind him. More men in suits stood beside them.

She placed a hand in her pouch of suspension powder, just in case—she doubted that someone with nefarious motives would have politely knocked, but it didn't hurt to be cautious. Slowly, she opened the door.

The light from the cottage fell on the man; he was older, with dark hair and a bushy mustache that were streaked with wide lines of silver, and he looked very familiar.

"I'm sorry to bother you so late, miss," the man said with a nod. "But I'm seeking High Wizard Arliss Bobydd on extremely pressing business. No one is answering at his tower—this is his daughter's house, is it not?"

The moment she heard his voice, with its English accent and somewhat nasal tone, she recognized him. Neville Chamberlain, the royal minister himself. She realized that she was staring with her mouth open.

"Um, yes . . . yes, sir. I'm his granddaughter. I'll, um . . . I'll go get him." She turned and began walking toward the kitchen, and then stopped in her tracks. Had she just left the royal minister standing on her doorstep? Red-faced, she hurried back to the door and pulled it open wide. "I'm sorry, sir. Please come inside and make yourself at home."

The royal minister nodded with a polite smile, though it seemed to her that beneath the smile his face was tired and worried. He stepped inside and stood beside the door, making no move to sit. With a glance out at the cars and men along the street, Dwyn shut the door and hurried to the kitchen.

She was surprised to find her grandfather awake and nibbling at a sweet pasty. He didn't hear her approaching, of course, but when he saw her out of the corner of his eye, he quickly stuffed the half-eaten pasty back into the bread box as though he'd been caught doing something he wasn't supposed to.

"I'm going to head up to my tower for the day, Mair," he said, moving to the sink. "Let me know if any petitioners come looking for me."

"For the day?" Dwyn repeated, caught off-guard. "Grandda, it's midnight."

Her grandfather looked at her with a mixture of confusion and fear that broke her heart. He glanced out the dark kitchen window. "Oh . . . I . . . all right," was all he said. He lowered his head and turned away.

Dwyn wanted to give him a hug and comfort him—she suddenly realized that she couldn't remember the last time she'd hugged her grandfather. Instead, she pointed toward the sitting room. "Grandda, there's . . . the royal minister is here to see you."

Her grandfather looked at her, his brow furrowed. For a moment, she thought he hadn't heard her; and then he suddenly swept past her out of the kitchen, walking more quickly than she'd seen him move in a long time. She followed.

"Neville?" her grandfather said as he entered the room.

The minister stepped forward from the door with a smile, extending his hand. "Arliss, it's good to see you."

Her grandfather was grinning. He shook the minister's hand enthusiastically. "Goodness, Neville, how long has it been? I haven't seen you since you were made minister of health . . . the first time."

"Yes," the minister said, his smile fading. "That was ages ago." He released the handshake and cleared his throat. "I'm sorry to bother you so suddenly, and so late, but it is urgent."

"What is the matter?"

The minister glanced at Dwyn and licked his lips. "Would you mind if we headed up to your tower? These are matters best discussed alone, and behind wards."

"Oh . . ." Her grandfather's face fell. "Well, there's . . . there's not much room up there . . ."

"I'll step out, Minister," Dwyn interjected quickly. "You won't have to climb all those stairs, and the whole cottage is protected against eavesdropping by my grandfather's wards, just as the tower is." In a way, that was true. She'd placed the wards, of course, but they were her grandfather's design.

"Thank you, miss," the minister said with a nod. Dwyn curtsied and then hurried away to her room, a looming feeling of dread enveloping her. There were no pleasant reasons why the royal minister would be visiting her grandfather in the middle of the night.

As soon as her bedroom door was shut, she ran to the mirror on her dressing table. She spoke a few words of Old Welsh, and the mirror lit up, showing her the sitting room. She'd put the same eavesdropping spells in the cottage wards as in the tower, just in case. Suddenly, she was glad that she had.

The minister had opened the front door again. After a moment, a man in a double-breasted blue suit stepped into the room, thin and slightly taller than the minister. Dwyn touched the edge of the mirror, swinging the view around so that she could see the man better. It was the king. He nodded to her grandfather.

"Your Majesty," her grandfather said, bowing. "You've gotten much taller, Albert."

"High Wizard," the king replied, nodding. He smiled slightly. "It's George, now, actually. Thank you for receiving us at such a late hour." He stepped aside to let in another man, one decidedly wider than he was. "Have you met Lord Wizard Churchill?"

"I have not," her grandfather replied, bowing again. "It is an honor."

"The honor is mine, High Wizard," the lord wizard replied in a gruff voice. He shook her grandfather's hand. Unlike the others, he wore a set of midnight-blue robes. "I am sorry that I've never had the opportunity to come and meet you before."

Dwyn stared as the men seated themselves. Some part of her had always known, of course, what kind of people her grandfather had once worked with. Everyone knew. But seeing the royal minister, the first lord of wizardry, and the king himself sitting in her cottage was quite another matter. She winced—her rumpled grandfather looked so out of place.

"I'm not going to waste time, Arliss," Minister Chamberlain said. "Early yesterday morning, the German Empire invaded Poland."

Dwyn gasped, then covered her mouth before remembering that the men couldn't hear her. It wasn't really a surprise—rumors had been spreading for months. But still, hearing it so suddenly was a shock. Her grandfather simply frowned.

"They attacked without a formal declaration of war," the minister continued, "and, as far as we know, they've completely over-whelmed Poland's defenses. Information is still scarce."

Her grandfather was silent for a moment longer. "What will you do?" he finally asked.

"We will go to war, this time, if we must," Lord Wizard Churchill replied. "The Germans have pushed too far—we can't allow this to continue."

The minister sighed and nodded. "Tomorrow, we will issue an ultimatum for the Germans to withdraw from Poland or face war, as will France."

"But . . . will they listen?"

The lord wizard scoffed. "It's obvious they will not—they mean to have all of Europe, perhaps even more."

Her grandfather shook his head. "What is Wilhelm thinking? He swore to us that he wouldn't follow in his father's footsteps."

"Wilhelm might be kaiser," Churchill replied, "but I do not believe he still runs the empire. That chancellor of his is disturbingly ambitious, and he's somehow obtained the favor of the imperial hexmasters."

King George sat forward suddenly. "Whoever is b-behind the invasion, it is of n-n-no . . ." He trailed off with a sigh, and the lord wizard quickly handed him a small vial. Dwyn squinted at the potion as the king gulped it down—the king used smoothspeak?

The king coughed and then continued, handing the empty vial back to the lord wizard with a grateful nod. "The fact is, war is upon us—and this time, if we allow it to progress, it will be worse than before."

The room went silent. Dwyn stared at her mirror. Worse than the Great War, the war to end all wars? How could that even be possible?

"Worse?" her grandfather whispered.

Minister Chamberlain nodded. "It seems likely. The Germans and Italy are allied—Mussolini will join with Wilhelm, or whoever is running the empire. He'll likely make another grab for Ethiopia, and perhaps more of Africa."

"Japan has already invaded China—they'll take advantage of the chaos to push further." Churchill sighed and rubbed his face. "And we all know that Stalin fellow can't be trusted one whit either. The Soviets will move west while the Germans move east. I doubt we can count on them to wipe one another out."

Dwyn pulled her feet up onto her chair, hugging her knees as they continued to outline the precarious position the world was in. Another Great War. She closed her eyes, trembling, recalling the few memories she had of the war. Waving to her father as he walked away from the cottage, wearing green-and-black magical forces fatigues. Her mother enchanting fighter planes down at the factory. A late-night phone call, and falling asleep in her mother's arms as both of them wept.

She opened her eyes, blinking back tears, and shook her head. Why were they even discussing it? The German Empire had been acting increasingly belligerent for months. Surely the Ministry of Wizards had long since prepared a new peace ward. Why had they come to her grandfather?

Her grandfather was shaking his head. "But . . . the Peace Ward. You just need to get into Poland and make another peace ward, and things will calm down."

There was a brief silence, and then Chamberlain sighed. "That is why we've come to you, Arliss. The Ministry of Wizards, they . . . well . . ." he trailed off and glanced at the lord wizard.

"We cannot create a peace ward," Churchill said.

Dwyn stared. The expression on her grandfather's face was the same as what hers must have been.

"Why not?" he asked.

The lord wizard sighed and seemed to deflate and droop. "You may not have noticed, High Wizard, but . . . magic is on its way out, these days. Fewer and fewer new wizards come to the academies each year, and each of them is a bit weaker than the one before. I'm one of the most powerful magic-workers in the ministry, and I can barely manage to perform the simplest of the spells you left with us."

He shook his head and ran a hand over his balding scalp. "There are several theories as to why it's happening, but it doesn't really matter why right now. The fact is, you're the only man in Europe—possibly in the world—who can make a peace ward."

"High Wizard Arliss Bobydd," King George said, leaning forward with a grim expression, "you once saved the world from the greatest destruction that it had ever faced. Now, as your king, I must ask you to do it again."

Dwyn felt herself begin to tremble. They couldn't really be asking her grandfather to do that. Not at his age.

Her grandfather seemed thunderstruck, staring at the king slack-jawed. Then, after a moment, he pushed himself to his feet, his joints creaking and popping. He straightened his back, adjusted his robes, and then nodded. "Well, all right. I mean . . . of course. I'll do it."

* * *

"You can't do it," Dwyn said, trying to keep her voice level.

Her grandfather dug through a pile of books and newspapers. "You had no right to eavesdrop on that conversation," he said, his voice muffled by papers and years of dust. "What did you do to my wards? They should have kept you from prying."

"You don't have any wards, Grandda. I've told you a dozen times that I replaced them all after you let them decay."

They were in the top room of his tower, which was illuminated by a single lantern that Dwyn had enchanted months before to float over her grandfather's shoulder when it was lit. He, of course, thought that it was the lantern he'd enchanted himself over a decade ago. Outside, it was still night—the king and his retinue had returned to London, where her grandfather was to join them in another day.

"I know that book is in here somewhere," he muttered. "Mair, did you move it?"

"No, I didn't." Dwyn pulled him away from the pile and turned him to face her, trying to be patient. If she got mad, he would just become stubborn and ignore her all the more determinedly. "Grandda, you can't do this. When you made the Peace Ward, it left you bedridden for over half a year. Even if you could somehow get into Poland right now . . . if you try to make a peace ward in your current health, it could kill you."

"It will be fine, Mair," he grumbled, pushing her hands off his shoulders and turning back to the pile. "It will be easier to cast early in the war, before the fighting begins in earnest. I can handle it."

"I'm Dwyn," she said, more loudly than she'd intended. "Grandda, this is—"

"Where is that book?" he said, cutting her off. He glanced at her with a sudden look of angry realization. "I know what must've happened to it—it's those goblin neighbors of mine. They took it when they broke in here!"

Dwyn clenched her teeth and her fists. Of all the times for him to start in on that again . . . "No, they didn't, Grandda. It's just deeper in one of these rooms somewhere."

"Well, I can't believe this," her grandfather said, moving to the window that faced southeast over the rest of Cardiff, overlooking the cottage and their neighbor's house beyond it. "It's bad enough they've been taking my tools and ingredients, but I'm not going to stand by while they steal my books."

"The Jameses aren't stealing your books, Grandda!" Dwyn said, stalking over to stand beside him at the window. "They're good people, and far nicer to you than you deserve, the way you talk about them. Besides, the tower is warded—there's no way they could get in here without me knowing about it!"

"Well . . . you don't know goblins like I do," her grandfather replied, cupping his hands to peer out the window, as though he were going to catch someone in the act of sneaking through his garden. "They're tricky. I guess I'll have to go over there and get the book back—I just hope they'll give it up if I threaten to call the police."

Dwyn clenched her fists again. "No, that's a great idea," she said. "Let's call the police."

"What?" Her grandfather seemed taken aback.

"Let's call the police, Grandda," she repeated with all the insincere sweetness she could muster. "If they've stolen from you, then they should be arrested. We'll just call the police, and tell them the neighbors somehow broke into the warded tower of a high wizard and stole his spellbooks."

Her grandfather frowned. "Well, I don't want to get them thrown in jail. I just want my spellbook back."

"No, Grandda. If you're so sure that this is what happened, then we need to call the police."

Her grandfather looked back out the window and then hunched his shoulders. "Goblins would probably just trick the police, anyway," he muttered, turning back to the room. He shuffled to his bed and began digging through a pile of old clothing there. "I guess I'll just have to do it from memory, since someone doesn't want me to get my spellbook. You try to be good and decent in this world, but look what it gets you . . ."

Dwyn just managed to refrain from punching a stack of newspapers into the air. Instead, she closed her eyes and took a slow breath, carefully unclenching her fists and forcing the muscles to relax.

"Grandda, please listen to me," she said, opening her eyes. "You're not up to sneaking through a war zone anymore. You're not up to creating a peace ward again—you just aren't. It will kill you."

"Well, I have to try," her grandfather replied, frowning at her. "Even if I might die. The world is depending on it."

"Grandda . . ." Dwyn sighed and rubbed her face. "You can't do it."

"Oh, just stop it, Dwyn. You're as bad as your mother, always thinking about your own wants before the needs of others."

Dwyn froze, staring at her grandfather. "What did you say?"

"You just don't want me to leave." Her grandfather tugged a natty old robe free from the pile and held it up to the light. "Your mother was always doing that, after the Great War, stopping me from going out to help people like I used to. All she cared about was what she wanted."

"You think my mother was selfish?" Dwyn said. "You? You think that your daughter, who spent years looking after your needs and putting up with everything . . . you think she was selfish?"

"Oh, don't go acting like Mair was some sort of saint," her grandfather said. "She made me take care of the tower all by myself, even when I was sick, and I had to do most of the chores around the cottage too. Why, she once—"

"You can't perform a peace ward, Grandda!" Dwyn snapped. She was shaking.

Her grandfather rolled his eyes. "I already told you, I—"

"I'm not saying that you shouldn't, I'm saying that you can't!" Dwyn shouted over him. "You're not the lord wizard anymore— you are incapable! You can't tell when your wards have decayed; you can't even tell a weed from starleaf anymore!"

"Well . . ." her grandfather looked startled and confused. Dwyn should have cared; but she didn't.

"And this!" She stalked over to where his battered, cracked cauldron still lay on the workbench and dipped her finger into the remains of the potion he'd botched that morning—which he still hadn't cleaned up—holding it up for him to see. "What color is clearthought potion supposed to be, Grandda?"

Her grandfather stared at the brownish goop on her finger, his eyes unfocused and distant and his brow furrowed.

"It's supposed to be light blue!" she said, waving her finger. "This looks like you were trying to make a shapechange potion and failed completely! And you think you can create a peace ward again? From memory?"

Her grandfather hunched his shoulders and stuck his chin out stubbornly. "Well, that may be what you think, but—"

"What I think?" Dwyn shrieked. The room was growing blurry— there were tears in her eyes, she realized. The piles of junk were leaning in on her, and it was difficult to breathe. "Grandda, you blew up your tower today! I have to switch out all of the potions and spells you make for people with ones I've made, because the ones you make might kill them! You eat rotten food, you can't hear anymore, and you make up stories about the neighbors stealing from you . . . do you want to know what really happened to all of your missing things?"

Her grandfather simply stared at her.

"It's all buried somewhere in a senile old man's . . . useless . . . trash!" she screamed. She grabbed the table near the window and heaved, toppling it on its side. Dust-covered newspapers flopped across the floor, filling the narrow pathway from the worktable to the bed. Other odds and ends clattered into the wall and against her feet—glass marbles, forgotten cups and plates, a stack of old plaques and commendations, and a brown, decayed potted plant that had been covered up and forgotten.

Dwyn stared down at the mess. She put her hands over her mouth in horror, sobbing. After a moment, she forced herself to look up at her grandfather.

She caught a glimpse of painful, terrifying awareness on his face, and her breath stopped. His eyes were wet, just on the verge of spilling tears. Then his chin jutted out again and his eyes hardened. He turned away.

Dwyn ran from the tower, slipping and stumbling over newspapers and books.

* * *

She hid in her room. She didn't even make it onto the bed, instead ending up curled in a ball on the floor, crying. At one point, she heard her grandfather come into the cottage. He went to his room, and then his footsteps moved to the back of the house, to her workroom. Probably stealing supplies that he thought he needed. She didn't care. She just pushed herself into the corner and covered her face with her arms.

By the time the sun began to rise, she was cried out. Her body was sore, her head was pounding, and her face was plastered with crusty snot and the salt of dried tears. But she was finally calm enough to know what she had to do.

Her grandfather was going to try to create a peace ward; she clearly couldn't talk him out of it. But if he botched a spell of that magnitude, who knew what it would do. It wouldn't just put him in danger—the effects could cover all of Europe, perhaps more. She would have to warn the king, to let him know that her grandfather wasn't as capable as he'd once been. Maybe . . . maybe the king would keep it from getting around.

Dwyn stood, stiff and aching, and began to pack a small bag with a change of clothing and her toiletries. She would try to send a telegram to the king from the Cardiff station, of course; but she doubted that he would be taking messages from young dropout wizards at such a time of crisis, no matter who her grandfather had once been. She would have to go to London.

And then what? She paused her packing, thinking. Would her grandfather even want her around after she'd gone to the king? He had ignored her for days and even weeks over minor disagreements —it wasn't hard to believe that he wouldn't ever forgive her for ruining his reputation with the king.

Maybe Mrs. Reilly had been right—maybe she needed to find an elderly home for her grandfather. She certainly wouldn't mind having time for her studies; there was even the chance that she'd be able to get back into the academy, if she reapplied soon enough.

She sighed and shook her head, resuming her packing. Even after their argument, her stomach knotted up at the thought of sending her grandfather away, of taking away the last vestiges of his pride. But then, if he remained angry with her, it might be best for both of them.

With the bag over her shoulder, she left the cottage and began following the gravel path to the road. When she reached the gate, she glanced up at her grandfather's tower. The faint glow of his lamp still shone in the windows, only slightly washed out by the gray dawn.

Dwyn hesitated. If she did it, she wouldn't be able to take it back. For several minutes, she stood there on the path debating. She didn't want to face him again right then, but . . . maybe he would listen to reason. Maybe. At the very least, she felt like her mother would have tried again. Finally, she sighed and walked to the tower.

She climbed the stairs slowly and then paused in the doorway at the top. The table was still overturned, and the newspapers and other junk still cluttered the narrow pathway. But she was surprised to see that a new path had been cleared through the center of the room to the far wall.

The path led to a bookcase that she hadn't even known was there. Her grandfather sat beside it in a sturdy old rocking chair— her grandmother's, some distant part of Dwyn remembered. There was a pile of books beside the chair, and her grandfather held one open in his lap.

Hesitantly, Dwyn stepped forward to see what was in the book. She'd thought that maybe, somehow, he'd managed to find the spellbook that contained the peace ward. Instead, she was surprised to see that it was a dusty old photo album.

"You look so much like your mother, Dwyn," her grandfather said. He rested his hand on one of the photographs. It was of her parents at their wedding. "Did your parents ever tell you the story of how they met?"

Dwyn looked down at her grandfather, but his head was lowered over the book and she couldn't see his face. "Um . . . Dad was one of your students, wasn't he?" she asked. "He met Mum when you had her help you carry some equipment to the classroom?"

"I made her help me so that she would meet him," her grandfather said. She thought she could hear a faint smile in his voice. "He was one of my best students, so promising, but he was determined to remain a bachelor forever. I knew he'd change his mind when he met your mother."

"I hadn't heard that part."

"I never told them about it."

Dwyn smiled slightly. It wasn't often her grandfather was so lucid anymore; she'd forgotten how pleasant talking to him could be. It was a much better reaction than she'd expected.

Her grandfather turned a few pages; Dwyn noticed that he'd already had the spot marked with one finger.

"Do you remember this?" he asked.

She peered at the picture he was indicating—her, as a baby, sitting in her grandfather's lap and gnawing on a wooden charm.

"No," she admitted.

"That was an old flavor charm, for improving food and the like. Your mother let you play with it after it stopped working."

Dwyn squinted at the photo. "Wait, I do remember that. I carried that old thing around for years, didn't I? I still had it when I started primary school."

"Yes, you did."

"What ever happened to it?"

"One day, after you'd left for school, your mother found it hanging in the kitchen. You'd repaired it and put it there yourself."

Dwyn blinked. "Really? I don't remember that. How old was I?"

"Six." Her grandfather chuckled softly, shaking his head. "Your mother thought I had done it, at first. Then she thought I'd been teaching you behind her back, even though you were too young.

But no . . . you had been sneaking peeks at our spellbooks, and had figured out on your own what the flavor charm was supposed to look like and what it did. So you fixed it and hung it up in the kitchen."

He lifted his left hand, and she saw that he was holding the flavor charm itself.

"You still have it?" she asked.

He snorted. "Of course I do. It didn't work for too long, but for a child your age to manage that, without any instruction . . . we were so proud. Even your mother wanted to keep it, for the memory. We weren't surprised at how well you did when you went to the academy—you already knew most of the curriculum, by that point."

Dwyn blushed. "It's in our blood, I guess."

Her grandfather nodded. He looked up at her, and she was surprised at how . . . present his eyes were. She'd never realized just how distant his gaze tended to be lately. There was water in his eyes and faint tear tracks on his cheeks.

"Yes, that's the point I'm trying to make," he said. "The magic is in our family's blood. It's strong. You're strong, Dwyn." He set the charm on the photo album and then reached down beside the rocking chair, lifting a thick, leather-bound book from the floor. "You're probably the strongest wizard alive these days."

With a sad, slightly pained smile, he handed her the book. It was the spellbook that held the peace ward.

"You can perform it," he whispered. He leaned back in his chair, visibly exhausted. "I looked at the wards you have on the tower—they're excellent. A peace ward will be difficult, even agonizing . . . but you can manage it."

Dwyn stared at her grandfather. She looked at the book, then back at her grandfather, and frowned. Something was wrong.

"Grandda, what's going on?"

Her grandfather had begun to doze. He started and looked up at her, his eyes half closed. "You were right," he said, his voice slightly slurred. "I can't . . . can't manage it. S'why you have to go . . ." He began to nod off again.

"Grandda?" Dwyn stepped around the rocking chair to look him in the face, and her foot bumped something on the floor. She looked down—it was an almost-empty glass flask. One of her flasks from her workshop, not one of the old, stained bottles her grandfather used. And it held a few spoonfuls of pale blue liquid.

Dwyn went cold. "Clearthought?" she asked. "You . . . you drank the whole flask?"

"Was too much," her grandfather slurred.

"Grandda!" she shouted, jolting him awake for a moment. She grabbed his head and turned him to face her. "You can't . . . you have to stay awake! I'm going to get you some monkshroom, but you have to stay awake!"

"No," he replied, his voice faint. "Rubellum and some fae dust—should counteract the effect." He blinked, his eyes becoming alert for a moment. "I think. Double . . . double-check in that book there." He pointed weakly at the bookcase.

Dwyn scrambled for the book and tore through the pages, finally finding a list of overdose countermeasures scribbled in her grandfather's shaky handwriting. She squinted, trying to decipher the words. He'd been right—rubellum and fae dust, boiled in moonwater.

"Grandda, stay awake!" she shouted, shaking him. "Tell me more stories!"

"I was the lord wizard, once," he murmured, his head lolling back against the chair's headrest. "Did you know that?"

"Tell me all about it!" She stumbled across the room to his workbench and dug through his cupboards until she found the ingredients. When she hurried back to her grandfather, his eyes were closed again. "Grandda!" She forced some of the rubellum into his mouth, the yellow chunks crumbling across his lips. "Just a little rubellum should keep you alert without being poisonous, right? Right? Just chew that while I brew the rest!"

For a moment, he didn't move. Then, just when she was about to burst from holding her breath, he began to chew and swallow. It wouldn't be enough. Dwyn looked around for something that could buy her time. After a moment, she remembered her suspension powder. She pulled the bag from her waist and dumped some of the powder on her grandfather, whispering the words to freeze him in time. It would buy him twenty to thirty extra minutes.

The next half hour was a haze of lantern light and dust. She dug madly through the room until she found the cauldrons she'd given him for his birthday, still in the gift box. While the potion boiled, she lifted her frozen grandfather—he was frighteningly light—and moved him to his bed, clearing enough space with kicks and plentiful curses. He coughed as she set him down; the suspension was wearing off.

When the potion was ready, she spoon-fed it to him with his head in her lap. He had trouble swallowing, occasionally coughing it back up. She mopped his face with shaking hands and kept feeding him. He had to pull through—he was all she had.

When the potion was gone, she sat and held him, waiting for his eyes to open.

* * *

Her grandfather finally awoke around ten o'clock, when the sun through the window reached his face. Dwyn had moved to a chair beside the bed, and she sat forward and squeezed his hand.

"Grandda? Can you hear me?"

"Dwyn?" He turned his head, and his eyes slowly focused on her. "You need to go," he coughed. "I'll . . . I'll be fine with a little more rest."

"I know," she replied. She held his spellbook in her lap and had been studying the peace ward. As he'd said, it was enormously difficult, but . . . she did think she could do it. "Grandda . . . they're going to ask why you sent me to do it instead of coming yourself."

He looked at her, his expression confused and frightened. "Well . . . just . . . just . . ." After a moment, his face calmed and he forced a weak smile. "Just tell them the truth."

Dwyn tried not to cry. The clearthought was wearing off. Beneath the smile, she could see that he was sad, confused, and broken. She looked back at the spellbook, not wanting to watch him slip away again.

If she managed to create a peace ward and stop the coming war, she would be a hero. Her name would go down in history, just as her grandfather's had. The academy would probably welcome her back with open arms, if she decided to go, and it would be an easy path to being ordained a wizard of the realm and even a high wizard. Everything she'd wanted would all be within reach.

But things wouldn't suddenly be better between her and her grandfather; she had no illusions about that. He would forget, would argue and mishear, would be just as paranoid as before. Word would get around about his condition, and petitioners would stop coming. He would putter around the tower and wander the market, lonely and confused, upset by all the knowing looks that people gave him that he didn't understand. People would respect and honor the man he had been, but they would pity the man he had become.

"I saved the world once," he whispered, closing his eyes. "I think . . . now it's your turn."

Dwyn sat watching him as he dozed off to sleep again. She had years ahead of her to do what she wanted, but it was suddenly painfully clear to her that she didn't have years with her grandfather. She didn't care about saving the world—she just wanted to save him.

* * *

Dwyn spent the afternoon making potions. Most were for Mrs. Reilly to give her grandfather over the next few days—a little bit of fortitude each day, and some wellrest for the nights. She also made one other, an earthy-brown potion, which she took with her.

Her train ride was quiet, even grim. She only left her compartment once; as she moved through the passenger car, she saw newspapers bearing the grim announcement of invasion on the continent. She heard fearful, worried whispers of war.

Her train arrived in London late that night. Before she left the train, she drank the brown potion of shapechange she'd made that afternoon. The conductor seemed confused when the old man stepped out of the compartment that had held a young woman only a few hours before.

People pointed at her as she left the train station, whispering in awe and hope. "High Wizard," greeted the coachman that had been sent to pick her up. Dwyn nodded to him with a smile and climbed into the carriage. As the coach pulled away from the station, she clutched her grandfather's spellbook to her chest with gnarled, shaking hands.

High Wizard Arliss Bobydd would save the world one more time.

About Christopher Baxter

Christopher Baxter got in trouble for reading novels in class from kindergarten through high school. He began writing stories in class to stop his teachers from getting upset (since it looked like he was taking notes). He works as an editor and a writer, and he gives tips on common writing errors and composing better prose on his blog, *The Story Polisher:* storypolisher.blogspot.com. He is blessed with the best wife and two adorable little boys.

LADY OF WAR

By Caitlyn McFarland | 12,100 words

LEANING AGAINST THE cutting wind, Riona raised a thumb and closed one eye, then opened it and closed the other, gauging the distance to the black cloud that darkened the sky to the east. Her horse danced, its hooves crunching the brittle blanket of snow spread over the clifftop. Riona jerked down on the reins and heeled the dappled gray stallion in the flanks until he stilled.

She turned to the knot of people huddled fifty feet down the slope. Dagny, the dragonskin woman who'd been assigned to attend her, sat on a bay gelding apart from the gray-clad members of the Queensguard, who lounged on their horses as if at a picnic.

Riona couldn't remember the last time she'd lounged.

Slouching means a switching, girl, I don't care whose blood you've got! Riona bit down on her back teeth, raising a mental shield against the memories. A thousand willow switches, fire-heated pokers, shoves into the stale blackness beneath the cathedral. The voice, like a razor edged in ice. *No one likes you. Not the cinan, not even the guards. They think you're incompetent. I think they're right.*

Riona gritted her teeth and turned back to the black cloud, tying down the voice and shoving it into the deep recesses of her mind. It was a storm. Had to be. Though . . . it didn't move like any storm she'd ever seen.

The sound of hooves startled her. Dagny reined in at Riona's side and peered out over the sea of trees and mist beyond the cliffs. The dragonskin woman's eyes—like a rock lizard's, with their diamond-shaped pupils—darted across the horizon. Two years with Dagny had done little to acclimate Riona to her alien sort of beauty. Human, except for those eyes and the shimmering scales that dusted the angles of her face and flowed over her arms from shoulder to fingertip—both features a match for the blue of the winter-washed sky.

"Sweet Fires," Dagny breathed. "Those are birds. War-birds and crows and carrion eaters."

Riona glanced from the dragonskin to the cloud, a frown pinching the skin between her brows. "It is a storm."

Dagny opened her mouth, then, looking uneasy, closed it again.

Riona slid down from the horse, jarring her legs when she landed on the cold, stony earth. A thousand feet below, the city of Crann Laith tumbled like spilled bone dice from the black cup of the canyon. It was as siege ready as she could make it—almost. She still hadn't laid the pretend bloody wards.

"Do you worry for your mother?" Dagny asked.

"What?"

"The birds. They're right over the place where the armies must be. Do you worry for the queen?"

Riona cast her a disdainful look. "Queen Eilis is not my mother."

Dagny's voice went soft. "Morna Brannon is out there too."

Riona flinched. Her true mother's name was a needle beneath her skin. She turned away before Dagny could see that she'd struck a nerve. Riona should call up one of the Queensguard and have them take the woman away. The problem was, she hadn't bothered to learn any of their names. "I don't know Morna Brannon well enough to care. Nor you well enough to speak of such things."

The scales on Dagny's cheeks turned a deeper shade of blue, but her eyes did not look contrite, they looked annoyed. "Apologies, Queen-heir."

Awkward silence fell. When Dagny spoke again, it was either to the sky, or herself. "When birds black the skies, War is coming. When the blood-winds rise, War is coming."

Souls, not that miserable ballad. "Makkah's Rise" was the most depressing story in all the Wilding histories. Besides, it wasn't birds, it was a storm. And war wasn't coming, it was upon them. Ten thousand Andrisi invaders moved through the Wildwood. And here was Riona, left behind to "ensure the city's defense."

Riona turned her attention back to Crann Laith. Its blocky white-stone buildings flowed in a wide triangle out from the canyon mouth with the river Eyea. Talonkeep and the cathedral sat at its apex, the rest of the city spreading out into the river basin until it hit

DEEP MAGIC ANTHOLOGY ONE

the curving wall that stretched from one side of the canyon to the other, a dam that had leaked small houses and farms over the years.

Where to make a show of putting the powerless wards? Queen Eilis had only agreed to them to appease the cinan—the thirty-odd women who led the Wilding clans. And because she knew *she* wouldn't be the one to stand there for an hour with her hand on a wall while a charlatan chanted at her. All Wilding magic—when they'd had it—could only be channeled through someone with the queensmark. Only two people with the queensmark ever lived at a time—in this time, it was Riona and Eilis. In Riona's opinion, that meant it had always been useless, even when magic had mattered.

Riona frowned at the birds—no—the storm. Magic was dead, or close enough that it was completely obsolete. Despite her heart-mother's orders—Riona had left the wards for last. A small victory.

When it came to Eilis, she'd take what she could get.

"Get out of the way! Let me pass!"

Riona and Dagny turned. Below, a dark-haired man leaped from a sweating horse and pushed against the guards, who'd drawn their bronze swords against him.

"Did you expect a messenger?" Dagny asked.

Instead of answering, Riona urged her horse down the stony slope. The man was tall. A green coat showed in patches beneath a layer of muck.

"Faolan Cuillin? Why aren't you with your cinan at the front?" Riona waved away the women of the Queensguard and their swords.

Faolan surged forward. Twin brother to Brigid, the cinan of Clan Cuillin, the scout was a few years older than Riona. He was usually handsome, but now he was sweat soaked and wild-eyed. He dropped to his knees and pressed his forehead to the icy earth.

Riona yanked her stallion to a stop, her stomach lurching. That was not the greeting for the heir.

It was a greeting for the queen.

Oh souls. Eilis.

"Rise," she whispered.

Faolan lifted his head, but didn't stand. Riona's stomach twisted again. Beneath the mask of grime and blood, the man's face was contorted with terror and grief.

"Speak," Riona commanded.

His mouth worked, but no sound emerged.

"Speak!"

249

He met her eyes. In that look, Riona saw something akin to a dagger flying toward her heart, and she knew there was nothing she could do to stop it.

He pressed shaking hands into the snow, as if holding himself up. "A message from Brigid, cinan of Cuillin. Queen Eilis nich Dalaigh"—he swallowed—"is dead."

The mountain might have crumbled beneath Riona. Lightning could have struck. The breath been taken from her body. She pressed the heels of her hands into her stomach to stop the sudden sharp pain. "Eilis . . . is dead?"

You hate me, girl? I think you love me, and hate yourself because of it.

The guards dropped to their knees in the same bow as Faolan. Only Dagny remained standing, watching.

Faolan opened one of his clenched fists. A silvermask owl feather was nestled in his palm, the same size and shape as the birthmark on Riona's neck. Once a generation, a Wilding girl child was born bearing the mark of the feather somewhere on her body—the mark that named her the next Wilding queen.

Despite the journey, the feather in Faolan's hand shone bright, the silver marred by a few rust-colored specks. His voice was rough and low. "Long fly, Queen Riona nich Brannon."

As if pushing through pine sap, Riona took the mangled feather. Silvermask owls did not have speckles. Those spots . . . they were Eilis's blood. Riona's ribs closed around her heart like a vise. Her breath came in short, sharp bursts of fog, snatched in an instant by the wind. "How?"

Eilis is dead.

Mentor, heart-mother.

Ha. There had never been any heart in her. But there had been moments. Fleeting, rare. Once in a great while, Riona would catch the flash of approval in the hard queen's eyes. Every time she saw it, she'd craved more. For all she hated Eilis, she would have died to make the old queen love her.

The cloud caught Riona's eye, reminding her that the Andrisi were still there, invaders still tried to take the Wildwood. She had the sudden mad urge to scream. *What am I supposed to do?*

As if in response, the cold wind slapped her face hard enough to steal her breath and snatch back her hood. Dark brown hair escaped her braided crown and whipped her face. Riona grabbed the wolf-skin hood, clutching it hard.

Then, instead of drawing it back over her head, she let it go. She opened her palm, pinching the mangled owl feather in place with her thumb to keep it from the greedy wind. Reaching up with her other hand, she tugged one of the golden eagle feathers from the leather thong wrapped into her braid and slid the owl feather in.

Eilis is dead. Riona couldn't bear it. Her heart was a rock in her chest. Her heart was an empty void. Her heart was . . .

Lighter.

Eilis is gone.

For twenty years, her life had bent toward this moment.

No more queen-heir. No more powerless, lonely girl, to be whipped and burned and slapped and locked in dark tunnels.

Riona nich Brannon. Queen of the Wildwood and Mountain Reach.

Riona forced her back straight and marched to the cliff's edge, where she looked down on the city once more. She inhaled frozen air through her nose, filling her chest. "It's *my* time."

"Queen Riona?"

Faolan's voice called her back. He'd risen. As she approached, he pulled a long, cloth-wrapped bundle from the back of his horse's saddle. Tawny eyes downcast, Faolan settled the weight of the bundle into her hands. Riona flipped back the oilcloth.

"*Cravh*," she breathed. The bone-shard sword.

She pressed the pad of her thumb to the cutting edge. Even after a thousand years, Frenna's blade was sharp enough to draw blood. The droplet gleamed, poppy-scarlet against the frost-white blade.

"There is more," Faolan said. An expression crossed the scout's face that Riona couldn't name. "She was killed by Makkah. The Lady of War."

Dagny gripped her skirts in white-knuckled hands. "The birds. I told you. War comes."

Riona's grief and elation dissipated. Her lip curled. "You dare lie?" she hissed at Faolan. "In your sister's name? To *me?*" She had grown up cloistered, not stupid. Makkah was a myth children used to scare each other. One of the Incarnations—beings formed at the dawn of time by human desire. Makkah was the Incarnation of War, a creature comprised of bloodlust and death.

"I do not." In a shaking hand, Faolan held out a letter with Cuillin's seal: a long-haired maiden in armor pressed into moss-green wax.

Riona snatched the letter and broke the seal.

To Riona nich Brannon, Queen of the Wildwood and Mountain Reach:

Queen Eilis nich Dalaigh has fallen. You will not believe Faolan, but I swear on the souls of my clan mothers, he speaks the truth. Makkah, Lady of War, is real, and she killed our queen.

The rest of the letter spoke of the battle. How the Andrisi were retreating until a winged woman appeared in the sky and began killing Wilding warriors with her bare hands, then snapped Eilis's neck where she sat on her horse a hundred yards from the thick of the fighting. Riona rubbed her own neck, imagining Eilis in that last moment. Brigid continued.

"Deliver this message to Frenna," the winged woman said. "Our game has long lain neglected, but it is not ended. I give her the throne, and play resumes."

Frenna. Truly? A legendary monster had returned, and she thought Riona was the First Queen? Yes, Clan Brannon bore Frenna's blood, but it had been a thousand years since Frenna had lived.

Riona's fingers tightened, crumpling the letter. This nonsense would cause a panic. Divide the cinan, who'd already be in upheaval at Eilis's death. Some would use it to their advantage, swoop in and try to snatch power. There had been queens in the past who had been ruled by the council, or a few powerful cinan.

Riona would not be one of those queens.

She pressed her fingertips to her temples. She hadn't replaced her hood, and the tips of her ears felt like ice. "Obviously, the Andrisi have heard our legends and come up with a clever ruse. They've probably got some woman with false wings swinging from a rope they've flung over a tree branch. We must not fall for it."

Faolan stepped forward, stopping when the guards drew their swords. "No! I was there. I saw—"

Riona silenced him with a glare and a flick of her hand. "You will *not* cause a panic." She met the guards' eyes, then Dagny's. "Tell no one what this man has said. The Lady of War is a trick the Andrisi are using to make us afraid."

Hundreds of others would have had seen the trick too. Riona wouldn't be able to keep the secret once the main body of Wilding fighters returned. Rumor would spread, but she would slow it as much as she could. She wrapped her hand around Cravh's hilt. It felt good to touch the sword. "I can—I mean—our people can handle anything the Andrisi fling at me. Us." She would guide them.

Show them. Make them listen. Belatedly, she added, "For Queen Eilis."

A flicker of unease crossed the faces before her. Faolan looked unhappy, but he held his tongue. Good. Eilis had not taught her much, but Riona knew a queen had to be decisive, strong, and never bending.

"Go back down to Crann Laith," Riona said to him. "Give your message to Steward Keelin. Except for the part about Makkah." One of Eilis's lackeys, the old woman would take the queen's fall hard. Riona felt a pang of sympathy, but it didn't last long. Keelin had been just as quick with a slap as Eilis.

"Your word is my will, Queen Riona." Face a neutral mask, Faolan Cuillin swung into the saddle and rode down the mountain.

Queen Riona. The birds—they were birds, she saw now, but birds were to be expected when there had been so much death—massed over the place where Eilis had met her end. She'd heard the Andrisi thought the Wildwood was haunted—it was one of the reasons their invasion hadn't come years before.

Perhaps Riona would fill her forests with their ghosts.

Next to her, Dagny's mouth slanted into something that was neither smile nor frown. "So, it's your turn. Will you join the ranks of the great queens?"

"The great queens?" Riona pulled herself onto her gray stallion, rolling over the words. Her childhood had been full of pain. Her present was dark. But she had intelligence, iron will, political savvy, and independence. That was another of Eilis's lessons: Do not need anyone, do not trust anyone. Power shared was power lost.

Riona smiled at Dagny. The expression was unfamiliar on her lips. "Yes. I will."

* * *

Riona stood just inside the massive wooden doors of the entrance to the cathedral situated at the highest point of Crann Laith. Cold wind and muted morning light streamed in around her. Coupled with the murmurs—as soft as a breeze through the forest—Riona felt as if she were stepping into the Underwood.

Far ahead, an eternity ahead, Steward Keelin Mochain—an iron wisp of a woman and the second greatest tormentor of Riona's childhood—raised her hands for silence.

A thousand faces turned toward Riona. A thousand clanswomen and clansmen robed in white, with only flashes of clan colors visible on arms or shoulders, ever shifting, like jewels half buried in wind-driven snow.

So many people.

You think you *are fit to be queen, girl?*

Riona resisted the urge to swat at the voice in her mind as she might a buzzing fly. Eilis's words had always haunted her, even in life, but since the night before—since the burning of the old queen's body—it had been worse. As if Eilis knew her funeral had been little more than a few platitudes and a bonfire. As if she knew Riona hadn't been able to pull back the shroud and look at her face.

You're a coward, girl. You are weak.

Blue and violet light fell across the dais, slanting over the pedestal at its center where the tall urn containing Eilis's ashes sat. Fitting—the fallen queen present to witness a new queen's rise.

The air warmed with every step Riona took away from the open doors. The peeling murals on the ceiling and walls watched her. With every step, history pressed down on her. Watching, like the people.

You are nothing, girl.

No. I am Riona Brannon. The first of Frenna's line to bear the queensmark for a thousand years. The first Brannon to wield the bone-shard sword.

Riona touched the silken fabric of her white gown, glimmering at hem, neck, and sleeves with silver. The freedom of a skirt was strange, the train cumbersome and heavy. A band of silvermask owl feathers circled her head, with more feathers and silver threads woven into her dark braid, left long down her back.

All the women of the clans wore feathers—eagle, hawk, osprey, and kite—as a sign of rank. Before today, Riona had worn eagle feathers, marking her equal in rank to the clan leaders, though the queensmark said she had no clan.

Now, she had no equal.

Riona trained her eyes on the dais. She would not look for Clan Brannon. Would not check to see if Morna, their cinan—her blood-mother—watched. If she looked proud.

Souls, how Riona had dreamed of this moment. She would rise, and the darkness that plagued her childhood would be washed away in power.

Riona reached the dais and climbed the stairs with shoulders back, head high. On the pedestal next to the urn sat a silver circlet, sparkling with a single sapphire.

Keelin raised her hands. "Today we crown Riona nich Brannon, daughter of Eilis—"

Daughter of Eilis, indeed.

"—Queen of the Wildwoods and Mountain Reach, ruler over the Wildings and the remnant of the dragonskin—"

On the wall behind the dais, an ancient mural depicted Queen Frenna, lithe and dark haired, clasping hands with a dragonskin man. Torsten, the Sleeping King. Real gold had been used to pick out the scales on the backs of his hands, to highlight his shining hair. The artist had made Frenna as tall as he was. Ha. Dagny and Eilis's old dragonskin companion—an emerald-scaled woman called Thone—stood half a head taller than the tallest Wildings. Riona could only assume a dragonskin male would tower.

"—since the defeat of Makkah, when Frenna united the Wilding clans—"

Below the first mural, a second depicted the dragonskin king's tomb. He lay there, still. Not in death—supposedly—but in sleep. Waiting until he was needed, carrying with him the knowledge of how to defeat Makkah.

Bah.

"—never replace Queen Eilis, glorious and illustrious, beloved from the mountainous nest of Crann Laith down to the sea—"

Under different circumstances, Riona would be making a pilgrimage to that tomb tomorrow. Tradition and superstition dictated that every new Wilding queen visit the Sleeping King, lift the crystal lid of his coffin, and kiss his lips. Disgusting. She should thank the Andrisi for leaving her no time to trek to the ruins and kiss a scaly, thousand-year-old dustbag.

Riona started when Keelin placed the circlet in her hands. She jerked back from the older woman's clawlike grip. Tightening her fingers around the hard metal, Riona looked out at the crowd, their dark hair and pale faces interrupted every now and then by a tall, brightly scaled dragonskin.

Stop crying, girl. No wonder you are alone.

Their hungry eyes devoured her. Every single one of them. They needed her. To be wise. To do the right thing. To protect them. Their heavy stares joined the weight of those in the murals, pushing her down. The room tilted. *Breathe. Breathe. Breathe . . .*

There was a children's game in the Wildwood. The daring would climb two close trees and leap from the branches of one to the other. The person who jumped from the highest, leanest, farthest apart branches was the winner. For safety's sake, a net was strung among the low branches to catch the one who fell.

In that moment, Riona realized that Eilis had been her net. A net of razors, but still.

Eilis was gone.

I need no one.

Of its own accord, Riona's gaze searched out the ocean blue of Clan Brannon. Each of the seafarers wore an embroidered spiral of waves somewhere on their mourning white, or a blue band around an upper arm, or a vest of azure leather.

And there was Morna Brannon. There was nothing spectacular about her. Middle-aged, medium height, weathered face, sturdy build. But in her gaze—as there had been on the few occasions they'd met—Riona saw something that Eilis had never given her.

Warmth.

Riona set the circlet on her head, perching it amongst the silver feathers, and lowered herself into a bow to the assembled people.

"Long fly, Queen Riona!" shouted someone in the crowd.

The answering cry echoed loud enough to shake down the mountains. "Long fly, Queen Riona!"

Oratory was not one of Riona's strengths, so she skipped parts of the speech that Keelin had written for her. She glanced at the woman every time she did, watching the old snake's frown deepen as Riona glossed over a sentence or skipped an anecdote about the greatness Eilis had instilled in her. Candied-petal speeches had never sat well on Riona's tongue, and Keelin couldn't take a fogwood switch to her bare back anymore.

Riona finished and stepped down from the dais. The people bowed in a wave before her. She would exit the cathedral and make her way to the keep across the square. There, she would meet with her cinan. She would turn the tide of the war.

When she was halfway down the aisle, the dais exploded.

Riona flew forward. She landed hard on her elbows and tasted blood. Dust billowed, chunks of rock shrieked in every direction. A hot, stinging pain sliced her cheek, her shoulder, the back of her hand. Shouts of shock and pain ricocheted off the vaulted ceiling. Benches banged against the stone floor.

Riona rose. In the same motion, she drew the bone-shard sword. "Up, warriors of the Wildwood! To me!" She wasn't sure if anyone could hear her.

She took stock of what she could see. The dais had become a waist-deep crater. People clustered all around, clogging the aisle like a herd of terrified cows. If she wasn't careful, Cravh's blade would draw innocent blood. The skin on the back of her neck prickled. Where was the enemy?

A cawing laugh cracked the air. Riona whirled. In the center of the tall, open cathedral doors, her red-stained bare feet ten paces off the ground, a woman hovered. A woman with wings.

Riona's hand went slack. The tip of Cravh's blade clinked against the stone floor.

For a moment, everything was perfectly still.

"Makkah!" someone close on Riona's left wailed. Others took it up until it was deafening. "The Crow!" "The Lady of War!"

Riona wanted to shout at them to stop, that this was a trick. There was a rope, a wire. Panic would serve nothing except to kill them all.

Then, with a thrust of those powerful, night-black wings, the woman in the door swooped inside.

Riona's heart stopped. There was no wire, no rope that could allow the apparition to move like that—she flew.

"Where have you gone, queen child?" The monster's voice lilted so that every word was a song. It took Riona a moment to realize what she'd said, because she spoke the dead language of the ancient dragonskin empire. Hearing it out loud was nothing like reading it in books. Of the hundreds of people present, only a handful would understand. Eilis's lessons ensured Riona was one of them.

Makkah—Riona could think of nothing else to call her—circled the vast space, weaving through columns. As old as humanity itself, the legends said. But Makkah looked no older than Riona's own twenty years. Thick hair the color of night streamed to her waist in waves. Exquisite, feathered wings sprung from her back, black as a lightless void. Her dress was crimson, her feet and her hands stained to wrists and ankles with the rust brown of old blood.

Riona grabbed the closest fighter, a man whose face was ghostly with dust. "Go around the side. Get the artisans and children out."

He nodded, then crouched and shuffled forward. He didn't make it ten feet.

Makkah folded her glossy wings and slammed to the ground before him. With a glorious smile, she lifted a hand and intoned a line from "Makkah's Rise." "And without touch, men fell before her, dead."

The man's head snapped to one side, and he collapsed. A woman screamed. Riona clutched Cravh's hilt so hard its edges bit into her palm.

"Where is the child queen?"

Souls save me.

Makkah gestured sharply. The cathedral doors slammed shut, cutting off all escape.

Souls save us all .

There was a way out, but it was too small for all these people, and Riona's soul shrank from the memory of the stale air, of a darkness so complete she thought she could feel it clinging to her skin.

Thrusting aside the memory, Riona stood to her full height and raised the bone-shard sword. "Here I am."

"Aha! Yes. There you are." Makkah bent at the waist and presented both hands, palm up, in an ancient dragonskin greeting. She straightened, her terrible grin softening into something beneficent, something beautiful. The radiance of it nearly brought Riona to her knees. Beside her, one of the men did fall. Another stumbled forward. His cinan grabbed him by the collar and jerked him back. Another of the cinan—Morna Brannon, Riona thought—pulled the fallen man to his feet.

Watching how the men stared at the woman before them, eyes vacant, another line from "Makkah's Rise" sighed through Riona's mind: *And when War came in her glory, the kingdoms of men were the first to fall. The Wildings saw, and chose from the clanswomen Frenna, and Frenna chose from them her cinan.*

Makkah Bloodlust, Lady of War, Destroyer of Nations, gestured to Riona with slender, graceful fingers. "Come here."

Fear blossomed in Riona's heart, a poisonous flower. Anger at her own cowardice boiled through her, withering the sharp edges of the icy bloom. But it would not die.

She stepped forward anyway. Someone behind her made a sound. Morna? But it didn't matter. *This is my time.* Another step. Another. Until she was five paces from the Crow. She smelled like iron—like blood.

Riona lifted her chin. "Why have you come?"

Makkah's mouth twisted into a grimace of sympathy, as if Riona were simple, and her simpleness was sad. "You have called me."

Riona made a noise of disdain. "Called you? You are a myth. We have no more called you than we could call the Old Men of the Forest, or the water horses, or the dead."

"Your blood calls me. Frenna's blood. I've felt it for years. Here." She pulled aside the neck of her dress and indicated a long, jagged white scar just below her collarbone. "A gift given me by *that*."

Cravh glinted in the dull light from the windows, and Makkah glared at it as if it were a poisonous snake. "So I finished my game elsewhere, and then I came here. Besides," Makkah wagged a finger at Riona, "Your former queen thought she had conquered Mountain Reach, but Mountain Reach is mine. It's part of my dragonskin empire. It's where they hid Torsten and his nightmares." Her voice dropped to a growl, her eyes gleaming and feral. "He is mine too."

Riona almost laughed. "You want the Sleeping King? Have him!"

Makkah pouted. "There's no fun in that. We must have war!"

"Have it, then!" Riona leaped onto the back of a bench and threw herself at the hovering woman, Cravh flashing up.

She slammed into an invisible force before she could strike. The force plucked her away from Makkah and flung her back all the way across the cathedral. Her head and shoulder struck the wall behind the shattered dais with a hollow thud. Pain split her skull. Sparks exploded in her vision. People were screaming again.

Makkah laughed, a cawing, ugly sound. Feet slapped against the floor. A presence hovered over Riona. When she opened her eyes, Makkah crouched almost on top of her. She caressed Riona's cheek with clammy fingers. Riona flinched away, and the movement made her gag.

Makkah's nails scraped Riona's skin. "I like pretty things." The Incarnation of War sighed and smiled, as if remembering something sweet. "Death will make you beautiful."

"Why have you come?" Riona asked again, fighting the urge to vomit. "To warn me? We know the Andrisi are coming. To kill me in front of my people, the way you did Eilis?" Riona spat blood. "You missed."

Makkah leaned close, wide eyes fixed on Riona's mouth. "Eilis had to be punished for Mountain Reach. But you must live, because we are going to have a game. I must know who I am playing against. Opponents should meet."

The Lady of War brought one finger to the trickle of warmth leaking from the corner of Riona's lips. When the Crow took her finger away, it was stained crimson. She popped it into her mouth and closed her eyes, inhaling deeply, then let her hand drop. Her metallic tang stung Riona's nostrils, her hot breath caressed Riona's ear. "Tomorrow, I bring the Andrisi to your city, and the game resumes. Just a quick one, for old times' sake. Greater things call me south, but I have made time for you. Farewell, Frenna's blood."

The Lady of War vanished, leaving nothing but a few black feathers that drifted slowly to rest on shattered stone.

*　*　*

The Court of Eagles was misty and chill. Like the cathedral, the largest room in Talonkeep had mural-painted stone walls and a high, arching ceiling. Four living fogwood trees forked toward the ceiling in each corner, silver leaves long gone with winter. The great table and chairs at the center of the room were made of the wood as well, twisted and bound together, the table topped with a long slab of whorled marble.

In the hour since Makkah had disappeared, Riona had changed from the torn dress into a white tunic and leggings, over which she wore the royal armor—gray leather and hardened fogwood etched with silver. On her head, she still wore the circlet and silvermask owl feathers.

When Riona approached the table, the cinan stood, the gnarled wooden chairs scraping softly against the stone floor. As one, each clan leader touched the first two fingers of her right hand to her lips, then heart. Eagle feathers gleamed in braids of bark brown and mahogany and cloudy gray. "Long fly, Queen Riona."

"Long fly, cinan of the Wildwood." Riona's voice was clear. Good. She'd been having trouble with it since . . .

Makkah. Real. Souls, she was real.

Magic was supposed to be dead.

Riona shook off the numbing terror of seeing War up close and opened her mouth to speak. Before she could, Nessa Dalaigh slapped the tabletop with a sharp crack. "We must evacuate the people!"

Riona started, mouth snapping shut. The oldest woman there, Cinan Dalaigh's dark hair had gone stormy gray, and her wrinkles were deep enough to hide coins. Unfortunately, her eyes were still as clear as the distant blue sea.

Eilis had been from Clan Dalaigh. Eilis had had those eyes.

Riona opened her mouth again, but another cinan spoke first. "Are you mad, you old bat? Let the Andrisi beat themselves bloody against our walls. They'll give up and turn home once half of them are dead. Crann Laith has stood for a thousand years, and it will stand a thousand more!"

Riona clenched her teeth.

"Makkah makes them battle mad." Brigid Cuillin was stony faced, her voice resonant enough to be heard easily from her place halfway down the table. "I've seen it. They throw themselves at death like fish trying to return to the sea. She doesn't care to take our land, she cares about causing as many deaths as she can. That's her 'game.' This will be no ordinary siege. It won't end until every Andrisi soldier is dead or Crann Laith has been torn down stone by stone."

Another woman made a sound of disdain. "Impossible. We'll be in far greater danger if we leave. They'll hunt us as foxes who've lost their holes."

"If we stay, you will see the end of our people!" Nessa barked at the other cinan.

"It's the end of times!" wailed one of the women who stood behind the chairs, too minor to have a seat at the table.

"You would have us give up our homes, our walls, our greatest strength," another woman snapped at Nessa.

"Weak is better than dead!"

Heat spread through Riona's cheeks. She must take control. "I —"

"Queen Riona is young and strong. We can beat the Crow and anything she can throw at us."

Nessa barked a laugh. "The Lady of War can snap a neck and demolish rock without a touch. What will the infant queen do against that?"

Silence fell and all eyes turned to Riona. She should speak, but her words had gone. What *could* she do against that?

Souls, were the wards as powerless as she'd thought? If she had allowed the setting ceremonies, would the Makkah have been able to enter the city?

"There's the pilgrimage," Morna Brannon said. "The new queen has yet to visit the Sleeping King."

"The pilgrimage?" Riona repeated like an idiot.

One setback and this is how you react, girl? I knew it, you aren't fit to rule.

Riona shook herself, brows furrowing. *This is my time.* "You refer to the prophecy." She'd had no idea Morna believed in such things. The revelation was . . . disappointing. "One Incarnate doesn't make every myth into truth. If Makkah"—souls of the Underwood, she couldn't believe she was saying that name with a straight face —"spoke truly, the Andrisi will be here tomorrow. I must take that time to further improve Crann Laith's defense and see to the welfare of the people inside its walls. Not go traipsing around the mountains, hoping for a savior."

Morna frowned, perhaps as unpleasantly surprised to find Riona a skeptic as Riona was to find Morna superstitious. "The Sleeping King has fought the Crow before. He knows how to defeat her."

"If he wakes," muttered one of the cinan on Riona's left.

"I think—" began Morna Brannon.

Riona raised a hand. "Cinan Brannon, *we have no time*. The Andrisi arrive with the sun. It's a day's journey to the dragonskin tomb. By the time we get back—most likely without the Sleeping King and whatever powers he has—I might not be able to reenter the city."

Nessa Dalaigh snorted. "Are you necessary?"

Riona rose. For a second time, the women in the room fell silent. "Mind how you speak to your queen."

The old woman's lips pursed, but she didn't reply.

Riona allowed the quiet to stretch until it was uncomfortable. Perhaps they should send everyone who could run into the forest, get them on the road to Clan Cuillin's stronghold at Cahair Scoth. It was deeper in the forest. The Andrisi might not reach it before the winter snows drove them from the Wildwood for a season. It could buy them time.

But Eilis had never run. *Showing your back is weak, girl.* Riona straightened. "We will stay."

Nessa sneered. "You hesitate! You are uncertain. Queen Eilis would not—"

Anger flamed through Riona. She gripped Cravh and drew it halfway from its sheath. "Eilis is dead. And she never used half her brain if she could use her sword instead." Or a rod. Or a belt. Or her hand.

Nessa's mouth fell open. Clan Dalaigh was the most powerful of the Wildwood clans. In all her years, she had probably never been spoken to in such a way. Even Eilis had shown her respect. "You dare—?"

Riona's nostrils flared. The clans were hers. The Wildwood was hers. Riona would teach them to respect her, and then she would save them. Even if she had to drag them, kicking and screaming, to their salvation. "*I* am Queen of the Wildwood and Mountain Reach.

You will listen and obey, old woman, or you will leave this room without your tongue!"

A gasp. Mutters. Riona let her glare range the room, and the whispers ceased. She turned back to Nessa. "Well?"

Nessa bared what remained of her teeth. "As you say, my queen."

"Exactly. As *I* say." Strong leadership, unity. That was key. They would fall apart if she was not strong.

Riona took a calming breath. When she spoke again, her voice was even, and everyone listened. "We are the Wildwood. We stay and fight. Now, report. How many warriors do we have, and in what state are their weapons?"

Morna Brannon tried again, once, then twice, then a third time to speak, repeating her plea for Riona to visit the sleeping dragonskin king. Riona did her best to ignore her.

There was much to do.

* * *

Riona had expected the Andrisi to come from the east, not the west—Andris lay to the east, after all. She'd pulled men from the western curve of the wall to defend the city's eastern side. When the first soldiers emerged from the trees in the opposite direction, a trickling fear chilled her heart. Like angry bees in their yellow and black, the Andrisi were easy to see even through a flurry of fat, wet snow. "Send more bowman to the western wall!"

And still, hours into the battle, Makkah was nowhere to be seen.

The pages switched the flags on the east-facing side of the tower. Through her spyglass, Riona saw the soldiers on the eastern wall move, a contingent in Brannon blue leaving the wall top by the stairs and heading west through the city's streets.

The six most powerful cinan and a handful of cinan-heirs watched with her from the flat-topped tower that was the highest point of Talonkeep, Morna Brannon and Nessa Dalaigh among them. They passed Morna's spyglass between them, muttering and conferring. Next to Riona, pages stood ready to change the four sets of multicolored flags hung just below the lip on each side of the tower. Similar flags hung at intervals on the inside of the city wall, an easy way to relay changing commands.

"They don't even have ladders." Morna passed the spyglass to her daughter, Liadan. "And yet they throw themselves at us. Something is wrong with them."

Riona tried not to look at the girl who should have been her sister. At seventeen, Liadan wasn't quite ready to command the

Brannon fighters. So she shadowed her mother as Riona had shadowed Eilis.

Somehow, she doubted the experience was the same.

Boom .

"Souls of the Second Hell!" Nessa bellowed.

Riona whirled back to the western wall. A great, billowing cloud blocked her view, like the dust and smoke from the exploding dais, but a hundred times the size.

The dust streamed toward the forest in the breeze from the canyon. And when it cleared . . .

"I think we've left the Second Hell behind," Brigid Cuillin whispered.

Boom. Another deafening roar and the bone-jarring crack of breaking stone. Another section of the western wall fell. In the rising dust, Riona thought she saw the flash of midnight wings. Her throat seized. In her nostrils, the phantom smell of blood. *Makkah.*

"Was that magic?" Liadan asked.

"Magic, or dragon's powder." Morna's hand was steady on the spyglass. "The Crow is ancient enough to know the trick."

Nessa rounded on Riona. "We are all dead. We should have gone. I *told* you we should have gone!"

All of the cinan started gabbling at once. *Retreat no fight no hide in the mountains no send someone to the Andrisi camps by cover of night no are you mad we won't even last until sunset.*

"Silence!" Despite the strength in her voice, Riona's mind was a whirlwind. *I've done the wrong thing. We will all die. Eilis was right. I'm stupid. I'm weak.*

No. This was a setback, nothing more. Riona squared her shoulders. *I am intelligent, iron willed, unbending. I need no one. I will bring us out of this.* "We—we can hold the breach. Call the rest of the Queensguard. Send more warriors. Hold the western wall!"

* * *

The western wall fell in less than an hour.

When Riona sent the dwindling Queensguard to help hold the breach, a second wave of Andrisi soldiers started to flow from the forest to the east like blood from a fatal wound. At first, it looked as though the eastern wall would be safe. In addition to the city's usual defenses, Riona had ordered hasty pits dug and filled with sharpened stakes. Those of the first wave who didn't fall to crossbow bolts wound up in the pits.

But there hadn't been enough time to dig around the entire wall. The second wave of riders sent foot soldiers before them, testing the ground. Aghast, Riona watched the metal-clad riders prod the foot soldiers forward until they broke through the branches and grass covering the pits, screaming to their deaths. When they found the end of the hidden traps, the remaining Andrisi simply went around. So many had died, but they remained relentless. Any sane army would have turned back, even with dragon's powder.

Brigid Cuillin had been right. They were battle mad. Makkah had infected them somehow, and they lusted for death—others', and, from the way they fought, their own.

Another deafening boom. Chunks of the eastern wall flew into the air, smashing homes and skidding down streets. People ran from the crushed buildings. Through the spyglass, she could see the blood. The broken bones.

Riona dropped the spyglass. It hit the stone with a crack. "Get them out."

Nessa Dalaigh laughed. "Now? It is too late."

"No." Riona grabbed the older woman's cowl. She was a full six inches taller than the bent, papery ancient, but she shook her anyway. The cinan of Clan Dalaigh, for all the force of her glare, was thin-boned as a bird. "We must save them."

Morna Brannon came to Riona's side, tugged her fingers from Nessa's cowl. Riona winced out of habit, expecting the fingers around her wrist to tighten and pinch, but they remained gentle. The realization of what she'd done catching up to her, Riona let Morna lead her aside as two other cinan rushed to Nessa's aid.

A little away from the others, Morna let her go. "You've been given a hard burden."

Riona bristled. "I am up to the task."

"Of course." Morna's gaze went to the side of Riona's neck, where the white feather probably peeked from her collar. Morna half raised a hand, then let it fall. "Eilis was not kind to you."

Riona stiffened. "She made me strong."

Morna raised her brows. "Eilis's sort of strength is brittle. Her 'strength' left fractures in the bonds between clan and queen. There is more to leadership than being born with a feather on your skin."

"I know that," Riona snapped.

Morna gestured sharply to the ancient leader of Clan Dalaigh. "Then what are you doing?"

Riona didn't respond. She took a hard, heavy breath. The backs of her eyes burned. She looked out over the city. It burned, as well.

Souls, what a stupid girl you are.

She wasn't sure if the voice was Eilis's or her own. Her vision blurred. She blinked it away.

Morna touched Riona's arm. "There are better ways. There were better queens."

"I know." The words were a whisper. Riona had read all the histories. Eilis had forced her to read all the histories.

The cinan didn't respect her—they barely listened unless she threatened, and every threat made them whisper, made them balk. Despite her new defenses and best ideas, the Andrisi seethed through the city's broken walls.

Crann Laith was lost. In its thousand-year history, the Wildwood had seen several great queens.

Riona would not be among them, after all.

She let the despair burn through her. The embarrassment, the shame. Then she hid them away, at least for the moment. If she would not be a great queen, she could at least be a queen who made sure her people survived.

Riona looked at the cinan who stood with her. Cinan she'd kept close to make sure they did as she wanted. It was useless, having them here. Dangerous, with the way Makkah was knocking down walls. Why give the Andrisi one target when she could give them six?

"You three," Riona indicated Nessa and two others. "Find your warriors and evacuate the elderly, artisans, and children out the northern gate through the canyon—get them away however you must. Makkah might have led the Andrisi through the Wildwood, but she doesn't know it as we do. Take the canyon road around Storm's Head to Cahair Scoth and wait for me. It will be difficult. If you can think of a better way, take it." Riona clenched her jaw, then exhaled. "Cinan Dalaigh, I am sorry for losing control."

The old woman blinked in surprise, then grunted, the sound not precisely forgiving. "Your will is my command, Queen Riona. Come," she barked at the others. "Let us save who we can."

Riona turned to the other three as the cinan assigned to evacuate the people left the tower. "Cinans Cuillin and Ruane, take command of the remaining fighters and keep the Andrisi occupied while the people escape."

Brigid Cuillin's brow furrowed. "You must leave the city, as well. There hasn't been a babe born with the queensmark yet. Who will rule if you fall?"

Riona laughed with little humor. "Nessa will do the job, I'm sure."

The women remaining in the tower didn't seem to enjoy the joke.

In the settling dust by the city's crumbling wall, Riona caught a glimpse of black wings. The Andrisi roared like the sea. Even without a spyglass, Riona could see the yellow-and-black-clad soldiers surging, frenzied and chaotic.

Makkah had finally arrived.

Riona turned from the sight of the Andrisi, from the smoking city. Her chest was hollow, and so was her voice. Her pride had cost the lives of thousands, and she would try anything to save the lives that were left. "I will go to the city on the mountain." She jerked her chin at Morna. "Cinan Brannon will take me there."

Morna inhaled deeply, closed her eyes, and nodded. "Your command is my will."

* * *

Cravh caught on the cathedral's outer wall, its fine tip sparking across stone instead of cutting cleanly through the neck of an Andrisi soldier.

"So much for slipping out unnoticed!" Liadan slammed the hilt of her sword down on an enemy soldier's head, and he collapsed to the street, a crimson stain spreading from beneath his head into the churned, dirty snow.

Riona growled in answer, slicing into the gap in the Andrisi's armor between breastplate and armguard. He cried out and lurched back. Riona lunged, slipped, and had to use Cravh to catch herself. The courtyard before the cathedral was slick with red-stained ice. Night had fallen, but between moon, snow, and the burning city, there was abundant light. She recovered before the man, and her next swing ended his life.

She raised Cravh, ready to face the next foe, but the courtyard was empty of living Andrisi. Only Morna, Liadan, and their Brannon fighters remained. And Dagny, who'd found them, somehow, in the chaos. The dragonskin woman had proven adept with the needlelike throwing daggers she seemed to produce from thin air—daggers, Riona realized, that had been hidden in clever pockets in the woman's dress.

A screech from overhead. Riona grabbed Liadan and Dagny and hauled them into the shadows next to the cathedral steps, hunching down next to the frozen stone. At Morna's barked command, the other Brannon soldiers scrambled into the dimness, as well.

A shadow blotted out the moon—a woman on wings of oil and smoke.

"Souls of the Underwood consume her." Liadan spat into the snow.

"Does an Incarnation have a soul to consume?" Dagny asked as Morna appeared beside them.

Riona snorted. "If she does, it's made of ash and blood, and even the damned would choke on it."

Liadan and Morna gave her identical wry smiles. It twisted something inside her.

Riona cleared her throat. "Come. Let's get inside before she circles back or more of her berserkers find us."

They scrambled up the slippery cathedral steps. Riona shoved open the door and held it for the men and women sworn to protect Clan Brannon. So few. They'd left the keep with twenty, but just as they'd emerged, an equal number of Andrisi had appeared on the other side of the square.

Riona and the others were lucky to have survived at all.

She let the door swing shut. Morna crouched at a window, the stained glass and fire casting flickering, multihued shadows over her face. Riona bolted the cathedral's great doors and crouched beside her blood-mother. In the last hour, Morna had shown her more about leadership than Eilis ever had. She constantly put the lives of her fighters above her own. She knew them, seemed to love them, and made no secret of relying on each for their strengths.

Why Morna Brannon had not borne the queensmark instead of her or Eilis, Riona would never understand.

A troop of metal-helmed Andrisi went by. The gleaming armor was like nothing Riona had ever seen before. Lighter than iron, but strong. Far stronger than the bronze swords her people carried. Over the course of the day, that metal and the dragon's powder had obliterated the Wildings like straw set aflame.

Riona let her forehead fall against the cold stone, resisting the chasm of despair that yawned beneath her. It would be a miracle if any of the people of Crann Laith survived this night, and it was all her fault.

A winged shadow passed over the snowy courtyard. Another shrill call. The soldiers passing by paused, then turned.

Riona's heart sank. Makkah must have seen them, and now her men were headed directly for the doors of the cathedral.

Riona cursed the Lady of War and her game. "A quick one," she'd said. It had been quick indeed. Why did she not just come down and end Riona's suffering?

Perhaps, for the Incarnation of War, suffering was the point.

The soldiers tromped up the cathedral's steps. For a terrible, mad moment, Riona wanted to stand and fling open the door. Let it end.

Morna rose. "Hurry. The entrance to the tunnels. Where is it?"

Riona tried to focus. Scenes from her childhood flashed before her. Groping in the lightless dark, the damp, the chill. *Find your way out or starve, girl.* She suppressed a shiver. "In the northwest corner. I —I don't know if there's time to lift the stone and get away without them following us." There were two dozen Andrisi outside with their dragon powder. She, Dagny, and the Brannons wouldn't stand a chance.

"There is time for you." Morna's voice held no fear. With her face illuminated in the shifting, multicolored light, she looked more a queen than Eilis ever had. Than Riona ever could.

Liadan, standing nearby, laughed softly. "What better way to end life than in a glorious last stand?"

"None. But that is not for you. Not today, my little eagle." Morna removed one of the eagle feathers from her hair and wove it with deft fingers into Liadan's braid. "Fly long, Liadan, cinan of Clan Brannon."

Liadan paled. "Mother?"

Morna grasped her shoulders. "Protect your queen."

Riona's throat closed. The first Andrisi blows landed on the door.

Their deaths are on your head.

Another bang on the door, then silence. The Andrisi would be preparing their explosive powder. It wouldn't be long now.

Morna grasped her by the shoulders, taking Riona by surprise. "This city holds a fraction of the Wilding population. The fall of Crann Laith will not be the end of us." She tugged. Riona resisted— no one had ever touched her but in accident or anger. Then, giving in to a desire she'd buried long before she could remember, Riona let the woman pull her into a hug. Her hands went around Morna's waist, her face into the older woman's shoulder.

Something in her broke. Something in her healed. Too soon, Morna released Riona, pressed a kiss to her own fingers, then touched Riona's cheek.

A mother's blessing.

"I wish I had known you," Riona whispered.

Morna smiled. "When we meet beneath the branches of the Underwood, our souls will know each other, and rejoice. Be the better queen. The future is yours to shape."

Boom. Splinters of wood and shards of stone flew through the air. Shouts echoed from the front of the cathedral.

"Liadan," Morna grasped her daughter by the cheeks, kissed her forehead, and murmured something too low for Riona to hear. The girl had tears streaming down her face. Morna gave her a gentle shove. "Go!"

Soldiers appeared from the dust. Morna called to her warriors and turned to meet them.

Locking away a suffocating wave of grief for things that would never be, Riona ran for the back of the cathedral, Liadan and Dagny close behind.

Hidden in shadow in the northwest corner of the tower, she showed the other two which of the great floor stones slid aside. With no time for memory, for choking fear that wafted up with the dank scent of the darkness beyond, Riona slid through the hole and splashed into the tunnel beneath. A second later, Dagny's tall, slender form slithered through. And then, after one too many heartbeats, Liadan's boots hit the ground beside her. Together, the three women wrestled the stone back into place. Pitch darkness fell. And with it, silence.

"Is there light?" Liadan asked. Her voice was thick, her breathing uneven.

"No." Riona stilled, as she'd learned to do as a child. Listened. Put the fear aside. It was easier now that she wasn't alone. "But I know the way. Take my hands."

They did, Liadan's small and callused, Dagny's slender and cool.

For the first time since Makkah had appeared at the coronation, Riona knew exactly what to do.

They emerged from the dark into the frozen dawn half an hour later. The tunnels let out onto an icy pass on the western slope of Storm's Head. No Andrisi lay in wait for them, nor any winged, preternaturally beautiful women. The wind had blown most of the sparse snow from the ground, so they would leave no obvious tracks.

They had escaped Makkah, for the moment. But below them, Crann Laith burned.

Riona hugged herself, her gaze tracing the column of smoke into the sky. Then she turned from the sight of the city. She could not change what her pride had wrought. But perhaps, in the ashes of her failure, she could salvage hope. Even if she couldn't wake the myth, perhaps she could find a way. Perhaps it was not too late for the Wildwood.

* * *

By late afternoon the next day—after a day and night and day clinging to rock faces, traversing ravines, and nearly succumbing to hypothermia—Riona, Dagny, and Liadan walked among the empty-eyed remains of an empire.

The stone buildings were oddly shaped, too tall and slender. Too smooth, with thin windows that rose into graceful, pointed arches, their borders carved with things—perhaps they had been flowers and birds—that had faded to unrecognizable lumps. Despite the wear of time and weather, hints of bright paint hid in corners and cracks. Flaking remainders of sunset and sky, meadow and ocean. Dagny trailed her fingers along each with reverence clear on her face. Liadan's gaze flitted about, her eyes filled with awe.

In the stillness, Riona felt the first, faint stirrings of hope.

The roads were stone, straight and wide, but their boots were muffled by a thin layer of snow that had fallen overnight, once the cutting wind had died. More fell, fat flakes that stuck to the fur of the hood pulled up around Riona's face.

Despite its thinness, the air was heavy, the past pushing through the broken paving stones like the winter flowers that splashed color against the gray-and-white landscape. It had the feel of a house before dawn, a breath held. As if dragonskin might bustle around the corner, or as if Riona and her companions might come across a thriving market. The city on the mountain was old, but not dead.

It slept.

At last, they passed the last ring of ethereal buildings and faced the Tomb of the Sleeping King. The city's center was large and circular, paved with pale stones that sank in a series of concentric circles, forming steps. At their center, a waist-high platform rose, covered in a breathtaking, clear crystal dome.

The sun emerged, casting a sparkling glare that hid the dome's occupant, but Riona could make out the silhouette of a man in repose. Dagny came to stand next to her, and Riona tried not to look as though her stomach had just tied itself in knots. "Is there something I should know?" she asked the taller woman. "Something I should do?"

Dagny didn't take her eyes from the shadow of the man beneath the glass. "Pray."

The sun dipped behind a cloud again as the three of them descended. Riona stared, transfixed. She'd known about the Sleeping King her entire life, but the knowledge had been distant. She'd only half believed it.

But there he was, golden scaled and golden haired, his chest rising and falling, as real as Makkah and her night-black wings.

He wore dark boots, fitted pants, and a sleeveless tunic in sapphire blue that belted at the waist. Everything, from toe to shoulder, was embroidered or inlaid with some kind of gold. A dusting of golden scales covered the backs of his hands from his fingertips and ran up strong arms to broad shoulders.

His face . . . Riona swallowed. Dusty ancient, he was not. He was young. A thousand years old, and he didn't look more than two or three years her senior. A furrow creased his brow, as if his sleep was not peaceful. Even so, he was breathtaking. Life suffused cheeks and lips with a pink glow of health.

And yet, for a thousand years, he had not woken.

On either side of her, Liadan and Dagny each took one of the golden handles and lifted the dome. It opened on silent hinges, and the scent of summer rolled over them. Of sun and heat, leather and sweet hay. Of something namelessly masculine that clung to Riona's nostrils and made it hard to look away from the man laid out on the platform of stone.

Beside her, Dagny muttered what could only be a dragonskin curse. Or maybe it was a prayer.

"Well?" Liadan asked when Riona made no move.

This was ridiculous. It could even be a prank—some beautiful dragonskin man crawled beneath the crystal dome once a generation or so to fool another Wilding queen. The whole situation was just too stupid. A legend had destroyed Riona's home, and to combat it, she had to wake a man who'd slept for a millennium. With her lips. "Souls."

Something dark passed in the corner of Riona's eye, and she heard a sound that might have been wings. Her head snapped up, and she craned her neck, whirling around. Liadan and Dagny did the same.

Nothing. The sky was empty.

They exchanged looks. Dagny tipped her head toward the sleeping man.

Riona's gaze followed the motion to his face. To his lips. She licked her own.

He won't wake.

He will, but it will be a joke.

He won't, and you'll have to find some other way. She, Liadan, and Dagny would go back to the Wildwood and do their best, but in the end, they would all die. What else could they hope for against Makkah? At least, in doing this, she could say she'd tried everything.

Feeling more foolish than she had in her life, Riona leaned down and pressed her lips against the Sleeping King's.

He was warm. She'd never kissed anyone before, and she'd expected kissing to be . . . squishy. But his lips, though soft, were firm.

For a single, long second, nothing happened. Then the rhythm of his breathing changed. The sleeping man inhaled a sharp, long breath through his nose. His eyelashes fluttered against her cheek. Riona gasped and tried to straighten, but strong hands grasped her elbows, pulling her into him. His lips parted, hands traced her upper arm and neck, burying themselves in her hair.

She was kissing a myth, and he was kissing her back. Warmth bloomed in her chest, spreading until it felt as if she were lying in the sun on a summer day.

He released her. She stumbled back, catching herself on the edge of the platform.

The Sleeping King slept no more.

He watched her, lips still parted, chest heaving, staring with eyes the color of molten gold.

It had worked.

Riona touched a finger to her lips.

It had *worked*.

In one, graceful movement, the king—Torsten—pushed himself up, pivoting so his legs hung over the side of the slab. He blinked like a lost child, then shaded his eyes with his hands and looked around. His eyes swept the city. Liadan. Dagny.

Then he looked to Riona. His gaze clung to her, as if she were a rope and he was drowning. Hope cracked the hard shell of despair that had formed around her heart. It was painful. Beautiful. It had *worked*. The Wildwood didn't have to fall. Her people didn't have to die.

Morna and Eilis had not died in vain.

The Sleeping King—Torsten—opened his mouth, but nothing came out except a rough noise. His knuckles whitened on the edge of the platform.

Liadan took an eager step forward. "How do we defeat the Crow?"

The dragonskin man looked at her in confusion.

"He's been asleep for a thousand years," Dagny murmured. "He doesn't speak the Wilding tongue. Not as it is now."

As if to prove Dagny's words, he suddenly covered his face with his hands. Rocking back and forth on the edge of the stone platform, he whispered, "It's over," in the same ancient language Makkah had used. "It's over. It's over."

Riona's brow furrowed. Waking the Sleeping King was supposed to be glorious. Lights were to shoot across the sky, the horns of the ancient dead to sound. He wasn't supposed be so confused, so . . . haunted. So broken.

"What's over?" she asked.

He didn't drop his hands. "The nightmare."

A chill shadow fell over her blossoming hope. This was not the hero she'd been expecting.

"Riona," Liadan whispered. "The sun is setting. We either need to find a place to sleep here, or see if we can find a dragonskin family to take us in for the night. They live in caves all around here, do they not?" she asked Dagny.

Dagny hesitated, then nodded.

Riona thought she knew why the dragonskin hesitated, and she agreed. By now, Makkah could be hunting them, and she didn't want to endanger anyone else with her presence. "These buildings are well maintained. They'll offer shelter from the wind. You two see about firewood and something to eat." Torsten had not shifted. "I'll . . . see if I can get him to move."

They nodded. Though Dagny looked as if she wanted to protest, she went with Liadan.

"How long has it been?" Torsten's words took her by surprise, and Riona started. His voice was still rough, though not as much as it had been. He held Dagny's waterskin. Riona hadn't seen her give it to him.

There wasn't a point to sugarcoating things. "A thousand years."

He paled beneath the golden scales on his cheeks and dropped his gaze to his hands. "You will never understand the depth of the debt I owe you." He slid from the platform, knelt, and placed the tips of his fingers to his heart, then took Riona's hand in his free one. His palm was warm and callused. "What is your name?"

She swallowed. "Riona. Riona nich Brannon."

"I swear on the soul of the Dragon, Riona nich Brannon, I will do everything in my power to repay you."

A spiral of flames leaped from their intertwined fingers and up their arms. Riona gasped as the skin beneath her collarbone burned. She pulled her hand from his and pulled aside her coat to see a golden, flame-shaped mark just to the side of her heart.

Magic. Souls. The man could *do* magic.

He hadn't taken his eyes from her. His gaze unsettled her and filled her with heat. He gestured to the feathers in her hair. "I knew a woman, once, who wore feathers like that. I think there's more to your name than you've said."

Riona wasn't sure if there was, not after the way she'd failed. "I was—am—Queen of the Wildwood and Mountain Reach."

His brow furrowed. "The clans are united?"

Riona realized they were still holding hands, and she released his. "Much changed while you slept."

He looked to the horizon, where smoke from the burning of Crann Laith still smudged the sky. "Some things remain." A terrible knowledge filled his eyes. "Makkah remains."

Riona nodded.

"Is that why you've come?"

She chose her words with care. "The Lady of War and the Andrisi have destroyed Crann Laith. According to the histories, there was a prophecy that said you would wake when needed and fight —"

"Of course. The prophecy." He laughed without humor, then ran both hands over his face and pressed his knuckles into his eyes. "I'm sorry, Queen Riona nich Brannon. You have come for nothing."

Ice crystalized in her veins. "What?"

"I cannot help you."

She leaned close, her voice a low growl. "Are you so embittered by the fall of your own people that you would see mine destroyed as well?"

He dropped his hands, expression furious. "I would give my life if I thought I could save a single person from Makkah. I would die a hundred times if it meant she would die too. A thousand."

"Then why do you refuse to help?"

Torsten breathed deep once, then again. "The prophecy did exist, but not for you. It was for my time. The people I was supposed to save were my own." He dropped his gaze. "I've already tried to kill Makkah, and I failed."

Riona reeled as if he'd struck her. "Failed?" Perhaps she was misunderstanding the ancient tongue.

"I should have died. Instead, she cursed me to sleep. For a thousand years, I have relived the nightmares. I have watched my friends' murders a thousand times. Ten thousand. The deaths of everyone I loved, the destruction of my entire civilization. They are burned into my brain. I see them when I close my eyes . . ."

Hope died, its demise so painful that Riona pressed a hand to her chest. She'd been right all along, and Morna had been wrong. Hoping magic could save them had been wrong. Thinking that she, Riona, could be any better than Eilis—could be any sort of leader— had been the greatest error of all.

At the same time, she couldn't help feeling a terrible empathy for Torsten. Like him, she had failed her people, watched them die.

At least she had only lived it once. "So . . . this is it? Nothing can defeat Makkah."

His returned his face to his hands. "I'm sorry."

The sun set. Liadan and Dagny returned to tell them that there was food and fire, but Torsten didn't leave the platform, and so Riona remained. Something about him pulled at her. Something familiar, something lonely. Perhaps it was only the knowledge that he had failed far more spectacularly than she had—Riona had lost a city. Torsten had lost a civilization.

But whatever the connection, it felt like more.

As the first stars were rising, the wind snatched back Riona's hood. Her hands went up to catch it and brushed the band of feathers woven into the wind-whipped strands. With a cry, she snatched them out and tossed them away. As her hands dropped, her fingers brushed the raised skin of the silver feather marked on her neck.

She laughed—or maybe it was a sob. *Riona nich Brannon, Queen of the Wildwood and Mountain Reach.* Her fingers curled, nails scraping skin, but there was nothing to grasp. This reminder she could not pluck out.

Riona left the silent dragonskin and walked all the way to the edge of the city. From its perch, high in the Spire Mountains, she could see the whole of the Wildwood spread out below. Crann Laith was hidden by the bulk of the mountain. From where she stood, the Wildwood seemed at peace.

Another sob tore from her throat. *This cannot be how we end.*

Morna Brannon's voice whispered in her mind. *There are other ways. There were better queens. Be the better queen.*

Riona thought of Nessa's vitriol, and her loss of control. *Are you necessary?* Eilis's mocking, and a life lived in fear. *Run, girl.* She touched her cheek, remembering Makkah's fingers, remembering Morna's final blessing.

A silver feather she had missed fluttered to the ground, loosened from Riona's braids by the breeze, and she stooped to pick it up.

The past was part of her. The loneliness, the pain, the failure.

The future is yours to shape.

Life had made her into a bone-shard blade. She was not perfect. Even with her intelligence, her determination, she could fail. Had done so, with horrifying consequences. But in the days since Eilis's death, Riona had learned. She was teachable, and flexible enough not to break.

"This is my time. I will not let it go to waste." She returned to the tomb and stopped before Torsten. Quick as thought, she took his hand and yanked him to his feet. "I will not stop trying."

The dragonskin man blinked. He *was* tall.

"Whether or not you failed in the past, you woke." Riona touched the little flame over her heart. "The magic is not what I expected, but it's alive, and so are we. Even if there isn't hope, we can't just give up."

Torsten's fingers tightened over hers. He looked over her head to the horizon, where the waters of Sythespine Bay would be gleaming orange and crimson in the setting sun. He seemed to wrestle with something inside himself. Finally, he dropped his golden gaze back to hers. "If you go to fight Makkah, I will go with you, and tell you what I know."

"Thank you." Riona looked to the warm flicker in one of the ancient building's windows, where Liadan and Dagny had built a fire within. Even if there was nothing she could do to stop Makkah, she would give her life to try.

And now she knew she didn't have to try alone.

About Caitlyn McFarland

Originally from the Midwest, Caitlyn McFarland currently lives in Utah with her husband and three young daughters. She has a Bachelor's degree in linguistics from Brigham Young University. When she's not writing about dragons or running around after her daughters, she can be found hunched over a sewing machine making elaborate princess costumes.

BETWEEN EARTH AND EXILE

By Laurie Tom | 9,100 words

WE HAD CAPTURED the Alcaltan frigate a week ago. It should have been an easy job. We chose that moment for a reason. The ship was being towed for decommission and only had a skeleton crew for defense. But that hadn't mattered. They still killed Kellen.

Sometimes no amount of planning or preparation is enough. Most of us, had we lived anywhere else on Earth, would not have had the opportunity to escape on the *Bloodborne*. We understood how some things came down to a matter of luck.

But luck still had to be dealt with. And Kellen was gone.

I knocked on the door to my Captain's quarters, telling myself that my plan was sound, even logical, and not that I was homesick after all this time. I was twenty-one and had served under the Captain for six years. Age did not matter in the face of survival.

"Come in."

Even while we were docked at Pyre Rock, the Captain preferred his quarters aboard the *Bloodborne*. It was quieter than the base most days, given all the construction and the wailing from Emma and Daiki's new baby.

I pushed open the door and it squeaked in protest. The *Bloodborne* ran on limited power while docked. The only reason we still had normal Earth gravity was because we were at Pyre Rock, where we could take advantage of the stolen generators we'd installed in our base. The Alcaltans' command of gravity had been one of the deciding factors in the war. It was nice to make it work for us.

"Alexa," he said, with a glance in my direction, "isn't your team lining the walls of the new wing?"

He sat behind a rough desk of our own construction, dark hands rotating a display of Pyre Rock on the holo. It was a draft of the construction. We hadn't burrowed into that much of the asteroid yet.

"Finished, sir. If I might have a moment of your time?"

The Captain gestured for me to take a seat at a small table a meter from his desk. He did not get up to join me, nor did I expect him to. The Captain had never been much for coddling his crew, or himself. His quarters were spartan, save for the rack of shelves on which he kept keepsakes of our victories. They were a reminder that against all odds, we still survived.

"Captain," I said. "Right now, the crew has its hands full. We're trying to expand our base and man the *Bloodborne* at the same time. And I hate to say it, sir, but Kellen's death has hit us hard."

He nodded, silent. I don't think he wanted us to know how much he missed Kellen. If the Captain was the head and the heart of the *Bloodborne*, Kellen had been the limbs to make everything happen. We'd lost crew before, but the second-in-command of the *Bloodborne* had been a sharp, intuitive man. Replacing him would not be easy. Not that we could really replace anyone, but even pulling from what we had, no one was Kellen.

"We need more people," I said. "I know there's a chance they're not even alive, but if we're building a colony here, I would like to rescue my family. My mom was a structural engineer before the war —she could help build Pyre Rock—and now my brother is old enough to crew."

The gaze that met mine betrayed neither surprise nor anger, but it was unflinching, hard. The Alcaltans had tried to break us many times, but even with Kellen's death, I knew they would never break *him*.

"We have been exiled," he said evenly. "You know you can't go back for them."

That was the agreement, the only reason the *Bloodborne* had been allowed to leave.

"I don't need to go back to Earth itself. Just the solar system would be enough. We *need* more people, before there aren't enough of us left . . ."

It was selfish to want to rescue my family. I wasn't supposed to care about things I could not change, people I could no longer see, but no matter how I wanted to be like the rock that was my

Captain, I could not be that strong. He had gone into exile with his head held high and a willing crew at his back. I had gone in tears.

My Captain studied me, and I tried to still the twinge in my gut. "And how do you propose to get your family off planet?" he asked.

"I have an idea," I said, and I felt very small sitting in the office across from the man to whom I owed everything. "I think I can get them smuggled out on a carrier. It won't be easy, or cheap, but I believe I can manage."

The Alcaltans were not a hive mind any more than humans. Though in exile, and officially hunted by Alcalta, there were a few rogue outposts where we, the crew of the *Bloodborne*, were tolerated despite what we were. We had connections, and if I pressed them hard enough, paid them well enough, I was reasonably certain I could arrange something even on occupied Earth.

"I'll handle all the arrangements," I said. "I just need your permission to borrow a shuttle."

I prepared myself for his refusal, because with a crew of a hundred, two on leave caring for a child, and no way for us to gain new recruits, he could scarcely afford to lose anyone to a whim, to a purpose that arguably served the individual more than the crew.

"If I offer this opportunity to you, I must offer it to everyone," said the Captain finally. "Find out who is interested and how many people that means you will have to rescue. If you think you can manage, you have my permission. However, I think you will find that a shuttle will not be enough."

"Thank you, Captain."

* * *

My life had changed the day the Captain's ship landed on the outskirts of Concord Grove, bringing the last human colonists home in defiance of Alcalta. It had stayed grounded for only a few hours.

The police, the *human* police, had surrounded the ship, as though they could hold a dreadnought and its crew at bay with tiny tanks and a handful of rockets until a representative of our government could arrive—the same government that had surrendered to Alcalta once they realized that the aliens only had an interest in keeping humanity contained and not in obliterating us.

Captain Jonathan Mercer had been an officer in the Earth-based fleet, but he didn't roll over when the war ended. He and his crew stole an Alcaltan dreadnought to rescue the survivors of a colony that would have died without help, survivors who would probably die anyway on a depleted and overpopulated Earth. Our government called it a pointless venture, but for that, the Captain and his crew were branded a threat to the peace.

If not for the fear that murdering the Captain would have turned him into a martyr, I had no doubt they would have executed him on the spot.

Instead the sentence was exile. He and his crew were to take that blasted ship and leave Earth, forever.

I remember seeing the Captain, standing so tall and proud that I doubted they could have forced him into exile if he had not agreed. He didn't belong there on Earth. To the rest of us, to those who crowded around his ship despite our fear, he issued a warning, that the Alcaltans would not hesitate to eliminate us the moment we became too great an inconvenience, that we might discover ourselves unhappy with the sacrifices demanded in a life of appeasement.

So he extended an offer, to any who were willing, to join his crew. At first only a handful dared to walk past the police, and when they weren't shot, a handful more. No one knew what kind of future a life in exile promised, but the Captain seemed so assured, so strong, that we knew he would not limp into the stars and fade away. I had no future on Earth, where every day revolved around finding enough to eat. With the new refugees, there would be even less.

My mom refused to go. She did not believe we could survive on a ship without a port, in the face of aliens that had made it plain they would only tolerate our existence if we remained on our home planet. I was afraid too, but I was more afraid of what would happen if I stayed.

I still remember her fingers in my hair, how her body shook as I hugged her good-bye and told her I had to go. She said she understood, though I don't know that I believed her. Without me, there would be one less mouth to feed, and she could care for my younger brother without worrying about what could happen to a teenage girl in a broken city. We'd fought so much—over school, over food, over curfew—that I could barely believe she let me go.

For a moment, I reconsidered, but fear was stronger than tears. When I darted past the police line, I did not look back. I fell in behind the new crew members preparing to board, the last to join.

In retrospect, we should have found it strange that we had been allowed to leave Earth on a stolen dreadnought, that the Captain had been allowed to take dissenters with him. The Alcaltans did not let us go so easily. Our first battle as a unified crew was shortly after we cleared Earth's orbit, once we were far enough away that we were out of sight of those on the ground below.

The Alcaltans planned to kill us where there would be no chance of martyrdom or inspiration to those who remained behind.

We were terrified, outnumbered, running a ship many of us had never served on before, some of us not even familiar with ships at all. I considered it a testament to our Captain that we escaped. We then understood what measures we needed to take simply to survive.

Our crew was alone in a universe where we were the only humans outside of Earth. We named our ship the *Bloodborne* and took to raiding for food and supplies. It wasn't out of rebellion, or a patriotic desire to show the Alcaltans that humanity was not done. We were pirates, and we could only rely on each other.

But as I relayed our Captain's offer to rescue our families back on Earth, I soon discovered that, though I trusted my fellow crew, I hadn't really known them.

Peter had a sister, three years younger than him, who'd lost an eye in a crossfire. Valerie had left behind her husband of only two months, not realizing that helping Captain Mercer in the colony rescue would result in her exile. Manuel wanted to know if his parents were all right. And Justin had asked me to find his son. I hadn't known he was a father.

Hitomi and I had even gone to the same school, though being in different years, we had never met. Richard's mom owned the store where I used to buy slushies before the sky fell, and if I thought hard, I could remember seeing him there on Friday afternoons.

When they learned the Captain had approved smuggling their families off planet, their lives came tumbling out, and by the time I finished speaking with everyone, I had a list of just under two hundred names. Not all the crew had family they could speak of, some had lost everyone in the war, but there were still more people than we could fit in a single shuttle.

I knew that the chances of all of them being alive would be negligible though. Perhaps a quarter would be, and we could work with that.

The amount of money needed to bribe our contacts to get information on two hundred people was astronomical. The crew chipped in whatever they could, even those without loved ones to rescue.

We used the Alcaltan *lumil* when dealing with the outside world, each member of the crew getting a share of the spoils after a successful raid, but we didn't use it with each other. There was no such thing as paying for room and board. You served on the ship, you got a room and three meals in the mess. Any *lumil* we kept was just gravy, and yet I couldn't account for more than half of what we needed.

People started talking about pawning their belongings the next time we visited an outpost. Human goods were nearly worthless to Alcaltans in their intended forms, but a diamond from a ring could be repurposed for manufacturing, the metal from old electronics could be salvaged.

"I can arrange the necessary information gathering," I told the Captain, when next I met him in his quarters. "The only problem is the money. Not everyone can afford it, but it doesn't seem right that we should restrict rescuing family to only a portion of our crew. And how would we choose? It's easy to say those who can afford it should get priority, but what about the rest? Would we hold a lottery?"

A part of me regretted conceiving this plan at all. If no one was rescued, we'd be no worse off than before, and I couldn't imagine what it would be like to see someone else's family come home while mine was left behind.

Once again I sat at the small table while the Captain remained behind his desk. The distance may as well have been the entire ship. I was just a part of the crew. I wasn't Kellen. I couldn't expect sympathy. After all, I was the one who'd dug myself into this mess.

My Captain spoke. "Would you consider it right to leave a few people behind, when by the luck of the draw they could have been the ones you save? You can't give hope only to take it away."

"It wouldn't be right, but it would be fair. I just didn't think this would happen—that we wouldn't have the money to even find out if the people we want to rescue are still alive. I thought the crew would have saved up a little more. It's not as though we've needed a personal stash of *lumil* to survive."

Indeed, we ate better on the *Bloodborne* than we had during our final year on Earth.

"And what did you save for?"

"I . . . I wanted to buy my own ship," I replied, feeling silly to admit it. "When I was in school, I had this idea I would buy my own ship, see the galaxy, go to Alcor, Yukikawa, and all those planets we don't have anymore. Of course, now I know I wouldn't be able to afford much more than an oversized shuttle, but it would have been less recognizable than the *Bloodborne*, so we could have used it . . ."

The Captain stood and walked over to the shelves suspended along the wall. "For years we've stolen everything we needed to survive, and used the ship's communal funds to procure what we could not. There are no longer such things as homes, vacations, or retirements to save for. It's unsurprising that the crew should spend the majority of their earnings on the rare outpost entertainment."

He retrieved a small brown box from the top shelf and offered it to me. "Not everyone is as industrious a saver as you. Here. This should cover the rest."

Had he known? I had contributed the largest donation to the smuggling funds, but I hadn't told anyone, feeling sheepish about how much money I'd saved. The crew already made light of my spending habits whenever we docked at an outpost.

"It's what is inside the box," said the Captain.

Remembering myself, I popped the lid and found a recorder inside. I flicked it on, bringing up the display, and stared.

"The schematics to an Alcaltan battle cruiser?"

"The new one, put into service in the past year," he replied. "I had intended to wait before bargaining with it, so that the Alcaltans would be less likely to tie it to the attack we made six months ago."

This would certainly pay for everyone's families, not just for the information, but to smuggle them out as well. There would probably even be money left over. Certainly there were some Alcaltan malcontents who could put this to use and would pay handsomely for it.

"Thank you."

He nodded and walked back to his desk. "That is only to pay for costs remaining after the crew has contributed all they can. Anything left over is to be added to the communal funds for the *Bloodborne* and Pyre Rock."

"Understood."

I turned to go when a sudden thought occurred to me.

"Captain! I forgot to ask. Do you have family back on Earth?"

"No."

"Oh. I'm sorry. Thank you, again."

* * *

I didn't tell the rest of the crew of the Captain's contribution, especially when it occurred to me that the only person on the *Bloodborne* more miserly than me was the Captain himself. The battle cruiser plans had come from his personal collection of trophies, which shouldn't have been much larger than any of ours, except that we tended to pawn things we didn't want as quickly as possible, and the Captain tended to dispose of his spoils as gifts or bargaining chips.

Finding a buyer for the schematics was the frightening part. I didn't know how the Captain could stand it, trading for ship parts and illegal weaponry on a regular basis. I did have connections, though, and a few inquiries took me to an Alcaltan weasel who claimed to have a wealthy client.

My mom wouldn't have recognized me, haggling over battle cruiser plans as if they were a scarf at a swap meet. I struck a deal, and with several members of the crew present for protection, we exchanged the schematics for two large crates of *surya*. The Alcaltans used the rainbow crystals to perform large, untraceable transactions, but I'd never seen so much at once.

With the profit, we doled out cards of *lumil* and handfuls of *surya* to individual weasels, but never in sight of each other, never letting them know that while we asked one to look into ten people, we were asking another to look into eight. The Alcaltans did not value familial relationships as much as humans did, and we counted on them to not piece together the reason for our inquiries, but as we waited for news, we could not help fearing that they would.

When their reports arrived, I was grateful.

Roughly a third of our list could not be tracked down, their whereabouts unknown even to the weasels. Others they confirmed dead, but they were able to locate forty of our family and friends in varying degrees of health. My mom was alive. She was over fifty now—despite everything she must have endured, she was still alive! She hadn't moved from Concord Grove, terrible though it was. My brother was in a labor camp. The Alcaltans were comfortable with exchanging food for work, so my brother was probably healthy, but for how long?

A sense of malaise settled over the crew. For some, they had lost family all over again, and we worried over the state of affairs on Earth in a way we hadn't since the earliest days of our exile. No matter that we had been forced off the planet—we didn't hate our home—but if I could not have Earth, I at least wanted my family.

We were overdue for a raid, but the Captain refused to launch the *Bloodborne*. He didn't tell us why with any words, but I knew from a look and his silence that we were in no shape for combat. I found myself doubting again whether I should have brought up my plan to the Captain, but I remembered his words about offering hope only to take it away, and I wasn't going to be the person who let the Captain down.

I told the crew to prepare for a rescue. Maybe we couldn't save everyone, but we could save someone.

Hush was my favorite information weasel, and the only one that I trusted enough to handle my family, so much as I trusted any of them. He was still an Alcaltan who made a living as illegally as we did, an opportunist. I just hoped he would consider our dealing with him beneficial enough to keep his end of the bargain.

Forty people, I told him, on one Alcaltan transport, to rendezvous with us on Varuna in the Kuiper Belt. I didn't care how he got everyone on board, but it had to be safe passage for all of them, intact, without harm. To this weasel I gave enough *surya* that his bulbous eyes misted a milky brown in contentment, with the understanding that he would get an equal amount if the selected humans arrived safely. Alcaltans had faces like earless elephants, and Hush signaled his approval with the shaking of his long snout.

The *Bloodborne* had come equipped with two shuttles, both with meager weapons and limited range. They were designed to convey guests to and from a planet's surface while the *Bloodborne* remained in orbit, though in an emergency they can and have been used to hop between planets in the same star system. If passengers were willing to get cozy with each other, we could squeeze forty people plus crew onto two shuttles for a short trip from Varuna's surface.

"We just need to get the *Bloodborne* close enough to launch them," I told the Captain.

We stood in what had once been an Alcaltan officers' meeting room. The ceilings were high and rounded, built for the aliens' greater height and sense of aesthetics, but we'd torn out their furnishings and replaced them with our own, fit for human dimensions. Kellen and the Captain had often met here to discuss strategy. Now the Captain and I had a map of the greater Sol System displayed on the holo before us and I pointed him to the ovoid ball of rock that was to be our rendezvous point.

"I would have liked carrying them out farther than the Kuiper Belt, but that would have required export clearance, and it wouldn't have been likely we could have gotten forty people past security for that."

The Captain nodded in approval. The Alcaltans weren't concerned about intrasystem smuggling, only between stars. A transport out in the Kuiper Belt could easily be on mining business. It was good cover. Humans had been occasionally used for that kind of labor.

"Still," he said, "the Alcaltans have early warning probes at the edge of the star system. They'll recognize the *Bloodborne*'s drive signature, even in the Kuiper Belt. The dreadnought's too large a ship to slip by without notice."

"Even if they have patrol ships in the area, it will take them time to react. It always has. We've never worried about them recognizing us before."

"We don't normally hit star systems this secure," said Captain Mercer. "Earthspace is still heavily fortified from the war. They know the *Bloodborne*, and you can bet they will send more than six ships after us if we get close to Earthspace again, but they might not react to a different ship, especially a smaller one that isn't on their most wanted list."

"The frigate?" I asked.

We'd finished the retrofit, but no crew had been assigned. A few of us had gone out on test runs, and though dated by Alcaltan standards, it was perfectly serviceable for us, if a bit cozy compared to the cavernous *Bloodborne*.

"Caleb says the test flights have gone well," said the Captain. "All systems check out, and he commended your handling of the bridge. Even if the Alcaltans identify it as the one stolen en route to decommissioning, they will not know that renegade humans are aboard. There's a decent chance they will wait for you to identify yourselves."

"Ourselves? Captain, aren't you going—"

"The *Bloodborne* is my ship. This is your plan. I want you to take the frigate to Varuna and handle the rescue. You may bring enough crew to staff the key posts on your ship and maintain a security team on the ground. Volunteers only."

"Yes, sir," I said, my voice cracking. "Of course."

So when I boarded the frigate for our mission and stepped onto the bridge, I did not go to the helm as my training would have suggested, but to the command dais in the center of the chamber. It had already been made over with chairs and consoles to our height.

The main screen was a wide wraparound display in the Alcaltan fashion, since the aliens' eyes rested on the sides of their heads. I would have to swivel the captain's chair to see everything around me.

This should have been Kellen's, I thought, as I stood looking at the high-backed chair. I had no doubt that if he'd lived, the Captain would have given him command of the frigate. Instead, the first person to sit in this chair for a real mission would be the relief pilot of the *Bloodborne.* I'd only helmed the ship once in combat. I wasn't part of the Captain's regular bridge crew.

But the rescue had been my idea. The Captain was right. I had to be the one to see it through.

My volunteer crew filed onto the bridge, taking their places in the stations that ringed mine. Valerie had the scanners, Peter was weapons lead, and Manuel, our helmsman. Hitomi was our best Alcaltan mimic, so we placed her on the comm, to delay any hostile response for as long as possible. Caleb insisted on being the frigate's engineer. He had overseen the retrofit, so it only made sense to take him along, and he'd brought three assistants with him.

In total, we had twenty crew on board, a fifth of our entire population. We had to come back.

With a deep breath, I sat in the chair meant for Kellen and ordered us out.

* * *

Varuna loomed before us, a pale red egg tinged with crisp bits of ice. Manuel put it up on the wraparound as he guided the frigate into high orbit. It looked sedate enough, but I knew better than to trust my eyes. The planetoid itself was a blind spot, blocking our view of anything that might be hidden behind.

"Anything on the scanners?" I asked.

Valerie shook her head, barely even looking up from her console. "No ships registering in our immediate vicinity, but we'll want to complete a full circuit around the planetoid to be sure."

I looked at the time set to Alcaltan standard. We were early, a habit born of the need to lie in wait for our prey. It would have been nice if the transport had been early as well. I couldn't stop the uneasy twinge in my gut, knowing that the safety of our families could not be guaranteed until they were on board with us.

"Manuel, prepare to take us down to low orbit once we finish our circuit, assuming nothing turns up. Peter, drop a missile pod."

"Sure thing, Alexa."

"On it, Alexa."

I watched the pod fall away, carrying a compliment of missiles with it. It would settle into its own orbit, away from us, and ready to launch a single salvo. It was a good way to catch an enemy off guard, striking it from a direction it did not expect.

"Alexa!" said Hitomi. She cradled a hand against the ear of her headset. "There's chatter on the Alcaltan emergency band."

My gut turned to ice. "What's it saying?"

"It's hard to tell. The speaker's very excited. Not military, but it's trying to alert them. Something about a chase with three ships. No, four. They're all in our sector of the belt."

Four ships racing through the Kuiper Belt? They must be lighting up the Alcaltan warning systems like fireworks.

"Valerie! Can you find them on our long-range scan?"

"Already checking," she said.

Manuel caught my eye but didn't say anything. We were still in high orbit. Low orbit would hide us better from a long-range scan, but we wouldn't be able to scan as well either, not with a planetoid blocking our view.

"Any luck?" I asked.

"Nothing yet," she replied.

If the ships weren't heading our way, we could ignore them. They would have nothing to do with our smuggling run. But if our transport was involved, we couldn't afford to stand by.

"Cargo ship," said Hitomi, eyes unfocused as she concentrated on the audio feed. "Mining-class transport. Smugglers on board."

"That sounds like it could be ours," said Peter.

"I know," I said.

What could they have done to arouse suspicion? I thought I'd offered enough *surya* that there would be no reason for the smugglers to risk the safety of their passengers. We'd paid double for the forged paperwork, and Hush would not get his bonus if the transfer was not complete.

"I still don't see them," said Valerie.

And that meant that we couldn't run to their rescue.

"Hitomi! Have they given out coordinates on the emergency band?"

She shook her head, but I could tell by the way she curled into herself that she did not like what she was hearing.

"A heading, please!" I said to her. "The tattler must be giving some frame of reference. Manuel, get us out of orbit. We can't stay here."

Valerie inhaled sharply. "Cap—" She turned to me wide-eyed, with reflexes telling her how to address the person in the captain's chair, but Captain Mercer wasn't here. It wasn't even Kellen, whom we'd called Lieutenant. It was just me.

"Commander!" she said, recovering. "I've sighted the transport! It's being pursued by two cruisers and a corvette."

Peter turned in my direction. "Alexa! I can have all weapons online in two minutes. What do you want us to do?"

The energy from the charged weapons would give us away. We could handle a single corvette, the frigate was big enough for that, but against two cruisers, we were just outclassed, outgunned.

"Alexa!" someone shouted. I didn't know who. "Alexa!"

"Commander!" Peter snapped.

I hadn't realized I'd stopped breathing.

The odds were bad, but the *Bloodborne* had faced worse escaping Earth. If we didn't try to rescue our families, they wouldn't have any chance at all. The Alcaltans would execute them for trying to escape. We knew that.

"Valerie, you have coordinates now?" I asked.

She nodded. "Already sent to Manuel."

"Manuel, set a course for the lead cruiser. Peter, keep the weapons offline a little longer. We need to be sure of the situation first."

The frigate shuddered as Manuel gave us a good burn. My gut turned all sorts of somersaults, none of which had to do with the motion of spaceflight. Yes, the *Bloodborne* had faced worse escaping Earth, but the *Bloodborne* had had Captain Mercer in command.

"Valerie," I asked, "can you bring up a combat map of the four ships on the main holo?"

"Done," she replied.

The three-dimensional grid displayed our potential battlefield and the four ships, all of which were headed in the direction of Varuna. I grimaced. One of the ships matched up with the schematics of a Mezzen freighter. That would be our transport.

"We're almost in missile range. How much closer are we going to get?" asked Peter. "Chances are their crews are preoccupied with trying to catch the transport. If we fire now, we'll be able to catch them by surprise."

"But if this isn't our transport, we're going to be jumping into a fight with the odds against us," I said. "Hitomi, have they noticed us?"

She shook her head. "Nothing as far as I can tell. The emergency band has gone silent. The situation has been reported as 'under control.'"

"That's a good thing," I said, with a confidence I didn't feel. "It means we won't have to deal with more than these three ships."

Peter was right. We could fire first and strike them before they could react, but if we didn't score a fatal hit on more than one of them, we'd still be outnumbered, and I doubted that we'd down a cruiser in an opening salvo. Those things were armored enough that we'd only bust a few bulkheads, with no guarantee we'd break through to the vitals. I couldn't risk such an attack for less than absolute certainty of the transport's identity, and there was no way to determine that without hailing it.

"Hitomi," I said. "Open a channel to the Alcaltan patrol ships and ask them under what circumstances they are chasing that transport. If they need our ID, go ahead and use the real one assigned to this ship. As far as they are concerned, we are a frigate returning to Earthspace for evaluation after being retrieved from pirates. Our goal is to give ourselves an excuse to hail the transport without drawing fire from the patrol. If it's not our transport, we'll withdraw. You know the pass phrase."

She nodded, hesitation melting away as she slipped into character. A languid expression crossed her face as she hit the comm and burbled out a salutation that sounded like a phlegm-filled mutter. I couldn't follow Alcaltan as well as Hitomi did, but she did a remarkable job of sounding as though she had just stepped into an undesirable problem she could not avoid.

The exchange passed for an intense two minutes, then moved to an extended pause. Turning off her mic, Hitomi explained that the Alcaltans were verifying our ship ID.

"Are they concerned about us?" I asked.

"Not yet. Seems within protocol."

Peter sat ramrod straight in his seat, hand resting on the lever that would power the cannons. His other hand had one finger on the comm that connected him to all the gun crews on the ship. He spoke softly, notifying them that they were on standby and should prepare to open fire on the lead cruiser at any moment. In the event that communication with him was compromised, they should assume hostilities with the Alcaltan patrol and use manual override to return fire.

"I have permission to speak with the transport," said Hitomi. "Opening a channel now."

She launched into another broadcast, her attitude miffed and domineering, and I knew the patrol would be listening in.

"You must have interesting cargo to come all the way out here," she said.

After a lengthy pause, the Alcaltan freighter replied, *"It is like home out here."*

Hitomi made a noncommittal statement as though nothing was amiss, but the rest of the bridge held its collective breath, the air so still that the silence was only broken by Hitomi's inane chatter.

This was our transport!

"I've got target locks down the length of the lead cruiser," said Peter. "Their distortion field will probably knock out the first volley, but we'll have a second before they can redirect."

"Should I continue approach, or turn the ship?" asked Manuel.

Peter shook his head. "Don't turn until after we fire the first two volleys."

"We can't use the side cannons from this position though."

"If we turn, they're going to notice we're up to something. We'll lose any chance of surprise!" Peter swung in my direction. "Alexa, do I have permission to power up the weapons?"

I gave a stiff nod. "Do it."

Hitomi continued to speak over the comm as though nothing was amiss, but I could tell something had changed in the demeanor of the freighter. It sounded eerily like hope, and if it was clear enough for a pidgin speaker like me, it must be blazingly obvious to the patrol.

A harsh voice cut in demanding to know why our weapons systems were online.

Hitomi insightfully pointed out that the Alcaltan patrol already had their weapons up, and we were only trying to help.

They probably wouldn't be able to recognize that our cannons were directed at them at such a distance, but our weapons coming up at the same time as the transport was getting optimistic wasn't a good sign.

"Weapons charged!" said Peter.

All the moisture went out of my mouth. "Fire."

A wave of long-range *Fulmi*-class missiles launched from half our forward cannons, then a moment later, the second round fired from the other half. The high-energy exhaust cones of the first wave made for the ideal smokescreen for the second. It was a tactic we had developed late in the war in an attempt to overcome the Alcaltans' distortion technology. Their command of gravity allowed them to warp space at points around their ship, diverting the direction of the missiles and causing them to miss.

Common sense said the Alcaltan cruiser would shunt the oncoming missiles at its flank above or behind it, so they wouldn't endanger the other ships in its patrol group or accidentally shoot down the transport. Once the hidden second wave of missiles closed in on the Alcaltan cruiser, they would execute a burn to redirect themselves around to the front of the ship, bypassing the warped space before the Alcaltans could see the new threat and set up a second gravity well. It should be a solid hit. Peter had done this before on the *Bloodborne* as Nathan's junior.

"Five minutes until impact," said Peter.

"Any reaction from the Alcaltans?" I asked.

"The targeted cruiser is changing its heading," said Valerie. "The other cruiser and the corvette are still in pursuit of the transport."

Manuel muttered a curse.

"They've cut the line," said Hitomi. "I can't raise the freighter anymore."

I grimaced. "It's not going to be able to outrun them."

"The targeted cruiser has returned fire!" said Valerie. "They've got better propulsion than us. We're looking at ten to twenty missiles in three minutes!"

"Distortion field is ready," said Peter. "I have gravity-well creation set to staccato just in case they try our own tactic on us."

"That's risking a hit! We're a frigate, not a dreadnought."

He grunted and shifted in his seat. "We should be able to take one or two hits without compromising the hull, but we won't want to risk an unprotected second wave. I'd rather take a fifty-fifty chance of minor damage than a ten percent chance at a fatal hole in the hull."

"Nathan wouldn't go for that," said Valerie, but she shot her glance at me rather than Peter.

When I did not immediately reply, Hitomi asked, "What should we do?"

And I realized that I needed to be the one to answer that. The cruiser we had shot at was turning to engage. It had been traveling lengthwise to us, allowing the use of its more numerous side cannons, so it if was turning, that could only mean that it had a fixed main cannon it wished to engage. I thought of the *Bloodborne*'s own implosion cannon, and a chill settled around me. The cruiser should be too small for such a weapon, but that didn't mean it couldn't be lethal.

"Two minutes until impact," said Valerie.

"Three for ours," said Peter.

Staccato creation would be no good against a main cannon. A grav cannon would be capable of powering through all but the strongest of gravity wells. The staccato defense was like slapping willy-nilly at the missiles. It allowed the space distortion to be done quickly by making smaller wells with little strength behind them, so it was capable of reacting fast enough to catch a stealth wave, but also risked not being powerful enough to divert any one missile.

"Commander!" This time it was Manuel.

"One minute," said Valerie.

Hitomi echoed her countdown, broadcasting to the rest of the ship and calling all crews to secure themselves.

"Change it!" I said, turning to Peter. "Change the distortion to full!" I could see him hesitate and shouted, "They're firing the main cannon!"

He was on it before the last word came out of my mouth.

"Impact in twenty seconds," said Valerie.

"Distortion set," said Peter. "We'd better hope they don't have a stealth wave."

"Ten seconds!"

"Don't forget to secure yourself too, Commander," said Hitomi.

I'd forgotten, and I quickly snapped on my harness.

If there was only one wave of missiles, they would be shunted aside by the well and we would feel nothing. But if there was a stealth wave . . .

"Missiles deflected—"

Peter did not have a chance to finish before we felt the impact of the stealth wave rocket up from below us. The lights flickered as we teetered in our seats. Then a second impact rippled through us, turning stomachs and making more than one of us hold our heads from nausea. The distortion field had dampened the full force of the main cannon.

"Heads up," said Valerie. "I'm registering heat from their main cannon. They're going to give us another shot."

"And this time they'll time it better with the missiles," said Peter.

Die by a rain of missiles or die by the main cannon. We couldn't divert everything.

"Damage reports are coming in," said Hitomi. "Internal teams have sealed the bulkheads to the damaged areas. It looks like we've only lost—"

"The corvette has changed course to engage. The other cruiser has almost caught up to the transport," said Valerie.

The lights flickered again.

"Lost what?" I asked Hitomi.

Before she could reply, the comm to the engine room lit up and Caleb's sweaty face peered up from the screen by my station.

"Alexa," he said, "we've got a problem. That hit took out some of the wiring to the ship. We're trying to reroute as much as we can to take the load off the damaged areas, but we're looking at several local power failures."

"Which systems were affected?"

"Gravity control. That's the biggest one. The grav drive itself is fine, but we're going to have to throttle it to make sure it doesn't short out. We're doing everything we can to make a workaround possible, but you're going to have to be extremely careful—"

"We're dead," said Peter. "If we have to throttle the grav drive, we're not going to be able to run the distortion generator at full."

No. We can't be. Not yet.

"Missiles incoming," said Valerie. "Three minutes. Main cannon hasn't fired yet, but it's safe to say it's being timed to arrive at the same moment."

Peter shook his head. "I don't know what I can do. I can put up a well for the main cannon at the last second to avoid straining the electrical grid, but it won't be very strong. It's still better than nothing . . ."

"Cut artificial gravity to the ship," I said. "Countdown in one minute."

Caleb had left the comm open, and he barked an affirmative.

Hitomi broadcast the warning to the rest of the ship.

"You'll have your power, Peter."

"Commander," said Valerie, "the corvette has opened fire as well!"

We couldn't do this. There was just too much. I could hear the different countdowns, to loss of gravity, to impact, all of it a gray haze. What was I doing there? And then I felt my stomach lift and my hair rise. Gravity was gone. We had only seconds left, then the missiles hit.

My harness cut deep into my shoulders as the ship rocked. I don't know how, but Peter must have pulled a miracle with the gravity well, because we were still alive.

"More casualties reported," Hitomi was telling me.

"One of them mine," Caleb cut in.

"Dead?" I asked.

"Not yet, but she's got a bad concussion."

"Three dead, two critically wounded," said Hitomi, as if she hadn't heard Caleb's interruption.

"We can't take another barrage," said Peter. "I could feel the distortion generator give just as I changed from full to staccato for the stealth wave. The ship's shedding plating. Too many bulkheads busted, and the forward guns have been heavily damaged."

"Then the casualties?" I asked.

"Mostly my team," he said.

Faces flashed before me. Without asking names I couldn't be exactly sure whom Peter had placed at the forward guns, but it didn't matter. I knew everyone who had come aboard. They had volunteered because I had a plan, because they wanted to rescue their families as much as I did and they believed I could do it.

I looked at the scanner display, at the ships heading toward us and the cruiser suddenly on top of the transport. The freighter would never get away unassisted. What would the Captain do?

"They're readying a third salvo," said Valerie.

Peter raised his head. "This is it."

"Manuel," I said. My voice couldn't have been more than a whisper, but I felt it thunder on the bridge. "Take us out of here, fast as you can. Peter, whatever shreds of the distortion generator you can get working, use it to cover our rear."

"We're leaving?" croaked Hitomi.

"We have to," I said. But no matter how hard I tried to put my family out of my mind, I could not help but picture my mom and brother cowering in that freighter, hoping to be rescued. I'd let them down, and I was sorry, so very sorry.

But I had other lives depending on me, and they still had a chance to escape.

"We're too badly damaged," I told Hitomi, "and I'm not going to risk the lives of any more crew."

"I'll try to wag our tail as we go," said Manuel. He would not turn around to face me. "If we're lucky, the energy cone from our thrusters will smear on their display, make it a little harder for them to target us."

The frigate shuddered as the ship turned around.

"Will we have enough power to get range on pursuers?" I asked.

"Maybe," said Caleb. "I'm more concerned about our hull integrity. It looks good enough for flight, but just barely."

I could see Varuna before us again, now that we had turned around. If we could duck around the other side, we might be able to earn a breather long enough to escape into deep space.

"Speeding up," said Manuel. "We're gaining distance. The cruiser has changed its heading. It does not appear to be pursuing."

"But the corvette is!" said Valerie.

"That thing's moving fast. If it wants to fight, it's gonna catch us."

"Peter," I said, "can we hold against the corvette?"

He shrugged. "You know what our systems are like."

Our display showed the corvette chasing us out of the solar system, closing in. In a fair fight it would be a close match, but it wasn't fair anymore. Its crew knew we were limping, they might even be contemplating boarding. Did they know who we were?

This was my fault. If I hadn't come up with this crazy idea, our families would have continued living on Earth, not free, but at least alive. We wouldn't have casualties on top of a failed rescue.

"They're gonna fire on us at any moment," said Peter.

"I know," I said. We weren't going to get around Varuna in time. "How are our rear cannons?"

"Fully functional, but with the distortion generator compromised, I don't know if we'll be able to get any gravity wells up again once we let the field down. You can forget staccato."

"If we don't take out this corvette, it's going to be over for us anyway."

I looked at Varuna on the wraparound and then down at the monitors at Peter's station. There was one reassuring green glow. One hope.

Peter noted the same thing I saw and said, "I'll time them. Distortion field coming down. Give me thirty seconds and we'll be ready to fire."

"Manuel," I said, "stop wagging. Let Peter line up his locks. We're going to need to make these shots count."

"They've opened fire," said Valerie. "Missiles will land in three minutes."

"Are we ready, Peter?" I asked.

The missiles lit up Valerie's screen. The corvette crew hadn't even bothered with a stealth wave from the looks of it. They might have seen our distortion field come down and assumed it would never return. They could have been right. We were wide open.

"Ready!" he said.

"Then fire."

The ship shuddered with the force of the cannons. Our frigate did not bother with a stealth wave either, because from orbit around Varuna, Peter had triggered our missile pod, the second attack that the corvette would not anticipate.

"Two minutes to impact," said Valerie.

"Distortion field is coming up," said Peter, but it wasn't rising fast enough.

On the holo, I could see two sets of missiles tracking for the corvette, timed to land at the same moment from different directions. It would not be able to block both.

"I think we got them," I said. "If we make it out of this, thank you, everyone, and I'm sorry."

Valerie's screen flashed red when the missiles hit us and took out what remained of our electrical systems.

* * *

The damage was not fatal, though for hours the ship was completely without power. We looked like a piece of space junk, which was just as well. If either of the cruisers had decided to take a spin back, it would have been over for us.

Caleb was eventually able to jury-rig something once we no longer had the threat of death hanging over our heads, and he thought it would be enough to get us back to Pyre Rock. On our way, we were met by the *Bloodborne*, and our sorry frigate pulled into its shadow, accepting the escort home.

The Captain requested my presence aboard the dreadnought and I took a shuttle over. The halls were largely empty, the crew focused on the execution that Earth broadcast into the depths of space just for us. I could not watch. I was the one who failed, the one who had risked everything and lost our families. I'd almost gotten the crew of the frigate killed. I was no Kellen.

When I entered the Captain's office, I found him sitting behind his desk as he had so many times before. He was watching the execution proceedings, but minimized the display with a gesture. I would have remained standing for the dressing down I expected, but instead he motioned for me to take a seat at the round table.

"You knew we'd fail, didn't you," I said. "That's why the *Bloodborne* came out to meet us. We aren't late by any means."

My Captain stood and walked over to me. His face was stern and I cringed beneath his gaze.

"I would not have wasted the schematics on a fool's errand," he said. "You know how much those were worth. You sold them yourself." He looked at me. "I did have some doubts about your success, but there is a difference between doubting and believing in failure. The important thing was your initiative."

To my surprise he pulled back the other chair from the table and sat across from me. "Ever since we lost Kellen I've been considering who would be best to replace him. It would have to be someone who knows my mind. Someone whom I can trust as an extension of myself. This was your test."

"But I lost! And some of my crew even died."

My Captain frowned, a shadow cast over his eyes. "How do you think I felt when we lost Kellen? Yes, you failed, but I think that is one of the most important lessons for a captain to learn. Think about what you've done in pursuit of this mission. You spoke with the crew. You bartered with the rogue Alcaltans. You commanded a frigate in actual combat and survived. You even took out an enemy ship. Sometimes you have to make choices, and they aren't the ones that you want, but that is part of what it is to be in command."

He paused.

"Did anyone ever tell you what happened when I first took the *Bloodborne* to rescue the colonists? The Earth government, afraid of what the Alcaltans would do to us, threatened to kill my family if I went ahead with the rescue."

"But . . . you did."

He nodded.

"I had to choose between four lives and four hundred, and either way I would lose. I think you know some of what that's like now."

"Captain, I—"

"The frigate is yours if you wish to command it. I know morale is low, but don't hold it against yourself. It was a worthy goal, and remember that every member of the crew who went with you volunteered knowing the danger. You did a fine job under the circumstances, and you now have a tested crew."

The frigate? Mine?

"I don't know what to say."

He regarded me, and I thought I detected a flicker of warmth that hadn't been there before. "How about picking a name for it?"

I thought about the battered ship, what hopes it had carried and what we had tried to do with it, and then of the burden it bore as we realized that there was nothing at all left for us on Earth. There had never been a chance of going home, but now even the dream of that was gone.

"The *Exile*," I said. "I want to call it the *Exile*."

"Very well." My Captain stood and pushed in his chair. "I understand your crew calls you Commander now. It's a good title. We'll talk again later once we get back to Pyre Rock and make the transition official. For now, dismissed."

I left his office, my heart a little less heavy, but understanding the direction he had given me. However much it hurt, I knew I had made the right decision. It was the decision the Captain would have made. My Captain and I—we are more alike than I thought.

About Laurie Tom

Laurie has been entranced by science fiction and fantasy since childhood and has been writing ever since. When not visiting other worlds she can usually be found gaming, reading books, or watching anime. Her short fiction has appeared in venues such as Strange Horizons, Intergalactic Medicine Show, and Galaxy's Edge.

WHAT HE OFFERED THE RIVER

By *Aimee Ogden* | *3,100 words*

JASON FOUND THE pieces of the broken boat down by the water just before the rain started.

Anger surged up first—Laurel should know better. Then doubt, undercut with guilt—hadn't he taught her to be more careful than that? Such a little thing, but still too much and too dangerous to leave beside this river. He let cool rain wash the self-recrimination from his clenched shoulders. He got to his knees to collect the pieces, and tucked them into the hem of his shirt to carry. Discussion could come later, would have to come later. First he had to prevent the damage that could have been done, if he wasn't too late already. He combed through the grass carefully to make sure he hadn't missed a stray bit of plastic. Rain soaked his shirt and blurred his vision, and he used his fingers to search for what his eyes might miss. When he was satisfied, he got up and turned his back to the river.

A small face peeped at him from the kitchen window. She must've gone up to the house when the rain started. He ducked his chin against the rain and started up the hill. His feet carved long muddy wounds in the sodden grass, and he counted each one he left: . . . *four, five, six* . . .

She was still watching, leaning against the kitchen doorframe, when he came in through the back door. His daughter had always been a quiet child, growing up solitary and a little wild, as likely to be caught trying to build a houseboat out of cast-off boards as perusing Jason's old nursing school textbooks. He sat down at the table, and she studied him as if he were one of those anatomical drawings, something to be picked over and thoughtfully analyzed to some obscure purpose.

He kept her waiting while he bent to take off his wet shoes. Six years of practice hadn't made him any abler at speaking to his daughter in a way that she'd understand. Or maybe she was just evolving faster, finding new ways to tune him out or misunderstand or let her big blue eyes gleam with unshed tears. He sighed and let the boat pieces spill out of his shirt and onto the table. The wet string tied to the cracked prow fell in a near-perfect circle around it, a ring of protection that had arrived too late. The little plastic fisherman who could sit in the prow was missing entirely—lost at sea, Jason supposed. "What happened?"

She bent her neck, carefully studying the scabs on her knees. "I don't know."

He pressed his thumb against one of the broken edges on the boat. It wasn't sharp enough to draw blood, but it did leach the rising tide of temper. "Laurel."

She looked up to meet his gaze through a tangle of black hair. That was her mother's look, and her mother's hair too. She huffed, and the snarl of bangs fluttered out of her face. "I wanted to see if I could fill the boat with water and swing it around in a circle so fast that the water would stay in." A flash of pride. "And I did it! But then I let go and it hit the tree and it broke." And her gaze dropped to the floor again as she toed the pattern in the linoleum. Her feet were dirty; they were always dirty. She loved being outside as much as she hated shoes. "And I remembered what you said about the river granting wishes and I thought maybe the river could fix my boat—"

Jason stood up too fast. The chair canted backward and banged into the wall. He let it fall, and strode to the sink. Both hands clasped the cold stainless steel as he breathed deeply of the draft from the open window. Granting wishes! As if the river was some beneficent genie, a simple mender of broken toys and finder of lost things.

Well, perhaps she had been that, from time to time. But nothing was ever that simple, not completely. Jason closed his eyes. Down by the river, the wind chimes sang arrhythmically, and the carnations he'd planted that spring shone pink and red in between the shrubbery. Despite his best efforts the words dripped out of his mouth, like the leaky faucet he'd never fixed: "Do you realize what you could have done?"

She held so still he could feel her lack of movement, the sudden absence of six-year-old wiggling and bouncing. He drank down a cool damp breath from the window, held it in his lungs for as long as he could, blew it back out. "Laurel," he said. Maybe she was ready. Not to offer a broken toy boat, no. But he couldn't keep her from giving things to the river, not forever. Not unless she understood. "Do you want to hear a story?"

A shuffle of bare feet on linoleum. When he looked over, a sharp crease pinched between her brows. "Okay," she said.

They sat down at the table with the superglue and the pieces of the boat scattered atop a towel. Jason worked his tongue in his mouth and tried to find the story's beginning. "Once upon a time," he said, "there was a man."

Laurel stared down at her hands in her lap under the table. "What kind of man?" she asked her scabby knees. "What was his name?"

"It doesn't matter." He passed her the tiny cap from the glue to hold, and ignored her scrunched face. "What matters is that he was lonely. He lived by himself, worked alone. No else to talk to. So he was lonely."

The cap rolled across the tabletop under Laurel's fingers. "So he left something for the river," she said, and darted a glance at Jason's face.

He nodded. The tip of the glue bottle traced the jagged rectangle where the boat's cabin had sheared off. "He didn't know that was what he was doing. But he planted mayflower down by the water, and left things lying around. Forgotten fishing lures and sandwich crusts, and maybe even a rake. Things the river liked, as it happened. He was still lonely, of course. But he started to have strange good luck, maybe even before he noticed anything was different. Sunshine on his shoulders on a cold day, or a good catch." He pressed the cabin into the line of glue he'd drawn and held it there. "You have to be careful, Laurel, what you offer the river. Because she'll take it, whatever it is, whether you mean to offer it or not." He leaned over the half-mended boat. "Did you know your aunt Kathy left a couple of cigarette butts down by the water the first time she visited us here?"

A scandalized giggle from Laurel. "Dad! Aunt Kathy doesn't smoke."

"Not anymore, she doesn't." He'd warned Kathy, of course, but she hadn't listened. He wasn't sure he would have believed his sister either, if the situation had been reversed. "Now every time she puts a cigarette in her mouth, it's as soggy as if it'd been lying on the riverbank for a week."

Laurel didn't say a word as she processed this, but her feet kicked against the seat of her chair. Finally she said, "Well, why doesn't she just leave a new offering and ask the river to stop doing that?"

"She's tried." Jason twirled the boat's mast against the tip of the glue bottle until it gleamed. It slid neatly into the jagged slot that it had come from, and he held it there. "If the river doesn't like your offering, that's the last one she ever takes from you. Whether you meant it as an offering or not. There's a kind of . . . symbolism to offerings, things they mean and secrets they hide. And it's hard for people to really understand what it is they're saying to the river, or asking her for." Even when it had been explained to him, he hadn't really understood. Human ears weren't made to hear that kind of language, and human eyes weren't meant to see it. You could get lucky with an offering, certainly. Or you might be left standing by a silent shoreline. His fingertips squeezed the mast, painfully. "I didn't want to tell you that. To make you afraid that she'd stop listening to you. But I've told you a thousand times, Laurel—"

"To be careful what I leave by the river." Her head was bowed and her messy curls cast her face in shadow. Her hands clutched the seat of the chair, and her feet had stopped kicking. "I'm sorry, Daddy."

Terrible silence stretched out between them while Jason fumbled for the right words to say. *There's nothing to be sorry about* wasn't quite right, and *I forgive you* was too high-handed. *Go add superglue to the grocery list* was totally unacceptable.

But Laurel saved him from that struggle. She peeked up through her tangle of hair, and he froze under her blue-eyed stare. "Daddy?" she asked. "What did the lonely man leave for the river, so that he wouldn't be lonely anymore?"

"Ah." He looked down at the boat. "Well, that's between the man and the river. But what he gave, the river liked. And so she came to live with him."

Her mouth hung open, and then she pushed back her chair so that it tilted onto two legs. Her knees kept her anchored to the table while she shook her head at the ceiling. "Dad, that's silly. This is a made-up story! How could a river live in a house?"

"Well, she didn't look like a river anymore." He smiled down at the mast, which held true when he let go. A glossy line of glue had dried on one fingernail too. Now there was just a crack left in the top of the boat. He traced it with the tip of the glue bottle. "She looked like a lady, with eyes like cornflowers and the thickest black hair you've ever seen."

The front legs of Laurel's chair dropped back to the floor with a one-two clatter. "Was she pretty?" Laurel whispered, and Jason nodded.

"As beautiful as the river. And the man wasn't lonely anymore. He loved the river. And she probably loved him too." He squeezed the outside of the boat's hull to bring the edges of the split together. The boat wouldn't be fully watertight after this, but it should hold up unless it capsized. It would have to do. "For as long as she could."

Laurel sat as still as a windless day. "What happened to her?"

"Nothing happened, really. Years went by, and I think maybe it's not easy for a river to be a person instead of a river." To be small, to be weak, to eat and hiccup and bleed. He checked the boat over one last time, then slid it across the table. Laurel didn't pick it up. "Imagine going from being this thundering giant, full of life and power, to being one small person with just one ticking heart inside." Laurel's eyebrows drew into a frown, and who could blame her? He didn't understand it any better than she did. He shrugged, a little jerk of one shoulder. "Well, she managed as long as she could, and when she couldn't take it anymore, she went back."

"And the man was lonely again."

He studied her across the table, the familiar dark tangle of curls, those too-bright blue eyes like sunlight on the water. "No," he said. "He was never lonely again."

One of Laurel's hands crept out, then pulled the boat toward her chest. "Thank you for my boat, Daddy," she said, and slid out of her chair. "I'll be in my room."

"Careful with it," he said automatically, and she fled.

For the next hour or two, soft thumps and padded footsteps came through the kitchen ceiling from Laurel's room. Jason stayed at the kitchen table with a cup of coffee and the Sunday newspaper, and tried not to be too curious about what she was up to. Occasionally she emerged on brief excursions: to the bookshelves in the living room, where she grabbed a stack of beloved picture books. To the kitchen, where she stuffed something from the fridge inside her shirt before haring off again. When the sounds grew still, Jason couldn't pretend to read the letters to the editor any longer. He left his coffee to cool, and padded up the stairs.

Laurel's door stood a few inches ajar, and he leaned against the jamb to peer inside. On the carpet lay hints of her mysterious project: the spine of her favorite book, a Jazz Age retelling of Cinderella, with only a jagged line down the middle to show where all the pages had been torn out. A Styrofoam tray of hamburger meat, open to the air and oozing reddish-brown. An old bottle of ladies' perfume, pilfered from the top of the dresser in Jason's bedroom. And no Laurel.

He came all the way into the room, and peered down through her bedroom window. There she was, sneaking outside in the rain with her secret handiwork clutched close to her heart. She meant to offer something to the river, he realized, purposefully this time, and his heart thundered in his chest like the rain against the windows.

He took the stairs two at a time. The screen door, well oiled, did not screech to announce his approach, and Laurel didn't turn to look as he followed her several paces back. When his ankle turned on a hidden obstacle, he stifled a curse and looked down to see what had almost given him away. It was Laurel's toy fisherman, head-down in the grass and the mud—not lost at sea after all. He stuck the little yellow-suited man into his pocket and kept on after Laurel.

She pushed between the riverside shrubberies, and crouched down with whatever treasures she carried. Jason recognized her plastic cup from the bathroom as he watched her dip her finger inside and use the contents to draw on her face. What was she drawing? "Having babies," she said. "That means blood. I know that." She had her back to Jason, and he didn't dare move closer. He couldn't interrupt her, not now. Next she bent and picked up one of the pages of her Cinderella book. She tore it into strips, and the strips disappeared into her mouth. "Bedtime stories and secrets," she said. This was the river's language, Jason knew, could feel it prickling the hairs on the back of his neck. Laurel spoke it unflinchingly and instinctively. What did she think she was asking for, and what exactly did she mean to give?

Now she stood up and shredded the rest of her book's pages like confetti, letting the wind take them from her hands. One clear laugh rolled through the rain to Jason. And then Laurel took one great step over the edge of the bank and into the river.

He cried out before the sound of the splash even reached him. The grass was slippery under his feet and the tangle of mayflower grabbed at his ankles as he leaped over. Cold water closed over his head like a finished storybook, and with it came panic. Water filled his mouth, but all he tasted was the bitter sting of adrenaline. It was all too familiar and too strange all at once. He'd been here before and shouldn't have survived to have another go. At least the river was full of warm summer rain this time rather than the last of the snowmelt. It wrapped him in its too-familiar embrace.

No. No time for the drag of memory now. He kicked off his shoes, reached forward, pulled himself through the water. His head broke the surface and there was Laurel, only a few yards out. She struggled to keep her head above water. When he shouted wordlessly to her, she spun, arms thrashing. He dived under once more, reaching, reaching.

She slipped under the surface just as he reached her, and her tiny arms locked around his neck. He yanked her, not gently, around to his back. He wished for a moment to simply hold her—but instead of riding the current, now he had to fight sideways across it to make for the riverbank. Leaden arms pulled against the water, weary legs thrashed. They went under together again, half a dozen times, tumbled relentlessly by the current. In his ear, between sputters, Laurel pleaded for him not to be angry, Daddy, please.

They finally floundered ashore just south of Buckthorn Island. Laurel huddled, small and shivering, under his arm while he tried to get enough air into his lungs to say: *What were you thinking, why did you do this, don't you know what could have happened?* But she wrapped her fists into his shirt and said, "Dad, Daddy, it's all right, don't be mad! I know what the man offered the river."

"Laurel," he said, and now the cold that soaked him was more than physical. Terror had frozen him to a psychological absolute zero, and there was no breath for more words, no movement in his lungs.

"I knew how to ask, just like you said, Daddy. Just like the man did, but not exactly the same. I don't need the same thing as he did. And I knew what I was asking for." The weight of her head on his chest, a million miles away, the soft reminder of sunlight on a cold and distant planet. "He offered himself. Maybe he didn't know that's what he was doing then, but that's what he gave her. Isn't it?"

"Laurel," he said, and his arms folded around her like a convulsion. She went still against him, holding him as tightly as he held her. *What did you ask the river for?*

"Daddy," she said. Her voice was small, confused. A little hurt. Close by, the waters of the river had begun to stir and froth. Jason knew the answer even before Laurel spoke it aloud, and his eyes squeezed shut against the burn of tears. "I asked her for my mom. Do you think she'll listen?"

About Aimee Ogden

Aimee Ogden lives in Wisconsin with her husband, three-year-old twins, and very old dog. A former software tester and science teacher, she now writes stories about sad astronauts and angry princesses.

LULLABY FOR THE TREES

By Sarina Dorie | 10,000 Words

A SINGLE NOTE rose out of Mama's throat. It was so beautiful, I forgot my cold and only felt wonder. The high, sweet song wove a pattern in the trees around her, brilliant sparks of magic bursting like fireworks in the dark shadows under the ancient boughs. I rubbed my eyes in awe. This had to be my imagination playing tricks on me, something inspired by watching too much television.

Mama's voice could melt hearts and sing the forest awake. At least, that's what Papa said. Tonight she sang, and the great oaks shivered. The twisted apple tree above her unbent his trunk and straightened to his full height. The air filled with the perfume of apple cider and autumn, making me feel safe and content.

I watched from behind a cluster of birches some distance from the immense apple tree. In that moment, I came to believe the folktales from the old country. My parents had told me about vilas, the maidens who were nature fairies, and leshii, the tree people. The grandfather apple tree came alive. His cracked bark smoothed, reminding me of human flesh, and the surface of his trunk gathered into an expression of admiration. He spoke with a voice as resonant as church bells, and when he sang, I knew I was in a sacred sanctuary.

The twisted limbs remained still, but they creaked and groaned as if dancing in a windstorm. Mama raised her arms, and her cape fell open, exposing the pale gown she wore underneath that looked like it belong to another time. Papa often teased her about being a romantic. Only being six, I wasn't sure what a romantic was. I suspected it had something to do with kissing, something my parents were quite fond of.

Mama danced around the tree, singing with joy. A percussion of pops and clicks echoed around us and vibrated through my body. My fingers twitched, and my toes, numb with cold, warmed in the embrace of music. She and the tree sang a duet. The grandfather apple tree's roots shifted as she danced around him. Any moment it felt as though he might uproot himself and twirl her in his arms.

I found myself swaying to the melody. When the first note escaped my lips, the forest music soured into silence. The magic died. The tree was just a tree. The air no longer smelled of hot apple cider and merriment, but rotting apples and wet mildew.

My mother leaned against the gnarled trunk, out of breath and spent. She looked up at me and frowned.

Knowing I would be in big trouble for spying, I ran. She called after me, but I didn't heed her words. I raced along the moonlit path. My feet crunched past the caved-in shack and then through the field of our neighbor's farm. In a few more minutes, I rushed up the porch steps and snuck back inside. A floorboard creaked as I tiptoed to bed. The pounding of my heart was loud enough I was surprised I didn't wake Papa. I expected to hear Mama march up to the door, the creak of rusty hinges signaling her arrival. I waited to be chewed out.

In the morning, Papa woke me. He didn't question why twigs were stuck to the hem of my nightgown or why my bare feet were covered in dirt. "Dobryj ranok, Liliya," he said in Ukrainian.

Usually I greeted him with, "Speak English, Papa. Say 'good morning,'" but this morning I just swallowed.

He ruffled my hair like nothing was wrong and opened the avocado-green refrigerator. He set about preparing the kutya sweet porridge for breakfast. I peeked into my parents' bedroom. Mama wasn't there.

"She'll be back soon, my little flower." The corners of Papa's eyes crinkled as he smiled at me. "Don't worry."

Mama still hadn't returned by the time breakfast was ready. The third bowl of kutya remained on the table long after we finished dishes. I stared out the window at the muddy road. The crisp gold of the leaves contrasted with the gray gloom of the sky.

Papa laced up his old boots. I knew it was my fault she hadn't come back. I'd disturbed the magic. I'd heard Mama talk about not displeasing the spirits of the trees in the past.

"Stay put, my little one," Papa said. "Do your schoolwork. It is due tomorrow, ni?"

My gaze cut to the backpack in the corner made from a patch-work of jeans my mother had sewn together. Her embroidery looked quaint and old-world compared to the Spiderman and Barbie backpacks of other children my age. Of course, the other kids weren't immigrants like we were either.

"Or you could watch the television," Papa winked.

Usually that would have filled me with joy since my mother only let me watch three hours on the weekend, and I'd already filled my quota yesterday, but nothing could lighten the weight on my heart.

I watched from the window as Papa skipped down the muddy path through our field and into the neighbor's. He came back an hour later carrying her in his arms. His face was stricken, eyes glazed and unseeing. He'd wrapped her up in her cloak, but there wasn't enough fabric to disguise the crimson stains on her white dress. Her arm was covered in bruises. Gashes marred her skin.

Mama was dead. All because of me.

* * *

I didn't want to go to the funeral. The tree had been her execu-tioner. When Papa told me where she was to be buried, I realized it was also her tombstone.

"Don't make me go! Please," I begged.

"Don't you want to say good-bye to your mama?" Papa asked. "That's why people have funerals. To say good-bye, ni?" His voice was like a tired old man's. His cheeks were sunken, and his eyes aged with worry lines.

If they had buried Mama in the cemetery in the churchyard like anyone else, I wouldn't have minded. But the minister wouldn't allow it. I was too young to understand why, only that it had some-thing to do with hallowed ground and her not being baptized. Instead, they buried her under the immense apple tree.

I didn't know my mother had so many friends until the funeral. Women showed up in elegant black dresses and pillbox hats, look-ing like ghosts of another era. Men shuffled around, as tall as trees and just as silent.

Even with the heavy stink of roses and ladies' perfume, the damp earth and decaying fruit couldn't be drowned out. I tucked my chin down under the collar of my coat and hid my face to keep the bad air out. An apple plopped onto the fallen leaves next to my foot and burst into mush.

I hugged Papa's legs. During the entire service, the air felt so thick I thought I would suffocate. Every time I blinked, I saw the startled look on Mama's face when I'd broken the spell of magic. Every pink apple on the ground, bruised and marred, reminded me of her arm not quite covered by her cloak, covered in blood and bruises.

As soon as they lowered her coffin into the ground, the air changed. The out-of-season perfume of roses faded under the autumn scent of decaying leaves and decomposing apples. The shadows thickened, and trees creaked around us despite the lack of wind. I wasn't the only one who heard it. Townsfolk looked around.

Another apple plopped to the ground and then another. A nervous laugh erupted out of the crowd.

An immense crack echoed through the air, and a branch snapped in half. People dived out of the way as it fell. But the minister's wife was struck on the head and died on the spot.

The tree had been my mother's executioner. Then it became her tombstone. Now it wanted to kill others.

* * *

A few months later it was poor Mrs. Monroe, who died of food poisoning from the apples she picked, then after another year, it was the minister's sons. With the two teenage boys, their death was caused by falling out of the tree. That's what the sheriff surmised from the torn sweater in the tree and both boys concussed on the ground. They might have lived if not for the internal hemorrhaging.

The summer I turned eight, it was an old man ravaged by wolves. At least, that's what they said. I thought it more likely it had been the tree. The winter after that, someone was stabbed by an icicle falling from the apple tree.

"It must be a coincidence," Papa said. "Your mother loved those woods. I can't believe her leshii are hurting people."

He hadn't seen what I had.

* * *

When I turned twelve, my world changed. At first it was small things like seeing lights dancing on cloudy, moonless lights. Then it was the whispering trees that I could almost understand. Under the surface of my skin, my nerves felt on fire. My palms burned with energy. I had to wear two pairs of socks inside my boots to keep my feet from feeling the vibrations of music coming up from the mud-caked earth that made me want to dance. By the time I was fifteen, it was all I could do not to let my feet carry me into the woods on the way to and from school.

Every day I fought the urge. This day was no different.

I stared at my hands in the dishwater, opening and closing my fists in the hope the tingle would go away. Fleeting wisps of relief washed over my skin when I plunged my hands into the sudsy water. The water grew tepid as I stood there, lost in my own world. I closed my eyes and willed myself not to think about the lure of the lush shadows, of the trees whispering my name, or of the tugging under my breastbone.

"It's the vila in you," Papa said with a wink. I knew he was going to talk about Mama before the words escaped his mouth from the way his eyes lit up. "Your mama had it in her too. Anthousa was special. Different. People didn't understand her. But I did."

I rolled my eyes. I was tired of his fairy stories from the old country that didn't fit into the American world we lived in. I pretended I didn't believe them. And if I kept on pretending, I might be able to make them not true.

Papa went back to clearing off the table. He stooped like an old man and shuffled along without energy. I doubted his eyes would have been so dull or his cheeks so sunken if Mama had still been alive. I submerged my hands in the water and slumped against the sink. The tingle was still there.

Twigs from outside tapped on the windowpane, the rhythm more enticing than the songs on the radio other teenagers danced to.

Papa leaned against the counter beside me. He spoke in Ukrainian, the words lilting over the percussion on the glass.

I gritted my teeth. "Speak English. We live in America."

"Yes, my little flower." He stroked my dark hair away from my eyes. "You have her eyes and hair. Every day that passes, you're more like your mama."

I thought of the tree and her last moments. All my sorrow and melancholy swelled up inside me and exploded into rage.

"I'm not like her!" I shouted. "I'm not going to be like her."

I left the kitchen and slammed the porch door behind me. I meant to cool off in the balmy night, but my feet kept going down the steps and past the driveway. I crunched over dried clods of dirt.

I didn't know where I was going when I set out, but as I passed our field and the neighbor's, the forest loomed closer. I forced myself to slow.

The trees shushed lullabies in the wind. "Closer. Come closer. Closer," they said.

My heart felt as though it were being pulled by a string. I would not go to the woods. I would stop when I reached the edge and turn back. I just needed to cool off. It wasn't right to take out my anger on my father. He was trying to share the only bits of happiness left in him that hadn't yet melted away.

When I reached the edge of the trees, I found my way barred by hazard tape. A sign nailed to a tree warned me to keep out. I stepped back, but pain stabbed into my heart and made my breath come out in a gasp. When I eased forward, I felt well again.

I pushed aside the tape and squeezed through.

I didn't doubt that the tree called me here to kill me. I could hear him speaking in his foreign tongue of snaps and pops. The words reminded me of the Ukrainian language my father spoke, yet this was rougher, more gravelly. The tone was sharp and full of sinister intent. Ferns brushed against my bare ankles, and overgrown weeds caressed my arms. A chill shivered down my spine despite the balmy air. I would be like the child who had died last season. I would not be like my mother.

* * *

Old Mr. Shevchenko had once owned the land, before his house had been foreclosed. For years there had been talk of bulldozing the woods or selling the land to a rich developer from out of town. It would have made my mother sad, but I wasn't my mother. It didn't make me sad. I was disappointed the bank didn't follow through and sell the land. Sure, bad things happened to loggers who tried to cut down the trees, and it made people afraid to go in to bulldoze. It made me angry when they let the trees spook them away.

Especially now that I was about to be the next victim.

Turn away, I told myself. I wanted to run back, but my feet weren't my own. My heart thumped in my chest, a beating drum to accompany the melody of creaking wood and rustling leaves all around me. My throat itched, and I cleared it. All around me the trees hummed, and I wanted to join in. I wanted to sing. With all my will, I pressed my lips together.

The song of the apple tree grew louder as I approached. The words sounded more Ukrainian than ever. With each step, the meaning became clearer.

"With their life blood I will fill,
For each one of them I kill.

Help me rise in power.
I need you, my flower."

The tree serenaded me as though I were a long-lost lover. I stared, mesmerized. It was all true. My mother had been a witch from the old country with a gift for speaking with nature. I couldn't deny what I'd seen in my youth had been real.

A leaf brushed against my cheek, and I slapped it away.

Brown apples from six months before quivered on the ground. Each joined in a high-pitched chorus calling out to me. White blossoms shifted and rained down like snow. The intoxicating aroma of magic and the apple vanenyky my mother used to make coaxed me closer. It lulled me into complacency. I brushed my fingers against the map of crevices in the tree's bark.

Is this what it had been like for my mother the night she died? I yanked my hand back. I wouldn't let myself fall under the leshii's spell.

Stepping away was like walking through mud. My heart clenched with pain. I drew in a shaky breath and made myself back up another step.

"No, no, no! Do not go!" the rotten apples cried. A shriveled one rolled toward my foot.

I kicked at it and stumbled a few paces back. I choked on the overly sweet stench of fruit.

It was easier to breathe once I dragged myself out of woods.

I ran back home and vowed I would never return to the forest no matter how much it called to me. It was time to put a stop to the dark magic that dwelled there.

* * *

The trees had to go.

I was only a kid, but I knew something had to be done. I went to the town hall meetings and talked to people. The adults discussed stupid things like the need for new heating in the school or the problem the pesticides from the farms caused in the water table. Every time I stood up to talk about the woods and how dangerous they were, people exchanged nervous glances and whispered.

Finally the minister approached me privately and suggested I start a petition. His face was a stiff mask, like he didn't want me to see what was beneath, but I read the tortured anguish in his gray eyes even if he wouldn't meet my gaze. If anyone had suffered as much as my father and me, it would be him with the loss of his wife and then twin sons.

I was seventeen, nearly through my senior year of high school, when I collected signatures for my petition. When I presented them to the city council, the elderly group of men and women shook their heads like I was crazy.

"Those trees are dangerous. This is a public safety hazard," I said. "I've compiled a list of all the people who have died there in the last eleven years. A total of thirteen since my mother's death."

The minister's spine stiffened at the mention of my mother.

"We have signs up," the mayor said.

"We warned your mother not to go there," someone in the audience said.

I lifted my chin. "I'm not the only one who thinks we should flatten that land and get rid of the danger. I have three hundred and forty-six signatures of people who also would like us to get rid of the woods."

"We appreciate your concern, but we can't bulldoze it anymore," said Mayor Horobets.

"Why not?" I asked.

The mayor's stiff smile turned to ice. "The problem, you see, is that it isn't public land anymore. We just sold it. The new owner won't let us bulldoze."

"Yeah?" I imagined some big corporation must have snatched up the land. Wouldn't they want to flatten it so they could build a McDonalds and make this a real American town? "Who owns it now?" I asked.

The minister crossed his arms. His mouth flattened into a grim line. "Your father."

* * *

"You let me humiliate myself, collecting signatures for a petition while you bought up the property out from under my nose?" I shouted. "You made me look like a . . ." I stammered, trying to think of the right word. One of his Ukrainian ones came to mind. "Like a duren."

Papa sat in his chair facing the television. Intermittent static punctuated the *I Love Lucy* rerun. He took a slow sip of homemade samogon. "I told you to leave the trees be."

"How could you afford that land? You can't even buy the new tractor we need."

He waved a hand in the air, the gesture floppy from the strong drink. "Tak, tak. Forget about the tractor. Jak skazaty . . . ? I have already sold our farm." His words slurred together. He wove in and out of Ukrainian like his words were made of thread. "Vybačte. Soon we will move into a trailer on new property. Ja tebe kohaju."

"And you planned to tell me this when?" I threw up my hands in exasperation. "Why do you have to ruin my life?"

He stood up, taking me by the shoulders and stooping to look me in the face. His breath smelled like sour jam, the samogon heavy on his breath. "I'm not ruining your life. I'm saving it. Jak skazaty ... ? Your mother wouldn't have wanted her trees destroyed, ni?"

I pulled away from him. "What do those stupid trees have to do with me? I'm not my mother."

"You will be like her someday. Hmm? You must make peace with the trees."

"No. I won't. I saw the trees the night she died. They murdered her." All because of me. Because I'd interrupted their magic.

"Ni! I don't believe that." Papa crossed his arms and returned to his easy chair. "I visit her grave, and the leshii don't hurt me." He waved a hand at his drink. "I collect the apples, and I am not poisoned."

That was debatable. The samogon would kill him eventually.

"Dig your own grave, then." I stuck my nose in the air. "I have nothing more to say to you."

* * *

The next few weeks were intolerable. Every day, the trees beckoned. The minister went missing. He was eventually found dead under the tree. A can of gasoline lay next to him. A soggy book of matches remained in his pocket.

I lived in the same house with my father, but we never spoke. Or I didn't speak to him anyway. The day I graduated from high school I left and decided I would never go back.

* * *

I left for a college town two hours away. The moment I stepped off the bus I felt like I was in a different world. There were new cars and paved streets with sidewalks. People talked on cell phones, and there was even a Walmart. It was all so ... *American.* The buzz of people drowned out the whispers of the plants next to buildings.

I'd found the youth hostel online using the school computer and planned to stay there until I could afford an apartment. I needed a job and applied for thirteen different positions: cashier at the grocery store, clerk in the library, and so on. It was the Christian bookstore that hired me.

I smiled at the irony of that. My mother hadn't even been allowed to be buried in hallowed ground. Would my mother have disapproved? I didn't know and I didn't care.

Margie, my new boss, helped me find a closet-sized studio that someone at her church rented out to college kids. A month after being hired, Margie asked if I'd like to go to church with her on Sundays. I wasn't sure I wanted to go, but I didn't know how to say no. Outside the building, people smiled and introduced themselves. They weren't like the folk back home. These people were friendly.

Going to church, I felt like an imposter. Yet, I didn't burst into flames when I stepped inside, and the minister didn't scowl at me. I liked how quiet it was inside during the service. People sang with normal human voices. I didn't trust myself to sing and kept my lips sealed together.

After church services, Margie and her husband introduced me to young people my age. There were so many in her church, it was almost the size of my old town. Every week she introduced me to someone new.

"You should join the youth group. There's so many people your age," she said in that Pollyanna way of hers.

"People my age," I repeated. Yeah, I had plenty of experience with them. They were nicer when adults were around. And then they whispered about you and called you, "devil girl" or "suka" to your face.

After my first week of classes in September, Margie steered me over to a cute college-aged boy with dark hair that fell into his eyes. "Have you met Lucas yet?" she asked.

"Um, no," I said.

"Yes," he said.

Margie flipped her silver-blond hair over her shoulder. "Oh? When?"

"Biology 101." He toed the ground with a sneaker.

"That's a big class. Where do you sit?" I asked.

"In the back. You sit in the front. Not that I was staring or anything."

Another young man slapped him on the back. "Foot in mouth much, bro?" The boy laughed, and Lucas's face turned red.

I didn't know why I kept going back to church. I supposed it was peaceful there, like that one moment I had felt in the woods before everything had gone wrong. And maybe a small part of me—a big part of me?—wanted to prove I wasn't weird. I wasn't going to die a horrible death by an evil magical tree. My life could be peaceful and boring and normal.

I was not my mother.

Only, I suspected I was. Margie told me I had a magic touch with the displays. I jumped when she said it.

"I think you mean a talent," I corrected. "Not magic."

"Silly goose, you know what I mean! Look at how you draw people to look at those pretty arrangements you make." She nodded to the window where I'd set up the books on top of a table. A fake branch of autumn leaves poked out of a vase with a giant cross on it. I didn't mind the plastic branches. They didn't vibrate with energy in the same way real trees did. They didn't speak to me like when I walked by the towering alders that lined the sidewalks on campus.

Margie's husband, Rick, strolled by and heard us talking. "Not saying you don't do a swell job decorating the place, hon, but I have a feeling it ain't your book displays that are bringing them in." He nodded to a young man watching us through the window.

It was Lucas. He blushed when he caught my eye and hurriedly walked away.

"Bringing the boys in anyway," Rick said.

"Oh, shush!" Margie said, swatting at her husband playfully.

He hugged her and planted a kiss on her plump cheek. "I'm just saying, my girlish figure ain't going to draw in crowds."

Watching them made me smile. It made me wonder if my parents would have been like them if my mother had still been alive. Would they have been jolly and full of love for each other? How I wished this were my family and this town was my home.

* * *

Everything made me think of home. One day in class when the biology professor mentioned an apple blight in passing, it made me think of home. It made me wish an apple blight had taken out my mother's tree long ago.

The old homeless woman I saw on the street reminded me of my papa's stories about Baba Yaga. I tried not to think of him. I didn't miss him. He probably hadn't even noticed I was gone. Yet my heart ached for him anyway.

One day, the old baba shuffled into the store. Her silver hair stuck out from under a kerchief, and her long nose resembled a witch's. Her weathered lips curled around her toothless gums, silently working out words as she perused the A–D aisle.

The stench of urine and garbage followed her into the store.

Margie and Rick told me if the homeless woman came in asking for money, I was to offer her a pudding or applesauce from the mini fridge in their office. So far, she hadn't asked for anything, just read the Bible and used the bathroom.

She brought a box of matches to the counter, a book that had Jesus's picture on it. Usually the boxes said something inspirational like "be a light unto others," or "he who follows me will not walk in darkness." This one looked like a misprint. It said, "Be true to your nature."

A chill settled over me. I was being true to my nature—the nature I wanted to choose for myself. I wanted to be a normal girl with friends and a family. I wanted to go to church and live in a big town, not the farming armpit of America.

The baba counted out her change.

"Oh, so you're buying matches? Do you, um, smoke?" I tried to make conversation as I breathed through my mouth.

She shook her head and cackled. "Ni, ni. I have other uses for them." She nodded to the window. "He's watching you again. He's out there as much as I am."

Lucas stood at the window again, examining the preseasonal Christmas tree. It was hard to imagine anyone could be that interested in little light-up crosses. Rick sometimes teased me when Lucas came in the store, saying the boy had a crush on me. Considering Lucas spoke in one-word sentences, I doubted it.

"It's uncanny how much you two are alike," the old baba said.

"What do you mean?" I asked.

"I suppose you'll have to have a conversation with him and find out." She shuffled out the door.

I ducked behind a bookshelf and watched Lucas.

Lucas was bundled up in a red-and-yellow scarf that matched the autumn colors. He shivered in his denim jacket. His brown eyes reminded me of Mama's, so full of shining joy it could warm you with one glance. He greeted the old woman in her tattered rags and took something out of his bag and gave it to her. She smiled and shuffled along.

I suspected he was Eastern European like my parents, from his dark Slavic features. I hadn't ever been interested in boys back home. And why would I when they asked me insulting things like if I was easy like my mother? Only this young man wasn't like the boys I'd known.

What was I doing, hiding behind a bookcase? I could be anyone I wanted. I didn't have to hide from boys or a scary tree. I could be normal like everyone else here.

I slipped around the shelves and opened the front door. "Would you like to come in and look around?"

He smiled, and his cheeks flushed like ripe apples. He followed me in and stopped at a stack of books.

"Looking for anything in particular?" I asked.

"Um, no, not exactly." He cleared his throat. "I was wondering . . . Um, I hope you don't mind if, well . . ."

My heart fluttered in my chest. This was about to be the turning point in my life. A boy was going to ask me on a date!

He cleared his throat. "Um, do you have any books about Christmas in yet?"

I escorted him to the aisle we stocked for holiday merchandise, trying not to let my disappointment show. I wondered if I'd misunderstood his reason for standing outside for so long.

He picked out a book and lingered at the counter after he'd bought it, making awkward chitchat about science class.

Finally, Rick shouted from the back. "Lucas, ask her out on a date and get it over with!"

* * *

I stared at the looming trees shushing in the wind above us. "It's November. It's too cold for a picnic."

If I'd known Lucas's plan for a date was to sit in the park, I would have thought up an excuse ahead of time. Why had I even agreed to this? Because some old baba had said we were a good match? I was such a duren!

Lucas smoothed out a wool blanket over the grass. "That's why I brought warm things for us to eat." He took out two thermoses and Tupperware containers and grinned. It was hard not to smile back.

I sat down on the blanket. I would ignore the trees and the sensation of grass growing under the blanket. I could pretend I was normal. For him. I kept on pretending until I realized the cup he poured for me was apple cider. My stomach churned.

"I don't eat apples," I said. The branches above us creaked with laughter.

"Oh, yeah?" His eyes widened, and he looked mortified. "Apples, yuck. What was I thinking? I hate apples, unless we're talking about pie. Or strudel. Or crisp. Or fresh apples. Okay, I really do like apples."

I laughed at his nervousness. He was cute.

He opened the other thermos. "How about coffee instead? I brought that too."

We sat in silence. I tried to think of something to say, but it was hard to concentrate with the way the trees chittered above. Their words were half-formed, whereas the ones back home had been clearer, speaking in a tongue I could sometimes understand.

"So, what did you bring for lunch?" I asked.

He'd brought apple pie and peanut butter and jelly sandwiches. The jelly was apple butter.

"It's all right. I'm not hungry," I lied.

He twisted the edge of the picnic blanket. "Yeah, me neither."

"So, um . . ."

The conversation was full of awkward starts and stops. More than ever I wondered if agreeing to the date had been a mistake.

Lucas asked me about my classes and where I was from. His father was a professor at the college, and he attended for free. "This has always been my favorite place on campus, even before I started going here. It's peaceful in the park. I love the sound of trees in the wind."

If he heard their whispers, I doubted he would have felt that way.

"So . . . I see you at church sometimes," I said. "I go with Margie and Rick."

"Yeah," Lucas said.

"Do you remember when they first introduced us?" I asked.

"Yeah."

"I didn't think you liked me since you've never spoken to me there. Or in class."

"I do like you, but I felt too intimidated." He swallowed. "You know how it is when you look at someone and you feel drawn to them and you start making up this story in your head about how they're your soulmate and you already see yourself married and having children and then you realize you don't know that person at all and she probably has a boyfriend because she could have any guy she wants?"

I laughed and shook my head. He was even stranger than me, and that was saying something.

He laughed too. "Well, I guess I don't usually know what that's like, but I do with you." His cheeks flushed as red as apples again. "Do you know what it's like to want to do something, but you chicken out, and you're afraid everyone will notice how stupid you are? You keep trying to do all the right things and make yourself feel normal, but no matter what you do you feel like a fake?"

"Um . . ." A shiver stole down my spine. I wasn't sure where he was going with this.

He bit his lip. "Do you know what it's like to not belong?"

I swallowed. "Yes, I do." Suddenly the world made sense to me. I wasn't alone. There was someone else out there like me. Different, but the same.

I placed my hand on his and decided I would go on another date with him. The trees above me snickered again.

* * *

For Christmas Rick and Margie bought me a bicycle.

"It's so you don't have to walk everywhere," Margie said, giving me a hug.

Tears filled my eyes. "I've never had a bike before." This was what a normal American family would give their daughter for a present.

Rick teased, "And if you want, I can put training wheels on it too!"

They were the parents I'd never had. I didn't know what I would have done without those guardian angels.

Lucas's family was just as kind. They welcomed me at their house during Christmas. It was odd how much Lucas was like his parents and so opposite at the same time. Their features were fair compared to his dark ones.

"You look so different from your mom and dad," I said.

"Yep, he looks more like the mailman," Lucas's father said.

Lucas rolled his eyes. "I'm adopted."

"But we love you as much as our own," his mother quickly added.

I could see she meant it. They were a true family. Lucas and his brothers and sisters were polite and kind to each other. They showered me with presents and acted like an American family in a holiday special. It didn't feel real. I was afraid I would wake up at any moment and find myself back home in that little farm shack without a mother and with a delusional father who spoke in broken English and reminisced about his broken heart.

I was happy when I was with Lucas. He made me feel normal and forget about my past. The old baba winked at me when she saw us together in the bookstore, like she'd known what a good match we'd be all along.

* * *

"Don't you love how peaceful it is here?" Lucas asked, staring up at the trees.

The perfume of flowers laced the air. Alders murmured and yawned like they were waking up. The childlike voice of baby buds sang above me. Birds chirped, and the breeze sighed through the boughs. My park bench wasn't enough to protect me from the earth pulsing with magic, even when I tucked my feet underneath me so I wouldn't touch the ground.

Lucas draped an arm around me and rested his head on my shoulder. Light danced over the sunshine of his smile. "I love the way the trees speak to each other."

My back stiffened. "What do you mean?"

"Nothing. I was being poetic," he said quickly.

That's when I knew he heard them too. And he liked it. I pulled away from him.

"How can you stand it?" I asked.

He bit his lip. "Stand what?"

"How they talk to each other? How they snicker and chatter away."

"Are you saying . . . do you hear them too? Isn't it the most beautiful lullaby in the world? It's like hearing people sing hymns in Latin. It's like . . . what's wrong?" His enthusiasm evaporated like mist.

Was this what the baba had truly meant when she'd said we were alike? "You and me," I said. "We're different. We aren't like other people. Maybe there's a reason we get along so well." Papa had once told me Mama had been an orphan. Lucas didn't know about his true parents either. Like it or not, we came from something old. Something not normal. I didn't want to say we were both witches or vila or some Ukrainian fairy-tale creature, even if that was the truth.

"There's something I have to tell you." I took a deep breath and gathered up my courage. He didn't have to know everything, but I didn't think I could keep going on walks in the park with him and retain my sanity.

He took my hands in his. "I know," he said. "I feel it too."

My eyebrows twitched in confusion.

"I love you too." He dropped to his knees. "I knew it from the first moment I met you. Please, Lily, marry me."

"What?"

Now it was his turn to look confused. "Oh no, that wasn't what you were going to say, was it?"

"No, I mean . . ." I considered what I had been about to say. I did love him. That was the reason I wanted to tell him why I felt uncomfortable in the park. I wanted to continue to spend time with him. But it was more than that. I wanted to unburden my heart and confide in someone. Only, I didn't know how he would react.

I swallowed. "I have a secret. I don't know if you'll still want to marry me when I'm done. You might think I'm insane."

I only meant to tell him about the trees not being peaceful, but once I started talking, it all came out: the reason I hated the taste of apples, why I felt like such an imposter, my childhood memories of the tree, and my mother's death.

He held my hand all the while. His brows knitted together in concern, but he didn't interrupt. He didn't tell me I was weird or that I was a witch. He circled an arm around me and drew me to him.

"I'm so sorry," he said. "I'll never give you apple cider again. I didn't know the trees bothered you. I wouldn't have brought you here if I had."

My throat tightened, and I nodded. His arms squeezed me with a fierce, protective embrace. I felt safer than I had ever felt before. My heart swelled in my chest when I thought about how much I loved him.

"Lily, you know it wasn't your fault she died, right?"

"But it was. I told you. I—"

"No, listen." He pulled back enough that I could see the vehemence in his eyes. "Your mother was dabbling in magic, probably something she didn't understand. She shouldn't have been out there in the first place if it was so dangerous."

I looked away and wiped my eyes.

"It wasn't your fault she died." He repeated it a second and a third time. The words sank deeper, taking root.

I nodded. Silent tears fell down my cheeks. He lifted my chin until our eyes met. He kissed me, and the sorrow lifted from my heart.

Lucas reached into his pocket, pulling out a tissue. "That tree haunts you still, even here, doesn't it? There's someone I'd like you to meet. He's like us, but . . . different. I think he can help."

* * *

Over the last few months I'd met Lucas's friends from the youth group. But I'd never met Jared, the theology major. He reminded me of a laid-back surfer dude, so out of place in the Midwest. And out of place in how he glowed with sunshine. He was like Lucas, but not like Lucas.

"So, dudette, it sounds like we've got ourselves a tree with some seriously bad mojo," Jared said after Lucas introduced us.

My gaze cut to Lucas, who had apparently told Jared more than I would have liked. At least his friend didn't laugh and tell me I was crazy. Jared sat us down at a table in the cafeteria and explained his idea for overcoming evil.

I listened, becoming more suspicious by the moment. "Your plan is to kill the tree spirit with snowballs made with holy water? You do realize this is a nature spirit, not a demon?"

"We have to start somewhere. Process of elimination, little dudette."

Lucas introduced me to his other friends, the pagans he had befriended in his classes. Squished into a candle-lit dorm, they looked like a motley crew of goth hippies. A bear of a boy slapped Lucas on the back hard enough to send him stumbling into me.

The boy took my hand to shake it. I prepared myself for my fingers to be crushed, but his touch was gentle. "So, you're Lucas's sister?" he asked a little too hopefully.

"Girlfriend," Lucas said firmly.

Touching the boy's skin was like running my fingers through blades of grass, a strange electric pulse that made me uncomfortable. I pulled my hand away.

"So we hear you have a magical problem. Let's see if we can help," the bear boy said.

"Mother Nature has been angered," a girl with dyed purple hair said as she consulted a book.

"It isn't about Mother Nature," I said. "The tree is male. He's . . ." I hesitated, not wanting to show them how un-American my family was. "He's a leshii, a kind of Ukrainian tree spirit."

"Cool! Let's do an internet search on my phone," said a small, imp-like boy.

After a few hours, they had devised several ways to "uncurse" the woods and banish the evil from the apple tree by lighting candles and chanting.

Naturally, I was skeptical.

"Now you have to go home and see if it worked!" said an enthusiastic girl.

I frowned and looked to Lucas.

He circled an arm around me. "Don't worry. You don't have to go back."

I wasn't so sure.

* * *

What if the answer wasn't magic, but science? What if I found a fungus that could infest the tree to kill it? Of course, that meant I'd have to go back.

I took botany classes and horticulture. I didn't like the way the vines snuggled up to me in the greenhouse as I worked. I made myself concentrate on the professor's words, not the plants' exotic lullabies. I needed to learn more about my enemy's weakness.

"Wow, you really have a green thumb," the professor said. "What did you use to get these apple tree grafts to grow so fast?"

"Magic," I said, my voice sounding dull and dead compared to the songs around me.

She laughed and waved me off.

I stocked up on toxic herbicides. I collected samples of fire blight from infected trees. I prayed in church and let the pagan hippies chant their nature magic spells. During the first week of summer vacation, before my newfound friends dispersed to their homes across the country, we would pay the apple tree a visit.

* * *

I locked the door of the Christian bookstore and was about to hop on my bike when I noticed the palace made of cardboard boxes in the alley. I walked my bike over. The old baba sat in the shelter. She lit a candle with a match and then lit another.

"That's pretty dangerous. Your house might catch on fire," I said.

She cackled. "Tak, tak. Anything worthwhile we do has a sense of danger, ni?"

I leaned my bike against the alley wall. I felt bad for her. I reached into my pocket and pulled out a chewy granola bar. She might not be able to eat it since she didn't have teeth, but it was the only food I had with me. With the reverence of an offering, I set it down at her feet.

She dropped the match into a puddle. I thought she meant to snatch up the granola bar, but instead she grabbed my wrist. "You ask the wrong questions. Ni? Have you thought to ask why the forest kills?"

I yanked my hand back, and she released me. Her cackle followed me down the road. It clung to my skin like a film of dust. Only, I couldn't remove it, even with a shower and a whole bar of soap.

* * *

"Hey, dudette. I brought my Snoopy Snow Cone Machine. I'm ready to make some snowballs out of holy water," Jared said.

I didn't have much hope in holy-water snowballs, but Jared was the only one with transportation large enough to accommodate me, Lucas, and six pagans. His hippie van didn't have enough seatbelts, but we all squeezed in there anyway. It took almost two hours to get to my hometown. We stopped at the general store for a bag of ice.

Closer to the woods, the van kicked up dirt along the road. When I spotted the dumpy trailer outside the woods, I asked him to stop.

"Do you think that's where your father lives?" Lucas asked.

I hoped it wasn't. Maybe he'd sold the land to someone else.

"You don't have to talk to him if you don't want to."

He didn't understand. I did.

Lucas got out of the Volkswagon bus behind me and held my hand as I knocked on the door. There was no answer. I knocked again. I hoped Papa hadn't gone into the woods. That would be just the kind of thing he would do, collecting apples for his samogon. A crash came from inside, and the metal door creaked open.

The stench of sour sweat and strong drink made me choke, and I staggered back. I could tell already this had been a mistake. Everyone would see him and know what kind of family I'd come from.

Papa's nose was pink, and his eyes were rimmed with red. Food stains marred a threadbare shirt. It hung baggy around his emaciated frame. His dull eyes stared blankly at us, seeing but not seeing. A car door slammed behind us.

I swallowed the lump in my throat and greeted him. "Dobryj den, Papa."

His eyes widened. He uttered something in Ukrainian and stumbled down the metal steps. He threw his arms around me and hugged me. "My little flower has come back." He went on in Ukrainian, crying and laughing at the same time, making it hard to understand him.

When he let me go, I said, "I'm going to the woods. Don't try to stop me."

"I won't." He laughed and wiped away his tears. "I never stopped your mama from her trees. I knew you'd come back for them."

More than ever I felt bad for him. Especially once he found out what I was about to do.

* * *

The rustles and creaks of spoken words coming from the trees reminded me of the danger ahead.

Jared lifted his Snoopy Snow Cone Machine. "Dude, let's get this party started so you can live 'appily' ever after."

"You can't come with me," I said to Lucas's friends. My friends. "The tree might hurt you."

Lucas squeezed my hand. "It might hurt you. I'm coming with you." He kept his face calm and expressionless, but I heard the fear in his voice. For the briefest moment, the anguish in his eyes reminded me of the minister's expression that day he'd approached me with the idea of starting a petition.

I unloaded the can of pesticides and my kit of bacteria specimens. No sooner had we stepped onto the overgrown path than the twisted brambles caught onto Lucas's T-shirt and thorns raked over his skin. I didn't expect the path to be easy. Surely the leshii knew what we meant to do. Another step and twigs caught in his hair and he stumbled over a tree root.

I remained untouched.

"Go back," I said firmly. "The trees will hurt you if you don't." The tree. The woods. The leshii. I didn't know who to blame, but I knew he wasn't safe.

Lucas bit his lip. "The trees at home like me."

"Well, these ones don't." But they liked me. The grumble of their toneless song shifted to one more palatable to the ears. The music was sweet and alluring.

My feet danced forward. Lucas stumbled after me, but a blackberry branch snapped against his chest in warning.

Hurt reflected in his eyes. "I want to help."

"Join the others and pray for me," I said.

I stepped into the beckoning trees. I didn't remember the gnarled roots forming a stairway down to the apple tree. When I turned back, I could see Lucas standing at the entrance of the path above.

A snowball whizzed past me and splattered against the ground. Shriveled brown apples on the ground laughed. Dried roots lapped up the melting puddle.

What possessed me to remove my shoes, I didn't know. My toes squished into the cool mulch of leaves. Below my feet pulsed a heartbeat, slow and sad. An excited chorus welcomed me back.

I set down the can of poisons and the case of bacteria specimens and placed my hand on the apple tree's trunk. A low, mournful note rose and died away.

I thought of the baba's words. I opened my mouth, and my mother's voice came out. No, not my mother's, but my own. Rich and harmonious, it resonated with magic. The tree silenced. The tree listened.

I asked, "Why do you kill?"

The bark shifted under my hand. Crevices deepened into eyes. An elegant nose and sensual lips formed underneath. His expression was hurt, his song lonely. It wasn't the one of hatred and venom I expected. His voice reminded me of an old man's, of my father pining for my mother.

He sang:

"Come tell me a tale of ferns and moss,

And I will tell you one of sorrow and loss.

Come sing me a song of happier times.

I will only sing of humanity's crimes.

Come dance your dance and forget the past.

While I am haunted by the death of an outcast."

For the first time, I really listened to the apple tree's song. He unveiled the past for me, and I saw my mama's death. At last I understood how she died. It had never been the tree that killed her, but the townspeople.

* * *

His song painted vivid colors in my mind as he told me a story about a woman, half-vila living among humans, not even knowing what she was when she'd first arrived from the old country. Her suitors were many, as was often the case with tree nymphs. The minister fell in love with her, and they had a child, only he wouldn't marry her on account of her being unbaptized. She got rid of the child and years later married someone else. He hated her, and his jealousy grew. He accused her of witchcraft.

The night I had seen her dancing in the trees had been the same night the minister had led a group of townsfolk into the woods to stone her to death.

I listened to the song and saw the grandfather apple tree hadn't just randomly lashed out. He sought vengeance on those who had harmed her. It wasn't right, and I didn't agree, but I understood why. And I understood why he hadn't killed my father or me. The tree had tried to explain himself, but I hadn't understood.

Now I did.

Another snowball splattered against the ground, falling short of hitting the tree. The melting ice shimmered with love and prayers, the energy trickling into the ground. For the first time, I truly saw the world as it was.

I glanced back at my friends. Jared, the theology student, glowed like an angel. The bearlike boy resembled a troll more than a human. He danced with a fairy girl at the edge of the woods. Two smaller imps circled and stomped their feet. Their voices rose and joined the lullaby of trees and ferns. They chanted and prayed, and as they did so, I could see the sparks of power they fed the hungry woods.

Lucas stood tall and still. Twigs and leaves in his unkempt hair gave him a wild look. I sensed the leshii in him, the tree magic blossoming like spring around him.

I bowed my head to the tree. "I apologize for all the wrongs humans have done. I apologize for my ignorance and my refusal to listen. I didn't understand. I do now. But I ask that you stop killing people. It won't bring my mama back."

He responded in song. "With each death I grow in power, so that I might avenge my flower."

"But it isn't right! You can't just keep on killing innocent people who didn't have anything to do with her death."

His creaky voice grumbled, filled with the sound of wind rustling through leaves and twigs snapping.

"I will have their kin,

As penance for their sin.

You have come to help me.

You will make this be."

The ferns and lichen chanted a chorus to his song, "Join us, help us. Lure him, kill him."

I thought of all the kind and charitable things Margie and Rick had done for others. Did I want revenge, or did I want to forgive? "Hasn't anyone ever told you to turn the other cheek?"

"Do I mishear?" The pops and snaps resembled a dark laugh. "You have already brought him here."

The meaning of his words rolled off me. My gaze followed a quivering branch pointing to the path. Leshii magic sparked and rose from Lucas as he prayed, not so different from the time I'd seen my mother singing to the tree.

The others danced around him, lost in their own frenzied magic.

My mind revisited the apple tree's words. Mama had gotten rid of the minister's son. He didn't mean she'd gotten an abortion. He meant she'd given him up for adoption.

I'd been drawn to Lucas from the start. His presence was comforting and familiar like a blanket warmed by the fire and wrapped snug on a cold winter night. Not because we were soulmates, but because we were related. My stomach cramped.

It couldn't be true. I didn't want it to be true. I loved Lucas. Tears filled my eyes.

"No!" I fell to my knees. "You can't have him."

Lucas must have heard me. He immediately started forward. In his hands he held an axe.

"Go back. Stay out of the woods!" My voice wasn't my own. It was made of wind and scraping wood.

Lucas swiped twigs aside, but they tore at him to keep him back. They cried out in warning, but he didn't heed them. I realized too late, they were trying to help him, not hurt him. It was the apple tree that wanted him.

The ground vibrated and rumbled like the apple tree might unearth itself. Twigs popped all around me, little bits raining down. The song of the tree became chaotic and garbled. Only the thunder of hatred came through.

"No!" I pounded on the ground with my fists. The tree wasn't listening. I took in a deep breath and exhaled all my sorrow and regret into my song. "He's her child too. He's my brother. Please, anything but him. Let him live. I'll do anything. I'll give you anything. Take me instead."

"Very well, I will let him live," said grandfather apple tree. "I will tether you to my woods as servant and set him free."

I ran to Lucas. Twigs grew out of his hair, and leaves sprouted from his arms, tearing at his clothes. His shoes shredded as his toes turned to roots. Anguish pained his face. Each step was a slow process while his roots planted themselves in the earth, only to be torn away as he planted a new step. He dropped the axe to reach out to me with spindly limbs, but his arms were no longer human arms.

"Stop it! You're killing him," I screamed at the tree. "You said you would let him live."

"I am setting him free."

This was the tree's idea of freedom? Loathing flooded through me.

I picked up the axe.

* * *

I rose from my seat inside the trailer and pushed the screen door open with a weathered hand. The sunset painted the sky with streaks of blood.

"Servant," I spat out. For many a year I had kept that title, kept that curse, and wore it around me like an old cloak.

I trudged down the path to the trees. With each step I felt like I descended further into my self-made hell. The trees greeted me with their usual lullaby. The ferns played a melody with the moss and lichen. The heartbeat below my naked feet kept time. I passed the stump where the first apple tree had been, the tree I had chopped down.

The new tree was young still, his limbs smooth and straight, unlike the previous one. Ripening apples hung from his branches. My tree. My brother. I plucked a red apple from above my head and inhaled the heady perfume. My mouth watered, but I didn't taste the forbidden fruit.

My tree sang to me, a voice full of love and longing. When I opened my mouth, it wasn't the voice of an old baba that came out. I had found my siren voice. It was one that could melt hearts and sing the spirits of the forest to sleep. It was a vila's voice that could waken my leshii and make him dance in my arms when the moon was full and our magic was at its strongest. I sang my lullaby, awaiting the day I would join him.

About Sarina Dorie

Sarina Dorie has sold over 100 short stories to markets like Daily Science Fiction, Magazine of Fantasy and Science Fiction, Orson Scott Card's IGMS, Cosmos, and Sword and Laser. Her stories and published novels have won humor and Romance Writer of America awards. Her steampunk romance series, *The Memory Thief* and her collections, *Fairies, Robots and Unicorns—Oh My!* and *Ghosts, Werewolves and Zombies—Oh My!* are available on Amazon.

A few of her favorite things include: gluten-free brownies (not necessarily glutton-free), Star Trek, steampunk aesthetics, fairies, Severus Snape, Captain Jack Sparrow and Mr. Darcy.

By day, Sarina is a public school art teacher, artist, belly dance performer and instructor, copy editor, fashion designer, event organizer and probably a few other things. By night, she writes. As you might imagine, this leaves little time for sleep.

LEVI'S PROBLEM

By Brendon Taylor | 9,300 words

WHEN MY MIND finally began to clear, I took solace in the thought that I had expected my memories and cognitive processing to work like a bicycle with square wheels. It was a funny thing to think because I had never ridden a bicycle. At least from the puzzle of my memory, I thought that was true. Yet it was comforting because I recalled my grandfather using that phrase often. My second thought was less comforting. With my mind otherwise a mess, my mission beaconed like a solar flare – I had landed on an alien terra to explore a potential alternative to Earth for the survival of my species. Such prospects came with the definite possibility that death might find me at any moment. I pushed that thought out of my mind and remembered another phrase, "One man's exploration is another's invasion." I could only hope my work here would not be viewed as the latter.

My first problem was to find a safe place to rest while the gears in my mind fully engaged. Unfortunately, I had no idea how long that would take and whether parts of my faculties would be permanently lost. My heart told me that the great risk had been worth taking, and that the sacrifice I was making came at a price worth paying. This was yet another thought about as comforting as a paper parasol in a thunderstorm.

The terra was dense, the atmosphere thick and viscous, and the ground beneath me clung and released my steps like tapioca pudding. No, more like flan. Now, those were unusual thoughts. In the decades since genetic modification had begun, food, nutrition and hydration had changed. The thoughts of those "foods" seemed like they belonged in my grandfather's head because they had never been in mine.

At that thought, a piece of my mind puzzle snapped into place. I should have a neurolink to allow communication. I searched my thoughts trying to will a connection to someone. Anyone.

"Levi?" a voice whispered, resonating not in my ears, but within my mind. A familiar voice.

"Grandfather?" The word formed as a thought. At least the neurolink seemed to be working.

"Hearing your voice feels better than April sunshine in a daffodil meadow."

I laughed in my mind and the sound caught me by surprise. It sounded different in the neurolink, like a chipmunk chittering. "Do you keep a bagful of folksy phrases with you at all times, Grandfather?"

"Do you think I should?"

"You never seem to run out." My mind was still more porous than a sponge, but connecting to my Grandfather's strong, happy voice soothed me. A calmer mind would mend faster.

"Statement!"

"What?"

"You can't recover with another question now. You made a statement – I win."

Another memory fit into place. Grandfather loved to play a game of questions that came from an old play, "Rosencrantz and… somebody… Are Dead." I was not familiar with the play and couldn't remember who that somebody should be, but the game of questions was a favorite of Grandfather's.

"You shouldn't pick on me when my brain is mush, Grandfather. Besides, shouldn't I be connecting to a commanding officer about the details of my mission?"

"Of course, how rude of me… don't you think?" Grandfather waited until I chuckled before moving on. "It is precisely because your brain is mush that you are communicating with me first. Until you regain your faculties, protocol dictates that you link with a familiar person who can help you recover."

I searched my mind for any other neurolink and found none. Admittedly, I was not sure how to even search for other neurolink possibilities. Guildenstern. That was the other somebody in the old play. "I'm trying to recall how the neurolink works. You put the thought about the square-wheeled bicycle in my brain, didn't you?"

"I've been trying to reach you for a while now. We weren't sure of when you would reach terra and arouse from stasis. I could only communicate once you were conscious, and could only speak to your active mind. Perhaps your sub-conscious felt me reaching for you and my genius wordsmithing was its finest option – the persimmon among the pigs, if you will." Grandfather's chuckle sounded familiar, not at all like a chipmunk. That was unfair, but welcome.

"Since when is a square-wheeled bicycle 'genius wordsmithing'?" What Grandfather said about only being able to communicate with a conscious mind rang true. I was also pretty sure that only willing participants could neurolink. You could not force a connection if a person did not want it. At least I thought that was true.

"Harumph."

"You said the word, 'Harumph,' Grandfather. You're supposed to just make the sound." My laugh still sounded like chittering in my mind.

"Very well, Levi. We might as well continue through the protocols before I make any more mistakes." Grandfather's tone said he was not offended. "First, however, are you someplace safe and comfortable?"

I had almost forgotten I was on alien terra, and surrounded by new wonders. The viscous atmosphere seemed to sway a little around me. I was glad my feet were anchored so I would not be swept away, but even more relieved when I tested and found I could move them. The landscape was lush with formations of purples, lavenders, reds and salmons. I could not tell if it was flora or some other form of biota. The thickness of the atmosphere limited visibility, but I felt as though I was in a beautiful cave, with no apparent threat of harm nearby. I chose a dense pinkish-red formation and sat, finding it squishy, but firm enough to support me. "I'm comfortable now, and see no sign of danger."

"That's good. Research indicated you should not face hostiles, but research from this distance is not always as accurate as we would like."

"How long was my transport? My mind is very fuzzy about my travel."

"Ah, protocols, Levi. Let me go through the questions to assess your recovery. Then, we can cover your questions."

"How was the question game you played on me earlier part of the protocols?" I protested in jest, hoping my tone translated through the neurolink.

"I will humor you by reviewing the first two protocols. One, establish connection with subject and confirm subject is aware of who he and his contact are. Two, using familiar words or phrases, bring up a memory that will comfort the subject. Really, Levi, I am very pleased with how quickly you are recovering."

"Well, I don't want to be the gnat thinking he's a mosquito." Yet another of Grandfather's phrases. I was not particularly troubled that I could not think of what that phrase actually meant. I suspected with my full faculties intact, I would still be at a loss for that one, but it seemed to be an appropriate thing to say to Grandfather.

He chuckled. "I should think not. Progress, I tell you. You'll be back to your old self in no time."

The light in the vicinity darkened slightly as the atmosphere thickened. I tried to locate the source of light to determine why it was growing darker by the minute, but failed. I was considering whether it was some sort of ambient light when a dull humming grew louder and changed into sounds that resembled language. "Hold on, Grandfather. Something is changing around me."

"Are you safe where you are? If not, move on." Concern quavered his words.

I yearned to hear the language, but it was like the muffled sounds of speaking under water. Then, movement caught my attention. At first, I caught only glimpses, like the shadow of a cloud, but then I saw an actual form. I felt the numb thrill of discovery tempered with the terror of facing an alien in its world alone. It was small, which was only a minor comfort. It was the size of a large rabbit, which also happened to be the size of a wolverine. Other than sharing the same size, this creature was in no other way similar to a furry mammal. A shiny, slick coating of silver and amber gleamed from an internal light within the thing. It had neither limbs nor head, but seemed to move with purpose by some unseen method of propulsion. The sound of language returned, but I could not tell if it originated in the creature or elsewhere. Direction of sound was difficult to distinguish. Of course, that might be because my brain was still spinning like a gyroscope.

"Levi?!" Grandfather's voice was frantic. "What is happening?"

"I'm not alone, but I believe I am safe." The lack of fangs and claws was definitely comforting.

"Do not engage it. Get to a safe place so we can coordinate. You are not ready for contact yet." Grandfather's voice was a forced calm – the kind of tone a parent used when a young child strayed too near a river's edge.

I checked for my gear, to secure a weapon or other protective device, not knowing what I had. I discovered I had nothing. Aside from a hard suit, that somehow allowed movement, I possessed no gear. "Grandfather, can you tell me why I have no gear, or does that question have to wait until after your blasted protocols, too?"

"Retreat to a safe place and we will get through your questions and the protocols. You have all the gear you need, even if it is not with you immediately. I will guide you to your base of operations very shortly. Please get to a safe place."

If it was not for Grandfather's concern, I would have felt almost comfortable with this little alien. The small creature seemed to have a level of intelligence that was intriguing. If it was capable of communication, I needed to know and find some way to assure it that I was not a threat. The last thing I wanted was to provoke it into acting rashly, or gathering the other proverbial villagers with pitchforks to deal with me. I decided Grandfather was right about gaining my wits and regrouping before engaging. If I had a base of operations to find, that would be a far better place to gather my answers and acclimatize. I made the universal, well Earthly, sign of peaceful assurance by raising both hands and speaking calmly to the shiny, little thing, "I mean you no harm."

Honestly, I was a split second away from promising that I came in peace when the cliché choked in my throat. The words I spoke sounded garbled to my ears. I worried that my brain might have the effects of a stroke that would allow thoughts to flow more freely than my motor skills could handle. The fact that I actually spoke or attempted to speak Earth-based English and expected my words to be recognized caused me even more concern. Grandfather was definitely right about retreating.

I stood and took several steps back, cautiously placing each foot to make sure I had the coordination and dexterity to move without falling. I was successful. The formations around me loomed taller and thicker the further I moved back. I felt like I was retreating to the depths of a cave. The shiny thing followed. I saw more movement behind it, and other, similar forms followed us in. At least they did not have pitchforks. The rumble of what I perceived as language grew louder. It did not sound threatening, but neither did a hunter's soothing tone sound threatening right up to the instant he pulled the trigger.

"Levi? What is happening?"

"I'm pulling back and searching for a safe place to communicate. I don't think these things mean to harm me, but I'm being careful."

"Let me know when you are secure."

That was when my back reached the wall of the cave, and I found myself between two large formations that felt firm to the touch. I gripped the sides, thinking I might try to climb up, or launch myself out if the aliens got too close. I thought I could jump over them, but I decided that would be a last resort. I had never been much of a jumper – realizing that felt good in the sense that I was remembering more, but bad in the sense that my limited physical skills left me with fewer options.

The creatures came closer, moving at a slow, but steady pace. There were at least five of them, all bobbing along toward me, perhaps fifteen feet away. They were now close enough for me to see how they moved. The shiny surfaces were covered by hundreds or thousands of little hair-like appendages that moved each creature along like a millipede in the shape of a globby duffle bag.

Subconsciously, I pushed my back against the wall. I expected it to feel hard as rock, but it was more the texture and firmness of cheese. It was not lost on me that much of this planet was reminding me of food. No doubt the long transport to this world was accomplished in a form of stasis that deprived my body of real food for a long time. I still had no memory of the trip, but if I was in stasis, that would not be surprising. Cheese, I could work with. The wall was soft enough that I could push into it. I thrust my arm in, and was pleased that my hand reached through the thick resistance into an opening beyond.

The creatures were almost upon me as I took a deep breath and pushed into the wall. As soon as I took it, I realized the deep breath was pointless as my suit had a breathing function built in that would allow me to survive on the new terra until a safe atmosphere could be established in the base. Although my conscious mind did not recall the mechanics of my suit, my logical brain knew it had to be true. I pressed into the wall. At once, I was enveloped in darkness with a tinge of maroon. Perhaps it was the pressure of the walls threatening to burst the vessels in my eyes that made me see maroon, because a moment later, I was through the solid barrier and found myself on a far brighter landscape.

I looked down, and located what I hoped was the ground many hundreds of feet below. I clung to branches of strange plants secured to a vertical wall that was otherwise smooth. I longed to find memory of climbing skills in my brain, but suspected I would find little there. Fortunately, the trees seemed to offer an easy route down, as long as my arms or grip did not give out before I reached the bottom. The air was thinner and brighter in this area. Better yet, the strange creatures seemed to be stopped in the cave. I kept an eye on the wall next to me and saw that it had sealed back upon itself – nothing else came through.

As I began a cautious descent, I reached out via neurolink. "Grandfather?"

"Levi!" His voice dripped with genuine concern. "Are you safe?"

"Yes. I am now. For a moment there, I was feeling about as safe as a termite in a pocket watch." Another Grandfather phrase, but one that sparked a real memory. I knew that pocket watches were all antiques, but recalled Grandfather talking about having one as a child. I struggled to remember how old he was, but could not place it.

"Well, I'm glad you are past that now. Have you hunkered down somewhere?"

"Not yet, but I have good visibility and no threats are nearby. Grandfather, can I ask you an odd question?"

"I suspect you will whether I allow it or not. How about we make a deal – you get your odd question and then we continue with the protocols?"

"Agreed." My foot nearly slipped as I lost focus on my climb. I had already realized the branches were wet in some places, which led me to wonder about rain or other climate issues I might encounter. "How old are you, Grandfather?"

"Older than a Neanderthal's uncle." The old man chuckled.

I groaned at his less than funny deflection.

"I suppose if I want real answers from you, I should give you the truth, rather than wit." I opted not to correct his mischaracterization, which I am sure he paused to allow. Grandfather continued, "224 years. Next year, I will be nine quarters of a century old."

I chuckled at that. "Well, when you say it that way..." Yet, realizing his age helped put more of my mind puzzle together. I knew people had not lived that long since the fabled ages in the Old Testament. At least, they had not lived that long until genetic science uncovered the key to slow the aging elements of the human genetic code.

"Alright, wise anus, we had a deal. Back to the protocols. What is your last memory prior to awakening?"

I realized I did not have a clear recollection of events in transport, or even immediately prior to leaving Earth. More troubling than that was the cloudiness of the memories I had of preparing for this mission. It was like pulling out of a deep sleep and immediately trying to recall which memories were dream and which were real. Only, I had been awake long enough that I should be able to tell the difference. "I'm struggling with that one."

"Don't fret, Levi. Let me help you. Do you recall anything about your ship?"

"No."

"That's fine. Do you recall anything about your squadron or commanding officer?"

I searched for memories and panicked when I could find none. Again, a foot slipped, and my body dangled in the air for a moment before I found another foothold. I was surprised my arms were not yet weary, and my grip felt strong. "No, I recall none of them."

"Very well. Let me move on to the fourth protocol and we can come back to this later. What do you recall about the reasons for interplanetary exploration?"

This question created a tickle in my mind that was frustratingly out of reach. Some of the blurriness was dense, while other parts were tantalizingly out of reach. "I feel like this is a question about which I should be able to write volumes."

Grandfather chuckled again. "A thumbnail sketch of history may clear this up for you. More than a century and a half ago after the threat of nuclear war was neutralized, the civilized nations and educated people of the world feared two things: global warming and depletion of resources. Near that time, American scientists cracked the genetic code more fully than had been done before, laying bare the flaws of humanity: disease, illness, deformity, and aging. Brilliant minds from around the world found solutions to these problems, and people began living longer and healthier. My father lived to be 152, and my generation has the hope of living far longer than that. Yours may live without limits of time."

Every word rang true. Memories came together like the pieces of an exploded building in a movie when the video was played in reverse. The holes of my memory began filling and I was thrilled to remember more. Realization struck me that I was 162 years old myself, though my aging had effectively stopped when I was in my twenties.

Grandfather continued. "Well, the governments of the world realized the Earth is far more resilient than expected. The planet regulated itself to the point where global warming was no longer a primary concern. That left the issues of resource depletion and overpopulation as the last global crises. More and more people occupied the planet because of longevity and optimized health. Even with renewable energy, maximized crop production, and animal cloning, there was simply not enough space to house and feed 94 billion people."

Light filled other dark corridors of my brain. I recalled studying complex systems as it related to the Earth and how the planet made adjustments in flora, weather patterns, and tectonic shifts to accommodate the issue of global warming. In effect, through millions of biological, geological and geographical adjustments, the Earth healed itself. I remembered reading dozens of studies in this field when I was in college at the American Science Institute. But I remembered more than just reading them. "Grandfather, I wrote a doctoral thesis on complex biological systems as it related to changes in the Earth in the mid twenty-first century, didn't I?"

"Trust the protocols, Levi. Yes, you did. Not only a thesis, but a collection of articles and studies that were peer reviewed, published and canonized. Is everything coming back to you, then?" Grandfather's tone was hopeful.

"I feel like a leaf on a branch being asked if the tree is done growing yet. I don't know if I'm a sapling or a mature oak, yet, Grandfather. But, at least I know I'm a leaf… or a scientist." That realization left me with a greater concern. "What went wrong in our transport or landing that one of the scientists in the exploration party was separated from the rest of the squadron? You mentioned something about helping me find my base and the equipment I would need."

Hope diminished in his voice. "That is a serious concern. I also mentioned that I don't have as much information about your landing as I would like. My team is searching for the answers you seek, and I will help you."

"You don't know what happened to the rest of the party, do you?" My stomach knotted and my mind began to race. "These protocols you're following are the ones designed to keep me calm and occupy my mind while you and your team try to figure out what to do, aren't they?" I felt sick at accusing my own grandfather of deceiving me, but I also realized my mind was not yet able to function properly and the danger I faced was likely dire.

"Slow down, Levi. I can feel your mind begin to panic through the neurolink. I am confident that you will be okay, and that together we will get you to your team. I can also assure you that the protocols were designed to help you put your head back together after the long period of stasis you experienced. Keeping calm is part of the process, but only because it will help you regain yourself."

"What if the damage to my brain is irreversible?" My doubts calmed but a little.

"One more promise, then I would like to continue the protocols. I can assure you that the technology that put you where you are was designed by the brightest people who have ever lived. There is empirical data to prove that. When you undertook this adventure, you were thinking clearly and trusted the science behind your mission."

My breathing steadied. Logic was the tether to safety, and I felt more anchored. "Alright, let's continue." As soon as the thought was out, the footing on the branches beneath me gave way. I slipped and found myself falling. I reached. I flailed. My body dropped, and picked up speed as it bounced off several other branches. I expected to be scraped, or break a limb, but the suit protected me. My mind latched onto the reality that the drop was going to end soon, and with a very quick stop. I grasped and felt branches go by. I focused on a larger tree below that seemed sturdy enough to catch me. I had to move myself to my right. I timed a kick and pushed hard against a branch on my left and made enough contact to change the course of my fall. I expected the branches to snap, or at least knock the wind out of me. My vision darkened as the branches held, and my deceleration halted quickly, but the branches also had enough give to sway down and flex before swinging back up to their original position. My lack of death was a welcome surprise.

"Dear Lord! What happened? Are you alright?" Grandfather asked.

Panting more from anxiety than anything else, I caught my breath before responding and then remembered what an idiot I was. Neurolink communication did not require breath. "I just took a shortcut to the bottom of the cliff. But, I think I am whole. I cannot believe I didn't break a bone."

"You are made of tougher stuff than you thought. If you're in a safe place now, let's continue. Otherwise, I do not want to distract you."

"I think I will stay where I am for a minute or two." I lay there, looking up and marveling at the distance I had fallen. It must have been more than a thousand feet. From this angle, the branches above me reminded me of the thorn and briar barrier surrounding Sleeping Beauty's castle.

"I'll continue, then."

Grandfather's voice through the neurolink beckoned a memory of his face – laugh lines around bright blue eyes. His hair was still mostly dark brown, but at his temples and sprinkled throughout the rest, his age shone with silver. His brow had the creases of one who spent a lot of time in deep thought, but it did not detract from the levity in those eyes. Oddly, I tried to recall my own face, and struggled to remember it. Strange which memories came easily and those I thought should, but wouldn't. I realized I had not been paying attention. "I'm sorry, Grandfather, I was lost in thought for a moment, would you begin again?"

"If you're sure the fall did not do more damage than you thought."

Although I may very well have sustained a concussion, I felt my cognitive processing was intact. "Please continue. I will pay better attention." I felt a growing darkness in my mind, a feeling of foreboding that I was in danger, but could not perceive the threat. I remembered stories of people killed centuries ago by carbon monoxide poisoning in their homes, caught unaware until it was too late. Detectors and elimination of fossil fuels greatly reduced these problems in modern day, but that was on Earth. Who knew what poisons might exist in this terra.

Grandfather's voice pulled me back to reality. "Very well. As we discussed earlier, the preeminent global concern for most of the last century was the sustainability of the ever-growing human population on the Earth. The initial research and development centered on food production, water purification and desalinization. Food engineering made great strides and surpassed the needs for several decades, but the projections showed that the ability to increase productivity and the trend of ever-increasing demand would cross paths by the year 2225. We are now less than thirty years from that point.

"Other approaches to the problem became essential. Some factions supported the idea that human nature would solve the problem. While it is true that starving people will fight and kill to survive, the vast majority of the civilized world rejected this theory. One theory that gained considerable momentum was adaptation to live and cultivate resources underwater. That is still an open branch of research, being pursued primarily through centers in Brazil, Argentina, Chile and Central America."

Absently, I thought, "I've never much cared for swimming." I continued to look up into the branches above, watching them sway on a strengthening breeze. I wondered if I should be concerned about the wind picking up. Atmospherics in this world may vary to extremes. I realized I would likely need to find firmer footing soon. Great, something else to add to my worries.

Grandfather chuckled. "You swim about as well as a racehorse flies, Levi. No, you were never interested in that field of study."

The winds continued to build, and the branch I was on swayed in an orbital motion. I was not in immediate jeopardy of being thrown off, but I was at risk of nausea and vomiting. "You have the subtleness of a sledgehammer, Grandfather." I turned onto my stomach, taking care to place each hand and foot on a secure branch, and located a reasonably safe path down the last fifty or sixty feet to the bottom.

"I like that one, Levi. I'll store it away to use later without giving you credit. It seems like you are moving again. Shall I wait until you are settled before I continue?"

"No need, I am nearly there." I had to drop the last eight feet, and found the landing to be relatively soft, but a little sticky. My mind went to honeycomb, continuing the obsession with comparing this terra to food. "I hope you are able to guide me to food and water soon, Grandfather. I keep comparing the landscape to food in my mind. I imagine even if my body is fully hydrated and fed, I will be in need of both in the near future."

"It is a priority. But, your immediate needs should be met by your suit."

I should have guessed as much. At the base of the cliff, I found a fairly dry spot under a tree-like structure and sat down to let Grandfather continue. My arm brushed against the trunk, and even through the suit it felt wet and slick. Again, a sudden panic ripped through me. I hoped it was the mental fog that caused me fear, but my logical brain could not sweep the concern away like a patch of dust. My instincts cried out in warning.

Grandfather continued, "As I was saying, scientific centers around the world have struggled with numerous approaches to solving the problem of a growing populace with ultimately finite resources. A popular theory is the alternate or multiple planet discipline. It originally gained prominence when global warming was a primary concern, but never lost momentum when resource depletion and overpopulation demanded attention. The romantic notion of finding another world viable for cultivation into sustaining a human population has drawn the largest grants and private donations of any scientific field. Although this field of study demanded many successes, including discovery of a suitable planet, travel, establishment, atmospherics, and countless other logistics problems, it has remained a favorite of scientists across the globe."

Although much of my recovery to this point had involved pieces of my memory fitting back into place, Grandfather's words drew together a sense of purpose that resonated in my heart and soul, chasing away the grip of panic squeezing me. "Space exploration is my passion. That is why I am here." It should have seemed obvious, given where I was, but this specific realization beckoned a wave of memories and thoughts related to decades of study and work in the field of space exploration. Theories and calculations flashed rapidly into place. I was lost in a torrent of recalled discoveries, feeling my passion attached to each success and disappointment in the failures. Many failures. When the rush subsided, I was glad I had sat down, and wondered how much time I had spent recovering. I realized there were still many holes in my mind, but I had gone from more holes than solids to a sturdy frame of myself with gaps in the structure left to fill. The task seemed manageable. The foreboding was muted, but still there, scratching to find purchase in my mind. I pushed it away.

"Wow, that trip was like a flea hitching a ride on a bullet!" Grandfather's chuckle was like a cozy blanket.

Yet, the feeling of elation was fleeting. "I didn't know the neurolink allowed that depth of shared thought." With my brain function improved, awareness expanded the boundaries of thought and recollection. I realized more about my circumstances, including discomfort about pieces of reality that did not fit together.

Before I could complete my train of thought, Grandfather continued. "You left your thoughts open to me as your pathways and experiences connected. This healing is good and important – you have just made an incredible amount of progress. However, I think you still have a substantial amount of work yet to accomplish. Your comment that space exploration was your passion may be true, but no more so than a childhood hero of mine, Michael Jordan, who once declared baseball to be his passion."

"Michael who? Before you answer that, Grandfather, I want to discuss the neurolink with you. I do not recall any personal involvement with the science behind the neurolink, but I believe I understand enough of the basic tenets to know that a connection spanning the distance between Earth and the closest potentially viable planet is not possible." Discomfort about this realization firmed into a certain level of distrust. Perhaps this was the source of the foreboding I felt. Something told me there was more. I continued, "My two most logical theories are that either you are with me on this planet or you are artificial intelligence and I am linked to the transmitting computer from transport or the base on this planet. Please tell me you are here, Grandfather."

"Levi, I can sense your heartrate and blood pressure rising. You must stay calm. I will help you figure this out, but there are other possibilities. And, you will see the whole truth very soon. The protocols have brought you this far, please trust in them to bring you the rest of the way." Grandfather's guarded tone left me even less trusting.

"You did not travel with me through space, Grandfather. I know there is very little that would pull you away from Earth and the family you love. Unless the planet is in chaos, and survival were imminently at risk, you would not take part in exploration. That leaves me with the most likely option that you are artificial intelligence. Very convincing, with all of your trite phrases, sense of humor and inflection. However, I am familiar with artificial programming and the level of complexity and reality that has been accomplished in that field. The true give-away for me was your reliance on protocols. Grandfather is a much more liberal spirit and would not be bound by protocols. But, a machine certainly would."

I felt sick. I worried about vomiting in my suit and wondered what I would even be able to produce. I doubt my stomach held much of anything. In addition to nausea, I felt stupid. Not just the kind of stupidity that followed recovery from stasis, but an additional personal dose of foolishness in being duped by a computer, and the brazen degree of risk I took by transmitting that very doubt. It probably would not have mattered. The kind of neurolink I would have with a computer would allow the machine access to all active thought. Ultimately, I decided, even though I was not really talking to my grandfather, I was connected to a source of information that I would have to use to get me to a base of operation, if there was one. If there was no base... If the transport failed to land safely and I had no team to meet... Icy panic streaked across my consciousness. I was still missing something important, perhaps many things.

"Levi, your concern is understandable, but it is also anticipated and I believe a necessary part of your healing. Will you extend a little more faith?" Grandfather's voice seemed so genuine. The technology was convincing.

As I weighed the limited options available to me, I also longed to recall the details of my mission, the planning for the transportation and to at least know which of the planets I had reached. *Grandfather* might be able to help me with that. "Perhaps not faith, but I will at least entertain my scientific curiosity by communicating with you further. Will you admit that you are artificial intelligence?"

Grandfather's chuckle felt warm. "Levi, if I was artificial intelligence, don't you think I would be programmed to believe I was real. Only the programmer or authorized user would have access to an acknowledgement such as you seek. Of course, if I was artificial, I would not be able to tell you that much."

"Unless that kind of bullspit was the kind of logic Grandfather might have used, and then that is exactly what an artificial intelligence of high sophistication would be programmed to use." My brain ached. I wondered if the suit had medications for pain, anxiety and other foreseeable ailments.

"No sense arguing with you that I'm real. You have always been stubborn (my word) or determined (yours) once your mind was made up. I have said on more occasions than a porcupine has quills that once you set your path, if a mountain stood in your way, it was more likely the mountain would move than you would change course."

"Can you just guide me to the base? Unless our landing was so compromised that a base does not exist, I want to begin moving toward it. I am confident I have recovered sufficiently to allow safe travel." I doubted this request would work, but it was worth trying. Feeling gullible, combined with a banging headache, I was ready to move past the ridiculous protocols and learn the critical information about my mission and the landing party. The thought of finding a safe place assuaged the ice crystals in my mind.

"I think it is best to complete the proto-"

"Don't say it!" I interrupted, perhaps sounding more harshly than I intended.

"Levi. Do you remember when you were a young boy, say nine or ten, and you wanted to learn how to drive my old Ford truck?"

I remembered.

"Do you recall how I promised to teach you to drive in a field just as soon as you were able to reach the pedals and see over the dashboard?"

"Yes." I was glad that memory was intact. I had thought I was big enough before Grandfather believed I was. I snuck out early one Saturday morning, found the keys above the visor, and fired the truck up. By the time Grandfather reached me in the field, the truck had both front wheels stuck in the irrigation ditch and the rear wheels digging holes in the mud as they spun.

"Well, the stakes are even higher this time. Can you be patient and trust this old man, just a little?"

He almost convinced me that he was my Grandfather. Whether it was trust or resignation, I decided it did not matter. Until I finished the protocols, *Grandfather* was not going to direct me to the base. "Proceed. But, I really think I need to find base, so let's make this quick."

"Excellent. I was reciting the various approaches the governments of the world and scientific community were taking to address the problem of overpopulation and depletion of resources. The last of the highly funded approaches was genetic modification and species redesign. Labs in Australia, Europe, along the United States East Coast and New Zealand worked together to find ways to manipulate DNA, and change the nature of humankind further."

I felt a wave beginning to build within my head. The pain behind my eyes grew. I knew I was close to something big. "Grandfather, who wrote the protocols?"

"That is the right question to ask." Relief saturated his words. "You did."

The wave that hit me this time was like a sunburst, illuminating the dark recesses of my memory and burning off the fog. My headache waned, and my anxiety lifted. The terror of not remembering my mission was gone. The fear of what had happened to the landing party removed. The drive to know answers I believed could be found from my Grandfather, rather the AI posing as my Grandfather, subsided.

I could feel the trembling in my neurospeech as I called out, "Grandfather. I am sorry I doubted you..." With my mind cleared, the sense of foreboding came clearly into view. I knew exactly where I was, and I was not safe.

Not sure of when it began developing, a gel of some kind pooled around me. I scrambled to my feet and felt the ground beneath me shake. It was not gel, but mucous. I began to climb. Quickly. The winds blew, and death tickled on the breeze.

Finding a thick branch, I searched for an opening. Desperation replaced panic and pushed at my logic centers to stall thought. For what seemed like minutes, I searched, knowing my death could come at any time. There. A small gap opened in the branch base. I reached in with both hands and pried a gap wide enough to slip my entire body through. As I started to pull with my arms, the structure shook and the wind blew in a torrent, ripping at my body and testing my grip. For a moment, I worried that my grip would not hold, but my strength persevered, adrenaline boosted me into the branch and fully into the opening. Immediately, my body was pulled deeper into the structure by a flowing wave of a thick, dark liquid through a series of pipes. This was better, I thought.

"I am dying to know how you did it, Levi. But, if you need to reach your destination before we talk, I can wait a little longer."

I let my heartrate slow and checked through a quick series of relaxation techniques before responding. "You may have already noticed – I can be a bit stubborn. When my application to join the space exploration teams was rejected, I was furious. Just because I had accomplished more in the field of genetics, I should not be forced into that discipline by bureaucrats. There was only one thing I could do about it. Solve the problem for both disciplines at the same time." I navigated the arteries, moving from one vessel to another. Several pinkish orbs began to treat me like a groupie at a Beastie Boys concert. Another Grandfather cliché based upon an embarrassing affinity to a fossil from the twentieth century. A groupie at an Orange Death concert would be more apt to the current day. I was able to keep the groupies away, but noticed more were following. By the time I reached the internal carotid artery, I was getting pressed by dozens of the pink orbs. I continued on, warily.

"But how?"

"The formulas, which I will be happy to share with you after I am restored, would fill every glass-board in every lecture hall in the American Science Institutes along the Eastern Coast. The short answer is that the Australian and New Zealand teams had the right idea, but they did not take it far enough. By modifying the genetic code, human beings could be shrunk, thereby reducing the space needed and resources required to sustain humanity. Perhaps it was the romantic tie to the works of Tolkien that limited their thinking, but New Zealand envisioned a hobbit-sized population, which would double, or possibly even triple, the number of people the Earth could sustain.

"I thought, why stop there. If genetic manipulation can shrink people to half their normal size, further reduction is possible. The difficulties arise when one is shrunk beyond a factor of ten, and the normal skeletal structure of the individual becomes an infeasible model. That is where my studies in complex systems provided the answer. By calculating and inputing data for the environment into which the person will be placed and the size of the reduction, the models I developed allowed the human genetic code to become a living program that worked with my own algorithms and models to find a solution. If a solution could be found, the programs would find it and the proverbial green light would beacon."

I looked down at myself as I rode the wave of blood through the artery, white cells converging on me, pressing harder, causing pain. I struggled to relax, worried that fighting against them would trigger a frenzied response. I forced my mind away from the discomfort, ignored it. I found it interesting that my brain had concocted the idea that I was already on the space exploration team. No doubt, it was the easiest explanation for my landing in what appeared to be an alien terra. Additionally, my preoccupation with space travel must have played into the delusion. More interesting is that I had perceived my modified body to be a space suit. I could see now that my form was less human-like than I supposed. That was off-putting to a large degree. I had limbs, but they were covered by a hard exoskeleton-like shell. My hands had digits, but only three, and they were more like hardened claws with dexterous pads. I also realized I was not breathing through the suit, but drawing in oxygen and nutrition through my *skin*. I wished there was a way for Grandfather to put me under an electron microscope and photograph this form before I restored. Perhaps I would solve that dilemma next time.

My eyes jerked back to my claws. Upon them were the shredded remains of several white blood cells. Bugger.

Grandfather's interruption was timid. "How did you know that your mind would be lost, but could be recovered?"

I willed myself to continue as I felt the surging pressure of more cells attacking me with purpose. Pulling my limbs close to allow passage through the artery, I wished I was closer to my destination. "That was the most difficult part of my coding. Many failed experiments on cloned mice showed that behaviors taught to the creatures were lost upon shrinking. Any time a substantial modification of DNA took place, the memories and cognitive process were disrupted. Ultimately, I turned to the field of neuropsychology for the answer. That's also the path that led me to the protocols. I found that if the subject was prepared ahead of time, with a series of keys and prompts that connected to specific memories, the mental recovery was not only possible, but accelerated. This became readily apparent with the first human testing in New Zealand. Our first hobbit took months to recover his memories. I knew that shrinking a person down to the size of an insect, or smaller, would cause far greater trauma to the mind."

"And, you knew it was likely the subject would be confused about where it was and perhaps even who it was?"

"Yes. The first hobbit, believed he was actually a hobbit in Tolkien's Middle-earth. I suppose he was so obsessed with the writing, that when he was transformed, his restructured mind created a reality that made sense. I had no idea I would think I was an astronaut, but I knew I would not likely be myself when I woke up. One thing I do not know is how long it has been since I initiated my transformation."

The cells jammed against me, dying, clogging the pathway ahead. This was dangerous, not only for me, but for Grandfather as well. If I did not reach my destination, his immune system might kill me and block an essential artery in the process. Spinning to create space, I looked down, hoping to find a means of propulsion. I kicked my legs and found they were limber and chuck full of fast twitch fibers. I lurched ahead, clearing my path.

Grandfather felt my anxiety. "What is happening, Levi? What's wrong?"

I lied. "Just a minor hitch on my transportation, Grandfather. No need to worry. Please go on."

Grandfather's tone sounded unconvinced, but he continued. "One week. I would have appreciated a little more warning and preparation for what was happening, Levi. You only spent one day with me to explain what you were doing and obtain my consent. Were you worried that I would change my mind?"

I was swimming like I had a propeller in my legs, but the white cells seemed like an endless curtain ahead of me. At least I was making progress. "Not really. I was more worried about the safety of my technology. I have all of the programming bio-locked in my computer. Nobody but me can access everything, but I still worried that others would try. Grandfather, the possible applications for this technology are endless, and many of them are very dangerous."

"You didn't tell me that your programs, formulas, data, etc. were all locked away on your device!" Grandfather's tone was heated. For him, that was unusual – about as common as a rabbit playing harmonica.

"I do not trust others with this technology until I am able to secure accords regarding the ethics to govern its use." The curtain in front of me thickened and I began to slow. I did not want to damage any more cells, but if I stopped, I would have no other option.

"Something's not right, Levi. Your heartrate is a snare drum."

I was about to lie again, to keep him calm, but then it hit me. I needed more pressure. "Grandfather, your white blood cells are attacking me, and threatening to stop me altogether." I let my mind apprehend the pain my body was feeling and share a portion of it with Grandfather. Behind me, a wave of pressure built and I surged through the blockage. "That's it, Grandfather, don't get too upset. But, your blood pressure is keeping me going."

"I'm not done arguing with you about your decision to keep the programming secret. What if you had not awoken, Levi? I would have had no chance to restore you if I could not have gotten into your computer! You would have been lost forever!"

I laughed. "Some scientist you are, Grandfather. I have discovered the solution to the greatest dilemma facing humanity – technology that may save billions of people, but you worry over the loss of one life."

"That's because I love you."

The sincerity of his words hit me like a bowling ball to the gut. I think I may have cried if I had tear ducts. I hoped I was getting close as I was beginning to slow again. "Grandfather, if I had not awoken and recovered my mind, I would not have been able to be saved. The only way to restore me fully is to reach your neurotransmitter at the base of your brainstem, and connect to your computer, then through it access my own computer. I was able to program into the DNA the basic ability to communicate with my host neurologically, but to transmit a connection to a computer still requires a bit of hardware. When I shrunk, my neurotransmitter was left behind.

"That was why it was essential that I develop protocols that I could use as keys to unlock the doors to portions of my memories, but which would allow me to make those mental connections myself. Had you tried to simply tell me everything, my mind would likely have rejected it – like when I believed you were AI. The most successful way to restore the memories and intellect was to pre-program the brain and allow it to heal on its own with a progression of triggers to stimulate the recovery." Within a cluster of white blood cells, I neared the Circle of Willis Artery, and quickly sped to the brainstem.

"Levi, you said before that you solved the space exploration/ alternate world approach with this technology. How is that possible?"

"Now, this is where my withholding of the program files was perhaps a bit selfish. As a condition of me making all of my work available, I will negotiate a place on the first mission to colonize another world. I solved their biggest remaining problem. The first problem was the amount of time and fuel it would take to reach another planet. With genetic modification, aging is not a problem. Explorers now live the hundreds or thousands of years it will take to reach whichever world we decide to colonize. The renewable fuels, and conversion from the gasses, and radiation in space will provide the means to travel, but the space required to feed, hydrate and otherwise sustain a crew were insurmountable problems. Even if the crew were all put in stasis, the equipment needed to maintain stasis would be substantial, and the possibility that the crew would not be recoverable after being in stasis so long is a real concern.

"Yet, if the crew is shrunk down to the size of viruses, all can ride in one pilot, the plasma needed to restore the matter of the body can be incorporated into the structure of the ship, which would protect it from excessive radiation and extreme temperatures in space. More importantly, the computer modeling will allow the atmosphere of the new planet to be analyzed and the data calculated to allow the crew to be restored to a form genetically modified to live in that atmosphere."

I approached the neurotransmitter at the base of Grandfather's spinal cord, but could not get to it without fighting through an army of white cells and more of the lumpy duffel bags with millipede legs. Time was fleeting and options few. I channeled my inner Bruce Lee and whirred into motion, slicing through the first wave of cells and launching myself forward. Progress was slow and very painful. I imagined myself wading to shore in Australia through scores of box jellyfish. Somehow, I reached the transmitter and latched onto it. Once I touched it, I could feel the connection to his computer. I realized how much I had missed the connection to my own. Forcing the pain of the onslaught to the back of my mind, I connected to my own computer. Like a robotic octopus with nitro-fueled limbs, my mental probes clicked through the biolocks and coding to the regeneration program, and found it waiting to be executed with a simple command. Through the camera on my computer I could see Grandfather standing in my lab before a tub of pink plasma. He turned and sat in the chair. I was about to start the sequencing that would transmit the restoration code to my DNA.

Grandfather's tone was concerned, "I am feeling a lot of pain through the link and my own head. Are you there yet?"

"Yes, it's nearly over."

"If my body attacks you when you enter, the test is still a failure is it not?"

I sighed. "If something goes awry in my restoration, my computer is now unlocked and the programs are available. I'm confident we can counter the immune system by coating me with a layer of the host human DNA. Then, the body will perceive the small intruder as tissue from the host. I worried that this might be a problem, but I did not want to add too many variables to the programming."

"Always seven steps ahead, Levi."

"I need to tell you two more things before I start the program. Grandfather, I love you; and I am very grateful you agreed to help me with this test."

I clicked start.

Grandfather continued. "So, when do you think you are going to leave me for that long space journey?" The sadness had returned to his voice.

"Who said anything about leaving you behind? One of my terms will be that you are part of the team."

"But I'm not a pilot."

I chuckled, and it still sounded metallic and odd. "You aren't, but by the time we leave, I will be. You get to do the downsizing next time."

Grandfather started to argue, but the sequence kicked in and I began to grow. I slipped through the port at the base of grandfather's skull, ready to land in the tub of plasma. That kind of convincing would require a face-to-face conversation.

About Brendon Taylor

Brendon is an attorney during the workweek, a writer when he can find time, a food and camping enthusiast often, a frustrated Miami Dolphins fan each fall, and a loving husband and father all of the time. He has been at Merrill & Merrill, chartered in Pocatello, Idaho, since he became an attorney in 1999, after graduating from Washburn Law School in Topeka, Kansas. He was an original founder of Deep Magic in 2002 and has written many articles, short stories and contracts since its inception.

HER GLIMMERING FACADE

By Eleanor R. Wood | 6,000 words

MY AUNT TOSHIKO disappeared two days after my wedding. She was beaming at the ceremony, seated beside my parents at the banquet, hugging my beautiful bride and welcoming her to the family. She waved us off on our honeymoon, cheeks flushed with champagne, her glossy black hair trailing from its bun. It was the last time I saw her.

Gia and I spent ten days basking in the glow of love and warm pearlescent beaches. Until I saw the lavender seas of Pathos 5 for myself, I didn't believe the brochures. We stayed in a beachfront chalet overlooking a bay ringed by teal-forested mountains. Bright parrot lizards perched in the trees, lending their colour to the vista's rainbow palette. We ate spicy fruits and fresh seafood and watched psychedelic sunsets. Gia taught me yoga; I taught her to surf.

Dad picked us up from the spaceport. He smiled and hugged us, but with quiet tension. He let us tell him about our holiday before he brought us fully back to Earth with his news.

"I hate to spoil your mood so soon, Carlos." He threw me a sad glance from the driver's seat. "Ma and I didn't want to worry you on your honeymoon. But it's Toshiko. She's missing."

"What do you mean, 'missing'?" Gia asked over my perplexed silence.

"No one's seen her in over a week. She's not home. Her car's outside. Her purse and phone are still in the house."

I found my tongue. "Are you saying she's been abducted or something?"

Gia squeezed my hand, in fear or reassurance.

"We just don't know. The police haven't found anything unusual. They've traced her last known movements, and nothing seems out of the ordinary. We're just waiting for news. Any news."

The honeymoon glow was already a fading memory. While my wife and I had been on an exotic planet, captivated by each other and its surreal beauty, tragedy had befallen my family. Toshiko wasn't my aunt by blood. She was my mother's dearest friend, and I'd called her "Aunt" my whole life. She'd always been there for me, in her warm, levelheaded way. She used to take me to basketball practice, let me hang out at her place after school, listen to my woes about unrequited crushes. She'd encouraged me to study engineering. She'd introduced me to Gia.

"How's Ma?" I could imagine her anxiety.

"Much as we've all been. Searching. Alerting missing persons sites. Uploading posters. Worrying for her friend. But she can't wait to see you." He smiled at me in the rearview mirror, but I couldn't smile back.

"You okay, bear?" Gia asked me, caressing my palm the way she did when she was worried. Sorrow had replaced the joy in her green eyes.

I put my arm around her shoulders. "I don't know."

Dad took the skyway route—more traffic than the road, but faster. When he pulled up at home, Ma was sitting on the front porch, book in her hand as ever, beside a jug of blackberry wine and a tray of snacks to welcome us. She threw her arms around Gia and me in turn.

"How was your honeymoon, my loves?"

We smiled and told her of the wonders we'd seen, but I was distracted. Gia sensed my impatience and took Dad aside to show him our photos so I could sit with Ma.

"Dad told us about Aunt Toshiko."

Ma's face fell, and she reached for my hand. "There's been nothing, Carlos. No news at all. Not even a hint as to where she's gone. It's as if she vanished into thin air." I heard the hitch in her voice.

"Have the police spoken to her family?" She had few relatives, but her elderly uncle lived nearby and she had a brother in Japan.

"They haven't heard from her. Her poor uncle's fraught with worry. I feel so helpless. I can't think of anything else to do ..." She broke down in tears and I held her, feeling numb.

I visited Toshiko's house the next day. Nothing seemed out of the ordinary. Her hanging baskets decorated the cottage with clusters of colour and bustling aromas, while her roses bloomed red, pink, and orange in their beds below. I stood before her front door and had to believe it was all a mistake. Surely she was inside, preparing food or weaving on her loom or designing some miraculous technology to be shared only when she'd got it just right?

But when I let myself in, the house was silent. Only the ticking of her clocks broke the stillness, like tiny ripples on a pond. I walked through the rooms, watering her neglected bonsai and picking up fallen petals from an orchid. Her rear garden was as lush and bright as the front, but she wasn't sitting at her patio table calculating ratios or pruning potted trees. Her absence rang loud in the silence. I opened her patio doors and let in the sounds of birdsong she couldn't hear, and I finally knew that she was gone.

I let the dread wash over me. Every memory I had of Toshiko assailed me at that moment. I longed for her to breeze through the door and laugh at our foolish worries. After a while, I longed for her to appear so I could chastise her for terrifying us all. But I knew she would never do that to us, and my tears flowed with fear that she might never come back.

My phone chimed. When I answered, Gia looked up at me from the screen and halted whatever she'd been about to say.

"Oh, bear. Don't do this to yourself. Come home?"

I wiped my face with one hand. "I'm coming back now."

"Good. I love you." She smiled sadly and hung up.

As I locked the front door, a wave of dizziness hit me. I stumbled against the porch frame and struggled to get my bearings as the world whirled about my head. It passed after a moment, leaving me light-headed. By the time I got home, I was ravenous.

"It's just the shock and worry," Gia assured me as she cleared away the supper dishes. "Have an early night and see how you feel tomorrow."

I kissed her and apologised for not helping clean up. Sleep sounded great. I dozed off wondering why I still felt as though I hadn't eaten in days.

* * *

"Sorry to hear you're not feeling too good, sport." Dad looked concerned.

"Probably just something I picked up on the trip home. Space flights are basically germ dispensaries, right?"

"Plenty of bed rest!" I heard Ma's voice from the background. Dad pointed his phone at her, and I had a glimpse of her shaking a finger at me before he came back on screen. I had to smile.

"The police want to speak to Gia and me. Apparently, we're the only ones from the wedding they haven't interviewed yet."

"Well, it was the last occasion Toshiko attended. They're trying any lead available."

"I know. It makes sense. They might come by today, although I've told them I'm not feeling great. I'm sure we've got nothing new to tell them, but everything helps, I guess."

"You bet. Heard you went by her house yesterday."

"Yeah." I closed my eyes against a new onslaught of vertigo. "Yeah, that was tough. Had to see for myself, though, you know?"

"I know. Listen, bud, you look pale. Get some rest. We'll talk again later."

I waved good-bye and bent my head between my knees, fighting unconsciousness. I lost and blacked out.

* * *

There were wires, and tubes, and something covered my face. I was too weak to pull it away. Dark metal. Plastic ... rigging? My hands felt thick and cumbersome and the ringing in my ears wouldn't stop. I shook my head and giddiness spun me into the black again.

* * *

I woke up in bed. Gia stood over me, with Dad just behind her.

"He's coming around," she said, relief on her face.

"The doctor's on her way," Ma said from the bedroom doorway. "Oh, love, you're awake!"

"Don't crowd him, Rita," Dad said. "The lad needs to breathe."

"What happened?" I asked, still feeling faint.

"You passed out," Gia said. I'd always teased her about the frown line between her eyes. It didn't seem so cute when she was worried. "I couldn't wake you ... I called your parents. Your dad helped me get you up here. How do you feel?"

"Weak ... hungry. I had the strangest dream."

"I'll get you some soup and bread, love," Ma called, already on her way downstairs.

"I didn't know you could dream while passed out." Dad looked puzzled.

"It was horrible." I leaned back into the pillows. "Frightening and claustrophobic."

"It's all right, bear." Gia kissed me on the forehead. "You're safe. You're going to be fine."

I closed my eyes for a while and wished Toshiko were here. Much as I loved my family, their fretting wasn't helping. Toshiko would have ushered them all out and delivered remedies in her sensible, pragmatic way. Where was she? I fought tears, feeling miserable and pathetic. I wasn't myself. This wasn't right.

"The doctor's here!" Ma called from below.

I struggled to haul myself upright, and the room spun a dance around my bed. *No ... please ... not again ...* Nausea crept up my throat and my consciousness dissipated once more. Gia's anxious face was the last thing I saw.

* * *

Can you wake up in a dream?

That's how it felt the second time; not as though I'd fallen into the sleeping awareness of a dream reality, but as though I'd regained consciousness and found myself somewhere else entirely. The ringing in my ears was louder this time and I plunged into claustrophobic panic. Disorientation fuzzed my brain as I sought my bearings. Everything looked dim, as if through sunglasses. *Goggles.* I pulled at them, but they remained in place, and my fingers felt nothing as I touched them. My hands weren't my hands. My motions were slow and fluid, as though I was suspended in something. My heart fluttered in increasing terror as I flailed and yelled and tried to free myself, aware of nothing but the blank, all-consuming panic shoving out any rational thought.

After a minute or an eternity, I ceased my struggling, exhausted and breathless. I forced myself to calm, to breathe, to extend my senses and figure this out. The ringing wasn't in my head, I realised. It sounded like some kind of alarm. I lifted my clunky hands in front of my face and saw they were encased in firm gloves. The backs looked like plastic robot hands, and the fingertips and palms were padded. My T-shirt and shorts had been replaced with a skintight suit. When I yanked off one of the gloves, it dangled from the sleeve by wires like a child's mitten on a string. My skin looked pasty. With my fingertips free, I felt for the goggles again and discovered they merged with the suit, which covered my head. Only my mouth and nose were exposed. I scrabbled at the back of my neck, searching for a fastener that would release me from this inexplicable second skin.

I found it. A tiny concealed zip began under my chin and wound around my neck and down the back of the suit. Despite my trembling fingers, I managed to unzip the hood, peeling it back from my face and ridding myself of the clumsy goggles. I looked at them in bewilderment. Their surface resembled a screen rather than a clear lens, and there were more wires and exposed microchips on the inside.

I could see properly now, although my surroundings made no sense. The dizziness, worse than ever, didn't help either. I was rigged up to some sort of mesh hammock, inside a black metal frame with wires and screens and tubes running along the inside. My feet were locked into boots connected with more wires to what looked like a sophisticated treadmill. To my left was an opening. Beyond it, I could make out a metallic floor and dusky, yellowish lighting.

I pulled off the other glove and twisted to work out how to free myself from the hammock contraption. Elastic clips joined it to the suit, so I unclipped them and managed to stand up in the weird, springy boots. My head spun and I clutched at the framework in order to remain upright. Something heavy hung at my side. I looked down and saw, to my horror, that I appeared to be attached to a large bag of my own waste. Had I slipped into some sort of coma? Was this a hospital? Repulsed, I tried to pull the bag away, but a sharp, gurgling tug in my gut dissuaded me. I had no idea how to disconnect the tubes entering the suit and my flesh beneath.

I swayed as nausea bulged up from my stomach. Just how ill was I, anyway? And where were the nurses who'd clearly been caring for me? No one had come at my panicked yelling, and that alarm was still ringing.

Still leaning on the frame, I freed my feet from the boots and stepped out through its opening. I emerged into a room that looked nothing like a hospital. The walls were the same dull metal as the floor and supported several banks of machinery. The dim yellow light came from a panel in the ceiling, and the incessant alarm emanated from a computer bank to my left. Directly opposite was a machine framework identical to the one I'd woken up in. Its opening faced me, and I could make out another patient suspended inside. At least, I hoped we were patients. My mind tried to suggest alternatives, but they left a frightening chill in the pit of my stomach and I pushed them away.

I no longer believed I was dreaming.

DEEP MAGIC ANTHOLOGY ONE

I turned to the alarm's source. A red light blinked in time with the high-pitched beep. The display panel flashed an Urgent Message alert. I looked around, still half expecting someone to come in and take over. There was a door panel at one end of the room, but it remained closed. The effort to extricate myself from the mechanical structure had drained every last drop of my energy. I didn't even have the reserves to walk the few paces to the door. I turned back to the display instead, and touched the screen.

The alarm stopped, although the light continued to blink. The message appeared on the screen, pale text against a dark background. I read it three times before it began to register.

Carlos, if you're reading this, something must have happened to me. You need to do three things immediately. First, open the panel below this screen and remove one of the nutrient packs inside. Unhook the spent pack from your feeding tube and replace it with the new one. Second, repeat the procedure with the colostomy bags on the shelf below. Third, you'll find a datacard secured to the inside of the panel door. Remove it, insert it into the slot below this screen, and return to your harness unit. Hook yourself up, and I'll explain everything. I'm so sorry you have to face this alone. —T

My body shivered. The combination of fatigue, hunger, and bewilderment had dissolved my nerves and I wondered whether I was hallucinating. *Feeding tube?* I looked down and saw a nozzle protruding from my abdomen. Reminiscent of a hose connector, it was clearly designed to attach to something. I stumbled over to my contraption and saw a squat mechanism tucked behind the hammock mesh. A loose tube dangled from an empty bag attached to it. I must have dislodged the tube during my initial panic. The mechanism whirred softly, and I deduced it was a pump for pushing the bag's contents into my digestive tract. I felt queasy.

T.

T ...

I didn't want to think about it. A horrible, creeping certainty uncoiled itself from my stomach and tingled up my spine. My back was to the other unit. I told myself I was imagining the scent of decay that lay over the barren room. Dread seemed to permeate the air as I turned towards what I'd assumed was my fellow patient. With leaden feet, I approached the unit and looked in at the figure hooked up to a harness identical to mine. The goggles were in place, the gloves and skintight grey suit encased the body, but it hung limply in the harness, the mesh hammock loose around it. The stench of death clung to my nostrils and I gagged.

I tried to look away. I tried to tell myself the sunken cheeks and sallow flesh made her unrecognisable. I tried to believe her remains belonged to someone else, someone I'd never met and had no reason to mourn. But I knew. I knew as soon as I saw her. I knew when I looked through the dim screen of the goggles and put her features together, however lifeless and hollow. I'd known her face all my life.

I sank to the hard floor and let the pain take me.

Toshiko ...

I clutched my lank hair in my hands and wept, long and hard. I had no reserves to draw on, save the agony of grief.

* * *

The wave of sorrow receded and left me drained and aching. I had never felt weakness like it. Toshiko's message flooded back to me, and I knew I had to meet my body's needs before it failed me altogether. I crawled to the panel below the computer screen. Inside were stacks of pouches, fat with nutritious fluid. Below them were empty bags, ready to receive the fluid's remnants after my intestines had processed it. I didn't understand why I couldn't have food. Was there something wrong with my stomach? I felt the warm weight of the bag against my hip and supposed maybe there was.

Swapping empty and full bags was straightforward enough, though surreal. I wondered again just how long I'd been out cold and who had performed these surgeries. My brain was too hazy to decipher my predicament, but I needed answers. Had someone kidnapped me and Toshiko? What had happened to her? She'd clearly been alive when I got here, or she wouldn't have left me her message.

It was time to fulfil the final part of that message.

I found the tiny datacard and inserted it into the slot. Returning to the harness contraption, I connected the feeding tube to the port in my abdomen and set about clipping myself in. I attached the hammock, pulled on the hood and goggles, and donned the gloves. I had no idea what to expect, but Toshiko's instructions were all I had in this bizarre, alien environment.

The goggles darkened to opacity. A disorienting sensation washed over me, from my fingertips to my toes, with a dip of fresh vertigo. I think I passed out again.

* * *

I stood at Aunt Toshiko's front door on a bright, sunny day. The intoxicating scent of her hanging baskets would have placed me there even if I'd had my eyes shut. I looked around. Was I home, safe, as if nothing had happened? The accursed blackouts were messing with my brain. The door stood open, as if inviting me in. I entered, expecting police or detectives.

But it was Toshiko's voice that called to me from the garden.

"Carlos? I'm out here. Come through."

I had to be dreaming. I walked through her cottage, as real and familiar as ever, and found her on the back patio, secateurs in one hand, a straw hat on her head, and a bonsai on the table before her. She turned to me and smiled.

"You made it."

Emotion choked me. "You ... you're here. You're all right."

Her expression saddened. She put down her cutters and came to me, wrapping her arms around my chest. Her head reached my chin, and I placed my cheek on her hair and hugged her.

She pulled away gently. "Come, sit with me. I have things to tell you."

I sat on a patio chair and she took the one beside me. "I got your message. But I don't understand how you're here. You were ... I *saw* you." My voice trembled at the memory and the discrepancy of her sitting with me now.

She took a breath, as if steeling herself. "I died. Didn't I?"

"Yes, but ..."

"Carlos, I'm so sorry. I tried to protect you from all this, but I should have told you before now. I just couldn't bring myself to shatter your world. And now I have to, and it breaks my heart." Her eyes shimmered with tears. My belly was a knot of ice.

She gazed around her fragrant garden and caressed one of the bonsai's gnarled branches. "This world—our world—is an illusion. It's a simulated environment, a place I created for us to live. Everything you've ever known was designed just for you. Every moment of your life since toddlerhood has been spent inside a virtual reality. This reality.

"I built it. I've maintained it. I've kept our bodies healthy while our minds have lived here, experiencing a life we could never have had otherwise. I always knew you'd be in trouble if something happened to me. That's why I set the alarm and coded the program to infiltrate your perceptions if I failed to come around at my weekly time. I wrote this program, the one we're in now, to provide you with answers. I'm a simulation, Carlos. Until now, you've always interacted with the real me, just as I've interacted with the real you. But now I'm a message I left you in case you needed it."

I couldn't breathe. I could barely take in what she was saying.

"You're not making any sense, Toshiko. You're telling me, what, the world isn't real? How can that be? I've lived in it all my life!"

She took my hand in that immediately calming manner she had. "I know you have. I designed it for that very purpose." She paused. "Where did you think you were when you woke up?"

"What, when I found your message?"

"Yes."

"I thought it was a dream. When I realised it wasn't, I thought it was some kind of hospital, that maybe I'd been in a coma or something."

"It's not a hospital. It's a room in the real world. Your body's there right now. So is mine."

My head was spinning again. I pulled my hand from hers and stood up to pace her lawn. The garden was a sensory banquet of colour and scent and birdsong. The grass felt springy under my feet. The air was soft and cool in my lungs. How could it be an illusion?

Yet the cold room in which I'd awoken, stripped of life and colour, had felt just as real. Its hard walls, blaring alarm, yellow light. The claustrophobic suit. The weight of my own waste against my leg. The sickly odour of death. I suddenly understood that if one was real and one designed, the designed one would be bright and safe and welcoming. If reality was bleak and harsh, what better way to escape it?

I turned back to Toshiko. Her expression was patient and sad.

"Why?"

She sighed and spoke in slow, measured tones. "You and I are all that remain of an extraterrestrial colony. Our parents were scientists who left Earth with two dozen others to found a satellite habitat to orbit and study Venus. I was a child when my family emigrated into space; you were one of the new generation born on board the space station that became our home. We established ourselves and thrived above the yellow planet for decades before a catastrophe destroyed us.

"Venus doesn't have the protective magnetosphere of Earth, and of course it's nearer the sun." She took a deep breath and met my eyes. "A massive solar storm hit the planet and swept us out of orbit. It knocked out our communications, destroyed half our solar panels, and left us hurtling through space. We were helpless, adrift, with no means to contact Earth and no way to know how badly they had been affected by the storm. As a satellite, we had no long-range propulsion. Our power source was halved. We had to crowd into a fraction of the station's living space to conserve energy.

"Some blamed the crowded conditions, others said our radiation shields had been damaged, and without the power to grow enough food we were certainly malnourished, but whatever the cause, illness took hold. Contagion spread. I managed to fight it off. You seemed to have a natural immunity and escaped it altogether." Her voice faltered. "By the time it finished its rampage, we were the only two left alive. Me, a thirty-one-year-old programming engineer, and you, an eighteen-month-old boy at the very beginning of life. There was still no contact with Earth. I couldn't maintain the station's full systems on my own. I couldn't face a blank, lifeless future, and I couldn't consign you to one.

"So I adapted the station's VR equipment and built onto its existing software to develop the most sophisticated program I've ever encountered. I programmed the surgical bots to fit us with neural implants and digestion tubes. I created us somewhere to live."

I slumped back into my seat. Numbness crept over me. I didn't know how to begin processing what she was saying. I cleared my throat and grasped the first coherent thought that came to me.

"What about Gia? And Ma and Dad? Are they on Earth, or in another colony, hooked up to other machines?"

Toshiko closed her eyes before answering. "No ... Carlos. I told you. Even if Earth escaped the brunt of the storm, we have no way to communicate with them." She took my hand again. Hers was slender and warm. "Your family, my family, all of our friends and loved ones ... they're part of the simulation. I wrote them. For us. So we could live normal lives and engage with other people. You and I are the only ones with physical counterparts."

My insides felt as though they'd been plunged in freezing water. I couldn't register Toshiko's words. "Are you saying they're not real?" My voice came out as a whisper.

A tear rolled down her cheek. "They're as real as I could possibly make them. They're as real as they are to both of us. I wanted you to have a family, Carlos. Parents to love and cherish you. I could have played that role, but ... I wanted you to know people of all ethnicities. I wanted to populate your world with as many kinds of people as I could, so you'd get to experience humanity. It was a sort of tribute to them too ... all those we've lost."

I thought of everyone I knew. I'd never noticed it before. My parents—Latino. Gia—fair-skinned and freckled, with auburn hair. My best friend at school—tall, with dark skin. Toshiko—petite and Japanese. She'd made our world a memorial for everyone she'd known. A requiem for humanity.

But how could I go back, knowing it was all fabricated? How could I begin to accept that everything I'd ever known was an elaborate pretence?

I realised I was sobbing. My face was wet, the salt liquid gathering at the corners of my mouth. Every sensation seemed acute, as though I had to feel it all in sharp detail, goading my mind to deny its existence. Its reality.

Toshiko was crying too. She reached to pull me into her embrace, but I couldn't take it. I couldn't let myself feel her warmth and essence and know she wasn't real. I saw her putrefying remains, stark in my mind. She'd left me. She'd created a universe for me and then left me all alone in it.

I walked away from her then. I didn't want to hear any more. I couldn't begin to consider what I was supposed to do now. I went back through her house and out the front door. I don't know where I was heading. But I jolted back into my clinging harness, in the dark, metallic confines of my VR pod. The disorientation was nothing like the first time, but it still hit me with its wave of vertigo. The program had ended. She hadn't written anything besides herself, in her home, talking to me.

I yanked myself free of the suffocating tangle of suit and webbing and stumbled out of the unit, landing painfully on the steel floor. My tube came free again, but I felt stronger for the nutrients coursing through my bloodstream.

I stood cautiously. The insipid light still coated the walls. The stench of decay still choked my nostrils. The closed door still occupied the wall beyond Toshiko's unit. I couldn't bring myself to confront her remains again ... but the door. Behind that door lay a deserted space colony. The place I'd come from.

My knees felt weak as I approached the door. I set my shoulders and opened it. A waft of cold, stale air gusted past me. Beyond was darkness. When I stepped through, some long-abandoned power source flickered to life as my motion woke the lights.

I wandered those corridors and chambers that still came alight as I entered them. I found grey bulkheads, and empty quarters, and the remains of a community that had grappled with survival and lost. I found dust, and debris, and chilly dampness. I found evidence of the living, and no one left alive. When I came upon a wide viewport, I stumbled in shock at the raw expanse beyond. Space travel had never frightened me before, but I wasn't travelling now. I was stranded.

I knew Toshiko would have exhausted every possibility over the last twenty-five years. But it was one thing to hear my fate from her simulation. Surely there were records. Computer logs, video diaries, something to confirm everything she'd told me.

The station's computer was easy enough to boot. Obviously the remaining solar panels were keeping some systems alive. *Including your whole world*, a snide voice whispered in the back of my mind. It took me a few moments to find log entries, but there were dozens of them. Some were password protected; others had public access. I scrolled back to the last cluster of entries and opened the top one.

It showed a recording of a gaunt man, pale-faced, with sores on his forehead.

"Magda died this afternoon. There are five of us left. Two children, three adults, and all but one of us are showing symptoms." He coughed, a hacking wet sound that made me wince. "I've tried one last time to mend the communications array, but without Anwelo's skill, we're screwed." A child began crying in the background. The man looked on the verge of joining in. He opened his mouth to continue, but swallowed hard and signed off instead.

The next entry was three days later. I opened it, and a young Toshiko looked out at me. There were tears in her eyes. She held a dark-haired toddler.

"We're the last two," she said. "I jettisoned Will's body this morning. It's just me and little Carlos." She held the child close. He was all she had left. "I can hardly believe it, but I'm better. It's as if I was meant to survive to help this little one. If I'd died too ..." She broke off and kissed the side of his curly head. A lump blocked my throat. That was the end of her entry.

She'd left later accounts of the VR development: her excitement at the initial idea, programming glitches, physiological and hygiene issues, descriptions of fitting me with new suits as I grew.

I stepped away from the computer, hit by the depth of Toshiko's love. I wouldn't have survived without her. I wandered away in a daze.

* * *

As I stood beneath the flickering light cells of a large communal chamber, gazing at abandoned furniture and discarded personal items, it assailed me. The hideous weight of a loneliness so crushing I thought I'd never be able to stand again. It bore me to the ground and I crouched, cowering like a frightened animal, my arms over my head and my breath choking out in hoarse gasps. I felt eviscerated, hollow, terrified. Out here, I was the only human. Utterly alone.

I don't know how long I huddled there, but after a time the lights went out due to my stillness. Even then, I couldn't bring myself to move.

It was the thought of Gia that roused me. My wife. My wife who consisted of binary coding and artificial, programmed intelligence. A fresh sob strangled me at the thought, which was also the realisation that artificial coding was all I had in the world. It *was* my world. Not this cold husk of an extinct population. That complex, all-encompassing, glimmering facade was all I would ever have. I could return to it, immerse myself in it, and share my life with the people Toshiko had fabricated for me ... or I could stay here, in this cold, lifeless reality until I lost my mind to it.

It was no decision, really. I retraced my steps to the only room I'd ever lived in and hooked myself back up. Later, I would find a way to jettison Toshiko's body and perhaps learn how she had died. Later, I would reload the program she'd left me and ask her how to maintain my equipment and keep myself alive, as she had always done for me. I could return to the station and scour the diagnostics for something the colonists had missed. If that proved fruitless, I could consume myself with overseeing my personal reality. But now, all I wanted was my beautiful wife. She was waiting, mercifully alone, when I came around. I pulled her into our bed with me and lost myself in her sweet, tangible reality. For that moment, there was nothing else in the world.

* * *

It's been years since Toshiko taught me everything I needed to know. I've quizzed her virtual persona on everything she could possibly impart. She helped me write the satellite program, establishing a place in my world where the colonists are thriving in their Venusian orbit, making lives and discoveries and babies. I've railed at her, and wept with her, and done my best to express my gratitude for everything she created for me when she was alive. There's nothing left to ask her now; nothing else to say.

But still. Every now and again, when I miss her the most, or need to touch the last remaining link to my physical past, I bring myself back to the metallic room and load her datacard. Her front door is always open, and she always calls,

"Carlos? I'm out here. Come through."

About Eleanor R. Wood

Eleanor R. Wood's stories have appeared in Pseudopod, Crossed Genres, Urban Fantasy Magazine, Flash Fiction Online, and the Aurealis-nominated anthology Hear Me Roar, among other places. She writes and eats liquorice from the south coast of England, where she lives with her husband, two marvellous dogs, and enough tropical fish tanks to charge an entry fee.

THE TARIFF

By Allen Shoff | 6,100 words

DIMITRIOS ELEFTHERIOU IDLY twirled a medal around his finger, disinterestedly watching the graven image of the bearded bishop spin in the microgravity. Like the illusions of a zoetrope, St. Nicholas seemed animated, appearing to extend his hand and offer anew his three bags of gold with each revolution. Dimitrios smiled thinly at this, humor dimly reflected in his dark Grecian eyes framed by sun-kissed Levantine skin—the latter a gift from his mother, God rest her soul. A nervous cough interrupted his reverie, and he turned his head to look at the timid clerk strapped in at his right.

"A problem, Yuri?"

The young assistant, barely twenty years of age, shook his head rapidly.

"No, Captain Eleftheriou, none. None at all," he quickly stuttered.

The older man snorted aloud.

"Yuri, please, Dimitrios. Call me Dimitrios. To the porters and the technicians, Captain, but you, young Yuri, are no mere hired hand—this is, after all, your father's ship."

The youth forced a humorless laugh and continued to watch the lazy revolutions of the medal in the captain's hand. Dimitrios, following his gaze, grinned and splayed the chain across his fingers, abruptly halting the necklace's orbit.

"Oh, this? This is what has you worried?"

"Well, Capta— Dimitrios, sir, yes. What if you lost it?"

The captain shrugged his broad shoulders dismissively.

"What if I lost it? Where could it go?"

"She's a large ship, sir. What with free fall, I don't think you'd ever be able to find it—"

He trailed off, interrupted by Dimitrios's hearty laugh. The ebullient Greek reached out and slapped the youth on the shoulder before settling back into his command chair with a well-practiced slide.

"Have you ever been out of atmo, Yuri? Been out in the black?"

Yuri, averting his eyes, responded sheepishly.

"No, Dimitrios, sir. This is the first time."

The captain's eyes widened.

"Your father is the deputy guildmaster for Saturn and her moons, and you've never left the surface of Titan?"

"No."

Dimitrios opened his mouth as if to say something—twice—but then finally closed it and shrugged.

"Well, then, first lesson: lost and found."

He held up the medal again and made a gesture as if he were tossing it, causing the youth to twitch unconsciously. Dimitrios half smiled and explained.

"In free fall, air only moves when we move it, and we move it through the air vents. If I drop this, it'll make its way through the ship and end up at a return. Nothing is ever lost up here, lad, just temporarily out of place."

He twirled the medal once more around his finger before clasping it again to his neck and dropping it under the collar of his jumpsuit. He smirked.

"You'll find spacers don't have much recourse to St. Anthony, Yuri. At least where their shipboard possessions are concerned."

The deputy guildmaster's son nodded thoughtfully, clearly trying to absorb as much knowledge as he could from the older spacer. Then he lay back in the chair, struggling briefly with the harness that kept his limbs from floating freely, before casting a sideways glance at the captain, trying to learn something about the man without attracting too much attention. The *Doukas* had been underway for the better part of the day, but her captain had thus far eluded categorization. His mood and his manner shifted from euphoric to melancholic in an instant, his bearing from breezy to stiffly formal—yet his penetrating gaze remained unchanged. The captain's eyes betrayed an intelligence far beyond that which was customarily displayed by a merchantman's master—always calculating, forever analyzing, and never dulled by indecision.

"—Yuri! You want to learn something about astrogation or not?"

The assistant, startled, stammered an apology, unaware that he had drifted off into his thoughts, but the captain continued without pause, quizzing his young pupil.

"We've arrived at the Titan-Saturn L2 EGR. Why do we care?"

The youth thought for a moment, desperately wishing he had paid more attention in secondary.

"Uh, EGRs are equipotential gravitational regions—calculated solutions to the n-body problem. We can ghost only from these regions; the translocation drive won't work anywhere else."

Dimitrios snorted.

"If by 'won't work' you mean *if we bypass the safeties and try anyway, every atom of this ship will be torn asunder*, then yes, full points."

He cleared his throat.

"And now, young master Yuri, are you familiar with Schliemann's first law?"

The guildmaster's son was ashamed that he had to shake his head. Dimitrios considered making a remark about scholarship on Titan, but he abstained.

"Schliemann's first states that momentum is preserved across a translocation. Remember: the drive bridges two points in space. Our velocity and heading don't change as we push through in that brief instant the bridge exists."

He pulled the console down from above him and began tapping commands into the screen.

"The art, my boy, is getting gravity to work for us. For today's run, we chose this particular EGR because Titan's position takes it on a heading that will work out nicely to slingshot us into Mimir orbit with only a brief burn on the far side."

He looked back at the youth, who seemed to feel physical pain as he tried to work out the physics of the maneuver, and chuckled.

"Save yourself the work, Yuri. Take a look at the astrogation computer's plot simulation and you'll see what we're doing." He tapped the microphone that clung to the side of his face.

"Shipwide. Now hear this, now hear this: translocation maneuver in thirty seconds. Take your positions."

An automated klaxon wailed, and the computer began calling out the countdown. The captain adjusted the harnesses at his chest, and Yuri did the same. Dimitrios looked back at his young charge, and saw the sun-shy youth's face blanched even paler than normal.

"First ghost?"

The youth nodded. The captain grinned.

"Close your eyes. Trust me."

The boy shut his eyes tightly and gripped the arms of his chair with an uncharacteristically ferocious strength. A low whine, almost imperceptible at first, began to build throughout the compartment. Outside, in the void, the radiators abruptly glowed a dull red, dissipating the waste heat as the reactor pumped more and more reactants into the sun-hot fusion chamber. The wire-thin superconducting coils encircling the *Doukas* began to vibrate as the current increased, fields growing stronger and stronger, enwrapping the vessel in a frighteningly powerful electromagnetic display. Few on board could have explained how exactly the drive worked; even fewer of those millions who lived in Terra's scattered colonies understood the mathematics necessary to allow this travesty of relativity. And yet, inside, the roiling crescendo of sound, so loud as to be almost deafening, reached its peak, and the computer performed the final half billion calculations necessary to precisely fix the point of arrival. The drive activated.

CRACK

To the hypothetical observer orbiting Titan, it all happened too quickly to perceive: in an instant, the nascent bridge swallowed the *Doukas* and vanished just as quickly, leaving nothing but a ghostly afterimage of the vessel burned on the retinas. Near the L4 Lagrange point of Mimir and Alpha Centauri B, the *Doukas* appeared just as suddenly, the crackling energy in the coils entirely spent. Panel radiators extended all along the ship's spine, liquid lithium within already heated to near boiling. The reactor's fire slowly died down to manageable levels.

Inside, Yuri sat blinking, head lolling as he tried to comprehend the sensations assaulting his mind. His hands seemed delayed as he moved them, and his thoughts felt sluggish and unrefined, like those immediately after waking. Dimitrios too, veteran traveler that he was, waited several moments to get his bearings before again taking to the shipwide circuit.

"Now hear this, now hear this: acceleration maneuver in thirty seconds, maintain your positions."

While Yuri continued to shake his head to clear the fog, he and the captain felt themselves thrown back against their chairs as the engines ignited, their harnesses tightening for safety. The acceleration far exceeded the leisurely burn from Titan; this time, the men felt their weight double as the thrust from the engine clawed at their cheeks and their eyes, pulling their skin taut and blurring their vision.

The *Doukas* was an old ship, to be sure—a long, narrow, almost skeletal, titanium frame, capped at the bow by a cluster of habitable compartments, and at the stern by a massive filigree of superconducting wire. The rings of wire formed an invisible but potent magnetic nozzle, directing the torrent of plasma blasted out by the sunlight heat of the fusion reactor. The blade shield protecting the wire coils, an exotic combination of graphite for heat resistance and tungsten for strength, glowed so brightly as to give the vessels both their distinctive look and their obvious name: torches. Although her discolored spine and pockmarked Whipple shielding betrayed her ripe old age, the *Doukas* could *move*. Her owner had made sure of that.

As she burned hard for orbit, the captain rapidly scanned the system for any sign of other vessels. Yuri looked concerned, and spoke through gritted teeth as he felt his lungs struggle to process enough air.

"Dimitrios, sir, what if the Republic sees us? We've got to be giving away our position, burning like this."

The captain took the time to turn to the youth and grunt out a laugh before looking back at the board.

"Your old man really told you nothing of the spacer life, did he, Yuri? Second lesson: stealth in space is a myth."

His fingers flashed over the panel, tapping buttons and tracing over the sensor data, looking for any incongruities that might reveal the presence of a hostile vessel. He continued.

"What's the background radiation of the universe—its temperature? Do you know?"

"No," heaved Yuri.

"We're talking under three kelvins. Even if we shut off every system and froze to death, the crew modules would still be at several hundred kelvins, and would be for months, until we slowly reached equilibrium with the surrounding space. Our radiators are above a thousand kelvins, and our engine's plume is—well, unfathomably hot. We're bright as a sun, Yuri, and there's no way to hide that, not from the cheapest of sensors on the rattiest of freighters."

He looked almost philosophical for a moment, even as the brutal pummeling of acceleration continued.

"The smallest ship is visible the moment she ghosts in system, so it's never a question of hiding. It's a question of running."

The console beeped an ugly warning tone, and Captain Eleftheriou winced.

"What's that?" gasped the young trainee, cheeks vibrating as the old ship rattled.

"Republican signature burning hard for co-orbit. Looks like a frigate. Kali's blazes," muttered the captain, eyes glued to his screen. He reached up again to his microphone.

"Giannis, what can you give me on mass flow? Another two, three, kilos a second?"

Yuri could almost hear the engineer's profanity through the captain's earpiece; under any other circumstance, it would have been humorous to witness the exchange.

"I understand, yes—yes—no, I really do. A kilo, then? We need to grab another few meters per second here; can you do it?"

Yuri listened intently, trying to overhear the other side of the captain's conversation. He saw all he needed when he saw the captain's face darken, and the man sullenly respond.

"Counting on you, Giannis."

The captain threw his head back in the chair and ran a hand through his black hair, eyes closed and face set in a look of aggravation. He spoke through clenched teeth.

"Third lesson: all propulsion engineers are liars."

* * *

The Alpha Centauri trinary system was awash in conflict, and the *Doukas* was rocketing into a political minefield. More than a century ago, a half-dozen independent entities—joined by a hodgepodge of national and supernational governments—dived wholeheartedly into the business of interstellar colonization in the wake of the invention of the translocation drive. One of the first of the fledgling colonies was the planet Mimir, an all-encompassing archipelago of islands dotting a single world ocean, the product of overeager terraforming caused by impatient arrogance. Many different entities founded their own small outposts on the low islands, and as the population grew, conflicts began to develop between the different factions over mineral rights, territory, and borders—no different from the squabbles that infected every other group of humans throughout history. After years of fruitless talks, negotiations failed and whispered threat exploded into a brutal, internecine bloodbath. But as the troops of the Republic of American States set boots in cloying Mimir mud, many of those that had managed to avoid taking sides—the Sol Merchant Guild among them—tasted the opportunity for profit.

And so, along her venerable spine, clustered between the vast hydrogen propellant tanks and the clusters of radiators, the *Doukas* carried containers filled with her trade goods: platinum-group metal powders, refined for printing from Saturn's dizzying array of moonlets; helium-3, that most valuable fusion reactant; and a wet container brimful of water melted from the gas giant's majestic rings. Besides the helium-3, most of the rest of the goods would be worthless in the Sol System; the water-production and metallurgical facilities of the Belt were far closer to the shipyards orbiting Terra and Mars, and so their goods would always outcompete those of Cronus. But the guildsmen who worked the skies of the old titan had a trick up their sleeves: extrasolar colonies lacked the sophisticated technology necessary to maintain a modern society, and while the Republic's colony-wide wartime blockades were in effect, those goods became that much more valuable. And so the *Doukas* arrived at Mimir, a streak of light deep in the black of space, laden with forbidden metals and cryogenics carved from the grasp of another star.

"—Dimitrios, sir, I don't understand."

Yuri's face had slowly drained of what little color it originally held as the strain of the acceleration gnawed away at him, and now he looked expectantly at the captain. Dimitrios had been resting his eyes, content to let his crew and computer handle the minor course corrections. He opened them slowly—regretfully—and looked over in the vague direction of the deputy guildmaster's son.

". . . understand?"

"Obviously we need to make orbit before the Republican ship catches us—Father has explained their rules of engagement, how stations and orbital hubs are neutral ground. We get there first, we're home free."

"I fail to see the question."

"But it's not like it's a mystery who will win this race, sir. That's my quandary. We can see how fast they're going, and they can see how fast we're going, so don't both of us already know who will make it first?"

The *Doukas*'s master grinned, impressed for once at his young pupil's comprehension.

"So your old man did teach you something. You're right, we both know just about everything we need to know about the other, just from our heat signatures: exhaust temperatures reveal thrust power and reactor configuration, and adding acceleration gives mass and even a good guess about likely cargo and crew complement—with a bit of math. No, they know we'll beat them to orbit with hours to spare; they likely started their burn the moment they detected ours, but they were out of position and on an outbound heading, so they have much more ground to cover."

"So why does Giannis need to push the engine, if we'll beat them handily?"

The merchant captain stroked his thick black goatee thoughtfully, for a moment almost forgetting the rumbling of acceleration from the ship's potent engine.

"That, my dear lad, is because you've forgotten one thing. We're not racing the Republican frigate, Yuri, not exactly; we're racing light."

The youth's look of immoderate consternation at the older man's words left little of his confusion to the imagination.

"Think it through, Yuri. We're not at war with them, and we sure as blazes don't want to start one. If they warn us to stop, we'll have little choice but to obey. But—" At this, he twisted his console toward the youth, pointing at the low ebb in their hyperbolic path traced around Mimir. "If we can move our periapse to within shuttle range of that station, we've won, even once they tell us to stop. Ordering us to abandon orbit violates the Delhi Accords: they are required to let us circularize rather than risk us flinging off into interplanetary space or burning up in the atmosphere. So we'll circularize and casually discard our shipping containers within range of a shuttle; there's just about nothing they can legally do to stop the station, and that shuttle will have our cargo aboard before the Republic ship arrives." The captain ran some calculations on his screen before continuing.

"Our scans showed that if they fired off their message immediately after we ghosted in, we have another minute or so before it reaches us. And we'll be where we need to be in about the same amount of time." He winced. "It's going to be close."

Captain Eleftheriou twisted the console back toward himself, muttering to himself as he pushed against the imposed gravity of acceleration.

"If Giannis could have given me another half kilo of mass flow, we'd have nothing to worry about."

As if on cue, the console beeped angrily, and the youth immediately looked over to his own screen. His face fell.

"Priority one message, sir. From the frigate."

Eleftheriou wistfully looked at the burn timer counting down for a few long moments before huffing at Republican impudence.

"Looks like they've improved their detection speeds. Good to know, I suppose."

He picked at a piece of lint that had somehow managed to affix itself to his jumpsuit and flicked it toward the air return. With an ironically grandiose gesture, he tapped the button on his screen and the frigate's message began to broadcast throughout the compartment.

"Attention unknown vessel. You have entered a restricted area subject to military interdiction by the Republic of American States, under authority of the Declaration of Martial Law, article seven, section B. You are ordered to cease your burn immediately and stand to for cargo inspection. Failure to submit will result in immediate offensive action. You have thirty seconds from receipt of this message to comply. There will be no further warning."

Dimitrios looked at the clock again and tapped at his mic.

"Giannis, we've done what we can. Shut her down. Pop the white flag while you're at it."

The captain and the clerk immediately felt the burden of acceleration lift, replaced at once by the unsettling sensation of free fall. The pulsating waves of plasma blasting from the wire-formed nozzle dissipated, leaving the *Doukas* drifting calmly through space. All her radiators—fragile as rice paper under any sort of assault—unfurled to their maximum extent, the international signal of meek compliance. Captain Eleftheriou absentmindedly wrapped the chain of his medal around his finger, eyes still flashing with constant calculation. He turned to the deputy guildmaster's son.

"Well, Yuri. Now we wait."

* * *

"Sir, it's been one minute since they've received us."

The captain's aide looked nervously over at the master of the *Gibraltar*, awaiting his reply. Captain Peter Gregory bore the face of a world-weary cynic: tired-eyed, gray-tinged tonsure ringing his prematurely bald pate, the beginnings of wrinkles now thinly stretched by the cruel tug of acceleration. His flight suit—the famous dark blue of the Orbit Guard—bore the ignominy of casual neglect, the golden striping of the collar tarnished by sweat, the pant seams having long abandoned their crease. The captain sighed heavily and waved his hand at the aide.

"Patience, Ensign. They'll comply."

True to his word, the incoming vessel's exhaust trail evaporated, leaving the glowing-hot signature's course unchanged. The captain grunted.

"Guidance, will their final orbit be within range of the station's shuttles?"

His guidance officer, a hawk-eyed Bostonian, shook her head after a moment's analysis.

"No, Captain. After circularization, they won't have time to adjust heading for rendezvous before we arrive."

The captain made a self-satisfied sound and turned to the officer.

"Maintain present course, notify me when we're within fifteen minutes of boarding."

"Aye, Captain."

The captain tapped on his screen and sent a command to his tactical officer.

"Lieutenant Alvarado, as soon as we end the burn, I want a squad of your men armed and ready at airlock one. I will join you there. Prep another two squads and pods to inventory the cargo."

The voice over the ship's comms answered with cool professionalism.

"Yes, sir. Expecting trouble?"

The captain sighed.

"No, Lieutenant. Just a precaution."

"Very good, sir."

* * *

Hours passed in silence as the crew of the *Doukas* anxiously awaited the rendezvous with the Republican frigate. Once the two ships had come in range for real-time communication, the*Gibraltar* had transmitted a series of instructions for the crew, and Captain Eleftheriou had betrayed no intention to disobey. His young charge expressed dismay at the captain's mild-mannered obsequiousness, but a single stern look from Dimitrios silenced any further muttering.

Gradually, carefully, the *Gibraltar* came alongside the *Doukas*, maneuvering thrusters gently prodding the much smaller frigate into position adjacent to the old trading ship's port airlock. Far below, the swirling, rain-heavy clouds of Mimir hugged the churning world-sea, and the occasional bolt of lightning sent momentary flashes glinting through the billowing masses, like the glow of far-off fireflies swallowed in the gloom of early evening. Captain Eleftheriou watched dispassionately through a tiny porthole, imagining the sheets of rain falling on Collins City or Endeavor.

"Captain? What are we going to do?"

Dimitrios turned away from the window and looked at the source of the ever-wearying voice, young Yuri.

"What else? We'll 'yes, sir' and 'no, sir' and 'have a good day, sir' until we're blue as their suits. You'll learn, Yuri, that much of guild work is knowing when to remain silent—a fact that I trust you will grasp, preferably sooner rather than later."

The youth finally caught on to the captain's jab, and shut his mouth pointedly. The captain turned back to the window, looking for a final moment down at the planet below, and then back up to the approaching airlock of the *Gibraltar*. The frigate's universal docking port made short work bridging the gap between the two vessels, latching on to the *Doukas*'s airlock with a decisive click and booming thud. Captain Eleftheriou took a deep, calming breath and spread his hands and feet out wide, palms facing forward toward the airlock. The deputy guildmaster's son mimicked him.

The muffled sound of the pressure alarm on the far side of the airlock sounded, and the door cracked open, followed immediately by the angry muzzle of a boarding carbine. A suited figure followed the weapon through the door, eyes flitting back and forth behind a clear helmet as the guardsman scanned the room for threats. He took up a position immediately inside the door, sliding his foot into a hold on the wall, and gestured another three soldiers through, who took up positions above, below, and in front of Captain Eleftheriou. The merchant captain smiled as pleasantly as he could, keeping his position with a foot wedged against the side of the module, hands still. Captain Gregory came through the airlock next, irritable expression visible even behind a mask and pressure suit. He grasped a handhold and halted himself with practiced skill immediately in front of the trader.

"I am Captain Peter Gregory of the Republic frigate *Gibraltar*, acting by and for the authority of the Senate of the Republic of American States. State your business in the Alpha Centauri system."

The merchant led off with a smile and a formal bow of his head.

"Captain Gregory, a pleasure. I am Dimitrios Eleftheriou, and this is the *Doukas*, a licensed and bonded free trader of the Sol

Merchants Guild. This is my second-in-command, Yuri Levin. We're here to trade, of course."

The Republican captain looked over his nose at the two men with a barely contained look of disdain.

"Do you gentlemen realize this system has been under martial interdiction for the better part of three months?"

"I do recall seeing something of the sort in the spacer bulletin."

The captain snorted loudly enough that his suit's internal microphone broadcast the sound. He pulled a tablet from a holster at his side and began to skim through the data on it, drawn from the *Doukas*'s registration information on the ship's black box.

"Would it be too much to presume, then, that your passing familiarity with the bulletins includes an understanding of what goods are prohibited merchandise?"

The merchant captain raised his eyebrows and responded quickly to the guardsman's sardonic barb.

"Well, I would assume weapons, of course—that goes without saying."

"Yes, it does," muttered the captain, flipping through the screens of data. He continued his queries without looking up.

"You left Titan late yesterday?"

"Yes, sir."

"No other stops along the way?"

"No, sir, this is a direct-route transaction."

"And what is your cargo? I remind you, *Captain*, misleading or otherwise inaccurate responses to my questions will be deemed intentional and you will be charged with providing false information to a Republican officer in time of war."

As if to accentuate his point, a thudding sound reverberated through the hull as an EVA pod airlock connected to the external loading bay of one of the shipping containers aft of the crew module. The merchant captain grinned disarmingly.

"I wouldn't dream of it, Captain Gregory! No, this is a fairly standard cargo run. Titanium, palladium, platinum metal powders, helium-3, and good old H-2-O."

The captain looked up from his perusal of the ship's manifest.

"I see," he remarked, a hint of amusement—or disgust—creeping into his voice. He switched off the broadcast microphone and spoke inaudibly inside his suit. The young assistant had watched this entire exchange with a growing sense of dread, and he fidgeted nervously with the flight-suit fasteners at his neck, causing the guardsman nearest him to gesture roughly with his carbine.

"You there, hands in front of you."

Yuri obeyed instantly, eyes wide with fright. Captain Eleftheriou spoke soothingly, attempting to defuse the situation.

"Guardsman, my apologies, my young second officer is green as Terran grass. Would you believe that this is his first trip in the black? Unbelievable, I know—to live your whole life on an icy orange popsicle like Titan."

The guardsman glared and lowered the carbine's muzzle, and Dimitrios quietly exhaled, tension momentarily relieved. Captain Gregory switched his headset back on again.

"Mr. Eleftheriou, I am happy to report to you that my men have verified that your cargo checks out with your manifest and your statements to me."

Dimitrios smiled and bowed slightly.

"Of course, Captain Gregory. I wouldn't dream of—"

"I was not finished, Captain."

"My apologies, sir—"

"All of the items on the manifest, however, are illegal goods carried in direct violation of the Declaration of Martial Law, article three, and notice posted in 'Bulletins for Spacers,' numbers four thirty-one and four thirty-five."

Captain Eleftheriou's face drained of color.

"Well, that's, that's—all of them?"

"Yes, I can provide you with the citations if you like."

"Yes, I would, actually," stammered Captain Eleftheriou, sheet-white face now slowly coloring red.

"Titanium, palladium et al metals, powdered or ingot form: prohibited by article three, section one, subsection seven. Potential use in military weaponry or vessel construction. Helium-3, in gaseous or liquid form: prohibited by article three, section one, subsection three. Potential use in restricted reactor technology. Water, in gaseous, liquid, or solid form—"

"Now wait just a moment. This is outrageous, Captain! I mean, yes, you could use titanium for military applications, but you could say the same about any material in existence!"

"Are you quite done?" The Republican captain's icy retort stopped Eleftheriou midbluster, and the middle-aged guardsman cut in.

"Mr. Eleftheriou, my job is not to argue with you. These restrictions were clearly posted in the proper channels, and I find that you had sufficient notice."

"What is this, a magistrate hearing? I want to appeal that finding, this is ludicrous."

"Mr. Eleftheriou, I advise you to stop before I have you arrested for contempt." The abrupt sharpness in the captain's voice was only accented by his imposing, suited form. He continued in the shocked silence.

"The *Gibraltar* is a vessel of the Republic under orders endorsed by the Triumvirate in time of war. Frankly, Mr. Eleftheriou, I have the legal authority to do whatever I want."

Captain Eleftheriou opened his mouth to speak, closed it, and then tried again.

"So what is the fine? Can I at least pay it now?"

The Republican captain had looked back at the manifest when Eleftheriou began to speak, but now his eyes shot back to the Greek's, narrowing to a penetrating stare.

"Was that an attempt at a bribe? Do you want me to start a list of charges too?"

Captain Eleftheriou quickly raised his palms in innocent protestation.

"Not at all, I'm sorry, I expected that I would be able to resolve this unfortunate matter by a fine or fee of some sort."

Captain Gregory chuckled dryly, humorlessly.

"I'm afraid you are mistaken, Mr. Eleftheriou. My orders say that contraband and illegal goods are deemed forfeited and are to be seized."

"Seized? *Seized?* For the love of— Captain, there's almost a half a million—"

"—that won't fall into the hands of the Coalition or Coalition sympathizers," finished Captain Gregory smoothly, depositing his tablet back into its holster and tightening the strap. He continued detachedly.

"Thank you for your cooperation, Mr. Eleftheriou. My men will remove your cargo containers; we will signal when you are free to leave." He spun himself around and pushed off toward the airlock, pausing for a moment at the threshold to turn back toward the ship's master and his assistant.

"Enjoy your stay at Mimir."

The moment the hatch closed behind the *Gibraltar*'s master, Captain Eleftheriou let out a shout of rage, bashing his fist against the bulkhead. Yuri floated nearby, too shocked to speak, watching as Dimitrios raved like a madman, flinging anything he could grasp at the closed hatch. Yuri could barely hear the sound of the pressurization alarm over the captain's ranting, but he felt the shuddering thump as the airlock detached and the *Doukas* floated free once again. A series of echoing thuds followed as the cargo containers were wrenched free of their supports, leaving the *Doukas* denuded of her treasures. Soon, the sounds outside ceased, and the Republican vessel transmitted their promised signal and ignited their engine, vanishing into the distance in a matter of moments. The captain suddenly stopped his animalistic cries, so abruptly that Yuri almost gasped. Without any warning, Dimitrios flashed a Cheshire grin and twisted to look at the young assistant.

"Think I sold it?"

"Wh-what?"

"My performance! Not quite Olivier, but passable, I feel."

Yuri's expression shifted from shock to amazement and back again, without a single coherent word managing to cross his lips in the meantime. Dimitrios reached over and slapped the youth on the shoulder.

"Come on, lad, we've got a meeting in Collins City! Don't want to keep the guild rep waiting."

Yuri turned himself awkwardly and launched down the corridor after Eleftheriou's fast-retreating form, finally managing to stammer out a response.

"But, sir, Captain! We just lost all our cargo! You were—what in the worlds is going on?"

Dimitrios stopped himself against a hold and turned his head back to the clerk.

"All our cargo? Those containers? Oh, my boy, those were merely the diversion. The real cargo is untouched."

"But you said it was half a million—"

"And that was not a lie." The captain looked thoughtful for a moment, then shrugged and pushed off the wall toward the bridge. "Of course, it would have been best had they not confiscated it— the three-H would have certainly garnered a pretty penny—but no, that cargo's purpose was to keep them from looking too closely at their scans. Fourth lesson: one for them to find, one for you to keep."

Yuri shook his head in wonderment as the Greek, gleeful as a teenager in love, somersaulted off the bulkhead and deposited himself smartly in his chair. With a tap of the controls, he put the intraship circuit up on the speaker.

"Giannis, my good man, get me within range of the station, on the double. We've got ourselves a dirtside date!"

For the first time, Yuri heard the voice of the ship's engineer, undoubtedly in better humor than before.

"Aye, sir, shouldn't be long at all. Remember your umbrella."

* * *

As Giannis had imagined, the summer rains of Mimir's northern hemisphere were in full swing as the shuttle descended in a fiery streak of plasma down to Collins City. Yuri found the whole experience terrifying, made all the more unsettling by the captain's good-natured humming, and his ceaseless twirling of that blasted medal around his fingers. Yuri closed his eyes to combat the nausea in his stomach as the cyclonic winds of the upper atmosphere batted the shuttle around like a toy. When the vessel finally punched through the last layer of clouds, Collins City lay directly ahead, a brownish-gray cluster of new construction circling a central ring of cylindrical buildings, the obvious signs of a city built from the modules of landed vessels. Dimitrios noticed drifting clouds of black smoke from several points on the horizon, the telltale signs of distant battle, but said nothing. No sense further troubling Yuri.

A guild representative, dressed in understated finery, met the captain and the clerk at a local printshop, amid the whirring of cooling systems and the crackling of laser sinterers. With him stood one of the printshop workers, a tall, soot-covered man, clearly a welder or machinist by trade, and a local official, wearing a nondescript gray tunic. The guild representative, a portly man, clasped the merchant captain's hand with gusto.

"Ah, Dimitrios! I should have known the guild would send you —no one else is crazy enough to try to run a Republic blockade!"

Dimitrios grinned and slapped the man on his shoulder.

"Barnabas, you sly dog—why'd you colonials go and force the Republic to start one?"

The local official, clearly a nervous man at the best of times, interrupted.

"Gentlemen, if you please. I trust your presence here means you were successful at running the blockade, God knows how."

Dimitrios nodded and bowed his head. Without further ceremony, he unclasped the St. Nicholas medal from around his neck and handed it to the guild representative. Yuri watched, awestruck, as the guildsman's eyes lit up and, reaching into his tunic pocket, the large merchant produced a tiny ring, which he waved over the medal. The medal clicked electronically and split in two, revealing the tiniest of wafers nestled within. Dimitrios gestured broadly.

"Magistrate, as promised, your requested equipment."

The official's eyes widened to the size of two glistening moons.

"This . . . this is all of it?"

Dimitrios nodded curtly.

"Yes indeed. Full presliced printer models for five firearms, three laser telescopes, two dozen assorted sensor systems and reactor subsystems, and a miscellaneous assortment of circuits and boards you'll need to jumpstart your foundries and hydroponics facilities."

The printshop worker nearly danced with glee, and the official looked like he was moments from joining him. He stuttered out his gratitude.

"Mr. Dimitrios, I don't know if we can ever thank you enough."

Dimitrios shrugged, displaying an emotion Yuri had not yet seen: humility, pretended or otherwise.

"Magistrate, it's just trade. The guild hopes that you are satisfied with your purchase."

"I have no doubt, sir, I have *no doubt.*" He turned to the guild representative. "The funds will be transferred immediately."

The guild representative bowed and said nothing, and he, Yuri, and Dimitrios left, flipping hoods up over their heads to keep out the driving rain. The guild representative turned to Dimitrios with a shake of his head.

"You know, the Republican guardsmen are looking for printer chips—they are specifically watching for them, to prevent us doing what you just did." He shook his head in admiration. "I don't know how you do it, Eleftheriou. Good work, but I'll be 'locked if I know how you do it."

Dimitrios looked at Yuri with a wink, then turned his head toward the guildsman with a mischievous smile.

"Nothing fancy, Barnabas. I just remembered to pay the tariff."

About Allen Shoff

Allen Shoff lives with his wife and three adorable children in the high deserts of the American West. While he studied history and music at the undergraduate level, he has always nurtured a profound love of science, technology, and philosophy, something evident in his fiction. When he's not practicing law, he writes code, builds furniture, and creates universes.

Website: allenshoff.com

THE PRICE OF HEALING

By D.K. Holmberg | 8,600 words

Kira felt a cough building as she looked around the familiar streets of Amon. The town had changed little in the years since she'd left—not nearly as much as she had changed, especially as the wasting sickness had taken hold the past year—but enough that she didn't know the square like she once would have. Maybe that would help Father make a few sales; local merchants never got the same price as those from out of town. And the gods knew they needed the extra income before reaching Annendel.

"Watch the wagon. The square is notorious for thieves sneaking through," Father reminded her. "I'll see if Rubbles will buy anything." He grabbed a rolled package of paper and a small box of inks from the back of their wagon parked near the center of the town.

Kira nodded as the coughing fit took hold. The fit lasted longer than usual before finally easing off. She wiped a hand across her mouth, afraid she'd see blood again.

Her father didn't notice, frowning as he glanced up at the dark clouds. "Are you certain you will be fine?" Roughly, he placed his hand on her head as he'd seen the healers do, but didn't seem to know what he was looking for and pulled it away.

She shook him off, surprised that he bothered to touch her. Usually, he feared catching her wasting illness and stayed at least an arm's length away. Besides, he wouldn't find anything. None of the healers she had seen had been able to find anything.

"I'll be fine, Father. Besides, any sale you make will help," she said. After the fit, her voice felt weak. She forced a smile onto her face rather than let him know just how weak. If he knew, he wouldn't continue to trade. They'd head straight to Annendel, sales be damned, and worry about finding enough coin to pay for healing later.

"Well—if you're certain. Just watch the wagon. I think we're close to what we'll need. Another week, maybe two, and then we will be in Annendel." He took her hand and gave it a squeeze. "The parchment might bring us the rest, even without knowing its secret."

Kira nodded, afraid to say anything. In spite of all the hard work to find a way to get her help, nothing had made a difference. When she had fallen ill, he had become driven in a way that she had never seen from him before, determined not to lose her as they had lost her sister. But Kira knew time was getting short. Even were they to get enough money for the study in Annendel, it probably wouldn't matter. After everything they had gone through to get the money needed, she did not dare tell her father that.

He checked the locked trunk in the back of the wagon one more time before securing it. The trunk contained the entire savings from their trip, her last hope for healing once they managed to trade for enough money. As he ambled away, he clutched the items he hoped to sell to Rubbles under one arm, glancing back only as he neared the edge of the square.

Kira made a show of waving, but once he was out of sight, she let out a long breath and shifted over to the cart, slipping as she climbed up. Standing even a few moments drained her, but *that* was something her father would not learn.

Another fit of coughing hit her. Her eyes watered with it, and she tasted bile at the back of her throat. At least her father wasn't there to see it; he got so worried every time she broke into one of those fits. Eventually, she worried that he would stop taking her word that she felt fine.

As she sat, the dark clouds overhead finally made good on their threat of rain. Kira pulled her cloak up and over her shoulders, fighting the sudden shiver that worked through her. She had not been away from Amon long enough to forget the heavy rains so common that time of year, rains that made even simple daily activities difficult.

Thankfully the rain had held long enough for her father to take supplies for a sale. If nothing had changed, at least Ms. Rubbles could be counted on to purchase some of their supplies. Every bit helped, getting them closer to being able to afford the price the healers demanded. Soon it wouldn't matter—at least, not to her—but she kept fighting for her father. She worried what would happen to him when she finally succumbed to the illness. At least by doing something—anything—any guilt he might have could be lessened.

A loud thunk made her turn. A small figure streaked away from the back of the wagon, quickly disappearing into a small throng of people. She looked down and saw the back of the wagon open.

She climbed down slowly. The cold rain sent shivers through her, but her heart fluttered for a different reason. Hopefully, the wagon had just been bumped, but the reminder of thieves in the square made her heart pound. Rounding the end of the wagon, she nearly slipped, barely catching herself on slick rain-soaked wood.

A few items were missing from the back of the wagon. A small lantern. A roll of cheap silks. And the trunk.

All the money they had collected gone.

Another fit of coughing overwhelmed her, doubling her over, but all she could think about was how her father would react, already seeing the disappointment on his face.

* * *

When the coughing fit finally eased, Kira wiped tears away from her eyes and swallowed the lump that had formed in her throat. She knew she shouldn't be disappointed; having the Guild of Annendel study her illness had always been unlikely to succeed, but it had been hope that she could cling to. Suddenly, even that was gone.

She tried closing the back of the wagon to avoid everything else inside getting wet. Her arms trembled and it fell open. She did not have the energy to try again.

"Kira?"

She lifted her head and looked up. A tall young man with straight brown hair falling over his forehead looked at her with piercing blue eyes. She recognized those eyes. "Galen?" she asked.

A wide smile split his face, until she started coughing again. When she finally got it back under control, he looked at her with the same expression of concern she always saw on her father's face. "You are unwell," he said.

From Galen, son of Amon's most respected healer, that simple statement made her throat tighten again. "I'm fine." The familiar lie was easy.

He blinked and she could tell that he wanted to say something more, but he remained silent.

She sagged, her legs giving out as another shaking chill rolled through her. Had Galen not been there, she would have fallen.

Galen lifted her and carried her to the front of the wagon, setting her atop the seat carefully. Without asking permission, he pressed the back of his hand against her forehead, with more confidence than her father had managed. Then he touched her neck and twisted her head from side to side before resting his head on her chest and listening. Her breath caught at the familiarity and lack of concern for catching her illness.

"Don't," he said. "Take a deep breath."

She took a shuddering breath. Her chest rattled as it so often did. So far, her father hadn't noticed. Or if he had, he hadn't said anything.

Galen sat up and met her eyes. "How long have you been sick?"

"A long time," she said softly. She pushed up, leaning back on the wagon and turning away from him. The way he studied her made her uncomfortable, reminding her of every healer she had seen over the past year. But none had shared the same compassion that she saw in his eyes. After all the healers she had seen on the road, she wondered why her father had not taken her to see Galen's father, Aelus.

"You've been to Annendel?" he asked.

She shook her head. "We're traveling there now. The Guild has offered a study."

Galen snorted dismissively. "And how much did they quote you for the study?"

"A hundred silver marks." Saying it aloud made it sound ridiculous.

"A hundred?"

Seeing the disgusted look on his face, Kira pushed on. "The Guild is unrivaled in their knowledge, Galen. I don't have to tell you that few have such an opportunity."

"Even fewer can afford such an opportunity," he said, then climbed down from the wagon, as if suddenly realizing how close he sat to her. He wiped ink-stained hands on his brown pants, smearing crimson stains down the sides. The rain soaked them, making it look like blood running down his legs.

"I am fortunate," she said bitterly.

Galen shook his head. "Kira . . ." He paused. "I'm sorry. That was poorly said on my part. Blame my father for teaching me that healing should not be something only the rich can achieve."

Kira glanced to the back of the wagon. They weren't rich, but her father was determined. Nearly a hundred silver marks—half a year's hard work on a journey that Kira once had thought impossible—stolen. Any hope she might have at the Guild finding an answer stolen with it.

Would it have made a difference to the thief had he known?

"Would he see me?" she asked.

Galen frowned. "Who? My father? I thought you were traveling to Annendel."

"I was . . . Am," she corrected herself. "But we've seen every healer my father could find from Duras to the Western Plains. None has helped."

"And you think my father will do better than a Guild healer?"

Kira sighed. She didn't, but since their money had been stolen, she had no other options. "It wouldn't hurt."

Galen shook his head sadly. "I'm sorry, Kira. He's not here. Left to collect herbs and other supplies about two weeks ago. Doubt he'll return for another two weeks. He left me in charge, though that mostly means inventory." He held up his ink-stained hands.

Kira took a deep breath and forced a smile. "Of course. It was worth asking."

The rain started to taper off, turning into a fine mist that still left her feeling soaked. She stared across the square, worry for what she would tell her father when he returned growing stronger.

Looking back at Galen, she asked, "Is there anything I can do for you?"

Galen laughed lightly, still watching her with his piercing blue eyes. "I had just stopped at Rubbles trying to buy paper," he said. "Probably not the best weather to make such a purchase."

Kira wondered if he had seen her father. Would Galen even recognize him after his years away? But he had recognized her, even changed as she was, though she shouldn't be surprised since she had always known Galen had a crush on her. "You didn't find any?"

Galen held up his hands again. "Closed."

If Rubbles's was closed, then her father would return soon. And she would have to tell him what had happened. "Where else can you try?"

A small smile crept across his face. "Theran."

"That's nearly a day's ride!"

"Longer by foot," he said.

"Galen—" Another coughing fit kept her from finishing what she intended to say.

"I don't know what the healers have tried, but if you're visiting Amon for long, you should stop by the shop. Let me at least give you something for the cough."

Kira managed to suppress the cough long enough to nod. "I'll talk to my father about that," she said, seeing the top of his head weaving through the crowd as he made his way back to the wagon. Already she felt her heart pounding as she thought about how she would tell him what had happened. Would they just return home to Duras? At least that way she would have time with her mother before the illness took her.

"Do you remember how to find it?" he asked.

There was a sincerity in his voice that pulled at something inside her. She forced another smile as she nodded. "Thank you, Galen."

He studied her for another moment and then started away. Kira watched him until he rounded a corner. Only then did she hear her father opening the back of the wagon, and she began to prepare for his outburst, dreading the conversation as another coughing fit threatened her.

* * *

Kira clutched the roll of parchment in one hand as she looked at the storefront. Little about it had changed since she had lived in Amon. The paint had faded somewhat, and the lettering seemed smaller, but otherwise, the sign reminded her of those days so many years before when she had still been allowed to move around the streets alone. She'd never had the same freedom once her father moved them to Duras. The larger city had different dangers. Unfortunately, he hadn't been able to protect her from everything.

She had not had the heart to tell him about the chest. With the rain, he had slammed the back of the wagon shut quickly, not looking inside, but she had no doubt that he would soon learn what happened. And then she would be forced to endure his disappointment.

A fit of coughing set her shaking, then slowly eased. The fits seemed to be getting worse, each time taking her breath away for longer. That time, a little blood came up. How much time did she have left? At the least, she could take Galen up on his offer and see if he knew of anything that would suppress the cough. Perhaps his father had learned of something the Guild had missed.

A bell over the door jingled as she pushed it open. Inside, the shop itself looked neatly cared for, rows of shelves all well labeled. That, at least, seemed different. She remembered Aelus's shop to be more disorganized, a clutter of scents from the stacks of herbs practically overflowing the shelves. She wondered if the change was Galen's influence.

Voices near the back of the store made her hesitate. An older man, his voice high-pitched and shaky, spoke to Galen.

"Do you know when he might return?" the man asked.

Kira peeked around the end of one shelf. She saw Galen standing across from a well-dressed older man, a pained look on the man's somber face. A narrow table was all that separated them. "I'm sorry, Hyp, but he'll probably be another week or two. If there's anything I can do to help . . ."

The man gripped his stomach. "Well . . . I awoke to severe stomach pains and haven't been able to eat anything all day. I've never had anything quite like it." His voice sounded pained and his head swayed as he spoke.

"Never?" Galen asked. There was a barely masked hint of surprise as he motioned to the table. The man crawled on top, moaning as he did, and Galen pressed his hands into the man's stomach and twisted his ear down to listen. Once satisfied, he helped the man sit back up.

"The pain goes through to my back and neck." He stood up straight, letting go of his stomach. "Aren't you going to write this down, Galen? Your father always documents my symptoms."

Galen let out a soft sigh. "I'm sorry, Hyp." For a moment, Kira thought that Galen would dismiss Hyp. He clearly did not think his symptoms were too serious, but then he grabbed a piece of paper, dipped a pen into ink, and quickly scratched something across the page. He slid the paper quickly off to the side. "Maybe it's time you see the Guild," Galen suggested, looking back up at Hyp.

A sour noted entered Hyp's voice. "The Guild?" He grunted and shook his head. "Your father is a better healer than any Guild member. Quite a bit cheaper too. And don't you worry, Galen, pretty soon you'll be there as well."

Galen smiled and steered Hyp down the rows of shelves. Seeing Kira, he winked. "Try these," he said, taking a few loose leaves and stuffing them into a small bowl. "Mix them in water. It should help soothe your stomach at least. Let me know if it doesn't work."

Hyp nodded. "You'll tell your father?"

"Of course, Hyp."

Hyp dropped a few coins into a bowl on the table before leaving the store with a soft jingle of the bell.

Galen watched the door for a moment before turning to face her. Tension faded from his shoulders and his neck. When he smiled, she could not look away from his eyes.

"You see him often?" Kira asked.

Galen shrugged. "Hyp is a worrier. It's been worse since my father left. I haven't figured out what my father gives him to help him relax, but nothing I've given has helped so far."

Kira looked back to the door. "Then what did you try today?"

"Just barberry and chamoline." He shook his head and wiped a hand across his brow. A streak of dark ink smeared as he did. "The chamoline is soothing. Might help his nerves. The barberry may help calm his stomach."

Kira suppressed a smile. This wasn't the same Galen she'd known when she was younger. That Galen had been full of chaotic energy, determined to leave Amon and explore the bigger world. The Galen standing before her carried himself confidently, seemingly content to follow in his father's footsteps.

Another cough threatened to come over her, and she covered her mouth and took a few shallow breaths. That was the only thing that seemed to work when the fits threatened her. Galen's eyes narrowed as he studied her and then he put an arm around her shoulders and steered her toward the small table near the back of the room.

"Sit," he said. "Let me see if I can find you something."

"You aren't afraid that you'll catch this?"

He looked at her with a strange expression before shaking his head. "I knew as soon as I saw you that you weren't contagious. I just wish I knew how to treat the wasting illness that's taken you."

Galen left her and wandered down a few of the rows of shelves. Kira looked around as he did. The hard table had a clean white sheet covering it. A few heavy tan ceramic mortars, the kind she had seen used by every Guild member her father had brought her to see, rested nearby, each darkly stained but otherwise clean. Behind the table were a few sturdy pots. As far as she could tell, all were empty. A stack of papers rested on the desk nearby, the topmost with only a few lines written on it. In a neat scrawl, she saw what Galen had written about Hyp.

Abdominal pain. Nausea. No physical findings. Suspect hysteria. Given barberry, chamoline, and feverleaf.

Galen returned and pulled one of the smaller mortars off the shelf. Kira did not see what he poured in before he began pounding at it with the heavy pestle. He caught her looking at the page and smiled sheepishly.

"My father prefers to document all the symptoms and treatments. Thinks he can catalogue them sometime, make a reference that anyone can follow."

"So they won't need the Guild?" she asked.

"The Guild will always be needed for certain things."

Kira frowned, surprised that Galen would admit to the usefulness of the Guild.

He shrugged. "Can't operate on yourself. And sometimes there are unique cases that don't have a clear answer. But often enough there is much that simple herbs can heal. I think that is his goal."

"I thought you were nearly out of paper?" She clutched the roll of parchment under her arm.

Galen nodded. "That was the last sheet. Shame I had to use it on Hyp, but he was right—my father would be disappointed if I didn't document what I saw."

He moved behind a tall shelf and reappeared with a pitcher and cup. "Just a small spoonful," he said, scooping out a small amount of greenish powder from the mortar. Galen poured water over the top of the powder and handed the cup to her. "It won't taste great, but should help ease the coughing."

Kira brought the cup up to her nose and inhaled. "What's in it?" She caught a hint of mint and cinnamon, but something bitter as well that seemed to burn her nostrils.

"Codain leaves mostly. The pulp from the leaves helps suppress the cough. Everlind takes care of what codain does not. Everything else in it just makes the taste more palatable."

She took a sip. The lukewarm liquid tasted as bitter as it smelled, and there did not seem to be any of the cinnamon flavor the scent promised. She almost spit it out.

When she managed to get it down, another fit of coughing worked through her. "I thought you said it would suppress the cough?" she said when it had finished.

"Give it time." He pulled a metal canister out from under the counter and scooped the rest of the powder into it before handing it over to her. "Take this. If it works, use it. You can always have another healer mix more for you; just remember to tell them to use codain and everlind. They can flavor it however they please."

Kira took the canister. Already she felt the urgency of the cough easing, like a knot in her chest loosening. For a moment, she wondered if Galen were wrong. Maybe his concoction could heal her. Or maybe if given enough time, he could come up with something the Guild had missed.

Then the moment passed. Even if the medicine took away the cough, nothing else had changed. She was still dying. For some reason, losing the money—and the hope of healing in Annendel—made that easier for her to accept.

The canister wasn't anything fancy, but after spending as much time traveling with her father as she had, she knew the price of metal. "I don't have anything to pay you for this."

Galen waved his hand toward a small jar at the end of the table. A handful of coins—mostly coppers—rested inside. "That's not how my father runs his shop, Kira. Just pay what you can. It all works out."

She swallowed and closed her eyes. "That's just the problem, Galen. I don't have anything to pay you."

"I thought you were going to Annendel?"

She shook her head slightly and took a deep breath. "We were. The money was stolen."

Galen blinked slowly. "When I first saw you. You nearly fainted."

She nodded. "After every place we've visited. Bels. Chefe. Even all the way to Voldin. To have it all stolen here in Amon seems a cruel irony."

Galen put his arm around her shoulder. She tensed at first, but there was a comfort to the way he held her that she never felt from her father. Tears streamed from her eyes for a long while before drying. Kira took a deep breath and sat up, pushing away from Galen.

"Is there any way . . ."

She shook her head. "Not that much silver. Not with the time left."

Galen studied her again. The way his eyes danced from her head to her neck to her arms left her feeling almost as if he touched her. Then he nodded.

"If only my father were here," Galen said. "Maybe he would know of something different you could try. I'm sorry, Kira."

She sighed, shaking her head again. "No, Galen. I'm sorry. You're just offering help." She pulled the roll of parchment out from under her arm and held it out only to realize that she'd grabbed the wrong roll.

"What is it, Kira?"

"I meant to bring some paper to you. I thought I could use that as payment."

"That would be perfect."

"But it's not," she said. "I brought the wrong one. There's a small roll of paper that my father has said is practically useless. I figured you could use it. But this isn't that roll."

"What is it?"

"This parchment is something strange my father found somewhere on the plains. The mystics there claimed it has special properties. Father thought to sell it to the Guild. They always appreciate items like that."

Galen unrolled the parchment and ran his hand across the surface before pulling one sheet away, fingering the edge as he did. "Where did you say he found this?"

Kira didn't remember exactly. Much of the journey blurred in her mind, a combination of the various medicines the healers they encountered along the way wanted her to try and the strain of traveling every day. "Voldin, I think."

"Much nicer than Voldish parchment," Galen said. "There's an unusual marbling to it." He looked up at her. "Why can't you still sell it to the Guild? Maybe you can trade it for the study."

"It's not worth enough. Not like it is."

Galen frowned. "My father would love it. This is just the kind of parchment he would use to begin his record of ailments."

"Record of ailments?"

Galen laughed. "Book of maladies?" he suggested.

Kira laughed. It felt good to laugh. That she could do it without coughing surprised her.

"What's wrong with it?" Galen asked.

In answer, Kira reached across him, grabbing the quill and bottle of ink resting near the stack of paper. She dipped the pen into the ink and drew a long line across the parchment.

"Kira!" Galen reached toward the pen.

She only nodded toward the parchment. The dark line gradually faded, as if absorbed by the page. "There is no way to write on it," she said. "Father figured we could discover some method during our travels and make the parchment more valuable to the Guild, but we haven't been able to find anything that would work."

"Would it be worth enough if you could?" Galen asked. He leaned over the page, staring after the ink for a moment. Then he took the pen and started writing. The words quickly faded.

"Father thinks it might."

Galen looked up. His eyes seemed bright. "Enough for the study?"

Kira didn't know. Could a roll of parchment—even this strange special parchment—really be worth that much? Her father had always intended the parchment to make up any difference that remained when they finally reached Annendel. She didn't think he expected it to fetch enough to fund the study completely.

"I don't know. Maybe?"

She felt a surge of hope rising in her chest and knew that she needed to tamp it down. Even were she to reach Annendel, she reminded herself, there was little chance the Guild could find an answer in time to help her. Nothing could change the fact that she was dying.

* * *

Galen leaned over the page of parchment. Ink practically covered his face, staining his cheeks, with a small dot on the end of his nose. His bright blue eyes still held the same excitement as when they had first started searching for an ink that might work; so far, all the different inks that they had tried had absorbed into the paper just as quickly as the first one. Kira felt herself growing increasingly disappointed.

"We can stop," she said, leaning back in her chair. She felt exhausted, though they had only been at it a while. How much longer before her father began to worry? She had told him that she wanted to visit some of her old friends, but the only person she had seen from her days in Amon was Galen.

"The colorant is all wrong."

Kira looked up and saw an older woman, gray hair pulled into a swooping bun atop her head, her dress of a simple cut but heavily embroidered.

"Ms. Rubbles," Galen said, lurching to his feet.

She waved her hand and glanced at the sheet of parchment. "Stock that thick needs the right colorant, otherwise you will barely be able to see it on the page."

Galen shot Kira a look before smiling at Ms. Rubbles. "Of course, you're right, Ms. Rubbles. We'll try that." He made his way around the table and stood facing her. "Can I help you with anything?" he asked.

Kira hadn't seen Ms. Rubbles since she had lived in Amon. After all those years, she looked older but no less distinguished. Being one of the few female shop owners in the village likely made the difference; Kira remembered her as tough but fair. She looked sickly, with a slight sheen to her face as she leaned on a lacquered cane.

"Is Aelus available, Galen?" Ms. Rubbles asked.

Galen shook his head. "I'm sorry, Ms. Rubbles. He's gathering supplies." He swept an arm toward the shelves. Kira didn't think they looked bare, but Galen obviously did.

Something changed in Ms. Rubbles's posture as she learned that Galen's father was not available. She closed her eyes and let out a soft breath. "I see."

"Can I help with anything?" Galen asked.

She gave him a placating smile. "I don't think so, Galen. I'm sure that your father has taught you well, but I need a fully trained healer."

"Of course, Ms. Rubbles. I'll tell my father that you stopped in." She tilted her head forward. "But if I might offer a suggestion?" he asked as she started to turn. She paused and waited. Galen moved past her and grabbed a few items from the shelves before returning to her. "Steep these as you would tea. It should help until my father returns."

Ms. Rubbles glanced down at what Galen had placed in her hands. She frowned for a moment before nodding. Then she turned and limped out of the shop, leaving with a soft jingle of the bell.

Before saying anything else, Galen grabbed the topmost sheet on the stack and pulled it toward him. In his neat script, he made a quick note. *Arthritic knees. Faint sweat. Eyes slightly pronounced. Visible mass on neck. Likely glandular problem. Given methimanine seeds, buglebalm leaves, and motherwort.*

He slipped the page back atop the pile and gave Kira a wry smile. "Maybe she's right."

"About needing a better healer?" Kira asked, surprised. "From what I have seen, you're as skilled as any healer I've met outside of Annendel."

"Thanks, but that's not what I meant. I think she's right about the colorant. We've been using different inks, but none has worked. Maybe we need a darker colorant. Treat the ink like I would any other medicine I compound."

Kira bit her lip as she turned back to the page. They had tried the different inks that Galen had available but had not really tried mixing their own. "What do you suggest?" she asked.

"Taris berry?"

Without waiting for Kira to say anything more, he slipped out and around the table and hurried to one of the shelves and back holding a small cluster of cherry-red berries. Setting them in his mortar, he ground them quickly with the pestle and then spooned it into the ink, stirring it with a practiced motion. Kira could tell that the ink lightened as he did, taking on some of the color of the berry.

"I thought you said we should go darker?" she asked. "That seems to be lightening it."

"Maybe lighter here, but I think the color will be bolder on the page." He pulled the sheet of parchment close to him and dipped the pen into the ink. Then, slowly, he ran the pen across the page.

Both watched the line as Galen pulled the quill off the page. For a moment, it seemed as if the bright red line would remain on the page, but then it began to fade, slowly absorbed back into the page no differently than any of the other inks they tried.

"Anything else that you can think of?" she asked. "Maybe darker, not just bolder?"

Galen furrowed his brow while thinking. "Maybe parsap?"

Again he hurried over to the shelves and again returned, this time carrying what looked to be a small twig. He broke the twig over one of his other mortars. A small droplet of a thick, oily sap dripped out into the bowl. Galen took a few drops of fresh ink and added them to the mortar, mixing it together.

"It's usually used as a sealant. Helps bind wounds," he explained, then shrugged. "With as thick as it is, maybe it will work."

With a tight expression, he cleaned the tip of the pen and dipped it into the ink before making a long mark on the page. This ink seemed a little different, almost congealing atop the page and giving

Kira hope that it might work, but then it slowly started to fade, sinking below the surface of the parchment.

Galen lifted the sheet and looked underneath the page, frowning. "Interesting how that works." He ran his hand across the top of the parchment carefully, expecting the faded ink to stain his hand. His frown deepened and he held his hand up to his face.

Kira sat back, feeling defeated. Nothing they had tried seemed to work. And if nothing worked, then any hope she had at getting enough coin to pay the healers for the study was gone. She hated the lump that formed in the back of her throat and tried to swallow it back.

"Kira, there are many other things we can try. Caldric ash? Torch thorn?" Galen's eyes narrowed as he thought. "Pollyton seeds? They stain everything."

She shook her head and smiled at him sadly as she blinked back the tears threatening to well up in her eyes. "We can stop, Galen. It never would have worked anyway," she said softly. "I know that I'm too far along. There isn't the time for a study to help, even if I hadn't lost the money."

Saying it aloud felt freeing in a way. Finally admitting what she had grown to know over the past few months took away tension that she hadn't known was there. She might not be ready to die, but there was nothing she could do to change it. Nothing anyone could do.

Galen slipped an arm around her shoulder and held her against him again. She didn't tense that time. "You didn't lose anything."

She turned to see him looking at her with more affection than she deserved. "I should go, Galen," she said. "My father will be worried about me. Keep the parchment as a gift for trying to help me." She patted her pocket where she had the small canister of medicine he'd given her and started to turn away from him before he could see her cry.

As she turned, her hand caught painfully on something sharp resting on the parchment. The tip of the pen, probably, she thought, bringing her hand to her mouth with a soft cry. She tasted the parsap ink before realizing what she was doing and pulled her hand away from her mouth.

"Let me see that," Galen said.

Kira tried to stand but found that her legs were weak. "I'm fine," she said.

She didn't want him to learn that the bleeding would not easily stop. That had been happening for the past few weeks. Like everything else, it was getting worse. And Galen had already been more than helpful to her. The cough medicine really seemed to work; she hadn't felt a fit come on since she first took it. And he had willingly worked with her as she tried to find a solution to the parchment, probably knowing that even if they found an answer, there was nothing the Guild of Annendel would be able to do to help save her anyway. Best to simply return to Duras. Be together as a family before the sickness took her completely. Considering what had happened with her sister years earlier, even her father could agree to that.

The bell over the shop door jingled. Kira stood then, willing her legs to hold her up so that she could make her way out of the shop. She did not trust herself to look back at Galen, though she knew she owed it to him for all that he had done.

"Aelus?" a deep voice demanded.

Kira turned, recognizing it as her father's voice.

"He's not here," Galen said, coming around the table.

Kira wished for a moment that he would put his arm around her one more time, longing for one last touch. When Galen had comforted her, there had been none of the concern others seemed to have of catching her illness, none of the fear that even her father had, the way he always kept her just far enough away. Only those times when she nearly fell did her father touch her.

Her father appeared between the shelves. Galen stopped and glanced back at Kira. He saw something on her face—the anxiety of admitting what had happened with the money, or her acceptance of her fate.

"Master Benril," he said, turning back to face her father. "Thank you for allowing Kira to visit with me while you stopped in Amon. It has been wonderful catching up with her after all these years."

Her father looked over at Kira. "You did not tell me you were coming here."

Kira took a deep breath, smiling as she turned, hoping that it didn't look as pained as it felt. "I said that I wanted to visit friends."

His broad face seemed to darken. "What did you tell him?"

For whatever reason, there had always been friction between her father and Galen's. She'd never understood.

Galen answered for her. "Only that you were stopping briefly through Amon." His smile appeared much more convincing than hers. "We talked about your recent travels, and I asked if she happened to see my father while to the west."

Her father turned to Galen. His frown deepened. "We have most certainly *not* seen Aelus. And she will not." He looked at Kira. "Come, it's time that we be going."

Galen tilted his head. "Of course, Master Benril." He turned to Kira. "It really was wonderful to see you again." He took her hand. His fingers felt soft and warm. One worked briefly over where she had cut herself, smoothing the skin and briefly probing the wound. Satisfied, he squeezed again and released. "May we see each other again soon," Galen said to her.

Kira swallowed and nodded sadly. Both of them knew that wouldn't happen.

* * *

Outside the Aelus's shop, she glanced back. Dusty windows blocked her view so she couldn't tell if Galen watched as they made their way back to the wagon. The streets were muddy and she took care to stay on the uneven cobbles as she followed her father, but she slipped and had to turn away before she could see if Galen watched. Her father walked a step in front of her and did not look back.

Kira dreaded telling him about the lost money. She wondered if he already knew. Could that be the reason he'd come for her? She doubted that he did or he would be angrier.

"Did you think that Aelus could help?" her father asked, pulling her attention back to him. He finally looked at her briefly, and she read annoyance on his face and heard the derision in his voice as he said Aelus's name. "We're going to Annendel. Home of the greatest healers in the known world. There is little a village apothecary can do compared to some of the healers you have seen."

Kira didn't want to argue, but knew that many of the healers they had visited during the journey west paled in comparison to the skill she had seen from Galen. She glanced at her hand and shook her head. He had even recognized that she was bleeding and used the parsap to seal the wound. It still throbbed, but no longer bled as it had, and certainly not as long as it usually would.

They weaved through the streets and reached the wagon. The back was latched and the tarp pulled tight over the top. Everything was ready for their departure. Kira would have to tell him that the box had been stolen. They couldn't go to Annendel. She was not sure she really would want to even if they still had the necessary coins.

"Father . . ." She started to explain, but felt an irritant in the back of her throat as another coughing fit threatened her. It would be the first one since she had taken Galen's concoction.

He watched her with a concerned look on his face as he always did when the fits came on. She knew he felt helpless and hated waiting for the fit to pass, but there really was nothing else that could be done.

"Water?" she asked between coughs.

He frowned but nodded, reaching into the front of the wagon and pulling out a flask. He handed it to her.

Kira wanted to turn so that he wouldn't see what she did next, but her father stood watching her closely. As carefully as she could, she slipped her hand into her pocket, pulled out the small canister that Galen had given her, and quickly took a pinch of the concoction to put into the water.

Her father grabbed her wrist before she could mix the medicine into the water. "What is that?" he demanded.

The coughing fit hadn't completely eased. She took shallow breaths as she tried to work through it. When he didn't let go of her arm, she pulled back and mixed the medicine into the water, drinking it quickly before he could say anything more. It tasted no better the second time she tried it.

"*He* gave that to you?" he asked.

The spell finally eased and she nodded. "Just a suppressant," she answered. "But it works. I haven't coughed for hours."

Her father frowned suspiciously. "Are you certain that all he gave you was a cough suppressant? I've seen how his father works. Thinks he knows more than the Guild, he does!" He lowered his hand, suddenly aware that he had still been holding it up. Something in his face changed, softening. "Kira—I just want you to get well. That is all I've ever wanted." He let out a long sour breath. "Once we reach Annendel, we can finally start getting you the help you need. The study will find—"

"Nothing, Father. The study will find nothing." She took another drink from the flask and shook her head. "Why should the healers in Annendel succeed when the others have not? Can't you see that nothing has made a difference? The only thing that has helped has been this!" She held the flask containing the cough suppressant out in front of her and shook it at him. "And you can't get past your anger at Aelus to let me have this one reprieve!"

"It is because of Aelus that we lost your sister." His voice dropped to nearly a whisper.

Kira blinked and swallowed back what she nearly said next. "You can't believe that. There was nothing anyone could have done for Lisa, not after that injury. Even the Guild couldn't have saved her."

His eyes grew wide and he shook his head angrily. "But because of him, we'll never know. He told your mother that she would be all right. Offered her kind words, letting her think that Lisa would pull through. Had we only *known* . . ."

"What? You would have subjected her to the same journey that I've had to take? Trudge her across the countryside until you found someone else to take a crack at making her better?" Kira coughed once and wiped her hand across her mouth. "She wouldn't have survived the journey. No more than I will," she said, turning away from her father.

"I just want you to get well," her father said.

Kira tried to suppress the tears that came to her eyes when she answered. "I know that you do."

Then he touched her shoulder and squeezed, at least trying to show affection. Kira couldn't help but contrast it to the gentle way that Galen held her. They stood in place for a few moments. Kira let the tears fall while her father made every attempt to look away.

"I can't lose you too, Kira," he said. "Losing Lisa has been the hardest thing your mother has ever gone through. Don't give up on the Guild. There's still the chance that you might be healed."

Kira looked down at the wagon, wishing that she didn't have to tell her father about the missing trunk. Losing the hope of her healing would break his heart almost as much as losing her.

But she had to tell him. Better that they have some time left together as a family.

"Father . . . I am not sure that we can."

"What do you mean?"

She took a deep breath to answer.

As she did, Galen came running through town toward them, splashing through the muddy street. He called out her name as he ran.

Kira turned, wondering if he came to tell her good-bye once more, but his face looked too serious for that. He held out one of the sheets of parchment as he ran.

"Kira. Master Benril," he said as he approached, nodding politely to them both.

Her father looked at the sheet of parchment, his eyes growing from surprised to angry in the span of a few heartbeats. "You gave him *that* parchment?"

"A trade for the medicine," Kira said weakly.

"Don't you know what that is worth?" he asked.

"It is not worth anything, Father!" She tried to shout, but her voice did not cooperate. "Not without the secret of how to write on it. I thought Galen could help me discover it. That we could then sell it to have enough money to pay the Guild."

"But we almost have enough for the Guild, Kira."

She closed her eyes. "No. We don't, Father." She sobbed. "A thief . . . I was sick, coughing on the wagon . . . You were at Rubbles's . . ." Kira knew she was babbling but couldn't stop herself.

"The money is gone?" he asked.

Kira opened her eyes, forcing herself to look at her father. His face had gone white. All the anger that she had sensed from him had disappeared, replaced by an expression that he tried so hard to hide from her—grief.

"I'm sorry, Father. I should have locked the wagon. Should have protected the trunk. Now the Guild won't help."

Standing there, she knew the moment that his heart broke. It was overwhelming to her when it happened. The flat expression disappeared, turned into a look of devastation. "But we were so close. The Guild had agreed to take you into the study. We just had to make it to Annendel. Now . . ."

She saw on his face that he had already lost her. Like Lisa. "Maybe this is better," Kira said. It was her turn to try to comfort him. "We can return to Duras. To mother and Nathan. Be a family for the time that remains."

"That means that you will . . ." He couldn't even finish the words.

"I don't think that anything was ever going to change that."

"That was the whole purpose of this journey. That we would reach Annendel with the silvers needed for the study. That you could get the healing you need."

"Maybe this is best. Now we can just be a family. I don't know how much time I have left, but I would rather be with you and mother, not sitting in a cold room in Annendel while the Guild picks me over."

Her father stared at her and then nodded bitterly. He looked at Galen and waved a thick hand at him. "Keep it. Just like what Aelus did for her, the parchment is useless. Tell your father it's payment for what happened with Lisa."

"But that's what I came to tell you," Galen said. "We found the solution. Or really, Kira found the solution."

"What? How?" she asked.

Galen held up the page. Copied on it in his tight scrawl were the symptoms he had recorded for Hyp and Ms. Rubbles in richly colored ink. A large smear of ink ran across the middle of the page, darker than the rest. Kira saw another line and realized that Galen had recorded her symptoms there along with the others.

"When you cut yourself. The blood stained the page." Galen laughed a soft rich laugh. "Unlike the other inks, it stayed." He pointed to the long smear across the page. "I diluted some of my blood in plain ink and it still worked. The colorant we needed is just blood!"

He looked up the street and Kira looked after him. She thought she saw Hyp, standing with a disheveled appearance, his shirt untucked and his pants wrinkled. Something about him seemed different from the last time she'd seen him. He smiled and waved at Galen, pointing to his stomach. Galen seemed not to notice.

Kira thought she saw Ms. Rubbles hurry down the street as well, then decided she must be mistaken. When she had last seen her, Ms. Rubbles had needed a cane and had a soft sheen of sweat across her face. The woman Kira saw looked different, more relaxed and younger than Ms. Rubbles.

Her father took the page from Galen and held it up to the gray light, frowning as he read it. "If this works, then the Guild might pay dearly for the secret. I wouldn't be surprised if we can trade the remaining parchment for . . ." He looked over at Kira. "But you don't want to go to Annendel, do you?"

She coughed, feeling a bubble of blood come up with it. "It won't change anything. And I'm . . . I'm just so tired." She was relieved to finally admit it, but she hated the look on his face. "I'm sorry, Father," she whispered. She knew that the healing she could find in Annendel was not the healing she needed. What she needed —what her family needed—was nothing more than time together. No healer could help her with that. All that she wanted was to return to Duras, to be a family, for whatever time remained.

Kira grabbed her father's hand. He did not pull away as he so often did. She smiled up at him and, after a moment, he smiled sadly back at her, finally seeming to understand what she needed.

Her father handed the page back to Galen and then nodded. He stepped over to her and slipped his arm around her shoulders, holding her up. He let out a pent-up breath, deflated and defeated. His voice came out as a whisper as he said, "Then let's go home."

About D.K. Holmberg

New York Times and USA Today Bestselling Author D.K. Holmberg lives in Minnesota and is the author of multiple series including The Cloud Warrior Saga, The Dark Ability, The Endless War, and The Lost Garden. When he's not writing, he's chasing around his two active children.

AUTUMN AT THE DRAGON'S CAVE

By Kathryn Yelinek | 6,000 words

Shaya, my dragon, my master, my friend, had been away for two weeks when the storm hit. An early autumn squall barreled down the mountains and buried our valley in ankle-deep snow. Once the storm had passed, I drew on my boots, wrapped myself in my dragon-feather cloak, and went to check for damage.

Snowmelt dripped from bowed pine branches. It beaded off my cloak as I checked on Shaya's cave, its door still locked. The cattle were safe in their meadow, and the greenhouse undamaged, its glass panes glittering. Everything looked tidy.

Blue jays shrieked as I strode past the springhouse, on the way back to my cabin. Below their noise, a woman moaned.

I spun. In summer, villagers trudged the day's walk into the mountains to seek Shaya's healing. But for the last month, the only human voice I'd heard had been my own baritone.

Against the eastern wall of the springhouse, lit by golden sunlight, a woman huddled in a cloak too thin for the recent storm. Snow crusted the hem of her dress. Ice glistened in her black hair at the edge of her hood. Beneath it, her lips showed blue.

I dropped to my knees in front of her. "What's your name? Are you hurt?"

She muttered something incoherent. Her cloak rustled; it seemed she tried to turn toward me, but her movements were sluggish, uncoordinated.

"It's okay," I said, and hoped it was true. Shaya wasn't here. I could only pray my meager healing skills would be enough. I reached for her hand. "You're safe. I'll see you get warmed up."

Her fingers wouldn't grasp mine; her skin felt cold to the touch. She was past the point of shivering. In desperation, I lifted her bodily from the ground. As I did, her hood slipped back. I gasped. I was staring into the face of Bleu Chandler, daughter of the village's late candlemaker.

Bleu, the only woman I'd ever loved.

* * *

Dragons are funny creatures when it comes to trespassers on their land. Shaya tolerated the villagers who sought her out because she enjoyed their reverence, and they never stayed past sundown. Me, her latest human companion, she welcomed because I was useful. She needed someone to uncork the wine, dry the herbs, and corral the cattle—all tasks difficult to do with four-inch claws. The arrangement suited me. Still brooding over my broken heart, I preferred the company of a dragon to the pitying stares of villagers.

Or I did, until Bleu's pale face emerged from that hood.

What will I tell Shaya? I fretted as I peeled off Bleu's wet things (keeping my eyes averted as much as possible) and slipped her into my best tunic and trousers. Behind us, the hearth fire poured out heat. *When will Shaya be back?* I wondered as I tucked Bleu (and a bed warmer, not me) into the cabin's single cot, under my dragon-down blanket. Already I imagined Bleu staying.

My cabin suited a bachelor hermit who needed only a cot, a chest, a table and stool, and a hearth kept burning with dragon fire. Still, two could fit. Plus, my braided rug cheered up the room, and on a shelf over the cot, I'd laid out my collection of birds' eggs. Bleu had always loved things that flew.

While I boiled mint tea, thinking she would like the smell, I listed in my head ways to spruce up the cabin. As I poured myself a mug, Bleu shifted on the bed.

"Ryeland Baker? Is that you?"

Her voice was throaty, deeper than I remembered. My heart didn't care. It pounded against my ribs, and suddenly I felt seven years younger, a lad of eighteen.

I turned, wiping my palms on my trousers. She looked older than she should have for a woman of twenty-four. Gray streaked her hair, and her flushed skin stretched thin over sunken cheeks. Life with the Sisters of the Ever-Burning Hearth must have been hard. Still, she was more beautiful to me than any woman in the village.

And she was looking at me as she once had, as I'd hardly dared to hope that she would, as if she'd found the one thing that would make her happy. "How are you back in town? Did you leave the dragon?"

To my shame, I didn't answer. Let her think for a little while that she'd made it back to the village. "How are you feeling?"

"Warm." She nuzzled the top of the blanket. Once, she'd nuzzled me like that. "And pleased to see you."

That was my Bleu, direct as always. I poured a mug of tea to give myself something to do and took it to her. "Think you can drink something?"

She nodded and pushed herself up. She arched an eyebrow at finding herself in my tunic, but she took the mug. I sat on my stool and sipped tea, content for the moment to sit beside her, smelling mint. I remembered our engagement night, lying beside her by the village stream, watching stars shoot across the summer sky.

When only dregs remained in my mug, I asked, "Will the sisters come after you?"

She shook her head. "They let me go, said my service was fulfilled."

I coughed. I put my mug down quickly. I'd dreamed about that, but those dreams had faded years before. "I thought you had eighteen more years."

"I'd rather explain only once. Could you get my parents?"

I bit my lip. I asked, "Didn't anyone write you last winter?"

She frowned. Slowly, her gaze never leaving my face, she set her mug on the blanket, her fingers still wrapped around the mug's sides. "Why should they have?"

"Your parents"—how I ached, being the one to tell her —"passed at midwinter. Pneumonia."

Her eyes widened. She pressed a fist to her mouth. Seven years before, I would have gone to her, would have hugged her close and stroked her hair. Now, unsure of our relationship, I only cupped her hand in mine, feeling helpless and sad. They had been good folks, her parents, and had been as devastated as I was when the temple tither selected Bleu as payment.

"The house was sold to pay for the funerals," I said after a time. "There's nothing left, I'm afraid. But you can stay here. For now," I added hastily.

She stared out my window, her thin hand gripping mine. I wondered what she was thinking, if she could find solace in the sight of sun and sky. I hated to think of her alone in her grief.

She shook her head. "It's nice of you, but I can't stay, can I? The dragon won't let me."

Of course she'd figured it out. "You can for now. Shaya's away on research."

"How long until she gets back?"

My heart leaped. Maybe Bleu would consider staying. "I don't know. She's always back before full winter, but other than that, I can't say."

She chewed her lip. "I've imagined finding you again for so long. I can't believe I'm here. But I don't want to cause trouble."

"No trouble. I'd like to have you here."

"You never did have good taste," she teased, the same as she had years before.

And just like that, the years disappeared. She was my Bleu, I was her Ryeland, and our love was our own. Her lips looked as soft as ever. It had been so long since we'd kissed. I leaned toward her.

She stopped me with an upraised hand. "It's too late for that, dear one."

I blinked. Had I imagined the look in her eyes? "Why?"

She took a deep breath. "I won't stay here long enough to become a burden."

Instantly my body went on alert. I knew, in the twisting of my gut, that I wouldn't want to hear what she was about to tell me. Yet I couldn't turn away.

"You'll never be a burden," I protested.

She met my gaze. "Ryeland, the sisters let me go because I'm dying." She pressed a hand to her side. "I'll be buried alongside my parents by the solstice."

* * *

The hard lump in Bleu's side lurked just below her ribs. It was a ravenous lump, sucking her energy and appetite. And hope. Seven years cloistered inside a temple had withered her belief in miracles.

"I just want a little peace," she told me the next morning, her face turned toward the window. "I want to see the sky and the clouds and to watch the birds streaming south. If I'm lucky, maybe I'll see Shaya fly."

"You can't give up!" I banged my spoon. "It might not be too late. Shaya could still heal you."

She shook her head. "I know my body. This is beyond even dragon healing." She pushed her bowl away. "I don't want to prolong this. I'm not scared of dying. It's the long decline that terrifies me. Promise you won't let me linger."

"I can't promise that." Losing her once had broken my heart. I didn't think I'd survive a second blow. "At our engagement, I promised to care for you. Don't you remember?"

"You must have something," she continued. "Some plant to end my pain when it becomes too much."

"Just hold on until Shaya gets back. Please."

She pressed her lips together. "The pain's not too bad yet."

I breathed out. I wasn't going to lose her, not if I could help it. And for now: "Let's get you under the sky."

I wrapped her in my dragon-feather cloak and helped her hobble outside. We stepped into a world topped by a crisp autumn blue. She beamed. A man would risk much to see that smile.

At her direction, I helped her sit on a stump just outside the cabin door. With her back to the wall, the sky and the valley stretched before her. Her smile grew wider.

With that smile in mind and after I was sure she was tucked securely in the cloak, I walked to Shaya's greenhouse, glinting behind the kitchen garden. Almost too small for Shaya to enter, the glass ceiling reached twice my height. Inside grew our cold-hardy herbs and greens.

Usually I enjoyed puttering in the dirt and tending the dragon fire in the central clay oven. Never before, though, had I entered without some task from Shaya to do.

I paused at the entrance and scanned the sky. My fingers tingled; I felt as though I stood at the entrance to a king's unguarded counting house. Once inside, I stole through the heat to the raised beds with herbs that Shaya used for stomach pains.

I snatched sprigs of feverfew, licorice, and chamomile. Even though I was alone, I hid them in a basket and slunk back to the cabin. While Bleu dozed in the sun, I steeped them in a tea. Then I paced the cabin, twisting my hands. Yes, I had stolen the herbs, but I'd done so to fulfill my vow to Bleu. Surely I could care for her until Shaya came back. Then Shaya would cure Bleu and let her stay with me, right? I crossed my fingers and prayed to any god who would listen.

Around noon, Bleu shifted on her stump. She was awake.

I brought her a mug. "Something for pain."

She raised an eyebrow at the smell but accepted the mug. Before she took a sip, she pointed over my shoulder. "What's that?"

I knew what she was pointing at before I turned around. Sure enough, she pointed to the railed platform perched at a dizzying height in an orange-leafed oak tree by Shaya's cave. My head spun and my stomach dropped just thinking about its distance from the ground. I had to lean against the cabin wall.

"The treehouse." I was proud that my voice didn't wobble. "One of Shaya's former companions built it."

Her gaze lingered on it. I imagined that she breathed in the sight of it more than she breathed in the air around her. A cold dread crept down my spine.

"What's it for?" she asked.

"Fun, I guess." Although I could not imagine anyone *enjoying* climbing that high. "Get a dragon's-eye view of the world."

"Is it in good repair?"

I shuddered. I knelt beside her. "Please don't think of going up there."

She blinked. A frown creased her forehead. "You're still not good with heights, are you?"

I shook my head. My face grew hot.

"It's okay." She rubbed my shoulder. "I should be able to get up there without you going. A pulley, maybe."

"Half the boards could be rotted through!"

She scrunched up her face. Then her gaze swung back to the treehouse. I don't think she realized it, but she licked her lips.

"Don't," I said. Panic made my voice rough. "It's not safe."

The breeze blew feathers from her cape around her chin. I realized I'd grabbed hold of the cape edge, was holding on for dear life.

"All right." She slumped back against the wall.

I breathed a sigh of relief. Only later, after the heat had left my face, did I realize she'd never explicitly promised to stay away from the treehouse.

* * *

A dragon does as a dragon wishes. Shaya had winged away on many trips during my seven years with her. She left when she wanted and returned as she wished. Never before had I gone to my knees, praying for some sign of when she'd return.

Over the next three weeks, the nights turned colder. Skeins of geese honked their way south. The walnut trees dropped their leaves, and the sugar maples deepened from orange to red. Bleu grew thinner and thinner.

"I'm not hungry," she said one evening when I roasted chestnuts. Their earthy smell filled the cabin.

"You haven't eaten all day."

She shrugged. Her dress, which I'd washed and patched, hung around her like a loose blanket.

"You have to eat to keep your strength up."

She glared at me. "I'm not hungry. Stop asking."

Dread coiled in my stomach. The next morning, I took the iron key from the ring at my belt. It was cold in my hand, an accusation, and I knew I would pay for what I was about to do. Still I strode across dead leaves to Shaya's cave. For the first time, I unlocked its door without her beside me.

The cave was massive, stretching high overhead and deep into the mountainside. I felt as small and unwelcome as an ant without her there. I hunched my shoulders and stole past the towering bookshelves and strange models that littered the front of the cave. Toward the back, where the air grew cooler and smelled faintly of salt, I slipped into one of the niches that held the most valuable medicines.

I lifted my lantern to see the shelves. My hand shook, causing the light to scatter over the vials. I took a deep breath. Bleu needed this; my tea wasn't working, and the gods only knew when Shaya would come back.

Ancient labels named the contents of each jar: serpents' tongues, bezoar stones, even rock dust from the walls of her own cave, since dragon caves were said to have life-extending properties. Those I passed by, preferring a white stone jar at the far end of the second shelf. I pulled it down and uncorked the top. Inside was enough powdered unicorn horn to buy a castle.

My breathing sped up to hold such a treasure. Luckily, I didn't need much. Even a tiny quantity could counteract poison and seal wounds. What better than unicorn horn for an internal hurt that was eating Bleu alive?

"Shaya forgive me," I whispered as I helped myself to one of the small cloth bags she gave to visitors. Into it I poured about a dram of the powdered horn. All the way out from the cave, I dreaded a claw on my shoulder, a low growl of *Thief!*

Bleu, on the stump by the cabin door, caught one look at my face as I returned and asked, "What'd you do?"

I froze. The pilfered bag hung awkwardly from one closed fist. I should have made up a story. Yet it was a relief to be caught. I blurted, "I got you some unicorn horn."

Her face softened. She didn't ask where I'd gotten it. It must have been obvious. "Dear one, that was kindly meant, but I'm not going to take it."

Anger drummed in my ears. "You can't give up!"

"Can't I?" Sunlight gilded the circles under her eyes. "The tea's not working. What makes you think this will?"

"It's stronger." A statement, or a prayer? "Much stronger."

"All I want is to sit in the sun and enjoy what time I have left with you. Not run after every possible cure."

"Just try it, please. Shaya has to come soon."

She held out her hand, and I folded my fingers around hers. How very tired she looked.

"It means that much to you?" she asked.

I nodded fiercely.

"I'll try it for a week, not a day more. And no more tea."

"Thank you." I squeezed her fingers and hurried inside to make unicorn horn broth.

* * *

Ice lined the puddles the next morning when I went to haul water. The flocks of geese had dwindled to a few stragglers. Shaya had never returned so late before. I scanned the sky and tried not to imagine her in some unknown forest with a broken wing.

For five days, Bleu ate only enough broth to fill an acorn. I offered to season it differently, to ladle it over pumpernickel bread, to soak it with oats, if she would only eat a little more.

"I'm not hungry," she said, and stroked my cheek and turned her gaze to the sky.

I chewed my lip and pulled my hair and searched the clouds for Shaya's silhouette.

On the sixth morning, Bleu walked right past the stump by the cabin door. With the dragon-feather cloak around her, she strode to the base of an oak tree beside Shaya's cave. She sat, her back against the ridged trunk and tipped her face to the sun.

I wanted to pump my fist and crow. Who cared about buying a castle when unicorn horn could bring Bleu a different view of the clouds?

"Are you cured?" I asked, trying not to split my cheeks grinning. "Is the lump gone?"

"No." She rubbed her side and crinkled her nose. "But the pain's gone."

An excellent start. "Do you want more broth?"

"Later. Let me enjoy the view here." She patted the base of the trunk. "Go, shoo. You have chores to catch up on."

I'd neglected them, it's true. By now I should have checked the entire length of the cattle's meadow fence. So that morning I walked to the near corner of the meadow, where I had a clear view of Bleu, and squatted down to check the first boards.

Is there anything more glorious than whistling while you work under a crisp autumn sky? The mountainsides were bright with orange and red leaves. Late-season crickets chirped under logs, and a woodpecker tapped in time with my tune. All the valley seemed to celebrate the glory of the day.

Whistling still, I turned the corner of the fence and glanced back to Shaya's cave. Bleu no longer sat under the oak tree. The feather cape slumped empty at its base.

My song died.

"Bleu?"

No answer.

Maybe she'd slipped away to the privy, or gotten tired and gone inside. Maybe she'd simply moved to a different tree. But my mouth was dry, and I had to wipe my hands on my trousers.

"Bleu?" I held my breath to listen.

No answer.

I strode back up to the cave. "Bleu!"

"Ryeland?"

Her voice floated down from above.

I froze. Reluctant to look, but knowing I must, I tipped my head toward the treehouse.

It was empty. Sunlight gilded the wooden rails and set the house in stark relief against the rich blue sky. Below that, about a quarter way up the tree, Bleu clung to one of the oak's thick branches.

Cold sweat doused my spine. My knees felt as solid as snowmelt. "What were you thinking?" I yelled.

"I thought I was strong enough to get to the treehouse." Her voice was thick. She'd been weeping, but I was too angry to care. "I can't move. I'm too tired."

I should have chopped down the tree before she'd ever had a chance to climb it. I should have burned it.

I stripped off my jacket and prepared to climb. "I'm coming!"

Metal rungs nailed into the trunk made an easy ladder up the lower part of the tree. My fingers tingled as I grabbed the first one. It was reassuringly solid. Still, my heart slammed against my ribs as I took the first step up. I climbed a second rung, a third. Then my head spun, and my throat closed. I squeezed my eyes shut and hugged a rung at chin height.

"Ryeland?"

"Coming." My voice cracked like an apprentice's.

"Ryeland, it's all right. I'll find a way down."

"No, I can—" I gritted my teeth and forced myself up another rung. My knees buckled. My right foot slipped from its hold. For a moment, I hung, my foot flailing.

"Ryeland!"

I fumbled to jam my foot back. My breath was harsh in my throat.

"Hang on!" From above, there came a scrabbling sound.

My foot found its place. Breathing hard, I looked up, just as the scrabbling ended in a shriek.

Bleu plummeted to the ground in front of me.

I felt her landing like a blow to my chest. "Bleu!" I scrambled down.

She moaned. Dry leaves scattered around her in golds and reds. I dropped to my knees beside her. "Where are you hurt?"

She moaned again. I ran my hands over her legs and feet. She jerked—good, it meant she had feeling and movement there. One arm was pinned beneath her. She screamed when I made to move it.

"I have to," I said. "I think your arm's broken."

"Stupid arm," she hissed through her teeth. "Stupid body. Everything hurts again." Tears leaked from her eyes.

"It's okay," I murmured. I wondered how on earth to mend this. Where was Shaya when I needed her? I stroked Bleu's hair; there were twigs in it. "I'll take care of you."

"Why? I'm no good for anything."

"You're good for me," I said. She sniffled, and I stroked her hair some more.

I didn't know how to heal a broken bone beyond rudimentary splinting. I didn't know what it meant that her old pain was back. The only thing I knew to do was to take her into Shaya's cave for its healing powers. But that meant leaving her inside, depriving her of the sky. And what if Shaya came back while she was in there? Would Shaya be too angry to heal her?

"Maybe this is a sign from the gods." Bleu gripped my wrist with her good hand. "A sign to stop fighting."

I stiffened. "No."

"Ryeland, the plant I asked about—?"

"Not yet." I fished for the key on my belt. "Hold on."

I braced myself—please, gods, let me be doing the right thing—then gathered her in my arms. She sucked in her breath. I stood, cradling her against me, giving her time to breathe through the pain.

Then I let us both into the cave.

* * *

I mixed cave dust into a paste and smeared it on her arm before splinting it. Wrapped in my feather cloak, she curled up in a corner between two shelves. I'd given her poppy extract for the pain; she'd sleep for some time.

Then what?

I had nothing stronger to give her to help her hold on. If Shaya didn't come back—no, better not think about that. When Shaya came back, she'd be angry. Still, she would heal Bleu. Of course she would. Because if she didn't—

I busied myself hanging Shaya's two small mirrors on the walls so Bleu could awaken to a view of the sky. Then I went to retrieve my dragon-down blanket so she might have something soft to lie on.

A shadow darkened my cabin window.

Heat flooded my face. I dropped the blanket. I turned.

Shaya peered into the window with one black eye, her pupil a yellow pinprick of anger. She clacked her beak. "Come out. Now."

I hurried out. *She's back, she's back*, my heart sang. Below it, my gut churned. I didn't seem to know what to do with my hands.

Shaya didn't have that problem. She stood on four taloned feet. She was twice the height of the tallest horse and lithe as a snake, a sleek, sinewy bundle of red, yellow, and bronze feathers. Her tail lashed, and her wings flicked close to her body.

I wanted to hug her, and I wanted to scream at her. I said, "She's ill. I had to—"

"My cave. My horn. How dare you?"

"She fell. I didn't know—"

Shaya growled. "I smelled her. In *my* cave."

I wasn't explaining this right. "She's Bleu! My Bleu. The one I told you about. She's back."

The feathers of her ruff stiffened in surprise. "Your Bleu?"

"She's sick. Please go look at her. We've been waiting for you to come home. I'm sorry I broke your trust, sorry I took the horn. I'll do anything you ask, anything. Just please heal her."

Shaya eyed me, her tail flicking. "Your Bleu?"

I nodded. My throat felt tight.

She clicked a talon. "I'll see her. Wait here."

Whisper soft, she vaulted into the air. In a moment, she was over the cabin, winging toward her cave.

I wanted to run after her, stand by her side while she examined Bleu, listen as she pronounced a cure. But I'd broken enough of her rules. All these long weeks we'd waited for her to return. Waiting a few more minutes to hear the good news wouldn't matter.

I was worrying a thread on my shirt sleeve when she returned. She padded around the side of the house. Her ruff was down, her tail curled close to her body, an odd posture for one delivering good news.

I straightened and smoothed my shirt. "Well?"

"Do you love her?" Spoken softly, her words still sounded like an accusation.

"Of course!"

"Then why put her in my cave?"

"I said—"

"She wants the sky. You put her in my cave. This is love?"

"She's dying! Your cave—"

"Has no sky."

"You don't understand—"

She stamped one great foot. "All my companions go. You stay some years, you go. My heart breaks. I do not lock you in my cave."

I stiffened. "How dare you compare our comings and goings to Bleu? She's dying! It's not the same."

"Sometimes it is."

My jaw snapped shut. I sank down onto the stump where Bleu had spent many a day. How many of Shaya's companions had sat there? I'd not thought much about them, other than to curse the man who'd built the treehouse. Had Shaya sat beside him as he died?

"How do you stand it?" I whispered.

She tilted her head. Her pupils widened, softened. "I told you."

"You did? When?"

"I do not lock you in my cave."

DEEP MAGIC ANTHOLOGY ONE

I stared at her. My brain clicked. "You gave them a choice. You let them choose their end."

She huffed, a confirmation.

"I can't! Bleu wants me to give her—"

"Her choice. You love her, you give her her end."

I shot to my feet. My throat felt tight. "Cure her."

"I can't."

"You must! Please. I'll do anything."

"I can't." Her voice was soft. "She past my aid. I'm sorry."

"But—"

"You must have known. Bleu did. Why you not listen to her?"

I swallowed. My voice seemed lost in my throat.

"She not eating. Her lump so big. You not notice?"

I wrapped my arms around my waist. My throat felt raw. "I didn't want to know. Didn't want to admit she would really die."

Shaya bowed her head. "Her time runs out. Will you help her?"

"I—" My voice trembled. I'd fought so hard to care for Bleu. I'd done everything I could to make her comfortable, to inspire hope. But maybe I'd cared for her the wrong way. Wasn't that what Shaya was saying? Rather than caring for Bleu, I'd locked her in my own cave of hope.

Now Shaya was showing me a different way, a softer way. She stood patiently, waiting to learn my choice.

Choice. Bleu's choice. She didn't fear death, she'd said, rather the long decline. Though it pained me, I could save her from that.

"Yes," I whispered. "I'll help her. Give me a moment."

Shaya bobbed her head. She slipped away, whisper soft, around the side of the cabin.

My knees gave out. I sat down hard on the stump. I hung my head between my legs. I didn't want to go, didn't want to ground the herbs or make that final tea for Bleu.

It didn't matter what I wanted. Shaya had made that clear. Bleu was dying. My job was to see to Bleu's wishes, whatever they were.

A wren warbled in the afternoon sun, grating in its cheerfulness. The whole world seemed too bright, the leaves too red, the breeze too mild. My mouth tasted of ashes.

I could have sat on that stump forever, if it meant Bleu lived. But that was not the way of the world. I stood, creaking like a man three times my age.

The cave door stood open. I cleared my throat and knocked.

No answer.

Perhaps Bleu was asleep. I slipped inside. "Bleu? Shaya?"

The cave was empty. I wandered its length, as if Bleu or Shaya could have hidden behind a book or inside a vial. I felt dumbfounded. Shaya could easily have gone elsewhere, but surely not Bleu?

I shuffled outside. Laughter from above made me look up.

Bleu sat on the treehouse, her black hair a smudge against the blue sky. Wrapped in the feather cloak, she seemed a bird at home in the trees. On a limb beside her, Shaya clacked her beak in dragon laughter.

She arched her neck down at me. "Join us!"

"Don't tease him," Bleu said.

"I'm not." Shaya cocked her head at me.

A challenge. I gulped. My stomach shifted uneasily. Bleu and Shaya looked impossibly high. "I'll be with you in a minute."

I ran to the cabin and retrieved a length of rope. One end I tied around my waist. The other I tied to the highest tree rung I could reach.

I took the first step. My knees shook. Sweat coated my palms. I climbed another rung, and another. My head spun. I closed my eyes and pressed my forehead to the trunk.

"Keep going!" Shaya's voice flowed down.

I breathed deep. I could do this. Darker challenges lay ahead, but this I could conquer.

I hoped.

The lower branches of the oak hung around me, a red curtain to block the outside view. It was easier to focus on the trunk, on the bark, on the cool touch of the rungs under my fingers. To listen to the rustle of the leaves, breathe in the smoky scent of the wood. To remember that Bleu waited high overhead.

I untied the tree end of my rope and retied it higher. Then I climbed. Rung after rung, rope tie after rope tie. I reached a branch, swung the rope high and tied it off. Pulled myself up to the branch and hugged it tight until my arms stopped trembling and the breath returned to my lungs. Then pushed myself up and started over.

The sun crept across the sky. Leaves fluttered over my scratched wrists and against my sweat-cooled neck. The branches grew smaller. My arms trembled. Still I climbed, and I climbed, and I felt like my entire life had been climbing and Bleu would forever stay out of reach.

Then I looked up, and the next tie of my rope would snag around the railing of the treehouse. I lifted my aching arm to swing—and

Shaya plucked me from the branch to set me down in the middle of the treehouse.

I lay gasping. My arms and legs quivered. I squeezed my eyes shut, reveling in being alive.

When I opened them, Shaya curled her front paw in a dragon wave. "You two talk," she said. "I come back at sunset." She slipped off her branch like a leaf on the wind.

Bleu watched her go, wonder in her gaze. I would have climbed a thousand trees to see that look on her face.

I dragged myself to a sitting position in the center of the platform. The view was breathtaking, blue sky over autumnal mountains, but I felt better looking at Bleu's face. She slid over until our shoulders touched.

"You didn't have to come," she said. She cradled her splinted arm in her lap.

"Yes, I did." I leaned my head against hers. "I'm sorry I put you in the cave, that I didn't listen to what you wanted."

"Forgiven, but I won't go in any more caves."

I nodded. "I'll give you the herbs, since that's what you want."

"It's not."

I blinked. A green shoot of hope unfurled in my mind. "It's not?"

She took my hand, traced my knuckles. The wind whistled in our ears, and far away a raven croaked.

She took a deep breath.

The green shoot withered. I braced for what she was going to say.

"When Shaya flew me up here, it was marvelous! She carried me as if I weighed nothing. And the wind in my face, the world so small —" She squeezed my hand. "That's what I want in my final moments."

I stared at her. Her face was alive, as it had been when she first spied the treehouse. "You're going to"—I swallowed—"jump?"

"Not quite." Her thumb stroked my knuckles, soothing, entreating. "Shaya's willing to take me for another ride. A final flight."

My mouth was dry. "You're going to fall."

"Shaya will give me an herb. I won't be awake at the end." How serene her face looked. "It's what I want."

I bent my head over her hand. Already I felt the chasm of her passing opening inside of me. I could see the desolate days ahead, every one as bad as when she was first taken. Yet, this time I knew it would not break me. It would not send me scurrying to deeper isolation. I had climbed this tree and survived. I could survive the grief ahead of me.

I kissed the back of her hand. "Go, with my love."

"Thank you." She touched my cheek. "I didn't believe in miracles before, but finding you again, and now Shaya, this is a miracle."

"Let me stay with you," I said, "until sunset."

"I'd like that."

She shifted to draw the feather cloak around both of us. I held her close, my Bleu, until I had to let her go.

About Kathryn Yelinek

Kathryn lives in Pennsylvania, where she works as a librarian. She is a graduate of the Odyssey Writing Workshop. Her fiction has appeared previously in Daily Science Fiction, NewMyths.com, and Metaphorosis, among others.

MONGREL

By Maria V. Snyder | 4,800 words

THEY CALL ME Mongrel. I don't mind. It's true. My blood is mixed like vegetables in a soup. I've lived in so many different places and I never belonged to any of them. But the other homeless don't know that when they tease me. Say I waste food on my mutts. That I reek of dog.

So what? I like the smell of dog. Better than people. Better than the others I hang with. Not that I enjoy their company, but they're useful at times. Warned me about the police raid a few months back, let me know when the soup kitchen opened and the women's shelter—not that I would live there without my pups, but a hot shower is a hot shower.

As long as no one messes with my stuff, I don't care what they say. It's mid-January and I need everything I've scrounged to survive. My spot is near perfect. I sleep under the railroad bridge and I share my blanket with five dogs. The term hot dog has a whole new meaning for me.

The others huddle around a campfire on the broken concrete slabs of the abandoned parking lot. We're all trespassing on railroad property, but the owners only send the police about once a year to chase us away. So far, never in the winter. Nice of them. (Yeah, I'm being sarcastic).

That night, snarls and growls wake me. Animals are up on the bridge fighting. My lot is awake with their tails tucked under and their bodies hunched low. A yelp stabs me in the chest and I'm running toward the sound. Something rolls down the side of bridge, crashes into the brush, and lays still. Something large.

A wounded animal can be dangerous, but I'm next to him before my brain can catch up with my body. It's the biggest dog I've ever seen. He lifts his head, but the fight is gone. He's panting and bleeding from lots of cuts. I yank off my gloves and run my hands along his legs, searching for broken bones.

He's all black except for the tips of his hair. They shine with silver like he'd been brushed with liquid moonlight. No broken bones, but a knife is buried in his shoulder. Up to the hilt.

I spin around and scan the bridge. Sure enough a figure is standing there, looking down at me. My pups catch the stranger's scent and start barking and baying. I don't hush them, and soon the person leaves.

The noise brings the others. They tsk over the injured dog, but will only help me drag him to my spot after I give them cigarettes and booze as payment. They laugh and lay odds on how long the dog will live. People disgust me.

When the others go back to the fire, I open up the good stuff— eighty proof. By now the big brute is shaking and I grab the handle of the knife. He's either going to live or die quicker without it in him. I tug it out, scraping bone. The dog shudders once then stills as blood pours.

Staunching the wound, I use the eighty proof to clean it before stitching him up. He doesn't make a sound as the needle pierces his skin. I count them as I tie the string. Fifteen stitches in all. When I'm done, I lay beside him with the pups nestled around us and cover us all with the blanket.

He's still alive in the morning so I make my daily rounds, searching for food, checking dumpsters, and my usual haunts. Wearing layers of grimy clothes, I'm invisible to the normals. Slush covers the city's sidewalks and cars zip by, spraying water without care.

A couple businesses are aware of me, and once in a while, they'll add a few extra leftovers to their trash cans. I chuckle as I score a dozen hamburgers still wrapped up like presents in the dumpster behind Vinny's Burger Joint.

Vinny doesn't like me, wouldn't help me if I was starving to death on his sidewalk, but he's got a soft spot for dogs. People are funny like that.

I don't linger long—Vinny doesn't like that, but I spy a small terrier crouched next to the dumpster. Almost missed the little rat. She is trembling and wet. Dirt stains her white coat gray. I lure her with a bit of burger and have her in my arms in no time.

Back at my spot, I'm greeted with wagging tails and excited mutts that are all happy to see me. Can't get that from people. Not for long. Eventually they ignore you or abuse you, then leave you.

I split the burgers among my pups, counting heads. I got to be careful not to keep too many pups and the ones I keep are the littles who have no homes. The big brute eats half a burger—a good sign. I think he's one of those Irish Wolfhounds or Scottish Deerhounds I've read about.

The new pup isn't sure what to make of the pack. Doesn't matter. She's wearing a collar and won't be here long. I inspect my trash bags, arranged just so. Funny that foster kids use garbage bags to carry their stuff, too. I don't have much—a few clothes, some toiletries, a propane stove that's a life saver, and cigarettes and booze for paying for favors. Nothing's missing.

Most of the others won't leave anything behind, pushing their belongings around in stolen shopping carts instead. We're not a trustworthy bunch. But no one's stole from me since I've been sharing my spot with the mutts. I just smile when I sees one of the others limping around with bite marks on his ankles. Serves him right.

However, if the hound recovers, I'm gonna need more food than I can scrounge. So I grab my nicest clothes and head to the women's shelter for a shower.

* * *

The lady who answers the door is nervous. She keeps the chain on and looks at me like she wants to call the police.

I hold up the white dog. "Found your dog, Ma'am."

And there it is. The woman's face changes as if a button is pressed inside her head. Joy beams from her and I soak in it.

She flings the door wide and presses the pup to her chest, kissing and hugging the little squirming rat. "Thank you so much! We've been so worried. My kids will be thrilled."

She goes on, but I don't listen. It's always the same. What's not the same is what happens next. I'm polite and not demanding as I ask about the reward money. Just a gentle reminder. "Your flyer at the grocery store offered fifty bucks?"

The joy dies and she eyes my best clothes with scorn and suspicion. I smooth my pink sweater and tuck a strand of long brown hair behind an ear.

"Where did you find Sugar?" she asks.

"Behind Vinny's on Sixth Street."

"That's over two miles away. Sugar would never go that far. You took her from our back yard, hoping for reward money. That's why the gate was still locked."

"No, Ma'am. I—"

She slams the door in my face. No surprise just disappointment. Sometimes I'll get the money. Not often.

I hurry away before the cops arrive. Since I wore my best clothes, the library staff won't bother me. Pulling my favorite book, *The Complete Dog Encyclopedia* from the shelf, I flip through the pages until I reach the hounds. The big brute is thick in the body and tall legged like the Irish Wolfhound, but his long face doesn't match. I scan the various breeds. The Siberian Husky has similar eyes and muzzle, but not quite. I guess he's a mongrel like me.

On my way home, I do a sweep of the flyers hanging in the vet's waiting rooms, grocery stores, and churches. Looking at the pictures of lost dogs, I think they're easier to find than missing children.

Halfway home, I remember the knife and rush to get it. The dogs press near me, hoping for supper. I shoo them away, explaining about the ungrateful woman. Yes, I know they don't understand me. I'm not stupid nor am I crazy. It's just nice to talk sometimes. And the big Wolfhound (better than calling him a brute) peers at me with his intelligent gray eyes as if he does understand. He's sitting up—another good sign he'll be on his feet soon.

I find the knife, clean the blood off and hurry to the pawn shop before it closes.

* * *

"Stolen?" Max asks, examining the weapon. The silver blade gleams in the fluorescent light. The pawn shop smells of engine oil and mold.

"Found it," I say.

"Uh huh." Max sucks his teeth while he thinks, making slurping sounds that crawl over my skin like lice. "Cheap metal, imitation leather handle...I'll give you ten for it."

Never accept the first offer. It's crap.

"It does have a nice design...how about fifteen," Max says.

"That blade's got silver in it. A hundred bucks at least."

He gasps and pretends to be horrified. It's all an act and all I want is to go back to my pups. In the end, Max gives me sixty dollars. Enough for a fifty pound bag of Science Diet and a couple packs of ground beef. I carry the bag over my shoulder. It's getting dark and I'm almost home when I figure I've been followed.

A quick check confirms a man is trailing me, but I keep going. Not that the others will help me. They'll disappear as fast as the ground beef in my bag. Not like this hasn't happened before. I might be invisible to most people. And despite the smell of dog and layers of grim, the strays of society still find me. At eighteen, I'm young for a street person, and high school boys, college boys, and even foster fathers can't resist. My scent attracts them just like a female dog in heat.

The curse of developing early and curvy. My foster father called me beautiful. He named the dog Beauty, but never bothered her the way he did me. Lucky dog.

I reach my spot and my pups. Too bad the big Wolfhound is too weak to stand. Dropping the bag, I grab the metal baseball bat a kid left at the park and wait for the stranger. As long as the guy isn't armed, me and my lot'll do just fine.

Wearing khaki pants, brown loafers and a long wool coat, the guy resembles a lost professor. As he nears, the Wolfhound pokes his head out from under the blanket and growls deep in his chest.

The man takes his hands from his pockets. "Hello?" he calls all friendly like.

But my pups' hackles are up.

"I was hoping you could help me," he says, stepping closer. "I'm looking for my dog. Someone reported seeing him in this area."

Bull. I wait as his gaze scans the mutts and lingers on the baseball bat in my hands.

He tries a smile. "He's quite large."

"Haven't seen him," I say. "Go away."

"Are you sure?" He keeps coming.

I raise the bat. "Yep." By now all the dogs are growling.

He is unconcerned. "Settle your dogs."

"No."

He is close enough to see the Wolfhound. They exchange a glance and it reminds me of two competitors acting nice until the game starts.

"Settle them or I will." His right hand dips into a pocket and pulls out a gun. He aims it at me.

A bone chilling cold seizes my heart. "Quiet," I order. They're familiar with this command. It's the first thing I teach a new pup. They sit down on all fours and wait without making a sound.

"Drop the bat," he says.

I let it clang to the ground.

The man tries to comfort me. "I'm just here for my dog."

Yet the Wolfhound doesn't seem happy to see him. Go figure. Now the guy is under the bridge and the hound lurches to his feet. The dog's massive jaws are level with my chest. The blanket remains on his back like a superhero's cloak.

The man shakes his head as if he's amazed. "How many near misses, Logan? Four? Five? Only you would find some homeless person to nurse you back to health. Too bad I found you first."

And people call *me* the crazy dog lady.

He turns to me and says, "His injuries are too extensive, I'll have to put him down." He aims the gun at the Wolfhound.

The urge to protect one of mine is instant and hot. "Wait," I say. "Can you take the blanket off him? It's my only one and I don't want it full of holes and blood."

The man laughs. "I see your charm with the ladies remains the same," he says to the Wolfhound. He's careful to keep the gun out of the dog's reach as he pulls the cover off.

My pups are well trained. And while being quiet is important, I've taught them protecting my stuff is essential. They hop to their feet and attack his ankles and calves with their pointy little teeth. He yells. I scoop up my bat and slam it down on the man's arms. The gun fires, but no yelps so I swing again and again until he drops the gun. Until he rolls on the ground, shielding his body from my bat.

I taste the desire to pound him until he's a pile of broken bones and bloody meat. Coming here and thinking he can just take what he wants. Just like my foster father sneaking into my bedroom. But this stranger isn't him, so I pull myself together and call my dogs off.

"Go away," I say to the man.

The man staggers to his feet, but his gaze is on the Wolfhound. Odd, considering *I'm* the one holding the bat.

"Next time I won't come alone," he says to the Wolfhound before limping away.

That's bad. I look at the Wolfhound. "Does he mean it?"

I swear the dog nods a yes. Okay so maybe I am the crazy dog lady. I pick up the gun and unload it as I think. If I hock it, I'd have money, but no weapon. The bullets are shiny silver. Living on the street, I've seen my fair share of guns and bullets, but these are special. Expensive, too.

We could move before he comes back. But that rankles. Nobody's gonna run me off my spot.

"How many will come with him?" I ask the hound. "Two?"

A shake—no.

"Three?...Four?...Five?"

Five. Crap. "When? Tomorrow morning?...Afternoon?...Night?" Yes to the night. I've a day to plan, but the Wolfhound gives me a decisive nod (yep, this confirms the crazy), and he takes off. Well, he tries. Poor boy stumbles after two strides. The knife damaged his muscles and he's still weak. He also ripped his stitches.

Half carrying him, I bring him back and fix him.

"Look," I say. "I didn't spend all that time and energy on you to see you throw it away, trying to be noble. You're part of mine now and I protect mine."

* * *

A day isn't much time so I'm at the Humane Shelter's door as soon as it opens.

"Hey, Mongrel." Lily greets me with a smile. "Find another pup?"

She's filling bowls with generic dog food (such a shame!). I help her feed her charges. Excited barks and yips ring through the metal cages. Lily's the only normal person I talk to on a regular basis.

"Not today."

"Take a look at the flyers. There's a black lab missing. Owner's are offering a hundred dollar reward."

Lily sees my face. "I can be your go between and make sure you get the money," she says.

"How did you know?"

"Police came yesterday asking questions about you. They thought you have a dog napping scheme going on."

So much for earning money that way. "What did you tell them?"

"The truth. You're better at finding lost dogs than anybody in town. That you're providing a service to this city and should be paid."

Lily is good people. "Thanks. Now I really hate to ask you for a favor."

She straightens and looks at me as if I just told her the sky is orange. "In the two years I've known you, you've never asked for anything. If I can, I will. Ask away."

I blink at her a moment. Didn't she want anything in exchange? She insists not and I make an unusual request which she grants. Did I tell you Lily's good people? Well she is.

* * *

After a stop at the pawn shop, I take my littles to Pennypack Park—a tiny snake of green in the middle of the city. I find a nice safe place for them, ordering them to stay quiet. They're handy against one intruder, but against five, one of them is bound to get hurt.

I return to the Wolfhound about an hour after sunset. He's alert with his nose sniffing' the cold breeze. Somehow, I know the professor and his goons aren't going to arrive with the wind, so I sit close to Logan and keep watch downwind. The others are nowhere in sight. That homeless sixth sense accurate once again.

As I wait, my heart is chasing its tail, running fast and going nowhere. It's not too long before five black shapes break from the shadows and approach. They're easy to see in the bright moonlight.

My insides turn gooey, but I draw in a breath. Nobody messes with mine. Not anymore. I stand as they slink toward me. No, I'm not being dramatic. Slink is the perfect word. Five big brutes just like Logan. Massive jaws and shaggy hair. The professor isn't in sight, but a tawny Wolfhound leads the group (give him two pairs of loafer's and he'd fit the part of the professor).

Now you're gonna to tell me something like this just doesn't happen, and I'd agree with you every other night. But not tonight.

The pack fans out, and I've seen enough street fights to know if they surround me I'm dead. I raise the gun, aim, and fire. I'm a pretty good shot. Thanks in part to my foster father. Unlike all the others before him, he'd taught me a few life skills and I'd loved him until...well, you know.

The tranquillizer dart hits the shoulder of the far left hound. (If you thought I'd shoot them with bullets, then you haven't been paying attention.)

I squeeze off a couple more darts, picking off two more wide receivers before the remaining two catch on and rush me. Dropping the gun, I palm a dart in one hand and pull the silver knife I reclaimed from the pawn shop, exchanging it for the lost professor's gun.

Then it's all hair, claws, and teeth. The Wolfhounds are fast and it's like fighting a giant yet silent dust devil. I jab the dart into dog flesh and strike, stab, and slash at anything I can reach with the knife. The tawny grabs my wrist with his teeth while his last goon is overcome by the tranquillizer.

Tawny bites through my skin like it's paper. I yell and drop the weapon. He pushes me over and stands on my chest. Breathing with his weight on me is an effort, and my heart lodges in my throat. He stares at me for a second with regret in his gaze, giving me just enough time to thrust my arm between his sharp teeth and my exposed neck.

A bit of surprise flashes in his black eyes as he latches on. I'd coated my sleeves and pants with Tabasco sauce. Useful for keeping pups from chewing things. In this case, not so smart as the burn makes Tawny angrier. The pressure increases in my forearm and I'm convinced my bone's about to snap in two when the brute is knocked off.

Logan and Tawny roll together. And the fight's no longer silent as they growl and snarl. I worry about Logan's shoulder as I dive for the tranquilizer gun. Lily showed me how to wrap up his leg to support his weight, but it's not much.

I'm outta darts. With Logan injured, the fight isn't fair. Most things aren't. And I guess that's the only way Tawny can win.

I spot a glint just when Tawny pins Logan. Sweeping up the knife, I lunge toward Tawny and bury the blade in his hindquarters. Up to the hilt.

He yelps and bucks. Logan presses his advantage and regains his feet. In a blur, Logan strikes and silences Tawny. Logan's muzzle is dripping with blood. I meet his gaze and can tell by his expression that he's sickened and sad. He's not a killer, but Tawny forced him to be one. Why couldn't he just leave Logan alone?

I'd asked my foster father the same thing. He said I was too irresistible so I ran away when I turned sixteen, removing the temptation. I'd thought I was smart, but no one knows about his inability to resist. It's been two years. What if he has a new foster child? Staring at Tawny's ripped throat, I realize a person has to stay and fight until there's a clear winner and loser or else your problems don't ever go away.

The burning pain in my arm snaps me back to my current problems. I inspect the damage. Ragged, bleeding flesh too mangled for eighty-proof and Band Aids, but I don't have another option. Once Logan's cleaned up—his stitches have ripped again—and hidden under the blanket, I hurry to the Humane Shelter.

Lily's working late and I suspect she's there for me. She sends a couple volunteers to pick up the sleeping Wolfhounds. I return the tranquilizer gun.

"A pack of wild dogs that are all the same breed is so unusual," she says. "Usually they're a bunch of mongrels." She slaps her hand over her mouth. "I didn't mean—"

I smile. "I know. Nothing wrong with mongrels."

Lily sees my arm and insists I go to the emergency room. I almost laugh. Invisible on the streets, I'm nonexistent in an ER. No money. No insurance. They'd fix a cockroach's broken leg before attending to me. I lie and say I'll go, but she sees right through me. Despite my protests, she escorts me to the ER and stays until I'm seen. The ER doctor gives me thirty-two stitches. Funny how the number of stitches is always reported like it's a source of pride.

* * *

By the next day, my life returns to; well, not normal, but back to the same—taking care of the pups. Logan is healing faster than me and eating like a horse. I feed him my share most days. Don't matter to me, my stomach's upset anyways. Tomorrow—one week after I found Logan—I'm gonna tell the authorities about my foster father.

I'd rather face a pack of wild dogs, but I'm determined to grab the man by the throat and not let go, finally doing what I should have done two years ago.

* * *

Five days later, Logan takes off and doesn't return. The hurt cuts deep and reminds me of how I'd felt moving from one foster home to another. Crazy lady that I am, I'd been talking to him about the police and the lawyers and the questions. No one is quick to believe me, and I don't have much proof so it's been rougher than I thought. Somehow telling my problems to Logan made the whole ordeal bearable.

But he's gone, and my resolve to go after my foster father wavers. But there is also a tiny bit of relief inside me. Keeping the Wolfhound fed was hard. And with one of life's little twists of fate and timing, I find the missing black lab after Logan left. Lily handles the reward money. Without Logan to feed, there's plenty of money to keep my pups in Science Diet.

Three—maybe four weeks after the night I helped Logan, a stranger enters the parking lot. Wearing blue jeans and a leather motorcycle jacket, he doesn't hesitate, heading right for my bridge. His black hair hangs in layers to his shoulders, and his stride is familiar.

I'm searching my memories to place him when my pups race toward him. Good. Except they don't bite him. They dance around, tails wagging and yipping in excitement. He crouches down and pets them! I grab my bat.

He glances up as I swing and dodges the bat with ease. Strike one. I pull back for another.

"Mongrel, stop," he says. "It's me."

I freeze and study him. He's a few years older than I am, about six feet tall and lean. Good looking enough to attract the girls. His gray eyes don't belong in the face of a man though.

He opens his jacket, and pulls his collar down, showing me an almost healed scar on his right shoulder. "Fifteen stitches."

I lower the bat. "Logan."

"Yep."

He moves closer and I back up. Logan pauses. "You weren't afraid of five werewolves, but you're scared of me?"

Werewolves. Saying the word out loud made it real. Before I could explain them away as really smart mixed breeds.

"Guess I'm better at trusting...werewolves than men," I say.

"One man dooms the whole species?"

"What about the guy...wolf after you?"

"He wanted to be in charge."

"And that's my point. Dogs...or wolves'll fight it out. One dominates and the other slinks away. The human side of him tried to cheat. Right?"

Logan says nothing.

"He used a knife and then returned with a gun. Very un-wolf like behavior."

"Let me prove to you we're not all bad."

"Why?"

"You saved my life three times."

I tap the bat against my leg. "So buy me a couple bags of Science Diet and we'll call it even."

"No. I owe you much more than that."

He's serious and I suspect stubborn as well. "Go away, Logan. You don't belong here," I say.

"Neither do you."

I huff and squash the sudden desire to take another swing at his head. He thinks my silence is an agreement 'cause he's now standing a foot away. And my heart's acting like it's scared. I expect him to crinkle his nose at the smell of dog on my clothes or for him to try to hide his disgust at my unkempt appearance.

Instead he takes my hand in his and pushes my right sleeve up with his other one, exposing the jagged purple scars on my wrist and forearm. I didn't heal as fast nor as well as he did. Logan traces them with a finger.

A strange teeter totter of emotions fills me. My first impulse is to flinch away from his touch, but his familiar scent triggers fond memories of the big Wolfhound I cared for.

Logan taps his thumb on my arm. "You've been bitten by a werewolf deep enough for his saliva to mix with your blood."

"So?"

He quirks a smile. "You accepted our existence with ease, yet you don't know the legends."

I gesture to his shoulder. "I believe what I see."

"You've been infected, but one bite isn't enough to change you into a werewolf." All humor is gone as he stares at me with a sharp intensity. "For you to become one of us, a bite from two different werewolves within a month is required."

He turns my arm over, revealing the light underside. His canines elongate. "I've never offered this to anyone, and it's a hell of a way to repay your kindness, but it seemed...right. Interested?"

My mind races. He's giving me a choice. "What about my pups?"

Another smile. "Only you would think of them first. They can stay with you."

"Here?"

"No. My pack has a network of places. We try and keep a low profile, but we'll support you in going after your foster father."

"Why?"

"Because you'll be part of mine and I protect mine."

I grin at the familiar words.

Logan adds, "It's not an easy life, and there is no cure. No going back. We don't belong to the human world or the wolf world."

"So you're a bunch of mongrels?"

"Yep."

"Then I'll fit right in." I raise my arm to his mouth, and he sinks his teeth into my flesh.

About Maria V. Snyder

Meteorologist turned novelist, Maria's been writing fantasy and science fiction stories since she was bored at work and needed something creative to do (shhh...don't tell!). Fifteen novels and numerous short stories later, Maria's learned a thing or three about writing. She's been on the New York Times bestseller list, won a half-dozen awards, and has earned her Masters of Arts degree in Writing from Seton Hill University where she's been happily teaching and mentoring students in the MFA program.

THE DRAGON BETWEEN WORLDS

By T.E. Bradford | 8,500 words

"He's a devil."

"He's a maester, and just what the boy needs. Training and discipline."

"I don't like it. The others won't go near him. It's no wonder he has no servants or acolytes."

"He's willing to pay, which is more than can be said of any others. Besides"—he drained his mug, banging it down onto the table—"what other offers have we gotten?"

In his hidden spot crouched on the grass outside the window, Cyril's hands balled into fists. He knew his father thought he was a failure. In spite of doing his best in all of his classes, none of the maesters had taken him as an acolyte. He wondered which one it was his father spoke of.

"They whisper that he calls on the dark magic."

There was a beat of silence. "The wagging tongues of cleaning women."

"Who have seen what is kept in the dark."

"Enough!"

The roar made Cyril flinch, even though he was safely out of sight.

"Ye'll keep yer tongue!"

The pounding footsteps that accompanied the growl filled in the scene well enough. His father would be looming over his mother, eyes red and face dark. His mother would be looking to one side. She knew better than to look him in the eye.

"I will not have you filling this house with gossip and lies." A fist landed on something, likely the counter. "He's offered to take the boy, and I've accepted. There'll be no more discussion on the matter."

Cyril felt a mix of fear and excitement fill him.

"Besides, it'll do the boy good to be out from under yer wings. Ye've coddled him long enough."

Footsteps, this time moving away, meant the tirade would not escalate, at least for now. He let out a breath of relief. Then soft sounds reached his ears. His mother was crying. He started to stand up, to go and comfort her, but stopped. His father thought he was too soft. That he needed to be more of a man. Maybe his mother did coddle him. Was that why none of the maesters had wanted him?

He felt guilty for thinking such thoughts about his mother. She had always been good to him. She'd tried to keep the worst of his father's anger away from him when she could. But when she cried, he felt strange inside. His father hated crying. That was why his mother did it only when he wasn't there to see. She hid her tears from his father. He wished she hid it from him too. It made her seem weak.

Maybe she was making him weak too.

He backed away quietly, careful not to step on any twigs or branches that might betray his presence. When he was far enough away from the house, he turned and ran. The feel of the grass whipping at his legs, of the air buffeting his face, soothed him. He ran until his legs felt unsteady and his lungs burned. When he could go no farther, he collapsed onto the ground, letting the grass and dirt cool him. He rolled onto his back and looked up into the sky. Clouds turned into shapes as he watched them. A pig shifted into a lion. A duck into an eagle.

These are omens, he decided. I will become something powerful. Something great. I will show them who I am. Whoever this maester is, I will stand beside him and learn all that he knows and more. I will be the best acolyte they have ever known, and then I will become a maester too. The greatest ever.

They whisper that he calls on the dark magic. He recalled his mother's voice in his head.

The idea of it sent a thrill through him. What did it mean, dark magic? What did it do? Could it call up demons and devils? Destroy cities?

His father was probably right. It was all just gossip from old women. Even as a student he constantly heard them chattering in the kitchens and in the halls. Most of the time it was just silly prattle about this couple or that leader or something they'd seen or heard. He'd never paid it much mind.

Above him, a cloud that looked like a lizard elongated, growing a great head and a roaring mouth.

A dragon!

He wondered if dragons had dark magic or not. Did they even exist? The old books at school said they had once, but that was long ago. Now they were just legends and dust.

He sat up, plucking a stone out of the grass and throwing it as far as he could.

Who cared what kind of magic the maester practiced? Either way, it was power, and that was something that could be learned. He would go, and he would be a good acolyte. He would learn, and if the maester did have some dark power, Cyril would find a way to have it too.

- 2 -

The wagon rocked as it rolled over the old dirt track. In the bed, two small crates contained all of Cyril's clothes, along with his sturdy boots. He'd tucked his one and only prized possession into a sock at the bottom so that his father wouldn't find it. He would disapprove.

"You remember to do good work for the maester," his father said, looking over at him with eyes that were such a light shade of blue they looked almost like the ice that formed on the river in winter. "He's paid good money."

"Yes, sir."

"Yer mother fill your head with idle gossip, boy?"

He shook his head no. She hadn't. Not really. He'd only heard it because he was listening in. That was a much graver offense, and one he wasn't about to disclose.

"Good." His father looked forward again. "She's not like us, boy."

He wasn't sure what his father meant, but kept quiet. It was always best not to say anything when he wasn't sure what would make his father mad.

"Some folks frown on Destructive," he went on. "Like it's not as good as Creative or Neutral, but that's far from the truth."

He glanced over at his son again, and Cyril saw something he'd never seen in his father's eyes before: excitement.

"You may not understand now, but you will. Destructive can do things others can't. You watch the maester, and watch well. If you're careful, you may find there are things you can learn that will serve you in ways you never imagined."

Cyril had seen a lot of looks on his father's face, but the one he saw next was the most frightening. The sides of his face stretched into a feral grin, lips spread back to reveal teeth that were yellowed by time and drink. His eyes glittered. The effect was terrifying.

As if the sun agreed, it went behind a cloud, casting a pall over the otherwise bright morning. Thankfully, the rest of the ride was mostly silent. They rode south, crossing the Casca River at a small bridge. As the sun neared its zenith, the heat reflecting off the ground in waves, they crested a ridge above a small valley. There was only one building, but the sight of it brought both of them to a halt as the horses shied nervously.

Made entirely of rock, it looked as if the earth had buckled upward, spewing out the foundation beneath it, erupting into the sky in razor-tipped fingers and jumbled deformities.

What maester is this?

His father flicked the traces several times before the horses were convinced to keep moving, dancing nervously down the slope toward the monstrosity. When they reached the bottom of the hill, the horses refused to go any farther, rearing up when lashed. They were not willing to get any closer to the unnatural place that loomed ahead. Swearing softly, his father set the brake and jumped down.

"We'll walk from here."

Each of them carried one of the crates. In spite of the heat of the sun and the weight of their burden, Cyril felt chilled. When they passed into the shadow of the rock, his fingers went cold. Up close, the rock looked even more bizarre, mottled and whorled as if melted and somehow resolidified. The front door was a solid slab of wood that looked thicker than most trees. He stared at it, his mouth hanging open, as a voice from inside beckoned them to enter.

"Maester Griven," his father said with a curt nod of the head.

Griven? Cyril had never heard of him.

"Come." The voice emanated from the shadows at the back of the room.

His father set the crate down to one side of the door, so Cyril followed his lead. The enormity of the space became apparent as their eyes adjusted to the darkness. It was a cavern, somehow aboveground. Glittering geodes in a dozen colors reflected from the ceiling that soared overhead. It was an impressive sight.

"Bring him here."

His father turned to him and waved a hand. "Go on, then."

Cyril took a few hesitant steps, his feet freezing, as a tall, dark shadow separated from the darkness and glided toward him. The maester's eyes were the same color as the rock. He had no hair. Instead, designs covered his scalp, the pigment of them a deep reddish brown. Cyril watched, mesmerized and horrified as a skeletal hand reached out to grip his left shoulder. The fingers were surprisingly strong, pressing into his skin, but he never had a chance to register the discomfort. Immediately on contact, his head exploded with pain. Crawling, slithering worms seemed to be invading his brain, tearing into it. His mouth opened to scream.

Griven dropped his hand, and the sensation stopped as quickly as it had begun. The pain in Cyril's head evaporated. The maester turned to Cyril's father.

"He'll do."

Cyril blinked, a wave of nausea rolling through him.

Griven held out a small bag. His father took it with another nod, then turned to go. Cyril watched, eyes wide, as his father headed for the door. Whatever this man was, whatever this place, he would be staying here. He would not be going home to his mother, or his bed, or the fields of tall grasses on the plains.

At the last moment, his father stopped and looked back at him. Cyril fought the urge to run, his body trembling.

"Learn," his father said, as if that one word conveyed all that was needed.

Then he was gone, and the door swung home, taking the light of the outside world with it, leaving Cyril trapped inside the great tomb of rock.

It was the roar that woke him.

Griven had picked up one of the crates with those oddly strong skeletal hands, and led him along a passage more like a cave than a hallway. It curved gently back and forth, the walls pitted and uneven. They passed several small openings before reaching the other end. There, the passage opened into a small room. A bed pressed against the far wall under the only window Cyril had seen. At the foot of the bed was a trunk made of some rich, burled wood. Along the left wall there was a table with several books stacked on top, and in the opposite wall there was a fireplace, fire already burning. It felt strangely soothing in the chill rock structure that was cold in spite of the heat outside.

Cyril was surprised. It was much nicer than his room at home. Of course, Griven was a maester, strange or not. It made sense that he had more comforts, but when Cyril had seen the strange rock building, he had assumed the worst: he would be living in a dungeon. This room was no dungeon.

Griven placed the crate beside the trunk. The back of the man's neck, Cyril noticed, had the same strange markings as his head. They traveled down his skin and disappeared into the dark cloth of his shirt. Cyril wondered how far down they went.

"You may store your belongings here," the maester said, indicating the trunk. "Since you've had a long journey, I will let you rest. I will come and get you when it's time to eat. We will begin work tomorrow."

Cyril found his tongue rather stuck in his mouth, so he just nodded. The maester turned to go, and Cyril found himself thinking that perhaps his strange appearance was not so frightening after all. It was Cyril's imaginings that had him fretting, not the man himself. Yet as the man passed by and those skeletal hands came into view, a shiver pressed through him. Griven may not be frightening, but he was certainly powerful. Perhaps the most powerful maester Cyril had ever met.

Once the boy was alone, he set to exploring the room more thoroughly. He put the crates into the trunk unpacked. It was large enough to fit a third alongside if he'd had one. Then he turned to the table and the books. There were several written in a language he didn't recognize. These he piled to one side. The others contained histories of plants, beasts, even legends and prophecies. One in particular drew his eye. On the cover was a serpentine form, with a large spiked head sporting a mouth lined with flame and filled with teeth. The coiling body circled behind, firelight dancing from the skin and glowing between the scales like lava as it circled and looped around to a pointed tail that curved into its mouth.

A *dragon*!

Cyril had dreamed of dragons since he had been old enough to know what they were. His mother had taught him a song once about a dragon.

"Don't let your father hear you sing it," she'd cautioned. "Keep it in your head and heart."

He had committed it to memory and only hummed the tune when he was alone, or when the lashes of storms thundered around their house, drowning out most other sounds. It was a song of power, and it soothed him.

The drawing on the book's cover was better than anything he'd ever seen before. The dragon looked real, its scales smooth and glossy. Even its eye seemed to be looking outward, filled with wildness. He ran his fingers over it, feeling the ridges and dips. There was an odd tingling sensation and he gasped. It felt as if the lines were moving. He jerked his hand away, eyes wide, breath caught in his throat. The picture looked just as it had.

Illusion.

Hesitantly, he put one finger back, just grazing the lines.

There! The tail moved! That was no illusion. Cyril backed away from the table, his heart pounding. He licked his lips. Was it a trick? Some kind of magic? How could a drawing move?

The backs of his legs hit the edge of the bed, and he sat down with a puff of breath. This place was so odd, yet so strangely exciting. Perhaps his father had been right. The maester was obviously powerful. He must have extraordinary magic here. All Cyril had to do was watch and listen and absorb all that he could.

Sighing, he lay back on the bed. The light from the window drew his eyes. Outside, the sky was a flawless, sparkling blue. The blue of summer. Lazy bits of cloud floated across it. As was his habit, he let himself see images in them. He drifted to sleep, soothed by the familiar game.

When he jerked awake, it was later in the day. The shadows were long, and the afternoon light hit his eyes, making him squint.

A loud roar shook the bed.

It was like nothing he'd ever heard. It was like screaming thunder. His first thought was that he was still dreaming, but then two of the books that had been too close to the edge fell off the table, thumping to the floor.

Cyril jumped out of bed, trying to orient himself. Beneath him, the floor vibrated. Then the roaring ceased, and all was still. He waited for a moment before walking to the doorway and sticking his head out.

"Maester Griven?"

There was no answer. He stepped into the hallway. It was much darker than it had been earlier. He put a hand on the wall to keep from bumping it, and slowly traced the curves back to the front room. It was empty. The fire had burned low. It was apparent that wherever the maester was, he had not been here recently. Perhaps he was sleeping too.

Could he have slept through that noise? It didn't seem likely, but perhaps it was familiar to him. It could be a machine of some kind that just seemed like a roar. The idea that it was nothing, that he was jumping at shadows like a boy half his age gave him pause. What would the maester say if he found him here, trembling and wide-eyed?

Be a man about it. His father's voice echoed in his head.

Taking a deep breath, he started back toward his room. He was halfway down the winding hall when another roar shook the stone. Dust and grit settled on his shoulders, dispelling any thought that it was just part of a dream. He placed his hands on the wall, feeling the rumble like an earthquake beneath his palms. The sound echoed and rang for nearly a full minute before subsiding. A blast of hot air surged over him.

Ahead, he could see the dim light from his room and the window. Around him, the hall was darker, but not completely black. Light was coming from somewhere else, he realized. He looked back over his shoulder.

There. One of the openings he'd passed seemed to glow. A reddish light flickered, making shadows dance just inside. Mustering his courage, he walked to the opening and peered inside. The stone floor curved to the left, then sloped downward. Heat poured out as if there were ovens down below.

Perhaps there were. Maybe in this odd house, the kitchens were in the basement.

"Hello? Maester Griven?"

His voice echoed back as if mocking him. Coddled boy, it whispered in his brain. Afraid of the dark like a babe.

His hands curled into fists. He was no babe. He pressed his lips together and stepped into the corridor. It wound slowly but steadily down, yet the temperature continued to rise. Sweat rolled down his face and sides. His shirt stuck to his back. He had gone far enough that any light from the hall would not reach, yet he could see. The light was coming from below. So was the heat.

Doubt worked at him. What if the strange stone had been pulled from the earth, and the corridor led to the fire-filled bowels where rock turned to liquid? Perhaps he should go back. His feet had already slowed when the loudest roar yet blasted. It hit him full in the chest like a lightning bolt, knocking him onto the floor. The air that washed over him was hot enough to singe his hair. His clothes began to smoke. Sweet Divide, he was going to burn to death.

The sound and the heat abated simultaneously.

From his seat on the rock floor, he looked up behind him. He could still go back. He probably *should* go back. Ahead of him, the shadows took on a new life as they danced. He stood up, dusting himself off and patting his clothes to make sure there was no flame. He was singed, but unharmed. At least the blast of air had dried his sweat. He licked his lips. There was little moisture left in him. Rubbing his face with his hands, he came to a decision. He couldn't turn back.

Around the next bend, a dark opening rewarded his persistence. The shadowed cavity looked as cool as a deep pool of water, but instead was hot as a furnace. Slowly, his heart pounding against his ribs, he approached it and peered inside.

Inside, the gloom and firelight revealed a cavern larger than the front room. It looked larger than even the whole house. It seemed impossible, yet there it was. Blackness danced along the edges in a rough circular shape. The walls were uneven, shaped by stalactites and stalagmites, but all of that was not what drew his eye. It was the beast at the center of the room.

It was as tall as a tree. Its sleek, silver scales glowed red around the edges, as if molten lava flowed through its veins. Chest heaving, Cyril followed the graceful lines with his eyes: up its studded back, around legs the size of boulders that ended in razor-tipped claws, and along the curved neck to its massive head. Its mouth was only slightly ajar, but flames licked from the sides. Its glowing eyes were locked on him. Even from across the room, he could feel its gaze. It penetrated him, laying him bare. There could be no secret, he knew, from the beast.

A shape moved near its feet, startling him. A man dressed only in pants, his torso bare, stood before the great dragon. His back was covered in symbols that glowed in the firelight. No, not symbols, spell forms.

Maester Griven!

As if drawn by Cyril's thoughts, the maester turned, his eyes quickly finding the boy standing in the doorway. What would he do to him? Should he run?

"Come, boy." Maester Griven's voice echoed across the giant chamber. "Come and meet our guest."

Still fearful of having been caught, Cyril obeyed. His desire to see the beast close-up overshadowed his fear.

As he approached, he noticed something he had not seen before. Great golden chains crossed the floor, attached to golden manacles that encircled the dragon's legs. This was no guest. This was a captive.

The dragon's glowing eyes burned, as if agreeing.

Griven looked between them, and then nodded as if approving of something unspoken.

"His name is Mnementh."

- 4 -

"What do you know of dragons?"

Cyril could barely gather his wits to answer. He knew what the song said, that the mighty dragons could see the unseen and steal away magic, but those words were vague, and came from legends and myths. Rather than say something wrong, he shook his head.

"It's difficult to put into words what dragon magic can do," the maester said, looking up at the great beast beside him. "Would you like to experience it? See with your own eyes what he sees?"

At those words, Cyril tore his gaze away from the dragon Mnementh and looked to Maester Griven's face. The heat in the air and the sweat on his bald head made the designs seem to writhe like red snakes. Was he serious? Could Cyril really see such a thing for himself? Or was the maester taunting him?

"Learn," his father had said.

Had this been what he'd meant? Had he known about the dragon? The idea of seeing such magic with his own eyes filled Cyril with excitement.

"Truly?" Cyril whispered.

His excitement was mirrored in Maester Griven's burning eyes. "Truly. I have perfected it." His smile was dark and triumphant.

He pointed to the gold manacles. "The gold contains the dragon's magic," he explained. "It's malleable. It holds it captive." He rubbed one hand across his head. "The taetaus allow me to pull it in. To focus it."

To control it.

The unspoken words echoed in Cyril's head. He blinked. Had Maester Griven said that?

"Come. I must make the connection."

One of the maester's skeletal hands clutched a gold manacle. The other beckoned the boy closer. Fear bloomed in Cyril's chest, filling him with a cold iciness that weighed him down like rock. Would it feel like the last time the maester had touched him? The agony of those probing fingers in his brain had nearly done him in.

Griven's face darkened. "Choose, boy."

Cyril licked his lips nervously. He wanted to know. Truly he did.

Are you strong enough?

This time, Cyril looked up. That was not the maester's voice. It was deeper. Richer. It was . . . liquid. He met the dragon's gaze, and a shiver worked through him. Before he could reconsider, before the fear could overcome him, he stepped forward and grasped the outstretched hand.

There was a sizzle and a snap. For a moment, he was sure he saw the lick of flames travel across those strange designs, the taetaus, and then the room disappeared. Everything was gone.

No, he realized. Not gone, just . . . different. Darker. He was higher up, looking down. Seeing . . . seeing an echo of light, blue against black. Two shimmering forms, connected. He realized he was looking at himself through the eyes of the dragon. Below, the glowing forms were he and Maester Griven. They pulsed. He could smell their breath, their . . .

Edah . . .

Ah, yes. The breath of life. The scent was familiar and wild. The magic in both of them was strong. One was Creative and Destructive. That was the captor. The usurper. The thief. That one thought he knew, but he was like a sightless bird, blundering through the air, flying without seeing.

The boy . . . the boy was different. The boy had Destructive, but he also had the balance. The void. Neutral. The boy could see.

Look, boy. Look through my eyes, and see your essence. Sniff through my nostrils, and smell the breath of life. Open your inner self, and see the magic.

The words thrummed through Cyril's soul.

Yes, the magic! It was like a current, running wild. He could ride it! He could fly, like—

His body jerked with a wrenching twist. He was being torn in half. A sickening pain flooded through him. He felt something hard knock the air from his lungs.

"Yes, the return can be difficult until you get used to it."

Cyril looked up. What was he doing on the floor?

"Could you see it?" Griven's eyes searched him. "Did you see it?"

Saw it. Felt it. Smelled it.

He nodded. Griven's feral grin filled him with loathing.

"What did it look like?"

He does not know, a voice whispered in Cyril's head. *He has looked, but he is blind to it. He does not have what you have. He does not have the balance.*

"I . . . I was looking down . . ." Cyril mumbled, not wanting to give away just how much he had felt. He didn't want Griven to know the kind of connection that he shared with—

Mnementh.

. . . the dragon.

"Such power," Griven hissed. "More than most imagine. It can be ours. Ours to control. To use."

Thief!

Mnementh's anger was palpable. It rolled along the boy's skin. Cyril knew then that Mnementh hated Griven. Hated the man who had trapped him and was using his power as if it were his own.

"Would you like that, boy? Do you want to taste that power on your tongue every day?" His greedy eyes glowed. "Will you help me?"

He tried to hide the suspicion that he felt. "Help you what?"

"Release it, boy. Release the power."

He would kill us both, Mnementh whispered in his mind. *Only you can give him the power to do what he wants. You are the key.*

He was the key.

He knew what he must do.

"Yes," he said softly. "I'll help you to release it."
Cyril's smile was grim. His father would be proud.
He was learning.

- 5 -

Dinner was one of the strangest things yet.

Appearing gleeful about Cyril's decision to help him, Griven had led the way upstairs and through one of the other mystery doors along the twisting hallway, revealing a heretofore unseen room dominated by an enormous table. The table's rich wood glowed red in the light from lanterns that were hung between heavy drapes, and the legs ended in carved dragon feet, replete with claws.

"Sit, boy." Griven said, sweeping his hand to indicate he didn't care where. "I'll check on our food."

He disappeared through another door in the far left corner. The smells that wafted in told Cyril that the food was indeed on its way. Who it might be making such delicious scents he couldn't fathom. He had seen no one else since arriving, nor heard other footfalls. Perhaps there were more secrets to this odd structure. All he knew was that he was ravenous. As if in agreement, his stomach rumbled.

He crossed to the other side of the table, the one nearest the wall. He was intrigued by the heavy drapes, and pulled one back to peek behind it. There were no windows. Instead, strange drawings marked the walls. Drawn in something dark, they looked as though someone had used charred sticks from a fire as an instrument. The designs were patterns, with spokes moving outward from a central point, surrounded by circles and webs at such an intricate level of detail he had to lean closer to make them out.

For reasons he couldn't articulate, the drawings made him nervous. He let the curtain fall and moved to another, feeling his insides clench as he drew it aside. Like the first, the fabric concealed no window, only more of the odd markings. If anything, these were even more intricate than the others, the tiny spaces between the spokes and the circling lines filled with images so small he couldn't make them out even when he narrowed his eyes.

Again, the crawling sensation of nervousness filled him at the sight. Were these spells? Had Griven drawn them? If he had, why here, on the rock walls of the dining hall? And why were they hidden?

Cyril heard footsteps approaching, and quickly let the curtain fall back into place, rushing to sit in one of the heavy chairs. His heart pounded, and his palms were wet. Why? What was he afraid would happen?

The door in the corner swung open, and a man carrying a heavy tray walked in, followed by a girl with a pitcher. Griven came in last, sitting at the head of the table even though it was two chairs away from where Cyril had seated himself. The man and girl laid their burdens on the large table, then left as quickly as they had come. Other than a faint impression of their age, Cyril could barely even say what they had looked like. A moment later Griven was lifting the lid away from the large tray, and all other thoughts and concerns were lost in the rich smell and dripping skin of the roasted meat in front of them.

A strange feeling tore through Cyril's body. It was more than hunger. It was beyond craving. It was a need. He wanted to plunge his hands into the meat and devour it, rip it apart with his teeth, and swallow dripping chunks of it. His throat worked convulsively as he tried not to let the strange feeling show.

Griven, however, appeared as lost as Cyril was. He grabbed two chunks of meat with his hand, using his knife to spear each one as he tore into it. The nature of it made Cyril's longing even greater. Unable to stand it any longer, he grabbed his own chunks. He didn't need a knife. He shoved the food into his mouth with his hands, pleased to find the meat still red and blood-filled beneath the darkened exterior. The flavors and scents filled him. Juices ran down his chin. He reached for more. Needed more. If only he could have caught it himself, been free to hold it down and tear into the tender flesh while it still pulsed with life—

No!

He dropped the meat he'd been holding, staring at it in horror. His hands were covered in fat and blood. He wiped at his chin, horrified to find more of the same. What was he doing? These thoughts were not his own! He was acting like some kind of . . .

Beast? Is that what I am?

Mnementh.

He shoved his chair away from the table, feeling suddenly sick and dizzy. Was that how it would be now? Would they forever be connected? He looked up to find Griven staring at him, his narrow eyes glowing, mouth pulled back in a pleased grin.

He knew! Griven knew Cyril and the dragon were connected!

Panic filled him; his heart thundered against his ribs. Did Griven sense it? Could he hear the thoughts that filled Cyril's mind?

He knows, but not fully. Mnementh's liquid voice soothed. *He is not as we are.*

Cyril stumbled away from the chair. He needed to get away from there. His stomach clenched angrily, yet the food did not come back up. His body wanted the meat, even if his mind didn't.

The door on the other side of the room wavered as he stumbled toward it, and his feet felt heavy and uncoordinated. He nearly fell twice, but finally grasped the latch and pulled it open. He fled into the dark hallway, hearing soft laughter follow him.

Griven.

He leaned one hand against the rough stone wall to keep himself from falling, and lurched toward the relative safety of his room. Once in it, he ripped away his clothes, using the material to scrub at his face and hands. He tossed them in a ball into a corner, then knelt before the chest, pushing back the lid. He dug through his clothes for something clean, something that smelled of home, and not this dungeon; this snake pit. He pulled on pants and a soft shirt his mother had made for him, and then his hands landed on the pair of balled-up socks near the bottom. The hard lump at one end told him that his treasure was still there, still safe.

Greedily he tore at the material, eager to have it in his hand. It dropped into his palm, the heaviness of it pushing his hand down. It was cool against his hot skin, feeling like a balm.

Riven stone!

So the dragon knew what it was.

Of course I know! His response was immediate and offended. *I am not a fool. Besides, I am magic-born. We know of such things.*

Yes, of course he would. He would know how the riven stone worked, and also what Cyril was planning to do with it. More importantly, he would know why.

We are of like mind, Mnementh agreed.

Cyril rolled the small dark silver-colored stone between his fingers. It was heavy, but perfectly balanced. It shifted easily between his fingertips as he moved it from one to the next. As he moved it faster, the silver color began to glow. Faster and faster he shifted it, until the rock moved through the air almost of its own accord, and the light blurred into a solid glowing line in the air.

With his free hand, Cyril summoned his Destructive magic. A ball of darkness rose above his palm, shifting and coalescing until it was a perfect sphere of midnight.

They were both perfect.

Cyril clapped his hands together sharply, striking the silver of the riven stone with the black Destructive magic. Lightning shot away in all directions, filling the room with an electrical charge that lifted his hair from his head.

Then it dissipated, and with it, the weight of the web that had been cast over him. Immediately his stomach settled, and his heart returned to a normal rhythm. He heaved a great sigh, then shook his head. He should have known. Should have suspected that Griven would not trust him so quickly, or offer something so powerful without a catch. He'd only realized it when Griven had grinned at dinner (if you could call what they had done something so civil as dinner).

Griven had not known what kind of connection would be made with the dragon, but he was no fool. He had cast a web spell over Cyril, trapping some of his thoughts and emotions, monitoring them.

You're good, Cyril thought, his mind finally his own again, *but I have some tricks of my own, old man.*

He tucked the riven stone back into its hiding place. He would have to be more careful from now on. The connection with Mnementh was temporarily broken as well, the riven stone doing its work completely, but he knew that would be easy enough to restore. They shared something Griven did not, and he could tap into it at any time.

He was almost ready.

- 6 -

"Sit still now," Griven said, his tone clipped and humorless.

He sensed it. He could feel that he'd lost his hold on his acolyte, but he didn't know how. Cyril fought to hold back a triumphant smile. Griven might suspect, but he could never truly guess. Riven stones were extraordinarily rare. There were only a handful in existence as far as anyone knew. After all, it was unusual enough for *people* to travel through the Divide, let alone a stone, but then for someone to find it and recognize it for what it was? Even his father had never suspected such a thing. Especially from Cyril's mother.

She had pressed it into her son's hand on the night before his tenth year began.

"I know not when you will need this," she'd whispered into his ear, leaning over him in the darkness, "but need it you will."

Her breath had been a tickle on his face.

"She's seen it."

She. The seer. The woman Father had forbidden her to visit. Oh, how furious he would be if he knew.

"You'll keep our secret, won't you?"

He'd heard the sadness in her voice, and the fear. He'd nodded then, accepting her gift and her secret. He hadn't realized yet what it could do, that small heavy stone, but it was a gift. The only one he'd ever gotten. He was loath to give it up. Later, when she'd explained how it worked, he was glad he'd kept it. Later still, when he'd first had need of it, he was even gladder.

No, Griven might sense that he'd lost his web of power, but he could not know how. Perhaps he thought that somehow Cyril was strong enough to break it on his own. If so, that was good. Let him be nervous.

The razor-sharp edge of the long blade slid along Cyril's skin, Griven's hand steady and sure. Cyril felt the soft sigh of movement as a swath of hair slid down his bare shoulders and onto the floor. Dark hair, he saw, with only a hint of his father's red. Good. His father had no place here. Not in this.

It only took a few minutes to shave away the hair, leaving his head as bald as Griven's. Next came the taetaus. Griven had ground some kind of red rock into a powder, adding other powders from small glass jars and vials, and then a drop of shining liquid. He stirred it all into a paste, dipping in a small brush and dragging it along the freshly shaved skin. A shiver rippled over Cyril, though whether it was from the paste or something more he didn't know.

"The taetaus will allow the use of your Neutral as a conductor," Griven had explained, "to infuse the magic into the ring."

A gold ring, as it turned out, that Griven had already prepared with spells, ready to capture and contain. Ready to be filled with dragon magic.

And your own, Mnementh cautioned. *He will do more than use your magic for this fusion: The circle to represent unending magic, the gold to contain my own, and the pairing of our balance and our breath of life to complete it. He will weave your essence with my own into the very soul of this object. Man with beast. Merged.*

Can it hurt us? Cyril sent his question silently.

Only in that one moment, when he holds the power between us and the ring. As he draws from us both, we will be vulnerable.

He hated that word, Cyril could tell. A creature as mighty as a dragon must loathe being vulnerable.

And after? Cyril asked.

Once it is done, it is done. The ring will contain the power, but we will be restored.

The ring would contain the power. Just the idea of it thrilled him.

He must not be allowed to have it. Even to touch it. Once it is complete, it will carry the combined power of us both, stronger than either.

No, he must not be allowed to have it, Cyril agreed.

He had opened his thoughts completely to Mnementh, and now the bond between them was uncluttered by Griven's clumsy intrusion. It was stronger than anything he'd known before.

What will you do with it?

The ring? I will hide it where Griven can never reach it.

Between worlds. Good, Mnementh approved. There was a pause. Then, *What will you do with him?*

Cyril felt a slow smile spread across his face.

Nothing. I will leave him for you.

The feelings that filled him then were not his own. Mnementh's pleasure, his anger, his fury at being held captive for so long, his desire for retribution of the theft of his power by Griven was so strong it was overwhelming. Cyril felt himself wobble and nearly fall from the chair.

"Be still!" Griven hissed. "The forms must be exact!"

With force, Cyril pushed Mnementh's feelings to the back of his mind. The forms must be exact. He didn't want anything to go wrong. Not now. Not when they were so close.

And when it was all over, he would return home and show his father exactly what he'd learned.

- 7 -

"It's time."

A pressure filled Cyril's chest. He wasn't sure what it was at first. Dread, excitement, fear, anticipation . . . It felt as though his whole life had led him to this exact moment.

"Don't worry," Griven said, misinterpreting his hesitation. "It's no worse than what you felt the other day"—his dark eyes burned —"and when it's done, you will be witness to the true power of the dragon."

He means to use it on you first, Mnementh said.

But Cyril had already known that.

It didn't take much of a leap to figure out why Griven had needed an acolyte, or why he'd paid so handsomely for one. How much, the boy wondered, had it taken for his father to sell his only son?

"Are you ready?"

He opened his mouth to form the word, to affirm his commitment to the plan, but at that moment a pounding echoed through the hall.

Both turned to look toward the front room. Who could it be? Who would visit this alien and profane place? There was a reason it looked as if it had been heaved up from the bowels of the earth. A reason it looked as if it had been melted and reformed. Griven was Destructive first, but he was also Creative. His unholy creation mirrored his blasphemous heart.

"Go and see who it is," Griven hissed, shoving him toward the door. "Send them away. I have work to do."

And with that, he disappeared through the doorway, down into the depths of his lair.

Cyril walked slowly into the front room. His mouth was dry. His heart beat like a rabbit's. He gripped the bar that secured the door, his hand closing over it on the far end. All he had to do was push it down. The counterbalance would lift the other end and clear the latch, allowing the door to swing open. It was just another way Griven used clever deceptions to impress and intimidate.

The knock came again, startling him.

Whoever it was, they weren't going away. This was stupid. Why was he afraid? He had nothing to fear. Not now, and soon enough not ever again. Annoyed, he pushed down on the bar. The door swung open. He paused in the shadow of it, but no one came in. Grinding his teeth together, he moved into the doorway.

The light of the sun nearly blinded him. He threw a hand up over his face. Not even a week he'd been here, and already he was like a cave dweller. The sun threw a swath of light into the room, as if sniffing out an adversary. Cyril took an uneasy step backward.

Standing outside the door, framed by the sun, there was a figure. His face was invisible, the glare a halo of brightness around him. Cyril squinted, ducking his head and turning it to try to get a glimpse of the stranger.

"Who is it?" he asked. "What do you want?"

"Cyril?"

He gasped, the use of his own name striking him like a hammer on a string, sending reverberations through his entire being. He licked his lips and tried to swallow, but his mouth was too dry.

"Who are you?" he whispered.

"I am called by many names," the man answered.

What kind of answer was that?

"Why are you here?"

The man's face began to appear amidst the bright light, Cyril's eyes slowly adjusting enough to see. The face was strange. It was twisted and pulled.

"Your mother sent me."

The words rocked him. His mother? How did she know this man? Why would she send him? Did she know somehow? Despite what his father said, she had always seemed like the stronger one. She knew things no one else did. For this man to show up now, it could be no coincidence.

He stared into the twisted face. The eyes were pulled in such a way that they looked sad, yet the mouth smiled. It was scars, he realized. His face was twisted with scars.

"Why are you here?" he asked again, only this time it meant so much more.

"You must choose," the scarred man said softly.

Cyril wanted to protest. He wanted to claim he had no idea what the strange, crazy man was talking about, but he would be lying.

He knew.

This man, this stranger covered in scars, was more than he seemed. He was Wardein; those of legend sent to guard and protect people in need. Cyril had always thought it no more than legend, yet as he stared into the man's face, he knew it was not. This man was a Traveler of the High King, sent to offer him pardon.

Like the bar on the door, his life was balanced on a fulcrum. In this one moment, it could still swing either way.

He could go home to his mother, his bed, and the fields of tall grasses on the plains. He could walk away from Griven and his dark schemes. He could walk away from Mnementh. He could even find another place. A place where he could start again, without the veil of darkness hanging over him that this place had created. He could wash away the stain that covered him. This man, the Wardein, was giving him what his father had refused to let him have.

A choice.

Right now, in this moment, Cyril could choose who he would become. He could choose the light or embrace the darkness.

He was young, and he was strong. Stronger than he'd ever realized. Stronger than his father had been willing to believe. He'd wagered money on it, and he'd been wrong. His son was as strong as . . .

A dragon.

Below his feet, the floor vibrated. Mnementh waited. The power waited. Griven would make his ring. The Ouroboros, he called it. The dragon between worlds, born of Neutral magic. It would be a ring imbued with all the power of a dragon, but also more. It would contain a piece of Cyril's edah. The essence of who he was. The two combined would create such power as he could only imagine.

"Choose," the man said again. His voice had the ring of finality.

The sun had lowered. Soon it would touch the edge of the world and disappear.

If he left, if he walked away, he would never know the kind of power that awaited him below, in the bowels of this place. He might learn magic and become a maester himself, but he would lose Mnementh. He would lose his chance. He would never feel the power of a dragon thrum through his veins.

Choose, Mnementh whispered into his mind.

That liquid voice filled him with a coolness that was like a deep river, flowing over and through him.

The plan was so simple, really. Almost too easy. Mnementh hated Griven. He hated the man who had chained him in this abomination of a place for so many years, using him at will like a hammer and nails. Griven must never be allowed to touch the ring. Keeping him from it would be easy. Cyril wouldn't have to kill him. All he needed to do was let Mnementh loose. Unlock the manacles.

Free the dragon.

Mnementh would take care of Griven, and then the power of the ring in all of its dark glory would be his to do with as he would. The blended magic of man and dragon, contained in a single band of gold, would belong to him.

Cyril looked back into the scarred face of the Wardein, framed by the setting sun. The twisted lips were turned down, his eyes sad. They pleaded with Cyril to change his mind, but he could not. There had never really been a choice. Not for him. His life had led him here. This was his destiny, and he was going to grab it with both hands. He was going to ride the dark wind.

Slowly but firmly Cyril closed the door, shutting out the light.

About T.E. Bradford

Tracy wrote her first complete story and her first song when she was twelve. They set an early tone for her desire to express faith and inspiration with words and music. Since then, she has continued to express herself, and to convey her beliefs in stories and song. She has published poems and articles in various literary magazines, and her column "Inside Technology" ran in the Harbinger out of Mobile, Alabama, for several seasons. As co-owner and a senior editor of ABC Editing Services, she helped aspiring and self-published authors achieve their goals, and is proud to have several books on her shelves at home that recognize her contributions to their success.

Tracy found her true writing voice when she combined young adult with fantasy, added a dash of music, and wove in a breath of spirituality. She will tell you that her husband once told her that kids today know more about fictional characters than they do about God. It is her deepest desire that through her words and stories she might be able to change that, and to shine a light that will help others find their way when the path is dark.

METAMORPHISTRY

By Jeff Wheeler | 7,500 words

The sun pierced brightly overhead, and the cobblestone streets were choked with dust and noise from the crowd of street hawkers and citizenry pressing to get into the giant arena in the heart of the city of Vaud.

Brandis noticed that his shadow had compressed beneath the soles of his boots and he paused and craned his neck, shielding his face as he squinted up at the sun. It was noontide and cheering had started up within the huge stone walls of the coliseum.

His valet, Roshaun, turned back and gestured at him to keep moving. "You can't stop in the streets, Brandis. You'll get trampled this close to the walls. I think I see the seventh arch over that way. Hurry, or you'll miss seeing her because of the crowd."

Sweat tickled the back of his neck beneath his mane of long hair. "I think she'll wait for me, Roshaun. She was more than a little interested, I think."

"Your title means nothing in this city," the valet said, laughing. "The Black Forest is hundreds of leagues away. Your father's castle is smaller than that inn." Another roar of cheers swelled from within. "The gladiators have started already? I don't want to miss all the fighting! Can we hurry?"

Brandis put his hand on the hilt of his sword as he walked. His tight white jacket was stained from the ever-present dust, and its epaulets bounced as he followed Roshaun up the steps. He stroked his goatee, having spent sufficient time grooming it earlier that day.

He wanted to look his best for her. He had made sure Roshaun had polished the family crest on his sword hilt.

The two approached the tall archway and found the gate beneath it was closed and locked with guards standing there. Roshaun held up his hands to Brandis to show he would take care of things, and he quickly walked ahead and spoke to the sentries posted. Brandis fumed with frustration. He had tried taking a carriage there, but the streets were so thick with people they could hardly move, and so the two had abandoned the driver to cross the rest of the distance on foot.

A groan from the crowd meant that someone had been struck down. Roshaun gesticulated to the sentry, speaking quickly and urgently. The sentry got the attention of his captain, who was watching the match in the heart of the coliseum, who then nodded vigorously and came to the gate with his keys.

"You have not missed much, Lord Brandis," the captain said. "Estenna informed us you were coming. She's waiting in her brother's box. It is one of the best views in the coliseum."

"I know," Roshaun said eagerly, clenching his fists. "Are there truly werewolfs in the arena, Captain? It's not just a tale?"

The captain snorted and laughed, which could have meant anything. "You foreigners are all the same, inventing foolish names—garwalfs, ulfhennin, weriuuolfs. They're *lycanthropes*. I work below the arena and have seen them transform. You won't believe what I tell you until you see it with your eyes. Well, satisfy your eyes, then. See for yourself. Meecham—take them to the Keltin box first."

The sentry bowed swiftly and brought them around the corner to a wide stairwell that zigzagged up the coliseum. The crowds gathered were cheering and waving kerchiefs. There were people of every fashion, every dominion throughout the lands who assembled at the lake city of Vaud. Brandis was nervous as they climbed the private stairwell, picturing her rust-colored hair and intriguing smile in his mind, trying to still the buzzing giddiness that threatened to make him grin like a fool when he saw her. Roshaun hastily climbed the stairwell, intent on aiding his master.

"This way," the sentry said, leading them up even higher. How many levels were inside the coliseum? Four? Five? Brandis's heart was pounding from more than emotion now. His legs were aching at the climb, but he was healthy and had the stamina to endure such an ascent. They reached the top ring of the stadium where he was impressed by the statuary waiting for them.

"By the arts," Roshaun said in awe, staring at the different poses of horror-stricken figures.

"Those aren't statues. They were all transformed by a medusa," said the sentry, gesturing. "Before she was caught and killed."

"Are you toying with us, man?" Brandis asked with a quirked smile, narrowing his gaze.

"Of course he is," Roshaun said. "It's fine work, but these were carved."

The sentry looked at them with contempt. "Think what you will. There is a reason that Vaud has the University of Metamorphistry. For a thousand years its sorcerers have studied that particular art. Are you a prince? From where?"

"The Black Forest," Brandis replied stiffly. "In Hennland."

The sentry sniffed and grunted. "Vaud stood here when your kingdom was nothing but twiggy saplings. And the Keltin family is one of the oldest." He stopped at a curtained door and bowed, gesturing for them to enter.

Brandis, feeling overwhelmed at the grandeur and the spectacle, mustered his dignity, straightened his posture, and waited as Roshaun brushed dust from his shoulders and back. Then his valet pulled aside the curtain and Brandis, gripping his sword hilt again, strode into the box where he saw Estenna and her brother.

"You came!" the girl said with enthusiasm, her blue eyes flashing with eagerness. He adored her eyes. "I was afraid you might have been stranded in the crowd." She wore a beautiful gown the color of dappled peaches, clasped at the shoulders with intricate brooches, that exposed her skin and the slope of her neck, where he saw a glimmering series of necklaces and medallions. Her long arms were bedecked with bracelets and her beautiful auburn hair was pinned on one side. She was a vision, and he felt his throat tighten with involuntary thirst.

"The crowds were eager to enter as well," Brandis said, giving her a little bow. "If you hadn't shared the secret entrance, we would have been lost in the throng."

"I know, which is why I told you. Gervase, he's here. The one I told you about who attended the lecture yesterday."

"Hmmm?"

Her brother was of the same height. He had dark brown hair instead of red, and it was spiked and askew. He hadn't shaved in days and a scrappy beard covered his cheeks and chin. His doublet was unbuttoned, revealing a lean chest beaded with sweat. He had a silk shirt and leather bracers that sparkled with inset gems the size of walnuts. Brandis felt his own attire paled next to both of theirs.

"He's the one I told you about," Estenna said coaxingly. "The prince from Hennland. I wanted you to meet him."

"I don't recall you asking," Gervase said, shrugging. He gave Brandis a dispassionate look. "So, you've come to see the wolf baiting?" He waved his hand to the balcony rail. "See it, then. Watch the populace gorge their senses in blood."

As if to bolster his words, another roaring cheer went up from the audience. Roshaun hurried to the edge of the balcony to witness the spectacle.

Estenna took Brandis by the arm to escort him. "It can be gruesome. Up this high, the details are difficult to see. The lower seats are the most popular ones. The closest to the fighting." Her touch, even gentle, sent a thrill through him.

He was hesitant to look, afraid of what he might see—the sight of blood had always made him a little squeamish, although he'd faced his disgust and had learned to master his reactions. Roshaun's eyes were bulging already, a look of euphoria on his face.

Brandis gazed down at the sandy bit of the arena floor. There were twelve gladiators battling fiercely below. Three had already gone down. One was dragging himself away with a spear stuck in his shoulder.

The gladiators were of various sizes and strengths. Some had whips. Some had axes. One hefted an enormous halberd. They wore armor on their shoulders and ragged loincloths that appeared to be wolf hide. Brandis squinted as one of the warriors struck down another from behind, earning a loud "Booo!" from the crowd.

"Those are the lycanthropes?" Brandis asked her, squinting in confusion. "I thought . . . I thought they'd be wolf men."

She laughed richly. "It's high noon, Prince Brandis," she said. "This is when their power is the weakest. This is when they are allowed to fight. When it is safest for them and for us. Can you imagine a full moon? They would all go mad with bloodlust. The walls are too tall to scale, but imagine if one did! The devastation they'd wreak in the crowd!"

Brandis was confused. "But how do you . . . what I'm saying is, how do you know they are really wer—lycanthropes. Have you seen them change?"

Gervase had wandered up and stood next to his sister. "You only believe that which you see?" he asked sternly. "How limited."

"It's not that. Where I am from, this *disease* is considered quite rare. No one has actually seen a transformation. We've only seen the evidence of it."

"The claw marks, the drool, the torn clothing," Gervase said dismissively. "It's not a disease, good sir. It is a magical curse. It is within the domain of Metamorphistry. Do you know what this means?"

Brandis bristled but he did not want to offend. "It is the art of transubstantiation. Turning one thing into something else. Like a caterpillar into a butterfly."

"Or a worm into a beetle," Estenna said approvingly. She squeezed his arm. "My brother is *the* expert of this art. He knows more than the chancellor at the university."

Gervase shrugged, but Brandis could see in his laconic smile that her praise pleased him.

"So you have seen the transformation yourself?" Brandis pressed, looking away from the battle raging below.

"Hundreds of times," Gervase answered flippantly. "I study it closely every moon cycle. I've documented the patterns starting from initiation to weakness that occurs after the regression. I know how long it lasts until madness, and I've measured its effects in ways you cannot possibly imagine."

Brandis's interest was more than piqued. "What have you written on your findings? I would very much wish to learn more."

Gervase turned to him, arching one brow. "It doesn't interest me to write it down."

"Why not? Such a work would be invaluable. Every university from here to Sangrall would want to know it, surely!"

Gervase scratched the corner of his mouth. "I care nothing for that."

Estenna's eyes gleamed. "He is trying to discover the *cure*, Prince Brandis. Would that not be of more use to your people in the Black Forest? Would that not be of greater use to the world?"

From the moment Brandis had met her, he had been entranced by her passion, by her determination. He had attended a lecture discussing the slavery conditions among the gladiators of the arena. She felt it was unfair that people inflicted with such a condition, lycanthropy, should be arrested and confined for the remainder of their lives to fight the blood sport of the city. She had believed that with treatment and precautions, those inflicted with the ... the magical curse could live freely, despite the mass prejudice against those who suffered from it.

At the time of the speech, he was not certain whether the malady was one of the mind—a sign of insanity. He had come to Vaud at his father's behest to learn more.

"Do you think it is even possible to cure it?" Brandis asked. "The legends say that once one is bitten, the doom is eternal."

"That's just a myth. If anyone can discover the cure," Estenna said proudly, "Gervase will find a way."

Brandis looked at the brother who smiled at his sister. Then Gervase turned his gaze on him. "You still don't believe."

He held up his hands. "It won't take much to convince me. The stories about the arena are that the gladiators use fake blood. The deaths are staged and then the warriors are brought back in different costumes or disguises. It's to entertain the masses."

Estenna's expression darkened. "I hate the gladiator trade," she said. "What they do to these victims defies conscience. They were people once, and now they've turned them savage."

"Or was it their savagery that made them transmute, Sister?" Gervase said, tapping his temple.

"I don't know what causes it," she said, turning back to Brandis. "But it is wrong to pen up these people and make them fight each other. Lycanthropes can be wounded, but they cannot die from their wounds unless the injury was inflicted with silver. They suffer, poor creatures, every time they perform in the arena."

"Surely you don't condone their execution?" Brandis asked.

"No! Of course not! For many it was no fault of their own. They were bitten. For some reason, a lycanthrope chooses a victim to carry on the curse. They are not killed as others are. We don't know why. No one does. My brother is closer to the truth than anyone has ever dared become because they have been afraid of being infected."

"Aren't you afraid?" Brandis asked Gervase.

The sorcerer shrugged. "I experience mild discomfort, but have hardened to the effects over time. A suitable series of precautions, in my view, has made it perfectly safe to work with lycanthropes. I'm not here for the sport, Prince Brandis. When the battle is done, I inspect the wounded and study the regeneration of their health. I assure you—the blood in the arena is not fake. So did you invite this prince to join us, Sister?"

Brandis glanced at Roshaun, who was still enthralled by the spectacle happening below. Brandis's ears were ringing with the sustained excitement. "May I?" he asked with growing interest.

Estenna beamed. "I did, Brother. He's come all this way from Hennland. You will see for yourself, then, Prince Brandis. These are pitiable creatures. We should help them, not fear them."

Gervase snorted. "But they represent our darkest fears," he said. "They embody it. So you do wish to join us? Do you dare it?"

* * *

Brandis was not sure what to expect as they descended into the bowels of the arena. Roshaun was edgy, his eyes darting to the sides as they entered the cavernous ground beneath. The stairs were wide and heavy, and there were scratch marks in the stone itself. Brandis stopped and traced his fingers in some of the grooves, imagining the strength it would take to leave such marks. He heard rattling noises, like hammers banging on well pipes, coming from different locations. The air was heavy and smelled of oil and iron. At the bottom of the steps, they reached a long corridor made of arches that shouldered the bulk of the massive weight of the coliseum.

Within the corridors, they saw servants wearing livery bearing stretchers, on which were the fallen gladiators. Some were groaning in pain.

"Can they transform down here?" Brandis asked, feeling his nerves growing more taut in anticipation. One of the pillars had a huge gouge in it.

"Those are marks from days past," Gervase said dismissively. "This coliseum is centuries old. Occasionally one of the lycan-thropes would escape confinement and try to flee. The panic that would cause! The people are terrified of these beasts. But there is a battalion of guards stationed here to prevent an outbreak, each man armed with silver-tipped spears and short swords and trained in subjugating their fear."

"Master Gervase!" one of the sentries called while carrying a stretcher. "Come see this one!"

Gervase quickened his steps, causing his sister and the others to hasten as well. When they reached the pallet being carried, the sentry looked excited.

"This is the one that was stabbed through with the spear. Nearly pinned him to the floor of the arena. Look, the wound has already closed! Nary a mark on him now."

Gervase squinted, looking at the man's back. Brandis saw that the fighter was heavily muscled, his skin a thatchwork of scars. "Of course it is. They cannot be killed save with silver. He will be walking in two days at the most. Even with such a wound. I've seen worse."

Estenna shuddered, her face twisting with sorrow and sympathy. She turned to Brandis. "Then he'll be compelled to go back into the arena again and again. It's brutal. It drives some of the poor fellows mad."

"Is it more merciful to kill them in the streets?" one of the carriers said. "Is it merciful to the poor families who lose loved ones due to their evil natures? The laws are strict to protect us."

"Yes, but if we can cure them," Gervase said, wagging his finger.

"Then no more coliseum?" answered the man with a snort. "I think not. The people will have their carnage. They must have it. They crave blood as much as these beasts do."

"Take him to his cell and I'll examine him later," Gervase said, waving dismissively. "My sister and I wish to show our guests some of the older ones."

The man chuffed and shook his head fearfully. "You couldn't get me down there. Not for thirty pieces of silver."

"How apropos," Gervase said with a cynical grunt. He turned to Brandis to explain. "The price of a slave. That is the reward when someone turns in a man who bears the curse."

"Are those who are turned in always guilty?" Brandis asked. They started walking farther down the corridor.

"What a terrible thing to say," Estenna said, looking at him with disapproval.

"He's honest, Sister. Do not fault him. As a student of human nature, I agree with the intent of your question. Let me answer it. There are simple tests we perform that can verify whether one is cursed. The captains of the night watch have all been trained to verify a lycanthrope. If someone is accused maliciously or falsely, there are consequences for the accuser. If it is an honest mistake, there is no harm."

"Are all lycanthropes men?" Brandis asked, trying to redeem himself in Estenna's eyes. He could see he had upset her and that made him anxious to appease.

"Not at all," Gervase said in annoyance. "Ah, here we are."

They reached another arched corridor, although this one was barred with silver. Gervase tapped one of the gems on his bracer and the gate began to life on its own or through some magic. Smoky torchlight wafted out from down the corridor.

"In we go," Gervase said eagerly.

Brandis turned to Roshaun who was visibly trembling with fear. Brandis gestured toward the gate, inviting him to remain behind, but his valet would never abandon him and quickly shook his head no.

Past the gate, they descended another series of stairs. They were in the catacombs now, the walls more rugged and containing rings with torches. The smell of pitch was thick in the air and it mixed with an earthy smell. Somewhere in the distance, Brandis could hear water running, like a brook.

"How deep do the caverns go?" Brandis asked.

"Farther than we will ever go," Gervase said. "We are nearly to the howling place."

Estenna sidled up closer to her brother, her mood even more somber now. The corridor narrowed.

A strange smell was in the air, the cloying smell of rancid meat. Brandis wanted to tug loose his collar. He was soaked with sweat beneath his jacket, and he gripped the handle of his sword nervously.

Gervase caught the gesture. "Little good that piece of steel would do you down here," he said with a smirk.

"Don't tease him, Gervase," Estenna scolded.

Some scuttling noises could be heard ahead. Then the echo of a mad laugh.

"What is this place?" Brandis asked, trying to keep the tremor from his voice.

"This is the lair, the howling place," Gervase said. "This is where they are confined after they've gone mad. It takes some time for that to happen. We've learned to feed their minds as long as we can. Inside, you'll see they revolt against any form of civilization. They rip apart any book that we send. They will no longer eat cooked meat. They'd drink blood if we let them."

Estenna looked back at Brandis encouragingly. "Don't be too frightened. They *are* behind silver bars."

"Silver bars," ghosted a voice from ahead. Estenna went quiet, her look darkening with sadness.

Brandis screwed up his courage and hastily wiped the sweat from his lip. As they turned the corner into another corridor, the way ended abruptly with another gate made of silver bars. There was a man posing there, leaning against the bars, gripping them hard. Little gusts of steam came from his hands.

"Good afternoon, Dracchus," Gervase said, stopping well away from the bars.

The man had feral eyes, unkempt hair. His tunic was slashed and ripped apart, nearly dangling from him. He twisted his head sideways, gazing at them hungrily, greedily, with all the ferocity of something savage.

"Is it afternoon, Sorcerer?" Dracchus asked, rattling the bars. "How should I know? There is no moonlight down in the howling place." He grunted and shook the bars.

There were more in chambers. Brandis saw smashed furniture, broken pieces of glass strewn everywhere. Books had been shredded and mangled, with bits and papers covering the floor.

"You don't need the moonlight anymore to transform, Dracchus," Gervase said simply. "This is a prince from the Black Forest. He'd like to see your form."

"From where?"

"The Black Forest. Do you know it still?"

The man shook his head, leering at them all. Roshaun was trembling, stepping back cautiously. Brandis's attention was riveted on the mad one. He reminded Brandis of the miller who had been bitten from the village. His insides twisted with disgust and intrigue.

"You wish to see my true form?" Dracchus asked him, grinning menacingly.

Brandis's voice was lost, but he nodded, swallowing, trying to keep his courage.

There was no convulsion, no gradual twisting, only an explosion of fur and fang and slavering jaws. Brandis's mind closed in terror as he heard it raving and snapping, trying to squeeze its massive bulk beyond the bars to rip his throat out. His mind went black, he was gibbering on the floor, and all reason and intelligence abandoned him in the urgent desire to flee. He whimpered and cowered in place.

He couldn't hear anything over the sound of his pulse, the mind-blasting terror. And then Estenna was kneeling before him, soothing him, bringing him back to himself with tenderness and sympathy.

"It's all right," she soothed. "They cannot hurt you. They cannot escape this place. It's all right. Gervase, drive him away."

As Brandis trembled like a frightened child, feeling humiliated at his reaction, Gervase grunted and snatched a torch from the nearby wall.

"*Shallic,*" he said, and the tip burst into smoky flame. He pressed the brand toward the silver bars, and the wolf fiend backed away, snarling and ravening, at the force of the flame.

"Come back to the surface," Estenna said, gripping Brandis's arm and helping him stand. "Now do you believe?"

Brandis trembled. The sound of Roshaun's steps faded into the distance. He nodded, still unable to speak. So it was real. It was very real.

* * *

That moment in the underground cave changed Brandis. Some might have run away in terror and fled to another city, never to return. For him, it opened vistas of possibility he had never considered. The Keltin siblings brought him to their mansion in Vaud, although Gervase and Brandis ended up spending most of their time at the coliseum where Brandis began to be tutored by the rich young man who had mastered the arts of Metamorphistry at a young age. Now it was Gervase's obsession to not only master them but to heal them.

Estenna was pleased by Brandis's ardent interest in the study and would participate in the discussions long after midnight. A fire had been lit inside of the young prince from the Black Forest. His valet, Roshaun, grew more and more worried.

Gervase and Brandis walked swiftly down the dark subterranean corridor, side by side. "So is the curse transmitted by the bite or not?" Brandis queried.

Gervase waved his hand. "Is that even the right question to be asking? A werewolf, as you still insist on calling them, eats prey of beast and man. Yet what stops them from slaying the victim that will transform? What about them is chosen to seed the curse into another generation?"

"Surely you've asked the gladiators and gleaned from their experiences?"

Gervase gave him another one of his condescending looks. Brandis had realized the man thought so quickly he became easily frustrated by others who could not keep up with the pace of his mind, let alone the pace of his walk. "Of course. Each story varies. I have found no commonality between them to link a cause. The cycle repeats itself over and over, as I've told you already."

Brandis turned to follow him into a cell where some guards were posted in front of an iron door.

The chief sentry, in his crisp tunic and armor, snapped to attention. "This one was brought in this morning. Turned in by his wife. She was a sobbing mess, horribly frightened, and hiding behind the guards as they took him away."

"Let me see him," Gervase said.

One of the guards opened the eyehole. "He's whimpering in the corner."

Gervase nodded curtly. The guard opened the heavy door and it groaned on the hinges. Brandis's pulse was quickening with excitement yet again, the thrill of facing danger. Beyond the iron door was a series of silver bars, as Brandis had seen before. The victim of the lycanthrope attack was sniveling. He was short, wiry.

Gervase touched a stone on his bracer, activating a magical ward. He stood at the bars imperiously. "What is your name, friend?"

"Moughton," said the man between sniffs. "Are you the sorcerer?"

"I am. Your wife turned you in?"

The man wiped his tears away. "She did. I tried to keep it secret." He looked up at the ceiling. "I didn't kill anyone, I swear it!"

"Not yet, anyway," Gervase snorted. "When were you bitten?"

"A month ago. I think. My memory is hazy now."

"That's usual. You thought you were sleepwalking at first." Gervase tilted his head to one side. "Then you woke up out of doors, without your clothes. You should have turned yourself in. The madness only grows worse without disciplined training."

Gervase had told Brandis earlier about the military regimen in the area underground.

"Am I going to go mad?" the victim hiccupped.

"Eventually," said Gervase without compassion. "Being here in the catacombs will help prolong your sanity. You'll be fighting in the arena, of course."

"I don't want to fight!" Moughton wailed.

"You don't really have a choice, now, do you? You're thin and quick. You'll do better than you think, especially as you get more used to the transformations. Some of the bigger ones will have a hard time catching you. That gives you an advantage."

Moughton sniffed. "Can you get me out of here, Sorcerer? I'd pay you. I'd pay you anything you ask."

"You cannot possibly pay me as well as the coliseum does, I assure you. Show me the mark where you were bitten."

Brandis edged closer to the bars. Gervase touched his chest and pushed him back. "He may look docile, but don't let it fool you. He can become savage in an instant. If you are within reach, he will try to attack you."

"Has that happened to you before?" Brandis asked softly.

Gervase nodded. "They'll try to trick and deceive a victim to get close. Sympathy is a powerful lure. Never succumb to it."

Moughton rolled up his sleeve and revealed a half-moon scar on his forearm. He twisted his arm around to show the other side.

Gervase stroked his goatee. "Most bites are on the forearm or the calf muscle. The calf if running away. The forearm if facing the creature and cowering. As you learned for yourself, it is very difficult keeping your presence of mind when one transforms."

"How do you do it?" Brandis whispered.

Gervase pursed his lips. "I've trained myself not to fear. The bars protect us. The distance protects us. The scent from the torches protect us. Fear is an irrational thing anyway."

"How did you master it?" Brandis asked, genuinely curious.

Gervase turned and started away. Brandis watched Moughton gazing at them. Just as Brandis turned to go, the young wiry man launched at the bars, reaching through with his hands, trying to snatch at Brandis. Steam began to hiss from the bars, and Moughton recoiled, scalded. He gave Brandis a cunning look. "You'll be one of us soon. Don't you see what he's doing to you? You'll be the next one in this cage."

Brandis backed away swiftly and exited the doors just after Gervase. The young sorcerer lifted his eyebrow. "Did he threaten you?" he asked.

Brandis nodded, feeling his skin crawl. He suppressed a shudder.

"They always do that. Don't mind it. They want to get into your head. You can hear a lie without believing it. You must have a will as strong as iron. Never let another think for you. Come to your own conclusions. Don't rely on me or anyone else. It is possible to break this curse despite what everyone says. The simplest remedies were once thought outrageous. We must tolerate the discomfort of not knowing."

Brandis followed him down the hall, nodding as they walked. Gervase was impressive. His mind was rigorous and disciplined. He was a genius, and he had fixed everything within himself on solving this problem. He sometimes missed eating for days as he pondered a problem. Food just wasn't important to him, which explained his gauntness.

Several days later, over supper, Brandis stared across the table at Estenna. He loved listening to her talk, the passion of her arguments in defense of the imprisoned gladiators. Gervase tolerated her discourse, but Brandis could see that the brother's thoughts were somewhere else. He sipped slowly from a goblet of wine, his eyes gazing into the hearth and its dancing flames.

"Sometimes I think he's not listening when he looks like that," Estenna confided to Brandis with a wry smile, "but then I ask him what I just said and he always surprises me by knowing the answer. He just thinks differently than anyone else I know."

"I like listening to you," Brandis said, feeling his cheeks flush with heat. "You've certainly inspired your brother's work. I asked Gervase a question, but he didn't answer it. How did he learn to conquer his fear?"

Estenna nodded and traced the rim of her goblet. Her lashes were incredibly long. "He's been bitten many times," she answered.

Brandis leaned forward, staring at her in surprise. "By werewolves?"

"No, of course not," she answered. "He's not that rash. Most people instinctively fear serpents. There is something about them that make us wriggle with horror inside. Well, Gervase said that fear is simply pain of the anticipation of something evil. We fear a snake because we fear being bitten. So he purchased snakes. He learned to handle them, to control his fear. After he had done so, he began handling poisonous ones. He was bitten sometimes, but always had a curestone handy. He conquered his fear of pain by willingly enduring the pain."

Brandis was more than impressed. "That takes phenomenal courage."

"Although it is powerful, fear is just a feeling," she said. She glanced away a moment and then met his stare. "There are other powerful feelings as well." She blinked at him, smiling openly. Then she scratched the side of her neck and rose from the table.

His mouth went dry. Her look was a little flirtatious, an invitation to follow her. Was he reading it right? Was she returning his interest at long last? His palms became sweaty.

Brandis leaned back in his chair, wondering how he could dismiss himself without rousing suspicion. Gervase was watching him, his brows needling in subtle vexation. That was the only mark, and it was very obscure. A flush of guilt crept into Brandis's chest.

"Is something wrong, Gervase?" Brandis asked him.

The young sorcerer's eyes did not meet his. No, he was looking across the room, not at an object, but at something within his mind. Then a brightening came, then a quivering smile. "It cannot be this easy. But perhaps ... perhaps ... but that does make sense. The moon. The stone gaze. All of them, it starts in the ocular recess. The eyes. Yes, the eyes. Is that it?" His fingers fidgeted on his lips. He was mumbling to himself, gazing down at the table, growing more and more agitated.

"I don't understand you," Brandis said, shaking his head.

"No, of course you don't. Of course you don't see it. *See* it." He rose suddenly from his chair and started to pace. "It's one of the philosopher sayings." He snapped his fingers in repeated fashion. "Yes! That might be it."

Brandis stared at him. He'd never seen Gervase so animated, so enthralled with himself. And while he was muttering under his breath, he strode out of the room in a hurry, heading toward his private study, the enormous library. That left the young man alone in the dining hall. It was Roshaun's evening off, and he was likely at a tavern enjoying his freedom. Brandis glanced at the door to the study and then to the door that Estenna had departed from.

He pushed his chair away from the table and followed the girl.

There was no one in the corridor beyond. The lamps were flickering and no servants were present. The house was quiet. Disappointment stabbed through him and he shook his head and started toward the stairwell to the row of guest rooms. Noises from carriages could be heard outside—the city of Vaud was always in high dudgeon regardless of the hour. He trod up the stairs, holding on to the wooden bannister, and climbed up in the dark toward the next level. As he reached the turn of the first landing, he heard a small noise behind him and turned back to look while his hand groped for the sculpted banister knob. When he set his hand on it, he touched skin instead, a hand already there.

Estenna was waiting for him on the midlevel plateau around the corner. Her sudden arrival had surprised him, but the jolt of fear quickly turned to more pleasant sensations.

"Is he distracted?" she whispered. Her breath tickled his cheek.

He was startled, pleased, and enthusiastic. "He just went into the study."

She took her hand away from the knob and then wrapped her arms around his neck and leaned up on her toes, kissing him. It was not the kiss of long experience. It was one from a girl who had been imagining what it might be like. Despite the brazen ardor, she was still shy and pulled away, giving him a hopeful look.

"Did you . . . did you like that?" she asked breathlessly.

Brandis pulled her close and leaned down, kissing her instead. He felt her lips pull into a smile as he withdrew. "Very much," he mumbled, his throat tightening as his feelings tugged loose and began running rampant in his chest. He watched her, mesmerized. The emotions were overwhelming and so exquisite. He didn't want to ruin the moment. He wanted to savor it.

After that small smile, she gave him another shy look. "I wanted that," she said. "Gervase is going to send you away. I just wanted to know what it felt like." She traced her finger down his chest.

"Why?" Brandis asked, shaking his head. The thought of leaving was painful. "I want to help with his work. With *your* work."

She smiled but glanced down. "Gervase doesn't want to share the credit of his discoveries with anyone. It must always be him. You're very clever, Brandis. I would like to visit the Black Forest someday. But that would not be possible. I will dream about you when you are gone." She pressed her cheek against him, pulling him into a possessive hug.

He was torn, the warm feelings dissipating like smoke. Conflict raged inside. "He cannot make me go," Brandis said, smoothing her wildfire hair, his voice rising in anger. She held her fingers to his lips to quiet him. He composed himself and lowered his tone. "If I cannot stay here, I will stay elsewhere. I want to be near you."

She looked up at him, pleased by his words. "It would be difficult to see each other," she said, biting her lip. "We couldn't keep it a secret long."

"Why should we?" Brandis asked. "I want to be your suitor, Estenna. I'm surprised you don't have several, but with such a guardian as Gervase, maybe it's not a shock. I will send Roshaun tomorrow to find other lodgings. This is a vast city. Surely he'll find something. I will not be far away."

She brightened. "I wasn't sure you felt the same way I did," she said, flushing. Then she leaned up and kissed his cheek and the dimple by his ear. "Send Roshaun to the coliseum. I'll leave notes for him where we can meet next."

Brandis's heart was racing with wonderment. "I'll come. I promise."

And he kissed her again.

And again.

* * *

Brandis's sleep was blissful. The bed cushions cradled him like feathers, and his dreams were of a soft mouth and eyes as shining as stars. Then his sleep was violently ripped away. A leather hood was dragged over his face, and burly men grabbed his ankles and wrists. He tried to wrestle, tried to yell, and a fist slammed into his stomach, doubling him over. Chains were fixed to his wrists and ropes bound his legs to the knees. He wriggled and struggled, panting, frightened out of his wits.

"He's a strong one," coughed a voice.

"All of the 'thropes are strong," breathed another.

Brandis felt the suffocation start because of his lack of air under the hood.

Then he heard Gervase's voice. "Take him to the coliseum."

He lost all sense of direction except that he felt them jogging down stairs. Was it night? Was it day? He hadn't been able to tell before the hood made it impossible. The bindings secured him and he finally quit struggling as his strength exhausted itself. The men abducting him were curt and uncommunicative. He was bundled away in a cage. He felt the metal floor and the bars pressing against his back. Then the cart jolted as the cage trundled down the road. Terror writhed inside his chest. He tried to banish it, tried breathing slowly. It was no use.

Hours later, Brandis found himself in a cell. The hood was finally ripped away and he glared at his captor, one of the coliseum guards who looked at him in disdain.

"You'll make a great one in the arena," the guard said coldly. "You've got the build."

"I am *not* a lycanthrope," Brandis said, his voice leathery. "What examination have you done? What pretext is this? Free me at once."

"A lycanthrope is easier to capture *before* he's bitten," the soldier sneered. His eyes were knowing. There was a stadium of spectators to appease. "Send word to the sorcerer that he's secure."

Brandis's stomach had compressed to the size of a walnut. He was hungry and fearful, his plight beyond imagining. Who would believe him in a city accustomed to werewolves in captivity? Even the legend of the founders of Vaud had been about werewolves. It permeated their culture. There were laws for such arrests, he'd been told. Was that merely deception? The gladiator games were a business, and men like Gervase held sway. Brandis had been utterly foolish and completely unprepared for the malice.

More time passed. The bonds chafed his arms. His resentment and fury built. It was murder. Sending him into the arena was murder. Putting him in a cage with a werewolf was just as vile. How was Gervase capable of something like that? How had Brandis not seen it in his eyes?

Time meant nothing in the dark. But eventually, there was the sound of locks and then Gervase stood outside the bars, staring at him as yet another specimen. None of the guards were there.

"Why are you doing this?" Brandis said.

Gervase's brow wrinkled. "Are you so daft as to even utter that question? There are two reasons and both are equally compelling. My sister, strangely, has fallen in love with you. Well, what she considers that emotion to feel like. She was sobbing at the manor for a while this morning. Quite hysterical. Her lover from the Black Forest was a werewolf in disguise. It couldn't be. Now she's determined to free you. She's at the gate right now with your servant trying to bribe one of the guards to admit her into the underground. They won't, I assure you. They've tolerated all her little speeches because of *my* work." He gave Brandis a cold smile. "But then last night I had the epiphany. Watching the two of you look at each other. Watching the bud of the flower open as you gazed adoringly at each other. It's rather sickening to an observer. But watching that, now I understand what causes lycanthropy. And it was you who taught me." He shook his head in amazement. "Not wittingly. You lack the knowledge and education. As I saw the way you looked at each other, it came to me. One of the philosophers' quotes. One I heard as a child. I haven't thought on it for years. The light of the body is the eye. If the light in your eye is darkness, how great is that darkness!" He started pacing in front of the cage. "Don't you see it, princeling? I couldn't deduce why some were spared and others not. It was in their eyes all along! It is *always* in their eyes! That is the key. How does a medusa turn someone into stone? Why was a weaver turned into a spider? Because she made things more beautiful than a goddess's! Jealousy, fear, lust—all exist in the eye. That is the answer to the riddle. A lycanthrope devours the good. It *spares* the evil."

Brandis was horrified. "I am not evil. What I feel for Estenna cannot be called that!"

Gervase shrugged, impassive. "What are feelings anyway? Truly, do you know? Can anyone know? We are controlled by them, like leashes. Except for me. I know the cure for lycanthropy now. I tested it on Moughton. The silver no longer burns him. The bite mark is gone. But what good will it do to overturn this order now?" Gervase stopped and stared down at him coldly. "I've spoken to the coliseum masters. They grow weary of the mundane, are always seeking something more exciting. And so I will give it to them. Wolves are not the only creatures that man can be transformed into. It wouldn't work for you anyway. A lycanthrope would *devour* you if I put you in a cage with one. Your motives are not the same as theirs. No, you will be the best gladiator in the arena when I am finished with you. What beast causes fear in all others? You wore the crest on your lapel when I first met you. A lion. That is what you really are, princeling. And you will rule this coliseum and rid us of the mad wolves."

He began an incantation.

"No!" Brandis said in despair. He squirmed against the bonds, but they were immovable. Unbreakable. He felt something inside his skin, something worming to get out. Gervase's hands began to glow as he continued the spell. He stared fixedly into Brandis's eyes.

Brandis tried to turn his head away, tried to shut his eyes, but he could not break Gervase's gaze. He felt his insides heaving, twisting, wrenching. He wanted to scream but couldn't find the breath. He was chuffing loudly, unable to groan, unable to express the agony as his limbs began to twist and contort. The pain was unbearable. He was stretching, each muscle twitching in spasms. His old life ripped apart, his sense of himself was gone in the chaos of rage and betrayal.

Gervase's eyes widened with awe, with glory, with exultation. "Look at you," he whispered reverently, magic darting across his fingers. "Look what I've made."

Brandis's chest swelled, his lungs filling with stagnant air. He needed to scream, to unleash the feelings inside of him. He opened his mouth to bellow.

And out came a roar.

The look of triumph in Gervase's eyes glazed away by sudden terror. The power inside Brandis was growing, equaling the rage, the ferocity. The metal was bending. Then it snapped.

Gervase staggered backward, falling to the floor, scrambling to get back, to get away. He heard a woman scream. There were footsteps running down the stairs, voices familiar and now totally incomprehensible. He stared down at his digits and saw the stubs of claws pressing out from the skin.

Darkness washed across Brandis's mind. He remembered no more.

* * *

Brandis awoke lying on the forest floor, nestled in pine needles. The sound of birds chirping came from overhead. He could hear every one of them in a glorious symphony. His stomach rumbled with hunger. Opening his eyes, he blinked. The colors—everything was new. He could see things he had never seen before. The colors were vivid, leaving trails before his eyes as he turned his head. Grunting, he shifted and tried to sit up.

Then he saw the fur on the back of his hands. His hands were bigger, the fingertips ending in pointed claws. Panicking, he started to breathe, filling his massive chest with air. His forearms were corded with muscle and tawny fur. Nearby was a small stream. His pants were shredded, his shirt was in tatters. He stood and felt the power of his leg muscles. There were no boots, only padded feet ending in claws. Brandis staggered to the edge of the brook and gazed down into the water.

A lion's face gazed back at him. Memories began to flash through his mind. A girl and a kiss. What was her name? He couldn't remember. But she had hair the color of fire. There was a man, a young man, shrinking in terror, gibbering, red slashes of blood on his chin, throat, and chest.

Brandis felt himself breathing fast.

How had he gotten to the woods? Where was he? He couldn't remember those details. But he did know some things. He was the Prince of Hennland. He was from the Black Forest. Where was he now? He stared at his paw-like hand, at the pads that were leathery and rough. Hands that had tried to kill.

Then he remembered. Gervase. Estenna. The cure.

Rage rumbled inside of him. Rage exploded inside of him and he lifted his face to the sky and he roared, and all the birds stopped singing.

About Jeff Wheeler

Jeff took an early retirement from his career at Intel in 2014 to write full-time and is now a Wall Street Journal bestselling author. He is, most importantly, a husband and father, a devout member of his church, and is occasionally spotted roaming hills with oak trees and granite boulders in California or in any number of the state's majestic redwood groves. He is also the founder of *Deep Magic: the E-zine of Clean Fantasy and Science Fiction*

A THEFT OF WORDS

By D.K. Holmberg | 13,800 Words

Novan the Historian secured the rope to the stone carving, wrapping it tightly before dropping the rope to dangle along the side of the building. If everything went as planned, the window would still be unlatched. Unfortunately for him, very little had gone as planned.

Checking that his pack remained clasped tightly to his back, he started down the rope. From the rooftop, he did not need to descend far. Not yet. That climb would be for later. He prayed his cloak disguised him, thankful for the cloudy night obscuring the sliver of moon. At least the darkness would shroud him.

As he climbed down the rope, his face pressed against the damp stone, which smelled of mold and the recent rain. His hands ached from clutching tightly to the rope, but he dared not relax for fear of falling. And then the historian would have to answer for his presence. He didn't dare risk drawing their attention, not until he knew for certain.

When he reached the window, he put a foot onto the protruding sill and carefully checked the window. It swung out. Some of the nerves he felt untangled then, and he sighed.

Novan climbed through the window, dropping to the stone floor on his soft leather soles. As he did, he froze.

Two lanterns still flickered in the library.

At that time of night, the library should have been empty. Nils, the ancient librarian, should have retired for the evening to his quarters on the second floor of the library. Had he simply forgotten to douse the lights? Novan brushed off that thought. The librarian would not simply forget to expunge the lanterns. That meant he was still there.

Novan looked back to the window. He didn't think that he could climb back *up* the rope—down had been hard enough. But with the rope left behind, the alarm would be raised. He would not get another chance at this. That meant it had to be tonight.

He crept along a row of shelves. Novan had been on this level before, but always accompanied by Nils, never left alone. A sign of Gomald's distrust of the guild. Rare that a historian would not be left alone to examine the works within the library, but it was also rare that a library possessed as many dangerous works as the Great Library of Gomald.

The lantern light flickered. Too late, he realized that he had failed to pull the window closed. A soft cool breeze gusted through the open window, carrying the scent of damp earth to mix with the musty odor of the ancient texts stored on the shelves.

He had to act quickly. Nils would know something was amiss. The librarian might be old, but he was astute and protective of the library like a merahl with her cubs.

Hurrying toward the back of the library, he found Nils straightening his back from where he was bent over a book. A lantern rested on the corner of the tall desk. The light flickered. Ink stained Nils's long face and hands, and the long quill angled in his arthritic hand bobbed on the page.

He looked up as Novan approached. Bushy eyebrows rose and a frown crossed his narrow lips. "Novan?" His voice carried a hint of confusion that turned to anger. "You shouldn't be here!" He shouted the last, loud enough that Novan suspected it could be heard near the guarded lower door of the library.

"I'm sorry, Nils," Novan said. He slipped his hand into the pocket of his cloak and grabbed the short knife he kept there.

As Nils backed away, he grabbed one of the books and turned as if to run. The old librarian was too frail to move quickly. That he tried made Novan wonder what it was he thought to protect.

Novan caught him and spun him. "Come sit. Be quiet and I will be done quickly."

"Is this how the guild operates now, Novan?" Nils asked. "You steal what you seek from the great libraries?"

Novan snorted. "Careful what you accuse me of," he said, flicking his eyes toward the stacks of books. Nils's eyes widened slightly. "Yes. I recognized most of these works. None should have been in

DEEP MAGIC ANTHOLOGY ONE

Gomald. Few should have existed outside the guild." That they had was a different issue, though one Novan would need to discover. The guild normally protected the original copies—those annotated by the historians themselves—but here, Gomald had a trove of such works. Either they were copies—rare enough, though known to occur on occasion—or there was another answer.

"These are the property of Gomald," Nils contested.

Novan sniffed, pulling Nils back toward the desk. That Nils didn't struggle should have raised Novan's alarm. "Property is interesting, isn't it, Nils? One can claim ownership as long as there is no objection. Interesting that the guild has not objected before now."

Nils narrowed his eyes but said nothing.

"Now, sit. I am not interested in that row of stolen documents." Nils looked at him, waiting. "But there are a few texts here that I *am* interested in."

Nils trembled. "And then you will leave?"

Novan nodded. "And then I will leave. The guild will learn of this collection, Nils. I will not be the only historian you will see."

"You think the guild does not know of this collection?"

Novan hesitated. The tenor to Nils's voice left him wondering. *Could* the guild know of this collection? He found the prospect unlikely, especially considering the fact that one of the works he had found came from Alaiht, and he *knew* that those had not been given to Gomald. That narrowed the options. But then, Novan wasn't exactly popular with the guild these days. Too many questions, and of the wrong variety.

"What I think is irrelevant," Novan answered. He knelt next to Nils and pulled a small roll of twine from one of the inner pockets of his cloak. Unspooling a few feet, he wrapped it around Nils's wrists and ankles, binding him tightly. "But there are a few texts that I need, so I will be borrowing them from the library. As we both know, they do not belong to Gomald, I do not expect you to come looking for them."

Nils frowned, his wrinkled brow darkening. "It is not me that you need to fear, historian."

As he said it, a loud rapping came from the door at the front of the library.

Novan jerked his head around, one hand gripping Nils's arms. The small man shouted.

Hating that he had to do it, Novan rapped Nils on the back of the head with the handle of the knife. He slumped to the ground, sprawled out.

He would have little time. Once the door opened, he would need to sprint toward the window and climb down the rope. Novan did not think he had enough time, not for what he had to do.

Starting toward the hidden stack, he glanced briefly at the book Nils clutched in his hand. His unconscious body was slumped atop it and Novan nudged him, sliding him over to reveal the small book. Pages of thick parchment were bound in stiff leather. Black ink appeared faded on the page, scrawled in symbols and runes that Novan had not seen before. The words written alongside the runes were familiar, though written in a tongue most had long forgotten. He wondered if Nils had recognized the words.

Novan grabbed the book. Not what he had come for, but he would look through it later. There were just too many questions for him to answer.

He jumped behind the tall desk and made his way to the stack along the back wall, hidden from the others. This was the reason he had come in the first place, the stack he'd struggled to get Nils to admit existed. Only after plying him with wine and hints of bribes had the old librarian admitted that he might have seen the works Novan sought. Novan had no confirmation until now.

A small shelf tucked into a wide stone pillar held seven books. None looked particularly special, and after glancing at the contents of the first few, some of them weren't. Three were. Each written in a tight hand that he hadn't seen in nearly a decade, with cryptic notes along the margins, making it clear to Novan that they were the originals. As far as Novan knew, no copies existed.

He grabbed them just as the door thundered open.

Novan sprinted past where Nils lay motionless, darting toward the window at the opposite end of the library. If he could reach it, he could throw himself out and down, slide down the rope and into the night.

A glint of light off armor caught his attention and he slid to a stop, jumping away toward a small table to hide. Novan ducked beneath the table just as the guard entered through the small doorway—far too small for a fully armored soldier—his oiled mail clomping across the stones. Gripping the stack of books he had pilfered from the library, Novan crept forward along the row of musty and ancient texts, mostly stolen copies of guild works that he ignored, careful to keep low, hiding the top of his head from view.

If he could just reach the window . . .

Something caught the guard's attention and he stomped toward it, running past the stacks of shelves with a rattle of metal. Dim lantern light flickered off his dull armor, but it was the unsheathed sword clutched in his hand that caught Novan's attention.

Novan froze, fingers gripping the thick leather spines, afraid to lose them after all the time he'd spent searching. These works did not belong in a place like this, no matter what reputation the great library of Gomald had. Had he another moment, he would slip them into the pack on his back, but he didn't dare risk making any sound or alerting the guard to his presence.

Soon the librarian would be found. Then the alarm would truly be raised.

It was his fault the guard had come in the first place. Novan had not managed to catch the librarian completely unaware, as much as he had tried, though he did not think it entirely his fault. At that time of night, this section should have been empty. What was Nils doing up anyway?

Novan shifted, drawing his cloak around him, trying to melt into the shadows. The guard made a few sounds near the back of the library. Where Nils was tied up.

He had to move. Waiting any longer risked capture, and the guild was not viewed favorably in this land.

Having no other choice, he unclasped his pack. The soft jingle of the buckle seemed to echo in the library. He slipped the books atop others.

Just as he heard the heavy clatter of mailed feet, he started toward the window. At least he had planned for his escape, had taken the time needed to open the glass. If only the rope held.

The guard drew nearer. Another dozen steps, Novan suspected, counting them off in his head. He reached the window and jumped over the edge, spinning and grabbing the rope to descend the three stories in darkness. Now if he could only climb down in time.

He worked his hands quickly down the rope. With Novan nearly to the bottom, the guard looked out the window. There came a shout from above him, though useless at that time of night as the rest of the castle slept.

The rope shook. Novan paused, looking up. The guard hacked at the rope with his sword.

Ten feet to the bottom. Too far to risk jumping, not if he wanted to walk out of the castle.

He slid. The rope burned through his hands, tearing flesh from his palms as he went down the last few feet. Just as his feet touched the soft dirt, the rest of the thick braided rope came coiling down around him.

Novan glanced up to see the guard straining against the darkness as he looked for him. The lanterns in the library flickered behind him. Novan swept his cloak around him, hoping the dense fabric shrouded him from sight, and worked his way along the wall.

* * *

Novan crouched along the side of the castle. A filthy stream of water ran alongside him, the fetid odor of the muck making him nauseated as he slid along the wall, his back pressed against the damp stone. Being so close to the water, the stone was even wetter than the other walls, but he didn't dare move away. At least there, his cloak kept him covered, protected by the ever-darkening night.

Somehow he needed to escape the city.

His pack felt heavy and full, pulling against his back. Novan did not dare open the pack, as much as he might want to, to look at the texts he had snared from the library. The others—the reason he had come to Gomald in the first place—sat at the front of the pack, but that was not the text that had his mind racing. Rather, he wondered about the book that Nils had spent the night copying. What would keep the ancient librarian awake long enough that he would copy into the night? And why would it be in Gomald?

Novan would need time to translate the words written in the book, but the runes would take longer.

Once free from the city, he would have all the time he needed. Especially once he reached Thealon. At least there they respected the guild, whether or not Novan truly represented the guild as he once had.

The stream of putrid water blocked him. More than that, the pair of guards standing alongside the city gates made him move carefully.

At least he had managed to escape the castle. Now that he was out, he needed to disappear, fade into the darkness, if only the guards would stop their patrols long enough that he could sneak away.

That they still searched told him more than enough about the value of what he had managed to secure.

Lanterns faded into the night. Novan waited until he heard nothing, not content that the fading lantern light kept him protected. Not after what he had seen in Gomald, not after the priests he had seen there. No—he waited until he heard nothing. Only then did he step through the thick muck of the stream, his pack held high overhead as he trudged through, holding his breath the entire time.

Once across, he darted into the darkness, running from the castle. He didn't know how long he'd run before he turned around, finally daring to look back. The castle blazed with hundreds of candles, but it was one on the topmost floor of the central tower that drew his eye, one that he knew to belong to the High Priest, a man he had intentionally avoided during his stay in Gomald.

Novan shivered. The idea that the High Priest knew he existed frightened him. But at the same time, he felt a small thrill. Defying the Deshmahne meant something, he knew. Especially if everything he'd learned about the religion was true. Even more if the High Priests were the ones that had wanted the text he now carried.

A gust of wind came in from the south. With it came the scent of the sea mixed with the stink of something unfamiliar. Novan shivered, fearing what that might mean, as he ran into the darkness.

* * *

"I just need passage."

Novan looked at the weathered riverman standing in front of him on the dock. The wide slats of the dock creaked under his feet and he did not look forward to the prospect of standing on the skiff as it crossed the river, especially with the gusting wind making the water swirl with whitecaps. At least his waxed bag should provide some protection from the water should the spray come up over the edge during the transport, but not enough if the boat capsized. There was nothing that would protect him then.

"Passage be ten coppers," the man said. He was missing half his teeth and those that remained looked blackened.

Novan sighed. Hurrying from Gomald had made him careless with his coin. A few coppers here for a night in an inn. Another few coppers spent on food. By the time he reached Rondal River, he had little remaining. Once back in Thealon, he knew ways a historian could earn money, but none that he could manage to do quickly.

First he had to cross the river.

The riverman had one hand on the rope barrier blocking access to his wide skiff. Thin wooden rails ran along the outer edge. In his other hand he held the long wooden oar, the flat blade streaked with mud from the river bottom. A few people stood on the deck of the skiff, most staring across the river. A younger woman watched him with curious eyes, her auburn hair pulled behind her head.

This would be the last transport across the Rondal River before sunrise. After everything that he'd been through, he wanted to put as much space between him and Gomald as possible.

"I don't have ten coppers," Novan began, "but I can get you something even more valuable." He pulled one of the texts out of his pack and prepared to open it.

The man waved him off. "Coppers, not paper," he said. "You got to be able to read to make paper worthwhile."

Novan shook his head. How could someone be unable to read, especially in a place of such high trade? He left the question unanswered and tilted the book toward the riverman. "This is the work of Alaiht. Original text," he whispered, careful about how loudly he mentioned his mentor's name. Novan hated bargaining with it, but knew that a copy existed, so if the original disappeared, the writings of Alaiht wouldn't be lost forever. "You take this to Thealon and you would be able to get ten silvers. Ten times what you're asking."

The riverman grunted. "Then you take it to Thealon. I want coppers."

An elderly couple pushed up behind him and Novan had to let them past. There was no use arguing with the man any longer, but he needed to convince him to let him pass. Somehow. Only he had nothing that he could trade.

"Is there anything that I can do for you?" he finally asked after the couple had passed.

The riverman began replacing the rope barrier. Soon the skiff would head across the river and Novan would be trapped for the night, left behind on the shore of Gomald. Much better, he knew, to spend the night across the border in the nation of Thealon, whether he spent it in town or sleeping on the side of the road. Even better would have been reaching the city of Thealon itself, but the capital was a long way off.

"Nothing other than coppers," the man said.

Novan sighed and slipped the book back into his pack. "I already said I don't have the coppers."

"Then you don't have transport. Head back to Gomald. The library there will buy your books. Then you can get transport from me."

The next place to pass was far upriver. At least another week by foot, probably more. Had he managed to borrow a horse, he could reach it in a day. But had he a horse, he would have been able to trade it for transport.

And he did not want any more delay. Remaining in Gomald left him nervous, fearful that Nils, and whoever requested the texts that Nils collected, would find him. Novan had the protection of the guild, but there were limits to that protection, and he had the distinct sense that Nils knew things about the guild that he should not. That made Novan even more cautious.

Beyond that was the book he'd found. He had not yet deciphered whatever Nils had been copying—the runes in the book meant little to him—but the wording made it clear that the runes had significance. If only he could learn what.

For that, he needed to reach Thealon. He knew people in the great university there, would have access to the library so he could research the runes. Other than the guild, he didn't know where else he might find what he needed, and he didn't feel comfortable returning to the guild without learning more.

Once, such hesitation would have seemed impossible for him to believe. Novan had always believed that the guild worked to further knowledge, but what he had seen over the last few months left him with new questions. Especially after Gomald.

"May I see that?"

Novan looked up to see the woman with the auburn hair looking at him over the shoulder of the riverman. The man turned and scowled at her but she ignored him. Eyes flashed with the color of the water as she smiled at Novan. She held her hand out and around the riverman. Novan noticed how delicate her fingers appeared.

He frowned at her. "You wish to see this?" He held Alaiht's text carefully in front of him.

Could she be from Gomald? Nils wouldn't send a woman her age after him, would he?

But the long pleated skirt of forest green and deep blue hung just past her knee, not to her ankle as was proper in Gomald. The embroidered cloak hanging over her shoulders looked more like a Rondalin weave. Strangest to Novan was the simple chain around her neck that looked to be Lakeliis made. A thick band of dull metal, which he did not recognize, hung around the chain. From her dress, she could be from anywhere but Gomald.

Her smile deepened and something about her face changed. "You were offering it for trade."

The riverman scowled and turned to step over the rope barrier. "Skiff is departing," he said gruffly.

The woman looked at him. "Then I will pay his transport." She reached one of her delicate hands into a pouch hidden beneath her cloak and pulled out a silver.

The riverman seemed to glare at her, but took the coin, pushing it into his pocket. Without a word, he opened the rope to let Novan pass.

Novan debated the offer for a moment, wondering if this weren't some kind of trick, before deciding to take the risk. If all she wanted was the book by Alaiht, he had been prepared to trade that to the riverman. If there were some deeper trick, then he would be caught anyway.

As the skiff pushed away from the dock, Novan stood next to the woman, making sure to stand as close to the middle of the skiff as possible. The gusts of wind sent occasional spits of spray up that splashed him in the face. Swells of water lifted the skiff uncomfortably.

"You are not accustomed to traveling by water?" the woman asked.

Novan shook his head. "Prefer a horse or my feet."

She looked completely at ease, shifting with each changing gust to ride out the change in the waves. "Not much different than riding a horse. You just have to learn the movements."

He laughed at that. "With a horse you can't end up drowning if you're thrown."

"Depends on where you ride," the woman said.

She gave him space near the middle of the skiff. Her arms crossed over her chest and she looked across the river, seemingly unconcerned about the swells that grew larger the farther they traveled into the river. Near the front of the skiff, the riverman worked his oar, steadily driving them forward, dipping down and then back up. Mud still clung to the blade as he lifted it from the water, telling Novan that the river was not too deep there.

"You seem nervous," the woman commented.

"Eager to reach Thealon." He could stay in Thealon for weeks if needed. There were places that the guild owned where he could stay, but he knew other places as well, places where the guild would not watch. Novan had not decided which he would choose. "Not eager to swim."

A surge of water splashed over the deck. In the middle of the skiff, water crashed over Novan's boots, splashing up and getting his pants soaked below the knee. The woman simply shifted, lifting her skirt to keep it dry, unmindful of the way she flashed her legs as she did. Novan could not help but stare.

"The river can be violent here. Some say that's why Gomald is so different from Thealon. That the gods wanted differences, so created the Rondal River to separate the lands."

Novan chuckled. "You think the gods care how men are ruled?"

Her smile faded. "You think that they do not?"

Novan chided himself for risking such debate. He should be thankful to the woman for paying his way across the river, not arguing the semantics of the Urmahne faith, but there he was, unable to help himself. "There are some who claim the gods do not exist."

"Those men are fools," the woman said with a decisiveness that surprised Novan. "Can they not look around the world and see the beauty the gods have created? Have they not seen the abilities wielded by the Magi and glimpsed a fraction of the gods' power? Even your Thealon, where the Tower of the Gods rises to the heavens, is evidence of their existence."

She watched Novan for a moment before turning and looking back out over the water. Her blue-green eyes skimmed across the surface of the water, flickering across every cresting wave and finally settling on the far shore where wide fields of massive grasses waved in the wind, swaying back and forth.

"I am sorry if I offend," Novan said, softening his tone. "Sometimes I forget myself and speak too freely. And after you have paid my fare, I should exercise more caution."

She laughed softly and turned to him, her eyes seeming reluctant to look away from the far shore of Thealon. "You think me offended?" She shook her head. "Not offended, though happy to debate the merits of your comment. Most who make comments about the gods are either ignorant or frightened. Since you carry the work of Alaiht with you, I assume that you are not ignorant. I would be interested in why you are frightened."

Novan started to answer but caught himself, slowly registering that she had identified Alaiht's text by sight as she'd been too far away to overhear. "I'm sorry. I did not catch your name."

Something flashed across her eyes briefly before fading. "I did not offer it."

Novan waited, thinking that she might say something more. When she didn't, he said, "I am Novan."

Her lips tightened. Another swell caught the skiff, sending more water splashing across the deck. The woman lifted her skirt, keeping it dry, unconcerned about the water that soaked her boots. "Just Novan?"

He shrugged.

"So a historian, then," she said, nodding. "I suppose that explains why you would care about the book. But not your fear."

That she recognized him as a historian based on name alone told him much about her. Suddenly her dress took on a different meaning. He had thought the clothing cobbled together, a cloak here, skirt there, the necklace from another place, all the result of wandering merchants. But perhaps that was altogether incorrect. If she recognized him as a historian, she probably had visited each of those places, regardless of how spread out they were. If so, she might be as well traveled as him.

Trying a different tactic, he asked, "You know of Alaiht?"

She smiled. "He has an interesting take, especially on the founding of Thealon, though I imagine you share his philosophy?"

"I would not call a historian's observations 'philosophy,'" he said, "but I share his conclusions."

"And about Vasha?"

Novan hesitated. The text by Alaiht he'd offered the riverman told much of the history of Vasha, the city of the Magi few understood well. As far as Novan was concerned, Alaiht's text was the definitive discussion on Vasha, one none of the Magi were willing to discuss. Or, more tellingly, refute. But it was not well distributed. Copies existed, though most were in the universities, like in Thealon or Vasha. A copy of his original text could be found in Masetohl, but only one of the guild would know about that.

"I think that he made some interesting observations," Novan said carefully.

"So you have read it?"

He nodded.

"Such observations leave you wondering *how* Alaiht managed to acquire such knowledge. The Magi keep their own records. Could Alaiht actually have accessed the Magi archives?"

"Where did you study?" Novan suddenly pieced together why the woman would know so much.

She laughed. Her voice sounded rich and melodic. "Many places. Though lately I would call Vasha my home."

Vasha. That meant the university in Vasha, so different from the one in Thealon. More selective. More secretive. Even Alaiht hadn't managed to learn much about the university, or if he had, he hadn't documented it.

"I have not known many scholars to travel so much."

"Then you must not have known many scholars."

Novan did not take the bait. The skiff had reached well over halfway across the river. Novan watched the riverman working his oar, swirling it in the water as he worked rather than lifting it with each stroke. He wondered how deep the water ran there. Many deep-keeled boats traveled the river, though most kept to the middle as they made their way down toward Riverbranch before it let out into the sea.

As the shore of Thealon loomed closer, the woman seemed tenser. Rather than flowing with the surging changes in current, she rocked more.

"Where are you traveling to?"

Her eyes looked toward the shore. "Thealon, same as you."

"The city?"

She nodded.

Novan wondered what would draw a scholar of Vasha to Thealon. "I haven't thanked you for paying my transport."

She smiled. "Oh? I thought the terms of transport were clear."

"You want the book."

She shrugged. It was the barest movement of her slender shoulders. "I would like to see the original."

Novan felt another moment of surprise. How could she have known that he carried the original work rather than a copy? "I assumed that you had read Alaiht's work on Vasha."

"I have."

"Then you would not find anything of value from the copy I carry. Let me repay you once we reach Thealon."

"We travel together now?"

Novan noted that she had not argued with him, wondering if she would still demand the book as payment. Would he agree to the demand if she did?

"We travel the same direction. The road can be lonely, and I think that I would find your company enlightening."

She turned away from staring at the shore and met his eyes. "Should I not fear traveling with a stranger?"

"I am a historian of the guild."

She studied his face, considering for a moment. "So you are. Then should you not fear traveling with a stranger?"

Novan laughed. "You said you were from Vasha. A scholar. What would I have to fear?"

She laughed and turned away. "What indeed?"

* * *

He did not learn her name until that evening.

They camped on the edge of the road. The woman showed surprising skill lighting a fire, twisting a small bundle of twigs together that seemed far too green to Novan before tapping on her flint. The small flame crackled softly, and she let it grow slowly. Once satisfied, she knelt across from him and pulled a few strips of jerky from a hidden pack and handed them to Novan.

"I am Lilliana," she said between bites.

Novan didn't say anything at first, trying to determine if he recognized the name. It didn't trigger anything for him and he knew of no scholars by that name, though he would not, especially from Vasha. "Just Lilliana?"

She smiled. "For now."

"Why do you travel to Thealon?"

"I imagine the same reason as you."

Novan clutched his pack close, careful to keep it next to him. He didn't distrust Lilliana, but she hadn't given him any reason *to* trust her either. And he did not want to lose the book before learning what the runes meant. "As a historian, I travel frequently."

She nodded, taking another slow bite. The firelight reflected off her hair and seemed to dance. "I imagine that is normally true. But you seemed in a particular hurry to reach the other side of the Rondal. Either you run toward something, or away."

"Which is it for you?"

She smiled and shrugged, shifting her cloak to keep her shoulders covered. The night felt chill, not as warm as they had been while in Gomald. "Both."

Novan laughed lightly and leaned back. He debated how much to share with her, but needed to establish some trust if they were to travel together to Thealon.

A gust of wind sent the fire dancing. Lilliana shivered and pulled her cloak around her, covering the necklace. She fingered the ring hanging from the chain as she ate, a distant look painted on her face.

"When were you last in Lakeliis?" he asked, considering her necklace.

Her eyes focused on him, and a slight smile played across her face. "Long enough that I suspect much has changed. What was it like when last you visited, Novan?"

"I haven't been to the south in many years," he admitted. "Though Lakeliis always welcomes those of the guild."

"Only because they don't know how to tell the difference."

Novan laughed. The guild had problems with imposters claiming membership, some even brazen enough to flash a forged mark to take advantage of the freedoms the guild offered. "And do you?"

"I have known enough historians to recognize when someone is not who they claim." She watched him as she spoke.

Novan shrugged. "With the abundance of imposters, it seems we are at an impasse."

"You think so? You think I doubt that you are of the guild?"

"Do you not?"

"You carry a book by Alaiht. Your pack is waxed, presumably to protect the contents from the elements. You make reference to works that only a few have seen. Either you are of the guild—and highly placed at that—or you are a skilled imposter." She smiled and laughed softly. "Either way, I think that it does not matter."

She fell silent and Novan didn't comment. Lilliana had sharp eyes and he wondered what else she had observed. A part of him wondered if she could help with the book he'd stolen from Gomald. A scholar from Vasha would be a useful resource in decoding the runes, but he didn't know if he dared allow the university access to it until he knew what it meant. Clearly Nils had felt it important enough to copy. Had Novan been thinking more clearly, he would have taken the copy as well.

Thealon. He could find answers in the capital. Another few days and they would reach the city of Chrysia. From there it would only take a week more. If he could manage to secure a horse, he could

515

make it in less time, but he had nothing to sell or bargain, at least nothing that he dared lose.

Novan watched Lilliana. She leaned back, away from the fire, her eyes drifting closed as the wind swirled around. It caught on her hair and pulled it briefly up and away from her neck, revealing a dark line, like ink tattooed onto her skin. Then the wind died and her hair fell back into place, covering her neck again and leaving Novan wondering if he'd only imagined it.

* * *

Lilliana spoke little the next few days. Occasionally she would ask him questions, first about his apprenticeship and then about his travels. After the first morning of such questioning, he realized that she was testing him, trying to determine if he really was a guild historian.

"I was first apprenticed to Bilnat. She preferred the southern lands and our travels took us from Voiga to Lakeliis and sometimes to the far east, beyond the mountains. I spent three years with her before her passing."

Lilliana nodded. "It is said that she fell to a wasting sickness."

Novan nodded, remembering the way that her once thick arms and legs had wasted away over several months, her eyes seeming to become more and more withdrawn. Even her gray hair thinned over time, leaving her looking aged well beyond her years. "After she passed, I had to find another apprenticeship."

"Is such a thing easy?"

They passed a copse of trees. The open grasses began to thin as the ground became rockier. A stream burbled in the distance, and they left the road to fill their waterskins. Both drank deeply. Novan spied a small village through the trees not far from the stream.

"Not easy," Novan admitted. He didn't recognize the village, though he had not traveled through this part of Thealon enough that he should. There were parts of the north, especially around Boastiin, where he expected to know every village. "Members of the guild are not required to take on an apprentice, and in fact, few ever do. I was the first that Bilnat had taken in twenty years. I do not think she cared for the disruption in her work."

Lilliana took a long drink of water and then crouched to refill her waterskin. "You were a disruption?"

She had turned to look up at him. Novan watched, hoping for her hair to shift so he could catch another glimpse of her neck, but it did not move.

"I don't think that I was any more of a disruption than an apprentice in general. There is a certain amount of teaching required when working with an apprentice. Some enjoy it and constantly have an apprentice. Others, only rarely." He took a long drink and wiped his sleeve over his mouth. "What is it like at the university?"

Lilliana splashed water across her face and wiped down her arms, throwing her cloak back over her shoulders after she finished. The early morning air still had a bite to it, not quite cold, but the occasional gusts of wind made it feel colder. She stood and wiped her hands on her skirt, smoothing it down. "As you can imagine, there is an expectation of teaching at the university. Each student is assigned a mentor who guides them through the early stages."

Novan could not imagine how there would be enough instructors for all the students. "How many students do you have each year?" he asked. In Thealon, the university took several dozen each year, but the classes were well structured, and the scholars were asked to speak to students no more than once a week.

"We can take three."

Novan blinked. "Three?"

"Some years there are fewer. The selection process is vigorous, not at all like Thealon."

Novan laughed. "You don't think that Thealon employs a vigorous screening process?"

She frowned at him and stepped away from the stream. "I think that Thealon is less selective. We allow only the brightest minds to enter the university in Vasha."

Novan knew not to argue, but he had seen the process in Thealon in person. Lines hundreds deep lasting all day for one of several dozen spots. He could not imagine Vasha was any more selective than Thealon.

He followed her back to the road. For a while, he thought he had managed to upset her, but she eventually turned and smiled at him.

"You never told me who you were apprenticed to after Bilnat."

"After Bilnat, I had to ask permission of the guild to seek a second historian. Such a thing is rarely done. Some who lose their apprenticeship fade away from the guild. Such is the risk of the apprenticeship."

Lilliana looked bothered. "That sounds as if the guild intends to prevent access."

"No more than the university in Vasha."

She did not look over. "And how many are apprenticed at any given time, Novan?"

"No more than six or seven, I would imagine. As I said, there are not many historians who take on apprentices."

"Yet you managed to secure not one but two apprenticeships," she commented. "You still have not said who the second was with."

"I did not," he agreed.

Lilliana smiled and said nothing more.

* * *

They spent that night in a small village. Lilliana seemed to know one of the families from the village and managed to secure them a place to sleep in a barn on the outskirts. Novan didn't argue, preferring the warmth of the barn to the chill of the night air.

The barn was simple. Five stalls. A small loft. Hay stacked in one corner and the air stinking of manure. But the walls kept back the blowing wind. Novan crawled into the loft, ignoring the soft whinnying of the three horses in their stalls. He considered stealing one of the horses and making his way more quickly to Thealon, but decided against it. As much as she had helped him so far, Lilliana did not deserve that.

As Lilliana spoke to the woman of the house—a thick woman with a severe jaw and jet-black hair—Novan made himself comfortable near the back of the loft. The boards were thick and rough but otherwise clean. A small lantern had been loaned to them, and he used it to give the loft a little more light. He pulled the stolen book from his pack and thumbed through the pages. Did he dare begin work on translating the writing? He had some skill with the language, but it would be tedious work and time consuming.

Then there was the matter of the runes. Scrawled across each page in different diagrams, some looking like nothing more than a string of words, others looked more complex, bound together as if creating a drawing. Something about the more complex pages pulled at him, as if he should remember why but could not.

When he saw Lilliana making her way up the ladder to the loft, he stuffed the book back into his pack and hurried to help her. She smiled at him and shooed him away.

"You know them?"

"I know many people."

"But here? How is it that you know someone here?"

She only shrugged and did not answer that question. "We have a warm place to sleep and food. You should not question the how."

"I always question."

Lilliana laughed. "In that we are similar."

They ate in silence the fresh bread and cheese given to Lilliana. When she finished, she claimed fatigue and rolled onto her side to sleep, placing her pack beneath her head and using her cloak for a blanket. Novan considered flipping through the book a little longer while she slept, but wasn't prepared for questions about the book were she to awaken and see him working through it. Giving it his full attention would have to wait until he reached Thealon. Then he would have access to the library and would be able to work on deciphering the runes. A nagging part of him told him they were important.

They left the village the following morning, rejoining the road with pockets stuffed with fresh loaves of bread and as much dried meat as the family could spare. Lilliana took a moment to say good-bye to the family, and the severe-looking woman gave her a tight hug before glaring at Novan as if to warn him from harming Lilliana. He did his best to smile as widely and warmly as he could, but her expression did not change.

Back on the road, the wind gusted with renewed urgency, blowing in from the south and east and carrying with it the scent of rain. The sky was a solid sheet of gray clouds spreading across the horizon. Novan worried about keeping the books dry. The pack had been freshly waxed before he departed, but there had been too many instances while still in Gomald where he had been forced through water that he worried the waxing would no longer hold.

As the day went on, one particularly strong gust of wind sent Lilliana's hair fluttering. Novan made an effort to look for the marking on her neck that he had barely glimpsed in the firelight. In the muted daylight, he saw the marking again, just as a flash of darkness, but enough that he swore it resembled one of the runes he had seen in the book stolen from Nils.

Lilliana caught him looking and pulled her cloak up around her shoulders. She remained quiet for most of the day, offering little more than a few words when they camped that night. They ate of the gifted food in silence.

In the morning, he awoke before her. The sun had already started cresting the horizon, sending orange slivers of light across the sky. The gray clouds had broken and with them the sense of the coming rain.

Novan stretched and saw that she lay on her side with her neck exposed. He leaned over her and stared at the marking on her neck. Definitely a tattoo of some sort. Set just below her left ear, the shape looked like interlocking triangles worked into a circle. He felt a sense of familiarity as he looked at it.

Lilliana opened her eyes then and saw him looking. "You could have asked."

He straightened quickly and took a step back. "Would you have told me?"

"Probably. When did you first notice?"

"As we were crossing the river, I think." She nodded, eyes drifting back as if she were remembering. "What does it mean?"

She frowned at him. "You do not know?" She seemed surprised that he did not.

He shook his head. "I feel like I've seen something like this somewhere. There aren't too many people with markings tattooed on them, at least not here." In the far southwest, such tattoos were more common, but even there he had never seen anyone with one on their neck.

She seemed to consider her answer for a long moment. "You might be surprised at how many are tattooed like this. But this," she said, placing a hand to her neck, "this was my test." Lilliana shifted her hair so that it fell back down over her shoulder, covering her neck. The necklace dangled across her chest, and she fingered the ring hanging from the chain.

"What kind of test?"

"One that I needed to take," was her only answer.

When Novan saw that she would not say more, he pressed. "Did you pass?"

She smiled bitterly. "I still live."

He felt taken aback by the comment. "There was a risk of you dying?"

"Others were at greater risk if I did not attempt it. That is why I took it."

"What does it mean?"

She pushed herself to stand, dusting off her dress, and swung her cloak up and over her shoulders. She slipped her tan pack back around her waist and buttoned her cloak. "I do not yet know," she finally answered.

Novan laughed, but realized she did not share in his laughter. "Why risk such a thing if you didn't know?"

She did not look at him when she answered. "Because I was the only one who could."

She started away from where they had camped and continued onto the road. Novan watched her, wondering what secrets she hid from him. He had thought her only secrets were about the university. The scholars in Vasha did not welcome outsiders, and he thought she simply protected the university, but there was something else there he didn't understand. And that made him uncomfortable.

As he trailed after her, his mind started working through what he knew. From her dress, Lilliana appeared well traveled. She had studied to become a scholar in Vasha. Now, like him, she traveled to Thealon. And she had been tattooed with a rune that reminded him of those found in the book he had stolen in Gomald.

What was he missing? There seemed to be some connection he couldn't place.

She did not speak much that day. Or that night.

They stopped in another small village and again Lilliana seemed to know some of the villagers, securing them lodging in the quiet inn at the center of town. The tavern held a few men dicing and drinking ale, but nothing like Novan usually saw in the larger cities. Most looked like village regulars simply out eating and drinking. The innkeep put them in a single room on the second floor toward the end of a short and poorly lit hall. A single mattress butted against the wall, a stained and chipped basin rested in the corner.

"I haven't thanked you for helping me along the way," Novan said as they closed the door behind them. Fading daylight filtered through a narrow window, and Lilliana lit the single candle that rested on the floor next to the mattress. "If not for you, I would have been camping along the side of the road each night."

With the chill to the air, he would have been increasingly uncomfortable, though he had traveled much since joining the guild and had known worse days. Had he not met Lilliana, he might have resorted to begging aid on behalf of the guild. Often smaller villages would put him up in exchange for stories or a chance to have their histories documented.

"If not for me, you wouldn't have crossed the river," Lilliana reminded him with a laugh.

She had spoken so little over the last day that Novan felt relief when she did. "You've been here before."

"I've made this journey many times. After a while, the people become friends. There is so little I can do for them, but I try."

Novan frowned, wondering what the people would have asked of a scholar. It was unusual for scholars to be afforded the same courtesy as historians, but then, he was beginning to think there was more to Lilliana than a simple scholar.

"What brings you this way often enough to develop these relationships?"

"You have been to Thealon. Is that not reason enough to travel this way?"

"But Vasha is farther north. You would have to come south first. There wouldn't be any reason to do that . . ." he started, then trailed off. "Unless you aren't coming from Vasha. And not Gomald, I do not think. That means you travel from the south, and often enough that you know people here. What would bring a scholar of Vasha to the south?"

He asked the question mostly to himself, trying to puzzle out what he had learned of Lilliana. She surprised him by answering. And laughing.

She sat on the edge of the mattress and looked up at him. The firelight danced in her eyes. Her auburn hair caught the colors of the fading sunlight. Sitting as she was, arms crossed over her breasts, Novan could not help but find her lovely.

"For a historian, you have taken a long time to reach these questions," she began. "When I first met you, I had already pieced together the fact that you were a historian, possibly separated from the guild—though I admit I cannot determine why—and were recently in Gomald, but were now running from there to Thealon. From the fact that you carry nothing but a small waxed bag, I presumed initially that you had nothing of value other than perhaps the work by Alaiht. Strange enough that you should have that. I imagined that it should belong with the guild, and likely in Masetohl if the rumors are true, or maybe in Voiga. Yet rather than returning to the guild, you seek Thealon and do not seem eager to have it known you are a historian. Most historians I have encountered are eager to announce they belong to the guild, flashing their mark as if to impress me."

When she finished, Novan didn't know quite what to say. He had seen that she had an observant eye, but this impressed him. Had she wanted to, she could have rivaled Alaiht, and he was widely considered the greatest historian in hundreds of years.

"How many historians have you known?"

She smiled, a hand coming to her neck and touching the ring hanging from the Lakeliis-made necklace. "Enough to recognize one of the guild. Enough to know that you were so distracted by what you were doing that you failed to behave like the others I've met." Her smile widened. "Though if the stories of Novan are true, then you seldom behave like others in the guild, do you?"

Novan stiffened. "What have you heard of me?"

"That you care less about class and more about knowledge," she answered. "In that, we are much alike. Part of the reason I helped you was that I wanted to know if that were true."

"That meant you knew I was a historian *before* you paid my fare?"

She nodded. "You carry yourself far too freely to be anything but a historian. Your dress is clearly ambiguous. You have a keen eye for detail. And you begged the boatman in a way that practically demanded he let you cross. I think that had I not intervened, you still would have found passage." She smiled slightly. "And there is something else about you that I cannot quite place. When I deduced that you were traveling to Thealon, I decided that it made sense that we travel together until I discovered what I wanted to learn."

"And that is?"

Her eyes shifted to his pack. "When are you going to show me what you have taken?" She looked up at him and smiled. "Don't be surprised. You do not hide it nearly so well as you believe that you do. The way that you covered your pack when the sky clouded over or the way you lean away when near water so as to keep it dry. And then there was the way you studied the markings. You had seen them before. Few outside have seen them."

"Outside of what?"

She sniffed and shook her head. "I should not have to tell you. As a historian, these are questions you should have been asking, seeking the answers on your own."

"I have many questions I ask."

"Not the right ones," she chided. "Not the questions you should be asking."

Novan frowned. It had been a long time since he had been chastised so. "And you think that you're asking the right questions? Is that why you make your trek from the south to Thealon often enough that people in these small villages know who you are and are willing to help?"

"That isn't the reason they help."

"And that wasn't an answer."

"No. And you still haven't asked the right questions."

Novan shook his head. "The guild feels the same way."

She smiled. "Is that why you went to Gomald?"

"I went to Gomald for answers the guild refused to give."

Lilliana studied him before sighing, pulling her hair to the side. The candle light flickered off the marking on her neck, making it appear to shimmer. "You have seen markings like this?"

She waited for him to nod.

"Few have. There is a certain power to the markings that, no matter how much I study, I cannot explain."

"Where else have you seen them?"

Lilliana shook her head and let her hair drop back down over her shoulder, covering the markings again. "I have only seen them one place. The same place that I acquired them. A dangerous place, and one that I am lucky to have survived." She shivered. "The risk was worth it, though. I have learned much by taking the test, much that can be useful to the others. What I would like to know is where *you* saw them."

Novan stared at her, debating how to answer. Already he knew that he could not simply deceive her—she had proven that she would recognize it if he did. He glanced at his pack, trying to decide what he should do. If he passed on this opportunity, he didn't know how long it would take him in Thealon to decipher the runes. Translating the words might take weeks by itself. And here he had someone who had seen the runes before. Shouldn't he take advantage of that?

"I traveled to Gomald to meet with the High Priest," he started. "I knew little of the Deshmahne, only that they had gained favor in Gomald as well as parts of the south. I thought to take some time to study and learn from them."

Lilliana's eyes widened slightly. "What did you learn from them?"

Novan shook his head. "Nothing. The High Priest would not meet with me, and none of the other Deshmahne priests would either. Before departing, I visited the library. The collection there had a growing reputation. I thought that I might visit with the man in charge of their acquisitions. Only . . . when I surveyed the library, I realized that something was amiss. They had books that they should not. Original works made by historians that only the guild should have possessed."

Lilliana nodded. "That is why you have the work by Alaiht," she said. "You took them back. But that isn't the reason you run to Thealon. Finding guild works wouldn't have driven you like this. You found something else—something you couldn't explain and didn't want to go to the guild for help with."

Novan pulled the book he'd taken from Nils out of his pack and sat next to Lilliana. After hesitating, he passed it over to her. She took it, looking at the cover with a confused expression. When she flipped it open, Novan saw that her face seemed to stiffen. She turned each page carefully, her lips moving as she read the words. Otherwise she said nothing aloud for long moments.

"You found this in the library?" She did not look up.

"It was late at night. I had snuck into the upper level where I had learned the guild works were stored. The library should have been empty—dark—but it was not. I found Nils copying this book." He shrugged. "I did not know what it was but felt compelled to take it. I have not been able to understand, but when I saw the runes on your neck, I recognized them as similar to what is in this book."

"Can you read it?" she asked, finally looking up and meeting his eyes.

"The ancient language?" he asked. "With enough time I should be able to translate it."

She nodded slowly. "And have you deciphered what it means?"

He frowned, reaching for the book. Lilliana looked at him, holding on to the book rather than passing it back. "Not completely. Do you know what it means?"

Her eyes closed and she nodded again.

"Will you explain?"

"I'm sorry, Novan," she started. Before Novan could protest, she turned and slid the book into her bag. And then, turning quickly, she struck him with her open hand under his neck.

* * *

Novan awoke with a painful headache. Darkness hung over the room so thick that he couldn't tell whether he rested on the mattress or the floor. The air smelled wet and damp. As he brought a hand to his head, he realized that his hair was wet.

With a jolt he remembered what had happened. Lilliana had stolen the book.

He staggered to his feet and fumbled toward the door. When he managed to reach it, he threw it open, letting light from the hall stream in, and stood in the open door, struggling to understand what had happened.

Propping the door open, he shuffled around the room until he found his pack. Rummaging inside, he discovered that the books he had taken from Gomald were still there. The only thing she had taken was the book of runes.

But he still didn't know why.

Novan grabbed his cloak and shuffled down the hall toward the stairs. Music drifted up from the common area. He smelled roasted meat and baked breads, both aromas making his mouth water but sending his stomach churning.

At the bottom of the stairs, he looked around the tavern. Most of the tables had a few people sitting around, either eating or drinking. Novan didn't know how long he had been out. Was it still the same night, or had he been unconscious for a full night? The darkness made him think that he had not been out too long, but he did not know for certain.

He looked around for the innkeeper. If he could find the man, he could ask about Lilliana. Already he had decided that he needed to follow her and recover the book. If it was valuable enough to be stolen—twice, he reminded himself—then he wanted to decipher the text and the runes to learn why.

As he surveyed the tavern, he saw a man dressed in a black shirt and pants near the corner of the bar. Novan had seen dress like that before, but only in Gomald and on a Deshmahne priest. That one of the priests would venture into Thealon surprised him, especially so close to the city. The Urmahne priests viewed them as a cult blaspheming the nameless gods.

As he weaved into the tavern, he watched the priest, looking as he did for the innkeep. Nearing the kitchen, he realized that the innkeep stood across from the priest. Sweat dripped down his bald head, which he hastily wiped away. Novan found a seat close enough to listen, keeping his back turned so that the priest could not see him.

"You said she was here." The voice sounded sandpaper rough, hoarse like some of the soldiers Novan had met over the years, voices strained from yelling.

"She was, but she left already. Listen . . . I've told you all that I know. I was asked to send word if she appeared, and I did my part. Now I want my reward." The innkeeper's voice had an edge to it, and his words were clipped.

The priest laughed. "You have done nothing worthy of a reward. Had you managed to keep her here, you might see what you seek, but you could not even manage that. Perhaps the next time you will be more prompt."

The innkeeper sputtered. "More prompt? I sent word as soon as I saw her. That was the bargain."

Novan shifted, trying to watch the conversation. He had no doubt that Lilliana was who the priest sought, but why would the Deshmahne priest look for her?

"The bargain was that you would notify us in time for her to be detained. You completed only half of the bargain. Now if you can tell me which direction she went, I might be inclined to offer a token reward."

"She went north," the innkeeper said. "By herself this time. Not sure what happened with the other that was with her."

"What other?"

The innkeeper hesitated. "Might that be worth more than a simple token reward?"

The priest laughed softly. "Only if what you can tell me is worthy of a reward."

"A man. Simple clothes. Carried little with him. Spoke with a northern accent."

"What did he look like?"

"Average height. Dark hair. Hazel eyes. Sharp fellow it seemed."

Novan heard something thunk onto the table and jingle softly. Coin. And plenty, by the sound of it.

"Where is he?" the priest asked.

Novan pulled his cloak around him and shifted in his seat. Had the innkeeper seen him?

"She left without him. They were on foot, so she couldn't have gotten far."

"Don't worry about the girl. I will find her. But where is this other?"

"Upstairs. Last room. They stayed together. I thought you knew?"

A chair skipped across the floor as the priest stood. "If he is no longer there, the reward is forfeit."

The priest started away, his feet making little sound as he made his way across the tavern. When he started up the stairs, Novan turned and looked at the innkeeper. He opened his mouth as if to say something, but shut it quickly.

Novan grabbed him. "Where did she go?"

"I thought she was with you . . ."

"Don't lie to me. I heard what you told him but not why."

"Then if you heard, you know that she went north." The innkeeper was not a tall man, and age had stooped his back. He wiped an arm across his brow, smearing dirt into his skin. He looked nervously over Novan's shoulder, toward the stairs.

Novan figured he had no more than a few minutes before the priest returned. And then he would either need to speak to him or keep hidden. Something about the priest made Novan nervous about facing him.

The innkeeper fidgeted with the sack of coins on the table. Novan grabbed his hand and pulled it up. "I think that you don't deserve this," he said, taking the coins and stuffing them into his pocket. "Violating the trust of your patrons."

"I violated nothing. The priests—"

"Are not recognized in Thealon. Would you like me to alert the church that you have aided the Deshmahne?"

The words had the desired effect. The innkeeper started sweating even more profusely. "Please. You don't understand. I had no choice, not after what they did the last time."

Novan frowned. He didn't have much time to delay knowing that the priest would return any moment, but the comment had his attention. "What did they do the last time?"

The innkeeper shook his head. His eyes looked past Novan's shoulders and widened.

Without turning, Novan released the innkeeper and slipped around him, unwilling to wait and see what would happen with the priest if he delayed. The door to the inn opened and a squat man came in, heavy jowls ruddy from the chill night. Novan squeezed past him, grabbing at the man's cloak as he left. As he shut the door, he pulled the man's cloak through with him, lodging him in the door.

As he hurried into the night, he heard the man sputtering. Novan suspected that might buy him a few moments, possibly enough.

He ran around the side of the inn. A small stable was there and he scanned the stalls. A mottled stallion looked at him from the nearest stall. Novan didn't hesitate and saddled him quickly before jumping on. He left the coins behind, hoping there would be enough to pay for the stolen horse. If he'd had another choice, he wouldn't have stolen, but instinct told him to worry about why the priest had come to Thealon.

Kicking the horse forward, he started out of the stable. In spite of the cool night air washing over him, he felt a flush of sweat as he headed north. A cloudless sky hung over him, the nearly full moon seeming to taunt him. Shouts sounded from behind but he did not stop to listen. He needed to reach Lilliana before the priest did.

Novan had not been atop a horse in months but felt it moving fluidly beneath him, as if sensing his urgency. He clung to the saddle, riding it hard as he followed the road. Trees lined the hard-packed earth, growing increasingly dense the longer he went. If he rode long enough to the north, he would reach the Great Forest. Somehow he didn't think that was Lilliana's intent.

When he had been riding nearly an hour, he saw movement in the distance. He slowed the horse but still hurried forward. The movement he had seen darted behind a thicket of trees. Part of him worried that it might not be Lilliana. What if he ran into someone else, thinking it her?

At that point, he had no other option but to try. "I saw you, Lilliana."

For a moment, there was nothing. Then he heard footsteps, but closer than he would have expected. A shadow emerged from near the trees only a few paces from him. Novan gripped the reins.

"You should not have come, Novan." She had her cloak pulled up around her shoulders, her hair spilling over it. A glint of moonlight reflected off the necklace she wore, not really catching the ring he knew was there.

"You stole the book from me."

She laughed lightly. "Then I think we're both thieves. Possession makes it mine."

"Why did you take it?"

"This book is dangerous. You shouldn't have seen it. There are others who can use it safely."

"Like the Deshmahne priest?" He suddenly wondered if she worked with him.

She stepped closer to him. "Why would you say that?" Anger danced along the edge of her voice.

"The innkeeper sent word. One of the Deshmahne priests looks for you." Novan exhaled softly, slowly piecing things together that he should have seen before. "Is that who you run from? Is that why you traveled to Thealon?"

She laughed bitterly. "For a historian, you have much to learn of the world."

"Then explain," he said. "I can be an ally or an adversary. And I would prefer to work with you."

She didn't say anything. Novan nudged the horse forward and Lilliana stepped to the side of the road, studying him with an unreadable expression.

"I told you of the test. The risk I took?"

Novan nodded.

"It was the Deshmahne who tested me."

"I don't understand. Why would the Deshmahne tattoo your neck?"

She sniffed. "The Deshmahne seek power. The greatest of them, the High Priest, seeks power beyond that of the Magi. There is something about the runes used in these markings and the ink used for the tattoos that conveys power."

Novan frowned. The High Priest of the Deshmahne had been in Gomald, but he had thought him there only to support the king. "And the book?"

She shook her head. "I don't know. I fear that there are runes found within that will give the priests access to more power."

"And you seek to prevent that?"

"Not just me."

"The university? Why would the scholars care about such things?"

"Not the university."

"Then who?"

Lilliana sighed and looked past him, staring into the night.

Novan turned in his saddle and looked, listening carefully. Distantly, he heard hooves thundering along the road. He had no doubt that the Deshmahne priest chased after him and searched for Lilliana. What would happen if they were caught?

Lilliana looked back at him, her eyes seeming to beg. "That's not for me to share."

Novan wanted to study the runes, to determine for himself just what Lilliana feared was found within the pages of the book, but he also wanted to help her as she had once helped him.

Reaching his hand out, he motioned to her, "Come on. We'll have to ride hard to stay ahead of them."

She grabbed his hand and started up and into the saddle but didn't make it.

A horse thundered up, suddenly there next to them. Lilliana jumped from the saddle and looked over at the rider. Novan twisted to see the same priest he had seen in the tavern. Moonlight reflected off his face. He held a long black-bladed sword in his hand. An inky black cloak hung over his shoulders.

"You should not have run, Lilliana," the priest said.

She shook her head, staying out in front of Novan's horse. "You should not have followed, Theran. You're not welcome in Thealon."

"As if you are. You should have remained in Vasha. Now you can't even return there."

Lilliana stepped away from the horse. One hand gripped the necklace she wore. "Are you so certain? You think that Vasha does not know why I left?"

"I know that Vasha does not know why you left." He laughed with a dark tone. His horse shifted as he brought his sword close to Lilliana.

Her eyes drifted to it briefly before looking back up at his face. "You know nothing."

He laughed again. "I know that you were exiled from Vasha. That the scholars discovered you reading forbidden topics, asking questions you should not have been asking. I know what you stole when you slipped away in the night. There is much that I know."

Lilliana tensed.

Novan frowned. He had thought Lilliana left Vasha on her own, but if she had stolen from the university before departing, she would certainly have been exiled.

Maybe they were more alike than he realized.

"You think you are the only one able to deceive?" the priest asked.

Lilliana didn't move, as if frozen in place.

"The Deshmahne have many assets in Vasha. As you can imagine, there are many who feel the Magi have too much power."

"I was not exiled." Lilliana's voice had taken on a different tone, more anxious.

"Perhaps not at first, but when the university learned *why* you traveled to Voiga . . ."

Uncertainty dawned on Lilliana's face. "There were many reasons I traveled to Voiga."

The priest smiled again. "Oh, I know those as well. Now that you have taken the mark, do you really think you can keep secrets from us?"

"I have taken nothing. It was given."

"Was it?"

The priest made a strange motion with his hand and the sword started forward.

Lilliana slid. Novan had no better word for what she did. One moment she stood in front of the priest, the next she had jumped ten paces to the side. She shot Novan a look that he didn't recognize.

The priest turned to face her again. "So you have learned to control it. Impressive. Even with the Deshmahne, few learn well enough to be of any use." With a sudden motion, he lowered the cloak from his shoulders and jumped from the horse, landing on the ground with the sword spinning before him.

Dark runes covered the priest's arms, working from the wrist up to his shoulder. Shapes that appeared to move slithered across his skin, so inky black that they seemed to absorb light. The priest moved faster than should have been possible, flickering the sword at Lilliana.

She jumped again, darting off to the side.

Novan knew little about the Deshmahne. That someone would attack Lilliana surprised him. That it would be a priest seemed absurd.

A dangerous determination spread across the priest's face. When he attacked again, slicing toward her, he moved with a strange grace. Somehow Lilliana avoided the sword.

Novan did not doubt that she would eventually fail. And after that? Would the priest attack him for simply being with her? Unarmed other than his small knife, he wouldn't be able to withstand the attack, not like Lilliana somehow seemed capable of doing.

But he had to do something.

The priest circled Lilliana, slowly backing her toward the trees.

Novan approached the priest's horse. At first, he tried to send it running, but the mare simply snorted at him. He hated the idea of harming the horse, but if he did nothing, the priest would catch him as well.

Novan slipped from his saddle. Kneeling next to the horse, he offered a silent prayer to the gods for forgiveness as he ran his knife along the mare's leg, severing the tendon.

She whinnied loudly and stomped her foot, trying to kick him in the process. Novan hoped Lilliana kept the priest preoccupied enough not to notice. He jumped back into the saddle and looked for Lilliana.

She held her arm strangely. The priest closed in, his mouth tightened in a grim smile. Novan doubted she would last much longer.

He had to do something.

Kicking the horse forward, he galloped toward Lilliana. He crashed into the priest, knocking him over. The dark blade went spinning up in the air as the priest fell. Novan turned the horse and Lilliana jumped on behind him, grabbing the sword out of the air as she did and then clutching him weakly.

Novan didn't wait to see if the priest would follow, heeling the horse and racing down the road, away from the priest and into the darkness of night.

* * *

Novan lost track of how long they rode. He finally had to stop when he noticed that Lilliana had ceased holding on to him and seemed to simply slump forward. The only thing she managed to hang on to was the dark-bladed sword.

They had reached thicker trees. When Novan had tried to turn off onto a side road, Lilliana had argued, forcing him to continue north. Toward the Great Forest. At first he had agreed, but he realized that he should have pushed back. She needed a healer, help that he couldn't provide.

Novan veered the horse into the trees, moving deep enough that the shadows around him provided cover, but remaining close enough that he could watch the road. They had not seen the priest since Novan had run him over, and he did not really expect to, but part of him worried about whatever strange magic he used that gave him speed. Could he outrun them even without his horse?

Once in the trees, he slipped Lilliana from the saddle and lowered her to the ground. She moaned softly. He touched her hair, smoothing it away from her face, and reached through her shirt to see how badly she had been injured, cursing himself for not having done it sooner. Of course, he had been more concerned about getting them to safety.

A wide gash split the skin near her shoulder. The edges had blackened, as if the blade had been burning when it struck her. Or poisoned, he realized. No blood drained from the wound. Novan knew little of medicine, but suspected that did not foretell a positive sign.

Lilliana's eyes flickered open as he touched her shoulder. "Has he followed?"

Novan shook his head. "I . . . I disabled his horse."

She coughed. Blood burbled from her mouth as she did. "That will not stop him."

Lilliana reached out her hand and found her bag, tapping it softly with her hand until Novan reached past her and grabbed it. Opening the bag, he found the book she'd stolen from him. Underneath it was another book with a similar cover.

"What are these?" he asked.

She coughed again and reached for her neck. Novan thought that she would try to cover the wound. Instead, she reached for the necklace and held it.

"Protection." She said the word softly. "The Deshmahne cannot have them. Ensure that they are safe."

"I don't understand."

She tried to smile. Novan saw the color had faded from her face. "Not yet. But you will." Lilliana pulled on her necklace and the chain broke. She pushed it into his hand. "Take this. There are others like me."

"Scholars?" As he asked, he knew that was not what she was. Perhaps she had been at one time, but now Lilliana served a different master.

"Of a sort," she said. "This will give you access, but you will have to ask the right questions. The Novan I've heard of will know the questions to ask." She squeezed his hand and then her arm fell away and rested on the ground, too weak to hold him.

"Lilliana," he started, touching her face. "What is this? Why did the Deshmahne have those runes tattooed on his arms? What power does that grant him?"

A faint smile twisted her lips. "That is a start."

"What start?"

"Seek answers to the questions you've long held. The guild will not provide. Neither will the university." She managed to reach his hand and squeezed it around the ring. "The Conclave can."

"The Conclave? Where can I find them?"

She coughed again and breathed no more.

Novan crouched next to her for a long time, feeling uncertain. The necklace in his hand felt heavy and cold. She said it would give him access, but access to what?

He took an unsteady breath. He had not known her long, but she had helped him. Had he only been able to help her in return, she might not be lying dead on the forest floor. But there were magics he had not known were possible, powers that seemed equal to what the Magi could achieve. The world suddenly seemed so different from the one he thought he knew.

Since learning of the book, he had planned on traveling to Thealon to research the runes. Now that Lilliana had gone, that changed only the urgency of his search. Now he had another book to study.

Novan gathered Lilliana's belongings, placing the books into his bag. He slipped the dark metal ring off the chain and tried it on his middle finger. It fit. A tingling sensation ran through his body and he shivered. The only other thing of value was the sword she had taken off the priest. Novan secured this to his saddle.

When that was done, he used his knife to dig a small grave. The earth came away freely, willingly, and he lowered Lilliana into the shallow hole. After heaping dirt around her, he stood and said a soft prayer for peace.

He sighed. There was much he didn't understand. Much the guild could not teach him. She had said that he had to ask the right questions. That meant answers existed. And he would find them, especially if there was this Conclave that could answer. Thealon to start, but from there?

He shook his head. From there it made little difference. Guild support or not, he would do what he needed to find those answers. Lilliana said there were others like her. Questions that needed answering. And he would find them.

About D.K. Holmberg

New York Times and USA Today Bestselling Author D.K. Holmberg lives in Minnesota and is the author of multiple series including *The Cloud Warrior Saga*, *The Dark Ability*, *The Endless War*, and *The Lost Garden*. When he's not writing, he's chasing around his two active children.

MOONBODY

By Scott Hughes | 7,500 Words

EVERY STORY *IS*. It exists. Whether a history or myth or some-where in between, whether a premonition or dream or fantasy, whether written a millennium ago or yesterday or a hundred years from now, you breathe life into its inhabitants as the gods breathed life into the first beasts and men. A story *happens* as it is told, and with every telling it happens again. And again and again and again. Stories *are*, my friend.

This one *is*.

Remember that.

* * *

Once there lived a boy who climbed trees and took their branch-es for fishing rods, pretend swords, or brittle structures he would later kick down. A boy who buried his mother's necklaces and his father's spare coins—treasures he could then unearth and rebury. Who set leaves on fire just to stomp them out. Who collected bugs in jars, where they either died forgotten or survived long enough to be set free. Who swam and ran and whooped and laughed. Who created and destroyed. Who did the things all boys do. And like all boys, Wick Longwall knew he was special. So he climbed and dug and laughed, and dreamed the dreams of a special young boy. Of all the wonders yet to come.

And one summer morning a wonder came. While Wick was digging a hole with his hands by the corner of the house, he heard the familiar rattle and clomp of an approaching wagon. He looked up. Two decrepit donkeys were pulling an even more decrepit wagon, and making slow work of it. Wick's family lived near the top of one of the large round hills that gave the region its name—the Knuckles. From afar, the green hilltops resembled knuckles on the horizon, perhaps of some underground titan thrusting his fists up through the earth. People often passed by on the dirt path that led up and away from the village—Knuck, it was called—that lay around, between, and upon the other hills.

Wick resumed his undertaking until the wagon clattered off the road and into his family's slanted yard. The driver wore a broad hooded cloak. The dark yellow cloth with swirling blue stitches shrouded the man's entire body, save for his hands. And although alone, he was talking. Wick couldn't hear any specific words, just the man's murmur. Unless a passenger was hidden under the stained canvas tied down over the back, he was talking to himself or to his donkeys or to the warm wind.

Beside the man on the wagon's seat sat a black bottle that came up to his shoulder. Its base was the size of a dinner plate, and it tapered up into a slender neck no wider than a finger, stoppered with what had to be the biggest pearl—or the tiniest moon—Wick had ever seen. In the morning sun, the bottle's obsidian surface reflected an aura of changing colors. First blue, then orange, then pink, then yellow, then green, then blue again. It reminded him of a toy spyglass his pa had bought him for First Harvest one year; he could point it at a lamp or candle or even up at the sun and peer into the eyehole as he twisted the other end, and every color in the rainbow would dance and whirl and blossom in front of his eye.

One of the donkeys honked like a goose, and the driver turned his hooded head toward Wick. Quickly the man hopped from the wagon, removed his cloak, and tossed it over the bottle. He was pale yellow from sole to crown, the color of the dust that covered everything in springtime. His stringy hair and short beard, his weathered skin, his wool tunic and pants, the braided belt around his gaunt waist, the boots that rose to his knees—all yellow. He looked like one of the scarecrows in the valley fields, made of sticks and straw and tattered burlap.

As the man approached, Wick could see his wrinkled hands and grooved brow and the pitchfork lines sprouting from the corners of his eyes, and then the only part of him not yellow: his eyes. The right was dark brown; the left, the cold gray of winter slush. The mismatched eyes didn't unnerve Wick. His own, although not as severe, were also different. Both were brown, but a thin silver halo ringed Wick's right pupil.

"This the Longwall home?" the man asked, his voice scratchy.

"Yes sir," said Wick.

"Your father here, boy?"

"Yes sir."

"Fetch him, and make haste."

Wick ran around the cottage to the woodshop to tell his pa of the traveler. Together they went back to the front yard. Wick's ma stepped out the front door as the two men shook hands.

"Benn Longwall," said Wick's pa, introducing himself. "And this is my wife, Tay, and my son, Samwick."

"Lovely family," said the traveler. "I am Valden Whitestrand. I come looking for lodgings for an indeterminate length of time. Hopefully only a few days, although perhaps a week or even a month."

"Then you've come too far, I'm afraid," said Benn. "There's an inn in Knuck—that's the village in the valley. As long as you have coin, they'll have a bed and a meal for you, though both are likely hard and moldy."

Valden smiled. "I passed through the village and stopped by that inn you speak of, but only to inquire about quieter lodgings, something more out of the way. Inns are never quiet or out of the way, I've found. The innkeeper told me where you live, Mister Longwall, and said you own another small cabin farther along the road. A cabin that presently sits unoccupied."

"Belonged to my mother. Now to me since she passed, gods rest her."

"Rest she well," Valden said lowly.

Benn scratched his chin. "Truly, I never thought of renting it. Nor selling. Planned to someday give it to my boy." He tipped a hand toward Wick. "Would you like to come in out of the sun, Mister Whitestrand? We could draw you a cup of water from the well and talk this over, and my son could see your animals drink as well."

"Both my jacks and I took drink at the inn," said Valden. "The cabin, Mister Longwall, is all I need, thank you."

Valden returned to his wagon, and his hand disappeared under the cloak tented over the bottle. Instead of the bottle, though, he produced a fat leather pouch. It seemed to float through the air from Valden's hands to Benn's. The pouch jingled when Benn caught it, and Wick could see his pa hadn't expected it to be so heavy. Benn undid the drawstring and peered inside. Wick knew from the sound that it held coins—and from Benn's widening eyes and open mouth, that it held *lots* of coins. Maybe even gold.

"That should be sufficient for a month, wouldn't you say?" said Valden. "Even if I stay only a single day, you may keep it all. Should I decide to extend my stay beyond a month—with your permission, of course—I will pay you more."

"Mister Whitestrand," said Benn, "with this you could rent—No, you could *buy* any house in Knuck."

"I have my reasons. I am an artist, and I travel to remote locations to create my pieces. I have been *fortunate*, shall we say, in my endeavors. I could crisscross the three kingdoms in a stately coach drawn by a team of mighty stallions, buying houses hither and yon. But as you can see"—he gestured to his battered wagon—"I prefer to live an artist's life. A humble life."

Benn stole one last glance inside the pouch, then pulled the drawstring and held it out to Tay. She eyed it as though it were full of scorpions instead of coins. Wick reached for it. Tay snatched the pouch and quickly dropped it into one of her dress's large pockets.

"One thing more, Mister Longwall," said Valden. "Do you know of a flower called a sirrodel, perhaps by one of its other names—godsbloom, shadow flower, dragon's maw?"

Benn cleared his throat and brushed the sawdust from his sleeves. "Most folks around the Knuckles just call it a local legend."

"Its legend reaches ears beyond the Knuckles, I assure you. It is known far and wide, and this is one of the few places in all the world where a sirrodel supposedly grows. The innkeeper told me travelers arrive every few months, searching for it, yet never finding it. Perhaps because they say only certain people can see it—those chosen by the gods."

"So I've heard," said Benn.

"Have you ever seen one, Mister Longwall, or know of someone who has? As an artist, it would be rather extraordinary to behold the rarest flower in all existence. To paint it, of course, nothing more."

"I haven't, sorry to say."

Valden looked from Benn to Wick, who lowered his eyes.

"Then," said Valden, "I will be off to my new lodgings."

"I'll ride with you," said Benn. "Open up and air the place out."

"No need. I will be—"

"I insist. No one's lived there since my mother passed, but it hasn't been empty. I'll wager there's mice and squirrels we'll need to chase off, maybe even birds or snakes."

Valden nodded. Then he added another nod to Tay and one to Wick. "Many thanks, Missis Longwall. And . . ."

"Wick," said Wick.

Valden repeated the name slowly, tasting it.

He gathered the cloak from the seat—only Wick and Valden himself knew what was under it—and gingerly secured it under the canvas on the back with his other hidden belongings. As he did so, Wick distinctly heard him whisper, "Not much longer." Valden stepped onto the wagon, then lent a hand to Benn.

"Can I go?" Wick asked.

Tay's arm wrapped around him and pulled him hard against her. The lump in her pocket jingled.

"Stay here, Son," Benn said as Valden took hold of the reins and got the donkeys to reluctantly begin moving.

Wick and Tay watched silently as the wagon followed the road over the hill and out of sight. Wick asked to see the money, wanting to dump it on the ground and make a city by stacking the coins into towers. Tay said no and went inside.

An hour later, Benn returned, his shirt darkened with sweat. Wick was still outside, although his interest had shifted from digging a hole to observing a spider cocoon a cricket in its silk. Benn passed his son and went inside. Wick left the spider and put his ear to the front door. Tay was saying she wanted to bury the pouch down by the creek and forget it had ever come to them. Benn said that was fool's talk and started listing all the things they could do with the money.

Wick turned and ran across the yard, up the road, over the hill, and down the other side until he arrived at his grandma's cabin. The wagon was out front, the donkeys no longer hitched to it. Gone too was the canvas, and only two large trunks sat in the back. Wick couldn't see the tall black bottle, or even the cloak Valden had wrapped around it, but it could've been pushed behind one of the trunks.

He climbed into the wagon, and as he got to his feet, his eyes landed on one of the cabin's windows. A small face, silvery white, was there looking out at him.

Valden appeared by the wagon. "What are you doing in there, boy?"

Wick hopped off and retreated several paces.

"Come to try to pilfer something, did you?" Valden eyed the trunks before shifting his gaze back to Wick. "Or were you just snooping?"

"Do you have . . . ?"

"Do I have *what*?"

". . . somebody with you?" Wick finished.

Valden looked stunned. Then his eyes narrowed. "What makes you ask that, boy?"

"I saw someone. There." Wick pointed to the window, now empty—no silvery face behind the glass.

"You saw someone, you say?"

Before Wick had time to run away, or even blink, Valden closed the distance between them and loomed over him. Valden stooped, and with his long yellow fingers held open Wick's eyelids as he studied the irises with his own mismatched eyes—first the left, then the right. He lingered on the right, then stepped back.

"Tell me, boy," Valden said, "have *you* ever seen a sirrodel?"

Wick glanced at the trees across the road, thinking of the promise he'd made to his pa a year ago.

"No sir," he said.

Valden tapped his fingers on his chin. "I have no one with me. What you saw was one of my pieces. The likeness of a young girl I sculpted from moonstone marble."

"Can I see it?" Wick hoped Valden might also show him the bottle; it must've been another of his artistic creations.

"Certainly not, boy. Now be gone with you. I will be out in the forest until nightfall, and I do not want some boy snooping around my very valuable artwork with his grimy little fingers."

Wick glanced again at the window. Still no pearly face.

"Gone!" Valden clapped his hands as though Wick were a mongrel to be frightened off.

Returning to the road, Wick imagined all the strange pieces of art Valden could have in the cabin, when a thought occurred to him. If that white face belonged to a statue, how could it have been at the window one minute and gone the next? Statues couldn't move, unless they were magic.

Wick stopped, wanting to race back to the cabin window to see if Valden did indeed have a marble statue of a girl, or if it was something else entirely. Then a figure came over the hill on the road ahead. His pa. Wick considered darting into the woods. If he could see his pa, though, his pa could almost certainly see him. More than likely Benn was coming for him, so running away now would only make worse whatever punishment he had in store. Wick walked gravely forward, head hanging and feet dragging. He might be going to meet his pa's belt, but he didn't have to go quickly.

Wick didn't get the belt, although Benn did swat him open-handed on the back of the head. At home, he perched Wick on a stool facing a corner for the rest of the morning. Even worse, Wick had to listen to his parents bicker about Mister Whitestrand and what Tay kept calling *his money*.

"*Our* money," Benn would say whenever she said this.

They stopped long enough to eat a lunch of leathery venison and pasty, tasteless beans. As they stared at the pouch on the table, Benn suggested they go to town for a huge feast, as much food and wine as they wanted. Tay said she would have no food or wine bought with *his money*. After that, they ate in silence. Wick picked over his food and daydreamed of marble statues and tall black bottles.

When he finished his meal, Benn said he was taking the pouch to the counting house in Knuck for safekeeping—before it ended up in a hole in the ground—and he would be back after dark.

"Going to flaunt that to everyone in the Knuckles?" Tay asked. "I'd tell you to try not to get robbed, but that might be a blessing."

Benn grumbled something as he left.

Wick helped his ma clean up, then asked if he could go too.

Tay narrowed her eyes. "What for?"

Wick looked down at his feet. "So he can buy me something."

Tay crossed her arms. "Well, you tagging along might keep him out of too much trouble, and you can make sure to get him back before sundown. Hurry along. And put on shoes."

Wick got his boots and was out the door. His ma would be watching him through the window, like the marble statue had, so he marched downhill in the direction of town. At the base of the hill, he left the road and headed through the woods until he reached the creek. He followed the creek bed, trekked up the wooded slope, and came out behind his grandma's cabin. The donkeys, eyes barely open, lay tethered to a nearby shade tree. They made no noise as Wick crept by, offering him only the occasional ear or tail twitch.

The curtains inside the back windows had been drawn, as were the front windows'. Wick checked the back of the wagon to make sure the old man wasn't hiding there. Empty. Then, making himself tall by standing on his tiptoes, he pressed his ear to one of the front windows. Hearing nothing, he went to the other—the one where the face had been—and listened. Nothing.

Hadn't Valden said he'd be gone until nightfall? If Wick was careful not to touch anything, Valden would never know he'd been there. Just to be safe, he knocked first. If the old man answered the door, Wick could say his pa sent him to ask how Valden liked the cabin or if he needed anything.

Valden didn't come to the door, so Wick pushed it slightly open and slipped inside. He had been there many times, though not since his grandma passed. Something about knowing she died there made his belly feel full of squiggling tadpoles. He felt them now as he took a few steps forward. All the curtains had been pulled to and no candles or lamps were lit, so the sunlight coming in through the cracked door cut a bright wedge into the dim main room. Wick saw nothing that hadn't belonged to his grandma. His parents had already removed the few items of much value, leaving only the dusty furniture and shelves his pa had made. The sole piece of art Valden had left in the open sat on the long wooden table: a browning apple core on a plate.

Then Wick saw the girl to his left and nearly cried out. She was a bit taller and older than Wick, but not much. Her straight hair fell past her shoulders, and she wore a simple long-sleeved dress, almost a nightgown, that went down to her ankles. Her left arm was at her side, her right hand behind her back. Her feet were bare. Except for one thing, one very strange thing, she appeared a normal girl. All of her—hair, eyes, skin, clothes—was the lustrous silvery white of a full moon. Wick had never seen any statues, not unless scarecrows counted, but he thought this had to be the most realistic one ever sculpted.

Then she blinked.

"Are y-you real?" Wick stammered.

The girl looked a little surprised. "You can see me?" she said.

Wick nodded, confused. "Yeah." His voice sounded weak, so he cleared his throat before continuing. "I saw you this morning, at the window. Mister Whitestrand said you were a statue. Are you some kind of . . . magic?"

The girl smiled sadly and shook her head.

"Then why do you look like that?" he said.

"You shouldn't be here," she said.

"This is my house. Well, it's my parents' house. It used to be my grandma's but it's theirs now and it's going to be mine someday and I can be here whenever I want."

"My father will be back soon. He'll be mad if he finds you here."

"Your father?" said Wick. "Mister Whitestrand? He can't be your father. He's too old. You must be his granddaughter or—"

"I'm his *daughter*."

"He must've been older than my pa when you were born, then. How old are you?"

"What does it matter?" The girl lowered her head, then looked back up. "How old are *you*?"

"I'm eight. Almost nine."

"I'm eleven, I suppose."

"You suppose?"

The girl said nothing.

"What's your name?" Wick asked. "And if you're not some kind of magic statue, why are you that color?"

The girl said nothing.

"If you don't tell me," said Wick, "then I'm going to go tell my ma and pa that Mister Whitestrand has a girl with him who's made of magic marble."

"They won't believe you," said the girl.

"They will too. And if they don't, I'll scream until they come here to see for themselves."

"They won't be able to see me."

"Why not?"

The girl said nothing.

"Well, if they can't," said Wick, "then I'll go tell everyone in Knuck, and they'll all come here, and if I can see you, then I bet some of them will too."

The girl began to look worried. "My name is Parin. I look this way because . . . because I've been eleven for a long time."

"That can't be. Nobody can be—"

"I died," she said. Her left hand went to her neck, stroked the silvery skin, and dropped back to her side. "That was many years ago. I was eleven, and I've been eleven ever since."

The tadpoles in his stomach returned, a whole wriggling swarm of them. "You *died*? Then how are you here? How are you alive?"

"I'm not alive. Not like you are, like I *used* to be. My earthbody, the flesh body, is buried. Has been for almost thirty years."

"That's not . . . You're not . . . You're . . ."

"What's your name?" Parin said. "I told you mine."

He cleared his throat again. "Samwick Longwall. My parents call me Wick."

"Wick, I'm going to show you I'm not like you. Don't be afraid."

She walked toward him. As Wick turned, intending to flee, one of his feet caught on the other. He didn't fall, but his back struck the door and slammed it shut. Before he could whirl around and escape, Parin reached out her left hand—her right still behind her—and her silvery fingers went *into* his chest, like smoke passing through a sheet. Her hand disappeared into him all the way to her wrist. Before Wick could scream, warmth spread throughout his body, from his chest out to his fingertips and down to his toes and up to the crown of his head. The aroma of cooking blackberries and honey filled his nose, and their syrupy tartness danced on his tongue.

When Parin withdrew her hand and stepped back, Wick no longer wanted to run away. The berries and honey were gone, as well as the warmth, but so were the tadpoles.

"How'd you do that?" he said.

"It happens when I try to touch someone. I could smell that too, and taste it. Was that blueberries?"

"Blackberries," Wick said. "What's it like being . . . not alive?" He didn't want to say *dead*.

Parin shrugged. "I've been this way a lot longer than I was alive. I've almost forgotten what it was like."

"So if you were buried, how are you here?"

"Have you ever heard of moonbodies?"

Wick shook his head.

"Everyone has two bodies," she said. "The earthbody is made of flesh and bone and blood, like you are now. But inside you, there's a moonbody. That's what people called it a long time ago, because they thought it was made of moonbeams." She held out her left hand and wiggled her silvery fingers. "I do look that way, don't I?"

Wick nodded.

"They believed when your earthbody died," said Parin, "your moonbody floated away to the moon and lived forever."

"So you're made of moonlight?"

"No more than you are. I'm not made of flesh and blood, either. Whatever it is, it does live forever, just not on the moon. Father calls it the Far Kingdom. It's a real place, but it's much farther away than the moon, and only your moonbody can reach it."

DEEP MAGIC ANTHOLOGY ONE

After Wick had found a dead robin by the woodshop when he was five, his pa told him that all living creatures one day die. "You go to sleep and wake up in a far-off land," Benn had said, "and everyone you ever loved is there." His pa had never mentioned earthbodies or moonbodies or the Far Kingdom, though.

"Why haven't you gone there, then, to the Far Kingdom, wherever it is?" Wick said.

"I can't."

Her head turned to the right and her eyes dropped as she brought her right hand out from behind her. The flesh—although not really flesh—was greenish-black and slimy, each finger like a fat, boneless slug.

Or tadpole.

Parin hid her deformed hand behind her. Wick saw shame in her silvery eyes.

"That's what happens when you can't go to the Far Kingdom," she said. "All of you turns into that, and you wander around that way forever."

Wick swallowed. "Is there anything you can do? Medicine or something?"

Parin smiled her sad smile. "Medicine can only help someone who's alive. But my father is a . . . a *sorcerer*." She whispered the word.

"He said he was an artist."

"He is. He doesn't make paintings or sculptures. He makes other things. Magical things. He made me something called an immanir. It's like a bottle."

"The tall black bottle!" said Wick.

She nodded. "It's where I stay most of the time."

"Where you stay? You mean *inside* it, like water or something?"

"Like that. The immanir is what keeps me from . . ." She looked down and to the right again, toward her greenish-black hand. "Being inside the bottle doesn't stop it, but it does slow it down."

Wick couldn't imagine living inside a bottle, magic or not. Then again, the girl wasn't really alive.

"Father found a spell to help me get to the Far Kingdom," Parin said. "It's very complicated and requires lots of elements, like ingredients. All of them are very rare, so it's taken him almost thirty years to find them all. Now there's only two elements left. One is why we're here. Father says the Knuckles is one of the few places you can find it. Some kind of flower called a . . . dragon-something . . ."

"Dragon's maw." Wick hesitated, then added, "I found one last year, right after my grandma passed."

This time when Parin smiled, it wasn't sad. It was an ecstatic smile, and her body glimmered like actual moonlight.

"Really?" she said, beaming. "You truly found one? You know where it is?"

He nodded. "It was in the woods, not too far from here."

"I would hug you if I could! Father will be so—"

The front door swung open, knocking Wick forward. He fell through Parin since he couldn't collide with her. As he did, he felt the same warmth from before and tasted the blackberries and honey, but he also must have passed through Parin's greenish-black hand. An icy spike stabbed at his chest, and the stench of a rotting animal carcass filled his nose. He could see the robin on the floor as he tumbled forward, exactly as he had found it when he was five: dead and crawling with ants that were eating away its feathers, its skin, its insides, its *eyes*.

He hit the floor; no dead bird was there. A hand grabbed the back of his neck and hauled him to his feet. The hand belonged to Valden Whitestrand.

"Father, he can help us!" said Parin. "He knows where a dragon's maw is! He found one!"

"I heard as much," said the sorcerer. "Is it true, boy? You can tell me where the sirrodel is?"

Wick wondered how long Valden had been listening at the door. Had he even gone out to look for the flower himself, or had he hid and waited, knowing Wick would come back to the cabin? Wick knew he had just been tricked by the sorcerer—and maybe the girl too—but Parin herself was no trick. He believed her, and if he could help her reach the Far Kingdom before her entire body turned into slimy tadpole skin, he would.

Wick breathed deeply, then said, "I can show you. It's not far."

"You can take me now?" said Valden.

Wick nodded.

Valden straightened up. "Let us be off, then. As for you, Parin, you know where you must go, only for a little while longer. Once we have the sirrodel seed, this misfortune will nearly be at an end."

"Do I have to?" Parin said. "I could go with you. Surely it can't hurt for me to—"

"We cannot risk it. We do not know the true nature of the blight on your hand. It could suddenly overtake you if you are not inside the immanir. You have been out today for too long already."

Valden went into one of the cabin's rooms and returned carrying the tall bottle. Away from the sun, the black glass gave off no colors, although it was still marvelous to behold. A work of art.

Valden pulled out the pearl stopper and extended the bottle to his daughter as if offering her a drink. "I love you, my dear. Now, in you go."

"Thank you, Wick," Parin said. "And if I don't see you again, good-bye."

"Bye, and you're welcome," Wick said. "I hope you get to the Far Kingdom, wherever it is. And I hope it's wonderful."

"It *is*," said Valden.

Reluctantly, Parin extended her left hand, keeping her right hand behind her, and stuck her forefinger into the bottle. Her body shimmered, like moonlight rippling on a pond's surface. Then she appeared to liquefy, her hair and face and body and clothes melting into a watery silver cloud that was drawn into the immanir like smoke going *into* a chimney instead of pouring out. Now, even without sunlight, the bottle began to shine with the same brilliant colors Wick had seen that morning.

Valden stoppered the bottle and took it back to the other room. When he returned, he said, "You're the leader now, boy. Lead on!"

They left the cabin, crossed the dirt road, and headed into the forest.

"A sirrodel lives for thirteen years, did you know?" Valden said as they walked. "Then it dies, and its single seed is carried on the wind until it falls back to earth and begins to grow. They say only one grows at a time in the Knuckles. Did you tell anyone where you found it, boy? I'd hate to have come all this way if someone else has come along before me and plucked it from the ground."

"We didn't tell nobody," said Wick.

"We?"

"I told Pa. I took him to see it too."

"So your father *has* seen one," said Valden.

Wick felt like he'd tattled. "No sir, not really. He couldn't see it, but he believed I could."

"You've got a godseye, boy. That gray in your right eye. It allows you to see things only the gods are meant to see, like moonbodies or a sirrodel."

"Pa made me promise not to tell no one about the flower. He said most people around here know it's got powerful magic and not to mess with it, but people come from all around to find it and they might try to take it."

"Your father is quite right," said Valden. "So why did you tell me?"

Wick wanted to say, *Because you tricked me.* "You're going to use it to help your daughter, right?"

"Yes."

"Then that's a good thing. I think Pa would think so too."

Wick closed his left eye and kept the right open. Then he switched, to see if the world looked different through each eye. It didn't.

"How did Parin die, Mister Whitestrand? Was she sick?"

Wick began to wonder if Valden had heard him, when the old man said, "Some may say you're too young to hear such as this, but no boy stays young forever. All boys must someday become men, and they must know the harsh ways of the world. The harsh ways of *men.* My daughter told you of me, yes? Of what I do. What I am."

"She said you're a sorcerer."

"*Sorcerer* is what most would call me, though I prefer *artist.*"

"You make things," said Wick. "Magical things."

"Yes, and I sell them. Years ago, there was a man, and one of my pieces was used to hurt someone he loved."

"Why do you make them if they can hurt people?"

"Well, like nearly everything in this world, my creations can be used for good or ill. Just because they can be used for nefarious purposes doesn't mean I shouldn't make them. Take a scythe, for instance. You know what that is?"

"Yes sir."

"In a farmer's hands, it harvests crops to feed families, whole villages. In another's hands, however, it can slice a man open from belly to neck. Does that mean we should no longer make scythes, that they are *evil*?"

"I don't know," said Wick.

"Of course not. But I could not explain that to this one particular man, that I was merely the one who created the piece, not the one who wielded its power for ill. So, to hurt me, he killed my sweet, innocent daughter. Strangled her to death with his bare hands."

The tadpoles had come back. Wick held his hands over his stomach. Since he was walking ahead, he couldn't see Valden, but he heard the man sniffle.

"That night I saw her," said Valden. "The *other* her, as you have just seen her, for I too have the godseye. I had known of moonbodies for some time, had even seen a few others, but I never thought I would see my own daughter's. Parin told you what moonbodies are, yes?"

"Yes sir."

"Being killed is what made her linger here instead of moving on, you see. Her moonbody was tainted by that brutal act, and so the gods will not allow her into the perfect paradise of the Far Kingdom. But after this spell, they will welcome her there this very day."

"Did they hang him?" Wick asked.

"Who?"

"The man who killed Parin?"

"He fled far away after his crime. I tracked him down a few years later, but alas, he had died in his sleep. It was too peaceful a way for him to pass, but who are we to question the ways of the gods?"

After that they did not speak until they came upon the sirrodel. Amongst the towering trees, the single black stalk stood as high as Wick's knee. The bloom, the size of a man's open hand, consisted of only two large black petals lined with pointy ridges that resembled fangs. A curly red stamen protruded from the center like flames. The flower did look like a dragon's gaping mouth.

"Can you see it?" Wick asked.

"Yes, boy," Valden whispered.

The sorcerer produced gloves and a small leather pouch, a tiny version of the one given to Wick's parents, and knelt by the flower. Wick wrung his shirt in his hands, expecting the sirrodel to transform into a real dragon and burn both him and Valden to crispy husks. After donning the gloves, Valden held the open pouch in one hand under the flower. Then he pinched the red stamen between two fingers of his other hand and carefully slid them outward until the single seed, black with orange spots, popped out and fell into the pouch.

"Can I watch the spell?" Wick asked after Valden tucked away the pouch and gloves.

"You absolutely must be there," said Valden.

When they returned to the cabin, Valden sat Wick on a stool by the door.

"Absolute quiet," the sorcerer said. "Even the most rudimentary of spells requires deep concentration, so you mustn't do or say anything. The tiniest mistake and this whole cabin could burn to the ground. Not only that, but Parin would never make it to the Far Kingdom."

Wick nodded.

Valden cleared the long wooden table and spread over it the large swath of canvas that had been on the wagon. Then he brought out the immanir containing Parin and set it in the table's center. It still shimmered colorfully.

Next he began arranging the first of the elements on the table: powders and liquids in small stoppered phials; leaves and flaky bits of tree bark and a bowl of berries; several candles, some long and thin, others as round as Valden's wrist; and various stones, both large and small. All of these, though colorful, appeared unremarkable.

Then came the more bizarre elements: a black, shriveled human hand; the pointy, curved tooth of an enormous cat or snake; a curling, hollow horn; and a dried tongue, forked and blue and the length of Wick's arm.

Then came the jars, which contained the most fantastical elements. One held gray flames—nothing burning, only the flames themselves. Another had a small bloody heart, still beating. In the next, a spider as plump as a field rat clattered its bristly golden forelegs against the glass and hissed. As Valden set the last jar on the table, the square of dark silk draped over it fluttered up long enough for Wick to see a tiny naked woman sitting inside. She had white hair, glowing red dots for eyes, orange skin, and papery white wings.

Finally, Valden took the pouch from his cloak, dropped the sirrodel seed into a bowl, and ground it into a fine powder. Then he stretched his back, which creaked like a rusty hinge. The elements covered the table like a strange feast, and the pulsing immanir was the centerpiece.

As Wick surveyed the many ingredients, he remembered something Parin had said. There were *two* remaining elements. The sirrodel was one, but the other . . .

"What about the last element?" Wick said. He clapped his hands over his mouth, afraid he might have ruined the spell.

"You know of the final element?" said Valden.

"Parin didn't say what it was. She said there were two left, but you only got the dragon's maw seed."

"She didn't say what it was because I never told her. She is a good girl, an innocent girl, so I didn't want her to know. The last element we need is actually the *first* element, the one that begins the spell. I wanted it to be the man who murdered Parin, but the gods took him already. Instead, they want you."

"Me?" said Wick.

"Why else did the gods give you their eye, to see their sacred flower and Parin's moonbody? Why else would they have commanded the wind to deliver the sirrodel seed so close to your home? Why else would they have led you to the flower or led me to your doorstep or led you to *my* doorstep, not once but twice? The gods want *you*, boy."

Wick slid off the stool. "For what?"

"You wish to help my daughter, yes? You helped her by leading me to the sirrodel, and now you may help her again. With this spell, I will be sending one moonbody to the Far Kingdom, a body that the gods saw fit to keep here. So to appease them, I must begin the spell with an offering—one moonbody for another." Valden stepped closer to him. "I am sorry, boy, and I will someday pay for my crime, but the gods want *you*. And compared to my daughter, what are you to me?"

Valden seized Wick's throat, his thumbs digging into the boy's windpipe. Wick kicked at Valden's legs and clawed at the man's arms and face, which only made the hands clamp down harder on his throat. Almost instantly his head began to throb from lack of air, and his limbs felt as though they were filled with wet sand.

Behind Valden, the immanir was still aglow, though now its color didn't change. It burned the bright red of a hot coal as it rattled on the table, close to tipping over.

Spots of color, like First Harvest fireworks, exploded in front of Wick's eyes. Through the color bursts, he could see Valden's mismatched eyes, the brown and gray irises now surrounded by red. The man was crying. Wick felt his own hot tears, barely, on his numb cheeks.

Wick was certain his pa would charge into the cabin and wrestle Valden's hands from his throat. That's how all the stories he ever heard had ended—a life saved by the brave hero. Benn Longwall, however, was still in the village buying another round of the finest brew the Thirsty Thrush had to offer, for himself and a dozen other men. At that very moment, Benn was proposing a toast to Valden Whitestrand.

The fireworks spread, swallowing the sorcerer's face. For a time, Wick watched the swirling colors. He no longer felt hands around his throat, no longer felt the need to breathe.

One by one the colors disappeared until only silver remained. Then that too faded away, and Wick could see the cabin again.

Outside, the insects and frogs were singing their evening chorus, and no sunlight was peeking in around the drawn curtains. In fact, there was no light at all inside the cabin, but Wick could still see. His grandma's long table had been cleared of the strange feast. The canvas was gone, as were all the spell's elements.

Except for one, the first element. His body—his former body, the one Parin had called the earthbody—lay on the floor with its legs straight, arms crossed over its chest, and eyes closed. If not for the purple marks on its throat, it looked as though it was sleeping.

The centerpiece had also been left behind, shattered into a thousand black pieces on the floor.

Already knowing what he'd see, Wick looked down at himself— at his new self. His clothes and skin were silvery white, the color of the moon. He held up his pale right hand and touched his thumb to each fingertip. Then he noticed a small greenish-black blemish in the center of his palm. He rubbed it with the fingers of his other hand, but he knew it wasn't dirt or food or blood. It couldn't be wiped off. It would spread. How long that would take, only the gods knew.

Wick didn't want to stay in the cabin any longer with the other him, the dead earthbody. Where could he go? Anywhere, he supposed. Except the Far Kingdom. He would never—could never— go there. He wanted to see his ma and pa—would they see him?— though not for some time. They would find *it* here, the earthbody, and they'd be very sad. He didn't want to see them sad.

He'd go to the sirrodel first, to see if it had died too after Valden stole its seed. From there, only the gods knew. They wanted *him*, after all. Maybe they would show him where to go.

Wick's moonbody took a deep breath, although not a real breath since the dead have no need for such things, and stepped through the closed front door.

* * *

You, my friend, have just committed murder. For this crime you will never swing at the end of a rope.

It's just a story, you say.

It is. All the same, murder is murder.

Me, a murderer? you say. *It was the sorcerer Valden who killed the boy, not I. Was Valden, that evil man. That* monster. *He, not I. Not I.*

But it was you.

Every story *is*, remember? Every story *happens*. You breathed Wick and Valden into existence once again. You brought Valden to the Longwall house. You sent Wick to the cabin, not once but twice. You led them both to the dragon's maw. You curled Valden's fingers around the boy's throat. *You.*

Do not be disheartened. We all are murderers, all destroyers. Yet we are also creators. There is one thing you can do for the boy, one small thing. Resurrect him, if only for a little while. Start at the beginning of Wick's story . . . then simply stop. Let his life linger in those sweet moments, suspended like a brittle leaf in an updraft, until someone else finds this story and snuffs him out again. And again. And again.

Here, we will do it together, we fellow murderers . . .

Once there lived a boy who climbed trees and took their branches for fishing rods, pretend swords, or brittle structures he would later kick down. A boy who buried his mother's necklaces and his father's spare coins—treasures he could then unearth and rebury. Who set leaves on fire just to stomp them out. Who collected bugs in jars, where they either died forgotten or survived long enough to be set free. Who swam and ran and whooped and laughed. Who created and destroyed. Who did the things all boys do. And like all boys, Wick Longwall knew he was special. So he climbed and dug and laughed, and dreamed the dreams of a special young boy. Of all the wonders yet to come.

About Scott Hughes

Scott Hughes's fiction, poetry, and essays have appeared in *Crazyhorse*, *One Sentence Poems*, *Entropy*, *Carbon Culture Review*, *Redivider*, *PopMatters*, *Strange Horizons*, and*Compaso: Journal of Comparative Research in Anthropology and Sociology*.

PAWPRINTS IN THE AEOLIAN DUST

By Eleanor R. Wood | 3,800 Words

REMAINING TIME: 6 hours 38 minutes

My boot prints look odd in the amber dust. It's been four months since the transport touched down, and I have been walking this plain nearly every day since we arrived. It's only just dawned on me what's wrong with the imprints I leave on the ground. They're missing their counterpart.

They're missing your footprints alongside them.

I haven't cried since losing you, but the tears are welling now, threatening to mist up my visor. I swallow to relieve my tightening throat, but it's no use. All I can see are the images of every Earth walk of the last fifteen years, superimposed over the rocky ground before me. My bare footprints in the wet sand; your pawprints in perfect outline beside them. My hiking-boot tread marks on the forest trail; your five-padded marks just in front. My shoe print in the wet, sucking mud; your footprint appearing for a brief moment before water fills it and the mud re-forms. I can see you looking back at me with your lolling grin, delighted to be outdoors with your pack mate, roaming, scenting, marking, *being*.

But I'm alone, and no walk was ever right without you. I took the mission after you died, hoping to leave the painful reminders behind and start new memories. I'd put on a brave face for too long: "men don't cry" and all that nonsense. I fled the planet to escape my grief. Foolishness. It was never confined to a single orb, but tangled up in my soul. I dragged it with me into space, and now, on Martian soil, here is a stark reminder that your loss still guts me.

There are no dogs here. We have no sheep to herd, no rats to hunt, no kills to retrieve. Our territory needs no defending. We have no blind settlers to guide or smuggled drugs to detect. Yet I miss you more keenly at this moment than ever before. I'm so far from home . . . so far from our shared haunts. You'll never again leave an imprint on Earth's surface, and neither will I.

Aeolis Mons dominates the horizon to my left; the sheer wall of Gale Crater is somewhere off to my right. And in front of me. And behind. The Aeolian Plain seems vast, but only from my vantage point. From space, I'm standing in a circular imprint with a small mound at its centre.

Remaining time: 5 hours 11 minutes

Jorge and I rode the buggy twenty kilometres out from Bradbury Landing this morning. Most of the settlement was still asleep, but we wanted to make an early start. Priya's tracking a dust storm headed our way, but she predicts it won't hit before early evening.

"Have you made it to site six yet, Huw?" Jorge's voice is tinny through my earpiece.

"On my way now, with samples from four and five," I reply. "How 'bout you?"

"The drill was stuck at site ten, so I'll have to bring Anders along next time to repair it. But I'm hoping to get a couple metres of core from eleven. We'll need plenty to keep us busy if we're gonna be stormbound for days!"

"That's for sure. I've gathered a few surface-rock samples too— there are some interesting fragments out here, possibly volcanic."

"Possibly?" Jorge laughs. "You seen this mountain?"

"Yeah, all right, smart alec." I smile at his infectious guffaw. "No harm in keeping an open mind."

"Well, there's no doubt in mine, man. The ground up here's littered with lava frags."

"Make sure you bring some down with you, then!"

Jorge's working the foothills while I take the plains. We need samples from both to see how they compare, but scouting Aeolis Mons itself is a task we haven't got to yet.

The thought transports me back to the Brecon Beacons, with you. The steep trails were easier for your four legs than my two. You'd be ahead of me all the way, urging me onward until we reached the top of a bluff and stopped to take in the magnificent view along with our sandwiches. Always fish paste for you . . . your eternal favourite. Sometimes we'd stay until dark to absorb the dazzling sky. I was ten years old when Brecon Beacons National Park became an International Dark Sky Reserve. I remember begging my da to take me up there after dark. That first camping trip was the night I decided to be an astronaut. The magic of that sky, unobscured by so much as a particle of light pollution, remains the most breathtaking experience of my life. I have never felt tinier, or more massive. I felt the entire universe was mine for that brief moment. The need to get closer to it, to see it for myself, to be more than a passive observer, etched itself onto my bones.

And here I am twenty years on, collecting geological samples on Mars. I shove aside your love of beach pebbles as I pick up an especially smooth rock fragment. I refuse to dwell on your penchant for digging as I nudge soil away from an embedded piece of possible haematite. I can almost feel the sharp sting of sand as your efforts spray my legs.

No. I'm not doing this. Not now. A warehouse door clangs down in my mind, shutting the memory off. It hurts to push you away, but not as much as it would to cling to those times and everything we'll never share again. I ignore my solo boot prints and continue my work.

The sun moves across the hazy sky as I move across the plain. The chronometer in my helmet tells me there's plenty of time before Jorge and I have to worry about Priya's forecast.

Remaining time: 3 hours 52 minutes

It's wrong.

The dust storm hits just after 1400 hours. It begins as a rusty haze on the horizon, quickly darkening the sky as it approaches. My heart begins to pound as I turn back toward the buggy, which I've managed to leave far behind.

"Jorge? Are you seeing this storm?"

"I see it." His reply is already fuzzed with static. "I'm on my way back, but I'm not going to make it before this thing hits."

"Me neither. Just fix the buggy's position and follow your display. I'll see you there."

His reply is garbled by static interference. It sounds affirmative, but I can't be sure he heard what I said. Jorge's experienced and level-headed; he'll be fine. I break into a run, not daring to look over my shoulder at the approaching cloud. My vision fogs up as the first powdery particles fill the air like smoke. There's no buffeting wind like you'd expect on Earth. The atmosphere is so thin here that I'd feel no more than a light breeze were I to strip off my suit. But in minutes I'm consumed by the cloud.

I keep level with the blinking light on my visor's display, guiding me to the trusty buggy. I'm breathing deeply to stay calm, knowing there's no real danger as I've already crossed this plain. I know there aren't any sudden drops or ledges to stumble from, but I'm still walking blind. I've been out in dust storms before, but never this far from the settlement. Waiting it out isn't an option—it could rage for days. My suit has already switched to its reserve oxygen supply, which gives me about two hours' worth at normal exertion. The suit's atmosphere compressors convert thin Martian air into gas dense enough to breathe, but with the air full of particles, the compressors have shut down to prevent the filters clogging.

I keep going, trusting my display and the ground beneath my feet. A warning blinker is telling me communications are down, but I'd twigged that following my chat with Jorge.

The dust swirls do funny things to one's vision. The mind's need to make patterns and sense from chaos creates images that come and go in seconds. It's hypnotic and disorienting. My feet are taking me forward, but my eyes tell me I'm standing still amidst a maelstrom of moving shapes and whorls. As the dust becomes heavier, the light fades, its dusty orange glow subsumed by the thick brown air.

Something brushes against my leg. It's the lightest touch through my suit. I look down and see nothing, of course; I can barely make out my own boot. I'm just about to dismiss it as a near-collision with an unseen boulder when I glimpse a shifting motion in the dust ahead. A bushy tail follows trotting brown feet into the curtain of gusting particles.

My treacherous heart leaps for an instant. I stop in my tracks as it falls again, hard. My throat clenches at the vision, so longed-for and so impossible. Curse this dust and my image-starved eyes. I take a breath, blink firmly, and trudge on.

The open-topped buggy looms out of the cloud a moment later. Dust has yet to settle on it, as the intense Martian breeze keeps it all moving. There'll be a dense layer everywhere when the storm stops, but for now objects in its path are merely stung with millions of tiny grains which then continue on their way.

There's no sign of Jorge. He must have gone farther than I did today. I take the driver's seat and wait for him, peering ahead into the storm. Several minutes pass. My senses report nothing but the constant scattered ping of sand against my helmet. I could start driving the buggy toward Jorge and catch him up if I knew his precise direction. But even with the headlights on, I'd risk colliding with him. Or crashing into an unseen ridge.

Remaining time: 3 hours 18 minutes

I switch off the now-defunct storm countdown. My chrono says it's been over half an hour since I spoke to Jorge. He should be here by now.

"Come on, Jorge," I mutter, sharply aware that he can't hear me.

I spot a defined shape in the dust. I lean forward, expecting Jorge's suited form . . . but it's smaller and nearer than I thought. The clogged air shifts, and my heart freezes.

You're standing there. Your chocolate fur, with its ruffles and tufts, is clear against the red dust. Your back is to me and you're looking over your shoulder, ears pricked, giving me your "What are you waiting for?" expression. The storm seems to hold its breath— or maybe that's just me—but only for a moment before the vision is obscured. You walk on just as the dense cloud swallows you up.

I'm rooted to the spot, knowing I'm seeing things but desperate to follow. My heart is thumping and there's a lump in my throat the size of a walnut. Even as I stand up and step away from the buggy my rational mind is demanding that I sit back down and get a grip. But your face . . . your eyes, dark and pleading, focusing their will on mine with an expression so familiar it's like I saw it yesterday. *Come with me.*

It's been over a year since I looked into that face. Your eyes were fogged with age, but they still regarded me with their depth of knowing, like you could see into my soul. You always could. It's why I'm walking away from the buggy now, back into the blanket of dust, in a direction I haven't walked today, over ground I have no reason to trust.

But I trust you.

I walk forward with a surety I didn't have earlier, even though my blinking sensor is telling me I'm getting farther from the buggy and its promise of safe return home. The ground is rocky, the dust is all-consuming, and I can barely see my gloved hands before my visor. But every few moments I catch a glimpse of something more: dust re-forming behind a gently waving tail, a ghostly canine shape just a touch darker than the raging motes all around me, poised to make certain I'm close behind.

We hike for a quarter of an hour, and my anxiety at the claustrophobic storm becomes a fading memory. I lull myself into the bittersweet familiarity of walking with you, just the two of us, on a jaunt of exploration and companionship, like all the old times. I can't see a damned thing apart from your occasional reminders that I'm not alone out here. You were always our scout on unfamiliar terrain; you could find a path if ever there was one.

The ground is sloping now, becoming slowly steeper, and I realise we're at the foothills of Aeolis Mons. This is craggy country, with dips and drops and gullies, and it's foolhardy to continue. I slow down, but there's a nudge of encouragement against my leg and I know you're guiding me. A rational thought intrudes, and it'll bring panic along for the ride if I acknowledge it.

Maybe this is crazy, but right now it's the only thing that makes sense. Later on I can marvel at my stupidity, but not now. Not yet.

I don't know if I'm following my loneliness and loss. I don't know if I'm hallucinating as my oxygen supply dips. I don't know if I'm lost on a distant planet, being led to my demise by a desperate dream that I know can never be. But I do know it's not just me out here. I do know there's still no sign of Jorge. I do know I've trusted you from the moment you chose me, the one puppy that was more interested in me than his littermates.

I haven't completely lost it; I know you're dead. I held you to the last. I buried you in the garden. I'd never known tears could pour out like that, in a broken-dam cascade of exhausting grief. I was helpless to bottle them up until that initial flood had passed. Your remains are hundreds of millions of kilometres away on the planet we once shared. But that doesn't change the fact that I can feel you here now, guiding me somewhere important.

And then, all at once, I'm there.

The bulk of a Mars suit is sprawled on the ground before me, just visible through the choking haze. I'm kneeling in a flash, reaching for Jorge's helmet, trying to see whether he's conscious. He grabs my hand.

"Huw . . ."

"Jorge, what happened?" Our radios seem to be working at ultra-close range.

"The ledge . . . I fell." He jerks his head upward and I realise he's lodged at the base of a steep drop. "I think my leg's broken."

His left leg is crumpled under him, twisted at a nasty angle. He cries out when I help him stand, and he leans heavily against me, favouring his right side.

"Come on. Let's get you back to the buggy." We wrap our arms around each other's shoulders and begin to limp back.

"How did you find me?" he rasps through the pain.

"Doesn't matter how. Let's just be glad I did." He could have lain there for days before the storm cleared enough to discover his body. You knew he was there. You led me to him, recognising an injured pack mate in dire need.

You're here again now, a gentle blur of movement in the stinging dust. My sensor will take me back to the buggy, but I feel safer following your lead. Even with the low Mars gravity, our return is slower with Jorge's dependence on me and it's nearly half an hour before the buggy looms through the storm. It's the most welcome sight I've ever seen.

I ease Jorge onto the passenger seat and climb in beside him. He can barely sit and I know every jolt of the vehicle will be agony for him, but there's nothing for it.

"What do we do now?" he asks. I can just about make out his face through the visor. He's gritting his teeth.

"We head back." I start the motor.

"What? You can't possibly drive in this, man . . . You can't see your hand in front of your face out here!"

"We don't have a choice, boyo. We've got to get you back, and our air reserves are dropping fast." Besides, I've got a feeling. "Just sit tight and trust me."

"Trust you? Don't give me that Kenobi line, amigo. You. Can't. See."

"Then you'd better lean forward and help me look."

The buggy's inertial guidance system will take us back to Bradbury no problem, but there are still an awful lot of boulders out here. Jorge's right—I can't see a thing. But you're waiting, right there in the shifting brown fog. You've led us this far, my old friend. Jorge's given no indication that he can see you, and I'm not about to explain and shatter my illusion of sanity.

I begin driving, easing the buggy forward, squinting ahead as if looking for unseen dangers. In reality, I'm looking for your beckoning shape. I follow your tail through clear passage across the plain, trusting your sure feet and keen nose to guide us past all obstacles. And you do. But it's slow going. It's a forty-minute ride back to the settlement at reasonable speed, with clear atmosphere. Under these conditions, we're looking at over an hour. It's time we don't have.

50 minutes oxygen remaining

My display is giving me regular updates now. I'm trying to stay calm, breathing as shallowly as possible, but I know I'm pushing my luck.

"How's your O2?" I ask, not daring to take my eyes off you.

"Getting low." Jorge's reply is tense.

"How low?"

"Twenty-five, thirty minutes."

My stomach knots. Our air compressors would have switched off at roughly the same time. Jorge's lower reserves must be due to his fall and the corresponding pain. He'll have been breathing harder than me.

"Hang on, mate. Short breaths. We'll get back." But I don't know if we will.

I speed up as much as I dare, watching your nimble form all the while. It's almost as if you recognise our new urgency. Your pace picks up along with the buggy's. You shift one way and I follow, realising moments later that we've bypassed a boulder hulking in the brown fog. We skirt obstacles I can't see, time and again, and I can almost feel Jorge squeezing his eyes shut as we rumble along in the blinding haze.

20 minutes oxygen remaining

I risk a glance at Jorge. His head is nodding.

"Jorge! Don't you pass out on me!"

"Light-headed," he mutters.

I'm feeling that way myself as I eke out my remaining supply. Your lithe shape seems to grow clearer even though the dust is as thick as ever. Your fur should be tinged red from the dust, but it isn't. It's not even shifting in the light winds. I suddenly long to feel its softness again. Your velvet ears. Your rough pads as you rest your paw on my knee.

Jorge's head drops against his chest. The movement startles me out of my storm-lulled reverie.

"Jorge. Jorge!" He doesn't respond.

15 minutes oxygen remaining

We're not going to make it. A swell of panic rises in me for the first time. I've never doubted your ability to get us home. But you can't help us breathe.

"Baskerville." I whisper your name, not sure if I'm seeking reassurance or a miracle.

You stop. You look right at me, and I'm pivoting on your gaze, my dizzy head finding an anchor in your eyes. I brake before I know what I'm doing, and suddenly . . . Behind you. The settlement lights, finally glowing through the dust, beacons of safety in the gloom. We shouldn't be here yet. Did you find a shortcut, my four-pawed scout?

I pull up beside the nearest airlock and press the activation control. The lock cycles and turns green, and the door slides up. Whooshes of dust precede the buggy inside, and we're home. Back to safety and clear vision and medical aid. The air clears as the chamber is flooded with breathable atmosphere. I pull off Jorge's helmet and am relieved to see he's still breathing, albeit in a ragged wheeze. He gasps in air and coughs on dust, and I tear off my own helmet and do the same. My head clears and I find myself looking for you as the dust dissipates and settles to the ground.

I don't know what I expect to see. You're not here. Of course you aren't. Yet the weight of loss threatens to swamp me again after following you all this way. Jorge groans in pain as he tries to move, and I'm back in the moment, glad of the distraction from my self-pity.

I manage to help him inside, where Priya, Anders, and Lucy are waiting. They welcome us with open arms and smiles of relief. They whisk Jorge off to sickbay and I head back to clean up the buggy and put it away before dust settles firmly into its mechanisms. Alone again, I lean against the bulkhead and breathe deeply, fighting waves of fresh sorrow. I miss you so much.

Standing here, under bright lights, breathing plentiful air, my face free of its visor and my vision clear right across the airlock, a twist of anxiety forms in my stomach. Was I completely mad to risk so much? Sure, I found Jorge, but I could have killed myself trying, or doomed us both on the journey back. What was I thinking?

The mind plays terrible tricks when one's senses are impaired. I recall I'd been thinking of you, missing you anew, only moments before the storm hit. Did I really just risk my own life and that of my fellow pioneer on the basis of dust visions and wishful thinking? We'd have been dead if I hadn't. But even that truth doesn't ease the lingering panic at the realisation of what an utter fool I've been.

I shake my head of the fruitless thought and grab the vacuum brush to clean up the buggy. There's a fresh layer of dust all over the floor too. My boot prints mark it as I approach, and there . . .

I choke back a sob. It can't be.

It is.

I kneel in the dust and cup its shape in my hands.

It's a single pawprint, perfectly rendered, perfectly yours, imprinted like none before and none to come, in the ancient Martian dust.

About Eleanor R. Wood

Eleanor R. Wood's stories have appeared in over a dozen venues, including *Crossed Genres*, *Flash Fiction Online*, *Deep Magic*, *Daily Science Fiction* and the Aurealis-nominated anthology *Hear Me Roar*. She writes and eats liquorice from the south coast of England, where she lives with her husband, two marvellous dogs, and enough tropical fish tanks to charge an entry fee.

FIRST COLLECTION

Visit us at: http://deepmagic.co

Printed in Great Britain
by Amazon

77426284R00338